A NOVEL

LES ROBERTS

"We have met the enemy and he is us."
Pogo by Walt Kelly ©
Circa 1955

This book is dedicated to all of you who struggle to overcome…
May God give you the will and the wisdom.

This book is a work of fiction. It is solely a product of the author's wild and fertile imagination. All characters and events are fictional. Any reference to actual persons, living or dead, actual locations, facilities, or establishments is made and used in a purely fictional context.

The guilty among you will know who you are.

Copyright © 2006 Les Roberts
www.poisonplum.com

Jacket Design by Yvonne Vermillion,
MagicGraphix.com

Text Layout by Lauren Simonetti,
RJ Communications

Library of Congress Control Number: 2007904805

ISBN 13: 978-0-9789659-0-7
ISBN 10: 0-9789659-0-6

Contents

1.	Tuskegee, Alabama—August 1946	5
2.	New London, Connecticut—Friday, July 3, 20__	12
3.	Plum Island, New York	14
4.	The Visitors	16
5.	Damage Control—The Pentagon, Washington, D.C	23
6.	Back to Work	29
7.	A Seed Is Planted	33
8.	Monday—The Doctor Is In	42
9.	Capitol Hill	50
10.	Talking Shop	58
11.	Back to the Constituents	62
12.	The Drive Home	65
13.	The Uncelebratory Gathering	71
14.	The Strategy Session	77
15.	Tuesday—Bad News Conference vs. Good News Conference	81
16.	The Forsaken	83
17.	Onward to the Community Center	85
18.	The News Conference	93
19.	Wednesday—"Bugs and Plums"	111
20.	Job Security?	113
21.	Thursday—Susan and Toby Visit the Ivory Tower	123
22.	Friday—Susan and Toby Visit the Emergency Room	135
23.	Surviving Hell	155
24.	Getting Back to Normal?	159
25.	Ben's Momma	183
26.	Friday in Washington	194
27.	Pennsylvania Avenue	197
28.	The Little Black Cocktail Dress	201

29.	An Eventful Day at the Office	225
30.	Tests and More Revelations	231
31.	The Dream	245
32.	The Performance of a Lifetime	260
33.	Operation Paper Clip	278
34.	The Package	284
35.	More Bugs	298
36.	Feeding Frenzy	307
37.	Calling in Markers	311
38.	Check-Out Time	317
39.	Storm Clouds Gather	323
40.	Picnicking with the Ticks	328
41.	Letters	339
42.	Sunday's Deliberations	346
43.	Pep Rally	354
44.	Dress Code	362
45.	Show-and-Tell Time	369
46.	The Arrival of Friday	376
47.	The Respite	384
48.	A Plan	391
49.	Under the Microscope	394
50.	The Return of the Lyme-Aid Express	396
51.	Hell Is Other People	398
52.	Contact Your Congressman	403
53.	Washington	406
54.	Big Brother Is Watching	413
55.	The Commuter	417
56.	Swift Injustice	423
57.	Bad News Travels Fastest	427
58.	America's Response	432
59.	The Hearings—Day One	434
60.	The Hearings—Day Two	446
61.	The Hearings—Day Three	453
62.	Operation Aerotick	455
63.	The Hearings—Day Four: The Living Dead	457
64.	Fly the Friendly Skies of	467
65.	Omega	468

Tuskegee, Alabama
August 1946

For almost five hours, Dr. Albert Pierpont and his three traveling companions had endured the sweltering heat and perpetual discomfort of a muggy, late summer day in the Deep South. Motoring from their offices at the Communicable Disease Center in Atlanta, they had traveled southwest along winding, two-lane U.S. Highway 29 toward their ultimate destination of Tuskegee, Alabama, which lay about forty-seven miles west of the Alabama-Georgia state line. Once intersecting the highway to Montgomery, about seven miles east of Tuskegee, the men again encountered delays due to a continuation of the repairs and uncompleted paving projects they had repetitively experienced every ten or fifteen miles of their journey.

Dr. Pierpont silently cursed the additional delay and the stifling heat and humidity of Southeast Alabama as their black, 1941 Ford sedan, now covered with dust, bounced and rattled its way slowly along yet another stretch of unpaved highway. The thick cloud of brown dust kicked up by the Ford's tires churned and swirled around the car, entering into the passenger compartment through cracked and worn gaskets of the trunk lid, doors, and windows.

Out of disgust for the uncivilized conditions now prevailing, Dr. Pierpont used his forefinger to wipe a swath through the layer of dust now covering the dash as if to dramatize his contempt for his surroundings. He and his three companions had long ago loosened their neckties and now sat quietly, skin glistening, hoping that around the next bend in the road, the community of Tuskegee would appear on the horizon.

"Quite a change from Boston, wouldn't you say, Dr. Pierpont?" spoke the Ford's driver, Dr. Walter Heller.

"Yes, Dr. Heller…you could say that. By the time we finally get out of this rolling oven, the combination of dust and perspiration will have us all looking like we are wearing pancake makeup! Throw in a little black face paint, and we'll look like a traveling minstrel show!"

"Welcome to late summer in south Alabama!" replied Dr. Heller.

God, what a shit hole! thought Dr. Pierpont. *Does it ever rain here? Is there ever a breeze? And are there any white people? All I've seen for miles now are Negroes. And do they actually live in those shacks I've seen? No wonder our bosses at the Public Health Service in Washington call this place the syphilis capital of the world! Hell, any germ known to man would thrive in these barbaric conditions!*

Shortly, to the delight of all of the passengers, the outline of buildings and houses appeared in the distance, and everyone knew they were approaching Tuskegee. As they passed the city limit sign and began entering what could loosely be described as the residential area of Tuskegee, Dr. Pierpont noticed a curious anomaly. The color of the road suddenly shifted from dirt brown to dark, very dark, almost black, and relatively free of dust. As he wondered how the transition from brown and dusty to dark and less dusty had occurred, he noticed a strange truck moving slowly along the opposite side of the road. It was fitted with a large cylindrical tank and a row of spray nozzles attached to the rear, spewing a black, viscous fluid that coated the surface of the road with a gooey slime.

"Would one of my learned companions please explain what the hell that contraption is all about?" Pierpont exclaimed.

"Certainly, my eager associate from the big city," replied Dr. Heller.

"That, my fine young doctor, is the local dust control mechanism. A few times a week, that truck, with its tank filled with used, burnt motor oil, sprays the streets in front of the houses in 'downtown' Tuskegee to keep the dust down. Quite a modern innovation, don't you think?"

"God, how primitive," responded Pierpont. "Trading dust for the stench of toxic petroleum fumes! Why don't these hicks just pave these streets?"

"M-O-N-E-Y," spelled Dr. Heller aloud.

"You have to realize that Macon County, Alabama, has the lowest per capita income in the entire state of Alabama. Indeed, it has one of the lowest, if not *the* lowest, in the entire nation, and the population is over 90 percent colored."

"Yes, and it appears that the 10 percent white get the oil, and the 90 percent colored get the dust." responded Dr. Pierpont.

"Have patience, gentlemen," Dr. Heller said. "In just a few minutes, we'll enter the campus of the Tuskegee Institute. See those large brick buildings in the distance? Atlanta or Boston it's not, but I think you will be pleasantly surprised as we make our 'leap back into civilization,' as perhaps you would describe our adventure, Dr. Pierpont."

"It's about time," responded Dr. Pierpont. "I was beginning to think we had discovered an alternate route to the Congo!"

"The large, three-story brick building you see at the end of this drive is Cassedy Hall. It houses the administrative offices of Tuskegee Institute. Further down and to the right is the impressive Carnegie Library."

"Is that where the money to fund this ambitious undertaking came from? The wealthy industrialist Andrew Carnegie? This all looks beyond the capacity of the locals to finance, that's for sure!"

"In part Dr. Pierpont, but not exclusively. Thanks to the generosity of Andrew Carnegie and other very wealthy benefactors, the campus, with its many fine buildings you see before you, has become a reality. Guided, of course, by the very capable hands of George Washington Carver."

"Incredible," muttered Dr. Pierpont as Dr. Heller steered the Ford into staff parking at the entrance to Cassedy Hall.

"Where did all the bricks come from to build these buildings? Hauling them in from Atlanta or Montgomery must have been an incredible undertaking!"

"Actually, Dr. Pierpont, the students themselves built all the buildings you see…and with bricks from a kiln located right on campus! Quite an exemplary example of self-sufficiency, wouldn't you gentlemen agree?"

Nodding in the affirmative while exiting the now parked Ford, the men began dusting themselves off before walking up the steps to the main entrance of Cassedy Hall. Once inside, the tall ceilings and large ceiling fans provided a cooling respite from the heat of their journey.

"Have a seat there in the study," said Dr. Heller as he pointed to a door down the entrance hall. "I'll make our presence known, and after you gentlemen are properly introduced to the staff, we will go over to the clinic."

"I assume there is water and a restroom somewhere?" questioned one of the doctors.

"Men's room is down the hall and to the right. Hold off on the water while I try to locate some large glasses of iced tea with fresh mint. Wouldn't that hit the spot?"

Within minutes, Dr. Heller returned to the study accompanied by four colored gentlemen who comprised the current administrative hierarchy. As introductions were underway, a colored female student of the university entered the room carrying a silver serving tray holding large glasses of refreshing-looking iced tea.

Dr. Pierpont remarked that since this life-supporting sustenance had been provided, he felt he would be able to survive at least another twenty-four hours. With that timely interjection of levity, the men thanked their hosts and hostess for their hospitality and adjourned for the clinic.

This was Dr. Pierpont's first trip to Alabama to observe what his superiors at the Public Health Service (PHS) in Washington had labeled "The Tuskegee Syphilis Experiments." Silently hoping this trip would be his last, he nevertheless sought to satisfy his curiosity, which had been steadily building since he first became aware of the experiments dubbed "a necessary evil to ultimately benefit mankind."

He was no stranger to the centuries-old scourge of mankind known as syphilis. "The Great Imitator," as it was known throughout the medical profession, had an uncanny ability to mimic many other diseases. As an infectious disease specialist, Dr. Pierpont had encountered the disease on numerous occasions throughout his residency at Harvard. Now largely preventable and easily curable in its early stages with the advent of the miracle drug penicillin, he had often wondered why Dr. Heller, the director of the syphilis experiments at PHS since 1943, had allowed the program to continue.

Bureaucratic boondoggle, he thought. *End the program and end the jobs and the income thereof…*

Maybe that's the answer.

But maybe not…too many unanswered questions remain for that pat answer to satisfy all the circumstances surrounding this program.

Greeting the doctors at the clinic was a smiling, colored lady, Nurse Rivers, who welcomed them enthusiastically and graciously offered her assistance should her services be required. Upon entering the clinic proper, Dr. Pierpont was struck by the incongruity of Nurse Rivers' smile as it contrasted sharply with the scene of misery, despair, and suffering unfolding before him. In that clinic were forty-two very ill Negro patients in varying stages of syphilitic deterioration…their bodies ravaged by the growth and dissemination of the causative germ, the bacteria known as a spirochete.

My God! thought Dr. Pierpont. *I didn't expect this! How many cases did I see as a resident? Two or three a year? This is an epidemic! I had no idea!*

As he and the other doctors began moving throughout the clinic to begin their exams, the scene that unfolded before them was as pitiful and tragic as it had been every month and every year since the experiment's inception in 1932. Most of the men were abysmally poor, ignorant Negro sharecroppers. Some were obviously dying; others wishing they were. Most were lying on cots, although some were sitting and some were feebly attempting to walk about with the classic, unsteady stumbling gait of syphilis known as ataxia. As the doctors began their examinations, the pleas for medicine to ease the pain and suffering became almost a din.

"Missa doc," began one patient obviously too weak to stand as he reached out for Dr. Heller's hand.

"I'se beese hurtin' sump'n bad an' I'se can't walk no mo'. Ain't yo got sum' mo' dem pills yo gimme one time?"

Another equally desperate patient asked Dr. Pierpont to "gimme sumptin so's I'se won't have the bad blood no mo'!"

Dr. Pierpont knew that the darkies were never told the true source of their sickness…only that they were suffering from a mysterious malady known as "Bad Blood." Treatments such as penicillin, which may have proved beneficial, were deliberately withheld from the patients. Instead, worthless placebos including sugar-flavored water were provided with the occasional aspirin. And all at the direction of the PHS superiors in Washington. Indeed, the purpose of these experiments was stated as a "long-term study of the effects of untreated syphilis on the human body."

Pondering what he already knew about this program while observing the ghastly scene before him, Dr. Pierpont's thoughts began waxing cynical and critical.

These wretches, these dregs of society, are little more than human guinea pigs in the eyes of the PHS and the CDC, he thought, *they are to be used until they die for the study and research of untreated, long-term, late stage tertiary syphilis! Of course beneficial treatments are withheld! How else to study this incredibly insidious disease to its inevitable fulminant conclusion? Penicillin would only interrupt and abort the progression of the disease. For whatever reason or reasons, our superiors don't give a tinker's damn about these primitive surrogates for a human being anyway. To their way of thinking, the world, even this shit hole called Alabama, would be a better place without them.*

Adjourning to the Carnegie Library at the completion of their examinations, the doctors began reviewing the charts of the patients' histories and compared them with their current findings. Obvious to all was the slow, inexorable progression of the disease as the months and years had ticked by. From the pool of patients in the clinics, every conceivable symptom and manifestation of syphilis had been observed. The ones rendered little more than breathing vegetables by the expanding brain lesions rotting away their minds…those with advanced cardiac involvement including congestive heart failure and the ubiquitous expanding aortic aneurysms…those with the inevitable central nervous system involvement of tertiary syphilis…some so far advanced the victims are unable to walk. They were all there in one single clinic…a veritable treasure trove of classic textbook examples.

Dr. Pierpont wondered if the cure for syphilis, penicillin, now so readily available, would be of any benefit to the victims with far advanced cases.

Probably not, he reasoned. *Too much damage already done. But at least it would stop the progression of the disease and perhaps provide some palliative relief. What about the several hundreds of additional syphilitics from Macon County Dr. Heller mentioned that were followed on a more or less regular monthly basis? Those that will report in, that is. Sure penicillin would help, maybe even totally cure, a large percentage of them. But somehow, I'm beginning to think the curing of indigent, dirt poor Negro sharecroppers is not the government's objective in these experiments. Even if the decision were made to begin penicillin treatments, what would be the incentive to encourage darkies to come in for treatment? Hell, I've heard that not even the promised $50 burial stipend is sufficient to ensure a high percentage of compliance for their monthly follow-up visits. Well, no damn wonder…who could blame them? I'm sure the news of those painful spinal taps probably spread like wildfire among the darkies!*

With every question my mind formulates, another surfaces. It's like I've got a diabolical Medusa inside my head producing questions instead of snakes. Or maybe the questions really are snakes but in disguise. I just don't know anymore! Why doesn't the government shut these macabre experiments down and stop this insanity? Why in the hell do we need to continue research into what we already know and understand? Do monthly exams and autopsy reports add one iota to the wealth of knowledge already accumulated about this disease? And what to make of this seemingly insatiable appetite the PHS and the CDC have for blood and spinal fluid samples and detailed autopsy reports? Hell, these experiments have been going on for twelve years now when they should have been terminated immediately after the development of penicillin! It all looks pretty damn simple to me…once the syphilis spirochete enters the bloodstream, it rapidly multiplies and disseminates throughout the body into every nook and cranny. Eventually, every organ is affected, and the victim endures a living hell until he or she mercifully dies. The lucky, more fortunate ones escape the nightmare of their unmitigated daily horror by dying of some other cause before the syphilis germ can complete its insidious destruction. How hard is all of that to understand? Whatever, one thing is for certain…damn certain! After this trip, I won't be coming back to this God forsaken part of America — ever! And as soon as I can find an opening somewhere in the vicinity of Boston, in private practice or teaching at a university, I'll be leaving the PHS. I had no choice at the time, but now that the damn war is finally over, opportunities will soon be opening up. At least the PHS stint beat the hell out of dying on some beach in Normandy!

New London, Connecticut

Friday, July 3, 20__

For the first time in a very long time, retired Colonel Gordon McClain was once again donning the full dress military uniform he had so proudly worn on the many special occasions throughout his illustrious career. Staring at his reflection in the full-length mirror, he was again starkly reminded of his debilitated condition by the appearance of the now oversized uniform hanging loosely from his gaunt, frail body.

"God, just give me the strength," he mumbled softly as he slowly moved about, obviously weak and in considerable pain.

Tomorrow is America's birthday, he thought. *And for all of my adult life, I have defended her from her enemies. Obviously, it was my destiny from birth. Why should today be any different?*

Colonel McClain was alone now since the divorce, the single occupant of a spacious, upper-middle-class home situated on three acres of wooded, beautifully landscaped property on the coast of Connecticut. From the large bay window of his tastefully decorated den and study, one could enjoy a spectacular view of Long Island Sound. The den walls were finished in rich oak paneling and were adorned with framed photographs and awards which chronicled the life of America's most celebrated living war hero.

Slowly looking around the room, Colonel McClain studied each photograph and each award for a moment before setting his gaze upon the next. From Richard Nixon to the present, he had been photographed with every president of the United States as well as many foreign leaders and dignitaries. Awards, medals, ribbons, and commendations filled a portion of one wall and included citations from England, France, Germany, Spain, Japan, and several other nations, each recognizing and expressing appreciation for his contributions to their governments.

THE POISON PLUM

His most cherished award, however, was the highest ever given by the United States of America—the Congressional Medal of Honor.

Vividly contrasting with the memories and mementos of a formerly robust and vigorously active lifestyle were the recent additions to the den. They brought sadness to the heart of Colonel McClain as the incongruity of their presence boldly reasserted itself. In one corner were the frequently used wheelchair and crutches. Nearby was the aluminum pole used to support plastic bags of fluids for intravenous infusions. On the large desk were dozens of bottles of prescription medications, vitamins, minerals, and herbal preparations. And the books…not of great battles waged by the brave men and generals of a bygone era, but instead there were dozens and dozens of medical books, as if the colonel was a doctor instead of a soldier. Indeed, one portion of that room represented a shrine, a living testimony, to a very brave man. The other portion, the incongruous portion, resembled the sick bay of a hospital.

"It's time," he spoke softly, as he took one last look around the room he had once enjoyed so much in the early years of his retirement. From a large, ornately adorned gun cabinet, a gift from the former president of Taiwan, the colonel removed his two favorite firearms. One, a gold inlaid Colt .45 automatic pistol, a gift from the Colt Firearms Company; and the other, a service issue M-14 rifle in .308 caliber, capable of full automatic fire. Pressing the thumb release on the frame of the pistol to release the clip, the colonel then removed a single cartridge from a box of fifty and loaded it into the clip. After reinserting the clip, he chambered the round before lowering the hammer to the part-cock safety position. The colonel's movements to the casual observer would have appeared almost mechanical because of his lifelong training and familiarity with the operation, handling, and functioning of each firearm.

Colonel McClain then removed a pistol belt and holster from the cabinet and a zippered bag containing ten 20-round clips for the M-14 preloaded with .308 cartridges. Slowly and with difficulty, the Colonel managed to place all of these items into the trunk of his car before beginning the short drive to the nearby ferry landing at New London. The time was 4:45 PM. He knew that at precisely 5 PM, the doctors, scientists, and other employees of the government's biological research facility on Plum Island would board the ferry for the ride to the mainland and the beginning of their July 4th holiday weekend.

Plum Island, New York

At the Animal Disease Research Center on Plum Island, formerly operated under the auspices of the United States Department of Agriculture, the employees were preparing to leave for the holiday weekend. As they began the short walk to the ferry for the ten-mile ride to the mainland, the prevailing mood was lighthearted and jovial. There was banter among them about their plans for the weekend…family cookouts, outdoor activities; short trips, ball games, and sleeping in seemed to dominate most everyone's list of priorities and discussion. Promptly at 5 PM, all the doctors, scientists, research assistants, and clerical workers responsible for the day-to-day operations of the lab at Plum Island boarded the ferry bound for the mainland. All but one however, for absent that day was Susan Collins, a single parent who had missed work again to take her sick son, Toby, to the doctors for more tests.

Colonel McClain sat quietly in his automobile at the ferry landing watching intently for any sign of movement in the direction of Plum Island. Shortly after 5 PM, he could begin to see the emerging, unmistakable outline of the approaching ferry. Moving like a very old man and with considerable difficulty, Colonel McClain managed to get out of his car and then removed the weapons from the trunk. Stepping to an outgrowth of vegetation nearby to remain unseen, he strapped on the holster with the Colt .45 and then loaded the first full clip into the M-14 rifle. After chambering the first round, he moved the fire selector switch to the full-auto position. Positioning himself so as to have a clear view of the parking lot and the ferry landing, he then dropped to his knees, a tear streaming down his cheek, as he softly began praying to God, begging for forgiveness for what he was about to do.

As the ferry docked and the employees disembarked, laughing and chatting, obviously looking forward to the festive weekend, Colonel McClain suddenly appeared about fifty feet in front of them, standing at full attention in his military dress uniform with the M-14 at parade rest. As the approaching employees noticed him, many at first thought he must be part of some patriotic holiday celebration or award ceremony. A few even began joking, asking aloud if the local VFW chapter had sent a war-grizzled veteran to welcome them back home for the Fourth of July.

Then, in one smooth fluid motion belying his physical condition, Colonel McClain suddenly shouldered the fully loaded M-14 rifle and began the systematic slaughter of the unsuspecting human beings before him. As rapidly as one clip was expended, another was smoothly inserted and the fusillade continued. At such a short range, the seemingly unceasing volley of bullets ripped through the startled targets shattering their bones and shredding their flesh while nearly cutting in half some and dismembering others. After what seemed an eternity, all was again quiet. Eighty-six people lay in a blood-soaked parking lot, either dead or critically wounded. Colonel McClain dropped the M-14 rifle with its smoking barrel to the ground and stood quietly for a few moments, sadly observing the carnage lying before him. Then, withdrawing the Colt .45 pistol from its holster, he placed the barrel to his temple, cocked the hammer, and pulled the trigger.

The Visitors

Susan Collins thought that Friday was one of the worst days of her life. She had spent the entire day in doctors' offices reviewing her son Toby's test results, listening to the doctors' opinions, submitting Toby to even more tests, and becoming even more frustrated. It was becoming increasingly evident that the doctors did not have a clue what was wrong with Toby. Today it was even recommended that Susan seek out a child psychiatrist for Toby. Over the past three months, Toby had been seen by Susan's family practice doctor who had, in turn, referred him to an internal medicine doctor who, in turn, referred him to a cardiologist, neurologist, and rheumatologist, in that order. The irregular heartbeats did not seem to concern the cardiologist. The slightly elevated liver enzymes and positive antinuclear antibody test did not concern the other specialists, and Toby was pronounced basically healthy. At only eight years of age, Toby was sick and getting sicker, and Susan could definitely tell something was wrong. As a mother, she knew it, too…that intuition that all mothers have. No, Toby's problem wasn't mental–it was something else…it was serious, and she was not going to stop until she had an answer. Susan was now becoming frightened and tired. The day had been exhausting, mentally and physically. The doctors' questions about her family life—did Toby start complaining about not feeling well after the divorce? Was she under a lot of stress at work, and was Toby sensing that stress? How was he doing at school? Did he "fit in" with the other children? Just reviewing Toby's symptom list with the doctors had left her drained. The list of symptoms seemed to grow larger and more bizarre with each visit to their offices. She even wondered if they sometimes thought she was crazy.

And if it seemed the day could not get any worse, it did. As Susan and Toby were leaving Toby's last appointment at the Children's Pediatric Center, she found herself and Toby in the middle of a monster traffic jam. She had never seen so many police cars, ambulances, and emergency vehicles in her life. All were rushing full speed in the same direction.

Just dandy, she thought, *I want to put Toby to bed, and I need a hot bath and a stiff drink. This traffic mess will mean at least another hour of driving time. Probably another pileup on the interstate. The way people drive now, no wonder.*

Finally she turned the SUV into her driveway. It was now almost 7:00 PM. Susan took Toby in her arms and carried him into the house. He was weak and fatigued constantly now and complained a lot about headaches and pains in his muscles. The doctors had prescribed muscle relaxers and sleeping medications to help him sleep. As she walked toward the bathroom to get Toby's medications, she grabbed the TV remote and turned the set on, more from habit and seeking a distraction than actually wanting to be entertained. Susan was about to realize that this Friday was not one of her worst days after all…it was her luckiest! The news report coming from the TV was blaring and frantic—on the spot reporters obviously agitated, excited, and shocked. As the words seeped into Susan's already overloaded brain, she was almost paralyzed by their significance, and it was as if every last ounce of strength in her body had suddenly been sucked away.

What was it that they were saying? A crazed gunman had massacred dozens of scientists, doctors, and support staff at the Plum Island Ferry that afternoon? Sixty-one people were confirmed dead and another 25 were critically injured, most not expected to survive their massive injuries?

"My God in heaven," Susan exclaimed! Those bodies were her friends and her co-workers. Faces she saw every day at her work at the Animal Disease Research Center on Plum Island. Susan's face would have been among the slain that afternoon at the ferry landing had she not taken the day off to be with her son. A chill swept her body, and she had to sit down. With her mind racing, she thought, *Why? What kind of a world is this we are living in? What kind of a crazy would do such a thing? Why can't we get the guns out of the hands of these lunatics? My God, what now? What? What? What?*

Susan stared in shocked disbelief at the television as reporters told the story, as they knew it, over and over. The facilities' staff was coming in on the 5:00 PM ferry from Plum Island to begin their weekend time off. The massacre began as they were walking to their cars after leaving the ferry. The only uninjured were the operating personnel on the ferry. The assassin was as yet unidentified and had apparently taken his own life. Details were sketchy and no motive was suggested.

Susan looked down at her hands and saw she was still clutching Toby's medications. She stood and began walking to his bedroom as if in a daze, while trying to assign some purpose and direction to her movements. Suddenly, the insistent, forceful pounding that began at Susan's front door at that instant jolted her like a bolt of lightning. Her heart leapt in her chest and she froze in her tracks. The pounding, if anything became more insistent, and it seemed to shake the entire house. Was someone knocking to gain entry or pounding to take the door off its hinges?

"Who's there?" spoke Susan, her voice quivering.

"Police," came the reply, "Open the door now!"

Susan opened the door and six large men in dark suits quickly moved into the room. Two flashed badges with some kind of official looking identification, muttered something about government security, or something of the like, and the other four men started moving through Susan's home. She could hear dresser drawers being opened, closet doors opening and closing and what sounded like furniture being moved around.

"Sit down!" she was ordered.

"But what is this all about?" she began.

"Shut up and sit down! We are asking the questions here." replied one of the men.

And questions there were, rapid fire and incessant.

"Are you Susan Collins? Where were you today? Why were you not at work? How long had you planned to be off today?"

As she tried to answer she was constantly being rudely interrupted and asked the same questions over and over again.

"Who were you with today? Who are your closest friends? Do you live alone?"

And then came the most bizarre question of them all.

"How long have you known Colonel Gordon McClain?"

"Who?" she responded.

"Ms. Collins, we are going to thoroughly investigate what you have told us this evening. Provide us with a list of the doctors you claim to have seen today with your appointment times. The consequences for not being totally honest with our investigation will be very serious indeed. Do not attempt to leave the area. We will be in contact with you if we determine travel will be allowed for you."

THE POISON PLUM

With that they were gone, and the house was quiet once again but messy.

Susan did not know what to do next. Her head was spinning constantly. She heard Toby's whimpering from the bedroom which reminded her she was still clutching his medication.

"God, those men must have terrified poor Toby lying alone on his bed!" she spoke aloud as she saw the drawers on the floor, closet doors flung open, and clothes scattered all over.

What a mess! Rude, uncaring, faceless, nameless men on a mission!

Trying to pull herself together, Susan moved to Toby's bedside and tried to comfort the obviously frightened, crying, and sick little boy.

"Mommy...those men scared me!"

"It's OK now, sweetie. They're gone."

"What did they want, Mommy?"

"I don't know Toby...I don't know what they wanted."

"But why were they here? I'm scared!"

"It will be all right Toby. They are not going to come back. Some people Mommy works with were hurt this afternoon, that's all. Maybe they were trying to find out why they were hurt."

"I don't understand, Mommy. How were they hurt?"

"I don't understand either, sweetie. Let's try to get some sleep now. I know you're tired... you've had a very busy day, and it's time for your medicine."

Tonight Susan was very grateful for the sleeping medication Toby's doctors had prescribed. Within a few minutes after swallowing the pills, Toby was sleeping soundly, and she was alone with her thoughts. Although exhausted mentally and physically, Susan knew she had to call her sister Cathy and silently hoped that she had not seen or heard the news reports of the massacre.

After only a few rings, Cathy, obviously recognizing Susan's number on her caller ID, answered cheerfully.

"Well, it's about time you two gadabouts decided to check in! And may I inquire as to exactly how you have managed to fritter away the entire day without inviting yours truly to join in your frivolity? Please tell me the doctors finally figured out what minor childhood ailment Toby has, and you spent the rest of the afternoon celebrating the good news."

"Not exactly. Have you been asleep?"

"No. Of course not! I don't sleep in the daytime, you know that. I've been busy cleaning house and sewing. What did the doctors say?"

"You haven't heard the news?"

"What news? Are you and Toby in the news?"

"No, and that's the good news. The fact that we, well especially me, are not in the news is a very good thing. You don't know? For real?"

"Stop the drama, Sis…what are you trying to tell me?"

"Some kook with a gun was at the ferry landing this afternoon and shot all of the facility's personnel as they disembarked."

"You can't be serious!"

"As a heart attack!"

"Why? What is going on?"

"I don't have a clue! And to add to the mystery, I had some very rude visitors from the government after Toby and I returned. They searched the house and asked me a bunch of questions in a very threatening manner. Hell, I think they were trying to find out if I had something to do with what happened at the ferry. Scared little Toby big time, and I had to give him sleeping medication to get him calmed down. And no, the doctors don't have a clue either. A total waste of time…well, maybe not…at least I was not on that ferry this afternoon."

"Yikes, Sis! Is there anything I can do to help?"

"No, we are fine. Toby is asleep, and I plan to join him very shortly. But you might want to check out the news reports on TV. It's all they are talking about. I'll call you tomorrow."

"I'll turn on the television, and I'll come over in the morning to make sure you guys are OK. Call me if you need anything."

"OK, Sis. I love you."

Sleep did not come easily for Susan that night. The many questions, the killings, the rude, insensitive men…*Entirely too much had happened for one single day,* she thought. After tossing and turning for over an hour and unable to sleep, Susan finally got up and poured herself a strong drink—a very strong drink. Shortly, Susan welcomed the calming wave of serenity and relaxation provided by the alcohol, and sleep overcame her.

THE POISON PLUM

As the sound of a jangling telephone brought Susan back to consciousness very early that next morning, her first thought was, *God what a short night.* Other thoughts of the previous day's events started cascading through Susan's brain as she was answering the phone. An authoritarian male voice boomed in her ear…

"Are you Susan Collins?"

"Yes, who is this?" she replied.

"Ms. Collins, this is Victor Perloff with the Department of Homeland Security in Washington. You are aware of the tragedy involving our personnel at the ferry landing yesterday?" he asked.

"Yes," she replied. "Did the authorities determine a reason and identify the…"

"Ms. Collins," the authoritarian voice interrupted, "it is imperative you assist the personnel with our team from Washington and Ft. Detrick in securing the Plum Island facility. An automobile will be at your home in one hour at 7:00 AM to transport you under security to the ferry landing. A special watercraft will then transport you to the research facility where you will join our teams already on site. Will you be ready at 7:00 AM?"

"Yes," she replied somewhat hesitantly, "I will be ready." Then the phone went dead. Susan's mind was a tangled web of emotions as she rushed around trying to get everything together to leave for the ferry landing. Toby was still sleeping, and she did not want to disturb him. Insomnia was a big part of Toby's symptomatology, and Susan realized the importance of rest for his weakening body.

"Got to call Cathy and get her headed in this direction. I'll just let Toby sleep, and Cathy will be here by the time he wakes up."

"Sis… I know it's early, but I just got a call from my superiors. They need me at the lab pronto, and they are sending a car for me at 7. Can you come on over as soon as possible?"

"No problem. I was already awake actually. I didn't sleep very much after watching those news reports. I'll be right over."

As Susan ended the call to her sister and hurriedly resumed dressing, she began wondering to herself how she would be able to help once she arrived at the facility. She had been at Plum Island for less than a year now, and her work as a microbiologist was somewhat isolated and focused. She knew the facility participated in research into animal diseases and was publicly identified with efforts to control and eradicate diseases such as hoof-and-mouth disease, which can decimate cattle populations. Recent problems with that disease in Europe have chillingly illustrated the vulnerability of a nation's farm-related economy and food supply. Even more chilling were the reports concerning another cattle-related disease with fatal implications for humans. BSE, or bovine spongiform encephalopathy, is a disease which damages the brains of its victims—punching holes in the brain tissues until a Swiss cheese appearance develops, and the patient dies. Exactly how many kinds of diseases were being researched at Plum Island, Susan had no idea. After all, security was a priority there, and a certain amount of hush-hush mentality was evident among her co-workers. *Well, her former co-workers*, she thought. The doorbell rang as she was trying to sort through those thoughts and others that were racing through her mind. The dark suit at the door presented Homeland Security credentials, and she was escorted to a waiting car just as Cathy was pulling into the driveway. *Perfect timing*, she thought and promised to herself to do something really nice for Cathy when all this settled down and Toby was, once again, back to his usual self.

Damage Control

The Pentagon—Washington, D.C.

The before dawn meeting that Saturday morning in the Pentagon was very, very hastily arranged and very urgent. The news of the Plum Island massacre had ripped through the nation's intelligence community like a hot knife through butter. Those in attendance were obviously upset, and the least of their concerns was the interruption of their holiday. They were all there; the top brass, upper-echelon management, doctors, biologists, virologists, and others representing the CIA, the Pentagon, Ft. Detrick, Ft. Collins, the CDC, the FBI's CNB Division, the Department of Homeland Security, and others. They were flown in as expeditiously as possible by government jets and helicopters from their homes and offices. Attempting to coordinate everything were several CIA personnel acting in liaison with the Pentagon brass privy to the inner workings and objectives of the bio-labs.

A review of the actual events with media film coverage was first on the agenda. Next, identification and discussion of the shooter. Most of those in the room needed little introduction to Colonel Gordon McClain. He was the very embodiment and personification of the all-American hero. He was well liked and respected by the military, the executive branch, the media, members of Congress, and the general public. He had a distinguished and impeccable career as a military officer spanning over four decades. There was no dirt or scandal in this guy's career. No Kennedy or Clinton here. Colonel McClain was a true, proud American representing all that is good and decent about America with no apology. God, family, and country...motherhood, baseball, and apple pie.

"The media is going to have a field day with this," boomed General Helms of the Pentagon. "Damage control is our number one priority until this thing blows over. Security at the remaining facilities is secondary. I have ordered all facilities armed to the teeth, and not even a gnat will be on premises without our knowledge."

CIA Director Steele moved to the podium with a thick sheath of documents under his arm. The assumption that everything that could be known about Colonel McClain was contained in the documents was correct. The assumption that the CIA already had an opinion as to "why" was also correct. Director Steele began.

"Colonel McClain was a sick man. Whether or not we will be able to use that information for damage control is highly debatable. We may add fuel to the flames. What is not widely known is that Colonel McClain became ill in 1996 shortly after moving to the Connecticut coast when he began semi-retirement. He presented with a bizarre array of symptoms, which included fatigue, paresthesias, meningitis, encephalitis, multiple neuropathies, focal myocarditis, heart block, mental confusion, weight loss, and muscle wasting. No, my memory is not that inclusive. Obviously, I am scanning the examining physician's notes from Bethesda. Colonel McClain left there in October of 1996 without a definitive diagnosis and was placed on prescription antidepressants and mood enhancers. After seeing about a dozen specialists, which included cardiologists, rheumatologists, neurologists, internal medicine, and infectious disease specialists, somebody ran a Lyme disease test on him, and it came back positive. He was immediately placed on powerful intravenous antibiotics. The guy should have died because the average person would have. But Colonel McClain was no average person; he was tough as nails and in superb physical condition at the time the illness began. He got better on the antibiotic protocol, but it didn't cure him. The doctors kept switching his antibiotics, trying to find something that would continue to work, but, of course, nothing did. And we all know why. The doctors and scientists that continued to develop the initial spirochetal research done at Tuskegee know what a splendid job of genetic engineering they have accomplished by developing a germ that can evade detection by antibiotics and the body's own immune system. An almost perfect biological weapon! And as we are all aware, the disease is capable of crippling and destroying not only human beings but a nation's infrastructure of health care and insurance services.

"Naturally, for Colonel McClain, deep depression set in. His wife left him, and for the last few years he lived, or more appropriately, existed, in his situation as a recluse. He avoided all media and all but the closest personal friends, to whom he was able to confide how ironic it was to have survived some of the most ferocious battles of several wars and conflicts only to find out he was struck down by an enemy he couldn't even see. How Colonel McClain made the connection between our facility at Plum Island and his Lyme infection is anyone's guess. The only employee not at work yesterday turned out to be an innocuous low-level recent hire with no connection to Colonel McClain and no connection to any of the areas of spirochetal research. She was assigned to the study of bat droppings removed from Carlsbad Caverns."

A few chuckles across the meeting room gave a momentary air of relief to an exquisitely sensitive and delicate discussion.

"Well, maybe not bat droppings, but something equally mundane, I can assure you. New hires are kept isolated for months, even years, and the big picture is never revealed, not even to most department heads. We are convinced the new hire was not the connection. And equally implausible would be any kind of connection to a member of the spirochetal team. Every single individual of that group was killed on the spot at the ferry landing. No, we think the link was something even more potentially dangerous to our work. Most likely, the link that provided Colonel McClain with some of the details of the activities at Plum Island was one or more of those damned ubiquitous Internet-linked Lyme disease support groups. The average person entering their chat rooms would most likely equate their paranoid ramblings with those sites devoted to UFO's, alien abductions, conspiracies, government cover-ups, and so on. The problem is, the longer one is sick with Lyme disease, the more desperate he or she becomes for answers. Why are they still sick after so much aggressive therapy? And these are the 'lucky ones'…the ones that have found doctors that refuse to give up trying to find something to help their patients. Frustration is the order of the day for those people. They feel alone and isolated and are willing to listen to almost anything that comes from another 'Lymie' or a 'Lyme literate medical doctor', an 'LLMD', as they are affectionately known among the Lyme community.

"We know that Colonel McClain was the chairman of a local support group until about six months ago, when he finally became too sick to continue. He probably had only a few weeks or months to live at the most when he blew out his brains at the ferry landing yesterday afternoon.

"Gentlemen, we have to leave this meeting today with some kind of viable damage control plan we can begin to implement immediately. We already have a few ideas at CIA, but I'll relinquish the podium to those of you who have already given consideration to plans of your own. Let's hear what everybody is thinking, and we'll wrap up it up with a distillation of all that is offered, and we will begin to take action immediately. General Helms will return to the podium now with thoughts derived from their years of media control at the Pentagon, necessitated by 'sometimes' publicly unpopular military activities and situations. General Helms…"

"Thank you, Director Steele. The situation before us this morning is both urgent and critical. As everyone in this room today clearly understands, we simply must not allow elements of the media to make a connection between Colonel McClain's Lyme infection and our biological research facility at Plum Island or any of our other facilities. We must expand our defense of Plum Island with an increase of our public relations work in the media and Internet. The portrayal of the facility as an Animal Disease Research Center that has been under the auspices of the USDA since 1954 must be communicated to the public. For decades we have been protecting livestock, cattle, and poultry in the nation's farms from diseases. Stress our efforts to shield our livestock from mad cow disease. Increase visitors' information and public-relation tours of *some* areas of the facility. Name some attractive middle-aged woman, a Martha Stewart type, to smile and be the director. The public must regard Plum Island as a facility devoted to the identification and eradication of diseases that affect the animal kingdom. *Animals not humans!*

"If the subject of Colonel McClain's battle with Lyme disease surfaces, make certain that his accredited primary physicians at Bethesda are unanimous in their affirmation that Colonel McClain was quickly cleared of any Lyme infection after appropriate antibiotic therapy. If he was seeing any other physicians seeking a cure subsequent to his initial treatments at Bethesda, those physicians shall be identified and discredited as quacks. Any lingering physical problems Colonel McClain may have been experiencing were certainly of psychosomatic origin, no doubt due to delayed post-traumatic stress syndrome complicated by his divorce. Trot out as many shrinks as might be required to cast doubt in people's minds. At this point, deny, deny, deny, ridicule, ridicule, and ridicule. Suppress any attempts at legitimate inquiry and label as conspiracy nuts those who try to make a connection. Do not acknowledge or refute any outlandish claims that may surface. Do not dignify the accuser with the courtesy of a reply.

"This is a tragic event in our nation's history. Colonel McClain shall be portrayed as a great American, one who gave so much for the nation he so loved. Such a tragedy.... We do not foresee any problems with the major media because they will be content to report for days on the human tragedy aspect of the event. Surviving family members, grieving husbands, wives, and children...we remember Charles, and so on. Interview after interview until everyone is sufficiently numbed into accepting that we just need to shut up and move on with our lives. The fringe media, supermarket tabloids, some late-night talk shows and Internet chat rooms will be a circus, we are certain. Plant even more ridiculous bits and pieces of erroneous information to muddy the waters, such as; alien mind control experiments, Plum Island is really a government-controlled portal to another dimension of lizard-like creatures, hence animal disease research, and so on, ad infinitum.

"Gentlemen, I think you get the idea, and should you all concur with our proposals, we at the Pentagon will begin swiftly moving in the directions I have outlined here. Today we also have representatives of the FBI's Chemical, Biological, and Nuclear Division present. I'll turn the podium over to Director Frey now."

"Thank you, General Helms. We at the bureau are of the opinion that we should not only discredit but move to arrest and shut down the Lyme literate medical doctors and also the alternative medicine practitioners that may be involved with the Lyme community. Anticipating a growing cohesiveness and political activation among the Lyme support groups, we have for months now stressed the importance of the various states' medical review boards' investigations into these doctors' practices. Where possible, charge them with 'over treatment' of Lyme patients. Seize their patients' files, effectively shutting down their practices, and find something, anything, to use as justification, for a formal review. These inquisitions can drag on for months or even years, and attorney's fees will force the physicians out of practice. Revoke licenses where appropriate and in those situations where the alternative medicine practitioners might be providing non-FDA-approved treatment protocols or modalities, have them arrested and jailed if possible.

"Those people are the problem, preying on innocent patients and spreading lies, which lead to paranoid delusions, which could possibly manifest in an event like what occurred today. We will dramatically increase our raids in conjunction with FDA personnel, and, of course, we will garner as much media exposure as possible. The media will be provided, in advance, the name of the doctor or doctor's involved, the office address, the time of the raid and a list of charges we will file. We will cite 'national security' in all instances, providing the ominous suggestion that this or that doctor was somehow involved in the massacre. 9/11 has provided us with the mandate to do whatever we please with no questions asked. A television report of doctors and their staff being led away in handcuffs while our agents tote out boxes and boxes of files will speak volumes to the viewers."

"Director Frey?" interrupted Kirkland of the CDC, "Should we involve the president in this?"

"Only to the extent that he makes public pronouncements to the citizenry proclaiming what a great American and dedicated patriot Colonel McClain was. Besides, he is in Europe as we speak, trying to pull the dollar out of the toilet before the international bankers pull the lever and flush it. His knowledge and understanding of the programs and agendas of the bio-labs is on par with his understanding of international finance… if your minds can conceptualize that. I say we hope this all calms down and blows over before he gets back…. It's best to let a sleeping dog lie."

Back to Work

The scene at Plum Island was chaotic. Officials from other bio-labs were scurrying about trying to figure out what experiments were in progress, reviewing employee notes, computer files, and lab results. The remaining survivors were in intensive care and certainly in no condition to explain their past work. Scientists and microbiologists to replace the slain personnel were being flown in as soon as possible from other facilities, including Ft. Detrick, Maryland; Ft. Collins, Colorado; and the Centers for Disease Control in Atlanta.

Susan's knowledge of the lab's operating procedures was limited to her work only, and as a consequence she lacked a comprehensive overview of the facility. Not knowing what else to do, she basically whiled the time away puttering about while awaiting direction from her superiors. About midmorning, Susan was surprised by the ringing of her desk telephone. Expecting instructions from higher ups, she instead heard Cathy's excited voice on the line.

"They didn't want to let me talk to you, Susan. I've been trying to get through to you for at least ten minutes…they asked me every question under the sun, trying to screen this call. I never had this much trouble before!"

"It's the security thing, probably…this place looks like an anthill somebody stepped on. Anyway, what's up?"

"Dr. Butler called. He said he had some news about Toby, and he wants you to call him."

"He's working on a holiday? It must be urgent! Did he say what?"

"Nope. Just said to call. Maybe you are about to get some answers."

"I'm all over it…thanks. I'll talk to you later."

Time to bypass that switchboard, thought Susan as she nervously reached into her purse for her cell phone. Moments later she was paging Dr. Butler on the number he had provided Cathy and was surprised when he answered immediately.

"Dr. Butler, this is Susan Collins. Thank you for calling. I hope you have some good news for Toby and me."

"Well, Susan, the tests we have done on Toby are still inconclusive at this point. The only test slightly abnormal turned out to be the test we ran for Lyme disease. It is probably nothing to be concerned about because the tests for Lyme are notoriously inaccurate anyway. But just to be on the safe side, I am going to refer Toby to Dr. Carlos Aventi, the head of the Infectious Disease Department at the Medical Center who is a recognized infectious disease specialist."

Susan's mind overloaded as she thanked Dr. Butler and began trying to sort through this latest news.

If it's nothing to be concerned about, she thought, *why is Dr. Butler working on a holiday trying to set up an appointment with a specialist? And anyway, what the heck do I remember about Lyme disease? Let's see now...it's a bacterial infection spread by an insect bite, it's endemic to the northeastern United States, and it was named after a small town on the coast of Connecticut.*

That would all make sense, she thought, *because Toby loved being outside and playing in the woods. And after all, Lyme, Connecticut, is only about ten miles away from our home in New London.*

Before leaving work that afternoon she appropriated a few moments for herself to access a computer database of medical information to review the symptoms and treatment for Lyme disease. She seemed to recall that the vector was a tick, and symptoms were primarily arthritic in nature, with fatigue.

Well, that might be part of Toby's problem, she thought, but she certainly did not think Lyme could be responsible for all that was going on with Toby. *Oh well, at least it was a place to start and, to date, the only significantly abnormal test result.* A cursory review of the database reminded Susan of other symptoms that could be associated with Lyme disease, but she was relieved to discover that even in advanced disseminated cases, two or three weeks of antibiotic therapy would eradicate the disease. *Oh well,* she thought, *a minor insect bite, nothing to worry about.*

A quick call to Cathy from her cell phone was in order to let her know what Dr. Butler had said and that she planned to be home at the regular time. Cathy answered promptly and said Dr. Butler had called back, and due to an unexpected cancellation, Dr. Aventi would be able to see Toby sooner than anticipated...Thursday at 8:00 AM to be precise at the Medical Center.

Great, thought Susan as she ended the call to her sister. *Finally we will get some answers. The Medical Center is also a teaching hospital and is world renowned for their cutting-edge medical research and treatments. The type of facility patients are finally referred to when the usual round robin of previous referrals and tests bog down with no definitive answers for the patients or the doctors.* Thursday couldn't come too soon for Susan.

Susan arrived home about 6:30 PM, mentally fatigued from the confusion and turmoil at work and the incessant uncertainty and worry over Toby's condition. Cathy greeted Susan with the usual warm hug and kiss on the cheek.

"How is Toby?" asked Susan as she started down the hall to his bedroom.

"He's sleeping now, thank goodness, but he complained today about hurting in his arms and legs and said his eyes hurt too. I took his temperature about 4:00 PM, and he had a low-grade fever. I gave him some children's aspirin and he shortly dropped off to sleep."

"Did he feel like playing or anything today?"

"Nope, he would just lie around and watch a little television, and said he was tired. It wasn't easy finding any children's programs for Toby. The media is devoting a lot of time to what happened at the ferry yesterday. Every news program is full of it, specials are popping up, and even the talk shows are buzzing with all kinds of speculation. For goodness sake, the president is scheduled to address the nation this evening. We are constantly being reassured that it was not a terrorist attack, but what was it? And why? Everybody wants answers, but there don't seem to be any. I guess the biggest question everyone seems to be asking is, 'Why would a man of Colonel McClain's reputation and stature do such a thing?'"

Susan was struggling to take her next breath.

"What did you say?"

"What do you mean?" replied Cathy. "Haven't you heard a word I've been saying? I've been trying to explain how difficult it was to find something for Toby to watch on television today."

"No, that is not what I meant. Colonel who?"

"Oh, I thought you knew. Colonel Gordon McClain was identified as the shooter. He was a big-shot career military guy, connected to the brass at the Pentagon and every president since Nixon it seems. The guy was a national hero with a spotless reputation. Surely you've heard of him, haven't you?"

Susan felt numb all over. Colonel McClain was the name the intruders asked her if she knew. *Was this all a bad dream?* she thought. *Will I awaken tomorrow in some mental institution?*

The rest of the evening was a blur. Susan just wanted to sleep. Thank God she did not have to return to the facility until Monday morning. Maybe tomorrow she could try to explain to Cathy what had happened in the last forty-eight hours but not tonight. Susan was mentally and emotionally spent. Sleep was the only thing on her mind.

A Seed Is Planted

Susan had hoped to be able to sleep in that Sunday morning to give her mind and body the rest that was so well deserved and required after the gut-wrenching events of the last several days. The bright Connecticut morning sun filtering through her bedroom windows, and the moaning and whimpering from Toby's bedroom brought Susan quickly to alert status much sooner than she would have desired. Upon entering Toby's room, she immediately encountered a pungent sweet odor that bordered on nauseating.

Now what? she thought and moved to open the windows for much-needed fresh air. As she hugged Toby to her, he felt feverish, and his pajamas and bed covers were wet from perspiration. Toby seemed half awake and half asleep at the same time. Susan managed to get him to his feet and gave him a bath and some breakfast, and then she changed out the bed covers. A check of his temperature revealed only a slight fever of 100.2, and he seemed a little better after the food and some juice. Susan tried to get Toby to watch some TV, but he said his eyes hurt and he just wanted to lie in the bed.

Oh, will Thursday ever come? Susan thought. *If I can just get Dr. Aventi at the Medical Center to examine Toby, I know we'll get some answers.*

Susan had asked Dr. Butler if he would prescribe antibiotics for Toby since the Lyme test had come back slightly positive. His response to her was prudent, explaining that injudicious use of antibiotics without confirmatory test results could do more harm than good. After all, he explained, the reason we are now experiencing so many drug-resistant strains of bacteria is because doctors have over-prescribed antibiotics for years, allowing bacteria to mutate to avoid destruction by the antibiotics. "Let's be on the safe side," he had stressed, "and if Dr. Aventi thinks antibiotics are warranted, well, we'll go from there." That all made sense at the time, but now she was beginning to wonder. Toby seemed to sink to a new, lower level every few days, and when she felt the rapid heartbeat and the pounding of Toby's heart in his chest, she knew that his little body was struggling to fight something…but what? The thought of taking Toby to the emergency room again crossed her mind, but every time before when she had become frightened and concerned and had taken Toby in, the answers were always the same: "We have no answers."

No, we'll just have to tough it out until our appointment next Thursday morning and then… Her thoughts were interrupted by the ringing telephone, demanding her attention.

"Hello," she answered.

"Hi, Sis," greeted Cathy. "Hope you and Toby got some good rest last night, and you both are feeling better this beautiful morning."

"I wish we were, Cathy. Toby seems worse, if anything, this morning. I don't think he slept very well last night, and when I looked in on him this morning, he and the bed covers were drenched from his night sweats. And, Cathy, there was this really foul odor in his room…it's like some kind of toxins are seeping out of every pore in his skin. I couldn't get the windows open quickly enough for some fresh air. Between my worrying and the uncertainty about Toby's condition and all of the things that have been happening at work, I feel, in the vernacular of today's young people, my brain is just about fried out to the max."

"I know, Sis… you have really been through the wringer lately. I only wish I could be of more help to you."

"Oh, Cathy, you just don't know how much you have helped and how much I need and depend on you now. I don't know what Toby and I would have done if you had not been here to help out over these last several weeks."

"Thanks, Sis, and you know I'll continue to do what I can, and I want you to call me anytime I can help. In fact, one of the reasons I called today was to ask if I could come over after church this afternoon. I want to see Toby, of course, but there are some things I've learned that I want to share with you. I could pick us up some sandwiches from that little deli you and Toby like over on 12th Street, and you wouldn't have to cook anything for lunch. Would 1:30 be OK?"

"Sounds great, Cathy. We'll see you then."

Susan spent the next several hours sharing time with Toby and trying to get organized to return to the facility the next morning. More scientists, research directors, and government liaison personnel were expected in during the week. Much confusion surrounded the daily activities at Plum Island, and Susan was not certain if any single group or entity had the slightest idea exactly what needed to be done next to perpetuate or terminate the work already in progress.

Maybe we're just going to kill each other and everybody else on Long Island, the coast of Connecticut, and New York City by inadvertently leaking some mysterious pathogen into the atmosphere, she thought. Sometimes an eerie, chilling sensation would sweep her body when those thoughts began to surface. Part of Susan's brain, the scientific rational part, would remind her how foolish that kind of thinking was and sternly remind her, *There is nothing to worry about!* But a deeper, more intuitive, more primal portion of Susan's brain was trying to surface. An unidentifiable fear and concern seemingly becoming more urgent and demanding. Susan remembered her grandfather talking about how certain events or situations gave him the "creeps" and made the hair stand up on the back of his neck. *Colorful descriptions of potentially unpleasant circumstances,* she had thought at the time. And now, with similar emotions seeping more and more frequently into her consciousness, she began to wonder.

Grandfather always seemed to have an awareness about him…almost a sixth sense some called it. Many, many times he had warned about this, that, or the other, and the passage of time would see his concerns vindicated. She silently hoped that portion of the gene pool had skipped her generation, but more and more Susan felt herself being swayed by emotions that seemed to be struggling for release and recognition, coming from some very deep and very private part of her very soul. Maybe grandfather wasn't as eccentric as some had perceived after all.

Susan was glad Cathy was coming over because she needed the closeness that only a family member can provide in trying, confusing times. Little Toby loved Cathy, too, and they always enjoyed being with each other. She had that special way of making Toby laugh, and a laugh on Toby's face today would really brighten Susan's day too!

Cathy was her usual punctual self and arrived promptly at 1:30 with the delicious-smelling deli sandwiches. Toby had not had much of an appetite lately, but he perked up when Cathy walked in, even managing a smile as Cathy hugged him close. Susan knew Cathy had something on her mind that she felt was important to share, but she also knew that the events of their visit together that afternoon would follow a priority of order. Enjoying each other's companionship and the food together would be the first thing they would do. With, of course, special emphasis on and attention to Toby and his needs.

Prevailing was a refinement of order and protocol so indigenous of their Old South heritage that the pleasantries and expression of concerns for one another were required before any attempt at discussion or conversation of a more serious vein. And the more ominous and important the subject matter to be eventually discussed, tradition would have it that the pleasantries were to be extended as long as practicable. And implicit also was the importance of shielding from the young, sensitive ears of Toby any dialog that might in any way contribute to his ongoing unease and anxiety. After their meal together and the visiting with Toby, Cathy finally asked Susan if they could talk privately. Susan was curious and eager to find out what was on Cathy's mind, so after making certain Toby was comfortable, they went out to the small patio that Susan never seemed to have time to enjoy. Once comfortably out of earshot of Toby, Susan began.

"Cathy, I know you have something to tell me, and I can't wait to hear what it is."

"I do, Susan, but I'm not certain where to begin. I've heard and seen so much in the past several days, my mind is spinning. I guess I'll start by telling you that our Bible study group at church has been praying regularly for Toby. I know you and I don't always see eye to eye on spiritual matters, but girl, it looks to me like you can use all of the help you can get at this time."

"I agree with that, Cathy, and I appreciate you asking the members for prayer support. I just have a hard time understanding how the God of this universe has any time or concern for one little sick boy. I see sick and dying people all around us, and I never hear any stories of divine intervention and healing. I just don't believe…I'm sorry, Cathy. I didn't mean to get off on a tangent. Please continue with what you are going to tell me."

"No problem, Susan. I told you about the prayer group so you would understand better where my information is coming from. In my discussion of Toby's problems with the members, a few of the ladies said it sounded like Lyme disease to them. Each had a family member that was sick for a long time before doctors finally discovered that they were suffering from a Lyme infection. Each related how serious the illness was and described how bizarre and confusing the symptoms could be. Apparently the tests are not that specific, and a great deal of controversy exists regarding diagnosis and proper treatment."

"Well, you know that a test for Lyme was done on Toby, and it did come back slightly positive. But Dr. Butler was not overly concerned. I think if he felt there was any possibility Toby did have Lyme disease, he would prescribe antibiotics without any hesitation. Toby's symptoms just don't match up completely with the medical literature examples. And besides, on Thursday, Dr. Aventi, a leading infectious disease specialist at the Medical Center, will see Toby. I just know he'll quickly get to the bottom of this dilemma. If it is Lyme, he will start Toby on the proper antibiotics, and in just a few weeks Toby will be cured. All of this will quickly be fading to a distant memory—a mere bump on the road of my life. Soon, we will all be able to get back to our regular schedules."

Cathy paused for a moment, and Susan knew she was collecting her thoughts for what she was going to say next. Her facial expressions were becoming more serious, and it was very obvious Cathy was uncomfortable with the message she was on a mission to convey.

"Susan," Cathy began after a long pause, "You know I love Toby as if he were my own son. My heart is breaking having to see Toby so sick. And Susan, having to watch you struggle daily with Toby's illness and the problems at work is tearing me apart. I thought that when we moved here from Birmingham, it would mean a new start and a better life for all of us. Instead, it has meant nothing but suffering, uncertainty, and disappointment. I really have a bad feeling about all of this. I guess I've got some of grandfather's blood flowing through my veins. You remember how he was always talking about his 'feelings.' Well, I've got some of that going on in my mind right now."

Susan briefly thought, *How strange it is Cathy is also thinking about grandfather at this time!*

"I'm afraid things are going to get worse before they get any better. I know you're the family optimist, and I'm sorry I'm being such a wet blanket today. Lord knows I want to help you and Toby, and I'll do anything I can to support what you are trying to do. I knew I would do a lousy job of trying to explain why I wanted to see you today. My emotions always get in the way of what I'm trying to say."

"I understand Cathy, but please don't worry yourself so much about us, because everything will be fine. We just have to sort things out, that's all. Things will soon be back to normal at work, the loony tune Colonel McClain will be forgotten about when the media feeding frenzy runs out of fuel, and whatever is wrong with Toby will be identified, and he will be treated. With modern advancements in medical science, almost anything is possible. Cures, which would have been unthinkable only a decade ago, are now commonplace. Nothing miraculous about it, just plenty of intelligently guided research and proper application of scientific principles."

Cathy paused with her head slightly bowed before looking up and searching Susan's face with her eyes before continuing. Obviously agitated, Cathy began.

"Susan, this talk of Lyme disease is what is really beginning to spook me. I understand what you are telling me about the medical literature describing how easily it is treated and cured. I know that medicine and science are your world, and you understand and embrace their discipline. But Susan, what you are telling me about that disease, and what I'm hearing from family members of Lyme victims at church are stories that are light years apart. I'm not hearing about an infection that goes away after a few penicillin shots in the butt. I'm hearing horror stories that are chilling me to the bone. I am really frightened when I think that this might be happening to us. I know you don't want to listen to this, and I don't want to relate it, but please hear me out. Susan, one of the church members has an uncle that developed Lyme after being bitten by a tick on Long Island. He had the classic bull's eye rash, and the blood test came back positive. He was seen first by an internist who referred him to an infectious disease doctor in New York. He improved somewhat on oral antibiotics, but when central nervous system involvement materialized, he was treated with powerful intravenous antibiotics. I think he was having trouble walking and also concentrating. Anyway, the doctors pronounced him cured after a month of intravenous treatments, and he was discharged. That was about three years ago. After a few weeks of being off the intravenous treatments his symptoms began returning with a vengeance. The infectious disease doctor refused to treat him with any more antibiotics, emphasizing that the Lyme infection was cured, and any remaining problems were most likely psychosomatic. Antidepressants were prescribed. The reaction of his internist was basically the same, and counseling was recommended. Well, Mr. Davis, that is his name, continued to have problems and was unable to return to work full time. I think he worked for the telephone company and may have been bitten by a tick while working on telephone lines out on Long Island. After a year or more of frustration and no improvement, he started seeing a Lyme disease specialist right outside of New York. That doctor is very controversial but seems to be helping a lot of his patients. He immediately put Mr. Davis back on a combination of IV antibiotics and also a mixture of vitamins, herbs, minerals, and some other alternative treatments. He also tested Mr. Davis for any co-infections he might have from the tick bite. It seems those ticks can be pretty nasty critters and can carry several other infections besides Lyme. Mr. Davis was diagnosed with two other infections; one was cat scratch fever if you can believe that, and the other was some exotic-sounding disease I've never heard of. But, the doctor treated him for those diseases and the Lyme. Mr. Davis is much better now and has high praise for that doctor. Dr. Glen Klinner is his name, I think."

"I don't know, Cathy," Susan said. "All this stuff is really overloading my tiny little brain."

"Well, Mr. Davis is better now but not totally cured. He has good days and bad days. The financial strain has almost wrecked that family because all this has been going on for a little over three years. We've taken several collections for them at church. The other story was similar in origin but didn't turn out as well. Mrs. Studdard is in our Bible study group and her husband also had Lyme disease. Initially the doctors treated him with the usual antibiotics, but the treatments were a failure. When additional antibiotics were withheld by the doctors, and Susan, those doctors were at the Medical Center, poor old Mr. Studdard, well not that old, he was only 53, finally deteriorated to the point he just couldn't take it anymore and blew his brains out with a pistol he and his wife kept in the bedside table. His suicide note had all the usual apologies to God and family but also some gallows humor. He wrote that Smith and Wesson had developed a cure for Lyme disease! I pray to God, Susan, that Toby does not have Lyme disease and that nothing like any of this stuff I've been telling you about ever happens to him.

"Susan, as if those horror stories were not enough, there's more. Some of the people at church and also at the vitamin/nutrition center where I shop are talking about where you work at Plum Island. They are saying that there is a connection between Lyme disease and the facility at Plum. The first outbreak was in the mid 1970s just a few miles from here at Old Lyme. That is where the disease was first identified after children in that area developed symptoms of arthritis. They point out that it is only about ten miles across the sound from Old Lyme to Plum Island. These people may all be conspiracy nuts, for all I know, Susan, but one thing is for certain. They are all extremely concerned and even fearful of what may be going on out there. Susan, they are claiming, and with great sincerity and emotion, that Lyme is just one of many diseases that are being researched at Plum. And get this, they contend that Lyme is a genetically engineered disease that either leaked out of the facility or was deliberately leaked to determine its effects on the population. Instead of working to ensure the health and safety of humans and farm animals, the facility is actually working to develop pathogens to be used in biological warfare."

"Jeez, Cathy!" responded Susan, "That's a bunch of crap! That is the most ridiculous thing I've ever heard! I mean, I'm sorry they had all those problems and all, but, Cathy, they are just trying to find someone or something to blame for their terrible experiences. It's sad that out of their sorrow, ignorance, and despair they try to assign the blame to an animal disease research center! For goodness sake, Cathy, those scientists are dedicated to eradicating diseases—not the creation of more diseases to plague mankind!"

"That is all probably true, Susan, and I hope that it is. I don't like having to talk about these very unpleasant topics, and I do so only out of my love and concern for you and Toby. I didn't ask to hear any of this information from the people I told you about, but when they heard that Toby was possibly infected with Lyme their response was immediate and intense. I was taken aback by their fervor. They were obviously determined to tell me what they knew or thought they knew. Susan, I don't know what is going on. I don't have a clue. I do know that I have a bad, bad feeling about all of this. Color me a reincarnation of grandfather if you like, but I want you to be careful out there. Maybe Colonel McClain was looney tunes as the media is telling us but maybe, just maybe, he did not think that research at Plum was as innocuous as we are led to believe. Promise me you will be careful, Susan. A lot of people besides me are praying for you and Toby now."

It was after 5:00 PM when Cathy left that afternoon. Susan hugged her sister good-bye and thanked her for her support while simultaneously trying to reassure her that everything would indeed be fine. *The blind leading the blind,* Susan thought.

Toby had slept a little that quiet afternoon, which Susan was grateful for. She was able to devote her attention to Cathy's visit. This evening she would spend time with Toby and also prepare for her return to the facility tomorrow morning. As she almost-robot-like moved about with her chores and activities that evening, she couldn't stop thinking about the things Cathy had talked about. Susan didn't want to admit it to Cathy, but she, too, was developing a distinct feeling of unease—that instinctive feeling that something is wrong, but you just can't put your finger on it. She wished now that she had asked Cathy to stay a little longer to watch over Toby while she went for a run to clear her head. About two or three miles would do wonders for her mood and ensure restful sleep and release of some tension. *Maybe tomorrow after work,* she thought.

Monday—
The Doctor Is In

The sound of the 5:00 AM alarm that seemingly began at a great distance, incessantly moved closer and closer until its soundly sleeping victim could no longer ignore it. *A rude intruder, an unwanted interloper,* thought Dr. Glen Klinner as the pleasant, peaceful dreams of the night faded like dissipating smoke and vapor before the onrush of consciousness.

I'm not ready to face another day…why did those dreams have to end so soon? thought Dr. Klinner as he ordered his well disciplined, athletic body to respond to his commands to get moving. He knew the day would be hectic. An already-heavy schedule included three new patients that had traveled to Long Island from considerable distances to see him. They had spent the night in area motels, and he would blend their appointments in with the existing daily load of his established patient base. The speed at which this disease was spreading across America was becoming truly frightening. He had surmised for some time that a very high percentage of the population was already infected with the spirochete that causes Lyme disease, and from a decade of accumulated empirical evidence and demographic study, Dr. Klinner strongly believed the current infection rate was at least 10 percent of the overall population and possibly even as high as 20 percent. Certainly the endemic northeastern region of the United States would reflect higher averages, but thanks to migratory birds and floating portions of vegetation transporting infected ticks southward down the great rivers, the percentages were rising steadily throughout the nation.

Many infected individuals were basically asymptomatic, experiencing only minor aches, pains, and fatigue. Easily attributed to advancing age, weakness, or a touch of the flu. Indeed, as he moved through the morning ritual of shower, breakfast, nutritional supplements, and dressing for the office, he could feel those tinges of residual aches and pains in his muscles and joints from his own bout of Lyme disease twelve years earlier. The stress of the previous week had triggered a resurgence of those symptoms he knew so well. As the established medical community encountered more and more patients exhibiting the APF triad of symptoms (aches, pains, and fatigue) the catch-all diagnoses of fibromyalgia and chronic fatigue syndrome became the diagnoses de jour.

What a crock, thought Dr. Klinner, *those terms do not identify a disease etiology, only the symptoms and manifestations of a disease syndrome.* Since diagnosis was elusive, prescriptions by the thousands were being written for the powerful antidepressants and pain relievers. *Got to find time to call my broker,* he thought, *and get some shares of those pharmaceutical companies producing the most commonly used products and put them in my portfolio.*

At some point in the future, selling short the stocks of the biggest health insurers might be a good idea also. If the existing APF patients, all these misdiagnosed multiple sclerosis, amyotrophic lateral sclerosis, and early Alzheimer's patients, were correctly diagnosed and properly treated, the resulting financial strain would probably bankrupt every major health insurer in the United States!

Sometimes, Dr. Klinner cherished the twenty-five minute drive from his home to his office in the Medical Professional Building and also the return trip much later in the day. A time for quiet reflection on the day's challenges and activities. For some reason, that particular Monday morning had him thinking how differently his life and practice might have evolved had it not been for that singular event twelve years ago that literally turned his world topsy-turvy. He and his wife and two sons had taken a few days off in late summer of that year for some camping in Upstate New York. It was there that the tick that would change his life forever bit him. The words of a long-ago rock 'n' roll song from his college days seemed very appropriate now. "'I wish I didn't know now what I didn't know then…'"

As an idealistic, young intern eager to develop a practice in internal medicine, the future looked very promising indeed. Having graduated in the top three percent of his class at Harvard Medical School and blessed with strikingly handsome features and a lean, athletic physique, the world was his oyster. After completion of his internship, his plan was to establish a good solid internal medicine practice near his childhood home on Long Island. His goal was motivated by altruism to sincerely help his fellow man while simultaneously providing stability and financial security to his family. Dr. Klinner had no intention of reinventing the wheel. He only wanted to practice solid "cook book" medicine in a responsible and conscientious manner. He clearly remembered the admonitions of several of his professors warning that when you hear the hoof-beats of an approaching herd, don't jump to the conclusion that the herd is comprised of zebras. In other words, don't expect the unexpected. *Most* medicine will be practiced in a routine environment. Expect the obvious and the repetitious. *What a 180-degree shift for my practice,* he thought. All day, every day, the thundering herd of zebras could be heard galloping into his office. When first infected with Lyme disease himself, Dr. Klinner quickly realized how relatively obscure that disease was. There was little in the medical literature of a definitive nature, treatment guidelines were obscure, symptomatology was ill defined, and case histories were clouded with contradicting reports.

Well, he thought, *how much has changed during the intervening twelve years? To hear the news media and the "established medical community" babble with their incessant prattle about Lyme, it is still a relatively obscure disease. Try telling that to the victims and families of the tens of thousands of sick and dying chronically ill patients.* Almost daily, he felt that they were all at his doorstep, begging for relief. And today was one of those days. By default, and certainly not by design, Dr. Klinner had become a recognized expert in the diagnosis and treatment of Lyme disease. He was praised by his patients and despised by their insurance companies as they sought to evade payments for the expensive long-term antibiotic therapies requisite for Lyme treatment. But never had there been any question in his mind of where his priorities lay. The patients always came first in his practice and always would.

As Dr. Klinner steered his BMW into the employee parking area at the rear of his office, a perfunctory scan of the vehicles already in place gave him the reassuring confidence that all six of his employees would be on duty that day.

Good, he thought, *we are going to be very busy today, and I'm going to need everyone functioning efficiently together as a team.* Little did he realize what lay ahead that fateful Monday morning. Some patients had arrived early for their 8:00 AM appointments, including one that had stayed the night in a motel, having traveled over 600 miles to be seen. Dr. Klinner settled into the normal office routine with his patients and staff and all was proceeding smoothly until precisely 9:00 AM. It was then that he heard a loud commotion in the receptionist/waiting area. The sound of heavy, rapid footsteps, loud voices, and then screams. He quickly leapt from the side of his third patient of the morning and opened the door of the examining room leading into the hall. Simultaneously entering the hallway from the direction of the reception area and swiftly moving toward him was a sight that would forever be branded into his memory. Abruptly he stopped, momentarily frozen by the shock and surprise of what he saw. Three large men dressed in black SWAT gear, complete with face masks, boots, and submachine guns quickly reached him, and one suddenly stuck him on the head with the butt of his weapon. The blow knocked Dr. Klinner to the floor. Dazed, he struggled to get up but was kicked several times in the midsection, and then his hands were handcuffed behind his back, with a booted foot pushing down on the back of his neck for good measure. Chaos and pandemonium swept the office. The employees were thrown to the floor as jack-booted SWAT team members surged through the office cursing them and holding weapons to their heads.

The patients were terrified, screaming, crying, some obviously in shock. More law enforcement personnel poured into the building and started seizing Dr. Klinner's testing equipment and began throwing patient files and records into boxes. The dark blue jackets were emblazoned with the alphabet soup of the government agencies involved—IRS, FBI, ATF, FDA, CDC, and the DEA. As if to further emphasize the incredible risk to humanity Dr. Klinner posed, he was shackled with ankle and waist chains and bodily lifted out of the building into a waiting SWAT team van. His employees, all in tears, were handcuffed and led from the building into waiting government vehicles. To complete the surreal image unfolding, the office parking lot was teeming with media vehicles and personnel representing all area television and radio stations as well as newspaper and radio. The cameras recorded it all that day, except, of course, what had transpired inside the office. Some viewers might have gotten the wrong idea and become sympathetic to Dr. Klinner if television images revealed a SWAT team member striking Dr. Klinner to the floor with the butt of his submachine gun or all of the female employees being cursed, kicked, and beaten to the floor before being handcuffed and led away in tears to waiting vehicles.

A total of fifty-six agents from various government agencies participated in the raid on Dr. Klinner's office that morning and the number of media present represented another thirty-two people. Approximately two dozen additional raids were conducted across the land of the free and the home of the brave that morning with most occurring in the northeastern quadrant of the United States. Media coverage began immediately.

We interrupt scheduled programming to bring you this special report. Today authorities raided so-called health care clinics with suspected links to the massacre that occurred at the Plum Island ferry landing last Friday. Apparently the focus was the office of a Long Island doctor with close ties to Colonel Gordon McClain, the man responsible for the grisly slaughter. Details are incomplete at this time, but WKGF news has learned from reliable sources that the Long Island doctor was Dr. Glen Klinner. It is known that at the time of his death, Colonel McClain was a patient of Dr. Klinner's, and it has been reported that Colonel McClain and Dr. Klinner together attended certain meetings that promoted antigovernment sentiment among the attendees.

Dr. Klinner was no stranger to controversy having been investigated several times by the Medical Review and Licensing Board of New York for reportedly over-treating patients with extended courses of antibiotics and the use of non-FDA approved therapies. At the time of the raid, his license was under review by the board. We now have a live report from the Capitol where Attorney General Budenz and Chief of Homeland Security Dolan are to address the nation momentarily.

Attorney General Budenz and the Chief of Homeland Security entered the conference room at the White House surrounded by cameras and media personnel. This was obviously not a hastily arranged meeting. Preprinted information had been provided to all the media representatives, the remarks of Budenz and Dolan were carefully scripted, and the message conveyed to those in attendance that morning was simple; "As you prepare your stories of today's news conference, do not deviate from the remarks of Mr. Budenz and Mr. Dolan or the printed information sheets you have all received."

Attorney General Budenz approached the podium and began the meeting.

"Good morning. At approximately 9:00 AM today, representatives of several government agencies working together as a national strike force raided the offices of a number of illegitimate health care facilities with known ties to the massacre at the Plum Island ferry. A number of arrests have been made, and pending the outcome of our investigations, we anticipate more arrests in the coming weeks."

Chief of Homeland Security Dolan then approached the podium and began his remarks to the nation.

"Ladies and gentlemen, we have before us a situation clearly involving national security. Let me reassure you that the unfolding investigations into the activities of the individuals involved have yielded vital information for the authorities. We are confident that the act of terrorism committed at Plum Island has been contained, and at this juncture we do not have reason to believe that agents of Osama Bin Laden were involved. But make no mistake about it! *Terrorism is terrorism*! Innocent lives are lost, and we all become victims of the fear and uncertainty that is created. Whether the terrorism is of foreign origin or homegrown, the results are the same. Rest assured, we will search and investigate until all of the collaborators and co-conspirators are identified and apprehended. America can not and will not tolerate further acts of lawlessness."

The question and answer portion of the news conference was brief. The reporters in attendance, for the most part, didn't have a clue what questions to ask. Information provided by the government was very sketchy and attempts to explore the links between Colonel McClain and any of the doctors or clinicians involved led nowhere.

"We will keep you apprised of future developments as our investigations proceed," was the government's response to questions that did surface.

In attendance that morning was a feisty, crusty columnist for *The Chronicle* by the name of MacIntosh McAdams. Mac was an unbelievably anachronistic throwback to the star reporters of the twenties and thirties that always seemed to ask the most prying questions possible of just the right people. McAdams had few friends in government positions and fewer still among the entrenched politicos on the Washington scene. Mac sincerely believed that if a bureaucrat or politician's lips were moving, he or she was probably lying about something. Despised by his peers and idolized by his readers, MacIntosh McAdams was indeed the most colorful and controversial newspaper man on the contemporary American scene. A lot of words beginning with the letter *I* have been used to describe Mac down through the years and all for good cause; intelligent, intuitive, indefatigable, intrusive, intrepid, inquisitive, irascible, and probably most significant of all, iconoclastic.

As Mac rose to leave the conference room that morning, the inquisitive portion of his brain began functioning like clockwork.

What a crock! A genuine, twenty-four-carat, USDA certified crock! USDA? Hey, that's right! Plum Island was operated under the auspices of the Department of Agriculture until it was transferred to Homeland Security after 9/11. Neat! Maybe I can use that in an article. Seriously though, what the hell is going on over at Justice? And furthermore, what the hell is going on at Plum Island?

The Friday afternoon slaughter had really piqued Mac's insatiable curiosity. Today's raids threw gasoline on an already smoldering fire.

Somebody is trying to cover something up, he thought. Instinctively Mac distrusted all government programs, agencies, and personnel, and especially those affiliated with the Justice Department. *Hell, only a few years ago the bastards were frying little children with flame throwers in Texas, now what are they up to?*

And what about Plum Island? Mac had harbored deep suspicions and concerns about the programs and activities at Plum for years. *Sure, I've heard the rumors and read the stories about Plum…Anthrax Island, bug factory, level 4 pathogen reactor, bio-lab, and so on.* He even remembered the obtuse references to Plum in the dialog of the popular movie *Silence of the Lambs*. He had often wondered how long it would be before those egg-headed idiots leaked something out that soap wouldn't wash off.

And what about the government's acknowledgment that infectious agents had been sprayed from airplanes on American citizens back in the 1960s and 1970s over Panama City, Florida, San Francisco, and other locations? Was Plum involved in that crap? Or the reports and rumors that tens of thousands of infected ticks had been dropped from planes over Long Island and Connecticut?

Maybe the Centers for Disease Control should be renamed the Centers for Disease Census. After all, when the government spends taxpayer monies to spray populations with infectious agents and drop infected ticks on people's heads, somebody has to be responsible for tallying the total of sick and dying victims that show up in hospital emergency rooms and county health departments! How else to evaluate the effectiveness of the government's biological warfare program?

Mac briefly entertained the idea of skipping the rest of the day by beginning with a very liquid lunch. *Too many negative thoughts, too much anger, a world gone nuts that I can't escape,* he thought. *Nope, wishful thinking…got to stay on track and focused. There's a story here, a very big story, and maybe the biggest of my career. Got to be careful though. Somebody high up is pissed…really, really pissed! These guys are moving heaven and earth to make sure the buck stops here!*

The big picture—not the events at the ferry, not the sideshow of the raids or the Attorney General's news conference, and not the little individual seemingly unrelated pieces of the puzzle, but the big picture—that was Mac's world. He had that uncanny, innate ability to pick up on unfolding news stories and ferret out with incredible tenacity and accuracy exactly what was really going on behind the scenes. Another piece of the puzzle, and then another, and another until the picture was clearly revealed for the entire world to see.

But is the world ready to see this picture when it is completed? he wondered.

Make no mistake about it; in the world of journalism, MacIntosh McAdams was a different breed of cat. His peers knew it, his enemies despised him for it, and his friends (not many of those) respected him for it, and above all, his publisher knew it. And how very well the publisher knew and appreciated the devotion of Mac's readers. And how very, very well he knew and appreciated exactly how much that reader loyalty and devotion contributed to the bottom line of *The Chronicle*'s balance sheet. Mac was an institution, one of the few columnists alive today willing to tell it like it is regardless of whose toes get in the way.

Mac was deep in thought as he drove back to his office at *The Chronicle* that morning. He was uncertain of exactly where to start, but already he was sufficiently fueling his subconscious with ideas and suggestions. That portion of his brain never failed him. At work on the story, even while he slept. Yes, he knew even now that the ideas would come.

Capitol Hill

Congressman Harry McDonald had been in his Washington, D.C., office since 7:00 AM that Monday morning. As Chairman of the Health and Human Services Committee, the congressman always maintained a very heavy schedule of committee meetings, correspondence, speaking engagements, and meetings with constituents. He was very popular and respected by the electorate of the Second Congressional District of Connecticut which he represented and was serving his sixth term as congressman for that district. His first appointment that morning was with a constituent concerned about potential Medicare cuts and social security entitlements.

A ticking time bomb, Congressman McDonald thought, wondering about the day sometime in the future when the Ponzi scheme, known as the Social Security System of the United States, would collapse in a burgeoning tidal wave of unfunded liabilities.

As the meeting with the concerned constituent was winding down, the congressman glanced at his watch. *9:00 AM,* good, he thought, *still plenty of time to make it to the Health, Education, and Welfare meeting at 9:40.*

As Congressman McDonald was thanking his visitor for taking the time to come to Washington to share his views and express his concerns, the congressman's aide suddenly burst into his office obviously agitated about something.

"Mr. Congressman, Mr. Tompkins, please excuse me for interrupting. Mr. Congressman, I think it is urgent that you see the CNN report currently airing!"

"Certainly, Miss Giblon. Thank you again for coming, Mr. Tompkins. I'm sorry I have to go now."

Miss Giblon escorted Mr. Tompkins to the office exit as Congressman McDonald quickly stepped into the conference room just as the attorney general's news conference was ending. The usual after-conference dialog offered by the news reporters provided commentary, speculation, conjecture, and opinion.

Congressman McDonald sank into the nearest chair as he began absorbing the full impact of what he was seeing and hearing. As Erin Giblon returned to the room, she silently observed and listened very carefully to every media comment and subtle nuance. She sensed the congressman's apprehension and concern and knew that her role as his aide at this moment was to remain silent and await his reaction and direction. A look of abject solemnity swept across Congressman McDonald's face as the news report continued.

Even under the duress of the moment, McDonald's mind was beginning to compartmentalize the events described, the federal agencies involved, the attorney general's role and rationale, the extent of the raids, likely public reaction, media involvement, and last but not least, Dr. Glen Klinner's niche in the unfolding travesty of events. Yes, Congressman McDonald knew the name of Dr. Glen Klinner and knew it well. For over twenty years now they had been the best of friends. Long before McDonald had ever entertained any political ambitions whatsoever, he and Glen had gone through medical school together and had served their residencies at the same hospital in Massachusetts. They became good friends their first year in medical school, and that friendship had continued down through the years.

Dr. Glen Klinner was a straight-arrow guy, a good student, a good friend, level-headed, conscientious, hard working, a credit to the medical profession, and a lifesaver to his patients. Glen had gone into internal medicine, and Harry had continued in the footsteps of his family heritage, the field of cardiology. Even after beginning their respective practices, their friendship remained strong. At least twice each year, Glen, Harry, and their families would allocate the time to have an enjoyable dinner together. Ties and bonds were strengthened at these gatherings, and it seemed as if it would always be the same with lifelong friendships established and maintained, professional practices nurtured, maturing, and prospering, and a common interest in medicine providing an overriding cohesiveness to it all.

Approximately fifteen years ago, however, Harry had become increasingly concerned about the direction the nation was taking and had become more and more politically active. In conversations with friends, including Glen, Harry stressed the importance of returning to the constraints of the Constitution as envisioned by the founding fathers. Government had become too large, too omnipresent, too intrusive, and too powerful.

"We're on the wrong track," he would argue. "If something isn't done and done quickly to reverse the course this nation has embarked upon, we are all going to wake up one day in a world very much like the one described by George Orwell in his book *1984*!"

When Harry announced to his family, friends, peers, and the media his intention to forsake a very promising career in medicine to offer his candidacy for the U.S. House of Representatives, most probably thought a self-referral to a competent psychiatrist was in order. Especially critical and resentful was Harry's family.

"Harry, you are a member of the third generation of distinguished physicians in the McDonald lineage," boomed Harry's father. "Your grandfather founded the McDonald Cardiology Clinic that bears our proud name. Your two brothers are cardiologists in that clinic as are you and I. We have built, down through the years, an impeccable reputation and an extremely lucrative practice. And you, Harry, are willing to toss all of that into the waste bin of history to take a $120,000 per year congressman's job? And for what? To save America from itself?

"So what if you *are* right and America *is* sliding into a socialistic, totalitarian quagmire? What the hell do you think you can do about it? Take care of yourself and your family, Harry. Let the country and the political whores and gangsters that have always run it go in whatever direction they will. But, Harry, don't try to stop it. Get out of the way and be concerned with yourself and your family. You are sacrificing a career and a heritage, Harry. If that isn't sufficient to destroy you, the powers that be will do the job for you if you get in their way."

Harry's brothers were equally critical of his decision.

Glen was one of Harry's few friends that was openly supportive. Although not totally in agreement with such a radical decision, he respected Harry's decision and wished him success. As peers, Glen admired Harry's courage and tenacity.

Glen frequently reminded Harry that a congressional campaign would certainly not be an easy undertaking…a cakewalk it is not. It would take a lot of pressing the flesh, raising money, and organizing supporters.

"What a dedicated guy you are, Harry!" Glen had told him. "No way could I do what you are doing! But I guess somebody has got to stand up, quit acquiescing, and draw a line in the sand sometime. I respect and admire what you are trying to do. You are making an enormous sacrifice. I only hope that after all is said and done, your efforts have made a difference. Only time will tell."

The rush of memories of medical school and the very long friendship with Glen was momentarily overwhelming for Harry. Why would the government of the most powerful nation on earth descend with full force and fury on such a truly decent human being as Glen Klinner? Too many questions, too few answers!

"Miss Giblon?"

"Yes, Mr. Congressman," she replied.

"I want you and our new intern to immediately begin gathering whatever information you are able to obtain from all of the agencies involved in this mornings raids…IRS, DEA, CDC, ATF, FDA, and the FBI. Make full use of any contacts whatsoever we may have at those agencies to the maximum extent possible. Find out who, what, when, and where. Expect reticence and obfuscation at every turn and especially at the Justice Department. Find out what, if any, charges have been filed against Dr. Klinner and his staff. You know the drill. Report back to me as soon as you have anything tangible. By moving quickly we may be able to capitalize on the dichotomy of reports we would anticipate receiving. The inherent bureaucratic nature of the agencies involved will necessarily result in a lack of information sharing among them. Due to their lack of coordinated cohesiveness, we may get lucky and find out information from one source that might be difficult or impossible to obtain from another. Please move as quickly as possible and keep me advised."

"Certainly, Mr. Congressman. I think I have a good idea of what you are looking for. I'll begin immediately."

Erin loved a challenge and the excitement of the moment was an incredible stimulant to her motivation. She also loved her work as an aide to Congressman McDonald. While still in graduate school, she had become aware of his highly controversial and hotly contested campaign for the congressional seat he now holds. She admired and respected Harry McDonald, equally sharing his political conservatism, concern for preservation of constitutional principles, and disdain for status quo politics. Erin had no patience for lame excuses, prevarication, or lies. Straightforward, direct, and possessed with incredible tenacity, she was an invaluable asset to the congressman. With a master's degree in American history and a doctorate in political science from Georgetown University, having graduated *summa cum laude*, she was certainly also academically prepared as well for the work she loved so much. At five feet and ten inches in height, Erin's lean and well-toned body completed the image of a no-nonsense, hard-driving, very professional woman with no illusions about where she was headed in life or what she was dedicated to accomplish. Possessed with incredible energy and motivation, Erin could be found after a long day of work either at the gym or out running three to five miles, or both, almost every single day. A few hours of reading the major media before sleep was the culmination of her busy day. *The Wall Street Journal, The Washington Post, The New York Times,* and *Foreign Affairs* were her nightcaps. She often joked that she wanted to keep up with what the enemy was doing and thinking.

During the cooler months when the 5-K and 10-K racing season began, Erin would frequently participate competitively in those races, often winning or placing in her age group. She was like a finely tuned machine, seemingly always functioning at a near perfect and maximum capacity. The running shoes, running shorts, and gym attire of the evenings or weekends always faded away to the high heels and neatly appointed business suits of the workday. Standing almost six feet tall in her heels with a thick mane of dark red hair, Erin conveyed a striking image of intellectual and physical confidence. Little did she realize or suspect how thoroughly every physical and intellectual attribute she possessed was about to be challenged to the ultimate.

As Erin made her way back to her office, she could almost hear the words of her father echoing in her mind. Words first spoken after her mother had died unexpectedly when Erin was sixteen years old and again as Erin was preparing to leave for college that first fall after high school graduation.

"Erin, honey, make us proud of you in all that you do. There are only seven of us Giblons left in the entire United States, and it looks like the line ends with this generation."

Erin's father had no doubt Erin's mother was watching down from heaven constantly. Consequently, Erin was well accustomed to phrases such as, "Make us proud honey" or "We are proud of you, Erin," spoken as if her mother was in the very room with her and her father. As Erin had grown older, her father grew closer to her, and he seemed to be more and more concerned that the Giblon lineage would dead-end with her generation.

A glance at the blinking lights illuminating the office telephones brought an end to Erin's few moments of daydreaming and served to reinforce the intensity of the situation.

THE POISON PLUM

These would be calls from the constituents back in Connecticut—the first of many, Erin thought as she took a call to help out the suddenly inundated receptionist.

"Congressman McDonald's office, this is Erin Giblon speaking. How may we serve you?" The voice on the other end was obviously very distressed and sounded almost hysterical. Erin had to ask the caller to repeat her name and had difficulty understanding what she was trying to say because of the crying. Then the name registered. *Oh, my God, it's Glen Klinner's wife, Fran!* thought Erin.

"Yes, Mrs. Klinner, he is here. Please hold and I'll get him for you." Erin quickly paged Congressman McDonald, who had already taken another call.

"Mr. Congressman, I'm very sorry to interrupt, but I thought you would want to know that Fran Klinner is on line three, and she sounds very distraught."

"Thank you, Miss Giblon. Please tell Mrs. Klinner I will be right with her."

Harry, with apologies, quickly concluded the call from the *New London Herald*, promising to keep them advised of any information regarding the raids his office might be able to obtain. And no, he had no information on the status of Dr. Klinner or the reasons for the raid.

"Fran, this is Harry, I just heard, are you OK?"

"Harry, oh, my God, what can I do? Oh, Harry, this is horrible."

Fran was crying, obviously calling from a cell phone and obviously extremely upset. Between the sobbing and background noise, it was difficult to hear and comprehend what Fran was trying to say. Harry tried to calm and reassure her. Sentences were started and not finished, and explanations were too emotional to understand fully. Harry was finally able to piece together a sketchy picture of what was happening despite Fran's borderline hysteria.

Fran was currently standing on the lawn of her home, still dressed in her sleeping gown and robe. She had borrowed a neighbor's cell phone to call Harry. Agents of the government had entered her home within minutes of Glen's departure for his office. Armed with a search warrant, they had moved through their home like a whirlwind while agents forced her to sit on a couch, guns pointing at her head and denying her requests to explain their actions or allow her to change clothes.

What a blessing the children had already left for school, thought Harry. Fran had just learned of the raid on Glen's office from her neighbors, and at that moment, her world was as upside down as it could possibly be.

"Harry, what is happening? My God, what are these people doing to us? What do they think we have done? What do I do? Harry, I'm afraid! I'm scared!"

"I don't know, Fran. At this point, I am as surprised and confused as you are. But I know this…I will be there for you and Glen. I'll find out what is going on and soon. I am immediately devoting my full attention and that of my staff to getting to the bottom of this. At this moment we have calls in to offices of all the government agencies involved. I'm grabbing the first flight I can to get back to Connecticut. As soon as I am on the ground, I will call you with any information I may have acquired by that time. Fran, why don't you plan as soon as possible to come over and stay with Anna and me until we can get a handle on this thing? We need each other more than ever now, so I hope the answer is yes, and I hope to see you tonight. I'll call Anna now and tell her that we have spoken and I've invited you to stay with us for as long as necessary. OK, Fran? Try to be strong now, pull yourself together, and let's work together on this. Just let my office or Anna know when your ferry will be landing, and we will either be there to pick you up, or we will arrange for someone to meet you and bring you to our house. Don't worry, Fran, everything will be all right, I promise!"

"Oh, God bless you, Harry. I always knew Glen and I could count on you and Anna. I'll pick the children up at school and arrange for them to stay with our neighbors. Thank you! I'll gladly accept your invitation, and I will plan to come as soon as possible."

"Thank you, Fran, and God bless you too! I'll see you soon. I must go now to arrange and catch the next available flight from Washington. Take care!"

Just as Harry hung up, another call came in on the vacated line. *We are going to be buried in calls from our district, everyone wanting answers,* he thought. *I must arrange a news conference promptly. Might be a good idea to have Fran Klinner there as well as the wives of other doctors raided in the Connecticut area. It will be imperative to display to the media and the government goons that a high-ranking member of congress is not taking this trampling of constitutional rights lightly. Public sympathy and support for the doctors, wives, and patients must be cultivated at this time. And quickly, before the media unleashes the full fury of their government-scripted spin doctors.*

"Miss Giblon," he almost shouted into the intercom, "get me the first available flight back to Connecticut. I don't care if it is a private-service puddle jumper. Just get me there as soon as possible. Call our local office in the district and have them schedule an all-media news conference and try to include the wives of any and all doctors whose offices were raided. Schedule the conference for as soon as everyone can be brought together. I'll work on an outline of my remarks on the plane. Call me with any information you receive from our contacts with the agencies involved in the raids."

Adrenaline was flowing in copious quantities that Monday morning in the office of Congressman Harry McDonald. For Erin, the excitement was akin to beginning an athletic competition for which she had arduously trained. Consumed for months with long hours of training and dedication—immersing totally every fiber in her being for the completion of an athletic event whose starting gun had just sounded. Her years of study and preparation and her total commitment to the causes and principles so eloquently espoused by the congressman were now to be utilized and sorely tested. Her heart pounded in her chest as she plunged herself totally into the work that lay ahead. For Harry, the feelings he was experiencing encompassed anger, resentment, resolve, and the realization that the forces of evil he had so long opposed, the enemy he had long studied and observed, had revealed its evil, ugly, true nature by drawing first blood. For Harry, the battle lines had been drawn, commitments had been established, and there was no turning back for either side.

The bastards have finally shown their true colors, thought Harry as he collected his essentials for the flight. *And now there will be hell to pay!*

Talking Shop

MacIntosh McAdams had been back at his office at *The Chronicle* for about two hours when a call came in from Hank Sturgess of the *New London Ledger*, an old friend and fellow journalist.

"Hey, Hank," answered Mac. "What's happening up there?"

"Well not much…as you know, it's tourist season here, but we do have this flap over those government raids this morning. Mac we're getting a lot of calls from readers wanting to know what the hell is going on. It seems we can't get squat from any of our government sources other than that crap disseminated at that news conference this morning."

"Yeah, I know. I was there and just got back to the office a little while ago. It was crap all right, USDA certified. No pun intended, Hank."

"What do you mean?" asked Hank.

"You know, Plum was under the USDA. Pigs, cows, billy goats, chickens, and lots of other animals. The bucolic heartland of American farm stuff—health and safety and high production for the disease-free farm animals. As American as baseball and apple pie."

"Yeah right, there might be some bulls involved, that's for sure. In fact, I think I'm seeing some of their production all over this picture," said Hank.

"And I think I am beginning to detect the odor of that production all the way down here in Washington," replied Mac.

"Well, old friend, you might need a clothespin for your nose after I tell you the latest. Mac, these doctors that have been raided sure don't look like quacks or conspirators to me! Of the offices hit in this area of Connecticut, eight physicians were involved. I can't speak for their support staff, RNs, physician assistants, or their certified nurse practitioners, but these guys I'm talking about are the cream of the crop in the professional and social circles of Connecticut. Five of the eight graduated from Harvard Medical School *summa cum laude,* the remaining three from Emory, UAB at Birmingham, and Johns Hopkins.

"Mac, they sit on all the charity boards, belong to the best country clubs and civic groups, and they are highly respected members of their respective communities. They all have beautiful families, homes, wives—the whole nine yards. Something is not right with this picture. For these guys to be involved in anything jeopardizing national security stretches my credulity to Pluto and back."

"Dammit, Hank! I knew something was rotten at that press conference! I couldn't put my finger on it, but I felt that the government was trying to cover up something. And Hank, I think it's big whatever it is!"

"Yeah, I think so too, Mac."

"Hey Hank...Other than being intelligent, hard-working, successful professionals, do those guys that were raided have anything else in common? Other than being terrorists and co-conspirators, of course…"

"Yeah, Mac, they do. And this is the weirdest of all. You remember the trigger guy, Gordon McClain?"

"Of course," said Mac, "the national icon and hero."

"Well, you're going to love this! My sources tell me that guy was dying from Lyme disease. He was under the treatment of one of those doctors raided over on Long Island, Dr. Glen Klinner. And yeah, Klinner was a straight arrow, top-notch professional just like the doctors in this area. Klinner was doing all he could to save McClain but the Lyme germ developed a resistance to the antibiotics they were using, and there was nothing else they knew to do. Downhill he went. And Mac, hold on to your dentures, make sure they are tight, 'cause this will really rock your boat! Dr. Klinner's practice was almost totally dedicated to the diagnosis and treatment of Lyme disease, as were the practices of the eight doctors arrested here in Connecticut! I know what you are thinking…. Damn, do you people have that much incidence of Lyme in that area? Mac, the answer to that question is yes—an emphatic yes! It seems that this part of the United States is ground zero for that nightmare. Did you know the disease is named after a town on the coast here in Connecticut? Old Lyme? It's an epidemic here, and it is spreading rapidly throughout the rest of the United States from what I hear and read."

Mac's brain was already in overdrive, now rapidly beginning to sort and assimilate the information he was receiving from Hank.

"Hank, that town…Old Lyme? How far is that from the facility at Plum Island?"

"Maybe nine or ten miles as the crow flies."

"Oh really…. How about the immediate area around Plum on Long Island? Is the prevalence of Lyme disease high there also?"

"You betcha. The office of Dr. Glen Klinner was about thirty miles down from Plum on Long Island. And maybe this is just another coincidence, but, Mac, do you remember that outbreak of West Nile Encephalitis that killed those people out on Long Island back in 1999?"

"Yeah, it was the first outbreak ever of West Nile in the Western Hemisphere. I remember…. Even some talk at the time of Bin Laden, Hussein, whoever, shipping exotic infected birds into New York to spread the disease as part of a terrorist plot."

"Well, before those people got sick, some very expensive thoroughbred horses fell ill and died. Most within about a twenty-mile radius of Plum."

The bastards have finally done it, thought Mac. *Something soap won't wash off.* The pieces of the puzzle were beginning to fall into place.

"Mac, I think this story is something you need to sink your teeth and claws into. You could take it national. Hell, if I try to go anywhere with whatever we find, who is going to read and be concerned about anything we publish in the *New London Ledger*? You, on the other hand, could run with it and maybe turn over some apple carts. God knows there's plenty that need turning over."

Hank continued, "You remember our congressman from this congressional district of Connecticut that is always waving the flag and ranting about restoring America to Constitutional principles and limited government? Harry McDonald?"

"Yeah…I kind of like that guy. He may as well be pissing into the wind and certainly doesn't have a snowball's chance in hell of turning things around, but I admire his conviction and tenacity. An honest, sincere politician? Is that an oxymoron to beat all? What is this world coming to?"

"Well, Mac, you might want to clear your calendar. We just got notification that McDonald's office has scheduled a news conference with the public invited for tomorrow afternoon here in New London at the New London Community Center auditorium. So what, you might ask. A media presence and a Q & A for the public to demonstrate that he is concerned about the government's intrusions into the affairs of the medical community. Ninety-nine percent of the time that would be exactly correct with all of the politicians you and I have ever experienced. But I think there will be more to it than that, Mac. Two reasons you need to think about attending the news conference. Number one; I'll be there, and you and I need to talk and compare notes privately. And number two; Congressman McDonald was a doctor before he was a Congressman. Bet you didn't know that. And guess who his best bud was at medical school, and who he has been best buds with ever since?

"I give up…who?"

"Dr. Glen Klinner, that's who!"

"You have got to be kidding!" Mac retorted. "Klinner, the shooter's doctor, and McDonald are best friends? Are you putting me on? Jesus on a crutch! What time is the conference? I'm there already!"

"Four o'clock, Mac, and oh, by the way,"

"Yeah?"

"Don't forget to bring insect repellent!"

"Repellent, hell! If I'm coming that close to Plum Island maybe I'll need a biohazard suit!"

Back to the Constituents

Harry hated commuter planes. His tall, lean, athletic physique just didn't fit in any of the seating provided on those aircraft. The best he could ever hope for was an aisle seat providing the opportunity to stretch at least one leg out. On flights where he was unfortunate enough to be jammed into a window seat, his knees and legs were crying surrender by the time the plane arrived at its destination.

And why do the pilots always look so young? he thought. *Gosh, they are just kids. Do they know what they are doing? Are we safe up here?*

The importance of this particular flight quickly subordinated the momentarily negative sentiments Harry entertained about commuter planes. At least he arrived at his destination in New London safely, and his ringing cell phone during disembarkation was a reminder of the task that lay ahead.

"Mr. Congressman? This is Erin. How was your flight?"

"A-OK, Miss Giblon. Thank you. How are the arrangements coming for the news conference?"

"We have the auditorium reserved for a four o'clock conference tomorrow afternoon at the New London Community Center. I hope that will be satisfactory, Mr. Congressman."

"Excellent, Miss Giblon. We'll need the space if we have a good turnout from the constituency. How does it look for the media response?"

"Fine," replied Erin. "At this point, from what we can determine, response to our announcement has been very well received. I would anticipate a unanimous response from the press, radio, and television. Interest is high, there is a lot of confusion, and people want answers."

"And so do I, Miss Giblon. Any response from any of the agencies involved in the raids?"

"I'm afraid not. Our staff has been on the phone solid since you left this morning, as best they could. We have continuously had a high volume of calls coming in from the district. All callers of course were notified of your conference tomorrow and were invited. And the agencies we were trying to contact had a lot of busy signals, and even when we could get a human being to talk to us, the replies were basically all from the same canned, prearranged script. They quoted the need for diligence, secrecy, and caution, all in the name of national security, you understand. We're still trying, of course, but we've almost exhausted every contact we had or thought we had. Just nothing solid and tangible we can use or pursue at this point."

"Good work, Miss Giblon. Please keep trying. Maybe some low-level bureaucrat will let something slip out. Something we can use."

"I understand, Mr. Congressman."

"What kind of responses do you have, if any, from the wives of the physicians whose offices were raided?"

"Fortunately we have been able to contact all eight of the wives involved. Response has been mixed however. Some are obviously quite frightened and reluctant to appear publicly in a news conference questioning the government's justification and motivation for staging raids of their husbands' medical practices. I'll never understand, Mr. Congressman. People are reluctant to 'get involved' but those people couldn't become more involved if they tried. Tyranny has taken their doors off their hinges, and all they can think about is the pursuit of some policy of seeking the government's absolution for whatever sins they are perceived to have committed."

"I agree, Miss Giblon! Remember how during the American Revolution a large percentage of the colonists refused to 'become involved' and sought appeasement and reconciliation with the tyrannical policies of King George? The battle for independence was initiated, sustained, and finally achieved by a relatively small number of dedicated patriots. The cowards and appeasers lifted not a finger but received the gifts of freedom by *fait accompli*. Anyway, I'm sorry, I didn't mean to digress. I'm preaching to the choir here, I know."

"No problem, Mr. Congressman. I'm sure my blood pressure will return to normal shortly after my five mile run about ten this evening. Anyway, back to the wives. We do have five of the eight that are just as frightened and confused as the rest but with important distinctions—anger and resentment. The fire of combativeness has, in my opinion, been kindled among those five."

"I have an idea, Miss Giblon. Why don't we extend an invitation to all of the wives from a former doctor's wife, mine, to come to our home this evening for dinner and cocktails? I need some information and quickly for that conference tomorrow. Maybe some of those ladies will have experienced something related to their husband's practices that will provide some connection to what is transpiring before us…just maybe. I have already extended an invitation to Fran Klinner to spend the evening with us, and she has accepted. I hope she will agree to attend the press conference also. Please try to contact the wives and tell them of my desire to have them for dinner and cocktails beginning at 7:00 PM. I'll call Anna and get her involved with invitations as well. Time is of the essence, and we must move quickly. Perhaps Anna will know personally some of the ladies involved. That would certainly be a big help. And, Miss Giblon, I honestly do not, at this moment, know the exact direction I need to go with that conference tomorrow. I need more facts and more information. What, at this juncture, can I tell the media and my constituents? I'm trying to respond forthrightly, positively, and decisively, but frankly I feel like the blind leading the blind!"

The Drive Home

Renting a car at the airport seemed the logical thing to do in the interest of conserving Anna's valuable time. She would certainly have her hands full this evening coordinating Harry's abrupt request for a dinner and cocktail gathering of doctors' wives. Thank goodness for very capable domestic help acquired through the years of Harry's tenure in Congress. The many social gatherings required in the world of politics necessitated more or less continuous employment of these people. Tonight they would be a Godsend. Overseeing it all would be the very capable Anna, a real trooper when the chips were down and totally dedicated to the development and furtherance of her marriage and Harry's career.

Fran Klinner had arrived about three o'clock in the afternoon appearing disheveled, stressed, and anxious. Anna had immediately begun trying to console and comfort her as best she could. Anna thought she had never seen another human being appear as frightened and distraught as Fran. If a by-product of the raid was intended to be the inculcation of fear, confusion, and uncertainty, the heavily armed, masked, government thugs could certainly revel in the success of their accomplishments. *Cowards and bullies all,* Anna had thought as she patiently listened to Fran's retelling of the events that morning.

What a horrible experience for an innocent, helpless person to endure. Harry would be livid to hear this story, Anna had thought. *And what of Glen? What pain, suffering, and indignities has he been forcibly subjected to? A veritable nightmare from hell, I'm certain.*

A light drizzle had begun falling as Harry neared home.

Tears of God, Harry mused, *an expression of disapproval of the day's events by the Almighty.* How very appropriate it seemed.

The McDonalds' neighborhood was located in an older section of New London. The homes were large, spacious, and comfortable. The streets were lined with large, ancient oaks whose boughs had grown to form a canopy over the sidewalks and streets contributing to the image of tradition and stability that the neighborhood conveyed. The McDonalds' home was a roomy, two-story, Federal style that Harry and Fran had purchased while he was still in medical practice. Harry very much enjoyed the quiet, comfortable respite the home provided whenever he was able to leave the chaos of Washington to spend time in his district…precious little time, it always seemed.

At about four o'clock that afternoon, Harry turned into his driveway in the airport rental totally preoccupied with the events of the day and the obligations and responsibilities that lay before him. As oblivious as preoccupied, Harry paid scant attention to the innocuous-appearing van with darkened windows parked a half block from his home.

Anna greeted Harry at the garage entrance to the house, and in hushed tones told Harry of her concern for Fran, who was quietly waiting in the den.

"I can only imagine what she might be experiencing, Anna. It breaks my heart to think that such dear friends of ours have been so unjustly attacked and humiliated. And by a government gone berserk that we swear allegiance to! Anna, has Fran told you anything that might in any way explain why Glen's practice was a target? I desperately need information for that news conference tomorrow afternoon. Our efforts at gaining information from our usual sources within the government agencies have all come up empty. Blank, zero, zip!"

"Not to me, Harry. So far, all she has mentioned has been her surprise, shock, and humiliation at what occurred this morning. Rude, insensitive, armed men ransacking your home while you are still dressed in your sleeping gown has that effect, I'm sure! Harry, they forced her to remain seated on a couch while agents pointed pistols at her head for the entire time. The house was searched, and no explanations or apologies were given…only rude, arrogant, heavy-handed behavior. Harry, I am mad! Mad as hell. But I'm also frightened. If government thugs can do that to the Klinners and those other doctors, what is to prohibit them from coming in here? Into *our home*, Harry?"

"I know, honey. Believe me, I do. And don't think I don't think about it every single day. Wasn't that the message of my campaign, and isn't that concern the motivating force of my efforts as a congressman? It's all about why I gave up medicine for the thankless job of trying to arrest the onslaught of the New World Order. For you, our children, and the Klinners of this world, my die is cast. And now, I must face, and try to the best of my ability to help, our dear friend and victim, Fran Klinner."

Tears began cascading down Anna's cheeks as Harry gently took her hand, and they slowly began moving toward the den.

Fran was seated on a small couch under one of several windows, which afforded a view of the lawn and neighborhood. Looking up as soon as Harry and Fran entered the room, the expression of despair on Fran's face quickly faded to one of relief with a trace of a smile. She knew she was among old and very trusted friends, and she knew she was temporarily safe from the forces of evil that had ravaged her previously serene world this morning. And if anyone on this planet could help bring Glen back to her, it was Harry McDonald.

"Fran, I'm so glad you could come. Anna and I are so sorry for what has happened, and we want you to know that I am going to do everything in my power as a friend and congressman to help you and Glen."

"I'm just so grateful for our friendship. I don't know what I would do without you two. Harry, why us? We were not hurting anyone, and we're certainly not antigovernment terrorists or conspirators. All Glen wanted to do was provide the best medical care possible for his patients. Those people really need Glen. You just don't realize how much, Harry. What will they do now? The sick and dying? Where will they turn? The damn government won't help them, that's for sure!"

"Somehow, Fran, we've got to sort through all of this to try to figure out what is going on. Glen may have been the primary target of the government's raids, but you and Glen were certainly not the only targets. Fran, most of the raids were on medical practices here in Connecticut and over on Long Island. All totaled, over two dozen offices were hit. I don't know what the government is doing. I don't know what they are thinking. I don't know who in government is directing and controlling these activities and I don't know which way to turn to get the answers we need. For Christ's sake, Fran, I have scheduled a news conference for tomorrow here in New London and to be honest, at this very moment, I don't have the slightest idea what I am going to say or do at that conference. The efforts of my very capable office staff have yielded nothing. All we have are the lies and exaggerations disseminated by the agency heads at that news briefing this morning. Twaddle for the masses, but I don't think the average American, as gullible as he or she may be, is going to swallow this nonsense. We don't know why or where they have taken Glen, and certainly the government will not let me talk to him. We're in the dark, Fran! And what about the government's allegations of a supposed connection of Gordon McClain to Glen's office? Was Colonel McClain actually a patient of Glen's, or do you know?"

"Yes, Harry, he was."

"Interesting. Well, so what if he was. What does that have to do with anything? Does the government think Glen somehow programmed the colonel to kill those people at the ferry? Preposterous! What was wrong with McClain anyway? Why was Glen treating him? Glen was internal medicine, not psychiatry!"

"Harry, Colonel McClain was dying of an uncontrollable Lyme disease infection. Glen had been working with him for several years, but the disease was intractable. In the later stages of the disease, nothing seemed to help."

"What? I thought Lyme was curable with appropriate antibiotic therapy! Glen had it, when, fifteen years ago? He was cured, wasn't he? Why wasn't McClain cured? I don't understand, Fran. What's the connection here? Malpractice charges come from the appropriate medical review boards, not an alphabet soup of government agencies and agents with guns."

"You don't have the total picture, Harry. For the past several years Glen's practice has been devoted more and more to the diagnosis and treatment of Lyme disease. He never mentioned it to you, I know. Our infrequent times spent together were valuable and precious for all of us. The last thing Glen wanted to do when we were enjoying each other's company was to talk shop. And you recognized that as well, Harry. You didn't tie up our conversations with talk of your work as a congressman. Our friendships came first. Sharing of professional burdens and cares were not top priority for any of us. In retrospect, maybe it should have been. If not top priority, then at least on the discussion agenda. Maybe, somehow, the events of today could have been avoided. Malpractice was not in the picture here. Sure, Glen had had his battles with the medical review boards and the insurance companies for, ha, 'over-prescribing antibiotics.' Harry, after that disease spreads throughout the body, it becomes disseminated, and the only option left is long-term and I do mean *long-term,* antibiotic therapy. We're talking *years* for some of those people. And it's not just orals we are talking about. When I would visit the office and see little children with IV lines hanging out of their arms for the daily administration of antibiotics, it would just break my heart."

"My God! Are you talking about central intravenous catheters? That is an invasive, potentially very dangerous procedure! Very serious infections can easily occur."

"You are correct, Harry. But what choice do those people have? It's antibiotics or else!"

"But, Fran, antibiotics are not the reason for the hell unfolding before us. Insurance companies are concerned obviously because they have to pay for them. Professional review boards could be pressured by insurance companies to stop the doctors from 'over-prescribing,' but I can assure you, the government agencies involved in those raids today could have cared less. It's something else."

"I know, Harry. I'm confused, too. But how can I be expected to think even remotely lucid after this morning's events?"

"Fran, you said Colonel McClain had been a patient for several years. What else can you tell me about him? Did the guy just get so depressed and despondent he just wanted to kill people? It doesn't make sense."

"Glen told me that Colonel McClain had evidence that Lyme disease is a genetically engineered germ. Genetically engineered by scientists at the Plum Island Animal Disease Research Center, to be specific. He was of the opinion that the government had secretly researched the use of spirochetes during the syphilis experiments conducted on blacks for decades in Tuskegee, Alabama. The objective was to use the germs as a biological warfare agent. As you may recall, Harry, spirochetes are the germs that cause Lyme disease. Why is syphilis easily treated in its early stages with penicillin, and it takes a sledgehammer to treat Lyme? Colonel McClain was convinced the government's research on syphilis spirochetes had been sent to Plum Island for the development of a genetically engineered pathogen—one which could evade antibiotics and the body's own immune system, and one which could cripple and/or kill millions. Colonel McClain had a lot of contacts. When he got infected, he soon began looking for answers. He told Glen that his sources, electing to remain forever anonymous of course, had told him the details of the entire nefarious scheme."

"Did Glen believe him?"

"I don't know. After some people become ill with Lyme, their mental processes can get all screwed up. The germ crosses the blood-brain barrier and spreads throughout the brain and central nervous system. Mental confusion, loss of memory, depression, symptoms of meningitis, encephalitis, you name it, have occurred. Glen didn't know if Colonel McClain was on to something or just had a skull full of rampaging spirochetes. Maybe both. In McClain's view, the scientists and the research they were performing at Plum Island were the very epitome of evil. His world of war and combat utilized men and machines to achieve victory. Head to head, one on one. Let the side of truth emerge victorious. The thought of cooking up germs in test tubes to clandestinely kill people smacked of cowardice and callous indifference. No question about it. But Harry, even if McClain killed those people at the ferry because he believed they were working in a bio-warfare lab, why did the government come after Glen and those other doctors? What's the connection to Glen? It's true that the other doctors in this area that also were raided were treating Lyme, but they didn't have any connection to Colonel McClain."

"What did you say? The other doctors were Lyme doctors too?"

"Yes, they were. Glen knew them all. They would frequently compare notes on treatment protocols and so forth."

"Oh, my God, Fran! That's it! McClain was on to something. He had to have been. The government is trying to cover up any connection between Lyme and the laboratories. That's got to be the explanation. Nothing else makes any sense. My God, my God! How far has this thing gone?

"Fran, thank you, and God bless you! I think we've hit the nail on the head here. Please excuse me, ladies. I've got to reach my office."

The Uncelebratory Gathering

Every word spoken in the McDonald home that afternoon and evening, as well as both sides of all telephone conversations, was dutifully recorded by the skillful FBI agents operating very sophisticated electronic eavesdropping equipment from within the van parked nearby. The names of all in attendance were also carefully noted. Congressman McDonald's call to his assistant, Erin Giblon, was of particular interest to the ears of the government that afternoon.

"Miss Giblon, sorry to bother you so late in the afternoon. I know you are probably trying to get out of there. I know it has been a hectic day."

"Oh, no problem. Actually I was just wrapping up an afternoon of utter futility. No one, and I do mean no one, at any of those agencies involved in the raids is willing to deviate one iota from the established party line. 'National security, national security,' they all kept saying, like a broken record, over and over. I've been unable to determine where Dr. Klinner or any of the other doctors have been taken, nor can I find out exactly what charges, if any, have been filed. It's almost as if they have been swallowed up into a black hole. Frustrating!"

"I understand Miss Giblon, and thank you for your efforts. And please thank the other staff members for me also."

"Will do. What can we do next?"

"We may have something. Or something may have us. I'm not sure which. I have been talking for the past hour to Fran Klinner. I think I know what is going on. Brace yourself!"

"Mr. Congressman, what is it?"

"The shooter at the ferry, Colonel McClain, was indeed Dr. Klinner's patient. Fran told me that McClain had become convinced that the disease that was ravaging his body was a product of the facility at Plum Island. He was dying and had nothing else to lose. Miss Giblon, that disease was Lyme disease. Evidently, it is a much bigger problem than I ever thought. If he was correct, the government is operating that facility as a biological-warfare laboratory. That would certainly explain the raids on the other doctors because they were all Lyme doctors. The government is trying to cover up any connection to Lyme disease and Plum Island. It all fits! Here's what we do. Stop trying to get information from the agencies. Nobody is going to talk. They have put the lid on this entire operation from top to bottom. It is a waste of time to pressure those sources. Instead, let's try to find out what is going on at that laboratory. Get our people digging on the Internet. Get the 'official' USDA description of activities there. See if there are any conspiracy sites talking about Plum, anybody writing anything critical about the goings-on there, whatever. Also, dig into Lyme disease. I've heard of Lyme disease support groups scattered about. Maybe there's something there or in chat rooms."

"Fascinating and frightening, Mr. Congressman. We'll get right on it!"

"One more thing, Miss Giblon."

"Yes, Mr. Congressman?"

"During the Clinton presidency, it was admitted that the government had withheld penicillin therapy from poor black sharecroppers in Tuskegee, Alabama, that were suffering from syphilis. The government paid the survivors and their families millions in compensation for using them as guinea pigs as far back as the 1930s. Dig into that sordid affair also. Not the Clintons, but the Tuskegee thing. There might be a link to Plum Island."

Maybe it was his imagination but Fran seemed more relaxed and more like her normal self when Harry returned to the den. She and Anna were chatting quietly, and Anna had even taken a few calls from the wives that she knew personally, confirming that they would come for dinner and also attend tomorrow's news conference. That the dinner would be bleak and devoid of gaiety that evening was a certainty. The wives were not attending to be entertained. The purpose of their attendance would be twofold. First, they would be reassured that Congressman McDonald was going to help them and their husbands in their current plight, and secondly, they were expecting answers from the congressman. Answers as to why their lives had been so suddenly and seemingly capriciously devastated.

Seven o'clock was the appointed time for dinner, but it was no surprise to Anna or Harry when the first arrivals began at 6:30. Also not a surprise was their unanimous acceptance of pre-dinner cocktails, obviously pleased at the offer of libations after such a stress-filled day. By 7:00 PM a total of six of the wives involved were in attendance. Anna knew three of the ladies from medical auxiliary meetings, but not the others. However, there was no awkwardness of personal interrelationships after introductions were made, as might have existed in a typical social gathering. The women were bonded, forever, by the trauma of a common tragedy. They were the survivors that had to pick up the pieces, determine a course of action, and forge ahead. They were seeking answers, leadership, and support.

Harry began feeling weary as if a steadily increasing burden was being placed on his shoulders. Joining the ladies in a stiff cocktail was an intriguing attraction, but he knew that total alertness and lucidity would be required that evening.

Maybe a nightcap after everyone leaves might be a good idea, he thought as they collectively began moving to the dining room for dinner. After all were seated and before any food or beverages were served at the large dining table, Harry stood to thank them all for attending and once again offered his most sincere condolences for what had transpired today. He vowed to do everything in the power of his office and position to right the wrongs that had been so callously perpetrated by a government seemingly bent on the destruction of innocent lives and professional practices. He acknowledged that his office's efforts to determine exactly what was going on had been unsuccessful so far, but he emphasized that no stone would remain unturned until he had answers. The personal charisma, personal magnetism, and handsomeness Harry conveyed served him well this evening. Confidence in Harry's determination and resolve was unquestioned. He sounded and acted believable because he was believable. Harry was a man that said what he meant and meant what he said. Even when he acknowledged that currently he had precious little information to provide direction for what must be done, their faith in his abilities was unshaken.

Congressman McDonald was immensely capable of impressing his peers and charming the distaff side. He exuded a "can-do" attitude that exerted a calming effect on all present that evening. Harry asked the wives if they or their husbands had had any connection whatsoever, be it personal or private, with Colonel McClain. All acknowledged in the negative. Harry then summarized succinctly what Fran had told him about Glen's professional relationship with Colonel McClain, which had, of course, been revealed at the government's news conference. He also revealed the concerns that Colonel McClain had expressed to Glen about the nature of the research being conducted at Plum Island. Then he asked the ladies if their husbands had ever mentioned anything to them along these lines. Three hands immediately shot up. One by one the wives told how their husbands had had patients that claimed their infections were caused by infected ticks that came from the island laboratory. Two of the wives said their husbands had mentioned they had personal concerns that there could be a causal link between the Lyme germ and activities at Plum Island. All of the doctors involved were too busy with their practices and hectic schedules to pay more than a passing curiosity to the possibility of a connection.

There was unanimous agreement among all attendees that evening that there was at least the possibility that the United States government was involved in a cover-up involving the research facility at Plum Island. It was becoming more and more obvious that the only people who would have any reason to harbor more than a passing interest in Plum Island were the Lyme disease patients and their doctors.

A silence fell across the McDonald's dining room that evening as the enormity of the possibility of a conspiratorial cover-up began sinking into their collective consciousness. Facial expressions reflected solemn thought and consideration. Much of the food offered at dinner remained uneaten…mostly pushed around the plates aimlessly with whatever utensil one might be holding.

Harry's mind was heavily burdened with thoughts of what actions he should take. The choices were few. He could walk away, do nothing, abandon these hapless victims and try to forget about it, knowing they never could, but the rest of America would certainly have no problem in doing so. That was option number one and was in reality no option at all. The enemy had drawn the line in the sand, and there was no turning back. The school yard bully was puffed up, haughty, arrogant, cocky, and in your face. Up front and personal. Stand up and fight or turn around and run. There was no choice at all. At least not to a man like Harry McDonald.

And what of the other choice? Harry knew it certainly would not be and could not be a half-hearted commitment to fight these forces of evil. From this decision there could be no turning back. It would be a fight requiring total dedication, resolve, and commitment to the very bitter end. No half-hearted effort here. It was all or nothing, and Harry knew the consequences full well. At that very moment, words from the Declaration of Independence that had first stirred his heart while he was still in grade school appeared in his mind as vividly as if projected on a massive movie screen: "With a firm reliance on the protection of Divine Providence, we mutually pledge to each other our Lives, our Fortunes, and our sacred Honor."

That and more, thought Harry as he tried to swallow the lump that was growing in his throat as he carefully considered what he was going to say next to those in attendance.

Harry was fully cognizant that the choice he was about to make would forever alter the future course of his life and the lives of his family members.

What the heck, the buck stops here, thought Harry as he once again stood to address the room full of women whose husbands, their households, and their practices had just been taken from them.

Anna knew that look of resolve on Harry's face, and she knew it well. The look she first saw when, in college, Harry had told her he was going into medicine, and he would be committed to more years of study and education. The same look in his features and eyes also appeared when he, with staggering resolve, told her of his decision to abandon medicine to seek election as a United States congressman. The same look occurred when he told her that he would never join the "go along to get along" crowd in Washington, that she should expect the recriminations, the media attacks, the criticisms, and the snubbings at social gatherings among the Potomac elite.

Expect the confrontations, character assassinations, smears, and lies, he had told her.... Just expect it all because it goes with the territory. Do *not* expect the enemy to roll over and give up just because you have figured out what he is up to! Harry had come to congress to make a difference, to shake up the status quo. And by the grace of God, that was exactly what he was going to do. By the grace of God!

"Ladies, thank you all for coming on such a short notice to our home this evening. It has been a pleasure for both Anna and me to spend this time with you. We regret the less than auspicious circumstances that have necessitated our gathering, but it is my hope and desire that our time together has been well spent. From the conversations this evening, I will attempt to coalesce and forge a plan of action that will defeat the government's plans of intimidation, harassment, and destruction. I shall not rest until every husband is reunited with every wife, every medical practice has been restored, and a full exposé of the government's nefarious schemes has been accomplished.

"Tomorrow afternoon, as you all know, I will be hosting a news conference at the New London Community Center auditorium. It is my sincere desire that each and every one of you will grace us with your presence at that conference. I feel that it is vitally important to our cause that the public is provided every opportunity to attach a face, in this case nine faces, to this tragedy. The human side must be displayed for all to see. Two of the wives involved were not, for whatever reason, present this evening. I realize that there is a high probability that some of you present know these ladies personally, and I ask that you make a sincere, personal effort to contact them and encourage them to come also. As unpleasant as all of this is, I reluctantly must ask all of you to have your children in attendance also. The public must realize that the victims of the government's raids are real, live human beings and families just like themselves and the people next door. The national media can not be relied upon to evoke the sympathies of the nation with coverage favorable to the victims. From their viewpoint, the government is omniscient and always right, even when their policies are morally reprehensible.

"The government is faceless and nameless. We must seize this opportunity, our best and perhaps only, to create the very real distinction between a solid, honest, hard-working family unit and a nameless, faceless bureaucracy totally out of control. Interest in the raids is very high. A lot of questions are being asked, and the government and the portions of the national media that serve as puppets and mouthpieces for the government are providing no substantive answers. Please understand the importance of what we are all involved in here. We must act quickly, urgently, and decisively. Thank you all for coming and please make every effort to be there tomorrow. And by the way, please arrive early, so that I can arrange seating for you and your children in close proximity to the podium. We will not give the media any opportunity to exclude your presence."

The Strategy Session

At precisely 11:05 PM that evening, the agency phone rang in the bedroom of CIA Director Steele.

"What?" he gruffly answered.

"Director Steele, this is Frey at the Bureau. Sorry to bother you at such a late hour, but we have a problem."

"What kind of problem?"

"I have on the call with us General Helms at the Pentagon, Director Dolan at Homeland Security, and Kirkland with the CDC. Today we had authorized a surveillance team to monitor communications at the office of a congressman from Connecticut that had announced a news conference for tomorrow afternoon."

"What the hell is so important about a politician's news conference? They all do it on every opportunity they can get to attract media attention."

Director Steele was irritated and his impatience and abruptness was reflected in his voice. It had been a long and tiring day. He had been asleep only fifteen minutes when he was awakened by this call. He was in no mood for inane conversation regarding some insignificant congressman's frivolous news conference.

"Director Steele, this is no routine 'vote for me, I'm doing a good job' news conference and this is no routine congressman."

"Who is it, Frey?"

"Congressman Harry McDonald."

"That flag-waving, Goody Two-shoes, son of a bitch?"

"I'm afraid so."

"That overgrown Boy Scout is a perennial thorn in all of our sides. What is stuck in his craw now?"

"We authorized a surveillance team after our research uncovered a link to him and the target doctor of our raids."

"Klinner, McClain's doctor? Link? What kind of a link?"

"Oh, nothing much. Just that they became best friends while they were in medical school together, and they and their families have been best friends and very close ever since."

"McDonald is a doctor?"

"Yep."

"Dammit! I didn't need to hear this! Why hasn't someone discovered this connection previously?"

"I don't know. Looks like it just fell through the cracks."

"This could be a problem, a big problem. If McDonald sinks his teeth into this…we are all acutely aware of his tenacity, aren't we?"

"You don't have to remind me. We at the Bureau vividly recall the backlash we endured from his office after Ruby Ridge and Waco."

"Yeah, he is a feisty son of a bitch, that's for sure. And dammit, he has a lot of followers and supporters. People believe him. Even other members of congress! He is dangerous, there's no doubt about it! What did surveillance reveal?"

"Well, after announcing the news conference, he instructed his staff to contact the wives of the doctors residing in his congressional district whose offices we raided."

"What for?"

"Two reasons. One, to invite them to his news conference. Two, the McDonalds invited all eight, plus Klinner's wife, for dinner at their home. McDonald is going to try to promote a good-family, bad-government image to the media. He even wants the wives to bring their kids. We placed a surveillance van near the McDonalds' home, and we have recordings of all the conversations that took place this evening. Six of the eight attended, plus McDonald and his wife."

"Oh that's just dandy! A staunchly conservative congressman surrounded by the impeccably dressed Stepford wives with their freshly scrubbed, pink-cheeked offspring! Just dandy! Dammit! Why were those wives not fitted with ankle tracking devices and restricted to travel within a ten mile radius of their home?"

"No one felt it was important. These wives are country club, garden club, PTA, and medical auxiliary types. About as politically astute as a garbage can. These developments we are discovering were impossible to predict beforehand."

"First thing in the morning, let's have agents on their doorsteps. Get those tracking devices on their legs and slam them with the travel restrictions."

"What if some of those wives reside farther than ten miles from the site of the news conference? And are not able to attend as a result of the restriction?"

"Good!"

"Maybe not, Director Steele. Remember with whom we are dealing with here. McDonald is the kind of guy that would make a big deal of the wives' restrictions to the media. Innocent wives of incarcerated husbands denied the opportunity to meet with their congressman. Good family, evil government."

"Well, all right, maybe so, but do it first thing Wednesday morning then. Shackle the bitches…electronically that is!"

"Director Steele, McDonald is convinced that the government is involved in a massive cover-up of the operations at Plum Island. That much we are certain of. But the only question is, what the hell is he going to try to do about it? Obviously we expected this kind of response from the fringe media, conspiracy theorists, and the lunatic fringe. We are capable of handling those types of allegations in accordance with the protocol reviewed by General Helms at our initial meeting. Allegations from less than reputable, even questionable, sources are easily deflected. But when those allegations come from a squeaky clean United States congressman who is mad as hell that his best friends were the primary targets of government raids…well, that could precipitate problems we just don't need."

"That may be an understatement, Frey!"

"Let's shift to the offensive here. At 9:00 AM, to coincide with our prearranged news releases, I suggest we add one more tiny bit of information for the media."

"What are you thinking, Frey?"

"I suggest we formally charge Dr. Klinner with aiding and abetting a terrorist attack on the United States. Details, of course, will of necessity remain sketchy, but we will leak enough to the media that the following scenario will be assumed:

"Colonel McClain was a patient of Dr. Klinner. We all 'know' that his Lyme disease was long-ago cured by his doctors at Bethesda. We also 'know' that he was suffering from post-traumatic stress syndrome complicated by his divorce. Dr. Klinner harbored growing anti-government sentiment because of his experiences with the medical review boards charging him for over-prescribing antibiotics to treat Lyme disease. Klinner recognized McClain's mental instability and contributed to it by prescribing drugs known to have side effects, including aggravation of schizophrenic symptoms and paranoid delusions. McClain was encouraged to strike back at the government that Klinner had convinced him was the source of all of his problems. Dr. Klinner was without doubt an able, knowing, willing accomplice in the evil plot to massacre those innocent, dedicated scientists and support personnel at Plum Island. He will be held, interrogated, and prosecuted in accordance with the provisions of the Patriot Act. We will attempt, if possible, to involve as many of the other Lyme doctors as practicable."

"I concur," chimed in Dolan of Homeland Security. "Why don't Frey and I jointly announce those charges in the morning? What are you thinking, Kirkland? You haven't said a word so far."

"I am in agreement. If we can nail Klinner and at least some of the other doctors, very few infectious disease doctors will risk rocking their secure practices by taking on Lyme patients due to so much stigma and controversy. Hopefully, they will deny it is the epidemic it is and refuse to treat those seeking treatment. By the way, I have one more suggestion. We need to charge all of those Lyme doctors with over-prescribing antibiotics even more vigorously than we have in the past. Move beyond the medical review boards. Claim collusion between the doctors and certain pharmaceutical companies. Claim kickbacks and the defrauding of insurance companies and Medicare of course. Federal crimes, felonies, prison time!"

"Excellent, Kirkland! Why don't we simultaneously reveal those charges in the morning? And instead of news releases, let's get the media to come in for a conference. Then, when McDonald has his conference later in the day, he won't have a leg to stand on. The charges we will be levying are serious, very serious indeed. Hell, the public won't know, and most won't care. We are the authorities. Who else can they trust and believe?"

"OK gentlemen, we have a viable plan, and it appears we are all in agreement. Let's roll with it. Of course make sure that each of your agencies has personnel in attendance at McDonald's news conference. Try to have them blend in to appear as either media personnel or members of his constituency."

Tuesday—
Bad News Conference vs. Good News Conference

Harry slept fitfully and sporadically that evening. The responsibilities he had already assumed would pale into insignificance after the announcement he would make in the afternoon, and he knew it. A steely resolve had consumed Harry over the past twelve hours as his brain had assimilated the information at hand. His decision, in retrospect, was not that difficult. Actually, it was the only decision possible under the circumstances. No regrets, no regrets whatsoever. And if any further tempering of that steely resolve were even faintly required, all was totally consummated by the conclusion of the government's news conference Harry watched that morning. Even when he was not at his Washington office, Harry always managed to check CNN for developing news events and Bloomberg for information on the financial markets. The joint announcement by Frey at the FBI and Dolan at Homeland Security which was carried by CNN revealed that Glen would be tried as an accomplice to a terrorist act under the provisions of the Patriot Act. The announcement sent cold chills down Harry's spine.

"My God in heaven, Glen will be tried by a military tribunal without benefit of counsel! Oh, my God. Oh, my God!"

Comments from media talking heads at the conclusion of the conference confirmed the government's "leaks" to ensure the proper spin was put on the interpretation of the conference. Typical were the remarks of Jenkins of the Amalgamated News Network:

Dr. Klinner was involved in kickback schemes with pharmaceutical companies. He was committing insurance and Medicare fraud. He promoted antigovernment sentiment among his patients, alleging vast conspiracies because of being investigated on numerous occasions by medical review boards for flagrantly over-prescribing antibiotics. He gave dangerous drugs to Colonel McClain ostensibly for the purpose of controlling depression, but in reality he was promoting paranoid delusions and schizophrenia. Dr. Klinner goaded Colonel McClain into striking at the "enemy."

Harry sat in silence at the conclusion of the government's news conference that crisp, clear morning in Connecticut. Harry was stunned, annoyed, and dumbfounded by what he had seen and heard. After several minutes of reflection, Harry dropped to his knees and prayed to God above for guidance, strength, discernment, and courage. He also prayed for the doctors, their families, and the patients whose lives had been so dramatically impacted.

"Almighty God, vengeance is yours. May your will be done in the name of Jesus Christ, my Lord and Savior. Amen."

MacIntosh McAdams had made no effort to attend the government's news conference that morning in Washington. Many details remained unattended to at his office at *The Chronicle* and there simply would not be enough time to cover that and make the trip to New London. Those travel preparations did not deter him from watching CNN's coverage, however. The government's levying of terrorist charges against Dr. Klinner jolted Mac like a lightening bolt. A string of expletives cascaded from Mac's mouth as his anger raged. Then, with somewhat more cohesive dialog, Mac blasted for all to hear: "Those bastards are going to prosecute that doctor under the provisions of the Patriot Act? Try a U.S. citizen before a military tribunal without benefit of counsel? Mao, Stalin, and Hitler would have loved it!"

"Tell us how you feel, Mac…don't hold back," mumbled a co-worker nearby. Mac's co-workers were accustomed to his frequent, quite vocal outbursts, but today's outburst topped all the rest. Mac was visibly livid, and he didn't care who knew it.

"That guy, McDonald, better show some spine at his conference! If he caves in and wussie's out, I may just kick his butt! Put up or shut up, Mr. Defender of Freedom and Constitutional Rights!"

And out the door he went with rage and fury emanating for the entire world to see. "Maybe if I'm lucky I *won't* have a stroke before I get to New London. On the other hand, maybe if I am lucky, I *will* have a stroke. Whatever…"

The Forsaken

As tragic as the consequences of the raids were on the doctors, their families, and office support personnel, the greatest impact was felt by the hundreds of patients who were being actively treated for Lyme and the multiple co-infections that frequently occur after the initial insect bite. The full spectrum of patient involvement was represented in the ranks of those hundreds who suddenly found themselves foundering rudderless in the bizarre and arcane world of Lyme disease and its diagnosis and treatment. Some patients, very ill, now waiting helplessly for the completion and interpretation of their laboratory tests, would be the first to realize the seriousness of the government's actions. The office staff required to receive those lab results and the absolutely critical interpretation of those results by the Lyme-literate physicians would simply not be available for the patients.

Most, if not all of this group, had already spent many frustrating weeks, months, or even years being bounced from one specialty of medicine to another, desperately seeking relief from their maddening symptoms. The final discovery of a physician who could diagnose the disease syndrome involved *and* provide treatment for amelioration of those maddening symptoms was a Godsend indeed to these patients. It was also the end of the road for these pitiful people. There simply was nowhere else to turn. With the offices of practitioners closed by the raids within a radius of several hundred miles, the only option would be to seek out a qualified physician at a greater distance from ground zero. Indeed, this presented a very formidable obstacle for many. Even if other doctors could be located by contacting Lyme disease support groups existing to network essential diagnosis and treatment information, there would be additional expense and time involved in commuting to those distant sites. And for the more critically ill among the patients, travel was an impossibility. The raids would prove to be a death sentence for a significant portion of the patient population.

The patients who were midstream, those who had been evaluated, diagnosed, and were being treated with massive doses of long-term antibiotics, would simply see their treatment protocols concluded when their existing prescriptions expired. Try explaining to a conventional physician, unaware (as most are) of what Lyme is all about, that you are sixteen months into an antibiotic regimen that requires semimonthly liver and kidney function tests as well as complete blood counts (CBC) and that you will require a minimum of an *additional eight months of therapy* to hopefully cure the disease. He or she will, of course, be totally understanding, sympathetic, and supportive, and happy to write a prescription for you…for a complete psychological evaluation!

With the seizure of all patient records by the government goons, anyone seeking further assistance, treatment, and evaluation would be required to endure once again the batteries of expensive, time-consuming tests and some potentially dangerous invasive procedures such as cardiac catherizations and spinal taps. As a consequence of the current "C.Y.A." litigation mentality sweeping America, *no* physician is going to prescribe or treat without confirmatory tests to support his or her diagnosis. Starting all over with all they have already endured is not an appealing thought for these patients that already feel they have journeyed to the very gates of hell and back.

Perhaps the multitude of the suddenly abandoned victims would naively believe for days or weeks the very government that had so abruptly set them adrift would provide their necessary guidance. Any day now they could expect that direction would be provided by some government agency advising them when and how their treatments would be continued, not unlike thoughts probably entertained by Holocaust victims as they were being herded into the waiting boxcars, optimistically anticipating transportation to a new and better place.

Onward to the Community Center

That Tuesday afternoon the weather on the coast of Connecticut was clear and quite pleasant. So pleasant, in fact, that Harry McDonald wondered during the four-mile drive to the New London Community Center how a world so grievously convoluted could appear so deceptively normal. The residents of New London were going about their daily activities and errands without a visible hint of distress or despair. In stark contrast, Harry was emotionally overwhelmed and felt that he and he alone was responsible for shouldering an incredibly huge burden of responsibility and obligation. A responsibility to his friends, the Klinners, an obligation to the other families involved, an obligation as a United States congressman and as an American to recognize and oppose evil wherever and whenever it rears its ugly head. On the surface, Harry was the epitome of calmness—not a hint of concern. Observers would concur, saying, "Cool, calm, and collected, that guy McDonald."

Inside, Harry McDonald was seething with anger, resentment, and unswerving determination to right the wrongs that had been committed. Anna was, of course, by his side, and Fran Klinner was in the back seat as they made their way to the community center that afternoon. Conversation between them was sparse. Harry was deep in concentration during the drive, consumed as he had been all day with the task that lay ahead. Anna remained silent, recognizing that her presence by Harry's side during this time of crisis was more important than any words that might be spoken. Their togetherness, love, support, and dedication to each other was obvious to all who knew them and even recognizable to casual observers. Harry knew he could always totally and completely depend on Anna's support. And Anna always knew the same about Harry.

Anna's gaze shifted to Harry as they neared the community center. She was very proud of her husband this day…her heart brimming with pride and love. He was dressed in a conservative, dark blue business suit with a white shirt and matching necktie. A thick head of black hair with slight graying at the temples completed the image of a tall, muscular, very handsome man. He was the epitome of a successful doctor, lawyer, business executive, or congressman. Anna knew he could have succeeded in any field that he had chosen. Handsome, extremely intelligent, charismatic, dedicated, focused, loyal, and moral.

What a combination, thought Anna. *And today, Harry McDonald, my husband, will need all of those attributes and then some.*

Harry was thinking about Anna also that afternoon. He was very, very fortunate to have her as his wife. It always seemed that there was no challenge or obstacle too great for Anna. Whatever came down life's highway in their direction, Anna took it in stride with not a hint of negativity or defeatism. There was always that pretty smile on that very beautiful face and always the optimism that the glass was half full and not half empty.

A striking couple they made. She was of Scandinavian descent with thick blonde hair, striking green eyes, and fair skin. Today she wore a smartly tailored dark green suit, which complemented her beautiful eyes and attractive figure, all five feet and ten inches of it. In any social setting, it was always glaringly obvious to any bystander that they were a couple and belonged together.

Turning the last corner before reaching the parking lot of the community center, Harry could see that the crowd today would be large—very large. Arriving early as was his habit, he was surprised to see the number of media vehicles already there. He spotted CBS, ABC, NBC, CNN, Connecticut Public Television, National Public Radio, and others. The conference was scheduled for 4:00 PM, and it was only 2:20 PM now. Typically, the largest number of attendees would arrive the last thirty minutes before a conference began. Unless some other function was already in progress, today's crowd was going to be a packed house!

Harry had sensed for some time that the events of 9/11 had created deep suspicions and distrust in the minds of a lot of Americans regarding their government's true motives and intentions. More a nagging intuitiveness that something was just not right and ringing true than a palpable concern. A silent unease and apprehension was spreading across America, and Harry knew it.

"Harry! Look at all those cars and media vehicles! I've never seen such a big crowd. There must be a thousand people here already."

"I know, Anna. Looks like some folks are looking for some answers. And, it is almost a certainty that some government agents are going to be in attendance as well as more than the usual portion of the media that is consistently hostile to us. You already know how I feel … the battle lines have been drawn by the enemy. No quarter has been asked and no quarter will be given. We will do what is expected of us today. I shall not shirk my responsibilities."

Before entering the New London Community Center that afternoon, Harry, Anna, and Fran held hands, bowed their heads and prayed. Then they quickly and unobtrusively made their way in through the back entrance to the office of the community center's custodial staff. The efficient and courteous director of the center, Mr. Robin Waters, greeted them warmly.

"Good to see you, Congressman and Mrs. McDonald! The arrangements are already completed for your conference, and we can't wait to hear what you have to say to us. Have you seen the crowd that is already here? We've got a packed house for you today. A lot of these folks are angry. Just thought I'd let you know up front, and I guess I'm angry, too, Mr. Congressman. But not at you, that's for sure. We in this district consider ourselves very fortunate indeed to have you representing us. The government is out of control. Those doctors that got raided are all good people, and the residents of this area know it. We don't care what the news media and the government says, we know better. These folks are our own. They are respected members of this community. We all want answers, Mr. Congressman, and we support you! I'm sorry…I didn't mean to make a speech. It's just that a lot of folks are upset, myself included, and I just wanted to toss in my two cents."

"I appreciate your comments, Mr. Waters. Believe me, I do. And I'm certainly going to need your support and the support of every voter in this district. At the conclusion of my conference today, you will understand why. Thank you for your help!"

"You are welcome, and you've got it. Please follow me…we have room 3-A reserved for you and your staff. It has a telephone, television, rest room, and computer access, should you need it. And if you should require anything else, just let me know. You are familiar with the center's sound system, and it's all set to go—just turn on your mike. Will you require any of the audiovisual equipment, projection screens, or anything else?"

"Not at this conference. I think we have everything we need. Thanks again."

"Oh, by the way, maybe it's an indication of what some people are really thinking, or maybe just the work of pranksters, but I had coffee this morning with

Police Chief Myers at the restaurant. He told me that during the night somebody painted Nazi swastikas on some of the government office buildings in town. The office of the ATF and FBI had several painted on the doors and signs. Even the post office got a few."

"That's interesting. Thanks for sharing. I think before the day is over, we will have a very clear idea of what the mood of the people really is, especially after the conclusion of the question and answer session!"

"Well, here we are…3-A. A member of your staff has been here already for several hours working on the computer. A Miss Giblon, as I recall?"

As Mr. Waters swung open the door of 3-A, Erin Giblon turned from the computer screen and stood to greet Harry and Anna. On the computer table were stacks and stacks of papers, documents, and photographs.

"Hello, Mr. Congressman and Mrs. McDonald."

"Hello, Miss Giblon. What are you doing here? I certainly didn't expect or require your presence at this news conference. How did you get here?"

"I know, Mr. Congressman, but I thought you might need some help today because it looks like the big guns are here and you are the target. Also, I have some information you might be able to use. I knew of no other way to get it to you, so I caught an early flight out of Washington to Hartford, and then rented a car for the drive here. Got here about eleven."

"Thank you and you are probably right. I see now that I could indeed use some help today. That crowd out there looks pretty overwhelming, and I could especially use some pertinent information. But before we begin, I would like to introduce Fran Klinner, wife of Dr. Glen Klinner."

"I'm pleased to meet you, Mrs. Klinner, and I am very sorry to learn of the ordeal you must be experiencing. I am Erin Giblon, the congressman's aide in Washington."

"Thank you, Miss Giblon. I just appreciate so much what you are all doing to help us."

"Miss Giblon, I see a big pile of documents on the computer table. Are those products of your research?"

"Yes they are Mr. Congressman. It appears we have opened a veritable Pandora's Box."

"What do we have?" McDonald asked.

"Well, to begin Mr. Congressman, it seems there is two of everything. Each one is 180 degrees out from the other. Maybe you should title your news conference 'The Gemini Conspiracy'."

"Gemini Conspiracy? Two of everything? What on earth do you mean Miss Giblon? Two of everything?"

"It's just that Mr. Congressman, two of everything. There are two Plum Islands, two Lyme diseases, two recognized groups of Lyme disease experts, two recommended treatment protocols, and two expert opinions as regards treatment outcomes."

"Two Plum Islands, how can that be?"

"Well, not literally, but certainly figuratively. On the one hand, we have the official government Web site, literature, and public pronouncements praising the facility at Plum Island and extolling the virtues of the wonderful work and research being done there to protect America's farm animals from disease. Originally, the facility was operated under the auspices of the Department of Agriculture, but subsequent to 9/11 it was transferred to Homeland Security. You know, in the name of national security we have to protect our farm animals from terrorist attack to ensure the integrity of the nation's food supply. This is the 'for public consumption and dissemination version' offered to the masses."

"And the other Plum Island Miss Giblon?"

"It's certainly not difficult to get a 'second opinion' when researching Plum Island! All one has to do is type in Plum Island for a word search on any of the Internet search engines. You are immediately taken to a veritable labyrinth of information and links to other sites. And those sites are anything but complimentary Mr. Congressman. Conspiracy theories abound, books have been written, opinions and conjecture advanced by many, and seemingly a common thread connects all of these suppositions and suspicions."

"And that common thread is?"

"Plum Island is a top-secret, U.S. government biological-research facility. A level-4 pathogen reactor dedicated to producing the most lethal pathogens possible for use as biological weapons. The next war will not be fought with conventional weapons or even nuclear devices. The weapons of future choice with the greatest potential for massive extermination of human life will be numerous germs! Or so goes the thread of commonality prevalent on that end of the spectrum of opinion regarding Plum Island.

"To continue with the theme of duality I have encountered throughout my research, we have the two similar but distinctly different Lyme diseases. One of those diseases is described in the medical literature as an insect-borne infection, and it is relatively easy to diagnose because of its classic bull's-eye rash at the site of the insect's bite and a positive blood test known as the Western Blot. Once diagnosed, treatment is also a cakewalk. Usually two or three weeks of the appropriate antibiotics are all that is necessary to effect a cure. The 'other' Lyme disease presents with a bizarre array of symptoms that baffles established medical professionals. And as diagnosis is extremely confusing and difficult, treatment is even more so. Complicated and extensive courses of various combinations of antibiotics, vitamins, and herbals are used, which improve the patient's condition, relieving many symptoms but seldom, if ever, resulting in a cure. Indeed most patients remain chronically ill and desperately seek help."

Erin continued, "Perhaps what I am about to say is a very exaggerated oversimplification of Plum Island and disease, especially Lyme disease, but here goes.... We have the group known as the 'no problem group.' These are government spokespersons, certain members of the medical community, especially those in the government-sponsored programs at the agencies such as the CDC and the government-supported teaching institutions. We also have 'expert' opinions advanced by representatives of insurance companies and some media groups. All assiduously promote the concept of 'no problem.' Nobody here but us chickens.

"And just as we thought we couldn't encounter another two of anything, we have the 'it's a big problem group.' This group is made up of Lyme disease patients, or at least they think they have Lyme, and their doctors who are recognized as Lyme experts. And one must assume that those doctors are either in it for the bucks, or they actually believe they are treating Lyme patients. Collateral to these people are the caregivers, usually family members of the patients who also suffer daily with the misery of the patients' lives. Support groups have sprung up all over America linking doctors, patients, and caregivers electronically, providing some cohesiveness to efforts to warn, support, and advise the general public and Lyme victims. Most, if not all, of the groups are staffed and financed by Lyme patients—some so sick that they are only able to devote a few hours a week to the group's activities.

THE POISON PLUM

"Like a gigantic patchwork quilt, these groups have begun to blanket America. Information fervently disseminated by these groups is basically the same. Whether you are looking at the Lyme Support Group of Connecticut or the Lyme Support Group of Central Florida, or wherever, their message is identical…'*It's a big problem!*'

"Some advance notions of a conspiracy of silence regarding Lyme, and they believe that a massive cover-up exists. And, Mr. Congressman, Plum Island is the number one target of the conspiracy theorists."

"Well Miss Giblon, how you managed to compile that much information and still make it here to the meeting is incredible. Have you had any sleep at all?"

"Not much, sir."

"I appreciate what you have done. After what I have heard from Fran and the other doctors' wives last evening, I must say that I am not surprised by the information you have shared with me today. I am not surprised at all. It only serves to reinforce the decision I have made as regards the course of action we must take."

"Are we moving to insect-free Greenland, Mr. Congressman?"

Harry, Anna, and Fran couldn't help laughing. Erin had that rare ability to inject, at just the right time, a touch of levity into a conversation that needed a respite, however brief, from its theme of solemn concern and deliberation.

"Thank you, Miss Giblon," Harry managed, regaining his composure after the laughter. "We needed that! But to answer your question, maybe not. Possibly however, we can ship to Greenland or somewhere else, those in government responsible for this mess."

"Perhaps some location a lot hotter than Greenland? Sounds good to me!"

"Well, before we banish the infidels to eternal damnation, I guess we need to get on with our conference for this afternoon. The doctors' wives and their children should be arriving soon. I want them to join me on stage behind the podium seated in a semicircle. Anna, would you and Fran please locate everyone and direct them to that holding room at the rear and side of the stage? About ten minutes before the conference is scheduled to begin, I'll join you all there and then we will all walk on stage together. Remember that we are conveying to the media and the attendees an image of family stability, concern, and cohesiveness. Please advise the wives that during the question and answer session, we should expect highly critical comments from some members of the media and also government agents planted in the audience appearing as constituents. Ask them to remain focused, to not become dismayed by these attacks, and to maintain their composure regardless of how mean and cruel some of those remarks might be. And, by the way, Anna, would you please take a pad and write brief bio's of the wives? Their community involvement, their children's names, and their husband's names and type of practice?"

The News Conference

At precisely 4:00 PM that Tuesday afternoon, twenty-seven people walked onto the stage of the New London Community Center. Congressman McDonald assumed his position at the podium to begin the conference as the others were being seated. In addition to Anna and Fran, all eight of the doctors' wives were present with most of their children. All were conservatively and smartly dressed, and all presented with facial expressions that mirrored their apprehension and concern. The first several rows of the auditorium, as well as the spaces immediately in front of the stage, were clogged with media personnel and their equipment—cameras, lights, recording devices, etc. Every seat in the auditorium was taken, and another forty or fifty people were standing on the sides and in the rear. Harry had used these facilities many times before, and he recalled that the seating capacity was approximately 1,500.

Well, they are all here today, he thought. *All it took for motivation was eighty-two dead at the ferry landing and government storm troopers taking doors off their hinges at a couple of dozen medical offices! Brings out the crowds every time!*

The traditionally apathetic American was on vacation that afternoon for certain. The attendees were agitated and obviously wanted some answers…and soon.

"Good afternoon," Harry began. "I am Congressman Harry McDonald, and I appreciate your attendance this afternoon. I have called this news conference to address the events that have impacted this area and our lives over the past several days. We were all shocked and traumatized by the grisly massacre that occurred at the Plum Island ferry landing last Friday. Equally shocking was the revelation that the assassin was one of the greatest Americans this nation has ever produced. And why he or anyone, for that matter, could be motivated to commit such a ghastly deed is almost beyond comprehension. But especially Colonel Gordon McClain…a man who gave his all for the nation he loved. No man could have given more of himself to his country. Why would he, of all people, commit such an atrocious act? His life was devoted entirely to protecting us and our nation from those evil forces that were bent on our destruction. To seemingly without provocation turn on the very government he was sworn to protect staggers the imagination.

"We may never know the answers to these questions. But it is our legacy as survivors to try to the very best of our abilities to attempt to fathom what might have been going on in the mind of Colonel McClain as he pulled those triggers last Friday afternoon. Our government would have us believe that Colonel McClain was a very depressed man in severe need of psychological evaluation and treatment. The coupling of the trauma of his divorce with the post-traumatic stress syndrome he suffered was simply too much for one man to bear. Consequently, Colonel McClain went over the edge psychologically and the events that transpired were a very tragic consequence of his depression and suffering. This explanation for Colonel McClain's behavior provided the justification for the raids conducted on approximately two dozen medical practices, eight of which were in this immediate area.

"To continue with the government's line of reasoning and explanation of their actions, the medical facilities were bogus and were being operated by quacks and charlatans that were dangerously over-prescribing antibiotics to their patients while simultaneously defrauding insurance companies and Medicare. These same quacks and charlatans were co-conspirators in promulgating antigovernment sentiment among their patients. Colonel McClain was a patient of one of these 'quacks' and was easily manipulated to violence because of his precarious mental state. It is alleged by the government that the research facility at Plum Island became the scapegoat in the 'quacks' antigovernment tirades, as they blamed the facility for all of their patients' ills and sufferings. To a military man like McClain, retaliation with violence when attacked by evil would be a logical reaction.

"His mind was inflamed constantly by an endless repetition of antigovernment sentiment, and when his treatments by the 'quack' failed to bring relief, it was explained that the real enemy was the facility at Plum Island. Do away with the facility, do away with the problem. As I said, we may never know what happened that fateful afternoon, but as I understand it, I have summarized the government's position and accusations.

THE POISON PLUM

"The lives and families of hundreds of people have been dramatically impacted by the events of the past several days. With me today on this stage are human faces attached to these tragedies. We have the wives and children of the doctors that were raided yesterday. We also have the wife of Dr. Glen Klinner, Fran Klinner of Long Island, with us today. Her husband, Glen, was the apparent principal target of the government's raids. As many of you will recall, Dr. Klinner was treating Colonel McClain and is alleged to have given him dangerous mind-altering drugs to further destabilize his mental condition so that he could be goaded into committing an act of violence. At this time I would like to take just a moment to introduce the other wives, many of whom I'm certain you will recognize. I will ask each of them to briefly stand along with their children as they are being introduced."

Congressman McDonald then moved to stand beside the first of the wives as he began the introductions.

"First, I would like to introduce Mrs. Janice Stegall and her son, Benjamin, and daughter, Eileen. Janice is the wife of Dr. Eric Stegall, a local cardiologist. Many of you will recognize Janice because of her very heavy involvement in civic affairs. She is a member of the New London City Commission and serves also on the board of directors of the local YMCA. Thank you, Janice, Benjamin, and Eileen.

"Next, we have Mrs. Dorothy Jackson and her daughter, Sybil. Dorothy is the wife of our very popular local pediatrician, Dr. Robert Jackson. Dorothy is also active in community affairs. She serves as a member of the board of trustees of the New London Community College and is also active in the First Methodist Church, serving as treasurer and organist."

Anna never ceased to be amazed at the incredible ability Harry had to scan and retain copious quantities of dates, names, addresses, and other details with only a cursory perusal. She had provided Harry with her handwritten bio sketches of the wives and their families as they were making their way to the stage that afternoon. With only a quick, one-time read through, Harry had folded the notes Anna had written and slipped them into his pocket as he began the introductions.

Congressman McDonald moved to stand beside each of the wives as each introduction was completed. Occasional applause was heard among the members of the audience because of the popularity and recognition of several of the ladies.

"Next, we are happy to have with us Mrs. Kathryn Davis and her sons Tim, Frank, and Scott. Kathryn is the wife of Dr. Edward Davis, who is in the practice of rheumatology. Kathryn is the organizer each year of the Junior Miss Pageant, president of the PTA, and president of the Garden Club in New London."

By this time, Special Agent Litvak, one of the sixteen government agents dispersed throughout the audience, had heard all he could stand. He turned to Special Agent Rogers and whispered to him.

"Would you get a load of this McDonald guy? This is like Ozzie and Harriett with a side order of June Cleaver and *Leave It to Beaver*! What the hell is he going to do next? Drag out some ninety-year-old grandmother on a walker to tell how she had to take up knitting and selling Bibles door-to-door to finance her orphaned grandson's medical school education? Geeeez, what a schmaltz!"

"Take a look around, Litvak! These people are clinging to his every word. He practically has them eating out of his hand. Look at these people! He may be a schmaltz but he's got this crowd."

And indeed he did. But Congressman McDonald always had the crowd, except of course when he was surrounded by the yapping curs of the liberal media, ACLU types, government agents, rabid pro-abortion feminists, or gun control advocates. Harry McDonald was loved, trusted, and admired by the average American man and woman. He was despised and vilified by those on the liberal end of the political spectrum who would seize any and every opportunity to hurl their epithets and spew their poisonous venom in Harry's direction.

Harry continued with each introduction, moving clockwise around the semicircle of seated wives and children until every family had been courteously introduced to the audience. Of the remaining group, there were wives and children of four infectious disease specialists and one neurologist. And, as with the other wives, all had positions of involvement and commitment to community affairs… board of education chair, medical auxiliary, charity boards, Junior League, Salvation Army, Girl Scouts, and many more.

"Before I ask Mrs. Fran Klinner to stand with me for a more formal introduction, I would like each of you here today to once again recall the government's allegations against these wives' husbands. Remember that these families' livelihoods and reputations have been smashed as a result of the raids…at least for the time being. In addition, very serious charges have been levied…including aiding and abetting a terrorist act against the United States of America. Please understand all of you… we are talking *treason* here, which carries the death penalty!

"And so, we are asked by the government to believe that the perfectly normal-appearing wives and children we have before us today belong to husbands and fathers who are conspirators, co-conspirators, frauds, and medical quacks. Let us now briefly examine each of these categories of charges to see if there exists any degree of merit to any of them."

Harry moved to Fran Klinner's chair and briefly stood by her side before asking her to join him at the podium.

"Ladies and gentlemen, please allow me to introduce Mrs. Fran Klinner of Long Island, whose husband, Dr. Glen Klinner, is the linchpin of the government's attacks against the doctors. Because Colonel Gordon McClain was Dr. Klinner's patient, all charges and allegations stem from that association."

Harry continued, "Fran, how long have we known each other?"

"How long, Harry? Well, let me think…. Glen and I started dating while the two of you were still in medical school. We have been married now for eighteen years, so I guess we have been friends now for about twenty years."

"That's right, Fran. Glen and I became close friends while we were in medical school together over twenty years ago. In all those years, I have never heard Glen express any anti-government sentiment whatsoever. What about you, Fran? Did Glen ever complain to you or express a dislike for the government or its policies?"

"No, Harry, of course not! Glen loves this country! I can't imagine any citizen being more responsible and patriotic than Glen. Unless, of course, it's you, Harry! Glen is totally devoted to his practice and our family. All he ever talks about is trying to help people regain their health. You know how dedicated he is, Harry!"

"Yes, I do, and I certainly agree. But I do think there is a conspiracy at work here. There are conspirators, co-conspirators, and nefarious plots and schemes aplenty. But not with Dr. Klinner or the other accused, however. For you see it's the accusers themselves who are the real conspirators. The modus operandi of tyrants worldwide has been to accuse their victims of the very crimes that they themselves were committing. As for the charges of fraud, quackery, and charlatanism, these are heaped up by the accusers in an effort to add as much vile calumny as possible to their allegations.

"As a former practicing, third-generation physician, I can assure you that fraud, quackery, and charlatanism are not practiced by men possessed with the impeccable medical credentials of Dr. Glen Klinner and the other victims. Fraud, quackery, and charlatanism are practiced however, by ruthless government agents and their superiors bent on the establishment of an evil preconceived agenda."

MacIntosh McAdams was seated on the third row of the area normally reserved for media personnel. He was grinning like a Cheshire cat and was just as feisty. Or as some would say, "He was a grinnin' like a jackass eating briers" and just as stubborn, they might add.

Oh, this is good! This is really good, Mac thought. *I just wish I could see that pusillanimous scum over at Justice and the Bureau twist and turn when they see and hear this! I don't know where McDonald is going with this build up, but he's got a good head of steam cooking already…keep their feet to the fire, Mr. Congressman…don't let up. If only the American people had enough brains and guts to elect 434 more representatives like this guy!*

Harry paused for a few moments, turned from the audience, and directed his gaze slowly and individually to each of the wives and their children. Having done so, he then turned again to face the audience, which by now was almost mesmerized by Harry's words and his presentation. The auditorium, although filled to capacity, was as silent as a tomb. Every man and woman present was waiting with baited breath for Harry's next words.

Well, it's come to this at long last, Harry thought. *Here I am at the precipice, and there's no turning back now…for better or for worse, now is the time I must strike back at the enemy.*

"Ladies and Gentlemen…make no mistake. I am quite serious in my conviction that there exists a conspiracy encompassing an evil, omnipresent, preconceived agenda. No, I do not at this time know what that conspiracy entails. I do not know who the conspirators and co-conspirators are, nor do I know the scope of their agenda. But as God is my witness, I give you today my solemn oath to leave no stone unturned in my quest for the truth. We must make it our unwavering priority to exonerate the doctors who have been so maliciously attacked by their own government and we must not rest until our great American hero Colonel Gordon McClain has been vindicated and honor restored to his name. Just maybe, that in death he will have achieved martyrdom status after the truth is known, and those responsible for their evil deeds are exposed and brought to justice.

"Ladies and gentlemen, my office has discovered information, which if true, would provide an explanation for the actions of Colonel McClain. And if true, would also provide justification for the government's raids and news conferences so slanted with inaccuracies, bias, slander, lies, and exaggerations, even Hitler's minister of propaganda Goebbels would have been proud. I believe Colonel McClain *had* discovered the information I am referring to, and I believe the horror of it all led him to make one last sacrifice for the nation he so loved. By the taking of other lives that he felt were committed to the furtherance of an incredibly diabolical program, I believe Colonel McClain, with his last breath of life on this planet, opposed and fought to the death an evil he clearly recognized. In contrast to a mind described by the government as being paranoid and delusional as a result of mind-altering drugs being administered surreptitiously, we may find in retrospect that Colonel McClain's cognitive functions were never more lucid and focused! We may disagree with his taking of human life, but ladies and gentlemen, please remember that Colonel McClain was a soldier, an American, and a patriot. Soldiers participate in warfare. And wars are waged when there is no other recourse…negotiations have failed…diplomacy has failed. The enemy must be stopped at any cost, or freedom will perish. According to General George Patton, 'compared to war, all other forms of human endeavor pale into insignificance.'

"I think Colonel McClain saw the enemy at the gate, or perhaps more accurately, he saw the enemy exiting from the Trojan Horse strategically placed within our borders. He was a soldier first and foremost, and ladies and gentlemen, when all the facts are in, we may just come to the belated understanding that his actions at the ferry landing last Friday afternoon were quite possibly the culmination of the greatest patriotic commitment and sacrifice of his entire illustrious career.

"But how, you may ask, could any evil, no matter how reprehensible, justify the Plum Island ferry slaughter…almost one hundred people dead, including one of the greatest Americans to have ever lived? How, you may ask? How indeed can we justify the battle of the Bulge, D-day, Hiroshima, or Nagasaki? Only in the context of the preservation of greater numbers of lives by the immediate sacrifice of a smaller number of lives. Statistically cruel, you may say, and we may reason and debate the morality and consequence of these actions for the rest of our lives. Regrettably but inevitably all of recorded history clearly illustrates the consistency of human action when threatened by a clear and present danger.

"Ladies and gentlemen, in my humble opinion, Colonel Gordon McClain was guided throughout his military career by that time-honored history of consistency in human action. And what was his motivation? What enemy had he discovered? What foul, evil, nefarious scheme had he uncovered? What vile, treacherous conspiracy had been revealed to him? Had Satan incarnate appeared at the ferry landing last Friday?"

MacIntosh McAdams felt he was on the verge of some apex of escalating emotional response, not unlike a powerful orgasmic release.

Is he going after Plum Island? Does he have that kind of cojones? What information? Holy cow! What next? Hell, bring on the cavalry! I'm ready to sign up! This is incredible…This guy is speaking from the heart! He has not resorted to one single note or cue! He actually believes what he is saying! Oh man, just when I didn't think it could get any better. And look at these people! They look like they are about two pints of blood low and somebody just turned the thermostat down!

McDonald continued, "What if Colonel McClain had discovered a plot against mankind more insidious, more malevolent, more diabolical, and more hideously terrible than could ever be imagined by any normal, rational human being? If that were true, would his actions then be considered justifiable? What has transpired can never be reversed…only the history of Friday's massacre can be written, rewritten, reported, altered, and embellished by today's media and the history books of the future. But to what end? What happened is what happened. It is to us, the living, to sort through the available information and facts at hand to attempt, at least, to come to some kind of understanding as to what actually did occur. Armed with that knowledge, we have the moral mandate to take whatever action is required to ensure that an event of this magnitude can never again, even accidentally, overflow from a seething cauldron filled with evil intentions and schemes of megalomania run rampant. The eyes of God are upon us, and we will be judged by the Almighty for what we do or don't do today. The sins of omission are as great as are the sins of commission! May God Himself guide, direct, and strengthen our resolve as we go forward!

"Ladies and gentlemen, it is my opinion as a former practicing physician, member of the United States Congress, and Chairman of the Health and Human Services Committee, that there exists, within just a few miles from where we stand today, a top-secret government bio-warfare laboratory functioning at the direction and control of unseen and unrecognized government officials with the objective and mandate of creating incredibly virulent pathogens genetically engineered specifically to kill or maim untold millions of innocent human beings."

THE POISON PLUM

The crowd's response might have been slightly different, if somehow, several caskets had suddenly fallen through the roof of the New London Community Center and had spilled their grisly contents upon the stage where Harry McDonald stood…but not by much. Five full minutes elapsed before sufficient order had been restored to allow Congressman McDonald to resume his remarks.

"Colonel McClain was dying from pathogens developed by scientists in that very laboratory. He understood their source and the mission of those responsible for their development. He was not driven mad by doses of mind-altering drugs. He was driven to action by a motivation to stop an out-of-control evil plot threatening the very existence of mankind. Ladies and gentlemen, the facility to which I refer is located on Plum Island, a scant ten miles across the Long Island Sound from Old Lyme, Connecticut.

"The government is trying to protect and preserve the secrecy surrounding that laboratory. That is why their brownshirts have raided and incarcerated the doctors who have dedicated their lives and practices to the treatment of diseases caused by the Plum Island pathogens. Any connection between the facility and those diseases must be suppressed. You, the innocent victims of these schemes, must be kept unawares of the true source of your oppression. Until, of course, it is too late to resist. All resistance at that point in time would be futile at best.

"Ladies and gentlemen, it's show-and-tell time! One of the pathogens, courtesy of the creative scientists at Plum Island, is a bacterial infection known as Lyme disease. You have all heard of it. How many of you today are personally infected with that bacterium or have an immediate family member or close friend battling the disease? Come on now; let's see a show of hands. Don't be bashful, hold them high."

MacIntosh McAdams was aghast! As the hands were raised, slowly at first and then in rapid succession, a cursory observation revealed that at least 45 percent of the audience had a hand raised.

Holy cow! Mac thought, *what a headline this would make! 'New World Order Conspirators Conquer America With Rampaging Arachnids!'*

Mac could almost feel tiny nymph ticks crawling up the calves of his legs. And probably a very sizeable percentage of the audience began scratching locations that really didn't itch at all.

Congressman McDonald was also shocked. He did not even remotely suspect, until this very moment, that the prevalence of infection was as high as this.

My God, he thought, *this is an epidemic!*

Several members of the audience including some in the media section obviously quite agitated were trying to interrupt the proceedings with impatient comments or questions. Others were talking aloud to each other, contributing to the hubbub and din that began to prevail. Minutes elapsed before Congressman McDonald was able to resume his remarks.

"Ladies and Gentlemen, to say that Lyme disease is a problem is a massive understatement. You all saw the show of hands a few moments ago. By any definition or measure, whenever any portion of a population is impacted by a disease affecting a percentage of that group as sizeable as represented here today, it is, purely and simply, classified as an epidemic. Epidemics by definition are crises that demand a massive, immediate, coordinated, concerted effort to control. And logically, an epidemic created by a conspiracy, demands a massive, immediate, coordinated and concerted effort to control the epidemic by exposing the conspiracy that created it in the first place! The greatest threat to any conspiracy's continued existence and perpetuation is exposure. The light of day must be allowed to shine brightly, illuminating the conspirators, their agents, their schemes, plots, and modus operandi.

"Ladies and gentlemen, the task before us is incredibly formidable and fraught with peril. Failure may indeed be our lot, but try we must. Indeed, we have no other option before us. The battle to vindicate Colonel Gordon McClain, free and exonerate all the physicians incarcerated by the government, expose the government's bio-warfare schemes, and prosecute all of those responsible including the maniacally malevolent geneticists and scientists involved, will be a Herculean effort. We must not, however, shirk from our responsibilities and obligations as freedom-loving Americans. The effort to right these wrongs begins here, and it begins now. The buck stops with us!

"As your representative to the United States Congress, I am today, formally announcing that I will use my position as Chairman of the Health and Human Services Committee to launch an in-depth investigation into the activities and programs of the laboratory on Plum Island. I will use the powers at my disposal, which include, but are not limited to, the use of subpoenas for obtaining testimony and the Freedom of Information Act to the maximum extent possible. I am asking all of you, as my loyal constituents, to offer and provide your support in any way possible to my efforts. Immediately upon my return to Washington tomorrow morning, my office will begin our investigation and initiate the gathering of as much intelligence as possible. And I will, as soon as possible, begin the necessary organizational procedures to begin committee hearings. We will also move very aggressively to secure the release, as soon as possible, of all of the physicians wrongfully charged and incarcerated.

"I thank all of you for your attendance today. And I thank you brave wives of the doctors for your attendance. Before we begin the question and answer portion of our news conference, I ask for your prayers. Pray that the very hand of God Almighty will guide and strengthen our efforts and lead us to victory. Thank you!"

The audience's reaction was swift and dramatic. A standing ovation, complete with whistles and shouts, began immediately and lasted for several minutes. Conspicuously absent from participation in the enthusiastic support for Congressman McDonald were several members of the media and government agents planted throughout the audience who remained seated with glum, dour expressions. *Well, that's one way to separate the wheat from the chaff,* thought Harry. *Now we know who the Judases are in this crowd!*

McAdams felt a pride growing in his chest that he thought had been banished forever by the growing cynicism of American society. Almost as if he were experiencing a musical hallucination, he could hear within his mind the words and music of the *Star Spangled Banner*. Standing very erect and vigorously contributing to the applause, Mac at that moment felt very proud to be an American and could have very easily begun singing aloud the national anthem.

"I've seen a lot of senators, congressmen, assemblymen, and other assorted predators and parasites walk across the American political stage during my many years as a reporter for *The Chronicle*. Most were no more than political opportunists, hacks, and self-serving whores. This guy is real! In my opinion, the man on that stage today is the greatest true American in Congress this nation has seen since the turn of the last century! I feel humbled and proud just to be in attendance at this news conference today!"

Mac was speaking to no one in particular but to all of the other reporters within earshot. Every media representative present knew who MacIntosh McAdams was. Many, of course, vehemently disagreed with most of his editorial positions, likening Mac's frequent diatribes to some form of anachronistic musings. But agree or disagree, two things were for certain. Every single member of the media represented respected Mac, and every single person within earshot listened to what he said.

Almost like a fax transmission, the words for tomorrow morning's op-ed piece on today's conference began accumulating and positioning themselves within Mac's brain. It would be a long day for Mac, but it didn't matter. Sleep would not come until much, much later because there was just too much adrenaline and too much excitement. Mac couldn't wait for the question-and-answer session to be completed so that he could begin writing tomorrow's editorial on his laptop. Before the press deadline, Mac's editorial would be completed in time to be published in the morning edition. For, on this very day, Congressman McDonald's crusade had become Mac's crusade. The baton had been passed.

Mac found himself thinking, *"For on one man's soul a light hath shone which doth not depart..."*

And why am I thinking of those lines penned so long ago? Who wrote that anyway? I can't remember. The last time I read that was in my high school literature class! Seems to fit nicely though, considering the circumstances at hand.

McDonald turned to individually thank each wife and her children for their attendance as Erin Giblon stood and moved to assume her position at the podium.

"Ladies and gentlemen, my name is Erin Giblon. I am Congressman McDonald's aide in our Washington office. We want to thank each of you for your attendance today, and we ask that you please contact our office with any information you may have that you feel would be relevant to our investigation of the Plum Island facility. We will be establishing a toll-free hotline for your convenience as soon as possible. Until that line is available, please consider using the Internet to contact us at www.usrepmcdonald.gov. There you will find a link to forward e-mail messages to us. Your input is very important to our efforts, and we appreciate your participation. At this time Congressman McDonald will return to the podium, and we will begin the question and answer portion of our news conference. Congressman McDonald..."

"Thank you, Miss Giblon. We will now address questions you may have. Please stand as you present your question so that others in the audience can hear and understand your question clearly."

The first person leaping to his feet without waiting to be recognized by the congressman was an editorial writer for *The Times* by the name of Simon Snodgrass. Simon wrote a weekly column for *The Times,* entitled, yes you guessed it, "Simon Says…" His columns consistently espoused a liberal panegyrical viewpoint some thought was to the left of Karl Marx. McAdams could barely suppress a sneer when he saw Simon stand, all five feet nine inches and 295 pounds of his pathetically sweaty and corpulent self. Mac and Simon were enemies, had been for years, and made no secret of their dislike for each other. Mac had always wanted somehow to obliquely incorporate a reference to Simon in an editorial by referring to him as Simon Slobass but the opportunity had just never seemed to present itself.

Someday, I'll nail that pig, Mac thought, *unless he strokes out or has a coronary first from all that lard he is hauling around. Better yet, ship him off to the lab at Plum and let the ticks feast on him! Hell, the ticks would probably get sick first!*

"Congressman McDonald!" roared Simon. "I'm Simon Snodgrass with *The Times.*"

"I know who you are."

"Congressman McDonald, have you no shame, sir? Witch hunts died out in the seventeenth century! McCarthyism was repudiated by the American people in the twentieth century! We now live in the advanced, enlightened age of the twenty-first century, or haven't you noticed? Your entire news conference today is nothing more than an attempt to establish a pretext to justify plunging America into some atavistic world you grandiosely envision. We at *The Times* will have no part of your schemes of civil liberty repression, and we will oppose your witch hunts as vigorously as possible."

"That wasn't a question, Mr. Snodgrass, it was a statement. Do you have a question?"

"Yeah, I have a question! Are you going to spare your constituents and the body politic of America the shame and humiliation of your so-called committee investigations by resigning? One Joseph McCarthy ravaging America was enough!"

"No!"

Even as Simon was shaking his head and lowering his ponderous bulk into his chair, others were thrusting their hands skyward and vying for attention…dozens asking and signaling for recognition, and all quite emotionally agitated.

"Congressman McDonald! Congressman McDonald! Reeves with the *New England Banner* here. If what you suspect is indeed true, how did those germs get out of the laboratory? By accident or by design? And are all of us living in close proximity to Plum Island in jeopardy?"

"I honestly, at this time, do not know, Mr. Reeves. Perhaps the germs leaked out due to lack of appropriate security measures. Perhaps the germs were deliberately placed to attack the neighboring populations. Perhaps some brilliant but twisted scientist couldn't wait to test the efficacy of his creation. Why do creators of computer viruses use their genius and creativity to bedevil mankind with their creations? I can't explain or rationalize that type of behavior. As regards your continued safety residing in close proximity to Plum Island, you may wish to recall the show of hands demonstrated earlier and come to your own conclusions."

"Congressman McDonald! Lemke with *The Post* here. Your rabid, right-wing predecessors, of whom Senator Joseph McCarthy was a sterling example, warned us that there was a commie under every rock. And now you, obviously bent upon perpetuating your predecessor's legacy of fear tactics, are warning us that the government has placed an insect laced with dangerous germs under every rock."

It's a good thing I'm not standing in McDonald's shoes, thought Mac. *I would ask that bottom-feeder Lemke if the liberal media were being forced out from under their own rocks by the unprecedented invasion of insects!*

And so it went that afternoon in the New London Community Center. For the better part of an hour, lunges and parries, jabs and jibes, ideological axes to grind, and finally after the big guns of the liberal media had exhausted their arsenal of invectives, the local media and concerned citizens had their opportunities to question Congressman McDonald.

McAdams patiently held his silence and remained seated. Oh, he had something to say all right, but it would be later, after the crowds had thinned and after other media personnel had left. A private conversation with the congressman was definitely in order.

Mac's intense concentration was interrupted when he heard his name called. Hank Sturgess of the *New London Ledger* was making his way through the slowly thinning crowd to be at Mac's side.

"Hi Mac! Glad you could make it. What did you think of the news conference? Did you get your money's worth?"

"Yeah, Hank, I did. Even more than I bargained for. I think I have just joined a crusade."

"What do you mean?"

"I think McDonald is on target. That damn lab sitting out there in Long Island Sound is a ticking time bomb that should have been defused a long time ago. And there may be others like it—Ft. Collins, Ft. Detrick, China Lake, and maybe even the CDC. Who the hell knows?"

"Are you going to puff McDonald?"

"McDonald? No. I'm going to provide ammunition for his committee investigation. My staff at *The Chronicle* is going to dig into these bio-labs. We are going to tap into our contacts and sources. We're going to ask a lot of probing questions, both editorially and privately. And we're going to chase a lot of rumors, and we're going to piss off a lot of arrogant people at Justice, CIA, and the Bureau. You know how Joe Six-Pack and the so-called silent majority are always waiting for someone to give them a cause or issue to be concerned about?"

"Yeah, the media programs their minds with the cause de jour and off they march like little wind-up soldiers."

"Well, if they want a cause or an issue to occupy their minds, something to be concerned about, they're going to get it! Starting with tomorrow morning's edition of *The Chronicle!*

Maybe those otherwise vacuous people can focus on something important for a change instead of the routinely inane drivel they normally feed on!"

"Mac, I think the congressman has really pulled your chain! I've never seen you so agitated and intense."

"It's not just McDonald," said Mac, "this stuff with the lab is just the tip of the iceberg. We have been watching the moral decline of America and the concomitant demise of accountability for a long time, Hank. Hell, you and I have had birthdays Hank, more than we care to admit. It's easy to look back over the years with the luxury of 20/20 hindsight vision and wisdom and gauge the degree of deterioration of society. The trend and direction of deterioration can be ascertained with accuracy given the luxury of years to compare. You see it too, Hank. I know how you think. You are as fed up with this crap as I am. Enough is enough! It's time to fight back. What did they tell us in journalism school? The pen is mightier than the sword! Well Hank, let's unsheathe our pens and see what happens before we wind up in wheelchairs with drip bags pouring antibiotics into our bodies!

"Hank, I need to tell the congressman I'm on the team, and I need to establish a liaison with his aide or whoever. Do you know them well enough to introduce me with an endorsement of my sincerity?"

"Sure, Mac. I've covered all of his campaigns for the *Ledger*. I think he trusts me because I've always reported the campaigns fairly and accurately. I've never met his aide personally, but we've talked frequently coordinating his appearances in the district. I've always wondered if she was as pretty as her voice sounded over the phone, and now I know. She's a looker, that's for sure. Yeah, this is a great opportunity for intros all around. Let me see if I can get her attention first and when things slow down a little more, I'll introduce you to McDonald. Let's go over to the side and rear of the stage and wait our turn."

By this time, the television and radio media had stopped their cameras and recorders and for the most part had left the auditorium. Some area newspaper reporters and some of the concerned constituents remained with lingering questions. Hank and Mac approached Erin Giblon who was chatting with a few of the wives before their departures. Realizing that the two men were waiting to speak to her and were probably media representatives, she politely expedited the goodbyes and expressions of appreciation, and then excused herself to greet Hank and Mac.

"Miss Giblon, I'm Hank Sturgess with the *New London Ledger*."

"Yes, Mr. Sturgess, we've spoken many times. It's a pleasure to meet you, and the congressman and I appreciate your attendance today. What did you think of the congressman's conference?"

"Well it was not exactly what I was expecting…it was a pretty sobering message. He certainly raised some issues and concerns that are quite unsettling and obviously require immediate attention. We at the *Ledger* will of course be following closely your investigation and will duly report developments as they occur to our readership. Miss Giblon, I'd like you to meet someone. This is MacIntosh McAdams of *The Chronicle*."

"Oh, really," responded Erin. "I've been reading your columns since I was in grad school. Your trenchant and incisive reporting style is certainly unique in today's journalistic environment."

"Well I guess that's a compliment. I'll take it as one, thank you. I have something to say to the congressman, actually to you both, and I wonder if you could arrange an introduction for me?"

"Certainly, Mr. McAdams. No problem. The congressman also reads your columns on occasion and frequently comments on their content. Looks like the questions are just about completed. Let me see if I can get his attention."

Hank, Erin, and Mac chatted among themselves for several more minutes until finally Congressman McDonald was able to break away and began moving in their direction.

"Hello, Mr. Sturgess. Nice to see you again. Thanks for covering my conference."

"Nice to see you too, Mr. Congressman. I must say that your conference today was definitely out of the ordinary. Some would even say gripping and shocking."

"Well, be prepared, Mr. Sturgess. As our investigation goes forward, it may get a little rough out there. I plan to step on a lot of toes before we are done. I only hope that you will provide coverage of the committee hearings for your subscribers in the same fair and impartial manner as we have become accustomed to with your reporting."

"I'll do my best, Mr. Congressman. You can count on it. And I have a suspicion that the gentleman here with me plans to do his part as well. Mr. Congressman, this is my longtime friend, MacIntosh McAdams of *The Chronicle*."

"Ah, yes, Mr. McAdams. I frequently read your columns, and I especially enjoyed your recent exposé of the selective placement of government contracts for the rebuilding of Iraq and Afghanistan. And what did you think of the news conference today?"

"You confirmed a lot of my previous suspicions. Before I return to Washington, I was hoping for an opportunity to meet you and your aide. Could we talk for a few minutes?"

"Certainly, Mr. McAdams. Miss Giblon would you please advise Anna that we will be occupied in room 3-A for a bit, and I will join her shortly?"

After Erin, Harry, Mac, and Hank were seated comfortably, Mac began by saying that he only had a very short time to visit. His flight back to Washington was at 8:20 PM, and he would need to find time somehow to prepare his column in time for tomorrow morning's issue of *The Chronicle*. Then Mac quickly got to the crux of the matter by explaining his reason for a personal meeting with Harry and his aide.

"Congressman McDonald, I am going to use all of the available resources that can be provided by *The Chronicle* to begin our own inquiry into the research activities at the Plum Island germ lab. Also, we will begin an extensive inquiry into the charges levied against the doctors and the terms and locations of their incarcerations. And to the fullest extent possible, we will investigate Colonel McClain's background, medical history, and possible motivations for his actions.

"Also be advised that I will provide to our readers continuous and on-going coverage of your committee's investigations. If you have the opportunity, check out tomorrow morning's edition of *The Chronicle*. I will be firing our opening salvo with my column. I think you will be pleased. I propose also that our offices establish a liaison to exchange pertinent information. We at *The Chronicle* will be happy to work with Miss Giblon or whomever you choose to designate. I am joining your team, Mr. Congressman. Call it a tocsin bell, a call to arms; the Redcoats are coming, or whatever you choose. The bottom line coach? Send me in, I don't smoke!"

Laughter spontaneously erupted after that comment by Mac, and as soon as Harry could regain his composure, he responded by saying how much he appreciated the involvement of both Hank and Mac. And yes, he appreciated also the offer to exchange information between their respective offices realizing full well the abilities of the press to gather information that would normally be outside the purview of the average citizen or even a congressman's office, for that matter.

Harry also realized the extreme importance of garnering as much friendly media support as possible. The cannons of the enemy would begin their fusillades and broadsides with some editions of the evening news. But the full force and fury of the approaching battle would begin with the eleven o'clock news reports. And from then on for the duration of this battle between the forces of darkness and deceit and the defenders of truth and light, the attacks of lies, smears, misrepresentation, character assassination, guilt by association, and endless canards would continue unabated. Their intensity and viciousness would only increase steadily in ferocity as the battle raged.

Wednesday—
"Bugs and Plums"

After a perfunctory scan of the title of MacIntosh McAdams's regular Wednesday column, perhaps many of *The Chronicle's* devoted readers surmised that in his advancing years Mac was beginning to wax a bit bucolic. Do we have before us a column devoted to the field of horticulture and specifically to the protection of plum trees from the onslaught of marauding bugs? Certainly the title and the first few lines of text might indeed support that supposition. A brief reference was given to the history of Plum Island, New York; a once tranquil island off the coast of Long Island noted for its serenity and of course, plum trees. Mac explained that the island had been in years past a sportsman's paradise offering opportunities for hunting deer, ducks, geese, rabbits, dove, and quail. It also was a favorite respite for day trekkers, campers, and vacationers, offering natural beauty and peaceful solitude.

The casual reader began to wonder if the plum trees and their juicy, succulent fruits were somehow being jeopardized by a mysterious plague of locusts or other insects. And perhaps just before the average reader might have become unconcerned with an exposé of the condition of plum trees on an island off the coast of Long Island and moved on to the sports page, the trigger words and power phrases began falling like trip-hammers into the reader's consciousness. The words and phrases were all there, offered up by the author in rapid succession, brilliantly interwoven to achieve maximum psychological impact among the readership. All of course in the unique inimitable MacIntosh McAdams style of journalism. What began as a benignly bland-appearing article about plum trees infested with insects rapidly evolved into a gripping, probing summarization of the recent events at the Plum Island ferry and the government's dramatic raids on physicians and their offices.

The bloody massacre at the ferry, the impeccable career of Colonel Gordon McClain, the unanswered questions regarding his motivation were all delivered to the reader in staccato, machine-gun style and intensity. In a normal world the "Bugs and Plums" piece would have been a shoe-in for a Pulitzer, but in a normal world, the events which predicated the article's creation would have never existed at all. For the majority of Mac's devoted readership with brain cells functioning normally and neurons firing in the proper sequence, their world would never ever again be the same after reading Mac's column that day. Questions and concerns were raised that could not be assuaged by even the most clever spin doctors and apologists for the machinations of the New World Order.

A deep-seated and foreboding fear of the unknown was inculcated that day among certain of *The Chronicle's* readership. Coverage of Congressman McDonald's news conference was, of course, provided at the completion of Mac's column and served to reassure at least some of the readers that not all good men are standing idly by to allow evil to triumph unabated. Fortuitously, someone in a position of authority and responsibility is taking action.

Job Security?

Even if Susan Collins were not totally preoccupied in her free time with her son's health problems, she probably still would have missed Congressman McDonald's news conference. Having never been much of a news hound, she would also have been unaware of MacIntosh McAdams's incendiary column in that morning's edition of *The Chronicle*. She would have been oblivious as well to the left-wing diatribes offered up by Simon Snodgrass and others of his ilk representing an assortment of the liberal media. Susan had always concentrated on the furtherance of her education, her career, and the needs of her immediate family. National and world events were beyond her ability to influence, and as a consequence, she felt it a waste of time and energy to occupy her mind with matters totally beyond her control. Besides, she reasoned, most news today was depressing, rendering to the observer feelings of helplessness and impotence.

Susan's only personal source for news events and developments now that she had made the move to New London from Birmingham was her sister, Cathy. In all probability, Cathy would have picked up on something in the news referencing Congressman McDonald's news conference and his plans to investigate the Plum Island facility. But since the weekend, Cathy was now spending almost all of her time staying at Susan's place doing what she could to help with Toby. Television and radio remained unused except for brief periods when Toby might watch a children's show. Toby was by now even sicker, and Cathy's support was a Godsend as Susan tried to balance work and care-giving for Toby. Thursday's appointment with Dr. Aventi at the Medical Center was now only hours away, and Susan was doing everything possible to tough it out until then. Help was right around the corner, she felt. Arrangements had been made with her superiors at the facility to take the entire day off on Thursday to be with Toby.

The bliss of ignorance however was shattered for Susan within minutes of arriving at the facility Wednesday morning. She was greeted with an atmosphere of solemnity, as somber expressions prevailed on the faces of the personnel present. Very shortly thereafter came an intercom announcement that everyone was to convene in the conference room by 9:00 AM for an important announcement.

What now? she thought. *Is funding for the laboratory going to be suspended by the politicians because of the controversy surrounding the massacre? Be just my luck. Lose my job, my income, and my medical insurance just when I need it the most!*

Susan closed down her work in progress and moved to the conference room, arriving a few minutes before 9:00 AM. The facility's support personnel were engaged in lively and animated discussions as she entered the room. Phrases such as; "extremely conservative Congressman," "right wing ideologue," "conspiracy theorist," "paranoid fanatic," "investigation," and "Health and Human Services Committee" could be overheard throughout the din of voices, which seemingly were all speaking at once.

Oh, my God! It's true! thought Susan. *Some nut is going to cut our funding! I don't need this! Not at any time and certainly not now!*

A dark-suited government somebody was trying to get people to calm down and take their seats in order to begin the meeting. Several minutes elapsed before order was restored and Acting Facility Director Stephens took the microphone to introduce the official from the Department of Homeland Security in Washington.

As Susan recognized his name, a distinct feeling of unease spread throughout her body. The official was none other than Victor Perloff, who had called her at home after the massacre. His icy cold telephone demeanor was reinforced by his physical appearance. His dark suit hung loosely on a tall, gaunt frame. The pockmarked, sallow complexion without a trace of a smile and cold piercing eyes completed the image of a chilling and foreboding presence.

This guy looks like he could chop his dinner guest into small pieces and then store those pieces in the freezer for snacks later on, thought Susan. *I've never seen anyone that conveyed the essence of sinister more than this creep. I'm going to sit close to an exit in case I have to throw up! Looks like Halloween came early to this place!*

Susan had a habit of mentally speaking back to her thoughts which provided a balance in her life and she did so again on this occasion.

Shut up, Susan, and just sit down and calm down. You don't have to look at this guy. Just shut up and listen to what he has to say.

Perloff opened by saying that there were enemies among certain members of the House and Senate that were narrow-mindedly opposed to the good work and research being done at the government's biological research centers and especially the facility at Plum Island. He continued.

"The unfortunate massacre of innocent scientists, technicians, and support staff by a crazed gunman has emboldened certain of these enemies to take legislative action to investigate, with the objective of curtailing research activities at Plum Island. Unfortunately, the most vocal of these critical voices belongs to a right-wing Connecticut congressman who happens to chair the Health and Human Services Committee. That congressman's name is Harry McDonald, and as many of you are already aware, he used his news conference of yesterday afternoon as a launching pad for his vendetta against the valuable research being done by the very capable scientists of the Plum Island facility. Research which I am sure you all recognize is more crucial to America's freedom then ever before as a result of the 9/11 attacks."

Well, it's true, thought Susan, *stir up some stink with a bogus investigation, and funding will be cut that's for sure. Guess I'll have to dust off and update my résumé! I really need more challenges in my life at this time!*

Perloff continued, "We at Homeland Security are, of course, committed to the continuance and preservation of our valuable work. We will be forced to comply with certain subpoenas, but information about our work here will not be volunteered to Congressman McDonald or any of his staff. Because of the sensitive nature of our research here, there exists enormous potential for misunderstandings to develop among the lay population regarding our intentions and the direction of our research. These misunderstandings could be fostered and nurtured by the short-sighted congressman and his staff, and those misconceptions and misunderstandings could be magnified beyond comprehension by frenzy-feeding irresponsible members of the news media.

"America's security depends on the efficacy and continuity of our work here and at the other labs involved in similar research. It is therefore in our collective and individual best interests to avoid any contact with any members of Congressman McDonald's office or any representative of the Health and Human Services Committee. Your reply to any question or questions will be as follows: 'I am not allowed to divulge the nature of my employment with the Animal Disease Research Center at Plum Island because of national security concerns.'

"You will avoid any and all representatives of the news media and make no response at all to any questions they may pose and then immediately report to Director Stephens how and by whom you were contacted. To say that your future job security depends upon your cooperation is an understatement.

"If any of you are presented with a subpoena, report to Director Stephens as soon as possible with the subpoena you have received. We will attempt to deflect as many of these unjustified subpoenas as possible using national security as our justification for seeking judicial order to quash. If you are subpoenaed, and our efforts to quash are rendered unsuccessful, you will be counseled and instructed thoroughly prior to your appearance before the committee. Your government appreciates your dedication to our mission here, and rest assured that we will engage all means to shield you from undue interference that may jeopardize your job security. America's future depends on the continuation of our work here, and by working together as a cohesive unit, that work will continue unfettered into the future."

Susan felt even more insecure and troubled after listening to Victor Perloff. Certainly his appearance was not reassuring and calming. His demeanor was even less so, and his words only contributed to the confusion in Susan's mind.

Just let me get through this day, let me spend time with Toby tonight, and tomorrow will be a better day. Answers will be provided by Dr. Aventi, and a course of treatment will be initiated that will quickly have Toby back to his former self. The Toby with the big, easy smile...the Toby with the quick laughter and boundless energy. The Toby with the playful spirit and the inquisitive nature. All of those things and more Susan wanted restored in Toby.

The sooner the better, she thought, *but there would always be work...always a job somewhere...* Susan would not allow her mind to dwell and obsess on the "what ifs" and "whys" of whatever might happen to her job at Plum Island. *Whatever is going to happen, will happen. There's no sense in fretting about it. I can get another job,* Susan thought, *but I can't get another Toby!*

Susan would go home tonight and do what she could to coax Toby to eat something. She would also do her best to try to make Toby comfortable and optimistic that after tomorrow's doctor's appointment, feeling better was right around the corner.

Her day passed uneventfully, and she remained oblivious to the water-cooler gossip and speculation so rampant at the facility that day. However, she was not oblivious to that damned constant nagging feeling of unease that seemed to permeate every pore of her body.

Grandfather's curse, she thought. *Ever since we arrived, it has been one dilemma after another with no end in sight! I just can't feel comfortable with any of those things causing the never-ending turmoil in my life. Tomorrow will be different, though, because getting Toby on the road to recovery will take a huge load off my mind. And if I need to explore other employment opportunities after that, well, so be it. At least I'll be up to the challenge.*

The more Susan thought about her job with the facility, the more she seriously entertained the idea of seeking employment elsewhere. Certainly she would miss seeing Cathy if she had to leave the area for another position, and Toby would miss Cathy too. But regardless of how one might try to rationalize the congressman's decision to investigate the Plum Island lab, the fallout from a prolonged inquiry could only be negative. Sentiment to continue funding for the facility could, and most probably would, be affected. Then, recent hiring for all biological research laboratories operated by the government would come under intense scrutiny, and would be the most heavily impacted by a funding reduction. Last in, first out. And that certainly would include Susan. But perhaps most problematic of all would be the evaluation of her credentials and résumé by any future employer.

The Plum Island lab was her first job since earning her doctorate in microbiology at UAB in Birmingham. The cumulative stigma of the massacre, ongoing rumors, critical and inquiring media, and ultimately a congressional investigation would put the icing on the cake. Susan would be guilty by association—her career forever and inextricably linked to whatever the ultimate fate of Plum might be.

Can't risk it, thought Susan. *It's got to be sooner rather than later. Just as soon as Toby is well again, I'll update my résumé and start the job search all over again. If I wait until the crap hits the fan, finding a comparable position might be practically impossible. I can just see it now…I go in for an interview at some prestigious pharmaceutical company and my résumé is reviewed by some cocky twit of a personnel director ten years my junior with a B.S. in administration.*

"Ms. Collins, I see here that you graduated with honors from UAB in Birmingham and you hold a doctorate in microbiology from that institution."

"That is correct."

"I also see that your only employment since completing your education was with that bug lab off of Long Island that was closed down by Congress after a lengthy investigation."

"That is also correct."

"Is it true, Ms. Collins, that homeless people were routinely removed from the streets of New York, Chicago, and San Francisco to be used in medical experiments at that facility?"

"I have no knowledge of that occurring."

"What exactly were your responsibilities at the biological warfare facility, Ms. Collins? Did you oversee the autopsies? Or perhaps you supervised the regular cleanings of the crematorium? Hmmm? Ms. Collins, we here at the Genesis Pharmaceutical Company are devoted to the preservation and betterment of human life, not its termination. I honestly don't feel that your employment history is compatible with and complimentary to our mission here at Genesis. I'm afraid we will have no need of your services, but we appreciate your consideration of our company. Good day, Ms. Collins."

Well, maybe that imaginary scenario is a bit of an exaggeration, thought Susan, *but what if it isn't?*

For the rest of that Wednesday, Susan's productivity at the center was minimal at best. The double whammy of concerns for Toby and her future employment was taking top priority. The ferry ride back to the mainland presented a time for reflection. The heavily armed security guards at both ends of the ferry route, as well as armed guards onboard the ferry, only contributed to Susan's growing sense of urgency. Tonight, she wanted to share with Cathy some of her concerns and also a summation of the employee briefing at the facility. She, of course, wouldn't bluntly shock Cathy by suggesting that the solution to some of these problems might be relocation to another city.

One step at a time, thought Susan. *Toby first, then employment.*

She was glad to leave the mingling crowd of her co-workers and make her way to her car for the trip home. She wanted to see and spend time with Toby before their trip to the Medical Center tomorrow, and she wanted to talk to Cathy. As soon as she was seated and her door was closed, Susan was grateful for the confinement of the vehicle's interior as it provided a temporary barrier of insulation between her and any connection to the lab or to the outside world.

THE POISON PLUM

Arriving shortly at her modest home, Susan was pleased to see Cathy coming down the driveway to greet her with a hug and a kiss on the cheek.

"How is Toby?"

"I think he has missed you more than usual today. And I guess he is a little nervous about having to go to the Medical Center tomorrow. He's on the couch now, watching some afternoon cartoons. He slept some this morning but complained about the light hurting his eyes and said his back and legs hurt."

"Well," Susan said, "we had some crap dumped on us at the lab today. I can't wait to tell you about it. Some anal-retentive congressman wants to launch a full-blown investigation into the facility."

"What?"

"Yeah, I'll tell you later. Right now I can't wait to give Toby a big hug!"

Toby looked up when Susan entered the room and smiled as his mother gave him a warm hug. Susan thought Toby looked even more frail and weak then when she left for work this morning.

Is that possible? thought Susan as lines of concern were momentarily furrowing her brow. "How is my big boy feeling today? Any better? Have you been behaving for Aunt Cathy?"

"I guess so, Mom. Do I have to go to the doctor tomorrow?"

"Yes, Toby, and we are all excited! Dr. Aventi is a very good doctor, and after he gives you some new medicine, you are going to feel much better right away!"

"Mommy, I don't want any more shots. They hurt. Please tell the doctor not to give me any more shots."

"I will, Toby, I will. Just be a big boy for Mommy. Are you hungry or thirsty? Do you want Mommy to fix you something to eat or drink?"

"No Mommy, I'm not hungry."

"How about some hot chocolate and some cookies? You need to eat something...just for Mommy?"

"Could I have an egg sandwich?"

"Sure, sweetie. I'll fix it now. I'll scramble some eggs for you and put them on the buttered toast that you like so much. And I'll warm up some hot chocolate milk for you, too."

"Mommy, my head hurts."

"I'll get you some medicine."

"He's had six children's aspirins already today," Cathy said. "We're pushing it on those dosages."

"I'll let him have another one anyway. You know how his head and eyes always hurt more after he's eaten. Maybe if he has one before a meal, it will help."

Susan and Cathy continued chatting while walking into the kitchen to prepare Toby's food. Susan was breaking and scrambling the eggs while Cathy heated the chocolate milk.

"What kind of investigation were you talking about, Susan?"

"I don't know, but probably just some self-serving, two-faced congressman trying to use the massacre as justification for curtailing funding for the facility. He probably wants to appear thrifty, so he can push for some pork-barrel project in his own district. As he comes across as a hero to his constituents for minding America's purse strings, I wind up losing my job! America the beautiful! Bend and spread, it's time to sing the national anthem! I'm up to there, Cathy. My plate is full and overflowing."

"I know Sis, but maybe tomorrow your luck will begin changing. At least the doctors at the Medical Center will identify what's wrong with Toby, and having him well again would take a big load off your shoulders."

"You're right Cathy. I can deal with all these other problems handily once Toby is on the road to recovery. We've faced some tough times before haven't we? We'll get through this too!"

"And I'll be right there for you and Toby any way I can."

"I know you will. I just appreciate so much what you have already done to help us. I can't imagine the turmoil my life would be in without your help! I love you, Sis."

"And I love you, too, Susan. But right now the eggs are done, and the milk is hot. Let's get this to Toby."

Cathy had more concerns about Susan's announcement of a pending investigation, but she didn't exactly know how to frame her questions. After Toby had eaten and appeared comfortable for the time being, Cathy asked Susan if she knew the name of the congressman that would be conducting the investigation.

"I'm not sure," replied Susan, "let me think.... McDonald? Yeah, that's it. McDonald."

"First name or last name?" asked Cathy.

"McDonald? Last name... Congressman McDonald."

THE POISON PLUM

"Congressman Harry McDonald?" again asked Cathy.

"That sounds right. I think that's it. Harry McDonald."

"Well Susan, I have to admire and respect your ability to concentrate and remain focused on your career and Toby, but sometimes, just maybe, you might want to pull your head out of the sand and look around."

"What on earth do you mean?"

"Well, for example, you have been living here for almost a year now, and you don't even know who your congressman is. Your congressman, Susan, is Harry McDonald. He used to be a very well-known, highly respected doctor in this area. A cardiologist from the famed McDonald Cardiology Clinic. Several years ago he gave up a promising career in medicine to run for Congress."

"Maybe he should go back to being a doctor and quit messing with the source of my livelihood! I need that job, Cathy, and I need that health insurance. With Toby sick and medical bills piling up, I would be sunk if I lost my job."

"I know Susan but you need to understand that Congressman McDonald is of a different breed. He's not your typical politician. The man is on a mission to try to make a difference in Congress. Believe it or not, he is actually trying to return America to constitutional principles and limited government."

"Yeah, and limited government could mean I will be unemployed if he succeeds in cutting funding!"

"I don't know Susan. Since I have been here, what, almost three years now, I have had the opportunity to observe Congressman McDonald on several occasions, and I even met him once. I have been very impressed with his honesty, sincerity, and dedication. And I appreciate what he is trying to do for this country. We need more information, Sis, before we cast judgment on McDonald. Something is going on that we don't know about. I feel certain that if Congressman McDonald is launching an investigation into Plum Island, he has very compelling reasons for doing so.

"Wouldn't common sense tell us that as a doctor, he would be all about funding research into disease prevention? You would expect him to champion expanded research at Plum Island if anything, not curtailed research. This doesn't add up. Look, I'll tell you what. Stop worrying about what may or may not happen with your job. Spend time with Toby tonight, and I'll talk with you tomorrow after you two get back from the Medical Center. Toby needs you now, and you need to concentrate on what you are going to say to the doctor tomorrow.

"This evening is our regular Wednesday night prayer group meeting at the church. Most of what I know about the congressman I learned from my fellow church members. They love him and pray for him regularly. I'm sure someone there will know more about this investigation. I'll get the details as best I can from those folks, and when I get home tonight, I'll get on the Internet and search for any news reports I might be able to find. And certainly the congressman's Web site will have some kind of information. I'll look at that also. Just relax tonight, and prepare for tomorrow. I'll take care of the research, and I'll see you and Toby tomorrow."

Thursday—
Susan and Toby Visit the Ivory Tower

The 5:45 AM alarm ended a night of sparse sleep for Toby and Susan. Toby's insomnia problem had worsened during the last few weeks with the addition of frequent nocturnal urination, which complicated his pre-existing collection of symptoms that made sleeping difficult, if not downright impossible at times. By 1:00 AM, Toby's bedcovers were already drenched in perspiration, and the bedroom air was permeated with the pungent odor of toxins being excreted through Toby's skin. Muscle and joint pain would also frequently awaken Toby after he had finally dozed off. These disturbances of sleep were in addition to the overactive bladder problem, which seemed to manifest itself every hour regardless of Toby's fluid intake.

And each time Toby would moan, cry, or toss and turn in the bed, Susan would awaken to attend to Toby's needs. *But today is the day,* thought Susan. *Finally, it is the day Toby will be seen by extremely capable, even renowned, physicians at an institution that is at the very pinnacle of medical prestige. The ivory tower of the world of medicine, as it were. Whatever was causing the bizarre array of symptoms plaguing poor Toby would be quickly identified by those capable doctors at the Medical Center who have dedicated their lives to helping their fellow man.*

Yes, after today, Toby will be on the road to recovery, and within just a few short weeks Susan would have her once again happy and healthy son back. Susan's optimism over the outcome of today's appointment vastly overshadowed her own feelings of sleep-deprived fatigue, concern, and frustration. In the days prior to this appointment, Susan had attempted to cogently list each and every symptom Toby exhibited in the certainty such a comprehensive list would prove invaluable to the doctors, enabling them to swiftly identify and diagnose Toby's problem. Accurate diagnosis and evaluation coupled with properly directed treatment would be the magic combination for Toby.

As Susan dressed and prepared Toby for the drive to the Medical Center, she took a few moments to review the symptom list she had prepared to make certain she had not overlooked something that in retrospect would have been crucial to the doctors' determinations.

It's a good thing I didn't decide to pursue a medical career, mused Susan. *If a patient came to me with a list of symptoms as diverse as this list for Toby, I don't know what I would think. How could anyone sort through all of this? Oh well, I'll find out in a few hours what the gurus and real professionals will say.*

Toby's previous records, test results, and charts had been forwarded to Dr. Aventi's office at the time Toby's appointment was secured, and Susan was prepared to spend the entire day, if necessary, at the Medical Center should additional tests or screening be required. Whatever it took to get to the bottom of the problems with Toby, Susan was willing to devote all the time in the world.

Susan and Toby arrived without difficulty at the Medical Center at 7:45 AM. Within another few minutes they had located the infectious disease department and were comfortably seated in the reception area. The short walk from the parking garage to the main building and subsequent walking to the infectious disease department had left Toby laboring for breath. The morning sun shining through the large expanse of glass in the reception area illuminated a child's face that was very pale and drawn. Susan's heart was heavy as she sat observing Toby that morning. He was thin, too thin, obviously weak and obviously in pain and discomfort.

"Mommy, the sun hurts my eyes. Can we move over there?"

Susan hugged Toby's frail body to hers, trying to comfort and reassure Toby that everything would be all right. The tear rolling down Toby's cheek spoke volumes to Susan. There, before her, was a weak, tired, emotionally exhausted little boy that had bravely battled an unseen enemy to the point that only tears were left for expression.

Be strong, Susan, she thought, *don't cry now. Don't let Toby see you cry! Be strong. Help is on the way. Just a little longer now.*

Toby was pointing to seating in the corner of the reception area facing away from the windows. As they began to move there, Susan heard Toby's name being called by a nurse.

The long awaited hour has finally arrived! thought Susan as they were greeted hastily and ushered into a nearby examination room.

THE POISON PLUM

"Put this gown on your son and seat him on the examination table. The doctor will be with you shortly."

Obviously frightened, Toby whimpered, "Mommy, please don't let the doctor give me any more shots. I don't want any more shots. Please, Mommy…"

The minutes ticked by as she held Toby close to her. Voices and footsteps were in the hall. She could hear mumbled conversations between patients and the doctors as one by one the examination rooms were entered and examinations were conducted. Approaching footsteps and then silence told Susan that someone, most likely a doctor, was just on the other side of the closed door reviewing Toby's file before entering. And then, finally, Susan could see the door knob turning, and in walked a dark-skinned man with a clipboard who identified himself as Dr. Fayed. He was obviously of Middle-Eastern extraction and also obviously lacking in bedside manners.

"Wot rong son?"

"I beg your pardon?" replied Susan.

"Son…sick?"

"Yes. I think he has some kind of infection. Is there some mistake? Our appointment was with Dr. Aventi."

"No mistake. I see son. Undress. Get on table."

Me or Toby? thought Susan. *Where in the hell did they find this guy? If these people are going to live in this country, they at least need to learn to speak English!*

Dr. Fayed began his examination of Toby with all of the usual procedures…looking in his ears, eyes, nose, and throat and then listening to Toby's chest, taking his pulse, respiration, and finally taking his temperature.

Not knowing what else to do, Susan began describing Toby's symptoms and explaining how long Toby had been ill. Dr. Fayed began reading Toby's medical charts and seemingly was disinterested in Susan's explanations and observations. Occasional comments by Dr. Fayed were mostly unintelligible and barely audible. As the reflex testing was being concluded, Susan sensed Dr. Fayed's physical examination was coming to an end and she decided to venture a question to hopefully stimulate some dialogue between them.

"What do you think might be wrong with my son?"

"Dr. Aventi in soon."

With that terse announcement, Dr. Fayed turned and left the room. As Susan covered Toby's naked body, disturbing thoughts began eroding the veneer of optimism that she had developed about this institution and its doctors. Only the ticking of a wall clock interrupted the silence of that examination room. The seconds and the minutes crept by for about a quarter of an hour until Susan again heard footsteps in the hall, which stopped just outside the door. Moments later, in walked a man who identified himself as Dr. Aventi. He was in his late fifties, Susan guessed, wearing plaid pants, a light blue shirt with a white collar, brown bow tie, and suspenders stretched valiantly but failing to overcome the push of a bulging abdomen. With half glasses perched precariously on the end of his nose, the image of a sartorially disadvantaged middle-aged man was complete.

I'm not going to look at his shoes, thought Susan. *Besides, it's not his choice of wardrobe that concerns me. I'm here to find out what is in that brain of his that hopefully can diagnose and treat my son.*

"I'm Susan Collins, Dr. Aventi, and this is my son Toby."

"Yes, and what is it, Ms. Collins, that makes you think your son has some kind of infectious disease?"

As Dr. Aventi spoke, he moved to begin his own examination of Toby.

"Well, you may recall that Toby was referred by our internist, Dr. Butler?"

"And why did Dr. Butler think your son had an infection?"

Damn, thought Susan, *these guys haven't even talked to each other. All Butler's office did was send over copies of lab work with his records.* The veneer was beginning to get thinner with each passing minute.

"Dr. Butler told me that Toby's test for Lyme disease came back slightly positive, and he wanted me to bring Toby here for evaluation."

"I saw the test results in Toby's charts. That test was negative, Ms. Collins."

"I know, Dr. Aventi, but Dr. Butler felt Lyme should be ruled out because the test was slightly positive."

"There is no such thing as a 'slightly positive' Lyme test, Ms. Collins. Either it is positive or it is negative. Your son's test is negative, as are all of his other tests."

"But Toby is so sick. He is tired all the time. He has lost a lot of weight. His appetite is poor, he has insomnia and night sweats. Here, I have made a list of all of his symptoms. Maybe this will help."

Dr. Aventi took the list and after a very brief perfunctory scan, he tossed the list aside, shook his head, and mumbled something under his breath.

Is that a trace of a smirk I see on his face? thought Susan.

"Ms. Collins there is absolutely no indication that your son has any kind of infection whatsoever. Any and all of those symptoms you have listed could be attributable to other causes. They are certainly not specific."

"They may not be specific to you, Dr. Aventi, but they are certainly specific to Toby and me."

"Ms. Collins, would you step outside with me for a few minutes? Toby will be fine here while we talk."

Susan followed Dr. Aventi to a room across the hall where they could talk privately.

"Ms. Collins," he began, "you need to understand that there are many human conditions that can mimic conditions caused by infectious diseases. You also need to understand that in the absence of any kind of ongoing disease pathology, which is most certainly the situation here, other causes need to be identified and addressed. Now, Ms. Collins, aren't you recently divorced?"

"Yes, but what…"

"And Ms. Collins, haven't you and Toby recently moved from your home in Birmingham to New London where you accepted a position at the Plum Island laboratory?"

"Yes, but…"

"And didn't this transition contribute to and aggravate the daily stress level of your household? You are a single parent that has been burdened with the responsibilities of moving your home to a new location, finding a suitable school environment for your son, and assuming the obligations of a new career. Now wouldn't you admit that the stress you have been under has been substantial and has also contributed to the collateral stress that Toby has experienced?"

"I guess so, but I just don't understand how so many symptoms could be attributed to psychological causes. Aren't you going to at least retest Toby for Lyme disease?"

"No."

"Are you going to test him for any other kind of infection you can think of?"

"No."

"You are not listening, Ms. Collins. I told you that there is absolutely no evidence of any kind whatsoever that would indicate your son has an infection. And you need to understand that Lyme disease is, in today's medical environment, a grossly over-diagnosed disease. Physicians that don't understand the total mind-body connection and the manifestation of physical symptoms as a result of emotional trauma are attributing these conditions to the disease of the season… Lyme disease. A fad diagnosis if you will. You need to stop stressing Toby further by dragging him to different doctors, Ms. Collins, and you need to work to structure your home and career in a way that will not contribute to Toby's anxieties. It is most essential that you seek, as soon as possible, professional counseling for your son's depression."

Susan's mind was numb. Whatever comments that may have been made by Dr. Aventi from that point on just didn't register. Almost trancelike, Susan dressed Toby, and they walked to the parking area together. Toby was trying to talk to his mother, but it was as if his words were coming from far, far away.

"Mommy… Mommy…"

"Yes, sweetheart," Susan finally answered.

"Thank you, Mommy."

"For what, sweetie?"

"You kept the doctor from giving me shots. Thank you, Mommy."

Susan was fighting to hold back the tears. This was too much to bear. After all of the delay, frustration, and then eager anticipation, it was all for naught. Susan felt totally drained and depleted, both mentally and physically.

What the hell am I going to do now? she wondered.

The ivory tower of medicine, the pinnacle of medical authority, the apex of medical and scientific wisdom, had in her mind been reduced to the rubble of a dung hill. The veneer of respectability and veneration had been stripped away revealing an ugly, grotesque skeleton lurching through humanity, crushing life and hope in its wake.

Again the weak voice of Toby seemingly coming from a great distance began pushing through to Susan's consciousness…

"Mommy? Mommy?"

"What honey?"

"Mommy, what did the doctor say was wrong with me?"

What indeed, thought Susan, *What the hell was wrong with them should be the question.*

"Well, sweetie, the doctor said you were going to feel better real soon."

THE POISON PLUM

"I hope so, Mommy. I don't feel good anymore. I don't like feeling bad and being sick. And Mommy, I didn't like those doctors. They weren't nice like Dr. Butler. Mommy, don't take me there anymore…please?"

"I won't, sweetie. I promise. I didn't like them either. We won't ever go back there, Toby."

And you can count on that, Susan thought. *It will be a cold day in hell when I set foot in that place again, much less take my son there!*

Susan had never felt more alone, isolated, and uncertain of the future then she felt at that exact moment. Her choice of medical doctors that could conceivably offer hope had now been exhausted, and there was nowhere else to turn.

My God, thought Susan. *Toby could die if somebody doesn't figure something out and soon. He just can't get any weaker and lose any more weight. He has nothing left to lose as it is! Oh God, are you listening? Are you looking at this situation? I need help, and I need it now!*

Glancing at her watch, Susan saw that it was only 9:45 AM, and wondered how she possibly could have become so emotionally drained in such a short period of time.

She also began wondering what Cathy was doing. *I need someone to talk to. If I don't share what's on my mind, I think my head is going to blow off!*

"Well, this is why God invented cell phones," said Susan aloud as she pressed the memory key for Cathy's number.

"What, Mommy?" asked Toby.

"Oh nothing, Toby. I'm just calling Aunt Cathy. Would you like me to ask her to come over this afternoon?"

"I guess so Mommy."

"Hi, Sis!"

"Hey! Are you still at the Medical Center?"

"No, we are in the car on our way home."

"Well, that didn't take long! What's the verdict? What did the doctors say?"

"I'll tell you later. What are you doing? Can you come over this afternoon? Lunch is on me."

"What is wrong, Susan? What is it?"

"Nothing, I just need to talk to you that's all. Can you come over?"

"Sure, no problem. I'll be there about 12:30. Will that be OK?"

"That's fine. I'll pick up some sandwiches from our favorite deli with the usual toasted ham and cheese on rye for you."

"Hmm, no, my taste buds are going in a different direction today. I think I want the chicken salad melt. I'm kind of hungry. Better yet, do you think they would have a New Orleans–style muffaletta? We could split one."

"New Orleans–style in Connecticut? Get real."

"It is an Italian deli…Gino's…remember?"

"Well, guess it's worth a shot, but don't get your hopes up. I'll get us something though, and we'll see you later."

"OK, Sis. Whatever you bring will be fine."

"Toby, we are going to stop and get some sandwiches to take home for lunch, and Aunt Cathy is going to come over and have lunch with us. Would you like that?"

"Yes, Mommy. Mommy, are we going to stop at the drug store and get me some medicine?"

"Medicine? No, not just yet sweetie."

"But Mommy, how am I going to feel better, if I don't get any medicine?"

God in heaven, how does a parent answer that question? thought Susan.

"Don't worry, sweetie. Everything is going to be all right. You will be feeling better soon. You'll see."

And how will I back up and explain that lie to my beloved son, thought Susan.

Cathy was her usual punctual self and arrived a few minutes earlier than the appointed 12:30 time, obviously eager to know what the Medical Center doctors had determined. Susan greeted Cathy at the door and shared the first bad news of the day.

"Well, I tried, Sis. The staff at Gino's just looked at me with puzzled expressions when I ordered a muffaletta. But I did bring you a chicken salad melt."

"No problem Sis. Maybe that sandwich is indigenous to only the southern Italians, and the Yankee variants we have here have never heard of it. It doesn't matter… my primary mission is to find out about Toby."

"Let's get some food in Toby and ourselves, and then we can talk."

Susan then reheated the sandwiches in the microwave, and they ate in the den where Toby was watching television. Susan was grateful Toby had found something to hold his interest, and she was equally grateful that Toby had at least exhibited a semblance of an appetite and seemed to be enjoying his sandwich and drink.

Susan and Cathy took advantage of Toby's preoccupation with his television program to walk out on the patio to talk in private.

"OK, Sis, spill the beans. It's show-and-tell time. What did the doctors say?"

The look in Susan's eyes and the tear beginning to roll down her cheek caused Cathy's heart to sink. Like Susan, Cathy, too, was optimistic that today's appointment with a renowned specialist at the Medical Center would lead to a rapid diagnosis, treatment, and recovery for little Toby. But, deep down, Cathy's optimism had never quite reached the levels attained by Susan's. Deep within, Cathy had her reservations. She had heard too many stories about the doctors at the Medical Center from her fellow church members.

Cathy put her arms around Susan to hug her close as Susan's sobs and tears began in earnest, cascading down her face and beginning to wet Cathy's blouse.

She needs this release, thought Cathy. *After she has had a good cry I'll try again to talk to her.*

Cathy knew, understood, and loved her sister. Whatever had transpired at the Medical Center was certainly not good and had deeply affected Susan.

Not good. Not good at all, thought Cathy. *What if the doctors found something else? Cancer? Leukemia? A rare blood disorder? Oh no, please no!*

Cathy's imagination now began to run wild. Not enough answers and too many "what ifs." Would this nightmare for the three of them ever end? The shaking, the trembling, the sobs, and the tears eventually subsided as Susan pulled away from Cathy's embrace and began trying to speak.

"Cathy, I can't believe what happened with those jerks at the Medical Center! Oh, Cathy, what am I going to do? Dr. Aventi told me there was no indication of an infection in Toby's body, and that he does not have Lyme disease, and all of his problems are caused by some kind of emotional stress we are all under. I wanted to scream at him, actually at them, there were two of them: 'You are doctors; can't you see when somebody is sick?' Are they blinded by the glare from that ivory tower they occupy? I've never seen such a display of professional arrogance in all my life! I can't take it anymore, Cathy! I have no idea what to do next. I have nowhere to turn, not a clue!

"And look at Toby. He is beginning to look like an Ethiopian refugee. He's skin and bones—he has no more weight to lose. Whatever in hell is wrong with him, it's eating him alive! He doesn't have much time left. I know it; I can sense it. Somehow we have to find someone to help Toby, and we have to do it soon."

Susan broke down again and began sobbing uncontrollably. Cathy was trying to remain strong but then she, too, began to cry.

Why has our family been afflicted with this curse from the pit of hell? Cathy silently prayed. *Oh Jesus, please protect us from the evil one and lift this burden of sickness from our midst. In your name we trust and pray sweet Jesus. Amen.*

Both sisters had a good, long cry that afternoon which was much needed, long delayed, and totally fulfilling. Perhaps the quality of a truly beneficial tear fest can be measured by the quantity of tissues required to dry the tears shed. If so, today's crying jag was a roaring success. Almost an entire box of tissues was consumed by Cathy and Susan, and later, a renewed effort at cogent, rational thought.

"Cathy, I need to try to reach Dr. Butler. He asked me to let him know the outcome of our Medical Center appointment. But I'll probably have to leave a message with one of the nurses. He just stays so busy."

"OK, Sis, I'll check on Toby while you are doing that."

Susan must have called at the most opportune time before Dr. Butler began seeing his afternoon appointments. After only a brief wait on hold, Dr. Butler answered and after perfunctory greetings asked her what Dr. Aventi had said.

"Dr. Butler, I just can't believe what has happened. Dr. Aventi told me Toby didn't have any kind of infection, and he was just stressed and depressed. Can't he see how sick my son is?"

"Hold on, Susan. Dr. Aventi told you what?"

"He said Toby was not sick—at least from an infection. He said he was seriously stressed from my divorce, from our move here from Birmingham, and was even stressed because of my stress as a result of my new career. Dr. Butler, how could stress alone account for all of the symptoms Toby has? I don't understand? What is going on?"

"Why don't you bring Toby in tomorrow, and we'll run some more tests. There are some blood tests we haven't done yet that might tell us something. And I'll run the Lyme test over again if that would make you feel any better."

"I told Dr. Aventi the Lyme test was slightly positive, and he said the test could only be positive or negative. I asked him if he would run it again, and he said no."

"Hmmm…well just bring Toby by in the morning, and we will collect enough blood for the tests, including the Lyme test. It won't hurt, and maybe we'll luck up on something."

"I'm not sure I can take any more time off from the lab. My superiors didn't want me out today, but I told them I didn't have any choice. Would it be OK if my sister, Cathy, brings Toby in?"

"Sure, no problem. As soon as we have the results in, I'll give you a call."

"Thank you, Dr. Butler."

Susan hung up the phone and began reflecting on Dr. Butler's comment, "Maybe we'll luck up on something."

Is that it? she thought. *Is that what today's world of medicine has been relegated to? Luck? When all else has failed, let's turn to our tried and true fallback mechanism—Lady Luck! Works every time! Just peachy! Well, whatever, Toby and I could use a heaping helping of it! Right now!*

Susan joined Cathy and Toby in the den and once again noticed the sweet, sick odor that permeated the room as soon as she entered. She wondered if Cathy had also noticed the odor but said nothing.

"Toby, did you enjoy your sandwich and drink?"

"Yes, Mommy."

"Are you and Aunt Cathy having a good time?"

"Yes, Mommy."

"Good."

"Mommy, my head hurts. Could I have some more medicine?"

"It's not quite time sweetie, but I guess it will be OK. Tomorrow we will go back to see Dr. Butler, and maybe he will give you some new medicine to help you feel better."

"OK, Mommy."

New medicine indeed. Little did Susan realize what the morrow would bring.

Before moving on to the next appointment, Dr. Butler paused for a few minutes to reflect on the just-completed conversation with Susan Collins. After pouring a half cup of coffee, he took advantage of an empty examination room to sit and collect his thoughts.

What the heck is wrong with that kid? I can't prove it, but I think it's some kind of infection going on. I just don't know what. Those guys at the Medical Center are good, real good, but I think they have totally missed this one. Depression as the sole cause of all that kid's got going on? No way, no way in hell! Something is wrong with this picture.

Dr. Butler briefly entertained the thought of calling Susan back to ask her to bring Toby in that afternoon, but he remembered his already overloaded appointment schedule. Plus he had to make hospital rounds after the office appointments were finalized, and it would be almost midnight before he would get home that evening.

They will be in tomorrow anyway. I'll work them in and spend some time with Toby, he thought.

Dr. Butler moved on to the next patient, but for the rest of the afternoon and evening, he kept thinking back on Susan's call. The pieces just didn't add up for this puzzle. He knew something was missing. Whatever it was, it was the key to the entire picture. Sometimes all of those years of study, observation, internship, and practice faded away to gut feelings and instinct. Sometimes he just had to yield to those inner voices when all else had failed. And this was one of those times.

Friday—
Susan and Toby Visit the Emergency Room

Susan and Toby were both tired from the exertions and stress of that day, but sleep just wouldn't come. And when it did arrive, the stay was fleeting. Toby tossed and turned all night, whimpering and moaning, and Susan, even if asleep, would awaken with each sound from Toby. Susan felt guilty pushing Toby's medications to the limit, but she just had to get some rest herself or her job would really be on the line. With the facility understaffed and still in a chaotic mess, it was clear her superiors wanted her on duty as much as possible. Their attitude seemed to be: "Have somebody take care of your kid or we'll get somebody that can show up for work every day."

Finally, about three in the morning, sleep came for them both, and the remaining hours until the 6:00 AM alarm were a Godsend. Susan tried to prepare for work as quietly as possible so as not to disturb Toby. Sleep was a rare commodity, much needed and precious for Toby.

As Susan was washing the sleep from her eyes, she heard Toby crying for her from the bedroom.

"Mommy, Mommy, help me!"

Darn, I was being as quiet as I could. I was hoping he could sleep at least until Cathy came. Help me? Did he say help me?

Susan threw the towel into the sink and rushed to Toby's side.

"What's the matter sweetie? What is it? What's wrong?"

"Mommy, I'm sorry. I'm sorry." Susan saw that Toby was crying.

"For what, Toby? Sorry for what? Don't cry, it's OK"

"I wet the bed, Mommy. I'm sorry. I'm sorry."

"It's OK, Toby. Just get up and Mommy will help you clean up in the bathroom, and I'll put a dry liner and clean sheets on the bed."

"I can't, Mommy."

"What do you mean you can't?"

"I can't get up, Mommy. I had to pee, and I couldn't get up, and I couldn't hold it any more, and that's why I wet the bed Mommy. I can't move my legs. What's wrong with me?"

At that moment Susan felt as if every drop of blood in her body had been replaced with ice water. Her lips wouldn't move, her muscles were frozen, and her brain was paralyzed with shock and fear.

Oh, my God! Oh, my God! This can't be happening! What do I do? What do I do? thought Susan, frantically.

"Toby, can you sit up for Mommy?"

"I'll try, Mommy."

Toby used his hands and arms and managed to raise his torso erect, but try as he might, his legs wouldn't move. Susan lifted him from the urine-soaked bed and carried him to the bathroom to wash him and change his pajamas.

"Can you feel anything in your legs, honey?" Susan hoped her voice didn't sound as shaky and frightened as it felt in her throat.

"Mommy, they feel like they went to sleep."

"Just sit here on the counter for a few minutes, and maybe the feeling will come back. I'm going to pull on your toes now. Can you feel that?"

"Yes, Mommy."

"Can you move your toes for Mommy?"

"I'll try Mommy."

Susan and Toby stared down at his toes for several moments but there was no movement.

"Which toe are you trying to move, sweetie?"

"I can't get any of them to move Mommy."

"Can you raise either of your legs?"

"No Mommy."

Susan was terrified. She took a deep breath, swallowed hard, and tried to think what to do next.

"Toby, is any of the feeling coming back in your legs?"

"No, Mommy. They still feel like they are asleep."

"I don't know what is wrong, sweetie. We will get some clothes on, and I'm taking you to the emergency room."

THE POISON PLUM

"Mommy, I'm scared."

"It will be all right, sweetie. You probably just slept wrong, and the doctor will tell us what to do."

Susan was grateful the nearest hospital was not far from their home, and she was also grateful the emergency room was not crowded that early in the morning. Cathy was already dressing for the day when Susan called her en route to the hospital. By the time Toby had completed triage, Cathy had arrived, and together they were taken to an examination area where Toby was seen by the sleepy-eyed physician on duty.

He examined Toby, conducted, or more properly attempted to conduct, reflex tests on Toby's legs and reviewed Toby's medical history on their computer system. Susan thought he looked concerned, but it was hard to tell. Maybe he was just sleepy.

"Ms. Collins," he began. "How long has your son been having problems?"

"Several months now, but he has never had this problem. Just yesterday he had an appointment with the doctors in the infectious disease department at the Medical Center. They told me Toby didn't have any kind of infection, and he was just depressed and overstressed."

"Why were you seeing infectious disease doctors?"

"Our doctor, Dr. Butler, said Toby's Lyme disease test was slightly positive, and he wanted him referred there for evaluation."

"Ms. Collins, depression and stress doesn't cause frank paralysis. Your son needs to have a spinal tap to rule out an infection. He will also need to be seen by a neurologist. I have had some experience with Lyme disease, and I can tell you it certainly has the capability to cause all of the symptoms I reviewed in your son's history, including paralysis. I'm not willing to hang that diagnosis on your son yet, but the possibility needs to be explored."

"Dr. Aventi at the Medical Center told me there was no such thing as a slightly positive Lyme test. It was either positive or negative. There is no middle ground."

"That may be his opinion, but it certainly hasn't been my experience as an emergency room physician. Is Dr. Butler your primary physician?"

"Yes. Yes he is."

"I'm going to put in a call for him. If any further testing is required, in his opinion, he will have to authorize it, with your permission, of course."

"Should I take Toby back home?"

"No, just wait here until I can talk to Dr. Butler. He might be able to see you here while he is making his rounds."

Well, this is a twist, thought Susan, *see a hundred doctors and get a hundred opinions. But what if this guy is on to something? What if it is Lyme disease? No, surely those guys in the ivory tower have seen enough of that to recognize it when they see it! God, I'm so mixed up and stressed out, I don't know what to think.*

"Mommy?"

"What Toby?"

"Mommy, are the doctors going to give me some medicine so I can move my legs?"

"Probably, sweetheart. They are trying to call Dr. Butler to come and see you. He may want to give you some new medicine."

"I hope so, Mommy. I can't move my legs."

A nurse interrupted before Susan could reply.

"Ms. Collins? Dr. Rogers was able to page Dr. Butler. He is on his way to the hospital now and should be here shortly."

"Thank you, nurse."

"Susan, are we about to get some answers?" asked Cathy.

"Maybe, just maybe. And wouldn't that be ironic. The ivory-tower, self-anointed experts totally miss a diagnosis that a routine emergency room physician correctly makes."

"I don't care who gets the glory Susan. I just want this nightmare to end. And besides…do you know the difference between a doctor and God?"

"The difference between a doctor and God? No, no I don't."

"God doesn't think he is a doctor."

"Ha! That's for sure! That's for damn sure!"

After about twenty minutes, Susan could hear male voices talking in the vicinity of the emergency room's central desk. She recognized Dr. Butler's voice and assumed he and Dr. Rogers were discussing Toby's condition. She couldn't understand what was being said, but her assumption of the topic of conversation was indeed correct. After a few minutes Dr. Butler and Dr. Rogers entered the examination area where Susan, Cathy, and sick little Toby were waiting. Dr. Butler expressed a faint smile which instantly faded to a grimace of concern when his eyes rested on Toby.

My God, he thought. *It has only been a few days since I saw this kid last. How could he deteriorate this quickly?*

"Susan, what is going on?"

"I'm not sure, Dr. Butler. Toby couldn't move his legs after awakening this morning. At first we thought that he had slept wrong, and his legs were asleep from lack of circulation, but there has been no improvement."

Dr. Butler began examining Toby, lifting, twisting, and palpating Toby's legs and arms, listening to his heart with his stethoscope, and looking into his eyes. He asked Toby to follow the light from the tiny flashlight he carried in his shirt pocket and exercised other arcane procedures routinely practiced by physicians worldwide on a daily basis.

"Susan, let's step over there for a few minutes and talk. Toby, I'll bring your mother right back. Just stay here with your Aunt Cathy and rest."

"Susan, Dr. Rogers and I concur that Toby probably has some kind of infection that has begun to involve his central nervous system. A spinal tap will need to be conducted which could yield valuable diagnostic information. If a causal agent can be cultured from the spinal fluid, we will know exactly what pathogen to treat. We will also need to order a CT scan of the skull and spine to rule out lesions that may be causing his paralysis. The good news is the tests can provide very valuable information. The bad news is tests can consume valuable time. In the event an ongoing process of infection begins to involve the central nervous system, time is of the essence. It is absolutely essential that treatment be provided as soon as possible in an attempt to avoid potential irreversible damage to the brain and the spinal cord."

At this point Susan felt like she was about to faint.

Toby and I will make a cute couple on that gurney, she thought.

Dr. Butler continued, "We don't have much to go on—a slightly positive Lyme test, and a veritable plethora of nonspecific symptoms…until today, that is. Now we have frank paralysis to add to the list. Susan, I'm going to go out on a limb here. The risks I feel are minimal and are far outweighed by the consequences of inaction on our part. I am going to order that Toby be treated with a trial of extremely powerful intravenous antibiotics to begin immediately."

Maybe Susan was thinking about Toby's aversion and dislike of needles when she asked, "Aren't oral antibiotics just as effective? Intravenous therapy seems pretty extreme to me."

"Oral antibiotics are fine for some conditions but they just can't get the job done once the infection becomes disseminated and central nervous system involvement occurs. I'm sorry, but this is nothing to fool around with. We have to drop an atomic bomb on those bugs, if there is an infection, and we have to do it now. Of course there is a possibility that Toby's problems indeed stem from an infection, but not a bacterial infection. If it is viral in origin, the antibiotics will, of course, be of no benefit. A fungal infection severe enough to cause these problems would probably have already been fatal, so I think we can safely rule that out. I don't think we have any choice but to begin immediately. I recommend that the first infusion be given here in the emergency room. As soon as that is completed we need to admit Toby to the hospital for observation and the treatments will continue for a minimum of seven days and possibly twenty-eight days."

Susan was at a loss for words. This was too much news, too dramatic, and too soon for her to assimilate in a coherent manner. But an inner voice and instinct told her that Dr. Butler was probably right. And besides, her and Toby's list of options and choices was not exactly brimming over at this moment.

"I just want my Toby back. Whatever you feel must be done, Dr. Butler, let's do it!"

"I'll get started immediately, Susan, but there is something else you need to know."

"Yes?"

"By beginning these antibiotics we are going to either include or rule out Lyme disease. Let me explain. If there is an infection, and the cause is the Lyme bacterium, there will be a dramatic worsening of Toby's symptoms once treatment begins."

"He gets sicker? I don't understand. He is so sick now, how can he get any sicker? Why would we want that to happen?"

"It's not that we want it to happen, but unfortunately it will have to occur before Toby can get better."

"He will have to get worse before he gets better? That sounds like something I heard from my grandparents when I was a kid growing up in Alabama!"

"Well, Susan, sometimes there is a pearl of wisdom in those old wives' tales. In this particular situation it is called a *healing crisis*. You see, when the antibiotic enters the body, and the killing of germs begins, the massive accumulation of toxins released from the dying bacteria causes a very pronounced aggravation of symptoms."

"Isn't there some other course of diagnosis and treatment Dr. Butler? This all sounds pretty scary to me. How long does this last?"

"No, there is no other way that we are currently aware of. And is it scary? Yes, it can be, but so can lack of treatment. And how long does this healing crisis last? It, of course, varies, depending on the germ load being carried by the patient and the effectiveness of the antibiotics being used. But generally speaking, after two or three weeks, the severity of the symptoms decreases as the germ load is lessened, and the body is able to excrete the accumulated toxins."

"Two or three weeks? God, that sounds horrible! I hope and pray that Toby doesn't have Lyme disease, and he will not have to endure that torture!"

"I hope so too, Susan, but as I said before, the antibiotic we are going to treat Toby with will either include or exclude the diagnosis of Lyme disease. There are only two bacterial infections that present with an intensification of symptoms when treated with antibiotics. One is Lyme disease and the other is syphilis."

"Syphilis? Do you think Toby has syphilis?"

"No, Susan, he doesn't have syphilis."

Susan's head was spinning. There was too much information, too much to process and assimilate. *This is heavy, very heavy,* she thought.

Dr. Butler continued, "The process I have been describing is called a Jarisch-Herxheimer reaction, so named for the doctors that first observed the phenomenon when treating syphilis. It is actually a good sign because it indicates the treatments are being successful. And, of course, if the presumed infection is of some other origin, we will not see this reaction at all."

"Dr. Butler, I am beyond confused. Only yesterday the gurus in the ivory tower of the Medical Center were telling me that Toby has no sign whatsoever of any kind of infection. Today you are rocking my world by saying that not only do you think Toby has an infection, but it could be an infection that would make him even sicker if we treat it. Please pinch me now and tell me this is all a bad dream! I don't know what to say. This all comes as the shock of my life. I had no idea that a tick bite, if indeed that is what we are dealing with here, could be so serious!"

"Susan, do not allow yourself to harbor any illusions. Lyme disease is not a benign infection that eventually will self-resolve and fade away. I'm not trying to frighten you into making a snap decision, but untreated Lyme disease is eventually fatal."

"Fatal? Oh, my God! Do you mean Toby could die?"

"Yes, he could die. But being crippled and suffering daily with pain, fatigue, and the agony of Lyme could be an even worse fate."

"Enough…that's it! Do it! Go ahead! Do whatever you have to do! Let's get started. I'll tell Toby you are going to give him some medicine that will make him feel better."

"I'll call the hospital pharmacy and get the antibiotic down here right away. After the first infusion, we will monitor Toby for a while here in the emergency room, and then we will admit him for observation and monitoring. And, of course, we will continue the infusions daily for at least the first seven days. Tomorrow we will conduct the spinal tap and the CT scans. And Susan, there is one more thing…"

One more thing? thought Susan. *Hell, pile it on! Ever hear of the straw that broke the camels back? I'm there now!*

"Yes, Dr. Butler?"

"Susan, I want you to understand that Lyme disease is an extremely complicated disease that is difficult to diagnose and even more difficult to treat. It frequently presents with co-infections that can be as serious, or even more serious, than Lyme."

"Damn, this is just peachy! Let me see if I understand this correctly. Toby is the rabbit in the shooting gallery, and everybody has a gun trying to shoot him! If one doesn't get him, there are plenty more where that came from!"

"Susan, what I am trying to say is this. The more I learn about Lyme, the more I realize that I don't know very much about it at all. But, we have to start somewhere, and what I've outlined is what I think we need to do now. Let me get that call in to the pharmacy."

After Dr. Butler walked away to order the antibiotics, Susan sat motionless for several minutes trying to gather her thoughts. Should she be elated that finally she and Toby may be on the brink of a successful diagnosis and the beginning of treatment? Or should she be despondent and dejected that Toby may be infected with so serious a disease? Could both emotions coexist simultaneously in one mother so filled with love and concern for her son? After several minutes of very serious reflection and soul searching, Susan returned to the examination area to rejoin Toby and Cathy.

As she approached, Cathy and Toby both looked up, their eyes searching Susan's facial expressions for any indication, any sign of news, whatever it might be.

No time to be inscrutable, thought Susan. *Suck it up and put on a positive face, even a little smile would be nice and appropriate at this time. No problem, am I not superwoman? Can't I smile in the face of death? Sure! No problem... no problem at all.*

Cathy and Toby spoke as she approached, almost simultaneously, "What did Dr. Butler say?"

"Mommy, are they going to give me some medicine?"

"Yes, sweetie. The doctor and nurse are going to give you some medicine in just a few minutes."

"Will I be able to move my legs Mommy?"

"We think so, sweetie, but it may take a few days for the medicine to work." And then to herself Susan thought, *Or a few days to kill you, Toby, we aren't sure which.*

"The doctors think you are sick from a bad old tick biting you when you were playing outside. Do you remember seeing a tick, Toby?"

"No, Mommy. I don't like ticks, and I don't like spiders either."

"I don't either, sweetie."

"Do they think it is Lyme disease, Sis?" Cathy chimed in.

"Yep, they do. Dr. Butler said the antibiotics would prove or disprove it."

"How?"

"By Toby's response. I'll tell you later."

"Mommy, I like limes and lemons. Is that what made me sick?"

"No, sweetie. The doctors' think you were bitten by a tick."

"Why do they call it lime disease?"

"Lyme and lime are two different words that sound alike but they mean different things. They are spelled different. One is a disease and the other is a fruit."

"Can we go home after I take my medicine Mommy?"

"No, sweetie. We are going to have to stay here, so they can do some more tests."

And, of course, as Murphy would have it, just as Toby began to question if they were going to stick him with any more needles, in walks Dr. Butler and a nurse, the latter pushing an IV pole on its stand and holding a drip bag, lines, and catheter in her free hand.

Toby's eyes widened as the growing fear began to spread across his pale, sick face.

Not a good time to be a mother, thought Susan. *Not a good time at all.*

Predictably, little Toby began whimpering and trembling, and tears were beginning to flow as the nurse began positioning Toby's arm for the infusion. At that moment, Dr. Butler, exercising a bedside finesse developed by many years of dealing with frightened children, began to distract Toby with joking and comical actions that distracted him sufficiently so that when the nurse made the initial stick Toby barely noticed.

Oh thank God! thought Susan. *These people are true professionals.*

She remembered how nurses had stuck her four or five times on occasions past when having blood drawn, missing the target vein repeatedly. But this team was really efficient. By the time Dr. Butler had ceased teasing Toby, the nurse had found a vein, inserted the catheter and was taping the drip line to Toby's arm to prevent movement.

Dr. Butler began to reassure Toby that they were going to put some medicine in his arm that would stop the germs from making him sick.

"Will it hurt?" asked frightened little Toby.

"No, Toby, it won't hurt. I just want you to lie still here on the bed while we are giving you the medicine, and you can talk to your mother and Aunt Cathy. Then we will take you to your own room so you can rest."

Susan's mind was trying to sort through the possibilities, that what ifs, and what to do next.

What if Toby doesn't have any kind of reaction whatsoever and after seven days there is no improvement in Toby's condition? What if it isn't Lyme? What else could it be? What will we do if it isn't Lyme but some other infection we can't identify? What if the problem is viral, and we have no way to treat it, and Toby will just get sicker and sicker until he dies?

All these thoughts and many others were racing through Susan's mind, and as she considered their options, it was indeed frightening how very few there really were. Repudiated and rejected by the omniscient authorities at the prestigious Medical Center, Toby's fate was now relegated to an RN who looked like she was happy her shift was ending, a sleepy emergency room physician with a facial complexion reflecting years of depression and alcohol abuse, and a well-meaning, middle-aged family practitioner.

And what if it really is Lyme disease? thought Susan. *Dr. Butler freely admits he is only guessing and knows very little about Lyme disease and its treatment.*

Susan sat staring at the pale, amber-colored liquid slowly flowing from the flaccid plastic drip bag into a clear, cylindrical tube before beginning its journey down the IV line until finally entering a vein in Toby's thin left arm. The slow, measured drip visible in the small cylinder connected to the final length of tubing seemed to Susan to reflect a statement of grim finality to this long, drawn-out nightmare.

So here we are, she thought, *It's finally come down to this—a catheter sticking out of Toby's arm carrying God knows what chemicals throughout his pale, sickly body, ordered by a physician that means well but really isn't certain what the hell he is doing. Why don't we just put a list of diseases on the wall and pick one by throwing a dart at it!*

The irrationality and incongruity of it all seemed to Susan to be almost surreal. To cry or to laugh…that was the question. *Could I do both at the same time?* she wondered.

"Susan, have you had a chance to call in? Does your supervisor know where you are?" Cathy asked.

Susan glanced down at her watch. "Oh, damn," she replied. "No Cathy. No I haven't, and it is almost ten o'clock! I've got to find a phone!"

"I think there is one in the hall near the restrooms."

Susan quickly found the pay phone and placed her call to her supervisor at the facility. For a moment, she was unable to remember his name. He had been sent in from the CDC in Atlanta as a result of her previous supervisor having his brains blown out at the ferry last Friday.

God, she thought. *Has it only been a week? With all that has transpired, it seems like an eternity ago!*

Susan was grateful when the voice on the other end answered by saying, "Microbiology, Gallagher speaking."

That's it! Herschel Gallagher. Now I remember—the dork with the penguin physique and his britches pulled up to his breasts.

"Mr. Gallagher, this is Susan Collins."

"Yes, where are you, Ms. Collins? It's obvious you are not here at the facility."

"I'm sorry, Mr. Gallagher, but my son is sick, and I had to take him to the emergency room."

"I see. And what is wrong with your son, Ms. Collins?"

"I don't know, Mr. Gallagher. His doctor's aren't sure."

"His doctors aren't sure?"

"That's correct."

"Ms. Collins, as you may be aware, an extensive personnel profiling and review has been underway as a result of the unfortunate events at the ferry landing last week. This in-depth investigation was, of course, necessitated by the security concerns for the facility. Ms. Collins, the review of your employment history revealed a substantial number of unexcused absences that have created no small amount of consternation among your superiors here."

"But my son has been sick."

"You need to realize and understand, Ms. Collins, that the work we are engaged in here at the facility is vital to our nation's defense. Every employee's efforts are a contribution to our overall cumulative production. We are a cohesive unit. When one employee doesn't pull his or her load, we all are impaired as a result."

"I'm really very sorry, Mr. Gallagher but..."

"Ms. Collins, there are many, very eminently qualified pediatricians practicing in this area that I am sure could treat your son. You seem unable or unwilling to seek them out. You must recognize and attend to your responsibilities Ms. Collins or you will quickly find that the consequences of your indifferent attitude will be dire indeed."

Susan was incredulous. If she could have crawled through those telephone lines and out the other end, she was certain she would have had the strength to choke the life out of this jerk.

Too damn bad this bastard was not on the ferry! she found herself thinking in the passion of the moment.

"I suggest, Ms. Collins, that you make a very serious effort to return to your responsibilities Monday morning and at the proper time. I am scheduling a meeting for you with Director Stephens at 9:00 AM in his office. Furthermore, I am today placing you on probation, and after your meeting with the director on Monday, you will be placed on administrative review."

"Mr. Gallagher, I need to..."

THE POISON PLUM

A click, and then the line went dead. Susan was livid, so incensed in fact that for hours the security of her employment was of little concern. All she could think of was somehow getting back at that jerk.

That insensitive bastard! He's probably a homo and hates the concept of a mother-son relationship. Well I hope the SOB is a homo, and I hope he gets AIDS... and soon!

Susan couldn't remember the last time she got so mad. That creep really got under her skin. Seething with fury and anger, Susan returned to Cathy and Toby as Toby's first infusion was nearing its completion.

"Where did you go, Mommy?"

"I had to use the telephone, sweetie."

"Mommy, what's wrong?"

"Nothing, sweetie. Just a rude man on the telephone that's all. It's OK now. And how are you feeling?"

"I still can't move my legs."

"It will take time, honey. But it will be soon, I promise. We'll have to give the new medicine time to work."

"OK, Mommy."

Susan and Cathy had a lot to talk about that Friday in the New London Hospital emergency room. But it would have to wait until private time could be found, and especially away from Toby's young, sensitive ears.

A nurse appeared, obviously the night shift's replacement. She greeted everyone and checked Toby's pulse, blood pressure, and made a slight adjustment to the rate of the antibiotic drip. Within ten minutes the drip bag's contents had all been transported through the IV lines and into Toby's waiting body. And unbeknownst to anyone at the time, the antibiotics had begun finding their targets as the blood coursed through Toby's veins, arteries, and capillaries, and the tissues supplied by that blood. Millions and millions of infectious spirochetes began biting the dust, releasing their debilitating toxins into the bloodstream and lymph systems and overloading Toby's already compromised waste elimination system.

Within one and a half hours, Toby began to complain of headache, dizziness, abdominal pain, burning, searing urination, numbness in his legs, arms, and chest, and later, diarrhea. The nurse recorded heart palpitations, a galloping irregular rhythm, tachycardia, heart block, and shortness of breath. The next twelve hours were critical. His temperature elevated, and chills set in.

Concerned, the nurse on duty reported her concerns and observations to Dr. Butler's office. She had been an RN for over fifteen years and had administered many courses of IV antibiotics during her long career. But she had never experienced a patient's response to antibiotics like Toby's. At first, she thought she was witnessing an anaphylactic reaction to the powerful third-generation cephalosporin antibiotic being infused, but as more symptoms appeared, she realized that something else was occurring, but she didn't know what.

Dr. Butler made another hospital round about 8:00 PM that evening and stopped in to see Toby. After reviewing the nurses' notes and examining a very sick and suffering little boy, he asked Susan to step into the hall for a few minutes, so they could talk. Toby had been moved into a private room around noon and Susan and Cathy had been by his side ever since.

"Susan," began Dr. Butler, "What we are witnessing is a classic Jarisch-Herxheimer reaction. Understand that this is the healing crisis I explained to you. Understand also that this reaction Toby is experiencing is diagnostic. Toby has Lyme disease. There is no question!"

"Oh, my God! Will be he OK? Can you cure him?"

"Susan, the next several days are going to be pretty rough. It will be rough on you and rough on Toby. We have no choice but to continue. We, of course, will still proceed with the tests I have ordered, and rest assured that in a proper hospital environment, such as we have here, Toby will be carefully observed and monitored and provided with any support measures that might be required. Can I cure him? I don't know, Susan."

"But, Dr. Butler, how can any germs survive an antibiotic as powerful as this one obviously is? Won't they all be eradicated shortly?"

"I don't know Susan. I am sorry."

"I'm scared shitless, Dr. Butler."

"I know you are Susan and for good reason. Listen, I'm going to try to help you and I have ordered that Toby's treatments be continued for twenty-eight days should that be necessary."

"Will Toby have to stay in the hospital for twenty-eight days?"

"I hope not. Perhaps after a week or so, he will be well enough to go home, and we will continue the treatments on an outpatient basis. And Susan, as soon as Toby is better, he needs to be seen by a Lyme disease specialist. I am happy to try to help, but frankly, Susan, Lyme with its frequent plethora of potential co-infections falls far outside my fields of expertise. Toby is very ill and deserves the very best of treatment. I am just not qualified to provide that."

"Specialist? I thought that was what I went to see at the Medical Center yesterday. He turned out to be a specialist at being an SOB!"

"Forget him. What we have to find is a Lyme specialist that has devoted his practice to the diagnosis and treatment of Lyme."

"And I guess I can just look in the yellow pages under bug bites and find the sub-classification for ticks?"

"Well, up until a few days ago, there were several in this area and over on Long Island. Apparently they were quite dedicated and competent. Certainly their academic credentials were impeccable."

"Up until a few days ago? What do you mean? Were they all kidnapped by aliens?"

"Possibly…depending, of course, on your perspective of current events. Didn't you hear? Have you not seen the news?"

"News? What news? I don't have time for the news. I've been working and trying to take care of Toby. I don't have time for squat."

"Well, last Monday, government agents raided the offices of all the Lyme doctors in this area, seized their files and arrested all of the doctors. Didn't you see Congressman McDonald's news conference?"

"Raided their offices? What on earth for? What on earth did they do wrong?"

"I don't know Susan. I don't think anyone fully understands at this point. Rumors are thick and contentious. Some battle lines have been drawn, that's for sure. Perhaps a specialist can be found away from this immediate area—one who has escaped the government's dragnet. Hell, these doctors around here wouldn't touch a Lyme patient with a ten-foot pole. They saw what happened to their peers, and they have no interest in joining their lot."

"Oh, my God! If this situation becomes any more surreal you are going to have another patient…me!"

"I'll be back in the morning to check on Toby. I'll get my office staff to do some digging on the Internet and among some of my sources, and we'll try to find someone I can refer Toby to. In the meantime, you and Toby need to rest. I'm going to order a sedative for Toby. Would you like something also?"

"No, Dr. Butler. I can't sleep soundly. When Toby is sick, I stay half awake and half asleep… one eye and one ear always open."

"Toby will sleep once the sedative takes effect. Maybe you will rest then as well. Are you sure you don't want something?"

"No thanks, I'll be fine. Besides, as soon as Toby dozes off, Cathy and I have a lot to talk about."

"I'll see you in the morning then. Good night."

"Good night, Dr. Butler, and thank you."

At 9:00 PM, another nurse came into their room and added a syringe of clear liquid to Toby's drip line. Whatever it was, it did the trick. Within ten minutes, Toby was sound asleep.

"Oh thank goodness. Look, Cathy, Toby is finally getting some rest. He has missed so much lately. I just know this will do him a world of good! And Cathy, as grim as this situation appears now, I feel more optimistic and hopeful than I have felt since Toby first got sick. Maybe it's because somebody is finally doing something tangible, and we finally know for certain that a major component of Toby's problem is indeed Lyme disease."

"We do?"

"Yes. Dr. Butler told me that Toby's reaction to the antibiotic was diagnostic. It's Lyme, he's sure of it."

Cathy moved to hug Susan close. "Oh, Sis, I'm so sorry."

"I know, Cathy, I know. But at least the uncertainty in our lives has been removed. The enemy has been identified, and now we must fight it."

"Is he going to treat Toby?"

"Well, yes, at least for a while until Toby is strong enough to leave the hospital."

"What then?"

"Toby will still need to come in daily on an outpatient basis to receive his daily infusion. But Dr. Butler admitted that he knows very little about Lyme. He said it was an extremely complex disease process that was beyond his expertise and capabilities, and he didn't feel qualified to treat it."

"So if Dr. Butler doesn't feel qualified to treat Toby, who will take over?" Cathy asked. "Who will provide the treatment and care going forward? I think we can safely assume those turkeys at the Medical Center are out of the picture!"

"That's for sure. That's for damn sure! I wouldn't take a dead cat to those clowns.

No, I'm not certain what we will do. Dr. Butler said Toby would need to be treated by a Lyme specialist, but there is a problem."

"A problem? What kind of problem?"

"Oh nothing much. Just a minor thing. It seems that all of the Lyme specialists in this area were raided and arrested by the government last Monday."

"How did you know that?"

"Dr. Butler told me. Said he would try to find someone from outside this area. He said the doctors around here wouldn't touch a Lyme patient with a ten-foot pole. What the hell is that all about? Do you know anything about it?"

"I'm afraid I do. Do you remember me telling you that I would ask around at church and find out what Congressman McDonald's news conference was all about?"

"I guess…yeah."

"Well, I did the homework I promised. I even obtained a transcript of his conference from his Web site."

"So what does his news conference have to do with the damn government arresting doctors that I need to treat Toby?"

"One of the prominent doctors arrested was a longtime personal friend of McDonald's. They even went to medical school together. I mentioned his name to you once…Dr. Glen Klinner. He was also the doctor for our church member, Mr. Davis, that I told you about."

"So what are you trying to tell me? McDonald is pissed and has an ax to grind because his buddy got raided by the authorities?"

"That's not the whole story Susan. Sure, he's angry about that but the big picture is, he thinks the government is trying to shut those doctors down that treat Lyme disease because he thinks there is a connection to Plum Island."

"What? McDonald thinks the doctors are connected to the facility or Lyme is connected to the facility?"

"Lyme…. He thinks the government is trying to silence those doctors because they know that the source for the Lyme germ is the laboratory on Plum Island. He even had the wives and children of those doctors on the stage with him at the conference. The only connection with all of the doctors raided was that they all had devoted their practices to the treatment of Lyme disease."

"So McDonald wants to investigate the facility to try to prove that the Lyme germ was hatched by scientists at Plum Island?"

"You got it!"

"Holy cow! What a kick in the crotch that would be! Granddaddy always said, 'Don't bite the hand that feeds you.' What if the hand that feeds you is doing the biting? Wow! But I don't know, Cathy. All this is a big leap. Guess I need to read that transcript too. Looks like I'll have some time on my hands for the next several days, staying here with Toby 24-7. Would you mind bringing me a copy the next time you come?"

"No problem, Sis. There's a copy in my car."

"Great! You know, maybe better yet, perhaps I could hook my laptop up to the telephone line here in the room, and I could start some research of my own. Wonder if the hospital would allow me to do that? I can't see that there would be a problem—the dial-up Internet number is a local number. Would you mind swinging by the house tomorrow and picking up that laptop for me?"

"Sure Sis. I'll do anything I can to help."

"Dr. Butler said he would ask some of his colleagues if they could recommend anyone for Toby, and he said he would ask his office staff to check around also. I get the feeling that he thinks Toby will need to be treated, tested, and followed closely by a capable specialist even after this initial course of antibiotics is concluded."

"From what I've heard about this disease, that certainly sounds plausible to me," responded Cathy.

"You mentioned that Mr. Davis from your church was seeing Dr. Klinner. Do you know what he is going to do now? Maybe he has found someone that's qualified somewhere else?"

"He may have. I'm not certain though. I've overheard them talking about a Lyme doctor in, of all places, Birmingham. Of course they felt the distance involved was too much of a handicap, but the doctor certainly comes highly recommended."

"Birmingham? There is no Lyme disease in the South! That makes zero sense. Is the doctor so good that the infected travel all that distance anyway to be treated? How else could the doctor justify his practice, unless of course he has other specialties? Well, regardless, it's out of the question for Toby and me. I'm having enough problems already with my superiors at the facility."

"Why? What's going on?"

"No big deal. It's just that when I phoned in this morning to tell my boss I wouldn't be in today because I had to put Toby in the hospital, the jerk crawled up my epizooty. He said I was either unable or unwilling to find a pediatrician to treat Toby."

"So he thinks you are irresponsible and are using Toby as an excuse not to work?"

"Yeah, pretty much. That's about it, I guess. I know one thing…he had my temper tantrum pot boiling over. I was about ready to volunteer a free autopsy for that dork! The SOB placed me on probation, of all things, and when I go in Monday, I have to see Director Stephens. *If* I go in, that is!"

"Wow! You are hot!"

"You betcha, I'm hot! My son comes first in my life! That damn lab and the island it is sitting on can sink into the ocean and straight down to hell for all I care!"

Cathy sat silent for a few moments staring at the floor. When she raised her head to speak, a look of intense concern had covered her face. "Susan," she began.

"Yes?"

"You didn't tell your supervisor or anyone else at the facility what Dr. Butler suspected was wrong with Toby, did you?"

Susan paused before answering, carefully thinking back on the words she had used that morning.

"No, no I don't think so. Let me think. No! I'm sure of it. I told the dork that the doctors didn't know what was wrong with Toby. That's when he said I was unable or unwilling to find a suitable doctor for Toby. Why? What are you thinking?"

"What if Congressman McDonald *is* on to something? What if he *is* right? You need to be back at work Monday, Susan. I'll stay here with Toby. You need to walk in that place with a big smile on your face, all apologetic and everything, and express how happy you are that the only thing wrong with Toby turned out to be a garden variety case of mono. And comment what a sorry state of affairs it is when doctors can't even recognize something as simple as that! Anyway, tell everyone everything is fine now. Toby is OK, and you are just as sorry as you can be that you missed work. Tell them it won't happen again, by golly. And tell Director Stephens that you are ready and eager to get back to work fully focused and dedicated."

"Yeah, and then I will certainly be nominated for an Academy Award. As angry as I am right now, it will take a massive effort on my part to not go straight for the jugular as soon as I walk in!"

"I understand, Sis, but take the next few days to calm down and spend your time taking care of Toby. We really need to keep a lid on this Lyme disease diagnosis. I've got a really bad feeling about all of this. I just don't know what might happen if your supervisors discovered that one of their employees had a child ill with one of their homegrown diseases. They might do nothing…but then again, maybe not. Just keep a lid on it. You have nothing to lose by doing so and possibly a lot to gain."

"This all passed into the realm of surreal a long time ago, Cathy. Now it is just plain damn scary. There's too much to think about. I'm tired and emotionally exhausted."

"I know Susan. I feel the same way – it's almost 11:00 PM. I'm going to get some rest and I'll be back in the morning. Do you want me to bring you anything besides the laptop and the transcript?"

"Would you mind giving me a call before you leave in the morning? I'm so tired, I can't think of what I need or don't need."

"OK, Sis. I'll see you tomorrow."

Cathy took a final look at Toby sleeping, hugged Susan, and then she was gone. Susan sat quietly for several minutes staring at Toby and her surroundings trying to sort through her emotions and the events of the past forty-eight hours. She was dog tired…all the way to the bone, it seemed. But until the brain slowed down, Susan knew it would be futile to attempt to sleep. Now she wished she had accepted Dr. Butler's offer of a sedative.

Surviving Hell

Glen Klinner had not seen the light of day since he was clubbed, kicked, beaten, manacled, shackled, and unceremoniously thrown into a waiting government vehicle the morning of the raid on his office. He was almost immediately blindfolded and his mouth taped shut by what he assumed was duct tape. For what seemed like several hours, he was transported by motor vehicle and then bodily carried into what he later realized was a jet airplane. Conversations between his captors he overheard were mostly unintelligible or laced with undecipherable acronyms and coded phrases.

Deprived of the senses of vision and taste, but not hearing and smell, Dr. Klinner attempted to use the resources he had available to him to try and determine exactly what was happening. Calculating the passage of time was an impossibility but surely several hours of flight time had elapsed before the jet carrying Dr. Klinner and, unbeknownst to him, the other seven doctors raided in the area closest to Plum Island, landed somewhere. Still blindfolded and with tape covering his mouth, Dr. Klinner was once again lifted and bodily carried to another vehicle. This vehicle was much noisier and rough-riding than the vehicle that had transported him from his office to the airport. But whatever the journey's destination, the time required for arrival was obviously much shorter than his first trip.

Upon arrival, Dr. Klinner was lifted out of the vehicle and allowed to walk to his final destination while being held, led, and guided by what seemed to be several men. Wherever he was, Dr. Klinner realized that it certainly was not Long Island or any location nearby. The temperature and humidity were dramatically higher and very uncomfortable; the air was thick and perspiration began to soak his clothing. Abruptly, his captors stopped, and he heard the metallic sound of a lock and door opening. Suddenly, the tape and blindfold were yanked off, and he was pushed into a cell he later determined was only about eight feet square.

Stumbling from the shove and unable to compensate by moving his legs because of the shackles, Dr. Klinner fell to the floor which felt very dirty and even slimy in some areas. The stench of urine and fecal matter permeated the pungent air and humidity.

My God, he thought, *Will I be able to breathe enough oxygen to be able to survive in this place?* The metal door clanged shut, and the voices of his captors faded as they moved away from his cell.

Up until Dr. Klinner was shoved into the tiny cubicle, which reeked of the stench of previous incarcerations, his thoughts were concentrated on trying to figure out why and where all of this was happening. Within moments of that door clanging shut the fear began. From this point on it didn't matter why, and it didn't matter where. What mattered now was survival. As a physician he knew that under these conditions the human body would begin deteriorating very rapidly. To his credit, Dr. Klinner was in excellent condition, having recovered almost totally from the Lyme disease that had ravaged his body years earlier. Proper dedication to nutrition, vitamin supplementation, and regular exercise had yielded a well-honed athletic physique capable of handling an enormous amount of stress. Dr. Klinner sensed he was going to need all of those reserves and even more before this ordeal was over.

Even though his blindfold had been removed moments before being cast into the cell, Dr. Klinner realized it didn't really matter because he found himself in a windowless cubicle with no source of illumination other than the crack under the door. His only companions were the pungent stench, oppressive heat, and drenching humidity. For what seemed an eternity, he remained manacled and shackled and could only lie on the filthy, slimy floor. Unable to control his urination, his only option was to urinate on his clothing that he had worn to his office that fateful morning. He prayed that his captors would show at least a modicum of humanity and sympathy before the inevitable next bowel movement. When, finally, two men entered his cell to remove his manacles but not his shackles, he could see that they were wearing military uniforms, and they appeared American. But his attempts to question why this was happening were met with responses rude and harsh in nature but of a language unknown to Dr. Klinner. It sounded Russian, but he couldn't be certain. The brief illumination, albeit dim, of his cell revealed only four walls and a floor of concrete with a toilet and sink along one wall. No ventilation and no illumination—a tiny, tiny slice of hell on earth.

And, as Dr. Klinner was thinking over the hours that it couldn't get any worse than this, it did. From out of nowhere, the sudden incredibly loud blaring of totally discordant music began which continued until Dr. Klinner thought his head would burst. Then as abruptly as it began, it stopped. Minutes of complete silence followed, only to be interrupted again with the piercing cacophony of discordance. This continued on and on for what seemed an indeterminable period of time. Sleep was practically impossible, and Dr. Klinner realized that never in his life had he experienced such overall total discomfort and suffering as now.

Long periods of time would elapse between feedings which appeared in the form of a tray laden with some unknown mass of material shoved through a hinged rectangular slot in the door. Sometimes the food smelled and tasted rancid, and he would instinctively shun it. At other times, it actually seemed palatable and even tasty but curiously after some meals, copious diarrhea and violent vomiting would appear spontaneously. After this cycle was repeated several times, Dr. Klinner realized that his food was periodically being laced with chemicals to induce the vomiting and associated reactions. And also he realized that the incredibly loud sounds he was being subjected to were part of a program of planned sleep deprivation. Sometimes the hunger was so intense that even the rancid food was appealing, and he found himself greedily and hungrily gulping it down. On one such occasion, Dr. Klinner felt within his mouth small particles of what he had just eaten moving about. Thinking at first that what he was experiencing was just some sort of hallucination triggered by hunger and sleep deprivation, he stopped chewing and remained motionless for several minutes to ascertain what was happening. The sensation was of tiny particles of the food moving on his tongue and the inside of his cheeks. He immediately spit this mouthful into his palm and continued motionless until he distinctly felt those same particles of what he had thought was food begin to move across his hand, fingers, and wrist. And then the realization—his meal was crawling with live maggots!

Dr. Klinner began thinking about death. As a physician, he knew the limits of physical and mental endurance. He knew also that there comes a time when death, so feared by man and avoided at any cost, could be welcomed and even embraced if one's mental existence reached and maintained an unbearable condition. He also realized that an induced emotional and physical state of absolute exhaustion was exactly the goal of his captors, and once those conditions existed, the interrogations would begin. If these people had wanted him dead, he would already be dead. No, it was not death they were seeking, at least not now.

What crime have I committed? He thought over and over. *What heinous act of rebellion against American society warrants this inhumane treatment?* His mind searched for answers, but there were none.

A case of mistaken identity? Was the government really targeting someone else? Perhaps they were looking for a mass murderer or a terrorist in the adjacent office complex? No, not likely...but what?

The American penal system, to his knowledge, certainly didn't function this way. Whatever was going on here was certainly not normal incarceration protocol...it was out of control and out of bounds.

What about Fran and the kids? he thought. *My God, they must be worried sick! Do they even know where I am? And what day is it? How long have I been here?*

Continuity of thought once again became impossible as the blaring cacophony of discordance began anew. Each episode was seemingly louder, longer, and more intense than its predecessor.

I am a man held captive and tortured by my own government for a reason unknown and unexplained to me. I am a man now invisible and for all practical purposes, nonexistent to my friends, co-workers, and family. But surely someone, somewhere at this very moment is working to secure my release.

It was reassuring to Glen at this time to reflect on his long friendship with Harry McDonald. Having a United States congressman as a personal friend at a time like this certainly couldn't hurt. If anyone could and would help, it would be Harry.

For Glen, the minutes would pass into hours in his tiny suffocating niche of hell. And those hours would pass into days, and those days into weeks; miserable, suffering passages of time and existence. He prayed to God incessantly for relief, release, or death, as the days drug on with no means of a tally. Finally and inevitably, Glen Klinner reached the point of finality when the predominant emotional preference was death.

It doesn't matter now which kind of relief God brings, or does it? He thought. "Oh death, where is your sweet sting?"

Getting Back to Normal?

Fran Klinner returned to her home on Long Island after the conclusion of Harry's news conference Tuesday afternoon. Harry and Anna had, of course, asked her to stay another night, graciously, as always, offering to extend their hospitality. Fran decided not to stay because she knew Harry needed to return to Washington early Wednesday morning, and Fran realized that she needed to return to at least a semblance of what her life had been before the horrors of last Monday. Her heart was overflowing with love and thankfulness that Harry and Anna were such close and devoted friends, and she shuddered to think how empty, helpless, and directionless her life would be now at this time of crisis without the McDonalds by her side. For she knew and understood that Harry McDonald would do everything in his power to right this wrong and reunite her and Glen.

As Fran and her children re-entered their home, once so warm, comfortable, protective, and filled with so many wonderful memories of their lives together, the ominous feeling of violation permeated her very soul.

Would it ever fade? she wondered.

Fran busied herself that evening with the needs of the children, trying to maintain her composure and exuding a positive attitude, constantly reassuring them that everything that had happened was all a big mistake and a misunderstanding that would be resolved very soon, and their dad would be home again. She reassured them that all would be fine before they knew it, and all that they had experienced would just be a bad dream that would quickly fade away.

The house was a wreck, totally disheveled as a result of the uncaring, inconsiderate actions of the agents that conducted the raids. Fran tried to pick up and rearrange as best she could before retiring about midnight, mentally and physically exhausted and hoping for a good, albeit short, night of sleep.

Their household always came alive at 6:15 AM on school days. Fran would cook a healthy breakfast for the children, make sure they were properly clothed for the weather and all their supplies were in order before they left for school.

Maybe tomorrow, Fran thought, *after Harry returned to his office, he would be successful in finding out where Glen was being held. A telephone visit possibly could be arranged and would be a blessing. Or maybe even a personal visit if Glen is being held in a nearby facility.*

The not knowing and the uncertainty was what hurt the most.

But one thing at a time. Get the kids back in school and on their regular schedule, get the house back in order, and await direction from Harry.

At 6:00 AM that Wednesday morning and exactly fifteen minutes before the jangling of their alarm clocks would begin, the Klinner household came alive all right, but not in the expected, pleasant, prearranged, and orderly manner that was their daily weekday ritual. The pounding at their front entrance was of such force and intensity the walls of the entire house seemed to shake. Fran was immediately fully awake and quickly pulled on her housecoat and began making her way to the front door from her bedroom on the second floor of their home. As she moved closer, she could hear voices loud and impatient interspersed with the incessant pounding.

"FBI! Open up! FBI! Open the damn door! FBI, open up! We have a court order. Hurry up! Open the door now or we are coming in!"

Fran was moving as quickly as she could, heart pounding in her chest and almost tripping on the stair runners as she began her descent.

"We know you are in there. Get this damn door open, and get it open now!"

Fran reached the door, moved aside the night-safety chair, released the deadbolt, and turned the knob to open the door just as it was pushed with great force into her face and body. The blow knocked Fran to the floor in the entrance hall as six heavily armed men rushed into the house. There were three in suits carrying submachine guns and three officers in uniforms with pistols drawn. Two of the suits stood over Fran with their weapons pointed at her head. Two men ran throughout the first floor of the house while the remaining two ran up the stairs and into the bedrooms where the children had been sleeping. As Fran tried to pull herself up she was immediately pushed back down by the foot of the nearest agent.

Fran began crying and screaming as she saw the agents descending the stairs bodily carrying her children over their shoulders. The children by this time were terrified and began screaming and crying. They were taken to the living room, placed on the couch and told harshly and repeatedly to shut up.

"Please don't hurt them. Please don't hurt them," screamed Fran, crying frantically.

"Shut up, Mrs. Klinner! We're not going to hurt your damn kids, and we're not going to hurt you if you shut up!"

"What do you want? Where is my husband? What have you done with him?"

"We told you, dammit! Shut the hell up! We are here to serve you with a court order! Get it through your stupid head that we are in charge here! You are a material witness in an ongoing terrorist and conspiracy to commit terrorism investigation being conducted by the Justice Department of the United States. You are herewith being restrained by a court order that will limit your daily travel to a ten-mile radius of your home. Effective immediately!"

As these words were spoken an agent reached for her ankles and began pulling her housecoat up her legs.

Oh, my God, she thought. *Am I going to be raped by these brutes while my children watch?* She instinctively began trying to resist, twisting, screaming, kicking her legs, flailing her arms, and trying to get up. Other agents quickly grabbed her and their combined power held her motionless while a device was attached to her left ankle and snapped into place. *Not unlike a dog collar,* she thought.

"That, Mrs. Klinner, is an electronic tracking device to ensure your compliance with the court order. Your every movement twenty-four hours a day will be known to us, and should you attempt to move beyond the ten-mile limitation, you will be immediately arrested. And should that occur, don't count on our agents being as pleasant next time!"

Through her sobbing, she uttered, "Where is my husband? Why won't you tell me where he is? What kind of people are you? Don't you have a conscience, you bastards?"

As abruptly as they had arrived, they were gone, slamming the front door so hard some pictures on the living room wall fell to the floor. Fran managed to get up and rushed to her children to begin trying to console and comfort them. As soon as she and the children had calmed down as best as could be expected, she hurriedly placed a call to the McDonald residence hoping to reach Harry before he left for Washington.

It had been a short night for the McDonalds. Arriving home at approximately 9:00 PM from the news conference, there remained calls to return and details to attend to before any sleep could be attempted. Even when Harry and Anna were finally able to get their showers and stretch out in their large and comfortable king-size bed together, their minds were racing with the events of the day. Too keyed up to sleep, too emotionally intertwined with the battle raging around them to rest, the 4:30 alarm signaled an end to the tossing and turning and episodes of dozing that had plagued them both all night.

Harry had to return to Washington to begin what would be the busiest, most stressful, and most hectic period of his career. Anna would return to being the wife of a United States congressman and providing all of the support she possibly could to help that congressman in what she clearly understood would be the biggest battle of their lives. She would also return to being the very loving and very capable mother that she had always been. Life goes on, and go on it must in the McDonald household.

Maybe this is what the pioneers meant when they spoke of keeping the home fires burning, mused Anna that Wednesday morning.

When the phone rang at 6:20 AM in the McDonald home, Harry was preparing to leave for Washington and was hoping to get away about 6:30. Anna took the call in their den, and Harry instinctively knew something was wrong. After a few moments of muffled conversation, Anna called out to Harry.

"Harry! It's Fran. They have been raided again!"

"Again? Oh, my God. I'll take it in here in the bedroom."

"Fran, it's Harry. What's happened?"

"They came into our home, Harry…again! The bastards came into our home with guns! They terrified the children, Harry. Two agents went into their bedrooms and bodily carried them screaming down the stairs!"

"Fran, are the children OK?"

"OK? Physically? Yes. Emotionally? No!"

"You said there were agents. What kind of agents Fran? Where were they from?"

"They said they were FBI, and they had a court order."

"A court order to do what?"

"Harry, I thought the apes were going to rape me in front of the children. I was manhandled while another agent attached a tracking device to my ankle."

"A tracking device? What for?"

"They said I was a material witness in a conspiracy to commit terrorism against the United States government. I have been restricted to travel within a ten-mile radius of our home."

Harry was certain that the blood in his veins had been replaced with a scorching hot substitute. His emotion was not fear, it was not anger, and it was not revenge. It was an all-encompassing emotion of determination and calculated resolve to right the wrongs that had been committed and bring to justice those responsible. Harry knew the only recourse was through the legislative process, and he also knew that he and he alone would be the only congressman willing to spearhead such a formidable task.

"Fran, I am so sorry. I wish Anna and I could be there with you now."

"I know, Harry, and I understand. I know you are doing and are going to do all that you can to help us."

"Yes I am, Fran, and I will continue to do so to the best of my ability and the abilities of my very capable staff. I realize that this is a big order, considering all that you have been through since Monday, but please try to remain calm."

"Easier said than done! I'm about six feet over the edge right now!"

"I know, Fran, but realize that the agents Monday and these agents today are just cowards. And those cowards and bullies with guns are hiding behind the badges that provide their illegitimacy with legitimacy."

"Harry?"

"Yes, Fran?"

"I'll survive the thugs that call themselves special agents, and I'll survive the dog collar. As humiliating as that is, it's not the problem. I can live with all of that. But what I can't live with is the uncertainty of not knowing what they have done with Glen. Please try to find out where they have taken him! If only I could just talk to him. I need to know if he is all right, Harry!"

"I will Fran. I'll do my best. As soon as I get to Washington today, I will be calling the FBI's congressional liaison office and also the Justice Department. And as soon as I know anything, I will call you."

"I hope it will be soon Harry. I really miss Glen. My heart is heavy with dread and fear over what these animals might have done to him. From what I've seen, I wouldn't put anything past these people. They are amoral Harry and without a shred of decency!"

"I couldn't agree more, Fran. I'll call you as soon as I have anything tangible."

"God bless you, Harry."

"God bless you too, Fran…be brave."

Harry's mind was heavy in deep thought as he made his way, almost trance-like, back to his Washington office that Wednesday morning. Anna, as was her custom, drove him to the airport for his flight, and the unpleasantness of their impending temporary separation was especially painful today. He didn't want to leave Anna's side, and she certainly didn't want him to go. But they both knew and understood that Harry had no choice but to immerse himself in this battle, totally and completely, and as soon as humanly possible. And to maximize his effectiveness, the total and complete mobilization of his office and staff resources would be required.

By the time Harry's flight had landed at Dulles International, his priorities for the day had already been neatly compartmentalized in his mind. First, he knew that Erin Giblon would have already assumed the responsibility of bringing the rest of his staff up to speed regarding the details of his news conference, and certain staff members would already be at work arranging for the beginning of the committee's investigation. Secondly, upon arriving at his office, he would apprise his staff of the latest government raid on Fran Klinner and the subsequent terror and humiliation she was forced to endure. It was doubtful that Erin Giblon or any of his other staff members needed any further emotional motivation to do their best, but reports like Fran's from the front lines of this battle certainly couldn't hurt.

But Harry harbored no illusions that Wednesday morning about whose shoulders would carry the burden of the most important task facing the office of Congressman Harry McDonald of the Second Congressional District of Connecticut. The terms, conditions, and whereabouts of his friend Glen Klinner's incarceration would have to be learned and soon. And no one but no one in that office had the capability of securing that information but Harry. The buck stops here. It would require that Harry personally wade through the bureaucratic labyrinth that is the federal government in Washington, D.C., to learn of his friend's fate.

Oh, Harry knew what would be required, and he knew only too well how the game is played in Potomac town. Expect stonewalling at every turn, lies, misrepresentations, delays for requests of information …you name it, especially with a situation as sensitive as this. Entrenched bureaucrats, especially those in the Justice Department and at the FBI, know that a congressman, and especially a first-term congressman, can be ignored. After all, they are only elected for two-year terms, and as soon as they win the election, they have to start campaigning anew for the next one. They come and they go at the whim of their constituents, seldom in office long enough to develop either a loyal constituency or political clout on the hill and certainly not among the bureaucracy that doesn't have to face re-election. Just ignore the congressmen and their silly, grandstanding demands, and they will go away soon, and everything will be forgotten—whatever it was.

Now the congressman that had served long enough to chair one of the more powerful committees that could potentially cause irritation for the bureaucrats was to be taken more seriously. Their requests for information or dialog were to be handled more carefully. Of course, stonewalling and whitewashing of any sensitive or embarrassing information was always to be attempted but as cleverly and discreetly as possible. The powerful House Ways and Means Committee was always a nemesis for the career bureaucrats and was highly feared because of its ability to control the congressional purse strings. Perish forbid that some government agency or program incurred the wrath of that committee. Cutting off funding for any project or payroll is total anathema to the career leeches that litter the Washington landscape.

Well, Harry had a few aces in the hole, and he intended to play them very carefully. As a six-term congressman from a wealthy congressional district in the northeastern quadrant of the United States, he was extremely well-known and enjoyed a very high profile. It was glaringly obvious that he was no Johnny-come-lately and equally obvious that he was not going to go away anytime soon, much to the dismay of his many enemies among the left and the New World Order elite. And equally disconcerting was his chairmanship of the powerful Health and Human Services Committee, backed by a very loyal and growing constituency in Connecticut.

Yes, Harry had paid his dues, and he was now a survivor in the human jungle that is euphemistically known as our nation's capital. Today Harry would use those aces, and he would use the considerable clout he had at his disposal. No, he didn't expect to speak personally with Frey at the Bureau or Budenz at Justice, at least not today, not yet, as much as he would relish that confrontation. However, eventually they would speak to him, and they would answer his questions whether they liked it or not. The power of subpoenas and congressional investigations is still a very potent force if used wisely. No, he didn't expect to reach the top today, but neither did he expect to spend valuable hours playing shuffle and phone tag with the many layers of underlings at Justice and the Bureau.

I'm going for the jugular. I'll be as forceful, direct, confrontational, impatient, and demanding as required. I want answers from these wretched excuses for human beings, and I want them now. Right now! Today!

Harry had no patience with career bureaucrats. To him they represented sinister, growing malignancies of the body politic that needed to be excised as soon as possible. Forget the pathology report. It's obvious what is growing. Cut it out and cast the detritus in the waste can.

Harry opted for public transportation from Dulles to his office after landing. Usually Erin Giblon or one of the other staffers would drive to the airport to pick him up, and their time together could be utilized to review the current legislative agenda. Today Harry wanted his staff to remain at the office working without interruption, and he also wanted time alone to sort out his thoughts and attempt a distillation of those thoughts that were so hurriedly accumulated during the past forty-eight hours.

My God, has it only been forty-eight hours? he thought. *Last Monday morning seems like an eternity ago. So much has happened! And so much lies ahead.*

With each passing development, the enormity of the challenge he faced seemed to grow geometrically. To his mind's eye, the overall picture, as he understood it at this point in time, resembled a giant menacing octopus with its sinister tentacles extended in every conceivable direction. Harry realized that trying to chop off those ubiquitous tentacles, as appealing as that exercise might be, would certainly not result in a solution to the problem. For only new ones would sprout where the former had been, each one stronger and more far-reaching and all encompassing than its predecessor.

An exercise in futility, he thought. *Ignore the tentacles, strike at the head of the beast and destroy its brain, and then all else will no longer matter. Without central control and direction, the beast will be rendered impotent and will wither and die. Somewhere, buried deep within the myriad of intelligence agencies of the United States government, is a nucleus of organization, control, and direction for Plum Island and the other biological labs. Through the committee's investigation and our research, we will attempt to locate and identify that nucleus, and then we will expose this evil conspiracy to the light of day.*

Harry couldn't help thinking of how Count Dracula in the old vampire movies he had seen as a child had crumbled to dust when exposed to sunlight.

Perhaps an invidious comparison, he mused, *but perhaps not. Time will tell.*

The commute from the airport seemed very short for Harry this Wednesday morning. He was deep in thought when the taxi driver stopped, and Harry was surprised to see that they were already at his office. Within moments, he was greeting his staff, which true to form, were busily working on their respective agendas. And also as expected was the long list of messages piled on his desk that would have to be returned. Many from constituents responding to his news conference, several from representatives of the news media seeking additional information and, sadly, messages from the other seven wives with their tales of abuse and humiliation at the hands of the agents who came bright and early this morning to shackle them. Regrettably, the return of those messages would have to wait. The first order of business would be a brief review of the news conference for his staff and then a discussion of the government's raid at Fran Klinner's home this morning. After that, Harry would begin his contacts to the FBI and the Justice Department to attempt to determine the location and conditions of incarceration of his friend Glen and the other doctors arrested. At the completion of the staff briefing, a portion of those messages could be answered by Miss Giblon or some of the other staff members. After a cursory review of the messages deemed most important by his staff, Harry sorted out those to be returned by Miss Giblon and those to be handled by other staffers. The rest he would have to address as soon as time permitted. But first things first.

"Miss Giblon?"

"Yes, Mr. Congressman?"

"Would you please have everyone come into the conference room?"

"Certainly. Right away, Mr. Congressman?"

"Yes."

Within moments, the telephones had been placed on voice mail, and Miss Giblon, the other staffers, and the interns were assembled in the conference room. Harry began by thanking them for promptly assuming the responsibilities of organizing the upcoming committee investigation. Then he succinctly summarized the news conference of the previous afternoon. To his delight, he learned that Miss Giblon had obtained video of the local media's coverage of the conference and had played it for the office staff first thing this morning. Harry's comments served to "flesh out" the event so that everyone present had a complete picture of what had transpired and understood thoroughly Harry's objectives and motivations. Satisfied that everyone was up to speed on the conference, Harry then moved on to discuss the telephone conversation with Fran Klinner that morning.

"At 6:20 AM, as I was preparing to return to this office from my home, I received a very disturbing telephone call from Fran Klinner, whom you will recall is the wife of Dr. Glen Klinner, the principal target of the government's raids last Monday. The Klinner's house was stormed at 6:00 AM this morning by agents from the FBI armed with guns and a court restraining order. Mrs. Klinner was told that she was under investigation as a material witness in a conspiracy to commit terrorism against the United States government."

As Harry paused, murmurs of surprise and sighs of concern were heard, and staffers began twisting about in their seats, obviously uncomfortable with this latest revelation.

"Furthermore, Mrs. Klinner and her children were manhandled by these 'special agents,' and she was forcibly shackled with an electronic tracking device and restricted to movement within a ten-mile radius of her home. The agents would not reveal where her husband had been taken and denied her requests to be allowed to speak to her husband. As abruptly as they had arrived, they left, leaving Fran Klinner emotionally distraught and her children frightened."

"Mr. Congressman, may I briefly interrupt?"

"Yes, Miss Giblon?"

"This morning we received calls from seven of the other wives whose husbands were also raided and arrested. It seems that their homes were violated as Fran Klinner's was, and they, too, were fitted with tracking devices and restricted to a ten-mile radius of movement. In one incident, there were complications of a potentially serious nature, but we don't have any further details."

"What kind of an incident?"

"We received a call from a very upset Mrs. Janice Stegall, who was calling from Our Lady of Mercy Hospital's cardiac care unit. It seems that when her eleven-year-old son Benjamin heard her screams during the raid on their home, he rushed to help her and began hitting and kicking the agents."

"I remember that kid. Good for him! So what was the problem? Was an agent so terrified by the child's attack he suffered a heart attack?"

"Hardly. The agents used Taser guns to subdue Benjamin. He developed heart arrhythmias as a result of the electric shocks and had to be rushed to the hospital. The doctors told Mrs. Stegall that because Benjamin had suffered rheumatic fever as a child, he was very vulnerable to this assault on his heart."

"What is Benjamin's condition?"

"We don't know for sure. Mrs. Stegall said the doctors were attempting to stabilize Benjamin, and we haven't spoken to her since."

"Well, let's see. The big strapping government agents were unable to protect themselves from this eleven-year-old sickly kid who was trying to defend his mother and were forced to Taser him to regain control of the situation?"

"I know, Mr. Congressman. It's a sorry state of affairs. Let us hope that Our Lady of Mercy Hospital lies within a ten-mile radius of Mrs. Stegall's home. Otherwise she will be arrested for seeking treatment for her son."

"That would be the icing on the cake, Miss Giblon, but certainly not beyond the purview of the enemy we face. For all of you in this room today, let these incidents serve as motivation for the work that lies ahead for all of us. For this is not some sort of academic debate we find ourselves engaged in. It's a war between the forces of what is right, good, and decent and the forces of the evil, the dark, the sinister, and the subverters of all that we would bear allegiance to.

"I want everyone to continue with the work you are doing, I'll be occupied for the rest of the day as I contact the FBI's congressional liaison office and the Justice Department, trying to find out what they have done with the doctors. Trying to find out the status of Benjamin would be futile because of the patient confidentiality laws now in effect. We will just have to wait on Mrs. Stegall to call us, or perhaps I could call Anna and have her drive over to the hospital to talk to Janice. Please advise me of any further developments, and we'll plan to meet back here in the conference room at 4:30 to assess our progress today."

"Mr. Congressman?"

"Yes, Miss Giblon?"

"I doubt you have seen this morning's issue of *The Chronicle*?"

"No, I haven't."

"I took the liberty of placing a copy on your desk. I think you will find it interesting. It contains a very hard-hitting column by MacIntosh McAdams. True to his word, he is going after the lab at Plum Island…big time!"

"Oh, really! Thank you, Miss Giblon."

As soon as Harry had returned to his private office, he paused to offer a silent prayer for young Benjamin Stegall. As a former cardiologist, Harry understood only too well the seriousness of disrupted heart rhythm in any patient with a compromised heart. After the electric shock insult to the heart, the restoration of a normal rhythm can be very difficult indeed.

Harry's first call was to Anna. He told her of the government's raids on the other seven wives and the Tasering of Janice Stegall's son.

"Anna, would you please try to contact Janice at the Our Lady of Mercy Hospital to determine the status of Benjamin? You may even need to drive over there, if you can't reach her by phone."

Anna was incensed and appalled by these latest developments and volunteered to do whatever she could to help.

Harry's next call was to be to the FBI, but he paused for a few moments to collect his thoughts. It was then that he noticed the copy of the morning's issue of *The Chronicle* Erin had conveniently placed and opened to MacIntosh McAdam's column. For the rest of that entire day he was glad he took the time to read that column.

For the first time in a very long time, Harry didn't feel quite so alone in his crusade to return America to its roots. He had found an ally in McAdams, and he knew that as a result of his column, there would be others coming aboard to help pull on the oars of the ship of freedom.

"'Bugs and Plums!' Indeed! What a great column. Vintage MacIntosh McAdams! I'll get the staff to have it framed!"

That brief interlude did wonders for recharging Harry's batteries. When he did place the call to the Bureau's congressional liaison office, Harry was ready for the challenge, even relishing the banter and verbal jockeying for supremacy. After the expected delay of the typical voice-mail mosaic, Harry was finally able to reach a live human being.

"Congressional liaison office, Frank Porter speaking, how may I direct your call?"

"Director Frey. This is Congressman Harry McDonald, Chairman of the House Committee on Health and Human Services."

"I'm sorry, Congressman McDonald. Director Frey is in a series of meetings."

"Yes, no doubt planning raids on more innocent Americans and their families! Let me speak to the assistant director."

"I'm sorry, Mr. Congressman, but Mr. Hopkins is also unavailable at this time. May I ask what this is concerning?"

"Yes, Porter, you may ask. It concerns the capture and detention of innocent civilians. The families of those incarcerated would like to know where and why their husbands and fathers are being held without counsel."

"I don't understand what you are referring to, Mr. Congressman."

"What I am referring to, Porter, are the two dozen raids conducted Monday morning on the office and homes of prominent doctors located primarily in the northeastern quadrant of the United States."

"I have no information readily available, Mr. Congressman. If you will provide me with your office number, perhaps I can have someone get back to you."

"Well, let's see. American citizens have been arrested by agents of the IRS, FBI, ATF, FDA, CDC, and the DEA. They have been incarcerated for two days now in God only knows where, habeas corpus has been suspended, and you don't have any information for their families or their congressman. Furthermore, you deny their congressman the ability to speak with individuals in positions of authority. I know and understand the game you are trained to play, Porter, but 'perhaps' is not acceptable. Connect me with Director Frey's office, and do it now!"

"One moment, Mr. Congressman."

After a long wait on hold of at least three minutes, possibly five, a male voice finally came on the line identifying himself as Assistant Deputy Director Allen Hendricks.

"Mr. Congressman, as I understand your request, you are seeking to determine the location or locations where the doctors arrested last Monday are being held? Is that correct?"

"That is correct, Hendricks, and I also want to know why their rights of habeas corpus have been suspended, and why they are not allowed to communicate with their families."

"Congressman McDonald, their locations and terms of incarceration are matters of national security. As regards the issue of habeas corpus, you must realize that in matters of national security, which conspiracy to commit terrorism certainly involves, the provisions of the Patriot Act take precedent over civil law. And you, Congressman McDonald, of all people, should understand the time-honored protocol that controls the bulk of communications between our agency and the legislative branch. A congressman's or senator's concerns or requests for information are to be addressed to the appropriate Bureau chief and prepared in written format. After receipt and review, your query will be answered by the appropriate division within the Bureau. If Director Frey and his staff responded personally to daily telephone calls from 435 congressmen and 100 senators, that certainly wouldn't leave much time to enforce the laws of the United States, now would it, Mr. Congressman?"

"What about the concerns of the wives involved for their husbands' safety and whereabouts? What about the concerns of the children involved? We are not talking here about Ahmed and his cousin Benbar captured in the New York subway system with a container of radioactive waste and forty sticks of dynamite. We are talking about highly respected members of their communities without even a trace of criminal background!"

"At this point, Mr. Congressman, the families in question are regarded by the government as material witnesses. The investigation is ongoing, and I'm afraid there is nothing more that I can add. If you will summarize your concerns in the proper written format and submit them to the Bureau, you will receive a formal reply within a reasonable period of time."

"My office provided that inquiry in the 'time-honored protocol' format, as you fondly describe it, on Monday afternoon within hours of the raids. Of course my office has not received a reply nor do I expect one anytime soon. In the meantime, innocent civilians are probably rotting away in some hell-on-earth prison to which they have been relegated. Hendricks, make certain what I am

THE POISON PLUM

about to say is accurately communicated to Frey. I know the games you people play. I know all about your lies, cover-ups, whitewashing, and stonewalling. I know most of your dirty tricks, and with just a little time and imagination, I could figure out the rest. Very shortly you are all going to talk to me. But not only to me but to the entire Health and Human Services Committee, the media, and the American people. You love to issue subpoenas? Get ready to receive and respond to them!"

Assistant Deputy Director Hendricks didn't have to concern himself with attempting to accurately convey Congressman McDonald's words to Director Frey, for not only was the entire conversation recorded, but Director Frey personally listened from the point Hendricks answered until Harry left the line.

"Well Hendricks, how does it feel to have encountered the reincarnation of Captain John Birch?"

"Sounds like he has an ax to grind to me."

"Yeah, Mr. Goody Two-shoes always has an ax to grind. I would be delighted to personally show that son of a bitch where his buddy Klinner is, and if it were my call, I would throw his ass in with Klinner, and they could rot together until they choked to death on each other's vomit."

Harry paused for a few minutes to reflect on his conversation with the underlings of the FBI. It went about as he expected—standard operating procedure for the entrenched bureaucracies of Washington town. Perhaps even more so, considering the excessive degree of paranoia exhibited by the agencies involved. Toes have been stepped on, and some big projects are vulnerable to exposure. The efforts of Harry and others to bring their schemes to public review would be blocked at every turn.

Maybe it's time to turn the heat up a bit, thought Harry as he pressed the office intercom button for Erin's extension.

"Yes, Mr. Congressman?"

"Are you busy?"

"Steady, but I can turn loose. What do you need?"

"Could you step into my office please?"

"Give me just a moment to close this out, and I'll be right in."

As Erin entered Harry's office, she thought she detected just the slightest trace of a vindictive smile on Harry's face. As she seated herself into one of the comfortable leather wingback chairs facing Harry's desk, she had the very distinct feeling that whatever the congressman had to share, it was going to be good.

"Miss Giblon, I had an opportunity to read Mr. McAdam's column in *The Chronicle*. I thought it was very well done, and I appreciate you bringing it to my attention."

"I thought you would find it interesting."

"Yes. And I also appreciate you taking the initiative to locate and play for the staff a video of yesterday's conference. That helped to quickly bring our entire team up to speed. Miss Giblon, I've got an idea now that I would like to share with you. I think I would like to turn the heat up a notch or two."

"Sounds intriguing. I'm listening."

"I just got off the phone from talking, or should I say, attempting to talk to people at the FBI. I was trying to find out where Dr. Klinner and the other doctors have been taken. They, of course, smugly proclaimed national security and the power-grabbing Patriot Act to deny my requests for information. I doubt seriously that my efforts at the attorney general's office or Homeland Security this afternoon will be any more fruitful. I'm beginning to realize that an unprecedented cohesiveness of unity now exists within these agencies, and for the moment, I am at a loss of ideas on how to pry the information we need from these people, excepting of course with the power of subpoena and our committee's investigations. But by that time, serious emotional trauma will have been inflicted on those families. And not just emotional trauma for those hapless doctors that have been incarcerated, but depending on where they have been taken, the possibility exists that irreversible physical harm will have been inflicted also. We need answers, and we need them quickly. Miss Giblon, did you ever have the occasion to read the story of Major General Edwin Walker?"

"I don't believe so, Mr. Congressman. That name is not familiar to me."

"General Walker was an American patriot of decades ago that incurred the wrath of the government he was sworn to protect. He, too, was incarcerated against his will. The results were most unpleasant. But I'll have to save that story for another day. We have work to do. As I mentioned a moment ago, I think I would like to turn the heat up a notch. Let's make the enemy squirm a bit."

"What do you have in mind, Mr. Congressman?"

"Do you think any segment of the media is aware of the raids on the doctors' homes this morning?"

"I would seriously doubt it. I think those wives have been frightened and humiliated by the actions of the government agents. That is not the sort of experience one likes to draw the attention of the public to."

"I agree, but conversely, Miss Giblon, if others learn independently of your plight and stand up to fight for you, that is a different matter entirely."

"Are you thinking what I think you are?"

"I don't know…let's see. I propose that you give Mr. McAdams a call."

"And?"

"Oh, nothing much. Just thank him for his column, mention that I also had read it and commented on its quality. Let him know how very much we, in this office, appreciate his efforts."

"And?"

"Tell him of the raids this morning. Tell him of Benjamin Stegall's life-threatening Tasering. Tell him which hospital he has been taken to. Give him the names and addresses and phone numbers of all the wives. Provide a list of their children's names and the civic and community affiliations of the wives, exactly as you did for our conference. If nice, quality color photographs of the wives, preferably posing with their children, could be obtained, that would be a nice touch also."

"You are going where I thought you were!"

"Good. Once again, we are on the same page, you and I! Let's provide some fodder for Mac's cannon. Maybe if he loads it properly and aims in the proper direction, perhaps a hole can be blown in the boiler plate our enemy has shielded itself with. I think it's worth a try!"

"I'm excited, Mr. Congressman. I'll get right on it!"

Erin Giblon's smile as she left Harry's office reflected her enthusiasm for the task that lay before her that afternoon. Providing information and motivation for MacIntosh McAdams would be time well spent in this battle, she felt.

Less than enthusiastic was Harry as he faced what was certainly to be another frustrating series of unproductive telephone calls, seeking answers from an intransigent, inscrutable bureaucracy bent on its self-preservation and perpetuation. The first call was to the Justice Department attempting to directly reach the office of Attorney General Budenz. Harry knew Budenz personally and had zero regard for him as a fellow human being. On more than one occasion, Harry had locked horns with Budenz, most notably when Budenz was serving as an assistant attorney general during the Waco incident. As the government waged its battle against the men, women, and children unfortunate enough to be surrounded by heavily armed agents in full battle gear, even tanks, Harry pleaded incessantly with anyone he could reach at Justice for reason and restraint to prevail. Most frequently, it had been Budenz that Harry had pleaded with to spare innocent lives. The more Harry pleaded for calm and common sense to prevail, the greater had been the arrogance displayed by Budenz. As the body count at the religious community increased, so did the flaunting of haughty, supercilious attitudes among certain high-ranking members of the Justice Department. But as intensely as Harry disliked Budenz, that contempt faded into insignificance compared to his enmity towards Budenz's predecessor. For it was she, in direct violation of the U.S. Constitution, who had ordered the armed military assault on American civilians.

Harry had felt at the time and continued to believe that the entire horrible circumstances that unfolded at Waco could have easily been avoided without any loss of life whatsoever. If laws were being broken by the Christians of that community, their enforcement could have easily been effected by the local sheriff. There was no justification whatsoever for the escalation of an easily resolvable situation into a military and law enforcement slaughter of innocent men, women and children. The sitting attorney general attempted to justify her order to storm the community by arguing that she was protecting the children from sexual molestation. She protected them, all right, from whatever imagined threats they may have faced within the community by murdering them. Yes, murder is a strong word and not to be used carelessly, but in Harry's mind the slaughter of those men, women, and children at Waco *was* murder, preconceived and unadulterated. Harry believed that the then attorney general hated Christians and the faith of Christianity. Why else would she have stated publicly during her administration that the most dangerous people in America were evangelical Christians? Why indeed! To Harry, the most dangerous people in America were those comprising an out-of-control government, relentlessly pursuing the agenda of the New World Order planners.

Now that I am in the proper frame of mind for a productive dialog with the Justice Department, Harry mused, *I think I will try to reach Budenz and ask what*

THE POISON PLUM

he has done with my friend, Dr. Klinner. I am sure he will be most accommodating! Just as he has always been to me.

After about ten minutes and as many voice-mail prompts with submenus, Harry reached an operator for the section of the building that contained the attorney general's office. After identifying himself and making his request to speak with Budenz, Harry was once again placed on a long hold.

What are they doing? he thought. *Activating all the recording devices, stress analyzers, and location sensors?*

Little did Harry realize how correct his presumptions were. Finally Harry heard, "This is Nicolai Pushkin speaking. How may I direct your call?"

"This is Congressman Harry McDonald of the Health and Human Services Committee. I'm calling for Attorney General Budenz."

A click, silence, and another long wait on hold—a six to ten minute wait estimated Harry. And then, with a heavy accent, a voice identifying himself as Vladimir Tokarov answered the phone and asked what the purpose of the call was. Harry's patience, already frayed, was becoming thinner with each passing minute and with each telephone transfer to another faceless, indistinguishable bureaucrat.

"I'm sorry," Harry replied. "There must be some mistake. Obviously I have reached the Russian Consulate. I was trying to reach the United States Justice Department."

"No mistake, this is the Justice Department."

"Well, fine, Comrade Tokarov. I'm calling for Comrade Budenz. Tell him it is important."

"I'm afraid Comrade…err, Attorney General Budenz is unavailable. May I assist you?"

"Well, I don't know, Comrade Tokarov. If you can tell me where several of my constituents have been incarcerated as a result of your office's raids on their homes and offices last Monday, that would be a big help. Do you think you can do that, Comrade Tokarov?"

"I'm afraid I don't have that kind of information at my disposal."

"Can you get it?"

"I'm afraid I cannot."

"I see. You, of course, are going to defer to your supervisors, who are, of course, unavailable too."

"That would be correct, sir."

"I want to know absolutely as soon as possible where all of the doctors arrested during your raids last Monday have been taken."

"I will convey your request, and someone will get back to you."

"Will that be in my lifetime Comrade Tokarov, or in God's lifetime?"

Without even a good-bye, Tokarov had left the line, and Harry found himself bounced back to voice-mail hell.

"No humor, those Slavs…no humor at all. Too much vodka and too many potatoes, I guess."

Certainly Harry entertained no illusions about hearing back with any response of substance from either the FBI or the attorney general's office. *All the snakes are in the same den,* he thought.

Consequently, his call to the office of Homeland Security that afternoon was, at best, perfunctory. Expecting nothing, he nevertheless went through the motions. And as expected, the dictum of "expect nothing, receive nothing" was validated anew that afternoon.

A total waste of time, thought Harry, *but by God I had to try! These inquiries are going nowhere, and I don't expect a breakthrough anytime soon. But why the recalcitrance on the part of the agencies?*

The answer to Harry was almost unthinkable. A thought so abhorrent, he could barely frame it upon his consciousness.

Crimes of terrorism and treason? He thought. *Suspension of habeas corpus? Trial by military tribunal? Incarceration in a military prison reserved for foreign terrorists complete with all of the associated degradation, humiliation, and torture? A military prison? Please God in Heaven… NO! Don't let it be!*

Harry sat silent, motionless, and in deep thought. For he knew that for the moment, he was stymied. Seemingly every avenue was blocked with no resolution in sight. Harry prayed for direction and guidance. He had such a helpless feeling to want to help his friend and the other doctors and their wives, but he was powerless. But Harry firmly believed that direction and guidance would be forthcoming from the Almighty…but from what direction…and when?

The afternoon passed quickly for Harry. After the fruitless calls to the FBI, Justice Department, and the Department of Homeland Security, Harry had reached out to friends and contacts that he had developed over the years as a congressman. Most offered their sympathy and support and encouraged Harry to proceed aggressively with his committee's investigation of Plum Island. But sadly, no one had any inkling whatsoever of where the arrested doctors had been taken. All agreed those heavy-handed government tactics were unprecedented, but no solution was offered or suggested…other than the selective use of Congressional subpoenas. Harry knew that valuable time was being wasted while his friend Glen and the other doctors were suffering whatever their fate had become. Such a helpless feeling—wanting so desperately to help a very, very close friend and being powerless to do so. Even more ironic was to have been rendered so impotent while simultaneously enjoying the status, influence, and power of a United States congressman and the chairmanship of the venerable Health and Human Services Committee. Totally frustrated, Harry's final call of the afternoon before making his way to the conference room and the 4:30 staff meeting was to Anna. Harry was concerned about young Benjamin Stegall, and a positive report from Anna would be a blessing in a day otherwise seemingly devoid of encouraging news.

Harry's call to his residence aroused only the answering machine, but he was able to reach Anna on her cell phone.

"Anna, sweetheart, where are you?"

"Oh, Harry, I'm headed back home now. I just left the hospital a few minutes ago. I've been with Janice Stegall all afternoon."

"That's why I'm calling. How is Benjamin?"

"Not good, Harry. Several cardiologists have been working with him, but Benjamin is not responding satisfactorily to any of the medications or therapies that have been tried. He stopped breathing twice but was revived and now is on life support."

"Those are ominous developments Anna. I am very concerned that young Benjamin may not pull through. How is Janice holding up?"

"She is having a rough time, Harry. Sometimes she breaks down and cries uncontrollably. The uncertainty of her husband's fate and location combined with everything else that has happened is proving to be too much. She blames the government for not only taking her husband from her but for also trying to kill her son. She loudly curses the government between crying spells and shows everyone within earshot the ankle tracking device, saying it is the mark of the beast described in the book of Revelation. Her personal physician was by to visit shortly before I left, and he gave Janice a sedative, which she accepted. That is when I left, hoping that Janice, with the help of the sedative, could get some rest."

"My heart goes out to that family Anna. I will redouble my prayers for them that they might be guided safely out of the valley of darkness."

"I'll pray too, Harry, and if I hear anything else, I'll call you as soon as I can."

"Thanks, sweetheart. I love you."

"I love you too, Harry."

With a heavy heart Harry joined his staff in the conference room for their 4:30 meeting. A cursory glance at the expression on Harry's face as he entered the room spoke volumes to his loyal staff. They sensed his frustration, and had he not spoken a single word, they would have instinctively known that his day had been totally unproductive.

Nevertheless, Harry managed to exude a positive attitude for his staff and appeared as organized and focused as always as he asked for a report on the progress of the committee's organization so far. As expected, the thoroughness and professionalism of his carefully selected staff had resulted in very substantial progress, and all seemed to be right on track. Next was a report from Erin Giblon summarizing her successful contact with MacIntosh McAdams and also her efforts to collect usable information about Plum Island's laboratory. Harry felt a little better after those reports. At least some progress had been made, he felt.

Harry told his staff of his lack of success in determining the location and condition of the doctors that had been arrested in the raids. His personal calls to the FBI, Justice Department, Department of Homeland Security, and personal contacts had netted a big fat zero. Whatever information those agencies harbored was a very closely guarded secret, and he knew that he had no viable plan to help his friend Glen or any of the other doctors. A question from a member of his staff helped to put everything in proper perspective.

"Mr. Congressman, won't the officials and agents involved in the raids be forced by the committee's investigation to surrender that information under oath?"

"Yes, that is correct," replied Harry. "But the organization of the committee and the subsequent interviewing of agency heads and witnesses, will of necessity, take time—very valuable time, which we cannot spare. For if my assumptions and apprehensions are correct, those innocent, decent, law-abiding doctors have been incarcerated in some hell hole of a military prison in accordance with the damnable provisions of the unconstitutional Patriot Act. We and they simply do not have the luxury of time on our side. Conditions in those prisons are not conducive to the comfort and longevity of the inhabitants, to say the least. Physical and mental abuse, including, but not limited to, torture will be incorporated by the guards daily. You can be certain of that! Even more frightening is the very real possibility of irreversible mental damage occurring as a result of brainwashing, the long-term administration of mind-control drugs, or actual lobotomy operations. The good news is, the doctors are finally released and allowed to return to their families. The bad news is they don't recognize their families when they see them. Miss Giblon, please remind me to someday share with everyone the saga of Major General Edwin Walker. His story would certainly be germane to the situation I am describing."

"But, Mr. Congressman, the Patriot Act notwithstanding, how can the government capriciously and in total disregard for due process, seize innocent American citizens, and as you say, lock them away in some hell hole of a military prison? Where are the appeals judges to rule this sort of activity unconstitutional? The ACLU? Anybody?"

"Where indeed?" responded Harry. "Where is the furor and uproar over the provisions of the Patriot Act? Undeniably the greatest power grab by government since the unconscionable acts of Abraham Lincoln during the Civil War."

"Amen to that, Mr. Congressman," chimed Erin. "When I was at Georgetown studying for my masters in American History, I did extensive research into Lincoln's administration. I, as a result of my research, came to the conclusion that Lincoln was nothing more than a self-serving political opportunist, willing to say or do whatever was required to advance his career. His total disregard and disdain for the Constitution was an abomination only surpassed by the atrocities committed against the South by the Union forces. And how can we as a people ignore Lincoln's incompetence, the damage done to our Constitution and the Republic under his administration, and go on to eulogize the man, put his image on our currency, and build monuments to him? Mr. Congressman, if I had my wish, John Wilkes Booth would be awarded the Congressional Medal of Honor posthumously!"

"An interesting thought, Miss Giblon. But as we are only too aware, the victors in war have the luxury of writing the history of the battle. It was as they say it was. Besides, what would our friends Simon Snodgrass of the *Times* and Lemke of the *Post* think of your proposal?"

"Let me guess. Would I be editorially eviscerated for my heresy?"

"For starters. Then if you held employment in a publicly funded school or university you would be terminated; if you held public office, your next election would be your last. Such is the power yielded by the rewriters of history. And perhaps if you were fortunate enough to have survived all of that after your rather laconic expression of your sentiments, maybe you could be visited by our jack-booted friends who would be more than happy to use their Taser guns on you. Doubtless, a new attitude on your part would emerge. And speaking of Taser guns, I would like to close our meeting by bringing everyone up to date on the condition of young Benjamin Stegall. Shortly before our meeting began, I spoke with Mrs. McDonald who was returning to our home after spending the afternoon at Our Lady of Mercy Hospital with Janice Stegall. The news is not good, I'm afraid. Young Benjamin has not responded to the efforts of the doctors to stabilize his heart rhythm. He is in intensive care as we speak and had to be placed on life support. The Stegall family needs our prayers. Let us hope and pray that Benjamin will recover quickly and Janice and her husband will be reunited soon. The families of all of the doctors involved thank you, and I thank you for the excellent work you are doing. We have a long and difficult road ahead of us, but we have no choice other than to stay the course. Try to get some rest this evening, and I'll see you all in the morning."

Ben's Momma

Erin Giblon was, as usual, the first to arrive at Congressman McDonald's office Thursday morning. It was her habit to arrive early enough to review the newspapers that were delivered each morning in order to stay abreast of current developments. Typically she would start her day with *The Wall Street Journal* before moving on to *The Times, The Post, The Chronicle*, and others. But today would be different. Erin's primary interest was with *The Chronicle* because she wondered if MacIntosh McAdams had acted on the information she had provided.

Probably not yet, she thought. *Not enough time to do the research and put an article together.*

Erin gathered all of the publications under her arm and moved to the break room to enjoy her second cup of coffee while reviewing *The Chronicle.* Spreading the newspaper on the large table while sipping her hot coffee, she began turning the pages searching for Mac's column. When she saw that his column was not in its usual location, she logically assumed that if he had a column forthcoming it would be in a later edition. And then as she turned one more page, she was stunned by the appearance of a very large article occupying the entire top half of one of the two pages allocated for editorial comment and letters to the editor. What first caught Erin's eye was the appearance of two rows of four large, color photographs of the wives whose husbands had been arrested in the raids. Some of the photographs included their husbands and children. Beneath each picture was the name of the wife and any family members that might have been included in the picture. And then beneath that was listed all of the professional and civic affiliations held by the wife and/or her husband. For all practical purposes, the article had the appearance of a chamber of commerce membership roster or a listing of influential benefactors of the university or a large hospital. But once one's gaze shifted to the article's title, any and all resemblance to the mundane and ordinary ended quite abruptly in true MacIntosh McAdams style. For there, emblazoned in very large type for all to see, were the following words followed by the article's text:

The Real Danger to America!
Osama Bin Laden or... Ben's Momma?

My fellow Americans, the faces you see illustrated above are of the wives and family members of the doctors arrested by the FBI during raids conducted on those doctors' offices last Monday.

Warning!

Do not be beguiled by the seemingly normal and innocent appearances of these women! For if government investigators are correct, these women are material witnesses in a massive conspiracy to commit terrorism against the United States. Their husbands are charged as co-conspirators in an evil plot to kill loyal government scientists at the Plum Island ferry that fateful afternoon of July 3, and are awaiting trial in an undisclosed location. We must all be alert and ever vigilant! Forget the stereotypes of terrorists promoted by the media! As these photographs dramatically illustrate, terrorism can assume any identity or appearance. At this very moment, the families of your own next-door neighbors could be knee-deep in sinister, nefarious schemes and plots to undermine our republic. Thanks to the intrepid and ever-watchful loyal agents of the FBI, Justice Department, IRS, CDC, ATF, Department of Homeland Security, and others, our freedom as Americans is more secure.

Early Wednesday morning, very brave government agents, staring danger in the face every step of the way and with no apparent concern for their personal safety, raided the homes of these incredibly dangerous eight women to attach tracking devices to their legs. This was necessary because of the obvious flight risk involved and also to protect innocent American citizens and their institutions from further attacks. Apparently, even the children of these women had been carefully trained by their parents in the ways of terrorism. For it was at the home of Mrs. Janice Stegall, wife of cardiologist Dr. Eric Stegall, that events turned ugly for the agents involved. As Mrs. Stegall was being fitted with the tracking device, her fanatical eleven-year-old son suddenly and viciously attacked

THE POISON PLUM

the brave agents on duty. Unable to control young Ben Stegall, the agents, exhibiting incredible restraint, managed to subdue Ben by the use of Taser guns only.

This incident clearly illustrates the dangers our government's agents face daily in their efforts to protect you and I, Mr. and Mrs. Average American, from the onslaught of unbridled terrorism. It also illustrates the fanaticism of highly trained terrorists committed to the completion of their agenda at any cost.

It is not known at this time if Ben Stegall will be tried as an adult for assaulting federal agents and interfering with the duties of federal agents. Unfortunately for the incipient young terrorist, he had the misfortune to contract rheumatic fever at the age of six. The infection damaged his heart, and because of the damage, it was necessary to hospitalize him after the Tasering to correct arrhythmias which developed. Government officials stressed that the use of Taser guns to subdue violent criminals is a very safe and humane way to temporarily immobilize a subject, and complications as experienced by Ben Stegall are very rare indeed. Gone are the primitive and inhumane days of clubbings, beatings, and shootings commonly used by police forces worldwide. Now, in modern times, and as a result of technological advancements previously only considered science fiction, we are able to incorporate the latest scientific innovations in police work. The Taser gun is an example of these advancements in current usage. They are humane, safe, and highly effective.

Indeed, the task of protecting America is a very formidable one. As the government officials responsible for securing and defending our institutions and way of life stare into the yawning abyss of the growing menace of terrorism, they must realize that no stone can be left unturned if we are to be totally safe.

Clever are the ways of those who are dedicated to spreading their poisonous ideas into the mainstream of America. As evidenced by a partial list of affiliations of the identified co-conspirators and material witnesses, no institution, organization, or group, no matter how benign in appearance, is above suspicion. In subtle, seemingly innocuous ways, trained terrorists can infiltrate, influence, and subvert groups such as those listed below to ultimately achieve their goals of destruction. As you consider affiliation with groups such as those listed, be wary and ever vigilant. Report any suspicious or unusual behavior promptly to the proper authorities. Take, for example, that bulge you see in the purse of the normal-appearing housewife seated next to you at the garden club meeting. Is that (don't stare, she may become suspicious) her makeup kit? Or a loaded .357 Magnum revolver? Or a bomb? Or a vial of Anthrax? Beware of her normal-appearing ways, mannerisms, and customs. Still waters run deep. You never know!

A Partial List of Organizations Potentially Infiltrated by Terrorists*

> New London, Connecticut City Commission
> Junior League
> New London, Connecticut YMCA
> Salvation Army
> New London, Connecticut College Board of Trustees
> Girl Scouts
> New London, Connecticut First Methodist Church,
> First Baptist Church and Presbyterian Church.
> Boards of Education
> Junior Miss Pageant
> PTA
> Garden Club of New London
> Medical Auxiliary
> Big Brothers, Big Sisters
> Chamber of Commerce
> American Medical Association
> American Cancer Society

*Due to space limitations, the above listings are of necessity considerably abbreviated.

As the threat of terrorism steadily increases in America, it may become necessary for the Justice Department to rethink their long-abandoned policy of publishing a list of subversive organizations to help keep innocent American citizens from unwise associations. For those of you too young to remember, during the 1950s the attorney general of the United States compiled a list of organizations known to have ties to communist, socialist, anarchist, or fascist groups or individuals. The goals of these organizations were deemed to be subversive to the government of the United States. Condemned at the time by civil libertarians and ACLU attorneys, the Justice Department finally recanted and stopped the production and publication of the Attorney General's List of Subversive Organizations. It may be time to bring these lists back—to be forewarned is to be forearmed!

In conclusion, we all must recognize the very deep debt of gratitude we collectively owe the various government agencies that successfully pieced together the obscure and tenuous links between Colonel Gordon McClain, the identified shooter at the Plum Island ferry, and the doctors responsible for their mind-control experiments designed to incite Colonel McClain to violence.

~~~~~And now back to planet Earth~~~~~

No Dear Reader, MacIntosh McAdams has not lost his mind, nor have I sold out to the enemy. I have written the above to give our readers an example of the mindless garbage being disseminated by the liberal media of this nation. This propaganda serves the purpose of diverting attention away from the real threat to the safety of American citizens, especially the sinister, out-of-control experiments at the Plum Island laboratory. We must all rally around the efforts of Congressman Harry McDonald and the members of the Health and Human Services Committee as they begin a congressional inquiry into the activities and research being conducted at the Plum Island facility while there is still time! Contact your senators and congressmen and insist upon their support of the committee's investigation. Also voice your objections to the unconstitutional Patriot Act and demand its immediate repeal. And last but not least, demand the release of all of the doctors arrested and the complete exoneration of any and all charges levied against them.

So there you have it, Dear Reader—your tax dollars at work. In the name of national security and under the auspices of the Patriot Act, government agents raid homes and offices of innocent, hard-working, pillar-of-the-community doctors and their Stepford wives. Enough is enough!

Erin slowly leaned back into her chair after completing the article and began sipping her coffee. She was deep in thought as she contemplated the coming reactions of the various government agencies and certain media to McAdams's column. Would it be silence? The strategy of ignoring your enemy by not dignifying their attack with a response? Would it be an all out frontal assault in an attempt at total repudiation? Or something in between these two extremes? Certainly MacIntosh McAdams had to be rattling some cages after the publication of this second cynical attack. And what about the so-called mainstream media? Erin expected that quarter to rouse from their slumber, apathy, and myopia, to begin questioning the events of recent days. If government atrocities continued to escalate, some of the questions raised by mainstream media could be quite probing indeed as the editors and news directors posture on the side of morality and decency.

Very interesting, she thought. *Don't guess I'm going to get bored anytime soon or schedule a vacation.*

A noise in the hall and the sound of the office door being unlocked brought Erin back to matters at hand as she looked at her watch and realized it was time for the congressman to arrive at the office. She rose and walked to the reception area to greet Harry as he entered.

"Good morning, Mr. Congressman. How are you?"

"Fine, Miss Giblon, but I'm afraid I have some disturbing news."

"What is it Mr. Congressman?"

"Mrs. McDonald received a 5:00 AM telephone call from one of the cardiologists treating young Benjamin Stegall. It seems that an uncontrollable arrhythmia developed, and Benjamin died at 4:30 this morning. Mrs. Stegall has also been hospitalized, and she is under heavy sedation."

"Oh, Mr. Congressman! That is horrible news!"

"Yes, yes it is. An innocent, sickly eleven-year-old child valiantly tries to protect his mother and is murdered by brutal, ruthless government agents. They should be arrested and tried for their crime…and in a rational world not totally devoid of reason, sanity, and morality, they would be."

"What do we do next?"

"I'm afraid my anger and frustration is clouding my judgment and direction at the moment. I am furious!"

"And I, as well, Mr. Congressman!"

"We, of course, can and will expand our committee's investigation to include this unfortunate incident. We will subpoena and question the agents involved and press for their suspension and job termination. But, that will all take time. And isn't it frustrating that we can't take some form of immediate action on behalf of young Benjamin Stegall, his loving mother, and his father, wherever he might be?"

"Perhaps we can, Mr. Congressman. I've got an idea!"

"You do? Excellent! What is it?"

"Have you seen this morning's *Chronicle*?"

"*The Chronicle*? No, I haven't. Has MacIntosh McAdams written another column?"

"A column? Yes, you could say that. I think *vendetta* might be the more appropriate description, however, but I'll let you be the judge. The paper is in the break room, and I thought you would want to see it as soon as you arrived."

"Yes, I do want to see it. But you said you have an idea?"

"I do have one, but I think it would make more sense after you have read the column."

Erin followed Harry to the break room, took a seat across the table, and carefully scrutinized his facial expressions as he read through McAdams's column. It was always interesting to attempt to gauge Harry's responses, and today, as she had anticipated, a faint trace of a vindictive smile once again appeared on Harry's face as he neared the completion of the column. MacIntosh McAdams had accepted this challenge, had taken the ball, and he was running with it.

"Well, Miss Giblon, it would appear that Mr. McAdams is indeed true to his word. It certainly takes considerable courage and fortitude to take a position so firmly entrenched and contrary to the usual 'inside the beltway, go along to get along, mentality.' I believe we have a very valuable ally in this battle."

"And so do I, Mr. Congressman. Furthermore, I think he is raising questions and issues that certainly cannot be ignored by the mainstream media, other congressmen, congresswomen, senators, or even the president. I suggest we add more fuel to the flame. Let us continue to stoke the engines that provide the momentum for the McAdams's express!"

"Sounds good to me. What do you suggest?"

"Very simple. I'll just call his office and tell him Benjamin Stegall is dead, and his mother is hospitalized and under deep sedation. I don't think he will take this latest development quietly… if I know MacIntosh McAdams."

"Interesting. So you think this might be sufficient incentive for yet another blistering column?"

"I do. Maybe even a take-no-hostages, scorched-earth policy from the pen of MacIntosh McAdams. The man is obviously very intense, focused, and incredibly tenacious. I'm glad he is on our side!"

"Yes, so am I. And I have the distinct feeling that you are right. More help is coming our way, and soon."

"I take it then that I have your permission to proceed?"

"Absolutely!"

"What do you think about issuing a press release from our office to the Washington and national media?"

"Well, I don't suppose it would hurt, but I doubt if any of the major media would pick it up because Benjamin Stegall's death would be viewed by most as a local and not a national event. It would be deemed 'not news worthy' to a national audience."

"Mr. Congressman, I realize you have just returned from your district but have you given thought to calling another news conference in New London?"

"I have, Miss Giblon and I do think it would be appropriate and also expected of me by the constituency. Eric and Janice Stegall are very well-known throughout that area. They are popular and highly respected. Yes, I owe it to my constituents to provide support. And hopefully, someday, some answers will be revealed. All those people know at this juncture is that Eric Stegall has been hauled off by the government to God only knows where, Janice Stegall has been terrorized in her own home, and eleven-year-old Benjamin Stegall has been Tasered to death by brutal federal agents. Yes, I do need to go back to the district, and I need to go as soon as possible. Let's try to secure the New London Community Center, as before, and schedule the conference for tomorrow afternoon at the most suitable time."

"Wonderful! Mr. Congressman, the rest of our staff should be here within the next fifteen minutes. As soon as they arrive, I'll have them contact Robin Waters to reserve the community center, and we'll get the local media contacted. Do you want us to advise Hank Sturgess and the rest of the media that the principal reason for calling the news conference is the death of Benjamin Stegall at the hands of federal agents?"

"Yes, but not exclusively. I'll also call attention to the unwarranted invasion of the doctors' homes, the terrorizing of the inhabitants, and the humiliation experienced as a result of the shacklings."

"I'll get right on it. But first I'll try to reach Mr. McAdams."

As Erin made her way back to her office from the break room, her mind began seriously contemplating yet another idea that she had nurtured for several days now. It was an idea so brazen and so bold that she *dared* not share it with the congressman. Indeed, the idea itself was so out of character for her, she privately wondered what spark of fancy had triggered such a radical scheme. Consciously, she attempted to suppress the urgings and motivations that seemed to fuel her desire to rationalize this wistful chimera that just wouldn't pass. For it seemed that for every objection her conscious, rational mind constructed, two arguments were offered by the subconscious to proceed.

Erin had struggled with such decisions before in her life and career. And each time, when she had finally yielded to the insuppressible urgings and proddings from her inner psyche, the outcome inevitably was positive. But this time was different. For this time, real, very real, palpable potential dangers lurked in the wings, and not only physical danger to herself but embarrassment to the congressman should she be found out. As they say, the devil is in the details. For this would not be some asinine sorority prank, some juvenile spray painting of the high school mascot, or even cheating en masse via purloined test papers of the most important final exam of the semester…Nope! This was big boy, big girl, all grown up and serious stuff. But as they say, whoever they are, all is fair in love and war! Are we at war? You betcha! Desperate situations require desperate measures! Erin sealed her fate. Nothing ventured, nothing gained. She was going to do it, someway, somehow. *The first step,* she thought, *is to call MacIntosh McAdams.* Erin seated herself at her desk, took a few deep breaths, and dialed the number for the office of McAdams at *The Chronicle*. It was early, only 7:50 AM. *Would he be in?* she wondered.

"Office of MacIntosh McAdams. Nancy Holt speaking. How may I direct your call?"

"Hi, Nancy. It's Erin Giblon at Congressman McDonald's office. Is Mr. McAdams available?"

"Oh, hi Erin. He's only been here for a few minutes, but I'm sure he will want to talk to you. Have you seen this morning's column?"

"Yes, I have. And the congressman has also seen it. Very impressive!"

"Hold on. Let me get him for you."

"Thanks."

Elevator music played for about thirty seconds, and then the booming, very masculine, voice of MacIntosh McAdams filled the earpiece.

"Miss Giblon...nice to hear from you. Have you seen this morning's issue of *The Chronicle?*"

"Yes, Mr. McAdams. I have. And so has the congressman."

"Excellent! What did you think?"

"We both thank you for your efforts and support. And we both feel that it is only a matter of time before a groundswell of opinion and concern is manifested in other media as a result of your columns."

"Well, that's the plan. Don't hold out for a swing of allegiance from Simon Snodgrass though!"

Erin laughed. Something about Mac really struck a chord with her. She felt a kinship with him beyond the boundaries of this battle with the government. *If only he were thirty years younger,* she found herself thinking.

"Thank you for taking my call so early in the morning. I hate to interrupt your schedule, but we have something that you will find interesting, I'm sure."

"And what might that be, Miss Giblon?"

"We thought you would want to know that Benjamin Stegall passed away during the night."

"Dammit! No Shit? Those bastards!"

"It's true. The cardiologists were unable to restore normal heart rhythm to Benjamin's heart as a result of the damage from the Taser guns. At about 4:00 AM he developed arrhythmias that could not be controlled, and he expired. His mother, Janice Stegall, is under heavy sedation and had to be admitted to the same hospital. The cumulative stress of her son's death and the uncertainty of her husband's whereabouts were just too much for her, I suppose."

"Murder! The gutless bastards murdered that kid. As sure as shit stinks and the Pope is a catholic, they murdered him. May their bowels scorch in the pits of hell!"

"Well, Mr. McAdams, I guess the latter is one thing we can be certain about. Anyway, we wanted you to be apprised of these latest developments."

"And I thank you Miss Giblon. I know exactly what I am going to do. Call it a contingency plan, if you will. And I apologize for my French a moment ago."

"No problem. No problem at all, Mr. McAdams. Sometimes directness is the finest expression of eloquence."

"You like directness? Check out tomorrow morning's *Chronicle*!"

"I had a feeling that would be forthcoming, knowing you! Thank you!"

"My pleasure. Thank you!"

"Mr. McAdams, before you go, I have a request. Actually a favor if you will."

"A favor, you say? Name it?"

"Regrettably, I am unable to ask you for the favor over the telephone. It is of a rather sensitive nature, you see, and I was wondering if your busy schedule would allow time for us to meet personally. Preferably not in our offices but in some location where our appearances could be considered happenstance if observed. Perhaps we could meet in the Library of Congress?"

"That could be arranged. When did you have in mind?"

"I'm flexible. The congressman will be hosting a news conference tomorrow afternoon in New London addressing these latest developments."

"How about 11:00 AM at the James Madison Building on Independence?"

"Wonderful. That would be ideal. We can meet in the current periodical reading room on the first floor. Thank you for everything, Mr. McAdams. I'll see you then."

Ah, it's a beautiful thing, thought Mac as he hung up the phone. *Kick the new world order in the ass and meet with a beautiful woman at the same time! Sometimes life can be grand, and this is one of those times!*

Friday in Washington

Seven-thirty that Friday morning found Erin already at the office and Harry McDonald en route to Dulles for his flight back to the district. Erin's attendance at this news conference would not be required and she felt it fortuitous that Harry would be away while she somewhat furtively met with MacIntosh McAdams. It was totally alien to her nature and sense of team unity to operate even slightly independent of the congressman's cognizance and approval. But for certain, his opposition to Erin's planned course of action would be firm and unwavering, if only he knew. In Erin's mind, something of a drastic nature had to be attempted and soon. The usual avenues of recourse to determine who, what, when, and where had failed. A cork had been placed in the bottle of useful information by the heads of the government agencies involved, and it was their intention to keep it there. For Erin, her mind was set and damn the consequences. If the congressman could bravely put his career on the line, and possibly his life, by announcing his intention to pursue a full-scale congressional committee investigation into Plum Island, certainly she could do no less if indeed she were a dedicated component of the congressman's team, both physically and philosophically.

If Erin's confidence was even slightly wavering that beautiful, clear Friday morning in the nation's capital, the reading of MacIntosh McAdams's column in the morning *Chronicle* forever banished any lingering hesitancy, no matter how trivial it might have been.

Erin enjoyed the early morning solitude of the office before any of the staffers arrived and before any of the telephones were taken off voice mail. She always used this quiet time to review the morning newspapers, but today her interest was focused entirely on *The Chronicle*. She had no problem finding his column that day, nor would have any other reader. It filled almost one-half of a page and was strategically placed on the upper right-hand side where a reader's gaze typically lands as the pages are turned. Even more eye-catching was the color and appearance of the column. It looked, for all practical purposes, like a weathered and time-worn wanted poster from the days of the Wild West or a page from the *Tombstone Telegraph*. In contrast to the surrounding paper, the column was sepia toned with cracked, torn, and frayed–appearing edges that gave the appearance of a three-dimensional piece that had been inserted separately within *The Chronicle*'s pages. In bold, black type reminiscent of the late 1800s there appeared the word…

WANTED

And underneath that, in slightly smaller type, the crime's description ……

FOR MURDER

The pictures below resembled tintypes of individuals wearing business suits clearly of the bygone era, but through the magic of modern computer graphics, the faces were of FBI Director Frey, Attorney General Budenz, and ATF Director Aderholdt. Their names and titles were printed below each picture, and beneath that were pictures of the agents directly responsible for the Tasering death of Benjamin Stegall. The faces and names were of the actual agents involved but the clothing, thanks again to modern computer graphics, was of the style normally worn by U.S. marshals and sheriffs of old, complete with the five-pointed lapel star and twin six-guns jauntily protruding from their holsters.

The text of the article was unadulterated MacIntosh McAdams on a mission and mad as hell. Collectively he was judge, jury, and executioner, giving no quarter and accepting no specious arguments as rebuttal or justification. Unequivocally, in the mind of MacIntosh McAdams, not only were the agents guilty of the murder of Benjamin Stegall but their superiors were as well. No punishment would have been too harsh or extreme for these enemies of freedom and the American way. Sentence after sentence and paragraph after paragraph, McAdams relentlessly and graphically dramatized the completely unjustifiable raids on the doctors' offices and homes, their arrests and incarcerations, the inhumane and brutal treatment of the wives and their children, and finally the senseless, brutal, and cowardly murder of eleven-year-old Benjamin Stegall.

The average *Chronicle* reader, even those accustomed to the pithy editorial style of MacIntosh McAdams, would have been shocked, sickened, angered, and perhaps ashamed at the actions of government agencies and their thugs called special agents. So as not to leave the reader directionless and with unfocused resentment, Mac offered several courses of action at the conclusion of his column but not before lamenting the abandonment of the practice of guillotining public servants turned evil and corrupt, and the usually infallible logic and hasty resolution of the lynch mob, requiring only a sound tree and sufficient rope.

First, he demanded that the president of the United States publicly apologize for what had occurred. Furthermore, he demanded the immediate removal from office, with prejudice, of Attorney General Budenz, FBI Director Frey, and the acting director of the ATF, Aderholdt. He also insisted upon thorough, unbiased investigations into the actions of the agents actually at the scene of the Stegall Tasering. Criminal prosecutions should begin as soon as a new attorney general is named. The president should also authorize the release of every doctor arrested and publicly apologize to them and their families, initiate a full-blown presidential inquiry into the entire matter, and announce his support of Congressman McDonald's committee investigations.

Only one thing is for sure, thought Erin as she settled back into the break room chair after completing Mac's column. *Mac's readers don't have to guess what is on his mind. The man consistently tells it like it is with no apologies or qualifications, regardless of whose fat gets fried or how many skeletons fall out of the closet.*

Erin realized that Mac McAdams was a dying breed; a colorful anachronism rapidly succumbing to attrition and the apathy of the world. Today's replacements in the field of journalism step up to the plate thoroughly groomed and educated in the finer points of situation ethics and unprincipled opportunism.

Erin glanced at her watch as she heard the staffers and interns beginning to noisily fill the congressman's office. *Good, 8:00 AM,* she thought, *all right on time.* She planned to spend a few hours reviewing the Plum Island laboratory information collected so far and then leave shortly after ten for her appointment with McAdams. A certain measure of excitement was building for Erin, for no longer was she experiencing the detachment of observing someone else's battle. Today she made it her own.

Pennsylvania Avenue

Throughout Washington, in various locations and circumstances, there began a most unpleasant day for Attorney General Budenz, CIA Director Steele, Homeland Security Director Dolan, FBI Director Frey, and acting ATF Director Aderholdt. For precisely at 7:45 AM, a call came through on the designated lines with a terse foreword announcement: "Hold for the president."

Budenz was having breakfast with his Russian-born wife, Olga, who was adorned in rollers, facial crème, housecoat, and slippers. He was certain that in only a few more years and a few more pounds she would be a dead ringer for Nikita Khrushchev's wife. What the hell was he thinking twenty years ago?

Steele was dressing for the office at the apartment of his twenty-one-year-old mistress Crystal, whom he had kindly rescued from a career as a Washington stripper two years ago.

Dolan was nursing a king-sized hangover from a night of bar hopping and carousing and was wondering who the handsome young man was sleeping next to him.

Frey, to his credit, had actually made it to his office and was busy working.

Aderholdt had responded to an earlier call from a member of his staff tipping him off to McAdam's column, which he quickly acquired and read. As a consequence, the president's subsequent call was not that much of a surprise. But surprise or no surprise, it was still bad news.

There was the wait of uncertainty while one by one each of the participants was located and identities confirmed before the conference call could begin. Without a doubt, each mind was racing as they all entertained the same concern—"What is this about? Why would the president be calling at this hour?"

Then came the voice of the call's coordinator as he announced, "Mr. President, as per your request, I have on the line Attorney General Budenz, CIA Director

Steele, Homeland Security Director Dolan, FBI Director Frey, and ATF Director Aderholdt. You may now begin your call."

Almost in unison, the five recipients attempted to respond with their versions of, "Good morning, Mr. President." A brief moment of silence passed, and then came the voice of the president, obviously not in the mood for friendly greetings or banter.

"It may be a good morning where your toes are touching the floor, but it's not a good morning over here on Pennsylvania Avenue where the rubber meets the road. I have just returned from the G-7 meeting in London with my trouser legs worn out from being on my knees begging our trading partners to keep buying U.S. securities to finance our current account deficit. When the treasury secretary tells me that we require over three billion a day in foreign inflows of capital just to break even and avoid default, I get off my knees and start kissing asses while promising everything under the sun to people that hate us just to keep the bucks rolling in. And if sore knees from begging and sore lips from kissing butts were not enough, I now have the red ass from being told how to conduct American domestic policy by a newspaper columnist named MacIntosh McAdams!

"Sweet mother of Jesus! Have you people collectively lost your sanity while I've been in Europe? What in hell are you trying to do to those doctors and their families up there in Connecticut? We've got enough terrorists running amok on this planet without you guys trying to teach Bin Laden a few tricks!"

Several voices tried to form a response but it was Attorney General Budenz who prevailed. "Mr. President," he began, "we of course regret the unfortunate death of the Stegall kid, but it was a consequence of violent resistance to our agents performing their duties who, of course, had no knowledge of the attacker's previous history of heart disease."

"Come off of it, Budenz! You're not talking to the media here. You make it sound like that kid was a 280-pound NFL linebacker!"

"Mr. President, surely you recognize that our agents have a duty to protect themselves from harm."

"Yeah, right! And if you keep this shit up, we will all be looking over our shoulders and trying to cover our asses because some pissed-off good ol' boys will be gunning for us! Don't any of you remember how after Ruby Ridge and Waco, citizen's militias were cropping up like weeds after a spring rain? Your predecessors didn't want to wind up taking a dirt nap, and they backed off. Didn't you learn a damn thing from their mistakes?"

"But Mr. President, we have formulated a well-coordinated, cohesive plan to divert attention from the biological laboratory on Plum Island while preserving the integrity of Colonel Gordon McClain's illustrious career."

"And how, may I ask, have you geniuses accomplished that formidable task?"

"To avoid any possible linkage of Colonel McClain's Lyme disease problems to the lab, we have charged his doctor, Glen Klinner, with using mind-altering drugs to incite McClain to violence against the facility. While receiving the drugs, McClain was told repeatedly that the lab was the source of his sickness."

"Lyme disease? Is that one of the diseases cooked up at Plum?"

"Yes, Mr. President."

"If the bio-labs exist to create biological weapons to be used in warfare while simultaneously developing deterrents to similar weapons to protect us from the enemy, why are innocent citizens getting sick with Lyme?"

"We are not sure, Mr. President. Perhaps some of the infected insects escaped from the lab."

"You are not sure? You sons of bitches! My nineteen-year-year-old niece is sick as hell with Lyme disease! I ought to fire every damn one of you right now and shut those labs down myself."

"But Mr. President, national security mandates that…"

"National security my ass! What is the cure? What is the antidote? I know there is one! They never conjure up a doomsday bug without a cure. What the hell is it?"

"Well, Mr. President, there is a treatment room at the facility. I could arrange for your niece to be…"

"You're damn right you will 'arrange' and you will do it today, or I'll have your ass! My niece has been through hell, you bastards!"

"Mr. President, it is unfortunate that Lyme disease has spread so far from the laboratory, but our program of spraying, we feel, has contained the disease. And not only Lyme but West Nile Encephalitis as well."

"Spraying? What the hell are you talking about?"

"You know Mr. President, the large commercial jets that we had stripped and fitted with storage tanks to hold the insecticides? For several years now we have been crisscrossing America in a grid pattern spraying Ethylene Dibromide. It has been very effective."

"So you kill the bugs. What happens to people when they breathe it?"

"Well, Mr. President..."

"All right! Enough is enough! Why have those other doctors been arrested? We are going to stop this insanity, and we are going to do it today!"

"All of those other doctors were Lyme doctors as was Klinner. They, too, were making the connection to Plum Island, and we had to shut them up."

"So who were they telling? Were they going to the media?"

"Not yet, but now that Congressman Harry McDonald has announced that his Health and Human Services Committee will conduct an investigation into Plum Island, we feel confident that incarcerating those doctors was the right thing to do."

"In other words, you feel that by doing the wrong thing in the first place by attacking the doctors, you provided justification for McDonald to investigate, which in hindsight is a good thing because you already have the doctors in custody! I'll tell you what *is* a good thing! It's a damn good thing you all found jobs in the government! With that kind of convoluted reasoning, none of you would ever make it in the private sector! I'll tell you all this—when I started this conference call today every single one of McAdams's proposed solutions to this problem made damn good, if unpalatable, sense. The catch-22 you bumbling fools have created is the only thing saving your jobs. If I could, I would can everyone of you, and with prejudice, right here and right now.

"At this point I am too angry and disgusted to proceed further, but rest assured each of you will be hearing back from this office and soon! In the meantime, try not to do anything else stupid. I face re-election this fall, and I don't need this ballast trying to sink my ship of state. If I do go down because of your blunders, I'm taking each and every one of you with me! And that's a promise, by God! By tomorrow morning, 0900 hours, I want on my desk a copy of your quote, 'formulated and well-coordinated, cohesive plan,' end quote. Expect to hear back from me before that day is over!"

The Little Black Cocktail Dress

Erin had left the office a little early, having learned a long time ago the unpredictability of Washington traffic. By 10:45 AM, she was comfortably seated in the Library of Congress's current periodical reading room nursing her second cup of coffee while reading that morning's edition of *The Wall Street Journal*. The front page article about the massive derivative losses at Fannie Mae and Freddie Mac piqued her curiosity, but to divert her attention in that direction at this time would be impossible. Another government bailout would probably already be underway or even a thing of the past by the time she would be able to enjoy the luxury of exploring that debacle.

So many avenues of interest, so little time, she thought as she began hearing a very masculine voice approaching. She turned her head in the direction of the voice to see MacIntosh McAdams walking briskly in her direction.

"Miss Giblon, what a coincidence seeing you here! It's nice to see you again!"

"And you as well, Mr. McAdams. What brings you to the Library of Congress this fine morning?"

"I was just finishing some research I've been doing for a column I'm working on."

"Would you like to join me for a cup of coffee? I'm about ready for a refill."

"Thank you. I believe I will. May I sit here?"

"Certainly. I was just finishing an interesting article about problems with derivatives over at Fannie and Freddie."

"Yeah, the guys running those operations felt they were operating under implied government guarantees for their investments, and as a consequence, they were running those entities like a hedge fund—fast and loose. The top brass were getting paid very handsomely, but I'm not sure anybody else will get paid though, once the dust settles."

As Mac settled into his seat across from Erin, he quickly glanced around to see who might or might not be listening and or observing.

"I don't think any of these people here know or care who we are, Miss Giblon. What do you have on your mind?"

"I wanted to ask you if your office has had any success determining where those doctors that were arrested have been taken, and what is going to be done to them?"

"Zip. I've got some suspicions, but nothing I can prove. None of my sources have anything, and the agencies themselves are corked up tighter than Dick's hatband. I keep hoping something will fall out but so far, NADA!"

"The same thing goes with our office. The congressman spent the entire day yesterday trying to get somebody to talk to him, but he was stonewalled at every turn. And like you, our sources and contacts either don't know or aren't talking. To say that the situation is frustrating is an understatement. We feel certain that the committee investigation will uncover the facts, but that will be weeks away, at a minimum. In the meantime, the wives are going through a limbo hell and the congressman has deep concerns that the doctors may be tortured and suffer irreversible mental and or physical damage."

"And you, I, and the congressman would like to speed up this process of discovery. Do you have any suggestions how that might be accomplished Miss Giblon?"

"How is your Latin Mr. McAdams?"

"My Latin Miss Giblon? About like my golf game…lousy! Let's see," said Mac as he pulled out his billfold and extracted a one dollar bill. "With the help of the Treasury Department and the Bureau of Printing and Engraving, I see on the reverse, *'Novus Ordo Seclorum,'* new order of the ages…you know, the New World Order. Is that what you had in mind?"

"Apropos, but not exactly. I was thinking more along the lines of *'In Vino Veritas.'*"

"In wine truth?"

"Yes, in wine truth. Do you remember, not that you are that old, but perhaps you saw the pictures in books; the slogan from World War II…'Loose Lips Sink Ships'?"

"I remember."

"Well Mr. McAdams, I have a plan, a desperate, dangerous, and brazen plan. One that if found out by the congressman would certainly result in my termination. I'm asking for your help, and I'm asking for your oath of confidentiality."

Mac leaned back in his chair while his brain sorted through the information presented by Erin.

Is she going to try to use her good looks, charm, and alcohol to pry information out of some scumbag government agent? God, this chick has bigger cojones than most men I know!

"Well, Miss Giblon, you certainly have my undivided attention, and you also have my oath that whatever you disclose to me today will be kept confidential." But silently Mac was thinking: *I can't wait to hear this!*

"Thank you. Here is my plan. I want you to tell me where the most popular Washington watering holes are. Not bars for the working stiffs, but the hangouts for the sort of bureaucrats that might be privy to the information we need. I'm going to pose as a doctorate student at Georgetown, enamored with the power of law and the government. I'm going to dress and act quite differently than what you see before you now. I'm not a heavy drinker myself, but I once worked as a cocktail waitress to supplement my income while in graduate studies at Georgetown. I know how to smile, and I know how to use that smile to get men to order yet another round. And I'm going to try to use those same abilities to get men to tell me what we need to know."

This is certainly a different side of Erin Giblon, thought Mac. *God help the poor bastard she sets her sights on. With enough alcohol, how could any man resist those charms? If loose lips can sink ships, no doubt tight hips can loosen lips! My God what a combination!*

"In addition to the names and locations of the most popular spots," Erin continued, "I'm going to need bios and photographs of the top-tier directors within those agencies that would have access to the information we need. Some of that we already have at our office, but anything appropriate from the files of *The Chronicle* would be very helpful."

"No problem. And just when do you intend to start this walk on the wild side?"

"Tonight! It's Friday! Tonight is Friday night happy hour in Washington, Babylon on the Potomac. They will all be there, blowing off steam, hitting on the girls, hoping to get lucky before they have to go home to their wives…you know the scene. Where do you suggest I start?"

"That's the easy part—the most popular spot for the types you will be seeking is an Irish Pub called the Dubliner. It's upscale and classy and the most popular watering hole for the vermin you are tracking. But you must be careful, very careful. Sure they are amoral, opportunistic scum, but just because they are all of that, and horny and drunk too, doesn't mean they are stupid. They didn't achieve the positions they occupy based on their immorality and avarice alone. They are cunning, smart, and dangerous! Miss Giblon, there's something you need to know, and I hope you never forget it. The world runs on three things and three things only…gold, oil, and sex! Everything else is a derivative of one of the three. You are going into battle with only one of those three assets, but maybe the one will be sufficient. But be careful. Yeah, I can have some bios and pictures for you by mid-afternoon. How can I get them to you? How about a Washington Courier? We use them all the time."

"That would be perfect! What time should I expect your package? I've got some shopping to do before I make my debut this evening."

"Three thirty this afternoon at the latest. I'll start on it as soon as I get back to the office. What time do you plan to arrive at the Dubliner?"

"I was thinking around 7:30. Do you think that would be a propitious time?"

"You may want to arrive a little earlier. Most of the regulars will trim their Friday afternoon schedules so that they can be at the pub shortly after 5:00. Assuming their first libation is around 5:30, then after an hour or hour and a half or so, they will be sufficiently juiced to be ready for an attempt at a conquest. That's when you need to make your grand entrance."

"So I need to arrive in the 6:30 to 7:00 range?"

"Correct."

"Do you go there often?"

"Maybe once a month. That is about the most exposure to those government whores I can tolerate!"

"So why do you go at all?"

"It's like reading *Foreign Affairs* and the liberal press. I have a masochistic desire to know what the enemy is up to. But I have to take it in short, well-spaced doses. Hence, the monthly visits."

"What do you do once you get there?"

"I usually go on a Friday after work. By then, another hectic week has elapsed, and I'm ready for a stiff double at the bar. Mostly, I just listen and observe. A lot can be learned by watching who is talking to whom. Over the years of observing the Washington scene, you learn to recognize the more predatory types, and it's always interesting to follow their careers as they claw their way to the top or slide the slippery slopes into anonymity and failure. Typically, the bigger the whore, the higher his or her level of achievement in the government. Most of those types won't engage me in conversation. They know who I am, and they are afraid they will wind up in a future column. Other members of the press, however, will sometimes come by to share a drink and talk shop. Sure I have my disagreements with a lot of them, but it's interesting sometimes to debate the latest hot news items. Luckily, I've not gotten into a fight yet or been thrown out. Probably only because I haven't encountered that blob, Simon Snodgrass, yet."

"He is a piece of work, isn't he?"

"Yeah, he is. But there are a lot of people out there just like him and worse. And the problem is a lot of them are movers, shakers, holders, and wielders of power behind the scenes. Probably most are unknown to the average citizen and desire to remain so. Being in the limelight and enjoying public popularity is not their ambition. It's all about power for those people. Power and control."

Erin glanced at her watch and realized that she needed to get moving. A lot had to be accomplished before 7:00, but she also realized how very much she was enjoying visiting with Mac. Maybe someday in the future and after the conclusion of the committee's investigations, she and Mac could share a drink together and commiserate. *Someday…maybe*, she thought.

"Miss Giblon, it's been slightly over a month since my last happy hour foray at the Dubliner. I'm overdue, and I think tonight is the night."

"But Mr. McAdams…"

"Don't worry. I don't know who you are, you don't know me, and I will be a fly on the wall. You will be invisible, as far as I am concerned. I won't make any attempt to talk to you, sit near you, or stare at you. I give you my word."

Secretly Erin was glad that Mac was offering to be present. She couldn't put her finger on why, but just the thought of him being nearby was reassuring.

"Well, alright then, I'll see you, but I won't see you, around 7:00."

"I'll be there."

"And Mr. McAdams, thank you for meeting me. And thank you also for your columns, the bios you are going to send over, and your promise of confidentiality."

"You are very welcome. It is my pleasure. Good luck and happy hunting tonight!"

As Mac stood and watched Erin walk away, he reflected on what a truly beautiful and extraordinary woman she was. And he knew also that he wouldn't miss tonight's drama and Erin's performance for anything.

Will tight hips loosen lips? Mix a little alcohol in the equation and it's a done deal! thought Mac as he started to return to his office.

Erin walked briskly to her car, realizing that lunch would have to be a protein bar from her desk. Just not enough time to spare. Grateful that it wasn't raining, and the Washington traffic was moving without interruption, Erin quickly headed for the Cumberland Mall and the shopping that would be required to prepare for her evening out.

The clerk at the exclusive women's store in the mall was an attractive woman about ten years Erin's senior, who smiled knowingly at Erin's requests and seemed instinctively to know exactly what Erin required. The first item on her shopping list was a simple black cocktail dress. It is simple in design, style, and manufacture, but arguably when properly used, one of the most powerful and dangerous weapons on the face of the earth. How many proposals of marriage would history record had been elicited by the wearer of such a garment? How many state secrets sold out? Corporate takeovers arranged? Seductions and acts of infidelity? Of the eight or ten in stock, Erin chose the very first one suggested by the clerk, and she knew the choice was perfect when she looked at her reflection in the fitting-room mirrors. And if any further confirmation were required, the knowing and approving smile of the clerk was all the affirmation required.

"I really think that dress is perfect for you, Miss. You look absolutely stunning!"

"I like it! Thank you."

"Will you be requiring any accessories or essentials to complement your choice this afternoon?"

"Yes. I would like a black bustier, black panties, matching garters, and black sheer stockings with the seam up the back. Also a pair of black high heels about three or three and a half inches in height."

"Certainly. I think we have exactly what you will need for that dress. If you will follow me, I will show you what we have. And will you perhaps need a new and exciting fragrance or jewelry?"

"That's a good idea! I have sufficient jewelry, but I would like some perfume with a little bolder statement than what I normally wear, if you know what I mean."

"Certainly. We have several new fragrances that make a subtle but powerful statement. I'm sure we can find one to satisfy your requirements."

Forty-five minutes and $389 dollars plus tax later, a smiling, confident Erin Giblon returned to her car with several shopping bags adorned with the store's label. By 1:30, with Washington traffic continuing to cooperate, Erin had returned to the office. Once there, she promptly sequestered herself in her office, leaving instructions with the staff not to be disturbed unless the congressman called for her. She began to accumulate and review pictures and biographical sketches of those she could access within the Justice Department and the Department of Homeland Security. Erin decided to concentrate on those agencies for two reasons. Number one, time constraints precluded researching FBI personnel, and number two, she felt that of the three agencies she wanted to focus on, the FBI would be the least likely to be represented at the Dubliner that evening. And even if present, they would most likely be the most difficult group to pry information from because of their training.

True to his word, by 3:15 PM, a bulging package arrived from MacIntosh McAdams delivered by a Washington courier service. It contained approximately forty-five pictures and biographical sketches of top Justice Department officials and thirty groupings for Homeland Security brass. Mac's FBI selection encompassed about sixty individuals, also complete with pictures and bio sketches. She quickly realized how much more comprehensive his information was compared to what she was able to access through the congressman's office. Certainly the newspaper's "morgue" as it is called in the industry was a vast repository of information, but Erin had the distinct feeling that the personal hand of Mac had been responsible for many of the selections he had forwarded. His personal dossier of individuals to be watched if you will. And perhaps most intriguing of all were the photographs that had been circled by Mac with red ink. No explanation was attached, and Erin surmised that either those circled would be the most likely to be out on the town or most likely to have access to the information she needed, or both. Until 5:00 PM, Erin studied the faces and biographical sketches in front of her carefully cross-referencing those from the office files and computer access with those provided by Mac.

"Almost like cramming for a final exam," mumbled Erin as she stacked all of the papers in a neat pile before locking them securely in her desk. "But one mistake, one slip, and the word 'final' could convey an entirely different connotation."

Erin's rumbling stomach as she hurriedly drove to her town house to dress for the evening reminded her that the protein bar was not sufficient to satisfy the hunger cravings and offset the increased gastric acid production generated by the stress she was under. "But not enough time to eat properly. A peanut butter sandwich on whole grain bread and a glass of skim milk would have to do."

By this time Erin was talking aloud to herself as she continued with: "First the sandwich and milk. I'll gulp that down and then grab a quick shower, shave the legs, and wash this hair. God, I hope I can get it dry in time. I've got to hurry! I want to be walking into that place no later than 7:00."

By 6:30, Erin was standing in front of her full-length mirror, assessing her appearance, and she liked what she saw. Her thick mane of auburn hair cascaded across her bare shoulders and the tiny straps of the cocktail dress that accented her stunning figure. No time to measure, but the three-inch heels certainly increased her height to slightly over the six-foot mark and contributed magnificently to the shapeliness of her incredible legs. The touch of the sexy lingerie on her fair skin in the most private of places combined with the scent of the devilishly wicked new perfume had Erin feeling very, very feminine, very sexy, and very powerful. She doubted that her level of self-confidence had ever been as high as it was this very moment. She thought to herself that the closest would have been victory in some form of athletic competition or superior academic achievement. But that was different, very different, and almost no comparison in retrospect.

A work of art walked proudly out of the Washington townhouse that Friday evening. She emerged with a body by the hand of God, accessorized and embellished by the hand of man. A truly potent combination! Seven o'clock sharp found a beautiful and statuesque Erin Giblon standing in the entrance foyer of the Dubliner, calmly observing the scene before her and looking for an empty seat at the bar. She moved gracefully and erect to the one vacant seat that became available approximately in the middle of the main bar. The faint trace of a smile and the very fluid and sensuous motion of her walk quickly caused many heads to turn. And not only were the men spellbound, but many of the women were captivated as well by her beauty and grace. Settling in and acknowledging the presence of the men seated on either side of her with a brief smile, she ordered the most feminine-appearing drink she could think of, a Cosmopolitan, to complete the image of sexy but classy.

Leaving small imprints of her full lips on the clear glass as she took a dainty sip, Erin noticed the man seated immediately to her left briefly attempting to engage her in conversation, but he soon withdrew, obviously feeling his own inadequacies and intimidation. To her right was seated a well-dressed man, obviously wishing to begin a conversation, but the presence of his significant other seated to his right precluded any attempt on his part. As Erin slowly sipped her drink, she very casually began observing the patrons seated at nearby tables and other areas of the pub. The images of the photographs she had reviewed that afternoon were fresh on her mind, and one by one, as her gaze rested momentarily on those within viewing distance, she searched for a match.

At a large elliptical table about thirty feet from where she was seated and approximately in the center of the pub's main seating area, she spotted a few faces among the all-male group that triggered what was perhaps a faint flicker of recognition. But she couldn't be sure because the lighting was subdued, and the air was thick with cigarette smoke further obscuring her vision. Erin hated the entire unhealthy bar scene, and under no circumstances other than those that prevailed, would she be found dead in such an environment. The polluted air, pungent with the stench of burning tobacco, spilled alcohol, and the juxtaposition of male and female fragrances each vying for dominance, were just too much for her olfactory senses to absorb and endure. All of those emotions were subordinated and subdued beyond the point of any possible recognition by a casual observer however, and for all practical purposes, Erin very much appeared to be in her element this evening. Perched elegantly on her bar stool, casually sipping her Cosmopolitan and maintaining a faint smile on her face, she radiated an aura of attractiveness that permeated the entire area. As the more aggressively predatory males present slowly gathered their alcohol-fueled courage for their approach, Erin could sense that the action was about to begin.

The first such emboldened would-be male conqueror quickly arrived by her elbow moments later, somewhat tipsy but politely asking if she would like to dance. From the corner of her eye, Erin had watched his approach from an area remote from the large elliptical table, and on an instinctive whim declined the invitation. She decided to follow her hunch that at least a few of the faces at that table may indeed have been among the many she had reviewed that afternoon.

No sooner had suitor number one turned and, with a dejected look, began returning to his table than Erin noticed another suitor beginning to wind his way through the crowded room in her direction. This one was taller, not overweight, less tipsy, and somewhat handsome. His approach was courteous and direct.

"Hi, I'm Frederick Hamilton. I couldn't help but notice you sitting here. You appear to be alone, and I was wondering if you would like to join my friends and me at the table near the window?"

Erin's mind was rapidly sorting through the list of names and the faces she had attempted to memorize that afternoon. Failing to recognize the name or the face, Erin politely declined but in such a way so as to leave the door open if subsequently she decided to move to that area of the room.

"Hello, Mr. Hamilton. I'm Brianna McGuire. Thank you for your invitation, but actually I'm waiting for a friend. Perhaps later?"

"Thank you Miss McGuire! I'll look forward to it."

Among the group of eight men seated at the large table, a conversation was developing which centered on the tall, beautiful redhead in the classy, sexy cocktail dress. So attractive, so desirable they were thinking.

"Somebody has got to walk over there and get her before somebody else does! But which of us would have the charm, courage, and charisma to successfully lure that gorgeous temptress to our table?"

A debate raged as how to best approach her. "Should one of us go over? If so, who? Should two of us go together? Three? No, too intimidating." Finally Evan Marshall stood to his feet, asked his friends to wish him luck, and boldly began to approach Erin.

"I'll get her. You wussies watch a real man at work," he spoke over his shoulder as he was walking away.

"You go, stud! Drag her back, Evan! Don't come back without her. The tab is on you if you fail!"

THE POISON PLUM

Bingo, thought Erin. *One is coming from the big table. Whatever he says, it doesn't matter. That table is my best shot. I've got to check out my hunches. A couple of those guys may be on my dance card this evening. Nothing ventured, nothing gained.*

Erin smiled as Evan approached. *Give the guy a little more incentive,* she thought.

"Hello Miss, that table over there not only boasts the most handsome men in the entire room but also 135 years of cumulative legal experience. We would like nothing better than for you to grace us with your presence this evening."

"Well, I do believe that is the most creative and unusual line I've ever heard. And you are?"

"Evan Marshall. I'm pleased to meet you Miss…."

As Evan extended his hand, Erin responded with a handshake and a warm greeting.

"I'm Brianna McGuire. Very nice to meet you, Mr. Marshall."

"Please call me Evan and please accept our offer. We would be delighted to have you join our table, Miss McGuire."

"Well, thank you, Evan. You're very nice. I believe I will join you and your friends. Let me pay my tab, and I'll be right over."

"Don't worry about that. We are regulars here, and the bartender will simply put it on our tab."

With that, Erin rose to stand, assuming her full height of over six feet and stood equally as tall as Evan. Her striking presence coupled with a scent of her fragrance caused Evan to take a deep breath as he appreciated the beauty standing before him. Back at the table, jaws went slack as they saw what was happening.

"Amazing! I don't believe it! How in the hell did Evan pull that off? Man, I do not believe this!" As Erin and Evan approached the table, everyone present stood to greet her as Evan began introductions.

"Miss McGuire, I would like to introduce you to my associates at the Justice Department. To our left, the smiling gentleman before you is Hugo Steinmetz. Gentlemen, this is Miss Brianna McGuire."

Double Bingo! thought Erin. *The Justice Department! I've hit the mother lode, I hope! Be careful and don't blow it, Erin! Keep smiling, listen, and observe.*

"Hello, nice to meet you, Mr. Steinmetz."

"And you as well, Miss McGuire."

"And next to Hugo is Jacob Meyer; next to Jacob is Terence Watson."

Triple Bingo! thought Erin. *The face matched the name—Terence Watson of the attorney general's office. Tonight is his lucky night. I'm going to be talking to him, and more importantly, he is going to be talking to me!*

Evan continued the introductions in counter-clockwise sequence until the remaining four were identified. One individual's name and face seemed familiar to Erin, but she just couldn't be certain. Introduced as Bruce Taliferro, he stood about five feet ten inches in height, was of stocky build with a reddish, pockmarked complexion and deep set eyes that she was soon to discover were capable of an eerily intense, steely gaze.

"Mr. Taliferro, it's nice to meet you. Are you with the Justice Department also? You look vaguely familiar. Have we perhaps met somewhere?"

"No, Miss McGuire. Actually, I'm with the FBI, and no, we haven't met before. I am certain of that. No one could forget a woman of your attractiveness."

"Well, thank you, Mr. Taliferro."

"Miss McGuire, may we refresh your drink? What are you having?"

As Erin replied to Evan Marshall's offer, a seat was offered adjacent to his and directly opposite from Taliferro. *No problem,* thought Erin. *Watson is only three chairs away to my left...as the evening progresses, I'll close that gap!*

"So," Evan began as soon as Erin was seated, "What do you do, Miss McGuire, other than attract a lot of admiration as you walk into a popular spot like the Dubliner?"

"I'm continuing my graduate studies at Georgetown. My goal is the completion of a Doctorate of Law degree. After several weeks of intense study and burning the midnight oil, I felt it was time to have an evening out to relax and have fun."

"Well, we are certainly glad you decided to join us."

"How could I resist your invitation, Mr. Marshall, of a table boasting eight very handsome gentlemen with a cumulative total of 135 years of legal experience?"

"But, Miss McGuire," responded Hugo Steinmetz, "we would assume a young lady of your beauty and charm would be inclined to forgo the rigors of law school and perhaps find a handsome and up and coming intern to be your husband. Isn't the idea of being married to a wealthy and successful surgeon appealing?"

"Appealing perhaps to a shallow-minded female with little personal ambition and only her beauty to offer. I have no intention of becoming merely a trophy wife for some doctor that is constantly away working long hours or having an affair with his nurse or receptionist."

"Sounds like you are not very fond of the medical profession."

"Let's just say I have my reasons, and the few I just mentioned are only the tip of the iceberg."

"We are intrigued, Miss McGuire. As you are probably aware, we too, have a sometimes adversarial relationship with the medical profession. Could you elaborate just a bit? I'm sure we would all be interested in what you have to say."

"Don't get me started. I may not know where to stop. But here goes. First of all, when doctors tell you they are practicing medicine that may be the only accurate and honest statement you will hear during your appointment." Laughter and knee slapping erupted around the table after that remark as the attorneys present felt that another shark and kindred spirit had joined their group.

"It's true," said Erin. "When my mother became ill while I was still in high school, the attending physicians practiced on her until they finally killed her. It was only in later years that I realized her death was totally attributable to gross negligence and incompetence. The Hippocratic Oath that they profess to embrace as a code of ethics should be renamed the Hypocritical Oath. Ninety-eight percent of those vampires could care less about the well-being of their patients. It's all about the money. It's a good-news/bad-news world they live in. Bad news, the patient died. Good news, the doctor still gets paid. His incompetence and callous neglect is rewarded handsomely."

This time Erin was interrupted with clapping as several of the lawyers actually stood to applaud her.

Guess I'm laying this crap on pretty thick, but they seem to be enjoying it. Hope my nose doesn't start growing like Pinocchio's! thought Erin.

Terence Watson was next to join in the conversation with a question for Erin.

"Miss McGuire, may we safely assume that the medical professional is definitely not your career or marriage choice?" Again laughter erupted around the table as Erin smiled and responded with, "Why Mr. Watson, was it something I said, or are you just normally incredibly intuitive?"

At this point, the boys were having a jolly good time. Beautiful Erin was the center of attention, alcohol and laughter were flowing freely, and every man present wanted her. No lull in conversation was to be allowed, and at times it seemed that everyone wanted to speak to Erin at once. But the next voice to prevail was that of Bruce Taliferro who was seated directly opposite Erin.

"So Miss McGuire, precisely what is it about the legal profession that turns you on? The money? The prestige? What?"

Well, this guy gets right to the point doesn't he? thought Erin. *But so can I. If he wants it direct, I can oblige.*

"Yes, Mr. Taliferro, it is all of those things, but more."

"Please, call me Bruce."

"OK, Bruce. You want to know what turns me on?"

What an understatement, thought every man present as they waited with baited breath for what Erin was going to say next.

"I'll tell you what turns me on...the law, that's what, especially the study of the law, the application of the law, the interpretation of the law, and the enforcement of the law. The sexiest scene on earth is a courtroom with a jury trial in progress! The judge, the bailiffs, the court reporter, the jury, the prosecuting attorney, the defense attorney—men with Brooks Brothers suits and thousand-dollar leather briefcases. The power, the drama, the intensity, the starkness of finality as the verdict is read by the jury foreman! These are the things that turn me on, gentlemen. I'm going to be part of that scene someday. The money, the power, the prestige, and all the rest are going to be mine, and it's going to be sooner rather than later."

Every man at that table was enthralled with what he was seeing and hearing. And why not? Erin was very convincing and espoused the sentiments probably held in varying degrees by everyone present at least sometime in the early stages of their legal careers, and before the idealism of youth faded away to the reality and cynicism of professional plunder and greedy opportunism. Erin's attention was diverted by Evan Marshall at her left, who suddenly stood and began striking his glass with a fork to get the others' attention.

"Gentlemen," he began, "I think it is time we offer a toast to our very charming guest. How is your glass, Miss McGuire? Do you need a refill before we begin?" Erin glanced at her glass which was only down about one third. *Got to appear to fit in,* she thought.

"I apologize, gentlemen, but I have been talking so much, I'm afraid I've neglected my drink. But I have sufficient to join the toast now, and then I would like another. A Cosmopolitan, please."

With that everyone stood, broadly smiling, glasses in hand as the toast was offered. Glasses tinkled as they one-by-one touched, and down the hatch went the alcohol to further fuel the party in progress and embolden the participants. As everyone was seated, once again Erin noticed that Bruce Taliferro was staring at her, as were the others, but his was a stare of different intent. His eyes now were cold as they scanned the features of her face, and Erin began to feel uncomfortable under the scrutiny and intensity of his gaze.

"Miss McGuire," spoke Taliferro, "I have the distinct feeling that I have seen you somewhere before, and recently, but I can't place where or when.... There is something very familiar about you."

"Why Mr. Taliferro," Erin said with a warm smile, "have you been spending your free time admiring the coeds in the Georgetown student lounge? And besides, didn't you say just a short while ago that you were certain we had never met? And that you had never seen me before?"

"I said I was certain we had never met, not that I had never seen you before." As he spoke those words, his eyes grew colder, if that were possible, but Erin, despite her unease, continued to offer her warm smile. At that moment something occurred that diverted attention from Erin. The men began nudging each other, whispering intensely, and looking in the direction of the entrance foyer. Acknowledging recognition by all except Erin, Evan said, "Well, well, lookie who is on the prowl tonight. Miss McGuire, do you see that tall, older man that just walked in?"

Oh, my God, thought Erin, *it's Mac!*

"Do you mean the man that looks like he would have to borrow someone else's smile to have a good time?"

"Listen to that guys. Did she hit the nail on the head or what? Do you know who that is, Miss McGuire? He is a celebrity of sorts but mostly in his own mind!"

"A celebrity? I don't have a clue! Who is it?"

"That, Miss McGuire, is our perpetual nemesis. God put him on this earth to torment us. You are looking at none other than the infamous MacIntosh McAdams, star journalist with *The Chronicle*. He hates anything and anybody connected with the government and constantly concocts lurid tales of wrongdoing and evil intent to persuade his readership to share his rabid right-wing views."

"He sounds like an anachronism you would just as soon have fade away," said Erin.

"That is putting it mildly, Miss McGuire. But I'm sure you would be interested to know that he is a fervent supporter recently of the profession you abhor."

"The hypocritical vampire league? I don't understand. How so?"

"It seems that Mr. Muckraker over there took great offense at our department's efforts to shield America from further terrorist attacks. You said you had been burning the midnight oil a lot lately, and maybe you missed the news, but surely you heard about the out-of-control wacko that massacred those government workers at that ferry landing in Connecticut?"

Bruce Taliferro's gaze shifted from Mac back to her as his eyes narrowed and stared intensely at her every expression and response.

That brute is trying to put something together, thought Erin. *I can feel it. Damn, I wish he would drink more. He is way too intense. I've got to watch my step.*

"Yes, I did hear something about that. But what does that have to do with the medical profession?"

"We have evidence that the shooter's doctor was involved in a conspiracy with other doctors to foment violence against a government research laboratory. When we raided the doctors' offices and arrested the doctors involved, a certain Goody Two-shoes congressman and that yellow-dog journalist across the room went into league together to question our motives and actions."

"So some doctors were behind the scenes to actually cause that disaster to happen? What was their motivation? Were they denied employment at the laboratory? A research grant? What?"

"We don't have all the answers yet. Our investigation is continuing."

"I wish you every success! I hope you stick those guys somewhere dark and deep so they can never hurt anyone else."

Poor old Terence Watson. Too much alcohol since 5:00, too much lack of association with any woman of Erin Giblon's beauty and charm in years, and too much lust and desire. And he, so desperately wanting to impress her and be noticed, said something he would later come to profoundly regret.

"Let's just say we hope they like Cuban cigars."

Erin didn't understand Watson's comment and not knowing what else to say, responded after a few moments hesitation by saying, "They do have a uniquely obnoxious odor, but that doesn't seem like punishment enough for what they have done."

With that, Erin assumed a quizzical look on her face, took a healthy swallow of her new Cosmopolitan, and asked to be excused to powder her nose.

Wow, she thought as she made her way to the ladies' room. *I like the way this is going, but I don't like the way this is going. Getting into this situation is probably going to turn out to be a lot easier than getting out of it, I'm afraid. I need to start winding this thing down, but I certainly don't want to miss anything. Taliferro is spooking me. I know he suspects something, but I just don't know what. And Cuban cigars? What the hell was that all about?*

Erin was totally preoccupied as she mechanically made her way to the ladies' room and didn't even notice as she passed by Mac, who was now seated at the bar with his back to her table.

"Taliferro was there Tuesday. Get the hell out!"

A chill swept through Erin's body as Mac spoke those words, but she continued on to the ladies' room as if nothing had happened.

Oh crap! Tuesday was the news conference in New London! That's why he looked familiar. He was seated near the stage, conspicuous because he didn't participate in the standing ovation Harry received! That's it! Taliferro has either remembered who I am or he is about to. I can't risk being exposed. I'll return to that shark nest and begin structuring my graceful departure, hopefully without creating too much suspicion. Maybe all this subterfuge and deceit was not such a good idea after all. I don't feel as if I have accomplished anything except blowing $389 dollars on apparel I'll probably never wear again.

As Erin exercised the time worn and universally accepted female prerogative of taking forever to return from the ladies' room, Bruce Taliferro finally put the pieces of this puzzle together. Like a flash bulb popping in his brain, Taliferro's neurons completed the process of connection and recognition, and he remembered where he had seen Erin, aka Brianna McGuire, before.

That conniving bitch, he thought. *Wonder if her boss is in on this little charade also. Maybe McAdams too? Got to get everybody out of here before anybody else does anything stupid, like Watson. She wants to look and act like a high-class call girl? That is exactly the way I would like to treat her tonight before I choke the piss out of her!*

"OK, guys! Listen up! The party is over. That twist that just went to pee is Congressman Harry McDonald's top aide. She is playing you drunk and horny fools like a violin. You are all thinking with the wrong head, and it's time to get out of here. Let's just hope she doesn't figure out what you said Watson! That was really dumb! You guys leave. I'll take care of Miss America!"

"What? But how do you know, Bruce? She certainly seems credible and sincere to me, and I'm sure to the rest of us. Could you be mistaken?"

"No, Hugo, I'm not mistaken. That's the broad that helped her boss with his news conference in Connecticut last Tuesday. Hell, I sat in the second row. What kept throwing me off was the way she is dressed. On Tuesday, she had her hair in a bun and was wearing low-heel business shoes and a well-tailored dark blue business suit. And here? Well, quite a difference, wouldn't you say? No, it was her voice and the way she carries herself more than anything. I'm certain, no doubt about it. That's her! Get the hell out of here!"

Seven men, totally dejected, somewhat embarrassed, and with dour and sheepish expressions, stood and began to make their way to the Dubliner's exit. To a man they had each enjoyed the visit from the mysterious, captivating beauty that had graced their table that evening. No one wanted the party to end this abruptly and certainly not in this fashion. The alcohol and her warm response to their hospitality had fueled expectations of even more delicious pleasures to come as the evening progressed.

From across the room, seated at the bar, Mac was able to observe the mass exodus in the bar mirror's reflection. *Not good!* he thought. *All are bailing except Brucey baby. He made her, no question. But why isn't he leaving too?*

Mac silently hoped the evening was not about to turn ugly. He knew what Taliferro was capable of, but he was not going to stand idly by while that goon harmed Erin. As his anger and concern began to rise, the feel of the .38 caliber snub-nosed revolver tucked snugly in his shoulder holster and concealed by his sport jacket provided a calming reassurance. Grandfathered in with a "right to carry" permit, Mac, because of his high-profile position and a history of exposé journalism, never went anywhere without his "piece." Over the years, most of the District of Columbia residents had been successfully disarmed by the politicians to protect themselves and the entrenched bureaucrats from any potential dissent or backlash. Whenever Mac pondered the zeal with which gun "control" was promoted by certain politicians and members of the government, he always remembered the words spoken years ago by some guy down in Alabama.... "When the government starts worrying about its citizens owning guns, it's time for the citizens to start worrying about their government!"

As Erin exited the ladies' room and began making her way through the crowded room to the table, she was stunned to see the table empty except for Bruce Taliferro, who was seated and watching her approach.

This is not right, thought Erin. *Guys do not collectively go to the john together—that's a girl thing, not a guy thing... well, unless they are fags, which that group certainly was not. Taliferro obviously has figured out who I am. Now what do I do?*

Without turning her head, Erin gave a quick glance in the direction of MacIntosh McAdams. The look on his face as their eyes met was one of concern, and Erin then knew that her instincts were correct.

The festivities of this evening are over. The challenge now is to extricate myself as carefully as possible from this situation while I'm still in one piece. The coldness of Taliferro's stare chilled her to the bone, but Erin knew she would have to keep smiling and displaying an aura of confidence and self-control.

As she reached the table, Erin smiled, seized the initiative and said, "Why Mr. Taliferro, it appears we are all alone. What have you done with your friends? Have I been so boring and uninteresting that I have driven them away? I certainly hope I am not having that effect on you. I'm having a really nice time, and I hope you are sharing the experience!" Continuing to smile warmly, Erin picked up her drink and moved to take a chair adjacent to Taliferro.

Damn, this chick is good, thought Taliferro. *She would fit right in over at CIA...a regular La Femme Nikita...but too bad her priorities are all screwed up with that God bless America crap. She needs to figure out what the real world is all about. But too late for that now.*

"Don't worry about them, Miss McGuire. Do you have a twin here in Washington?"

Taking a sip of her Cosmo, she giggled, "I have a brother and a sister, not a twin, and not in Washington. Why do you ask?"

"Just wanted to make sure that I was talking to the congressman's aide, that's all."

"But I'm not employed. I'm a graduate student at Georgetown."

"Cut the crap, McGuire, or whatever your name is. You know I saw you on the stage with McDonald last Tuesday in New London. What's your game here? Did the overgrown Boy Scout whore you out and send you to do his dirty work? Are you a whore for him and to him as well?" Taliferro suddenly grabbed Erin's arm with a vice like grip. "You scheming slut! You are going to tell me what you are up to, and you are going to do it now, or I'm going to break your damn neck!"

Sometimes the Irish just can't help themselves—the tempers matching their hair color made all the more incendiary by alcohol can suddenly explode spontaneously. With Erin's free hand, she, with lightening speed, threw the remainder of her Cosmopolitan squarely into the face of Taliferro, now contorted with rage and anger. A split second later the same hand slapped Taliferro so hard the sound was heard throughout the room, and all eyes turned in their direction. Mac quickly stood and placed his right hand near his pistol ready for any eventuality. As Taliferro attempted to yank Erin to her feet, a tall man rapidly approached from the table near the window, obviously on a mission. It was Frederick Hamilton, who had earlier attempted to get Erin to join his table.

"Is there a problem here? Get your hands off the lady, asshole!"

"Shove off Buster! I'm with the FBI!" shouted Taliferro as he continued trying to yank Erin erect while at the same time striking the approaching Hamilton in the chest.

"You're with me now, you son of a bitch!" said Hamilton as he struck Taliferro on the chin with a left hook so powerful it broke his jaw. Taliferro crumbled as the gush of blood issuing from his mouth washed three teeth onto the floor. Hamilton, in a rage, pounced on Taliferro and continued to pummel him with incredibly powerful blows until Taliferro was unconscious. Free of Taliferro's grip, Erin was now vainly trying to pull Hamilton away from Taliferro.

"You've got to get out of here! He really is with the FBI. Let's go now before the police get here!" Hamilton just stood there with his clenched fists bleeding, straddling the body of Taliferro like some powerful jungle animal proudly standing over its fallen prey.

Erin's heart was racing as she snatched her Cosmopolitan glass and quickly used the napkin to wipe away her fingerprints. In a flash she was outside the pub and running to her car faster than she ever thought possible wearing high heels. She could hear the approaching sirens as she pulled her car into the traffic and headed east away from the Dubliner.

THE POISON PLUM

MacIntosh McAdams sat back down and smiled smugly as he sipped on the remainder of his double. *Ah, what an exciting evening in Washington town!* he thought. *A beautiful woman turns into a damsel in distress and is rescued from the evil ogre by a charming knight in shining armor...a regular Sir Galahad! Wouldn't have missed it for the world! And since I am so highly respected in the community and will prove to be a very credible witness, I'll stay to offer my unbiased eye-witness testimony to the police. Saw it all, yes I did. That stocky man on the floor viciously attacked that young lady, probably when she rejected his advances, and she was rescued by that tall, handsome gentleman. The unconscious guy is FBI you say? Hmmmm...not good press for the Bureau, I'm afraid. Yes officers, I'll be happy to help any way I can with a statement or whatever you might require. No, I've never seen that young lady in here before. Poor thing, she was probably terrified and ran for her life. Can't say I blame her.*

As Erin guided her compact car through traffic driving as fast as the speed limits would allow, she constantly checked her rear-view mirror, hoping and praying that the police were not after her. Hopefully no one at the scene saw her enter her vehicle and consequently would be unable to provide a description. And as far as she knew, only one other person in the Dubliner recognized her besides Taliferro, and that person was MacIntosh McAdams...certainly not one to identify her to the police. And Erin didn't think Taliferro would be talking either. The entire incident would not go down well with his superiors, especially since the intervention by the handsome stranger was required to protect the fair lass from being manhandled by the brutish Taliferro. The Bureau and Taliferro would just have to shut up, swallow pride, and acknowledge defeat in this skirmish. As for Steinmetz, Watson, Marshall, and the others, Erin felt certain their lips would be sealed as well by the circumstances and the thick layer of egg on their faces.

What had begun as an evening of excitement, mystery, and exotic intrigue had deteriorated into an event that left Erin feeling soiled, dirty, cheap, and ashamed.

Guess this wasn't such a good idea after all, thought Erin. *All that risk and effort and for what? Have I accomplished anything except potentially embarrassing the congressman? His plate is full enough without his top aide running amok initiating dangerous liaisons and potentially compromising situations. I need a shower, but will I be able to wash away my feelings of defilement? And my clothes and hair—gross! They reek of the stench of tobacco and alcohol.*

With each elapsing mile Erin was that much closer to the security of her townhouse. And with no blue lights yet in her rear-view mirror, her optimism and confidence grew that the police, at least for now, would not be coming for her. But would Taliferro send goons? Now or later? Probably not, she reasoned. Logically, he would assume that the events of the evening would be dutifully reported back to the congressman, and any subsequent retaliation against her would only add to the impact of the committee's hearings.

Dutifully reported back to the congressman, she thought. *And exactly how am I going to do that without appearing as a recklessly out-of-control subordinate taking dangerous chances that could undermine the work that we are all doing? A bitter pill, but I must swallow it. I'll have to tell the congressman everything. And sadly, everything must include the failure of not gaining one iota of useful information. Oh well, if I live that long, maybe someday I can tell my grandchildren the story of Erin's folly, which I probably would rather forget.*

Erin was glad to see her townhouse that evening and happier still when she was once again inside and the entrance door locked securely behind her. The first order of business would be to get out of the stinking clothes and scrub until pink in a long, hot shower. She was expecting the congressman to fly in this evening from his news conference because of the heavy schedule at the office, and she and several other staffers were expected to be in early tomorrow. Erin knew that she was too keyed up to sleep, but the shower would help. And maybe a glass of wine before retiring would be a good idea.

A little after midnight, Erin, sufficiently scrubbed and powdered, was relaxing in her terry cloth robe, meditating on the events of the day while sipping on a nice glass of Chablis and hoping the sandman would be coming soon. The very last thing she expected at that hour of the evening was the telephone call, which shattered her calm and repose.

Who could that be? she thought. *Is this trouble that has found me? Don't answer! But what if it's the congressman? What if something is wrong? His flight? Those damn commuter planes! Or is it the police? The FBI? Well, there's only one way to find out!* thought Erin as she reached for the phone.

"Hello?"

She was greeted by the now familiar booming masculine voice of MacIntosh McAdams.

"Are we having fun yet? Are you OK? All safe and sound?"

"Oh, my God, Mr. McAdams, you frightened me. I had no idea who might be calling at this hour. How did you get my number?"

"Ah, Miss Brianna McGuire, a very clever alias I thought, by the way. Never underestimate the capabilities of a seasoned, or is that jaded, I can't remember, journalist. I've got more contacts than a telephone switchboard. Are you OK? Would you like to hear what happened after your hasty and rather unceremonious departure?"

"Yes, I'm OK. No problems other than some jangled nerves. I'm sipping a glass of wine as we speak, hoping it will calm me down. I've got to get some sleep. We're going to be in the office bright and early tomorrow, but my curiosity is killing me. Will you bring me up to date?"

"No problem, but I suggest you follow my advice and stop sipping and start drinking. Grab the rest of the bottle while I'm sharing the juicy details with you."

"I don't guess that's such a bad idea. Hold on a sec….. OK, I'm back. So what happened?"

"Well, Washington's finest arrived moments after you disappeared, and yours truly became the star witness of the evening, enabling the gendarmes to piece all of the puzzle parts together. Your brave, valiant savior was charged with assaulting a federal officer, which charges will not stick, by the way, because Taliferro never produced ID. Taliferro was unable to give his version of what happened after he awoke because his jaw is broken, and he is hospitalized. Such a shame, don't you think? My version of the events served to only reinforce and corroborate the testimony of the gallant Mr. Frederick Hamilton, who interestingly enough, is a former Marine special ops officer now employed with the General Services Administration here in Washington. It seems he takes a dim view of men manhandling women because his younger sister was viciously attacked and raped by two thugs about four years ago here in Washington. I don't expect any of this to go any further—all inter-governmental as far as the D.C. law is concerned. It was self defense on Hamilton's part, no ID produced by Taliferro, and the mystery lady of the evening is nowhere to be found. No one knows except Taliferro, and he isn't talking, literally and figuratively, that is. Your performance was stellar, Miss Giblon, perhaps only eclipsed by your Houdini act at the end. I think you are clear."

"I certainly hope so. If I foolishly did something to embarrass the congressman or jeopardize the upcoming committee investigation, I think I would just die."

"Maybe in this situation, the end justified the means. What did you find out? Taliferro was behaving as if you had gained the keys to the temple."

"That's just it! Nothing, nada, zip! Maybe after a few more hours and liters of bourbon, scotch, and vodka, tongues would have loosened, and secrets would have poured forth. I just didn't expect to encounter anyone this evening that would recognize me. If only Taliferro had not attended that news conference in New London. Come to think of it, though, one of the guys did say something that didn't make any sense at all. And at the time it seemed to me that Taliferro shot him a look of disapproval. I shrugged it off because the guy was more tipsy than any of the others, and I assumed that Taliferro was irritated that he was showing his lack of control."

"Who was it, and what did he say?"

"It was Terence Watson of the Justice Department. I recognized him from the pictures you had sent over. He was my target for the evening. The conversation had shifted around to the medical profession, and I had expressed my deep dislike and mistrust of the entire profession while simultaneously confessing to be absolutely enthralled with, you guessed it, the legal profession!"

"Bravo, Miss Giblon. And then?"

"Well, the guys noticed you when you arrived at the Dubliner and mentioned, among other things, that you had taken offense editorially at their arrest of certain doctors connected to the assassin at the Plum Island ferry landing. I responded by saying something like, 'I hope you put them someplace dark and deep where they can never hurt anyone else again.' Watson's response made no sense at all, and it was then I excused myself to go to the ladies' room. As best as I can remember he said, 'Let's just say we hope they like Cuban cigars.'"

"Cuban cigars?"

"That's what he said. Guess he was just drunk."

"That's it! Now we know! Damn fine work, Miss Giblon!"

"What on earth are you talking about? Know what? I'm lost!"

"Cuba, Miss Giblon! Cuba! That's where the doctors have been taken! They are being tortured and are rotting away at the infamous prison at Guantanamo Bay. Gitmo…the bastards plan to try them with military tribunals without benefit of counsel—habeas corpus out, Patriot Act in. God in heaven! Your efforts this evening were not a failure at all, Miss Giblon! Au contraire!"

An Eventful Day at the Office

Erin slept little that evening. The events of the evening were repeated over and over and over in her mind like a phonograph needle stuck in the groove of a record.

And how to explain it all to the congressman? she agonized. If anything, Erin felt as dirty, soiled, and ashamed upon awakening as she did upon leaving the Dubliner hours earlier. The garnering of a valuable clue which might reveal the whereabouts of the doctors was of little solace, serving to only slightly mitigate the circumstances.

But Erin could not afford the luxury of a restful weekend to allow mind and body to recuperate. She had no choice but to appear at the office early as planned. For that Saturday morning in Washington found Congressman Harry McDonald and his entire staff hard at work at their office in the Cannon House Office Building. No luxury of a pleasant, restful weekend would be afforded these warriors either. Erin's original intentions were to ask the congressman for some private time together so she could attempt to explain the events of the past evening. But the intensity of the work environment already in progress as she arrived convinced Erin that if there would ever be a more propitious time for attempts at an explanation, it would certainly be later in the day after the other staffers had left for the evening. There was just too much on everyone's plate at this time. What was normally a busier than average congressional office had rapidly spiraled into a hotbed of frantic activity as a result of the massacre at the ferry. Erin had no choice but to immerse herself in the work at hand and hope for a suitable time to talk to the congressman later. She knew that there were the organizational requirements of the coming committee investigations announced by the congressman, there was the extremely focused and diligent research required to adequately fuel the investigations, and there was the effort to sort and assimilate information now arriving in copious quantities from concerned constituents via telephone, e-mail, fax, and conventional mail.

What began as a trickle had become an avalanche as stories and allegations began pouring into McDonald's office. Some anecdotal, some more or less firsthand, some well-meaning, some critical, and some obviously from kooks waiting for the next UFO to whisk them away to another galaxy. Just to accumulate the massive amount of information beginning to roll in was becoming a monumental task. Sorting, verifying, and attempting to collate the data was a staggering challenge.

And overseeing it all was Congressman Harry McDonald. Seemingly undaunted by the enormity of it all and seemingly never tiring, he was motivated by a driving force that appeared to consume every waking moment and every fiber of his being. Erin had never witnessed such motivation and determination as exhibited by Harry since their news conference. With Harry and the staff putting in twelve-to sixteen-hour days, the growing intensity of it all served to fuel and supercharge their efforts to even greater heights. No one appeared tired or fatigued, only eagerly, excitedly, and aggressively working cohesively toward a common goal. Each person's dedication and perseverance seemed to amplify and stimulate that of their co-workers.

Erin had concentrated her research by focusing on existing archival data that related to Plum Island. The Internet had proven to be a veritable treasure trove of valuable information and Erin relentlessly perused relevant sites and connecting links. Sorting the wheat from the chaff was a formidable task, but Erin excelled in that arena. Possessed with a piercing deductive reasoning, she quickly identified and retained that which was relevant and cast aside that which was not. She knew her target, and she knew what the congressman needed for his investigation. And intuitively, she knew already what the facility at Plum Island was all about.

It was all true, she thought. *All the allegations about a laboratory engineering germs with the capability of killing millions of human beings are true.* And just as intuitively, Erin knew that what she had already discovered was only the tip of the iceberg. *Surely Plum was not the only facility,* thought Erin. *There are certainly others scattered around the United States concocting God only knows what to bedevil mankind. And the mindset of those who implemented the plans and funding of those facilities would be the most frightening aspect of this entire horror story.*

For minds that are capable of conceptualizing programs that were implemented at the bio-labs would not limit their evil designs to that arena only. Minds insidiously clever enough to foist their satanic agenda upon an unsuspecting, trusting populace would certainly be sufficiently diabolical to have laid the groundwork for even more comprehensive programs and activities to accomplish their objectives for control and subjugation. Who are these people? What is the scope of their agendas? Are any of us safe? Can they be exposed? Stopped? How late is the hour? Is it already too late? Will our efforts make a difference at all? Will they be hoisted by their own petard or will it be us that will be splattered like bugs on a windshield?

Until this moment in her life, Erin's inherent conservatism and devotion to preservation of the Constitution, which she held to be sacrosanct, was reflexive and academic in nature. All that had changed, and dramatically, as the full brunt of the consequences of germ warfare began sinking into her consciousness.

And not just the concept of germ warfare, as horrible as that would be, she thought. *No, it was the realization that some incredibly evil, amoral people have achieved positions of extreme power and influence, obviously operating immune to detection, review, censure, or condemnation. They are untouchable.*

Erin had no illusions about the magnitude of the task that lay before her, the congressman, and his staff. Finding a veritable cornucopia of information pointing to a research laboratory out of control was one thing. But convincing a congressional delegation that the laboratory was not out of control at all but was instead totally in control and tracking a brilliantly and carefully prearranged course of operation was a different matter. It would require an indisputable accumulation of facts, proof of cause and effect, expert testimony, and last but certainly not least, witnesses.

Ah, yes, a smoking gun with a hand wrapped around it would be a nice touch, thought Erin. *Perhaps we can just run an ad in the classifieds for any and all current or former employees of the lab to come forward and serve their country by testifying in front of our committee. Maybe they will just surrender once we declare we caught them with their hand in the cookie jar. Yeah right! And I'm from the government and I'm here to help you.*

Erin continued thinking that even if a lower-echelon current or former employee were to come forward offering testimony, its value would be of a dubious nature. It would be assumed that only the top scientists and directors would be privy to the innermost secrets of the laboratory. Chances were slim that a member of the inner circle would be motivated to come forward. And if so, what would that motivation entail? Sour grapes maybe? A change of heart? A sudden manifestation of moral qualms about the work he or she had been or is involved with?

Not likely, thought Erin. *At that level, they would have known from the get-go what the program was all about. If morality was not an issue in the beginning, it would almost certainly not be an issue at a later date.* Barring an event as experienced by Paul on the road to Damascus, the appearance of a surprise witness laboring with a contrite heart would be a slim possibility indeed.

By five that afternoon, it was evident that despite intense and focused motivation, the level of fatigue among everyone present was significant and rising. Several staffers had gathered in the break room for a bit of a respite with snacks and feet propped up. Most, if not all, would continue working until after nine that evening. And then tomorrow, Sunday, most would come in after their respective church activities and resume work. A grinding, grueling schedule fueled by dedication, resolve, and tenacity. As Erin sat and watched her busy co-workers, her mind wandered and she began to ponder.

Was progress being made? Was all of this effort going to assure success for the coming committee investigation? And what defines success? Is it the closing of the bio-labs as a result of Congress cutting off their funding? The release of all of the doctors with public apologies made to them, their wives, and their families? What about the millions of people already sick and infected by some germ cocktail created by the government's finest scientists?

Erin's mind was heavy with these thoughts, and she was beginning to feel the cumulative effects of stress, fatigue, alcohol, and lack of sleep as she considered joining the others in the break room. Her day of research had convinced her that there was enough circumstantial negative information about the facility on Plum Island to sink a battleship. She silently wondered why God allowed such a menace and abomination to exist. If the ocean opened and consumed Plum like it has Atlantis and Port Royal, Jamaica, *Well, that would be a good thing and would save us all a lot of work,* thought Erin.

As Erin rose and made her way to the break room, she could hear agitated and excited voices from her co-workers. Soon, she heard the heavy footsteps of the congressman rapidly approaching the break room from his office.

THE POISON PLUM

What the heck is going on? thought Erin as someone increased the volume of the break room television which was constantly tuned to CNN. Apparently, coverage of a Justice Department news conference had just begun, and as Erin entered the break room, she saw on the television screen Attorney General Budenz standing at a podium saying something about the government's investigation into the ferry assassinations. Everyone sat quietly, listening intently as Budenz continued with his remarks. In typical government style and format, a review of events, beginning with the shootings, was given with the usual government spins and embellishments inserted where appropriate. Colonel Gordon McClain's illustrious career was again covered for the zillionth time, and again it was mentioned what a great tragedy had befallen our proud nation.

"In our time of sorrow and collective introspection," spoke Budenz, "we must all remain vigilant and united as we tirelessly seek out and search for those enemies of our way of life." And then after several more minutes of the usual contrived pap and tendentious drivel, Budenz dropped a bombshell.

"Yes, ladies and gentlemen and concerned Americans. I am pleased to report to you this evening that our thorough and comprehensive investigations have revealed that only one of the doctors arrested in the sweep we conducted in the Connecticut and Long Island areas was directly involved in attempts at mind control and manipulation of our great American hero, Colonel Gordon McClain. That doctor, Glen Klinner, is being held at an undisclosed location, awaiting trial by a military tribunal under provisions of the Patriot Act for crimes of terrorism against the United States."

At that point, a photograph of Dr. Klinner filled the screen as Budenz continued on with comments about how dangerous this diabolical doctor was and what a disgrace he was to his chosen profession. His wife, Fran, had also been arrested as an accomplice and would be tried by the same tribunal.

Erin glanced over at Congressman McDonald and saw a face as intense as could possibly be imagined. Unblinking, his eyes, now piercing, were fixed on the face of Attorney General Budenz.

It's a damn good thing those two are not in the same room together at this moment! thought Erin. The bulging carotid arteries and rising crimson in Harry's neck and face revealed a seething rage. To Erin, Harry resembled a big jungle cat crouched with muscles tensed, ready to pounce on its unsuspecting victim.

Erin turned her attention back to the television. Budenz was explaining that the release of the other doctors had been authorized, and they would soon be cleared of all charges and would be returned to their families. Budenz, as the representative of the Justice Department, of course regretted any inconvenience to the doctors involved or their families. The death of Benjamin Stegall was never mentioned.

Tests and More Revelations

Susan Collins slept better that Friday night in the hospital than she could have ever imagined possible. Thanks to the sedatives prescribed by Dr. Butler, Toby slept for hours at a time, relieving Susan of her motherly instinctive and reflexive obligation to awaken and check on Toby each time he moaned or awoke. Susan was only briefly disturbed by the night nurses as they made their rounds checking on Toby, but from 6:00 AM on, however, the daily activity of the hospital began increasing in tempo as do all hospitals with the routine changing of the nurses' shifts, breakfasts being provided for the patients, doctors making their rounds, patients being taken for tests, or preparations made for checkout. Sleep from that point on was impossible. Susan arose, freshened her face and prepared for the day ahead. Dr. Butler would be making his rounds soon, and Toby was becoming fully conscious as a result of the increasing hospital activity.

"Well good morning, sweetie. How are we feeling this morning? Are you hungry?"

"Yes, Mommy, I'm hungry. Could I have some pancakes?"

"Pancakes? I don't know, sweetie. Someone will be bringing breakfast soon. I'll ask if they have pancakes this morning."

"I hope so, Mommy. I'm hungry."

Well I guess that is an encouraging sign, thought Susan. *Toby's appetite has been almost nonexistent here lately.*

"Mommy! I can move my leg!"

"You can? Which one, honey? Show me?"

Susan noticed movement under the bed covers, and she pulled them back to reveal Toby's legs, which were motionless except for his right foot which was moving in what could be best described as a partial ankle pump.

"Mommy, my legs still feel like they are asleep. When will the new medicine work?"

"I don't know, sweetie. We'll just have to wait and give it time to work."

"Will I be able to walk today?"

How do you tell your son he may never walk again? thought Susan. *But keep smiling Wonder Woman, Toby needs to see a positive face!*

"We'll just have to wait and see Toby. And when the doctor comes in, we'll ask him. Will that be OK, sweetie?"

"Mommy, my head hurts, and I need to go to the bathroom."

"Just sit up, honey, and I'll help you use the bed pan."

As Susan was helping Toby with the positioning of the bed pan, she heard a gentle knock on the door and turned to see Dr. Butler pushing open the door and entering the room.

"Good morning, Toby, and good morning, Susan. How are we feeling today?"

Toby was the first to reply with, "I'm hungry," which elicited a smile on Dr. Butler's face. Susan responded with, "Good news, and good morning, Dr. Butler. Toby can move his right foot."

Dr. Butler moved to look at Toby's legs and feet while Toby resumed the movement, albeit limited, of his right foot.

"That's good, Toby! Can you move anything else?"

"No. My legs feel like they are asleep."

"Well, Toby, it will take a little while for this medicine we are giving you to work."

"Will I be able to walk?"

"We think so, Toby, but it will probably take a few days."

Dr. Butler moved to palpate Toby's abdomen and listened to his chest with his stethoscope. After a cursory examination and review of Toby's chart, Dr. Butler seemed pleased and asked Susan to join him in the hall for a few moments.

"Susan," he began, "I think what we are experiencing with Toby is a classic response to the antibiotics we are treating him with. I believe he will be able to walk again soon, but the tests we have scheduled for today will provide us with more definitive information."

"Do you still think it is Lyme disease?"

"Yes I do. Everything we have seen so far is just further confirmation. We have Toby scheduled this morning for a spinal tap, and then this afternoon we will do a CT scan of the skull and spine. If the spinal fluid we recover from the tap is cloudy, milky in appearance, that would immediately signal a serious bacterial infection of some sort. If the fluid is clear, it doesn't necessarily rule out a Lyme infection because frequently the Lyme germ cannot be cultured from the fluid, even when there has been extensive central nervous system involvement. Either way we will have to wait for microscopic examination of the fluid and for cultures to be run.

"What we are trying to do here, Susan, is rule out any other pathogen that might be involved. With the CT scans, we will attempt to determine the extent of any lesions either in the brain or spinal cord that could be inhibiting Toby's ability to walk. The results of those scans will need to be evaluated by a neurologist, but we will move as expeditiously as possible with these tests. I am encouraged by Toby's response to the treatment, and we will continue these antibiotic infusions on a daily basis unless Toby experiences some sort of untoward reaction."

"Is there anything I can do or anything I should watch for as Toby is being treated?"

"No. I don't think so. We have Toby on a monitor, and the nurses will keep a close vigil on him."

"How long before you think he will be feeling better?"

"Hard to say. From what we have seen so far, it looks like the antibiotic we have chosen is doing a pretty good job of clobbering those germs it can get to. I would expect he will be well enough to go home about the middle of next week or so, but it may be several weeks more before he starts noticeably perking up. Remember that he has deteriorated quite a bit lately, and it will take time to rebuild and recover. And, of course, we will continue the antibiotic infusions on an outpatient basis for at least twenty-seven more infusions."

"And what then Dr. Butler? Will that be the end of this nightmare? Will Toby be cured at that point?"

"Cured? I honestly don't know, Susan. Conventional medical literature says yes. Frankly, I personally don't know if any Lyme patient is ever totally cleared of the infection. It's a tough bug. We will go as far as we can here with diagnostic procedures, and we will continue to treat and monitor Toby to the best of our ability. But Susan, if Toby were my son, I think I would want to seek out a specialist to continue Toby's care after we have exhausted all of our options here. I promised I would have my staff make some inquiries for you, and I feel certain that we'll have some information for you soon. As we have already discussed, some of the finest Lyme disease specialists in the nation were in this immediate area."

"Yes, but 'were' is the operative word here. I find it incredibly ironic that I've lived my life up to this point never having any reason at all to even think about Lyme disease, much less have a need to seek out a specialist for my son. And now that I do, the damn government has arrested and hauled off to jail the very doctors I need the most. As Murphy would have it, impeccable timing has once again prevailed. Or perhaps more appropriately, some of the good ol' boys back in Alabama had a bumper sticker several years ago that summed this and a lot of other situations up rather nicely—until it was banned, that is. Maybe you saw or heard its message, Dr. Butler? Roughly translated, it said: 'Fecal Matter Occurs.'"

Doctor Butler was vigorously nodding in the affirmative as his spontaneous laughter erupted, causing heads of patients and nurses to turn up and down the hall. After regaining his composure, Dr. Butler assured Susan he would return that evening and check on Toby as he was making his rounds. Susan thanked him and as he turned to continue his rounds, she noticed Cathy coming down the hall from the opposite direction, carrying several large bags. Susan greeted her as she approached and asked what all the bags were for.

"Well, let's see. Mainly just some essential needables. I've got you some fresh clothes and toiletries, some fresh fruit and snacks, your own toothbrush, a hair dryer, and slippers."

"God love you, Sis! Now I can take a shower and get into some clean clothes!"

"There's more," said Cathy as she moved into Toby's room, seeking a place to put all those bags down.

"What?"

"As promised, I brought your laptop computer complete with a $29 wireless ethernet adapter card from the office supply store. This hospital installed wireless DSL Internet access during their latest renovation. You will be able to search the web until your little heart is content!"

"Wow! Thanks, Sis!"

"That's not all. I promised you a copy of the transcript of Congressman McDonald's news conference. Here it is, complete with the question and answer section."

"I can't wait to read that! Thanks!"

"Don't be so sure, and don't thank me yet. I've read it. We're not talking about the Cub Scout Handbook here Susan. This is heavy-duty stuff we're dealing with. And I know I promised to give you a call before I left, but I had a pretty good idea anyway of what you needed. And besides, I forgot. If you need anything else, I'll be happy to scoot out and get it for you. Well, look who's awake! Hello, Toby. Give Aunt Cathy a kiss! How are you feeling this morning?"

"I'm hungry Aunt Cathy. I want some pancakes."

"Hospitals don't have the best food selections, Toby, but I'll tell you what, if they don't bring you some pancakes with your breakfast, Aunt Cathy will go get you some! Would you like that?"

"Yes Aunt Cathy. I'm hungry."

As Cathy continued to visit with Toby, Susan removed the items from the bags Cathy had brought, reserving the laptop and transcript for last. Susan's mind was already deep in thought as a very aggressive inquisitiveness began to manifest within her mind and soul. She needed answers, and as she stared at the small rectangular black box and the sheath of papers adjacent to it, she felt as if she were looking at the entrance portal to another dimension. Before that weekend was over, Susan would feel as if she had indeed been transported to another place, another time, to a surreal world where black is white, up is down, two and two makes nine, and morality, if it ever existed at all, had been banished forever.

"Well tell me, Sis, what did Dr. Butler say? I saw you talking to him."

"Not a lot. He has scheduled some more tests for Toby—a CT of the skull and spinal cord and a spinal tap."

"Will those confirm his Lyme diagnosis?"

"Possibly, I guess, but he seemed to stress that he was looking for some other causative agent. No, he seems quite certain that Lyme is involved, he's just trying to rule out any other problems."

"Mommy, will the tests hurt?"

"No, sweetie," Susan responded as she almost bit her tongue.

The correct and most honest answer would have been: "No sweetie, unless we have an inept neurologist that strikes a nerve in your spinal cord as he rams that big needle into your back. Hurt? Oh yeah, sweetie. It will be like having 10,000 volts shoved up your epizooty. But no problem, the pains will stop after he leisurely fills the big syringe with your spinal fluid and finally withdraws the long needle."

Susan was thinking that perhaps after all of this turmoil was behind her, she would write a handbook for mothers entitled; *Raising Your Child in the Twenty-First Century…Needful Lies, Half Truths, and Misrepresentations for Every Occasion.*

"When will the tests be done and how long before we have the results?" asked Cathy, interrupting Susan's digression of thought.

"Not sure. I guess they will start right away. And I don't know how long before we have the results. I would think the CT results would be same day, but I think the spinal fluid would have to be sent to a lab somewhere."

"Why don't we send it to your employer Susan? They could lace it with the cocktail de jour and maybe the doctor could just shoot it right back in. Don't waste a drop that way!"

Precisely at this delicate moment of unbridled cynicism exhibited by Cathy, a cafeteria worker appeared bringing Toby's breakfast. The pushcart was a small buffet on wheels and contained a selection of juices, milk, coffee, eggs, hash browns, bacon, and yes, to Toby's delight, pancakes with butter and syrup. Susan was delighted that Toby's appetite had improved, and she eagerly helped Toby with his selections and plates.

"I've already eaten, Susan, so why don't I stay with Toby while he is eating, and you can go down to the cafeteria and get yourself some breakfast."

"That's a good idea Cathy. I'm kind of hungry too. If you don't mind, I'll go now. And I'll take this transcript with me. Pleasant or not, I've got to return to work on Monday bright and early, and the more I can find out about what might be going on out there, the better prepared I will be."

Susan appreciated this opportunity to get out of that room and be alone with her thoughts. She selected several items from the buffet and reflected on just how hungry she was. Choosing a less crowded, small table in a corner, Susan settled down, began eating, and turned to the opening page of the transcript. Her attention was immediately drawn to the color photograph of Congressman McDonald, and she was struck by his handsomeness.

Now that's a good looking man, she thought. *Why can't I meet someone like that? Oh well, looks aren't everything. Let's see what's on his mind.*

Having come from the congressman's Web site, the transcript contained other photos as well. There were pictures that were taken at the news conference showing the congressman standing at the podium, surrounded by the doctors' wives and children, pictures of the large crowd in attendance, and even photos

THE POISON PLUM

of the Plum Island facility, the ferry, and Colonel Gordon McClain. Susan began reading, and within moments it was clearly obvious that she was totally unprepared for what she was seeing. The words spoken by Congressman McDonald only last Tuesday at the nearby New London Community Center began searing her brain like a red-hot branding iron. She impulsively stopped eating as her jaw became slack and her eyes darted across the pages, flickering rapidly from left to right, not unlike the carriage return of a high-speed, electric typewriter.

Had Susan been but an ordinary concerned constituent of the congressman's, the impact of his speech would have been sobering and troubling enough, but to have a critically ill son upstairs with an uncertain prognosis, made ill by the outpouring of the devil's own wicked brew from a simmering cauldron, kept warm, stirred, and formulated at the very facility which provided her employment, was too much! Too much! Susan's appetite was now gone, replaced by a sickening knot in her stomach that felt like it was trying to pull the surrounding stomach into it. She sat quietly and motionless for several minutes after completing the transcript. She was too numb to stand, her mind filled with an abundance of emotions, each one vying for prominence. Perhaps it was fear which triumphed over all the rest as she realized that in less than forty-eight hours she would have to return to the Plum Island facility. Instinctively, she wanted to run, and right now! She wanted to unhook Toby from all the wires and tubing, cradle him in her loving arms, and flee from this evil place, never looking back and run all the way back to Alabama!

Cathy glanced up as Susan returned to their room and was struck by the look of intensity and resolve on Susan's face.

"You look like you just finished reading your autopsy, Sis. Didn't you even eat at all?"

"Not much."

"Well, you need some nourishment. You can't keep going on a diet of stress, resentment, and frustration. Get back down there for an early lunch for sure. While you were gone, a nurse came by and said they would be coming soon to get Toby for his spinal tap."

"Did she mention the other tests?"

"Only that they are scheduled to begin at 2:00 PM, and they plan to give Toby his antibiotic after the spinal tap."

"One thing is for certain, Cathy."

"What's that, Sis?"

"If I had even the slightest reservations remaining about terminating my employment at Plum Island, they are now unequivocally banished forever from my consciousness. After reading that transcript, I am almost in a state of shock. Granted, I don't know for sure what is going on out there, but something is, and whatever it is, as Granddaddy used to say, 'It ain't good!' My God, Cathy, I don't think I've ever read anything in my life that conveyed sincerity and heartfelt emotion like that transcript of Congressman McDonald's!"

"He knows something, that's for sure. He wouldn't be going out on a limb and staking his career on his congressional investigation if he were not fully convinced that something is rotten in Denmark. Plus the guy is a doctor, which gives him a big leg up on seeing through the mumbo jumbo that surrounds Plum. Yeah, I'm out the door but not just yet. I've got to go for the Actress of the Year award when I return Monday morning. I've got to be convincing and believable that I am truly, truly sorry for all of my recent absenteeism, and it won't happen again, I swear, and there is no place on this planet I would rather work at than Plum Island.

"I need time, Cathy. I need for that group insurance to pick up these hospital and doctor bills. I have no idea what all of these tests and treatments are going to cost, but I know that if they were piled on top of my unpaid student loans, I would be over the hill and into the poor house without my job and the insurance. Color me a prostitute if you must, but I have no choice."

"No argument from this corner, Sis. A girl's gotta do what a girl's gotta do, and right now, Toby comes first! And speaking of cost, the nurse remarked while you were out, that she had never seen an order for twenty-eight infusions of that antibiotic they are giving Toby. She said one or two maybe three infusions would cure almost anything because it's potent stuff! And it should be for what they charge for it! She said the hospital bills the patient $330 dollars for each infusion!"

"Three hundred and thirty dollars! Jeez! Let me see, that times twenty-eight? Yikes! That's almost $10,000 dollars! Holy cow! By the time those tests are totaled, and all the doctors' and hospital fees are included, this tab is going to be huge!"

"But, whatever it takes to get Toby well has to be done."

"I know, Sis. Whatever it takes."

"Mommy, what are you and Aunt Cathy talking about?"

"Don't worry, sweetie. It's just grown-up talk. We are just real happy that the doctors have figured out what is wrong with you, and they are giving you some medicine that is going to make you well."

"Will it be much longer Mommy?"

"I don't think so, Toby. You remember what the doctor said this morning?"

"I know, Mommy, but I don't like to feel bad."

"And we don't want you to, honey, but we just have to be patient."

Patient indeed, thought Susan. *At Toby's age, time crawls by almost imperceptibly. Christmas never comes, and the pot never boils. Tomorrow seems like forever! With the passing of years, some sadistic power geometrically increases the speed of clocks, and the pages of calendars begin flipping like someone fanning a deck of cards.*

"How much longer, Sis? Before you are out the door, that is?" asked Cathy.

"Well assuming they don't can me Monday…at least until sweetie pie over there is finished with the antibiotics."

"Let's hope and pray that whoever is responsible for coordinating and verifying your insurance claims doesn't make the connection between this diagnosis and your employer, until you are out the door that is."

"Oh peachy! I didn't even think of that! But hopefully that won't even become an issue. I think that is done by offices in Washington serving federal employees across the country."

"Let's keep our fingers crossed that nobody breaks out of the usual stagnant bureaucratic modus operandi and gets creative."

A knock on the partially open door signaled the arrival of a spectacled, tall, thin man in a white lab coat followed by an orderly pushing a gurney into the room.

"Good morning. I'm Doctor Thomas with the Department of Neurology here at the hospital. Which of you is Ms. Collins?"

"That would be me, Dr. Thomas," replied Susan as she stepped forward to shake his hand. "I'm Susan, this is my sister, Cathy, and this is my son, Toby."

"It's nice to meet you. So this is Toby. Are you ready to go for a little ride this morning Toby?"

"I guess so, but I can't walk."

"That's OK, Toby. We'll let you ride on this gurney here, and George will push you. Sometimes he might go a little fast, would you like that?"

"I guess," replied Toby as a trace of a smile appeared on his face.

"Susan, we will be taking Toby to the radiology department for the procedure Dr. Butler ordered. We have state-of-the-art imaging equipment there which eliminates the earlier challenges we experienced trying to ensure patient comfort."

"That's reassuring. I'm happy to hear that."

"You may accompany us to the facility, but you won't be able to be in the actual room where the procedure will be performed because of the necessity of maintaining a sterile environment. The sample we will obtain will be sent to a lab for culture and microscopic examination, which will take several days. I will interpret the results and communicate that information to Dr. Butler as soon as possible. Do you have any questions about the procedure Susan?"

"I don't think so. Dr. Butler explained why the test was necessary and what he was trying to accomplish. It all seems pretty straightforward to me."

"Fine. Well, if everyone is ready, next stop, the Department of Radiology."

Susan noticed that Toby actually seemed to be enjoying the attention and the opportunity to be mobile and go somewhere. Ten or fifteen minutes later, and after Toby had been taken into the sterile area of the procedure room, Susan and Cathy had a further opportunity to visit together. Susan began their private time by remarking again what a powerful impact the transcript had made upon her.

"Cathy, I admit I was skeptical when you first started trying to tell me what you had learned about Lyme disease and Plum Island. Now, after the furies of hell have ravaged our world, my skepticism has faded and has been replaced with furies of my own and an appetite to learn as much as possible about what is really going on. Between Toby's tests I am going to fire up that laptop and read everything I can find about Lyme and Plum Island."

"Well, good luck! You will need more than this weekend. Once you initiate a word search for either, you are going to be taken to site after site and link after link. And that's just for starters. If you get into some of the Lyme or government conspiracies chat rooms, God only knows how long it would take to even barely scratch the surface of the information available. And that's just for the credible sites. If you drift into the Planet X, Roswell, alien impregnations, abductions, and spontaneous human combustions, you will be bogged down ad infinitum. Start with the Lyme disease support groups of Connecticut and New York. You can use your own discretion about where to go from there. And besides

Susan, why do you even want to burden yourself with all the details? I mean, haven't you already decided you are going to vacate the premises at Plum Island as soon as you can? And haven't you already decided that there is a very strong possibility that these funky diseases we never heard of before are indeed homegrown at that place you work? Why cross the t's and dot the i's? What difference does it make now?"

"I don't know Cathy. I really don't. What you are saying makes perfectly good sense and, yes, I probably should just suck it up, take my lumps, and get on with our lives. But there is a voice deep down inside of me that is telling me to go all the way with this thing. After all, one of their damn, homegrown, as you would put it, bugs has almost killed my son and blown a hole in our lives big enough to run a truck through. I'm mad, I'm vindictive, and I have a voracious inquisitiveness raging inside of me I've never known before!"

"What do you mean 'go all the way with this thing'?"

"I mean I can't stop now. I've got to find out more. That much I know for sure."

"And then? After you 'know', what are you going to do with all of that newfound knowledge? What good is it?"

"I honestly don't have a clue Cathy. I really don't. I guess I'll make that decision when I get there."

"Lordy, girl. Sometimes that stubborn streak in you makes me think Granddaddy has been reincarnated in you!"

Seemingly, Susan and Cathy had only just started talking to each other when already they were rolling Toby out of the sterile area on the gurney.

"Well, hello, sweetie! That didn't take long. Are you OK? Were you a big boy for Mommy?"

"Yes, Mommy, but my back and my head hurt."

"Toby certainly was a big boy, Susan," remarked Dr. Thomas. "The procedure went fine, and there were no difficulties. The lower-back discomfort and headache he is experiencing should fade away after several hours. I see from Toby's chart that Dr. Butler has already prescribed a mild combination pain reliever and sedative which should provide relief."

"I understand, Dr. Thomas, that the fluid will need to be sent to a lab for evaluation, but Dr. Butler mentioned that if the appearance of the fluid is cloudy or milky in appearance, then that could denote an infection?"

"That is true. Luckily, Toby's was crystal clear. I could show it to you, if you would like. It's in a sealed vial."

"That's OK. I'll take your word for it."

"I understand Dr. Butler is trying to rule out Lyme disease?"

"That is true…or maybe rule it in. I'm not sure."

"Well, we certainly have our share of Lyme disease in this area. I wish both of you good luck!"

Susan and Cathy followed as the orderly wheeled Toby back to his room. Within minutes of their return, the nurse arrived and attached a fresh vial of the amber-colored antibiotic to Toby's catheter and began the drip for infusion number two.

Only twenty-six to go and I'll have Toby back again, thought Susan…. *Or will I?*

"Cathy, if you don't mind, my hunger is back, and this time it isn't taking no for an answer. If you will stay with Toby, I would like to run down to the cafeteria and have an early lunch."

"No problem, Sis. You need some food. We'll be OK. Take your time."

"I won't be long. Just for grins I'll take my laptop. Maybe it will work there too. I'm ready to get started!"

Just for grins? Did I say that? thought Susan as she started down the hall. *I must be ready for the psych ward!*

For a hospital cafeteria, Susan thought the food selection was excellent, and she hungrily loaded her tray with the most appealing offerings. Again taking a small, corner table, out of the traffic flow, she began eating while simultaneously positioning her laptop for viewing comfort. And to her delight, Internet access was immediate, and she was off and away to her first word search. Following Cathy's advice, her first selection was the Lyme Disease Support Group of Southern Connecticut.

This should be interesting, thought Susan as the Web site was accessed and words and images rapidly filled the screen. *Oh, isn't that just a dandy. A nice big, color picture of a tick! Excuse me? I'm trying to eat here!*

But as Susan soon found out, the tick picture was only for emphasis. The site provided names, addresses, and contact information for the support group's leaders. Also, names and contact information for Lyme-literate medical doctors within close proximity to the area represented. Susan wondered if any were still left after the government's raids. The site also provided a history of Lyme disease and a symptom list much more comprehensive than anything she had seen in the medical literature. As she scanned the list, she was struck by the complexity and diversity of the symptoms. For it seemed to her this disease was capable of mimicking any and every disease symptom known to man.

Everything perhaps but hangnails and irregular male menstrual cycles! she thought, expressing a little giggle.

Imbedded throughout the site were numerous links to articles, reports, suggested treatment protocols, testimonials, and other information perhaps of merit to a Lyme sufferer. But there was no mention of Plum Island and no mention of Congressman Harry McDonald. Susan scrolled to the bottom of the Web site where there appeared links to media articles relevant to Lyme. Most appeared to Susan to be garden variety articles mentioning Lyme but were devoid of any depth or substance. Scrolling on down she noticed what appeared to be the most recent updates to the site.

"Wait a minute," she said aloud as she continued munching a portion of a baked chicken breast. "What is this? A link to an article in *The Chronicle* dated this week, entitled 'Bugs and Plums'?"

Susan eagerly clicked the link while muttering under her breath, "What the hell is this all about? And who the hell is MacIntosh McAdams?"

Like many of *The Chronicle*'s readership, Susan initially thought that perhaps the article had something to do with horticulture issues on Plum Island.

What the crap does a sick Lyme patient care about bugs eating plum trees on Plum Island? Where is this guy going with this? she thought as her eyes rapidly scanned the article. And then it happened—Susan encountered, for the very first time, the sledgehammer, no-holds-barred, take-no-prisoners, inimitable writing style of MacIntosh McAdams.

Holy cow! thought Susan. *This guy is dropping a bombshell here! Wow! This is incredible! I've got to show this to Cathy!*

It would be later that evening that Susan's relentless search for information would uncover the other two articles written by McAdams with a vitriolic pen— 'Osama Bin Laden or Ben's Momma' and the article disguised as a Wild West wanted poster.

And still later, much later, Susan finally had the opportunity to stretch out and welcome some much needed sleep. The day had been a busy and stressful one for Susan, Toby, and Cathy. The afternoon CT scans had revealed minor lesions in Toby's brain and spinal cord which the attending neurologist seemed puzzled by. A more comprehensive evaluation was promised for tomorrow. Dr. Butler's evening visit during his hospital rounds was noncontributory but only because of the lack of additional substantive information. Susan was learning firsthand the world of hurry up and wait that all Lyme victims have been conditioned to endure, not of their own volition but necessitated by the bitter exigencies of their situations. Cathy had continued to be a Godsend and had attended to Toby between the antibiotic infusion and the tests, giving Susan more time to continue surfing for information.

Susan was hoping that the hospital would be quieter this evening because it was the weekend. Her mind and body desperately needed some solid restful sleep. With Toby sleeping more soundly thanks to the prescribed medications, she planned to take full advantage of the opportunity. Cathy had left about 10:00 PM with a promise to return tomorrow after church. Shortly thereafter, Susan closed her eyes and soon felt her body slipping into a deep sleep.

The Dream

What followed was a very realistic dream that Susan unfortunately would remember for the rest of her life. She found herself walking into a very beautiful, very old church with high, vaulted ceilings and beautiful stained-glass windows. A crowd of approximately fifty people dressed in black occupied the first six or eight rows of pews closest to the altar while an organist played softly, contributing to the somber and solemn mood that prevailed. The church reminded Susan of the St. Louis Cathedral on Jackson Square in New Orleans that she had visited while still a senior in high school. As her dream progressed, she continued walking toward the altar, and she wondered why she was there. As she approached, she saw two caskets adorned with and surrounded by beautiful flowers and wreaths. The dream was so realistic she could even smell the fragrances of the flowers. As she slowly approached the open caskets, the mourners in attendance seated on the left side of the aisle rose one by one and turned to look at Susan. Their faces were of the doctors and other health care providers that Susan and Toby had visited over the past several months. They were all there, including Dr. Aventi and his assistant, Dr. Fayed, from the Medical Center. But instead of bearing countenances befitting the occasion, each wore a sinister and knowing smile as they stared into Susan's eyes. As Susan continued to approach the altar and the waiting open caskets, those in attendance seated on the right side of the aisle also began to stand and turned to stare at Susan. Theirs were the faces of her co-workers at the Plum Island facility that had perished in the massacre. Last to stand and stare in her direction were her superiors at the facility—the ones who had been killed and also the replacements sent by Washington and the CDC. There was acting Director Stephens, Victor Perloff, and finally, her nemesis, Herschel Gallagher, each silently staring at Susan as she approached and each bearing the same sinister smile.

All eyes continued to follow Susan as she reached the altar. She stopped alongside the first casket to look inside. To her horror, the body she saw was her very own! Her eyes were wide open and fixed in a macabre stare. Susan tried to scream, but no sound was forthcoming. And then, as if some mighty force was directing her movements, she stepped unwillingly to the adjacent open casket, and there lay the body of her son, Toby. His eyes were also open and fixated in a blank stare. The screams wouldn't come, and somehow Susan knew this was a dream, but she was powerless to force its conclusion. Instead, with the mighty unseen force continuing to prevail, she was compelled against her will to continue staring at the caskets' contents while dozens of ticks of all sizes and colors began to emerge from beneath the corpses and slowly began crawling over the bodies of their victims. She watched in sheer, stark terror as the ticks began crawling onto her and Toby's faces, in and out of their mouths, nostrils, and ears. Their hair became covered with ticks, and then she could see the ticks one by one beginning to bite and dig into the skin. As the ticks crawled across the surfaces of Susan and Toby's open eyes, Susan's blood-curdling screams violently erupted, awakening a frightened and confused Toby. Immediately, three nurses rushed down the hall to their room to find Susan in a cold sweat, crying and shaking uncontrollably, and Toby sitting up in his bed obviously terrified and crying, "Mommy, what's wrong? Mommy what's wrong?"

The nurses didn't have a clue what was going on, and it was several minutes before Susan could be calmed enough to even begin an explanation. Toby continued sobbing and kept asking what was wrong. Susan moved to Toby's bed, cradled him in her arms as her tears mingled with his in their embrace.

"Mommy, Mommy what's wrong?"

"Just a dream...just a bad old dream. I'll be all right. It was just a dream. Everything is OK. Don't worry, sweetie. Mommy just had a bad dream. Nothing is wrong."

It is said that in the courses of their careers, nurses eventually see it all. But none of the three in attendance had ever seen anything quite like the scene that unfolded in the Collins' room that night. Totally sympathetic while trying to maintain their professional composure, they observed Susan to make certain there were no extraneous issues contributing to her borderline hysteria other than a super-duper, Grade A nightmare from hell. After she had calmed down considerably, a sedative was offered, which Susan gratefully accepted.

THE POISON PLUM

Later, as both were trying to return to sleep, Toby asked his mother what the dream had been about. Even as the calming waves of the sedative began sweeping her body, Toby's question once again brought tears to Susan's eyes.

"Don't worry sweetie, it's gone now. It was just a bad old dream that grown ups sometimes have. Try to get some sleep, honey. Your mother is very tired. We'll sleep, and we'll both feel better in the morning. I promise."

"OK Mommy, Good night."

"Good night, Toby. Mommy loves you."

Even with the sedative, it took Susan quite a while to return to sleep. Not only was the "bad old dream" vivid in her mind, but there was the fear that it would recur. *Maybe it won't be over the hill and into the poor house,* thought Susan. *At this rate it will be over the hill and into the insane asylum!*

When sleep finally overcame them both, it was mercifully uninterrupted until the light of the dawning sun began filling their room. Susan arose, and still somewhat groggy from the sedative, began dressing for the day and attending to Toby's needs. The remembrance of the nightmare was upon Susan's consciousness, albeit somewhat suppressed by the sedative, which she was grateful for. Throughout the day, Susan did her part to continue the suppression each time the dream tried to reemerge to gain prominence over her thought processes. Susan's inherent practicality and common sense gave her an edge in fighting the wispy, ephemeral, nocturnal invader that had mysteriously appeared and shaken her to the core.

If you can't see it, measure it, taste it, or feel it—forget about it! It ain't real! These are good words to live by, thought Susan. *It's just the practical application of those words that I'm beginning to have a problem with!*

Toby began coming fully awake, and the first words out of his mouth were, "Mommy, I hope you don't have any more bad dreams. You scared me."

"I know, sweetie. I was scared, too, but it was just a dream. Maybe it was something I ate in the cafeteria that gave me a little tummy ache. Sometimes that causes bad dreams."

"Why Mommy?"

Oh, my goodness, thought Susan. *Why did I go there?*

"I don't guess anybody knows, honey. Tell you what. After you are grown and become a doctor or a scientist, you can study that and find the answer. Would you like that, sweetie?"

"Look, Mommy! I can move my other foot! And I can raise my leg too! Look, Mommy!"

Susan pulled back the sheet, and sure enough, Toby was moving around his left foot and was able to raise his right leg and bend it at the knee.

"Do you want to try to stand up, Toby?"

"I think so Mommy. Will you help me?"

Toby swung his legs over the edge of the bed, and Susan helped him to his feet. Toby was able to stand unassisted but he was not able to take any steps because he said his left leg was still "asleep." Nevertheless, this bit of progress was very encouraging to Susan, and she tried to explain to Toby that this was a sure sign the medicine was working, and it wouldn't be much longer before he would be walking again.

"Mommy, I'm dizzy. I need to sit back down."

"It's OK Toby. I'll help you. You are getting better. It's just going to take a little more time."

"I hope so. Why do I have to be sick all the time?"

Why, indeed, thought Susan. *Why, indeed.*

That "why" was now irrevocably burned into Susan's brain. Until she unequivocally knew the answers beyond a shadow of a doubt, her every waking moment would be dominated by the all consuming desire to put the pieces of this gigantic puzzle together. She remembered how difficult it was as a child to assemble a large jigsaw puzzle that her parents had given her without being able to refer to the picture on the cover of the box for guidance. Otherwise, each piece was pretty much the same as the other pieces; splashes of color with irregular edges. And now with a picture beginning to take shape and form an image thanks to Congressman McDonald and MacIntosh McAdams, not to mention a mysterious visitor known as Lyme disease, the pieces of this mosaic were beginning to fall into place. But did Susan want to see the finished product with all the pieces in place? Did anybody in their right mind want to see it?

Whatever it is, thought Susan, *I'll deal with it when the time comes!*

The rest of that Sunday was relatively uneventful. And Susan was certainly grateful for the respite. Toby's third IV was around 11:00 AM and went well except for complaints of a worse than usual headache and eye pain afterwards. The attending nurse slightly increased Toby's pain medication, which seemed to help. At every opportunity, Susan would continue her Internet odyssey into the bizarre and mysterious world of Lyme disease. Soon after Toby's IV, Cathy returned from church, and Toby as usual was happy to see her. Toby excitedly showed her how he could move his foot and leg.

For most of the afternoon, Susan remained engrossed in her search and had made several pages of notes and references. Toby and Cathy, for the most part, kept each other occupied and entertained. As the bright daylight of the afternoon began fading into early twilight, Susan turned off the laptop and stood for a few moments before asking Cathy and Toby if they minded if she went for a little walk.

"I need to gather my thoughts Sis, especially after what I've read. I feel that it is going to take a Herculean effort on my part to just walk in that lab tomorrow morning and especially to appear all cheery, bubbly, and enthusiastic! I don't know what that will require, but I just know I've got to try. So, if you don't mind, I'm going to walk outside for a few minutes, get some fresh air, and sit by that fountain out near the entrance. I'll be back in about twenty or thirty minutes. Toby, honey, you and Cathy keep each other company while Mommy gets some exercise."

As Susan walked out of the main entrance and headed for the fountain area, she took several deep breaths of the fresh air, which was beginning to turn cooler as the sun was setting. Taking a seat on one of the benches facing the fountain, Susan began mentally reviewing what she had learned in the past thirty plus hours. There was no doubt whatsoever in Susan's mind now that the facility at Plum Island was one of the most, if not the most, dangerous places in the entire world. To Susan, it represented a portal to the very gates of hell. As frightening as the thought of returning to the facility was, there was an even more troubling development as a result of Susan's research. That development entailed the prognosis for Toby's recovery. Susan had discovered that there was a common thread in all of the Lyme sites and patient testimonials she had read. The common thread was that all of the patients were still sick, albeit improved, even after extensive courses of antibiotics were administered. For Susan, it was heart wrenching to read of their suffering, frustration, and despair. She could only imagine how the uncertainty of what the future held for those people could imprison them within their own bodies, creating a veritable hell on earth to endure daily.

Susan sat there, quietly thinking to herself. *Were these hapless victims only the very vocal minority of all of those countless thousands who had been treated and were cured? And for whatever reason… misdiagnosis, inept professional care, failure to adhere to rigid treatment protocols, or hypochondriacs, they were still sick or thought they were. Is treatment failure the norm or the exception?*

Susan didn't know. She didn't have a clue. But for certain she knew she wanted her son well and completely free of this insidious disease. To watch Toby suffer day in and day out, month in and month out, year in and year out, would for her be a fate worse than death itself. Her mind was filled with a mass jumble of information from so many different sources it was almost impossible to sort it all out. Did she read of one single testimonial where any Lyme victim claimed to have been cured after antibiotic therapy? *No!… The answer was no!… Not a single one, not a single one!*

Equally disconcerting to Susan were the testimonials and chat room discourses painfully recanting the tales of a search for a cure and the myriad of alternative treatment protocols discussed and suggested. Susan was amazed and aghast at the vast array of treatments that these unfortunate victims had experimented with.

Either these people are crazy as hell or desperate as hell or maybe both, thought Susan. *I've never even heard of most of that stuff that those people are using on themselves. Talk about being a human guinea pig! I could never subject Toby to any of that insanity! Those antibiotics have to work, and that's it!*

Susan had read of the megadoses of vitamins and minerals taken daily by the Lyme victims, which was scary enough but the suggested treatments went downhill from there. A large variety of different herbal concoctions were being used by some, most of which Susan had never even heard of, and especially one of their favorites, TOA-free Cat's Claw.

What on earth is that? thought Susan. She knew that the use of some herbs could be quite dangerous indeed. *Being sick from Lyme disease or dead from herbal abuse? Is that the question? My God, what are these people thinking?*

And then there were the discussions and testimonials of people being infused with intravenous hydrogen peroxide and or intravenous ozone!

Plop, plop, fizz, fizz, thought Susan. *Why not just shoot Clorox into your veins? Kill everything!* And how about the hyperbaric oxygen treatments at the facilities in California and Florida? She even read of patients receiving as many as 150 of these costly "dives" as they are called. And they improved, or so they claimed, but they still presented with symptoms.

One of the most bizarre treatments Susan encountered was called ICHT, which was an acronym for intercellular hyperthermia. The theory was to raise the body's core temperature high enough to kill the spirochetes, and, of course, sometimes the host. One could travel to Italy for that fun fest. Another therapy high on Susan's list of wacko protocols was known as ultraviolet blood irradiation. In this interesting procedure, blood was withdrawn from the body into a cylindrical glass tube, bathed in ultraviolet light and then re-infused into the body hopefully purified and rendered germ free.

Susan encountered several sites of testimonials where lists were provided of which therapies proved to be beneficial and those which were not. One patient from Alabama, in particular, had a very extensive list of what had worked and what had not. What was amazing to Susan was the fact that the gentleman was still alive after all that had been done to his body. She thought at the time that it would be interesting to meet that man for surely he must be as tough as nails to have survived all the physician-prescribed treatments plus self-experimentation! He had done everything, it seemed, except hyperbaric and ICHT. After seeing twenty-five or thirty doctors, including a Lyme disease specialist, he still suffered daily from the disease, even after four years of continuous antibiotic therapy.

Totally frustrated and seemingly devoid of all hope, his Web site told of how he had embarked on a dedicated mission of pursuing, evaluating, and experimenting with what Susan perceived to be very radical treatment modalities. Ironically, the ones he attributed significant improvement to were seldom mentioned by other patients.

Perhaps he was the only one desperate enough or crazy enough to try them, thought Susan. But somehow he had found a medical doctor somewhere that agreed to give him intravenous infusions of a colloidal silver solution. He claimed immediate significant benefit from those and also claimed considerable benefit from treatments with an electromagnetic frequency device call a Rife machine. The latter supposedly functioned by using selected precise frequencies to vibrate the spirochetes to death, much like sound waves shattering the wine glass.

It was all too much for Susan to bear. Never but never could she ever subject Toby to such witch-doctor remedies. From today on, the concept of a treatment failure is an impossibility as far as she and Toby are concerned.

"What was it that Cathy was always saying? Oh yeah, 'You've got to have faith, Susan. God sees you and knows your situation and your needs. He will provide for you and Toby. Just have faith'."

As Susan began making her way back to Toby's room, her thoughts shifted to her concerns over returning to the Plum Island lab tomorrow morning. In order to gather her thoughts and try to rest as much as possible before boarding that morning ferry, she began seriously considering asking Cathy if she would stay the night with Toby. Susan felt that if she could spend the night alone in her own place, she could concentrate on the possible scenarios she might face in the morning and devise strategies to deflect or ameliorate potential further damage. She thought she would quietly mention her plan to Cathy when she returned, and if she agreed, it would give Cathy an opportunity to go out for anything she might require for the evening and the following day. And then after Toby had received his evening sedative and dozed off about 10:00 PM, Susan would leave. She hated to impose further on her loving sister, but she knew she needed every possible advantage on her side tomorrow. Hopefully Cathy would understand because she knew that Susan would not ask this favor of her unless it was very important.

As Susan approached their room, she could hear voices through the partially open door that she recognized as Cathy's and Dr. Butler's. He had arrived for his evening rounds and had just begun examining Toby and was chatting with Cathy.

"Good evening, Dr. Butler. Thanks for stopping by."

"Hello, Susan. How do I find you and your family this beautiful evening?"

"We are all excited that Toby is regaining use of his legs. He was able to stand this morning but couldn't walk because his leg still felt asleep. Has he already told you?"

"Yes, yes, he has. And he showed me how he could move his feet and his leg. Toby, do you think you could stand up for me?"

"I'll try. Mommy, will you help me?"

Toby sat up in the bed as Susan helped steady him. Then he swung his feet over the edge of the bed and stood erect with Susan's help.

"Very good, Toby. Take your time. How do you feel?"

"I'm dizzy, Dr. Butler, and my head and my back hurt."

"How do your legs feel?"

"My feet are stinging. They feel like they are asleep."

"If you hold on to your mother, do you think you can walk for me?"

"I'll try."

As Toby began trying to move his legs, it was obvious that he had very little control over which direction they would take after the brain's signal was sent to stimulate the muscles involved. But, he was able to walk, after a fashion, from his bed, to the hall, and back to the bed again. And of course clumsily, even with Susan's help.

"That's good, Toby. Those antibiotics we are giving you will have you up and walking before you know it!"

"I hope so Dr. Butler. I don't want to be sick anymore."

"I know you don't, son. You were bitten by a nasty old bug that has made you very sick. But you are going to get better. We'll keep you here in the hospital a few more days, so we can keep an eye on you, and then if you are still improving, we will let you go home. Would you like that?"

"Yes Dr. Butler."

"Dr. Butler, do we have any results yet from the spinal tap and the CT scan?"

"Yes and no, Susan. I spoke late this afternoon with Dr. Thomas. Obviously we don't have cultures back yet from the tap, but he felt that the other findings were consistent with tertiary Lyme disease."

"The lesions?"

"Yes, and they, like the other abnormalities we are seeing, elevated liver enzymes, low white and red blood cell counts signaling characteristics of anemia, heart block, tachycardia, headaches, muscle and joint pain, diarrhea, bladder irritation, and so on, all come with the territory. And just as they come with the territory, we anticipate their departure as the antibiotics demolish their territory. The human body, Susan, has remarkable recuperative powers. Once the offending invader is removed from the scene, the body begins to rebuild, rejuvenate, and recover. Always remember that the darkest hour is right before the dawn. We have to remain patient and let the drugs do their job."

Susan's mind was remembering the testimonials she had read as Dr. Butler was speaking. She thought about how removing the "offending invader" was easier said than done. Even though attacked and wounded, the invader stubbornly refused to leave its host and would use any lapse of effective therapy to regenerate, regroup, and launch another debilitating assault on its host. A battle to the death, for eventually only one would survive. Either the host or the spirochete and its allies would be victorious. But for the moment there was no choice other than to continue the antibiotic therapy and hope for the best.

Whatever the outcome, thought Susan, *we'll cross that bridge when we get to it. For now, this is our mess of pottage, and we must partake of it.*

"Dr. Butler," spoke Cathy. "Is there anything else you can think of that Susan and I could do to help Toby?"

"As the feeling in his legs returns, try to help Toby walk up and down the hall, as he is able. And be sure to encourage him to drink plenty of water. It will help to flush out the toxins from the dying pathogens. And try to be patient. This is going to take time."

"Dr. Butler, I have to return to work tomorrow, but Cathy will be here with Toby."

"Work? Were you not able to arrange a leave of absence?"

"Hardly! To say that my employers have been less than understanding and sympathetic would be a gross understatement. The 'leave of absence' they prefer would be permanent."

"And I thought you government types could pretty much come and go as you pleased and still get paid."

"Well, not at that facility, and most assuredly not since the loss of personnel at the ferry massacre."

"That's unfortunate. But rest assured that Toby will be under excellent care here at the hospital. And I, of course, will be by to check on him at least once a day. Just do what you have to do, and together we will get through this."

"In the wonderful, miraculous world of modern medicine, Dr. Butler, is there some wonder drug that I could take tomorrow that would enable me to selectively tune out the unpleasant reception I am certain to receive while simultaneously allowing me to function normally at my job duties?"

"I'm afraid not Susan. The developer of that panacea, in addition to becoming obscenely rich, would also be awarded the Nobel Peace Prize and the universal acclaim of all mankind. I know also that if that drug did exist, I would have my personal prescription filled as soon as possible! But until the Almighty bestows that elusive formula on some fortunate recipient, about the best suggestion I have is to make it through the day as best you can while focusing on how relaxing that first glass of wine will be when you finally get a chance to prop your feet up and relax."

Susan managed a smile and a little laugh as she thanked Dr. Butler and wished him a pleasant evening.

As the sounds of his footsteps down the hall faded, Susan, Cathy, and Toby sat quietly for a few minutes just looking at each other. Toby was the first to break the silence.

"Mommy, when can we go home?"

"I'm not sure, sweetie. It depends on how you are doing. Maybe in just a few more days. Would you like that?"

"Yes Mommy."

"Cathy, let's walk down to the vending machines. I need to ask you a question."

"Sure, Sis."

Once out of range of Toby's hearing, Susan told Cathy of her need and desire to have some quiet time in preparation for her return to work tomorrow.

"Actually," responded Cathy, "I was going to suggest that you get out of here while I stay the night with Toby. I even brought some extra clothes and other essentials to enable me to stay until you get back tomorrow afternoon. We will be fine. Go and gird your loins or whatever you have to do to face those bastards tomorrow. We will be praying for you, and I am certain you will do fine with the supreme acting performance of your career. Just remember to not rock the boat by losing your temper. And, Sis, do not under any circumstances breathe a word, not one word, of Lyme disease."

"Oh, Cathy! You are such a sweetheart. I guess you are just the greatest sister a girl could ever have! Thank you!"

"I'm happy to be here with you and Toby. We will get through this thing. You can count on that."

"Well, if it is OK with you, when we get back to the room, I'll tell Toby what I am going to do. The nurse will be in shortly anyway with the sedative, and it will be lights out for Toby after that!"

"Fine. I've got to scoot down and get some things out of the car, and I'll meet you back in the room."

Toby had turned the television on while Susan was gone, and as she re-entered the room, she could hear the voices of the news anchors of a local television station. Toby was sitting up in the bed with an excited look on his face as he stared at the screen.

"Mommy! They are talking about what made me sick!"

Susan turned to look at the TV as one of the anchors began explaining to the viewing audience that an exclusive interview had been arranged with Dr. Barrett Simmons, who was one of the Lyme disease doctors from Bridgeport that had been arrested during the government's raids and released yesterday. Susan sat next to Toby on the bed, putting her arm around him as they both watched intently. The interview began with Dr. Simmons explaining that with the increase in prevalence of Lyme disease in the area, his infectious disease practice had, as a consequence, become almost totally devoted to the diagnosis and treatment of the disease. He explained that in the past ten years he had treated over 3,700 confirmed cases of Lyme disease, and new cases had been arriving daily.

"Dr. Simmons," began the distaff side of the news anchor team. "Do you have any explanation why you and the other doctors were arrested?"

"No, no I don't. I've asked myself that question over and over at least a hundred times. I don't have the slightest idea."

"Did you have any relationship whatsoever with Colonel Gordon McClain?"

"I never had the pleasure of meeting the man. I, like most other Americans, only admired him from afar."

"Do you have any idea what could possibly have motivated Colonel McClain to take such a drastic action?"

"No. I'm certainly in no position to try to put myself inside his head."

"Are you aware of the allegations that Colonel McClain was dying of Lyme disease and he blamed the government's biological research laboratory at Plum Island for his illness?"

"Yes, I am aware of those allegations."

"Dr. Simmons, you are obviously an expert in diagnosis and treatment of this rapidly spreading disease, which is now threatening our residents in epidemic proportions. What is your opinion, Dr. Simmons? Is Lyme disease indeed a product of the government's research at Plum Island?"

The camera shifted to a close-up of Dr. Simmons' face, which by now conveyed a grim, serious, and very stern expression. After a long pause came Dr. Simmons' terse response.

"I can't prove that…"

Holy cow, thought Susan. *He has been thinking about it. I can't prove it, but I would like to! Is that what he is saying?*

Absent from this interview conducted exclusively by local television personalities, were the snide, arrogant, and critical comments frequently offered up by representatives of the national media in their efforts to sway public opinion in whatever preconceived direction they intended. Even a non-news hound like Susan could easily see the difference. If a bias existed at all it would have been slanted towards a very suspicious attitude concerning the government's intentions and activities at the Plum Island facility. Indeed, but unknown to the viewers, each of the news anchors had personally interfaced with Lyme disease victims that were either direct family members or close friends. They, like many others of this area of the United States, had experienced first-hand what a serious problem Lyme disease had become. And certainly no one needed to convince Dr. Simmons of the severity of the problem. He, after all, had been on the front lines of this battle for years.

Susan felt Toby's body tense, and as she looked at his face, she saw tears beginning to roll down his cheeks.

"Mommy. Is that where you work? That place they are talking about?"

Oh boy, thought Susan. *Where is this going?*

"Yes, Toby."

"Mommy! Why do you work at a place that makes people sick?"

"Sweetie, I would never have anything to do with making people sick."

"But, Mommy, the lady said…"

"I know, honey. It's just a news program. Sometimes they talk about things they don't know anything about. Do you understand, sweetie?"

"Mommy, am I going to die?"

Susan pulled Toby close to hold him tight as her own tears began streaming.

"No, sweetie! Of course not. You are going to get better every day until you are completely well. I promise!"

So much for me being able to leave early to get some rest as home, thought Susan. *Now, for certain, I'll have to wait until after that night nurse gives Toby his nighty-night shot. I wish I could just crawl into this bed with Toby, get the same lights out shot and start forgetting forever about Lyme disease and Plum Island.*

"Hey, what's going on here?" asked Cathy as she returned with her overnight bag. "Have you two started your own private pity party without inviting me?"

"Come on in, Cathy. It's not a problem, just a news program that got Toby upset. Everything is OK isn't it, sweetie?"

"I guess, Mommy, but I'm still scared."

That was Cathy's cue to crawl into the bed on the opposite side of Toby. Together they hugged each other close until the nurse arrived to give Toby his infusion. And, predictably, a few minutes later Toby was sleeping soundly, and Susan was finally able to head for home, leaving Cathy in charge of taking care of Toby until she could return after work tomorrow.

The drive home for Susan was a time of reflection. A lot had happened to her, Cathy, and Toby these past several weeks. And indeed, a lot had happened to the nation as well. Susan wondered just how much stress her overloaded mind, body, and soul could endure before she would self-destruct. She felt that an inner strength was being tapped that she had never known before. She knew not its origin, only that its appearance was surprising, and she was very grateful, whatever the source. It reminded her of something her dad had said while she was in grad school and was continuing to pull down a 4.0 grade point average. "Way to go girl. I knew you had it in you!"

One thing was for sure. Call it grit, inner strength, determination, or stubbornness, she knew she would need all of the above and more for tomorrow's performance. Walking into Satan's cocoon would be a challenge enough; the appearance of being happy and delighted to be there was right up there with a one-legged man climbing Mount Everest. But, it will all happen in due time. Whatever is to happen will happen, and she would just deal with it as it unfolded.

Straight ahead, at the outer reach of her headlights, began appearing the familiar outline of her driveway. Susan was glad to be home and already had the rest of her evening planned to the very last detail. After a hot shower, a cold glass of wine, a sleep aid, she set not one, but two alarm clocks in failsafe mode, set for thirty minutes earlier than her usual wake-up time.

She knew that there was no wiggle room for any mistakes on her part tomorrow. Her career, such as it was, was on the line. And somehow, someway, she had to hold this tenuous liaison together until at least the end of Toby's antibiotic therapy.

Sleep finally came for Susan that night but not before she had played over and over in her mind every possible confrontational scenario and exchange of dialog she could possibly imagine that might occur between herself and her superiors the next morning. She used the thirty minutes of extra time in the morning to good advantage by consuming an extra one and a half cups of black coffee and carefully selecting the most professional outfit she could put together. Leaving nothing to chance, Susan left for the ferry at least twenty minutes ahead of her usual schedule. Traffic in that direction had never been a problem this early in the day, and today proved no exception.

The Performance of a Lifetime

The morning air on the coast of Connecticut that Monday was uncommonly cool for that time of year. As Susan made her way from the parking lot to the launch area for the ferry, she felt a chill sweep through her body. The day was overcast and the facility, which was normally visible in the distance, was obscured by a low cover of fog, which added to the chilly gloominess of the morning. Completing the scene of unpleasantness were the dozen or so soldiers present, wearing their camouflaged uniforms, boots, and each carrying an M-16 rifle. Another dozen or so men wearing suits were also milling about and were obviously security personnel. Before the massacre, there was normally only a morning and an afternoon ferry which connected the Connecticut coast to Plum Island. Employees and supervisory personnel alike would share those ferries as they made their commutes to and from work. As part of the elevated security procedures implemented in the wake of the disaster, two ferries were now employed. The first to leave in the mornings carried the director, supervisory personnel, and the employees immediately ancillary to them. The second ferry leaving thirty minutes later carried all other employees and the support staff. In the afternoons, the schedule was exactly reversed, with the upper-echelon personnel arriving last. And, of course, security was heavy on both vessels and at the launch sites.

As Susan stood quietly assessing the dreary scene unfolding before her, she reflected that only a few short weeks ago the cumulative impact of everything she was witnessing would have been sufficient to send her over the edge. But Susan was beyond those emotions now. The only thing that mattered to her on this chilly, gloomy Connecticut morning was that sick, helpless little boy lying in that bed only a few miles from where she stood. She was going to do whatever was necessary to prolong her employment until Toby's prescribed course of antibiotics was completed and covered by insurance. *And after that?* she wondered.

THE POISON PLUM

That bug lab and all the bug scientists in it can sink into the ocean and straight down to the pit of hell, for all I care. In just a few short weeks, these people are going to be looking at the back side of me. But thank God for small favors. At least I won't have to endure the smirks and sneers of my accusers, Stephens and Gallagher, on the ferry ride over!

Susan's respite was short-lived, however. For upon arrival at her work area, there sat Herschel Gallagher at her computer gazing intently at the screen. He stood as she approached and began addressing her with language purposefully incendiary in an effort to provoke a confrontation.

"Well, Ms. Collins. We are so grateful you decided to grace us with your presence this morning. I trust you have perhaps allocated sufficient time in your busy personal schedule to perform your duties today?"

Susan had seen Gallagher's type before. He was a physically unattractive social misfit of a man who, having acquired a position of authority, used that position to demean underlings in his pathetic attempt at superiority.

Well it's not going to work on this chick, thought Susan. *I'm on a mission here, and I'm not going to fail. At the end of the day, I will have succeeded, and you will still be a disgusting little twit.*

"Good morning, Mr. Gallagher!" responded Susan enthusiastically with the warmest smile she could muster. "I'm excited to be back to work with all of my conflicts successfully resolved."

"Obviously not all are resolved, Ms. Collins. You are aware, I am certain, of our policy forbidding personal e-mail messages. You are aware of that restriction, are you not, Ms. Collins?"

"Yes, I am, Mr. Gallagher but…"

"Ms. Collins, I count no less than forty-three messages on your "Out" box to your sister, and an equally large number from her in your "In" box. These flagrant violations of our security procedures will simply not be tolerated."

"I had to arrange for care for my son."

"Your problems with your personal life are expected to be resolved by you on your personal time. In addition to violating security procedures, you are wasting taxpayer's dollars by expecting to be paid for time you expend on personal matters. Your lack of dedication to our mission here is unacceptable Ms. Collins. As you already know, you were placed on probation and administrative review last week.

Today, I am going to recommend to Director Stephens that you be terminated immediately."

Susan was certain that if she took that freshly sharpened pencil from her desk and rapidly and repeatedly plunged it into the dork's fleshy neck, she would eventually pierce a carotid artery, and the arrogant bastard would bleed to death right on the spot. Perhaps it was the mental image of that event unfolding that enabled her to continue to smile graciously as she addressed Gallagher.

"I understand completely, Mr. Gallagher, and I somehow want to totally assure you that the problems with my son's health that distracted me and were responsible for any flagrant errors of judgment have been totally resolved. And I also want to assure you of my total dedication and devotion to the work we are all committed to here at the facility."

Susan's warm smile and steady eye contact with Gallagher never wavered as she continued. "I sincerely hope you will reconsider your evaluation of me, Mr. Gallagher. Certainly you recognize from a review of my academic credentials, the degree of focus and determination of which I am capable. And if you will only agree to give me one more chance, I won't disappoint you. By the end of my probation period, you will be proud of the degree of commitment and accomplishment I will have demonstrated. I am ready, willing, and able to totally dedicate all of my abilities to my position here at Plum Island. I am very proud of the work we are doing to make our nation safer and healthier, and I want to be a part of that team for years to come."

Wow, thought Susan. *Where did all of that BS come from? Guess I'm laying it on pretty thick. What was it Dad used to say? 'You can go to hell for lying just like you can for stealing'!*

Gallagher was obviously taken aback by Susan's response. His words were chosen to elicit a response of out of control anger bordering on hysteria. He delighted in pushing subordinates to that point, but Susan didn't take the bait.

What the hell, thought Gallagher to himself. *Just appear to be as condescending as possible, and maybe the bitch will be so grateful, she will give me a little someday.*

"Whatever, Ms. Collins. You make a compelling case for the continuation of your employment. However, the scenario you describe is not totally supported by and compatible with your employment history at this facility. Your meeting with Director Stephens is still scheduled for 9:00 AM. I will meet with him prior to that time, and I will review our meeting and my concerns. We will advise you of our decision."

Susan managed an even warmer smile as she moved closer to Gallagher, extending her hand for a shake while expressing her heartfelt appreciation for his consideration.

As Gallagher turned to walk away, Susan found herself wishing she had a third arm and hand to pat herself on the back with.

"And that ladies and gentlemen…" she muttered under her breath, "is the exciting conclusion of Act Number One. Stay tuned for Act Number Two coming to you live from the heart of America's biological warfare program."

Susan was relieved that the encounter with Gallagher was over, at least for the time being. Next, she would have to face no less than Mr. Clement Stephens, the acting director of the facility. She knew nothing of Stephens's background or his personality. She, for that matter, barely knew the previous director who like many others, had succumbed to a rather serious case of lead poisoning.

Well, thought Susan, *if Director Stephens is an unknown quantity, so is employee Collins. What time is it? Hmm… in precisely forty-five minutes, we will find out what we are each all about.*

Somehow, Susan managed to busy herself in the intervening minutes with review of and preparation for her job duties, which she intended to pursue aggressively at the completion of her "interview" with Stephens.

At precisely 8:59 AM, Susan arrived at Director Stephens's office intentionally conveying the image of a time-conscious employee desiring to be both punctual and not wasteful of work time. Time thrifty as some would phrase it.

Director Stephens appeared to be about fifty years of age, balding, and slightly overweight. *He was,* Susan thought, *cordial enough, obviously focused, highly efficient, and gave the impression of a man preoccupied with much weightier issues than the tardiness and absenteeism of a single employee.* He wasted no time getting to the heart of the matter once Susan was seated.

"Ms. Collins, your department supervisor, Mr. Gallagher, has conveyed to me his concerns about your frequent absences and tardiness. He has, I believe, explained to you the importance of each and every single employee fulfilling his or her responsibilities to enable the entire facility to function at optimum performance. He discussed your meeting this morning and related your apologetic and contrite demeanor. However, his concern at this point is a possible lack of sincerity on your part. I, as director of this facility, certainly realize that there can be two sides to an issue. I have seen your work review reports, which have been satisfactory, except, of course, for your absenteeism. I am thoroughly acquainted with Mr. Gallagher's opinions regarding your performance. The purpose of this morning's meeting between you and I is twofold. Number one is to reinforce our concern about the continuing viability of your employment here. And number two is to give you an additional opportunity to present your side of events."

So that's it, thought Susan. *The inconsiderate SOB Gallagher is ready to kick me to the curb. But for whatever reason, he is deflecting to Stephens for the final decision.*

"I understand completely, Director Stephens, and I appreciate this opportunity to explain the circumstances that have prevailed, which are responsible for my absences. As you are possibly aware, I am the single parent of an eight-year-old son whose name is Toby. My son, like myself, has been blessed with extraordinarily good health. To miss school or work because of sickness is unheard of in our family. We don't get colds, sore throats, viruses, or flu like the average population. However, that streak of perfect health for my son came to an end several months ago when Toby became ill with a debilitating sickness that baffled the pediatric physicians and specialists that I took him to."

Was it her imagination, Susan thought, *or did Director Stephens's attention to her remarks perceptibly become heightened when she mentioned Toby's sickness? Did one eyebrow arch slightly higher? Did his gaze become slightly more intense? Did his body shift slightly more to her direction? Was he suspecting Lyme disease or some other Plum potpourri as the cause of Toby's illness?*

Susan continued on. "Perhaps it was precisely because we had been blessed with such good health that I was totally unprepared for the situation that unfolded. The contributing complications of sickness, single parenthood, and new employment presented sincerely formidable obstacles in my life."

"I can appreciate that, Ms. Collins, but Mr. Gallagher and I have had difficulty in understanding why this problem with your son's sickness has been so long in resolution. To imply that an illness is beyond the ability of modern medicine to diagnose after such a lengthy period strains credulity and smacks of malingering."

"Precisely my point as well, Director Stephens. Allow me to explain."

THE POISON PLUM

"Please."

"When Toby first became ill, I took him to a respected board-certified pediatrician in New London who suspected some unidentified strain of the flu and prescribed a seven-day course of antibiotics, plenty of fluids, and bed rest. When Toby's condition worsened, the pediatrician began referring Toby to specialists, who in turn referred him to even more specialists. It became a case of not being able to see the forest for the trees. The doctors became so obsessed with discovering the arcane, they missed the obvious. And of course with each faulty diagnosis, my fear level rose along with my frustration and confusion."

"Mr. Gallagher remarked that the problems with your son's health have now been completely resolved, and you are in a position to return to work full time totally dedicated and focused. What did the doctors finally determine was wrong with your son?"

"Ironically enough, after all of the specialists and exotic testing we endured, it was finally a sleepy-eyed emergency room physician that hit the nail on the head."

"And the diagnosis?"

"Mononucleosis! That's right, can you believe it? An ordinary garden variety case of mono! It would seem that even a first-year medical student wouldn't have a problem hanging that diagnosis. And after all we have been through! I still can't believe it!"

"That's pretty incredible, Ms. Collins. Incredible indeed. And how is your son now?"

"Oh much better, thank goodness. He is still weak and has to rest a lot, but he is rapidly making a complete recovery. My sister, Cathy, is able to stay with Toby while I am at work, and everything is working out beautifully. I am ready to rededicate my efforts to our work here. I will give one-hundred and ten percent of myself if I am allowed the opportunity to do so. In fact, I would like to volunteer for any additional assignments or additional responsibilities that you feel I may be academically qualified to assume. The very fact that I am here today is a testament to my dedication to this facility. In yet another bizarre irony, had my son not been ill the day of the ferry massacre, I would have been among those pitiful victims. As it is, I am the only facility employee to escape unscathed from that terrible event. Now, ask yourself Director Stephens, how many employees would, after such a harrowing close call, even remotely consider a continuing employment relationship with this facility?"

"Ms. Collins, I am glad that we have had this opportunity to examine and review your situation. We are indeed shorthanded as a result of the massacre, but I would recommend a continuance of your employment even if we were not…predicated, of course, upon the outcome of your probation period. After what you have shared with me today, I don't foresee any problems going forward. I will review your request for the assignment of additional responsibilities, and it may well be that we will indeed be able to fill a developing niche with your capabilities. I'll let you know. In the meantime…"

Director Stephens was interrupted by his secretary advising him via the intercom that he had a call from someone with the CDC in Atlanta.

"Please excuse me, Ms. Collins. This will only take a moment."

"Should I step out?"

"No, you're fine."

While Stephens was occupied with the call, Susan took advantage of the opportunity to look around the director's office. During her employment, she had never before visited this particular office which was larger and more comfortably furnished than any of the others she had seen. Director Stephens had, of course, a large, attractive desk, which held several telephones and a computer monitor. Behind the desk was a large credenza and bookshelves, which housed additional computer monitors and numerous books, periodicals, and pamphlets. Adorning the walls were several large maps of the United States, the Caribbean, Africa, and Europe. She noticed lines and degrees of shading in certain areas of those maps, but, of course, had no idea what that represented. Also on the walls were framed photographs of various dignitaries employed at the facility and individuals she assumed were previous directors or other high-ranking doctors or scientists. Many of the photographs were obviously dated from the fifties and sixties because of the clothing styles represented or the occasional vehicle included in the photograph.

One photograph in particular was intriguing because it was significantly older, much older than even the oldest of the rest. She guessed from the style of the suits worn by the eight men pictured and the one black woman who was dressed in a nurse's uniform that the photograph was taken in the late 1930s or early 1940s. An automobile was visible at the left side of the photograph which appeared also to be late 1930s vintage. The participants were posed in front of a rather inconspicuous building of wood-frame construction that certainly did not look like anything she had ever seen at Plum Island. To her it resembled photographs of structures that had been built in the Deep South during the Depression by workers from the CCC or WPA. As she continued to scrutinize the photograph, she noticed the appearance of pine trees in the background, which reminded her of rural scenes from her home state of Alabama.

Interesting, she thought. *And just what is that photograph's connection to this facility?*

To Susan, the large number of photographs displayed represented a tribute, indeed a shrine, dedicated to the memory of the doctors, scientists, and support personnel who have in some way been connected with Plum Island.

Let us all genuflect and pay homage to those germ scientists that have bravely gone before, thought Susan angrily. *May they continue to rot in hell where they belong!*

As it appeared Director Stephens was concluding his call, her attention was redirected to the area of his desk where one would normally keep current work in progress. In his close proximity were several folded newspapers, which from her seated angle were difficult to see clearly. But awkward angle not withstanding, there was no mistaking the origin of the newspaper closest to Stephens. It was unmistakably the issue of *The Chronicle* which carried the sepia-toned article resembling an Old West wanted poster written by MacIntosh McAdams.

Very interesting, thought Susan. *I wonder if this guy feels like someone is rattling his cage....Hmmm.*

"Sorry about that, Ms. Collins. Let's see. Where were we? Oh yes, in the meantime I will advise your supervisor, Mr. Gallagher, that it is my decision to continue your employment, and I will recommend that he attempt to more fully utilize your abilities within his department. That certainly should not present too much of a challenge for him, considering our situation here. Regrettably the procedure of probation must continue because of established procedural protocol. Based upon your expression of sincerity, I certainly do not expect any difficulties for you."

"Thank you, Director Stephens. I will do my best to contribute to and enhance the work we are doing here at Plum. And again, I sincerely regret any inconvenience or misunderstandings that may have arisen as a result of my son's incapacitation."

"Fine then, we are in agreement. Good day."

"And good day to you, Director Stephens."

As Susan exited his office, she felt almost euphoric.

"Thank you, God" she muttered under her breath. "I feel as if I have been through a gauntlet of demons in hell's foyer, but somehow through divine providence, I have been vindicated!"

Susan couldn't wait to share her good fortune with Cathy, but she knew it would have to wait until she left the facility this afternoon. For sure, Gallagher the dork would be watching her every move like a hawk. *Nope*, thought Susan. *Keep smiling, and I'll briskly return to my work area and somehow concentrate on the work in progress.*

As she walked down the labyrinth of hallways past empty work cubicles and blank computer screens, she couldn't help but reflect back on the old photograph hanging in Director Stephens's office. She was now convinced that the photograph was taken somewhere in the South and sometime during the late 1930s.

And if all of that is true, what on God's green earth does any of that have to do with modern-day Plum Island? And what is on the hard drives of those dozens of unattended computers in those unoccupied cubicles throughout the complex? And what about those stacks and stacks of files and boxes scattered about? What are your secrets oh spawn of Satan? If only I could delve into the inner sanctum of your most private of privates, what revelations would unfold? Gee, what are all these references to God and Satan all about? I'm starting to sound like my sister. Next thing I know, I'll be dressed like the church lady on Saturday Night Live, jumping around with my hair pulled back into a bun! Slow that imagination down, Susan! You are becoming positively giddy. Concentrate on the work that needs to be done and keep that smile going. Get through this day; you have successfully jumped all the hurdles. Get back to the hospital to give Cathy the good news, relieve her to return to her place of rest, and spend time with Toby. That's the plan!

And what of Susan's work in progress? It was work she had been assigned by her previous supervisor, perhaps not so mundane as studying bat droppings retrieved from Carlsbad Caverns, as CIA Director Steele had sarcastically expressed it, but certainly not Nobel Prize material either. Somewhere and somehow her previous assignment upon completion would eventually be merged into a mosaic in progress by the grand planners and directors of the bio-labs. And where did her piece of the puzzle fit into the grand design? She would probably never know the answer to that question, and what difference would it make if she did? Susan cared, but she didn't care.

Was the AIDS virus genetically engineered at Ft. Detrick, China Lake, or Plum Island? Ebola, West Nile Encephalitis? Was the Legionnaire's disease bacterium spliced onto the prion that causes Creutzfeldt-Jakob brain-wasting disease so it could be spread pneumonically around the world, spliced down the hall or at the CDC in Atlanta? What damn difference does it make? she thought. *At this point in time, the only things I care about are my son's health and who is responsible for creating the bug that has wrecked our lives.*

Susan was confident the bodies would continue to pile up from all of that other stuff already out there, and whenever the time is deemed opportune by those in control, a massive discharge of pathogens into a selected population will result in the deaths of hundreds of thousands, perhaps millions of innocent civilians.

Let God sort that out, thought Susan. *Maybe the Almighty will send more like Colonel Gordon McClain! In the meantime, if little ol' me could somehow pull the plug on this insanity and inhumanity to mankind, I would. But what can impotent Susan Collins do? Talk about David and Goliath? I don't even own a slingshot!*

Susan managed, as she always had, to push inopportune and inappropriate thoughts from the forefront of her consciousness as she returned to her work. She even limited her lunch break to a hastily consumed sandwich and soda in the cafeteria in order to be as productive as possible. Around 2:00 PM, Susan was elbow deep in work when she felt the presence of someone standing behind her and looking over her shoulder. Turning, she found herself once again staring into the face of Herschel Gallagher.

What does the dork want now? she thought. *I was hoping I was finished with this SOB for the day at least.*

"Yes, Mr. Gallagher?" responded Susan with her warmest smile.

"I have spoken with Director Stephens, Ms. Collins, and I am aware, that at his request, your employment at this facility is to be continued, at least for the time being."

"Yes, Mr. Gallagher. I am grateful and eager to be of service in whatever capacity you feel appropriate."

"In that regard, Ms. Collins, I do have work that you should be qualified for that is of greater significance than your work in progress."

"Sounds exciting! What do you want me to do?"

"As you are probably already aware, or maybe you aren't, I don't know, the Department of Microbiology was the hardest hit as the result of the massacre. The previous supervisor and all employees, with the exception of you, were killed at the ferry landing. You are the only person in the entire facility that would have even the slightest idea of what work was in progress and the status of that work in this department."

Actually, I don't, thought Susan, *but I'll keep quiet and see where this is going.*

"I want you to temporarily shelve the work you are engaged in and begin attempting to consolidate and evaluate the work programs of your peers. I will provide you with access codes and PINs for their work stations and computers. You should be able to determine the direction and scope of their efforts to this point. As you move forward in the coming weeks, a single workstation at a time, I will expect you to report promptly to me your discoveries and determinations as you evaluate each workstation. In other words, you will assume the identities of each and every employee that previously existed in order to determine exactly where they were with their programs."

"This sounds exactly like the type of challenge I could sink my teeth into, Mr. Gallagher! When can I start?"

What's a few more lies piled on top of the dozens I've already told, thought Susan. *Tell them what they want to hear until I'm out the door and down the road!*

"Actually, Ms. Collins, there is no time like the present. You may begin immediately. On this piece of paper are the codes and PIN numbers of former employee, Eliot Steadman, who occupied nearby cubicle number 11. His work was related to viral pathogenesis and mutation. Provide me with an outline of that work as soon as you are able. After you have finished there, I will advise you which workstation to occupy next."

Hmmm, pondered Susan. *This could be interesting. What a coincidence that I was just fantasizing about exactly this! Maybe there is someone up there looking out for us after all. Cathy will get an earful tonight, that's for sure! This is almost too good to be true.*

Susan excitedly moved over to the number 11 cubicle as Herschel Gallagher had referred to a former living, breathing human being's work environment. As she began to access computer files, notebooks, e-mails, logs, and even a personal diary maintained by the former inhabitant as it related to his work, Susan felt a kinship with the departed Eliot Steadman, whom she scarcely remembered from before the massacre. Nevertheless, to be allowed to assume the identity of another person for all practical purposes was exciting and, for want of a better description, somewhat voyeuristic and intrusive. Susan felt almost naughty, the hand in the cookie jar experience, as she methodically ventured into the world of viruses as explored by Eliot Steadman. Mesmerized as she was, the remaining hours of the afternoon flew by as if they were minutes. It seemed that she had only begun to access computer files when the facility came alive with employees closing down their work and making their way to the ferry landing for the afternoon ride to the mainland. Susan's desire to continue her exploration was tempered by her desire to return to Toby and Cathy. And so it was with mixed emotions that Susan closed out her work and gathered her things to leave.

What a day! reflected Susan as the ferry churned through the murky waters with the mainland looming larger until she could begin to see the outline of automobiles in the parking area. Susan felt an enormous relief of tension as a result of her successful defense against a hostile supervisor and the amelioration of any pending misunderstandings or misrepresentations that may have existed in the mind of Director Stephens.

"Good job, girl! You done good!" as Granddaddy used to say, Susan mused to herself. But as much as Susan would like to take all of the credit for today's success, there was that inner voice that just wouldn't leave her alone.

Was today's success possibly accomplished by divine intervention, or were today's accomplishments solely attributable to my prowess and nimble negotiating skills? Was it coincidence? Good luck? Or was a higher power at work?

Susan was beginning to feel that through incredible misfortune, duress, frustration, and helplessness, she was being forged anew in some celestial, otherworldly crucible that she was powerless to resist.

A fitting topic for a late night philosophical discussion with Cathy, thought Susan, *sufficiently lubricated with a fine bottle of Merlot of course.*

But in the meantime, she couldn't wait to get back to the hospital to see her darling Toby and share the excitement and elation of today's experiences with Cathy.

Thirty minutes later, as Susan approached Toby's room, she could hear through the partially opened door, the voices of Toby and Cathy, as usual enjoying each other's companionship.

"Hi guys! What are you two up to?" spoke Susan cheerfully as she pushed open the door. "Did you miss me?"

"Mommy! Aunt Cathy and I walked to the end of the hall!"

"Oh, sweetie, that's wonderful!" said Susan as she rushed to give Toby a big hug and then Cathy a hug and a kiss on the cheek.

"He was a little wobbly, Sis, but he did fine. Didn't you, Toby?"

"Yes, and I really want to go home."

"Cathy, has Dr. Butler been by yet?"

"Not yet, Sis. It will probably be around 8:00 or 9:00 before he comes."

"Have you heard anything?"

"Nope. The only activity today other than the nurses coming in every few hours to record his vitals was to administer the antibiotic about 11:00 AM."

"Well, I have had enough excitement and activity today for all of us. I can't wait to tell you about it!"

"And I can't wait to hear about it," responded Cathy. "I know how stressed out you were! Is everything OK?"

"Better than OK, but I'll tell you later. Right now I want to see how my sweetie is doing! Give Mommy a kiss!"

"Mommy, why do I feel tired all the time?"

"It won't be much longer, sweetie, until the medicine has you feeling much better. See, already you can walk some. It won't be much longer. Would you like to show Mommy how you can walk?"

"I guess, but I have to pee again and my head and my eyes hurt."

"Well, let's tinkle first, and then you can walk for Mommy."

"He must have some kind of bladder irritation or something Sis. He has to go about every forty-five minutes. And he still complains about being dizzy and says his heart is jumping around."

"I'll be glad when that clears up. I think I'll ask Dr. Butler about the arrhythmias when he comes in."

Toby was able to get out of the bed and go to the restroom without Susan's assistance, but Susan's heart sank when she saw how pitifully pale and thin he appeared standing in his hospital gown. Somehow Susan managed a smile as she took Toby's hand for their walk down the hall. As Toby began taking the first few steps toward the door, Susan felt his body slump and she thought Toby was going to fall.

"Sweetie, what's wrong?"

"My legs, Mommy. Sometimes they feel like they are going to stop working."

After a few moments Toby got his balance, and together they walked out into the hall.

"Do you think you can make it to the end of the hall and back again, Toby?"

"I'll try, Mommy, but my legs won't go where I want them to."

Susan was holding Toby's hand and wrist as they continued down the hall, and Susan could feel Toby's very rapid pulse as the modest effort took its toll on Toby's laboring heart.

Toby was indeed weaving and lurching like a drunken sailor on shore leave. Susan bit her lip as she made every effort to suppress the tears that threatened to gush forth at any moment. The afternoon venture down the hall was not as successful as Toby's morning walk with Cathy. About half way to the end of the hall, Susan could feel Toby's little hand gripping hers even more tightly as he spoke in a trembling voice.

"Mommy, can we turn around? My legs are tired."

"Sure, sweetie. Mommy is here with you. Just take your time."

"Mommy, I have to potty."

"Number two?"

"Yes, Mommy."

And as Toby spoke, Susan heard what began as a little poot that rapidly deteriorated into an uncontrollable bowel movement which ran down the back of Toby's legs and splattered onto the tile floor of the hospital's hall. Susan scooped Toby into her arms and rushed back to their room.

"I'm sorry, Mommy, I couldn't hold it."

"It's all right, honey. Mommy will get you cleaned up."

As soon as Cathy saw what had happened, she pitched in to help as best she could while calling for the nurse.

"Has Toby had any diarrhea today?"

"His stool was a little loose at noon, but he seemed OK. Do you think the antibiotic could be the cause?"

"Who knows Cathy? That's one more question for Dr. Butler. And if we can be certain of anything about Lyme disease, we know that it has more twists and turns than the Blue Ridge Parkway and more tricks up its sleeve than Houdini."

Within moments a nurse appeared, and Susan, somewhat embarrassed, explained what had happened.

"We are very sorry, nurse. Dr. Butler had suggested we try to walk Toby up and down the hall a few times each day."

"Don't worry about it. We've got a new orderly on duty. This will be a good initiation for him. Sometimes, Ms. Collins, antibiotic therapy can cause bowel irregularities, constipation, or diarrhea, and sometimes alternating back and forth in a vicious cycle. I don't think it's anything to be concerned about, but I will note it on Toby's chart, and I will mention it to Dr. Butler when he gets here. He may want to prescribe an anti-diarrheal."

With the help of Cathy and the nurse, Toby was soon all clean again, and after being fitted with a clean gown, he settled in for the evening. After calm was once again restored to the room and Toby had received his nightly sleeping medication, Cathy took the opportunity to begin questioning Susan about her experiences that day.

"OK, Sis, the excitement is over, at least for the time being. Let's hear it! What happened out there at the bug factory today? I can't wait!"

"Cathy, you wouldn't believe it! Just like we planned, I got there right on time dressed in my most professional business attire, all bubbly, eager, and with a smile that would make any orthodontist proud. My first encounter was with my supervisor, Herschel Gallagher. You remember the guy that gave me such a royal reaming over the phone that morning I had to bring Toby here?"

"Yeah, I remember. He really got under your skin."

"That's just the kind of person he is. When I arrived at my work station, he was snooping on my computer, tallying up how many personal e-mails I had sent and received."

"Anal retentive."

"You got it. But anyway, I was all humble and apologetic and sucking up like a Hoover Deluxe. I know beyond a shadow of a doubt that the dweeb had already made up his mind to fire me at the conclusion of the probation period."

"So what happened?"

"That's just it. I was positively dripping with humility and presenting such a compelling defense, he deferred the decision to fire me to Director Stephens."

"So what's Gallagher's problem?"

"I don't know, but I suspect if a team of shrinks successfully picked away his layers of protective veneer, I wouldn't be surprised if they discovered he harbored a deep-seated resentment towards his mother, and by extension, all women."

"Why?"

"How else to justify his miserable existence on this planet other than by blaming the one responsible for his being here? Anyway, forget him. In a few weeks, he will become a fading, soon-to-be-forgotten memory along the highways and byways of my life. Good-bye and good riddance."

"You had to meet with Gallagher and then Stephens?"

"With about a forty-five-minute hiatus between the two, allowing Gallagher time to brief Stephens."

"And?"

"Oh, Cathy, it went great! I swear, I don't have a clue where all that bull shit pouring out of my mouth was coming from, but whatever the source, Stephens swallowed it hook, line, and sinker! I even began to wonder about that 'higher power' you are always talking about. Maybe after all this settles down, I will take you up on your long-standing invitation to attend Sunday School classes!"

"Now we're getting somewhere, Sis. I'll hold you to it!"

"Anyway, Stephens agreed to continue my employment, contingent of course on the outcome of my probation period."

"And we know that will not present a problem because you are going to be a model employee. Aren't you, Sis?"

"You got it! And especially since I have been blessed with a new assignment! They haven't seen enthusiastic and bright-eyed and bushy-tailed like they are about to!"

"What on earth are you talking about Susan? I thought you wanted out of that hell hole."

"Don't worry Cathy. I know what I am doing."

"Come on Sis. What is it?"

"Well, as part of all the sucking up I was doing, I asked to be allowed to assume additional responsibilities. After all, am I not the most dedicated employee ever? Who else would want to consider continuing their employment after narrowly missing having their brains blown out?"

"Additional responsibilities? What are you thinking? Are you sure there are any brains left in there to be blown out? Geez, girl!"

"It's a perfect opportunity. I couldn't have asked for anything better! They just dropped it in my lap."

"I'm listening."

"The supervisors don't know the status of the research and work that was being done by those killed at the ferry. There are dozens of computers standing idle in those work stations. Do you have any idea of the kinds of information that could be available on those hard drives and discs?"

"Yeah, I do, and that's what I am worried about."

"But don't you see Cathy? They have assigned me to access those computers to identify and evaluate work in progress. Look at it this way. I have carte blanche to snoop! I wanted answers, and this is my chance to get them!"

"God in heaven, Susan! Do you want to join your former co-workers in the hereafter? Do you have any idea how dangerous this nutty idea of yours is?"

"Dangerous? How? They assigned me the work. I'll just be doing my job. And boy will I ever be doing my job!"

"You ninny! Just what are you going to do with all of this newfound information and revelations from the germ doctors once you get it? Type up nice and neat memos and status reports to provide to your superiors and go home with a 'job well done' smile on your face? I know you, Sis, and I know what you are thinking. You are going to try to smuggle out of that vault of death the secrets of the inner sanctum! And that will result, oh sister of mine, in your imminent demise and departure from this earth. I won't have it! You've got to come to your senses before it's too late!"

Moments of silence ensued while each sister searched the eyes and face of the other. Luckily, Toby continued to sleep soundly, allowing uninterrupted, emotional, and intense discussion of Susan's plight.

"I know, Cathy, believe me I know. But do you see what's left of the love of my life over there in that bed with that line hanging out of his emaciated arm? We have been wronged, Cathy. Our family has been attacked by a sinister and stealthy invader. And not just us. Think about the hundreds and thousands already out there suffering from the same disease little Toby is valiantly battling as we speak. And what about the untold thousands who have already fallen victim to whatever germ cocktail that was unleashed on them. And how many more victims in the future will fall ill before this horror ends? You? Me? It's not much of a leap at all for me to imagine what might have been going on in the mind of Colonel McClain as he stood at the ferry landing on that Friday afternoon. Of all the situations and circumstances that have existed since the dawn of creation, God only knows I didn't request to be plopped down right here and right now in the middle of all of this. But for whatever reason and purpose, here I am. I disagree with Colonel McClain's, methods but not his intent.

"I will be careful, Cathy. I promise you that. I owe it to Toby and to you. But, Cathy, as God is my witness, I've got to do what I can with the opportunity presented to drive a stake in the cold, cold heart of this monster before it consumes us all!"

Operation Paperclip

Ingrid Schillinger sat quietly at the breakfast table of her comfortable, two-story New London home, gazing serenely through the expansive bay windows at the neatly manicured lawn and flower garden in glorious bloom this fine summer day. She reflected on how much joy and pleasure she had derived from tending to that flower garden and lawn down through the years while her husband spent his days working at the animal disease research center on nearby Plum Island. After coming over from Germany in the late 1950s, the early years in America had been happy ones for the Schillingers as they cherished the opportunity to begin life anew in the States.

Heinrich, Ingrid's devoted husband, was fortunate enough to have escaped possible Soviet retaliation for his work with biological warfare agents during the years immediately following World War II. It was because of his training and background that Heinrich was able to apply for and receive employment and U.S. citizenship through the Operation Paperclip program which had been implemented to focus on recruiting and acquiring the best scientific brains of the former Nazi Third Reich. Famed space pioneer and scientist, Werner Van Braun, and one of the founders of the Plum Island facility, former Nazi germ warfare scientist, Erich Traub, were among those brought to U.S. shores through the Operation Paperclip program.

Heinrich's U.S. career began with the CDC in Atlanta, and then in 1964 he was transferred to the USDA's Plum Island facility, where he became involved in viral research. Ingrid had hated the heat and humidity of Atlanta as well and the ingrained Southern culture and mentality she unavoidably encountered daily. Consequently, the move to Connecticut proved to be quite pleasing for them both. He was devoted to his work, and she found the climate and the indigenous population much more to her liking, especially the large percentage, relatively speaking, of peoples of German descent. Arriving too late to have participated in the pro-

Nazi rallies held at nearby Camp Siegfried in Yaphank, Long Island, she nevertheless immersed herself in the German culture and activities that remained. Sometime however, during the late 1960s and early 1970s, Heinrich's usually cheerful and expansive mood began to change. Almost imperceptible at first, the change eventually began manifesting in expressions of frank depression and moroseness. Ingrid, quite naturally concerned and simultaneously supportive, began attempting to coax Heinrich out of his self-imposed withdrawal.

During many a late night discussion as they shared the warmth of their fireplace during the long, cold Connecticut winters, a picture of discontent began forming that, in spite of the warming flames, chilled her to the bone. She knew that Heinrich was wrestling with a moral dilemma that grew stronger and more obsessive with each passing day. For the first time, Heinrich was even talking about his desire to leave the facility.

"But Heinrich," she would ask almost plaintively, "where would we go and what would you do? The world of viral research is your world. Your talents, your genius, your expertise, your acumen, it's all there, and probably the only place in the world today that can offer you employment. We live very comfortably here, and we are not getting any younger. It's not like we can be carefree and just throw caution to the wind and relocate to some unknown environment on a whim. Is it that bad for you, Heinrich? Can't you just turn a blind eye and pretend?"

"I try Ingrid. And each day, I try harder. And each day brings another thread in the web that is being woven. I try to convince myself that the work we are doing is not like the work during Hitler's reign. I tell myself repeatedly that we are working to eradicate disease and improve mankind's lot. But each day Ingrid, I see another milestone on the road to biological warfare. The viruses we are developing have the capability of eradicating entire populations, but our work is not focused on the destruction of viruses we discover. Our work is devoted more and more to the creation and engineering of new and even more virulent viruses than their predecessors. But I love my work, Ingrid! I have fulfillment and intellectual stimulation. How many men can boast of these accomplishments?"

"Could the inventors of the atomic bomb boast of fulfillment and intellectual stimulation? And would that be before or after Hiroshima and Nagasaki?" asked Ingrid.

And so it went, year in and year out until the relentless passage of time precluded any attempts at redirection of their lives. Life became even more comfortable with each raise, bonus, and cost of living adjustment. Dark hair began graying and late-night fireplace discussions faded to early night consumptions of alcohol in sufficient quantities to properly anesthetize the portion of the brain that thrived on moral qualms. Occasionally, especially after too much alcohol had been consumed by Heinrich, there would be a recrudescence of emotions Ingrid had thought long-since suppressed.

On one particular evening, Heinrich seemed even more despondent than usual. After a very long pause in their conversation, he posed a question to Ingrid.

"Ingrid, my love." he began. "What is the distinguishing difference between a germ laboratory operated in Nazi Germany and a germ laboratory operated in the United States?"

"The direction and ultimate objective of their work?"

"No. The design on the flag flying above the facility!"

"Ingrid, can't you see? I'm in too deep. I've been there too long. It's like the Sicilian Mafia…once in, always in. Or the American CIA—you can't quit; you can't leave. You are always a part of it. You don't quit it, it quits you. What was that American song that was so popular? 'Welcome to the Hotel California…You can check in any time you like, but you can never leave…'"

"Oh Heinrich, I had so hoped that the fear we endured in Germany would be forever eradicated by our moving to America and the embracing of the great American dream."

"And I as well, Ingrid. But the evil and immorality of man is never constrained by geographical borders, only by a belief in and subordination to our Creator."

Ingrid and Heinrich finally came to a workable solution to the anxieties that plagued them both. Heinrich agreed to begin his retirement the January following his sixty-ninth birthday in spite of the protestations of his superiors at the facility. Realizing that after the transition, he would be like a duck out of water, he and Ingrid began making elaborate plans to travel extensively, finally be their own bosses, and do the things they always wanted to do at their own leisure.

Ah, yes, mused Ingrid. *Those were the plans, but the best laid plans of mice and men sometimes go astray. Isn't that what the philosophers are fond of telling us?*

She took another sip of her glass of Liebfraumilch and allowed her mind to reflect back on that fateful day only two years ago when she had sat unconcerned in her doctor's office awaiting his interpretation of her latest mammogram results.

"Probably nothing to be concerned about Mrs. Schillinger," he had said. "But, to be on the safe side, I think we had better biopsy that area that has enlarged since your last examination."

That terse announcement was her first wake-up call. Then, as the weeks unfolded, each examination and each procedure indelibly forged her future. First there was the biopsy, then the pathology report of aggressive carcinoma of the left breast, stage three. Then came the suggested treatment protocols, each with their glimmers of hope. The radical mastectomy was followed by prolonged chemotherapy. With each setback and subsequent advancement of the insidious disease, the oncologists would offer more hope and different drugs in their attempts to eradicate or put into remission the disease process that was destroying Ingrid. And, like untold millions before, when faced with the immediacy of her own mortality, Ingrid turned to the Holy Scriptures for comfort, solace, guidance, direction, and finally, a measure of true hope.

Her body was by then riddled with metastases. Ingrid knew she had only a few months at the most to live, but she now knew a peace and calm that had eluded her throughout her life. The next January would be Heinrich's scheduled retirement date, but he had taken numerous leaves of absence to be with Ingrid during her illness. Ingrid had encouraged Heinrich to work and be active as much as possible so as to redirect his attention away from her illness.

While she was still strong enough to travel some, they had scheduled a short vacation to their homeland of Germany to begin the week after the Fourth of July. Ingrid and Heinrich had known it would be their last festive time together, and each had embraced their plan, eagerly awaiting the departure date.

Ah, yes, thought Ingrid. *The best laid plans…*

Ingrid reflected back on the shock and horror she had experienced when the news of Heinrich's death at the ferry landing reached her that fateful Friday afternoon.

Oh God, prayed Ingrid, *the bitter irony of it all. We both knew and acknowledged that I would be the first to go. Why, oh why, God! And God Almighty, is this your judgment on my husband's contributions over the years to Satan's design? And my judgment as well for my support of his work? Lord, please forgive us and deliver us from this evil and your coming wrath!*

Ingrid prayed a lot these days, especially after Heinrich's untimely death. She prayed for guidance, forgiveness, and the strength to endure what seemed to be impossible obstacles in the days ahead.

Lord, just let me get through this day and help me with the next one until you blessedly take me from this insane world and let me live eternally with you and my beloved Heinrich in your heavenly paradise. Amen.

Ingrid's actions after the funeral, in retrospect, seemed entirely logical. She had come to regard the Plum Island facility as a hideous monster, the spawn of Satan himself. Indeed, it was Plum Island that was maliciously spewing Satan's poison throughout the planet to destroy mankind. It was the destroyer of the happiness that she and Heinrich had expected in their later years, and, eventually, the destroyer of Heinrich himself. Logical? Yes! Retribution and revenge were in order. And would God have it any other way, would he expect any less of her? An eye for an eye, wasn't that the Old Testament admonition?

Ingrid recalled how Heinrich had started bringing, somewhat furtively, she thought at the time, papers and documents from his work. She assumed it was work he had brought home to finish, but she thought it odd that it never occupied him further except to lock it away in their home safe. Finally, after quite some time had elapsed and the accumulation of papers had grown to a rather respectable size, she one day decided to inquire of Heinrich exactly what was so important about those papers he had been accumulating.

"Heinrich, my dear," she had asked, "what on earth are you up to? Have you turned into a pack rat or a sentimentalist? What could be so important about a stack of papers you have brought from your work that would necessitate safekeeping? Don't you get enough of that place during the day? Why would you want to bring reminders into our home?"

"It's not what it seems, Ingrid. Those papers are copies of my insurance policy."

"Your insurance policy? But Heinrich, your group policy and our individual policies are in the filing cabinet. And they certainly didn't arrive piecemeal. Whatever are you talking about? I don't understand."

"Darling, of course you don't. And I don't expect you to. There are things better left not understood…dark secrets and designs of evil men of evil purpose that have no place in a mind and heart as sweet as that of my dear Ingrid. Those papers are indeed my insurance policy sweetheart...and I hope and pray they shall never be required."

Ingrid knew when to back away from an issue and that moment was one of those times. She didn't question Heinrich's motives, but she instinctively knew that those papers had the potential to reveal information about what was really going on at Plum Island that could be damaging if made public. For the first time, Ingrid inspected the trove of documents after Heinrich's funeral. She understood very little of what she saw but was astounded to see that the dates on the documents began in the 1930s and continued until 1975. Was security too tight for Heinrich to smuggle more out after that date or was that the culmination of whatever sequence had been revealed? Ingrid knew she would never fully understand, but that really didn't matter. What was important, however, was what she knew she had to do next.

Oh what a natural course of events...so logical. What else would I do? What else could I do? Maybe Heinrich went to all that trouble for just such a time and circumstance as this! And maybe my actions will, in the long run, make a difference and be pleasing in the eyes of God. And if someday I am found out, so what? I'll be gone soon anyway. At least I will have done what I could!

The Package

Since the Anthrax scare in the aftermath of 9/11, security had been dramatically increased in Washington to ensure the safety of all mail addressed to members of Congress or other government offices. The bulky package arriving that Monday morning for delivery to Congressman Harry McDonald's office raised eyebrows immediately among security personnel because of its bulk and also because there was no return address, only a New London, Connecticut postmark. X-rays and sensors detected no problems, and it was determined that the content was only unadulterated papers and photographs. Because of its postmark and unusual appearance, the staffer in the congressman's office responsible for sorting and directing incoming mail immediately notified Erin Giblon of its arrival that Monday morning.

"Miss Giblon? This is Angela. We received a rather large package this morning addressed to the congressman. It cleared security, but I think you had better take a look at it."

"OK," responded Erin from her office. "I'll be right out."

To Erin, the package appeared to be several legal-sized manila envelopes, taped together with masking tape and hand addressed. The envelopes were well stuffed, and the package indeed bore a New London postmark.

Oh, God, thought Erin. *I hope this is not another batch of 'actual un-retouched photographs' of reptilian aliens at the controls of spacecrafts circling Plum Island. We've been through a long week, and I'm not in the mood!*

Erin placed the package in the center of her desk and reached for her "unlicensed, unregistered, potential weapon of mass destruction," as she cynically liked to refer to her box cutter, to open the top envelope. It was obvious each of the manila envelopes had already been opened by the postal inspectors and resealed with their own tape.

THE POISON PLUM

So much for privacy and unreasonable searches and seizures, she thought as she methodically proceeded to remove sheaths of papers and documents and spread them across her desk.

Her jaw dropped as she saw the words: Confidential—For Director Use Only, Top Secret—Authorized Personnel Only, and the letterheads "CDC: Centers for Disease Control," "USDA: United States Department of Agriculture—Animal Disease Research Center, Plum Island." There were also photographs of people, buildings, apparent laboratories, and scientific equipment as well as pictures of objects taken under magnification, test results, laboratory analysis, etc.

"Holy cow!" Susan exclaimed, "What the hell is this? I'd better get the congressman in here pronto!"

"Mr. Congressman, this is Erin. I have something in my office that you need to see!"

"Can't it wait until after lunch, Miss Giblon?" he replied. "I'm pretty occupied at the moment."

"No, Mr. Congressman. I don't think you would want this to wait!"

Harry, recognizing the urgency in Erin's voice, immediately walked to her office. As he entered, she had begun opening the second sheath of papers and was spreading them across her desk.

"My goodness, Miss Giblon, what do you have? Did someone mail in the contents of their dumpster to protest government paperwork?"

"I don't understand what I'm looking at," she replied. "But no, I don't think it's someone's trash basket. Look at this…no return address and a New London postmark. Look at this stuff! CDC and USDA letterheads, lab reports, photos, and God only knows what else."

Harry pulled up a chair and began inspecting the papers Erin had spread across her desk. Erin could tell that within seconds the congressman's attention was totally focused on what lay before him as he rapidly scanned one document after another. Harry's ability to read and assimilate copious quantities of data was truly prodigious, and it seemed the more pertinent the material under review the more heightened his abilities to absorb and assimilate became. Erin remained silent while she opened the remaining envelopes for the congressman.

After several minutes had elapsed, Henry leaned back in his chair and then asked Erin, "And we don't know where this came from?"

"No. What you see is what we got."

"Do you have any idea what this is?"

"No, only that it has something to do with Plum Island, but I have no idea what. That stuff looks pretty technical to me!"

"What I've reviewed so far involves spirochetal research done at Plum and the CDC in Atlanta. This flies in the face of their continual denials of this type of research and experimentation. From whatever source, Miss Giblon, this could be the breakthrough we have been seeking. This appears to be a veritable treasure trove of classified information that no subpoena on earth could have ever dislodged. I certainly have no intention of looking a gift horse in the mouth, however. I am going to devote the rest of this day to reviewing these materials, and I want you to supervise the scanning to computer discs and the copying of everything you see before you. Also, take our digital camera and take pictures of what we have here, especially the packaging and that handwritten address and postmark."

"I understand, Mr. Congressman. I will begin immediately."

As Erin stood from her desk, the receptionist buzzed her intercom.

"Yes?" replied Erin.

"Miss Giblon? You have a call on line three," she heard through the speaker. "It's MacIntosh McAdams. He says it's urgent."

"OK, I'll take it," responded Erin as she pushed the button for line three to place the call on speaker phone. *Oops,* she thought. *What if he wants to talk about Friday night?*

"Good morning, Mr. McAdams. I hope you don't mind if I have you on the speaker phone. The congressman is here with me."

There, she thought, *that should provide me with some protection. Mac won't say anything.*

"Good morning, Mr. Congressman and Miss Giblon. I have something I think you should see."

"And what might that be, Mr. McAdams?" responded Erin.

"Oh, I don't know," he said. "I haven't completed my mail-order microbiology degree yet, but it looks like the Dead Sea Scrolls wrapped around the Holy Grail with a map of the location of the Lost Ark of the Covenant thrown in for good measure!"

"Did you by chance receive a rather bulky package in the morning mail?" asked Erin.

"Yeah, you could say that."

"Mr. McAdams, this is Congressman McDonald. We very much appreciate your call. I need to ask a favor of you."

"Name it."

"We need to ascertain if its Siamese twin is here with us. Would it be possible for you to have your staff scan each page and e-mail it to our office?"

"Yeah, but it will take a while. There must be hundreds of pages and photos here."

"Here too. We understand the inconvenience, but we need to make absolutely certain we have every single bit of information to compare to what we have received."

"I understand, and no problem on this end."

"We shall be eternally grateful, Mr. McAdams. And regrettably, I'm afraid, I need to ask an even bigger favor of you."

"Yes, Mr. Congressman?"

"Obviously, what you have before you is common fodder for enough editorial material to last until the next leap year. Until we know exactly what we have and can ascertain with a logical assurance it's authenticity, I am asking you to sheath your pen until we know where we stand. A very cursory review of these materials is sufficient for me to realize that even with my extensive medical training, I am unqualified to interpret and evaluate conclusively what I have already seen. What we will need is some third-party help we can trust, including, but not limited to, a microbiologist, an epidemiologist, a virologist, and an expert in laboratory analysis evaluation. That may be just for starters. Identifying the photographs may take an historian or two or at least a field day with the Bettman Archives and Google Images. And, finally, unless yours has a return address, we don't know the source. Does it, Mr. McAdams?"

"No, but it does have a New London postmark."

"Same here. We must be careful. It's possible this is a cleverly designed ploy by our enemies to attempt to throw us off course. I doubt that, considering the voluminous quantity of what we have, but we must never underestimate the creativity and deviousness of our friends at the CIA and FBI."

"Agreed. No copy will issue forth from my pen until we have a handle on this thing. I trust you will keep me advised of your research, and I'll reciprocate with anything we turn up on this end. But frankly, I'm chomping at the bit to splatter this story across the front page and turn it loose on all the wire services. Even at my age, I do derive a considerable amount of satisfaction out of being able to say, 'I told you so.' I'll be sure to send Simon Snodgrass of *The Times* and Lemke of *The Post* a sufficiently lubricated copy of my first column with instructions to insert where appropriate."

Ah, thought Erin, *Mac is Mac, 24/7. That brain and acerbic wit will never stop. But isn't that the charm of MacIntosh McAdams? In a world of boys playing at being men with namby-pamby personalities and directionless careers, lives, and marriages, it's refreshing to meet a true constant with no surprises. What you see is what you get when Mac is involved. Perhaps somewhere out there in this great world there exists a younger version, a veritable clone, if you will, that I could have for my very own.*"

Harry and Erin sat quietly for a few moments after Mac had left the line. Both were thinking of the enormous implications of the materials they now had in their possession. Erin knew her ability to assist the congressman in unraveling the legacy of this Pandora's Box was quite limited indeed. Short of searching for the qualified specialists Harry felt would be required, she simply had no idea how she could help. And besides, the last time she had a bright idea of how to help Harry…well, that didn't turn out so good. She wondered constantly when she would have an opportunity to tell the congressman at least some of the story of her wild Friday night escapade. It seemed each time an opportune moment was about to arrive, something happened which precluded any attempt at disclosure. With all the government's big guns brought to bear against Dr. Klinner, there would be nothing the congressman could do to secure his release or even relocation to another facility away from Gitmo hell. He is probably doomed anyway, so the location of his incarceration is moot at this point. But Erin still had an obligation and a responsibility to tell Harry, and she knew revelation time couldn't and shouldn't wait much longer.

Why, oh why, did I have to be so impetuous, she thought. *If ever I can get this behind me…* "Once burned, twice shy," *as someone once said! Good advice. Next time I'll listen!*

"Miss Giblon, before we begin the arduous process of seeking professional assistance with these materials, I am going to dedicate the majority of the rest of this day to reviewing what we have to the best of my ability. At the very least, I should be able to establish, with some degree of accuracy, the chronology of these documents because many predate the establishment of the facility at Plum, which was 1954. I spotted some papers dated in the mid-and late-1930s. What that is all about and its relevance to Plum Island is indeed a mystery. But every mystery has its beginning, and, for us, the beginning of this mystery is now. Please have all of my calls routed to your desk, and use your personal judgment in determining if I need to be interrupted."

"Yes, Mr. Congressman, I will. Can you think of anything else I might do to be of assistance other than the scanning, copying, and photos you wanted? I feel so helpless and unproductive at this time."

"No...no, Miss Giblon. I cannot. For the time being, this challenge has fallen squarely in my lap. But please be available if my research should uncover areas where you may be able to assist. Depending on what I am able to interpret and comprehend, I would like to discuss with you what approach we should take. Hopefully earlier, but considering the scope and bulk of those materials, I'm thinking around four or five o'clock."

"No problem, Mr. Congressman. I'll be here as long as you need me."

With that, Harry stood to return to his office where he would await the delivery of the documents after each had been scanned and copied.

Erin couldn't help but notice how grim Harry's facial expression appeared as he moved away from her desk. To her, it appeared that Harry had aged several years in only a little over a week. It seemed that any remaining vestige of happiness had been drained completely from his soul.

Erin called in two other staffers to help, and they rapidly began the process of duplication of the documents. Within only a few minutes, Erin delivered about twenty-five papers to the congressman, and it was obvious he was eager to begin his research.

By noon, all photographs had been taken, and the laborious process of scanning and copying had been completed. Not taking any chances, Erin made several copies of the CD where the images from the digital photos and scanned copies had been stored. Also, around noon, the first of many e-mails began arriving from the office of MacIntosh McAdams. Erin and the staff began reviewing and comparing the e-mail images with the documents they had received. After a cursory review of perhaps fifty pages, Erin thought that it certainly didn't appear they would be seeing any surprises. Whatever they had received, identical information had been received by Mac. She would bet on it.

Who else is seeing these documents? Erin wondered. *Are we the only recipients? Maybe so, maybe not. But one thing is for certain...if someone had an ax to grind with the government for its bio-warfare programs, where else would that kind of information be sent? Certainly not to Homeland Security, FBI, or the CIA. Anyone with access to that kind of classified, top-secret information would not, under any circumstances, entertain any illusions about those agencies. It would be understood from the get-go that they were part of the problem, not the solution. Nope, the mole that purloined those papers selectively chose the only two avowed enemies of the work being done at Plum Island and the other bio-labs. By sharing that information, the sender obviously hoped to inflict as much damage or revenge as possible. I wonder if we will ever know who our mysterious source and benefactor is.*

Erin had just finished a late, and light, low-carb lunch when a call came in for her from Mac.

"Miss Giblon, good afternoon. This is MacIntosh McAdams."

"Yes, Mr. McAdams. Thank you for the e-mails. We have received several, and so far they correlate exactly with what we received in the package."

"Good! I wanted to make sure they were coming through OK. I have an inherent distrust of electronic gizmos and the black hole of cyberspace. It will take several more hours, but by the end of this day, you should have copies of everything we received on this end."

"Wonderful! Thank you!"

"I've got something else you might be able to use...I think you will find this very interesting!"

Interesting? thought Erin, *If Mac thinks it is interesting, it must be right up there with a tsunami swallowing Seattle!*

"You have my undivided attention, Mr. McAdams...what do you have?"

"Well, while I was looking through the photographs, unable to interpret the printed material because my mail-order microbiology degree is still lost in the mail, I spotted a photograph that caused an alcohol-soaked neuron to begin to twitch. Just something about it rang a distant bell and, on a hunch, I checked out a column I had written back in the Clinton years. You don't know how much satisfaction it provides me, Miss Giblon, to be able to say 'back in the Clinton years.' I thought his presence and plague on this nation and the office of the presidency would never end. But Miss Giblon, it finally did, and if I have learned

THE POISON PLUM

anything as a result of having a lot of birthdays and keeping my eyes open, it's that everything eventually goes full circle if you wait long enough.

"Anyway, I'm drifting here. Back to the photograph. It was included in the aforementioned column I wrote about Clinton's public acknowledgement and apology to the nation for the government's syphilis experiments involving poor black sharecroppers in Tuskegee, Alabama, that began way back in the 1930s. It was a file photo taken of some of the doctors and a nurse involved in the syphilis experiments posing in front of a Tuskegee Institute building. The year was 1938. Do you have any idea what might be the relevance of that photo to Plum Island? That place didn't get cranked off until 1954!"

"Yes, Mr. McAdams…as a matter of fact I do. Our sources have revealed to us Colonel Gordon McClain had discovered that the accumulated research done on spirochetes at Tuskegee was sent to Plum Island for development into a biological weapon. Lyme disease is caused by a spirochete. It appears the syphilis spirochete has been genetically engineered by the government's scientists to resist treatment by antibiotics. You can't cure Lyme, but you can syphilis."

"Damn it to hell! Do those SOBs ever think about anything other than trying to figure out how to kill people? And with our tax dollars!"

"I'm beginning to wonder Mr. McAdams, if the materials we have received are going to establish a chain of continuity linking the research done at Tuskegee to the facility at Plum. I'll know more later today. The congressman is in isolation as we speak soaking up the information on those pages like a sponge. He might not understand one-hundred percent of everything he will see, but I'll bet you a double at the Dubliner, he will have a very strong opinion about the message contained in those pages before this day is over. He wants me to meet with him later this afternoon for us to plan our approach."

"So, Miss Giblon, if our packages contain irrefutable evidence the government callously experimented with helpless, innocent human beings in order to bring into existence a germ that has the potential to cripple and kill millions of Americans while simultaneously wrecking and bankrupting our health care system, your committee will have all of the ammunition it needs. And yours truly will have enough subject matter for an endless stream of earthshaking columns."

"I think that is a fair statement, Mr. McAdams."

"Well, I certainly have my homework assignment cut out for me. I'm going to research those Tuskegee years while my staff works on identifying those other photographs. The scientific mumbo jumbo, I'll leave to you guys to interpret."

"Mr. McAdams, I can't thank you enough for the work you are doing, and I know the congressman shares my sentiments. Together we shall persevere! Thank you!"

Erin was up to her elbows comparing images she could access on Internet sites with the photographs they had received when Harry buzzed her to join him in his office. A quick glance at her watch caused her to wonder where the afternoon had gone. It was already 5:30. Erin thought the congressman looked very, very tired as she entered his office. If anything, the look of grim resolve that seemed a permanent fixture of his face these days was even more intense than ever.

"Have a seat Miss Giblon. The stack of papers and photographs you see on my desk reveal a hideous, diabolical plot against mankind above and beyond the most evil schemes ever foisted by any tyrants and megalomaniacs that have ever walked the face of this earth. To my mind, there is no question regarding their authenticity. The only question, Miss Giblon, is the motivation of the person or persons responsible for collecting those documents and subsequently forwarding them to our office. And that question may forever remain unanswered.

"The documents encompass a time frame beginning in 1932 and culminating in 1975. One must not assume however that the story that they tell ends in 1975…quite the contrary. Their legacy continues and grows unabated until this very day. We have documents from the Public Health Service, the Centers for Disease Control, the USDA's Animal Disease Research Center at Plum Island, the Army's germ warfare facility at Ft. Detrick, Maryland, the National Institute of Health, the Air War College at Maxwell Air Force Base in Alabama, the World Health Organization of the U.N., the CIA, FBI, Pentagon, and others. Whatever Colonel McClain's sources were, they were right on target. We have an unbroken link of spirochetal research that began at the Tuskegee Institute in 1932 and continued until the U.S. government was forced, through public disclosure, to close that experiment down in 1972. The documents clearly reveal the flow of that research to Plum Island after that facility opened in 1954 and the subsequent development of a genetically engineered spirochete, which we now know is the germ responsible for Lyme disease and the ensuing epidemic."

Harry paused for a moment as he bowed his head and stared at the floor. Erin thought she had never seen another human being appear so sad and dejected. The burden of this disclosure was simply too much for one person to bear, especially if that one person was Congressman Harry McDonald, who felt his shoulders alone were responsible for its carriage.

Erin was next to break the silence, "So we have everything we need for the committee investigation to go forward. Pending authentication of those documents of course."

"Yes, it would appear so. If we wanted to limit our investigation to the role of Plum in the development of the Lyme germ, that is."

"What do you mean, limit our investigation?"

"Just that. Those documents are not limited to Lyme disease."

"There's more?"

"That would be an understatement. I'm afraid Lyme is just the tip of the iceberg."

"And?"

"HIV-AIDS."

"A genetically engineered virus?"

"I'm afraid so. And not just engineered to resist treatment and mutate when threatened, but also engineered to be more virulent among black and Hispanic populations. Race specificity…"

"That would explain why infection rates among those groups are so dramatically higher than the population at large!"

"And also reveal the grand design of its engineers."

"A grand design?"

"Yes, the ultimate decimation of the black races of Africa so that the survivors of the New World Order elite will have unlimited access to the incredibly rich and bountiful resources of the entire continent of Africa. With current infection rates of over 30 percent in some areas, that transition may be sooner than later."

"My God…and we were told that the AIDS virus was some previously undiscovered virus that had been hidden away in the deepest jungles of Africa until recently being spread to humans by monkeys."

"Yes…two-legged monkeys in the employ of the World Health Organization. Do you remember when the WHO announced their intentions to once and for all eradicate smallpox from the planet in a massive humanitarian inoculation program?"

"No."

"I guess that was a little before your time, Miss Giblon. The year was 1965. The World Health Organization, operating under UN auspices, of course, took enormous quantities of the smallpox vaccine to Africa and began inoculation of the indigenous populations. All in the name of eliminating the scourge of smallpox, you understand."

"I don't understand the connection between smallpox and AIDS."

"It's all there in these documents, Miss Giblon. The smallpox vaccine was laced with the AIDS virus. At least the recipients didn't have to worry about succumbing to smallpox!"

"I guess not! They were too dead from AIDS to care! But Mr. Congressman, if the ultimate objective is control of Africa's natural resources sans the indigenous black population of course, why are Hispanics targeted as well?"

"I don't know…there was some reference in those lab notes indicating attempts at using the skin melanin as a synergist for the virus's replication."

"Incredible!"

"We will still require the expertise of microbiologists, epidemiologists, virologists, and others to fully extract the secrets buried in those pages before we can take it to the full committee."

"Are you going to limit the scope of the committee's investigation?"

"No. When I made the announcement at the New London news conference, I stated that the committee would conduct an in-depth investigation into the activities and programs of the government's laboratory on Plum Island. And that, Miss Giblon, is precisely what we are going to do. Just because our efforts to clear all the snakes off the property revealed more than one under that first rock we lifted, doesn't mean we stop now. We have no choice. Our mandate is clear."

Erin sat quietly as the full impact of the congressman's words soaked into her consciousness, indeed into her very soul. Erin found herself suddenly wishing she could somehow be instantaneously transported to some distant location, far away from the surreal insanity of this world.

"Miss Giblon?" Erin heard the words but they sounded very distant… "Miss Giblon? Are you still with us?"

"Oh…yes…I'm sorry, Mr. Congressman. I guess this is a lot of very bad news to absorb in one fell swoop."

"I suppose so, Miss Giblon. I feel pretty overwhelmed myself."

"Well, I have a bit of news to further complete the mosaic, Mr. Congressman. MacIntosh McAdams has been sending over e-mails that are confirming the papers and pictures he received are identical to what we have."

"I expected as much."

"And he has been able to positively identify one of the older photographs. It is from 1938 and is a picture of doctors and a nurse involved in the Tuskegee syphilis experiments. They are posing in front of a Tuskegee Institute building, complete with Alabama pine trees and a 1938 vintage automobile at the side of the picture. He had used it in a column he wrote about Clinton's apology to the nation for the government conducting the experiments on those helpless black people."

"I saw that picture and wondered if it was taken in the South. One more piece of the puzzle."

It's now or never, thought Erin. *I've got to tell him about Friday night. Granted, a severely truncated version to be sure, but I've got to get it out!*

"Mr. Congressman, I have some additional information I've wanted to share, but, with everything that has been going on in this office, there never seemed to be an opportune time."

"What is it Miss Giblon?"

"It may be nothing…but on the other hand it may be a valuable clue regarding the whereabouts of Dr. Glen Klinner."

Harry sat erect as his eyes fixed intently on Erin's face.

"Last Friday night, I did something totally out of character for me. I attended one of Washington's premier pubs on the off chance I might be able to engage some bureaucrat in conversation or overhear some comment that might provide a clue as to what the government did with those doctors after their arrests."

"You did what?"

"I know, Mr. Congressman…as I said, totally out of character for me. As it turned out, I pretended to be a graduate law student from Georgetown and met several men from the Justice Department."

"I hope your out-of-character experiences do not recur, Miss Giblon. Do you understand the potential danger you placed yourself and our committee investigation in?"

"Yes, Mr. Congressman, I do. The frustration we both experienced as a result of the government's intransigence temporarily overwhelmed me, I'm afraid. But maybe something beneficial came out of it."

"You met some Justice Department officials?"

"Yes, I did. And with a little gentle nudging on my part aided by the generous quantities of alcohol they were imbibing, the conversation got around to the current news headlines of the government's raids on those doctors' offices. I pretended to be enamored with law and the justice system and conveyed the impression that whatever fate befell the greedy, incompetent doctors was justly deserved. It was then that one of the men, perhaps more juiced and loquacious than the others, made the comment, 'Let's just hope they like Cuban cigars!'"

"Cuban cigars?"

"That's what he said. I dismissed the comment as meaningless prattle from an intoxicated man at first, but as I continued to think about what he said, I began to wonder...Cuba? Have they been taken to Cuba? The prison at Guantanamo Bay?"

"God in heaven, Miss Giblon! It all fits! The subsequent announcement that Dr. Klinner would be charged with conspiracy to commit terrorism against the United States and tried by a military tribunal under the provisions of the Patriot Act...at Guantanamo Bay! It all fits perfectly!

"My friend, Dr. Klinner, if he is still alive, is rotting away in that hell hole of a prison. If we could get the physicians that were released to talk, they would doubtless confirm their destination was some tropical location. I'm sorry you subjected yourself to that kind of risk, but I'm grateful for this bit of information. Do you remember the name of the official?"

"Yes, I do Mr. Congressman. It was Terence Watson."

"Terence Watson? He is one of the deputy directors that reports to the attorney general...certainly in a position to have that kind of information. This adds considerable validity to your interpretation of his remark. But sadly, Miss Giblon, knowing the location of Dr. Klinner and being able to do anything to effect his release, unfortunately, are two very different things. We can only hope the committee investigation will proceed more expeditiously than the military tribunal, and a groundswell of public opinion will force his release!"

"I certainly concur, Mr. Congressman!"

Wow, thought Erin as she exited the Congressman's office, *I'm glad that's behind me. I just hope the myriad of omitted details don't rematerialize someday to bite me in the butt!*

More Bugs

As Susan prepared for her return to the facility that Tuesday morning, she paused to reflect on what a blessing her sister's support and assistance had been throughout this incredible ordeal. Cathy had left for her own place after spending the day with Toby and would return this morning to allow Susan to get back to work. She never complained, always seemed to anticipate what might be needed next, and never hesitated to offer even more assistance if she thought it necessary.

Earning crowns in heaven, thought Susan, *isn't that what the believers say about those laboring to help the needy? Cathy has a point, and I know she's right. I was too busy with school activities and boys in high school and college to take time out for church activities…and then it was a marriage that turned sour and a son to raise. I didn't have any time for a God, if there is one, but this all sure looks like a wake-up call to me. Yup, I've decided…Get out of that job, relocate to I don't know where, but find the time to get in that Sunday school class with Cathy, and see what that's all about. When I get half a chance, I'll tell her that's what I'm going to do.*

Right on time, Cathy walked into their room with a big smile, hugged Susan, and proceeded to join Toby on the bed.

"What are my favorite sister and nephew up to this fine morning? How's my sweetie? Are you feeling better, Toby? It's a beautiful day outside!"

"Will you take me outside, Aunt Cathy, while Mommy is at work? Can we go home today? I don't like being in the hospital."

"Well, sweetie, we can't go home until Dr. Butler tells us it's OK, but maybe tomorrow we can."

"Can I go outside?"

"I don't know, sweetie, but I'll ask the nurse if it will be OK to sit out on the balcony for awhile. Is that OK, Susan?"

THE POISON PLUM

"If the nurses approve...Toby could use some sun. Sounds like a good idea. Cathy, Toby... I've got to scoot...can't take a chance on being late. All eyes are upon me now. Give Mommy a hug and a kiss, Toby, and I'll see you both this afternoon."

Susan then hugged Cathy as she was leaving and thanked her again for coming in.

For Susan, the difference in her stress level compared to yesterday was astronomical. The day at work flew by quickly as she continued to absorb herself in the viral research done by Eliot Steadman, and there was no sign of or contact with either Herschel Gallagher or Director Stephens, which was truly a blessing. As far as Susan was concerned, she didn't care if flesh-eating bacteria ate their faces off as long as they left her alone. Susan was also grateful for the additional courses she had taken in virology to complete her PhD in microbiology for some of the information she was encountering was extremely intriguing, to say the least.

But Susan had not a clue how she could possibly smuggle anything larger than a pinhead out of the facility at the end of the work day. Security was tight, tight, tight, with cameras watching their every move, computers blocked to prevent file sharing with other computers on the outside and body scans performed on each employee as they entered or exited the facility. But Susan was watching, learning, and retaining information with a voracious appetite to discover some path or clue that would lead to the smoking gun of intent to engineer germs to kill people. In her review of Eliot's work, Susan had frequently encountered links and references to recombinant engineering. Susan had only a cursory knowledge of that technology, but she clearly understood it could be used as a double-edged sword. A virus could be either engineered to become even more lethal to its host or it could be engineered to be rendered harmless. Enormous implications existed for either procedure. Harmless viruses properly used could assist in transporting life-saving therapies to diseased tissues...cancer for example. On the other hand, a virus engineered through recombinant technology could be designed to be an extremely lethal, durable, and untreatable killing machine.

Hmmm, thought Susan, *AIDS, Ebola, Marburg, Avian Flu, West Nile? Who knows? This place has got to be the bug capital of the world! I wish the luck of the draw had placed me at an employee's work station that was dedicated to spirochetal research, but maybe that would be too much to ask for. I'll play my cards as they have* been dealt and continue looking for something, anything, I can use. And just exactly how am I going to use this deep, dark secret if and when I find it?

Susan had not thought that far ahead, but now, with the possibility of an actual discovery looming, she realized she needed to devote more than just a passing thought to the concept.

That newspaper guy in Washington? MacIntosh McAdams? How do I know he could be trusted? What are his loyalties? Those guys can talk out of both sides of their mouths or write with either end of the pencil. And what about the congressman? Cathy likes him and so do the members of her church. Does that mean anything? I remember how popular that Baker guy and his wife that overdosed on Mary Kay were with their TV evangelism programs before the crap hit the fan. And then there was that Swaggart guy from Louisiana that apparently did too much of the wrong kind of sightseeing in New Orleans before he fell like a rock. And besides, aren't politicians expected to lie and prevaricate at every twist and turn? I'm playing with the big boys here, and, if I'm going to stick my neck in a noose, I've got to know who to trust. Worry about all that another day, Susan.... You don't have a thing to use yet and you may never.

Returning after work to the hospital, Susan was relieved and delighted to see Toby sitting up and watching cartoons on the television. Cathy was absorbed in a novel she had purchased, and Susan thought that Toby looked better than he had in quite some time.

"Hi guys! What's up? Have you missed me?"

"Mommy! Aunt Cathy took me out on the balcony, but we had to use a wheel chair. I didn't mind, it was fun!"

So that's it, thought Susan. *Toby looks better because he got some sun on his face. That's OK—any improvement is a plus.*

"Sweetie, that's wonderful. Have you been a good little boy for Aunt Cathy?"

"Yes, Mommy."

"So what about it, Sis? Is our trooper here telling the truth?"

"You betcha...we've had a good time."

"And how are we feeling today?"

"Well, still some diarrhea off and on, still a little wobbly trying to walk, eyes and head hurting, burning urination, feet stinging, fatigue, and a nap in the afternoon. Other than that, Mrs. Lincoln, how did you enjoy the play?"

Susan giggled and hugged Cathy, wishing there were some other way besides words she could express her love for Susan and Toby. It was moments like this that she wanted to pull the both of them close to her and embrace them for a long, long time. For the first time, Susan felt she was beginning to see the light at the end of the tunnel, and at least a major part of this ordeal would soon be past.

"Has Dr. Butler been by today?" Susan asked.

"Not yet, but his nurse called and asked if you were going to be here after seven o'clock. She said Dr. Butler would be making his rounds, and he wanted to talk to you."

"Do you have any idea what about? Test results or anything?"

"She didn't say, but I told her that you would be here."

Susan glanced at her watch while silently wondering what could be on his mind. She couldn't think of any test results outstanding other than the spinal fluid cultures, but maybe something had turned up. Susan was a bit uneasy but managed to continue smiling until Dr. Butler, obviously tired, arrived about 8:30.

After perfunctory greetings and a quick examination of Toby and review of his chart, Dr. Butler asked Susan if they could go down to the cafeteria to talk for a few minutes. His justification was his need for a hot cup of coffee.

Susan wondered how many cups the man had already had today as they found a table for two and sat down. He looked like he was running on caffeine and little else. But Susan knew the coffee was secondary….he had something to say to her that he didn't want Toby to hear. She took a deep breath and told herself to be calm as she waited for him to begin.

"Susan, I asked you to come to the cafeteria so we could talk privately. I have some good news and some, well, not so good news."

Susan's heart sank, and she sat quietly, her eyes scanning Dr. Butler's face. Finally, after a long pause, she managed to respond with a reply which belied her fear.

"Well, we should start with the former first because goodness knows I've had enough of the latter!"

"I understand. The good news is I think Toby is well enough to go home tomorrow. He will still need to come in daily for his infusion, but that can be done on an outpatient basis. I will continue the prescription for the antibiotic for the full prescribed course of twenty-eight days."

"That is good news, Dr. Butler. Toby was asking just this morning when we could go home."

"Fine...and now for the not so good news. Toby has been improving clinically, albeit slowly, and I think he will continue to improve as the treatments continue."

"So what is the not so good news? This all sounds wonderful to me!"

"It's difficult to explain, Susan, but I'll try. Part of Toby is getting better on the antibiotic, but part of Toby is not. I know that doesn't make any sense, but bear with me. It would be like, and this is a greatly simplified example, you came in with a broken bone and appendicitis. I could set the bone, and it would be on the road to healing, but if I didn't also treat the appendicitis, you would still be a sick puppy. You could even die."

Susan felt her heart leap in her chest.

"My God, Dr. Butler. What are you telling me? That Toby is going to die?"

"No, Susan...that is not what I'm saying. What I'm saying is that I don't think Toby's problems are solely attributable to Lyme disease."

"Good grief! Isn't that enough of a challenge for an eight-year-old to handle?"

"You and I would agree, but our vector friend the tick obviously can have other ambitions."

"Other ambitions?"

"Susan, Toby has an enlarged spleen, liver function abnormalities, night sweats, and brown urine. These symptoms, other than the liver function problems, are not typical Lyme disease symptoms."

"What then, for God's sake, leukemia?"

"No, Susan, they are suggestive of a frequent co-infection of babesiosis. So frequent in fact that the literature describes co-infection rates of over 60 percent in Lyme patients. It seems our vector friend can be an enormous reservoir for a veritable plethora of nasty critters. In addition to Babesia, he can convey Ehrlichia, tick paralysis, Rocky Mountain spotted fever, Bartonella henselae, and God only knows what else. But I'm preaching to the choir. You already know this stuff. You have a PhD in microbiology, don't you?"

"Yes, but I don't know diddly about Babesia. It's an intracellular parasite, isn't it? Like Malaria?"

"Yes."

"So what's the problem? Run the test and treat it, if you suspect that's the problem."

"Here's the problem, Susan. There are over fifty variants of Babesia known. The tests currently used can only identify three of these variants. We ran those tests on Toby, and they came back negative. Because of his symptomatology, we have a potential clinical diagnosis of Babesia with no confirmatory test result."

"So why don't you just treat it empirically if you think that's what it is?"

"Because I don't know how, Susan. I hate to be so blunt, but I don't know any other way to put it. Great controversy exists in the literature regarding the most efficacious treatment protocol for Babesia. Outcomes with the available modalities have been inconsistent, and at times, have had very negative results. In all honesty, I'm just not qualified to venture into those waters. If we had a tried-and-true drug to go after that critter, then fine. But we don't. The existing anti-protozoals leave much to be desired, and in the interest of Toby's health, you need the advice and guidance of an expert specialist with plenty of hands-on experience, not just for presumed Babesia but the Lyme germ as well."

"So what do I do? Look in the Yellow Pages for Lyme disease doctors with a listed sub-specialty of Babesia?"

Susan's head was reeling by this time. Her earlier feelings of optimism about her job security at Plum and the eventual outcome of Toby's treatments began to pale in significance.

So what if I keep my job, and Toby's Lyme disease is conquered, but he dies anyway of a co-infection! she thought. *Why don't I just run up to the roof and jump off on my head?*

"Susan, I promised I would make some calls for you in an attempt to find a specialist to continue Toby's treatments. And as you recall, the government's vendetta against Lyme disease doctors resulted in the incarceration and subsequent release of all but one of the most qualified physicians in the Northeast."

"Great! If they have been released, which one do you recommend?"

"That's just it, Susan. The doctors had barely time to wipe the dust off their desks before the medical review boards in all the states involved suspended their licenses pending a review for 'over-treatment of Lyme disease.' Yes, I know it's a travesty, but that's what happened."

"I'll go somewhere else. I'll take Toby out of the Northeast for treatment."

"Unfortunately, the farther away from ground zero one travels, the lesser the incidence of Lyme and, consequently, the fewer trained practitioners to treat what Lyme there is. Toby needs and deserves the best, Susan, not some quack or an out-of-his-league chiropractor that thinks he can throw herbal preparations at it."

"You mentioned you had made some calls."

"Yes, but I don't think you are going to like what we discovered."

"I'm sitting down."

"Well, way down in Atlanta there is a self-proclaimed guru that talks the talk. Only problem is, some of his patients have died as a result of a procedure called intracellular hyperthermia."

"I've read about that treatment. No way in hell is anyone going to do that to Toby! Over my dead body!"

"Well, equally distant and, curiously enough, right in your hometown of Birmingham, Alabama, we have a highly respected, extremely capable physician. He has devoted the bulk of his practice to the diagnosing and treatment of Lyme and its associated co-infections. From what we have learned, the man has an impeccable reputation and could aptly be described as a doctor's doctor. He has been treating Lyme for over twenty years. But talk about the irony of full circle! Here you and Toby are in New London, Connecticut."

"I'll go to Siberia if I have to, Dr. Butler. Toby comes first. How urgent is this decision? Do I have twenty-four hours to talk it over with Cathy?"

"I think so, Susan, but realize you need to proceed expeditiously."

As Susan made her way back to Toby's room that evening, her mind was busily attempting to conceptualize various strategies and scenarios which would enable Toby to return to Birmingham for treatment. Susan felt she really didn't have a choice—either get Toby to that doctor or watch him slowly die. To Susan, it was a no-brainer as to what must be done. The logistics, however, presented a very formidable obstacle. Certainly she would not under any circumstances be able to arrange for more time off. She could hear the dork Gallagher now.

"You want more time off to take your son to a specialist in Birmingham, Alabama? But you assured us as a condition of continuance of your employment that your son was rapidly on the road to recovery from an ordinary case of mononucleosis. Everything had been resolved you said, and you were eager to give 100 percent to your obligations here at the laboratory. No problem! We will comply with your request, Ms. Collins, and you may consider your personal time to be totally available effective immediately. Your services are no longer required at this facility."

No, thought Susan, *it's not going to come to that. I'll somehow arrange for Toby to be taken to Birmingham to see that doctor, and I'll continue being employee of the year at Plum. Those paychecks and the insurance coverage will keep right on coming. Sure, it will be tough. Toby will want me there, and I'll worry myself sick until I can see and hold him again.*

Cathy was on pins and needles waiting for Susan to return. She couldn't wait to hear what Dr. Butler had told her. Toby had received his "lights out" medication a few minutes ago, and mercifully he was already soundly asleep.

Good, Cathy thought, *now we can talk openly.*

When Susan reentered the room, Cathy read the expression on her face like an open book.

Oh, crap, she thought. *Whatever it is, it ain't good!*

"Sis, you don't look so hot! What's going on?"

"Oh, nothing much. Only that I have to figure out how to keep my job at the facility while simultaneously arranging for Toby to be treated by a specialist back home in Birmingham. No problem, no problem...no problem at all. I think we are conducting some research on cloning life forms at Plum, so I'll just volunteer to be a guinea pig. Assuming the experiment is a success my clone can take Toby to Birmingham. No problem!"

"You have to be kidding. You can't be serious!"

"About the cloning? Yeah. About Birmingham? Nope...I'm dead serious. Did I say dead? Scratch that. That word is *not* to be used...unless it's in the context of Gallagher and Stephens."

Wow, Sis is torqued about something, thought Cathy.

"Sit down, Sis. Toby is sound asleep. Let's talk. What did Butler say?"

"Butler is jumping ship."

"What?"

"Just that. After the antibiotics have been administered for the requisite twenty-eight days, he's bailing out."

"You mean he's not going to continue to be responsible for Toby's treatment?"

"You got it!"

"But why? That doesn't make any sense!"

"I can't blame him. Only those scheming bastards at Plum Island! He is pretty sure Toby has a serious co-infection he's not qualified to treat. He says it's over his head."

"What kind of co-infection?"

"It's called babesiosis. It's an intracellular parasite like Malaria. Gets in the red blood cells and causes them to burst open. Frequently fatal if untreated and sometimes fatal if treated!"

"Oh shit! That's just peachy! From the same tick that gave him Lyme?"

"Oh yeah, he was a generous SOB, always willing to share it seems."

"And there's no one qualified anywhere closer?"

"Not according to Dr. Butler. Those docs that were specialists in this area had their licenses yanked by the medical review boards as soon as they were released by the government."

"So the government is responsible for making Toby and millions of others sicker than dammit and is hell bent and determined to make sure everyone stays sick?"

"Sure seems that way, doesn't it?"

"What's the name of the specialist?"

"Hell, I don't know. I was so upset, I didn't even ask."

"Tomorrow night is our regular Wednesday night prayer meeting at the church. I'm going to try to make it after you get back here from the lab. I'll ask around. I think someone has already been talking about some of the Lymies making plans to go see a doctor in Birmingham they've heard about. I'll try to come up with a name."

"It's all a test, isn't it?"

"What do you mean, 'It's all a test?'"

"Isn't that what you Christians believe? It's how we endure and deal with the endless trials and tribulations we encounter here on planet Earth that qualifies us for higher service in heaven? It's all one great big test, isn't it?"

Feeding Frenzy

Since the Saturday afternoon announcement by Attorney General Budenz that all the doctors arrested in the raids would be released except Glen Klinner, the nation's media had saturated America's consciousness with endless reports and interpretations of the government's actions. The medium of television in particular provided the most lurid images possible of the ferry slaughter cleverly interspersed with images of Colonel Gordon McClain and Dr. Glen Klinner.

The carnage at the ferry needed no embellishment by the most ingenious and creative minds of the fourth estate, for it was, after all, what is was—an unmitigated human tragedy of the highest order. Likewise, the career of the great and illustrious military hero Colonel Gordon McClain stood proudly alone on its own merits. No spin doctors were required to twist or whitewash any potentially embarrassing or contradictory periods in McClain's history for there simply were none.

The innocent and defenseless Dr. Glen Klinner proved to be fair game, however, and every attempt was made to fabricate, distort, and embellish any and all information from his past. From the media's perspective, Dr. Klinner's sins against humanity to this point included membership in the National Rifle Association, a long-lasting friendship with America's most controversial Congressman, Harry McDonald, and (gasp) the discovery that Dr. Klinner had once attended meetings of the John Birch Society.

It was impossible to pick up a newspaper or supermarket tabloid that didn't devote considerable ink and paper to the latest developments and conjecture involving the massacre, McClain, and Klinner. Likewise, the coverage also dominated radio news reports, talk shows, television reporting, and late-night talk shows.

The government line had Dr. Klinner pursuing a vendetta against the government because of repeated investigations by the Medical Review and Licensing

Board of New York. It was speculated upon, amplified, examined, and disseminated as justification for using mind-altering drugs on Colonel McClain to incite him to violence against the "enemy"...the employees of the lab at Plum Island. The mind of the average American was being conditioned to accept the only true terrorist to be Dr. Klinner, who with cold, calculated, evil intent goaded the psychologically unbalanced war hero to strike against innocent civilians.

Doubtless, the media was grateful for these developments to feed upon. In the absence of yet another killer hurricane slamming into Miami, Tampa, Pensacola, or New Orleans, and with the latest charges of sexual misconduct against Michael Jackson having been resolved, if only temporarily, the nation's media was like a gigantic carnivorous buzzard in need of more road kill. That road kill was generously offered up by a government intent on obfuscation and diversion of attention from its top-secret biological research laboratory at Plum Island. Dr. Klinner would be the required sacrificial lamb to satisfy the appetite for vindication being engendered by the media's relentless coverage. Someone has to be guilty for such a heinous crime against America, and it was simply unthinkable for that blame to be levied against one of America's greatest heroes of modern times, Colonel Gordon McClain.

Relatively obscure Dr. Glen Klinner would fill the bill and would be adjudged guilty, guilty, guilty, as a result of the massive media blitz, continuing unabated. To the mind of the average American, now approaching lynch mob mentality, it would be of little concern that Dr. Klinner would be denied competent legal representation in the kangaroo court of the military tribunal. Find a sturdy tree and sufficient rope...let's get on with the hanging. Justice must be done.

Indeed, the sophistry, calumny, misrepresentation, obfuscation, and outright deceit ingeniously employed by the major media would have put to shame the cleverest schemes of Hitler's minister of propaganda, Joseph Goebbels.

Simultaneous to the media's efforts to convict the innocent, documentaries and special reports began appearing, extolling the good work being done down through the years by the dedicated scientists and employees at Plum Island. Emphasis was given to the role of identifying potential disease threats to the nation's livestock and to the successful eradication or amelioration of those diseases. Images of herds of healthy cattle and smiling mothers pouring milk for their cherub-cheeked children filled the airwaves. A new director of the facility (in title only) was named, and she immediately began hosting news conferences and good will tours throughout college campuses and civic groups. Middle-aged, soft-spoken, and always conservatively dressed, she gave the appearance of an upper-middle-class housewife devoted to family and generously giving her time to charitable efforts and the local Girl Scout troops.

No one in their right mind could possibly charge or suggest that such a person could be in any way whatsoever involved in a plot or program to use germ warfare against innocent civilians. Such an assumption was ludicrous and preposterous. Equally preposterous would be the assumption that this public relations figurehead would have the slightest idea of the inner workings of the Plum Island facility. She was hired, trained, and coached to convey an image of motherhood and apple pie, and that, with the support of the majority of the nation's subordinated and prostituted media, is exactly what she did.

Like a wolf in sheep's clothing, the image of Plum Island was camouflaged to the point that the hearts and minds of America began to embrace with warm fuzzy sentiments the stated objectives of the facility and its new director with the all-American name of Martha Johnson. The sooner the memory of the ferry tragedy and final justice for the evil and manipulative Dr. Glen Klinner could be relegated to the trash bin of history, the happier we would all be. Lemke of *The Post* opined that the individual states should be stripped of the power to license and regulate doctors. It should be a function of the federal government, and all doctors should be licensed, regulated, and controlled by a new bureaucracy entitled the United States Medical and Professional Health Review Board. Had this highly efficient agency been in existence, according to Lemke, the loose cannon, Dr. Klinner, would have long ago been identified, his license revoked, and this entire horrific event would have been averted.

Snodgrass of *The Times*, in his infinite wisdom, proposed all doctors be bound by federal regulations, promulgated by the FDA, allowing the treatment of patients only in accordance with strict federal guidelines and established protocol. Any deviation from established regulations would result in professional review and possible censure. Patients and their caregivers would be provided with printed copies of the regulations applicable to their particular afflictions, and the regulations would be thoroughly explained to them along with their legal rights to pursue a doctor for noncompliance.

MacIntosh McAdams angrily consumed more Scotch than usual and gritted his teeth while staring at the pen he pledged to keep sheathed until given the go-ahead by Congressman McDonald.

"Now I know how General Patton must have felt when Eisenhower denied his tanks the gasoline to take Berlin. Here I sit on the brink of the biggest story of my journalistic career, and all I can do is hurry up and wait!"

Mac fully realized the impact his columns and the concurrent committee investigations would have when fueled with the irrefutable disclosures they had been provided. His long-harbored desire to watch the imbeciles Lemke and Snodgrass twist and turn in the fury of the public's repudiation and scorn was now within reach, and he knew it.

It won't be much longer now, thought Mac. *I've got at least twenty more columns cooking that I can't wait to get into print. The FBI, CIA, Justice, FDA, CDC, and all the rest are in my sights! It's time those lying vermin get their heads handed to them on a platter…slimy Snodgrass and lurid Lemke, too. Enjoy today because very soon, I'll be coming after you!*

I can hardly contain myself! This is worse than being a kid and waiting for Christmas! This damn country and its gullible inhabitants need a catharsis, and I'm just the one to give it to them. A wake-up call…the cold, hard light of day to dispel the fairy tales, pixie dust and accumulated myths spun by the government and its handmaiden media. Soon now, very soon…

Calling in Markers

Erin Giblon welcomed the opportunity to leave the office at the relatively early hour of 7 PM. She needed to get in a quick workout at the gym coupled with the therapy of a three or four mile run. A short shopping trip to the supermarket near her townhouse was also in order before crashing for some much needed rest of body and mind. Tomorrow would begin the process of attempting to ferret out qualified experts capable and willing to interpret, evaluate, and render opinions, eventually before the congressional hearings, of the documents which had been received at the congressman's office.

Erin was growing increasingly concerned about the congressman because of the incredible level of stress he was subjected to. It was written vividly across Harry's face and recognizable to even the most casual observer. She only wished there was some way she could contribute more and lighten the burden Harry was laboring under. Erin recognized only Harry would have the knowledge of which medical specialists in particular would be required to assess the documents and after having done so, provide the necessary acumen to sort out and link together the chronology. Proof of cause and effect would be required and more importantly, proof of intent. It must be established beyond a reasonable doubt that the government's objective in germ research was not simply identification and etiology but creation and development of pathogens for use as biological weapons. For without that thread of continuity, the committee investigations would be futile.

Another short night of sleep and rest passed all too quickly for Erin, and by seven, she had returned to the office at her normal time of arrival. It was also normal that she would arrive before any of the staffers. She appreciated the moments of quiet time to review the morning newspapers, the latest CNN headlines, and also the financial markets. What was not normal on this Tuesday morning was the presence of the congressman already surrounded by computer printouts and notes and obviously totally engaged in whatever he was doing with his computer.

"Well good morning, Miss Giblon. How are you?"

"I'm fine Mr. Congressman, but more importantly, how are you? Have you decided sleep and rest are unnecessary inconveniences?"

"Too much to do, Miss Giblon. Time is of the essence if we have any chance to save Dr. Klinner's life. The modus operandi of military tribunals is swift application of justice. Unfortunately, history reveals that true justice is frequently subordinated to the motives of the government in charge of the tribunals. And not infrequently, a careful review of history also reveals that tribunals are a convenient way to remove any potential opposition to a government and its frequently unpalatable agendas.

"In these circumstances, Miss Giblon, the public's thirst for speedy justice would be quickly satiated by a guilty verdict and hasty execution of Dr. Klinner. Never mind that true justice would never be served at all.

"By bringing a swift conclusion to the debate over who was responsible for the ferry massacre, attention can be diverted away from Plum Island, and America can once again go back to sleep."

"How much time do you think we've got?"

"Hard to tell. What we need are some unexpected delays."

"Delays, Mr. Congressman?"

"Yes…We need someone to toss a wrench in the gears. I've got a few ideas we can try, but I don't know if they will work. Anything to slow that tribunal process down."

"What do you have in mind? And what can I do to help?"

"For starters, I have some friendly contacts among some senators in the Senate Judiciary Committee. Or at least they seem friendly. We'll soon find out. I helped get some co-sponsors in the House once for companion legislation that came out of that committee. And believe it or not, a few of those senators actually seem to be strict constitutionalists. I'll make some calls to remind them habeas corpus is being suspended, and a United States citizen is being tried for treason before a military tribunal…not Osama Bin Laden, but a citizen of this republic! Perhaps they could prepare a letter to the president with several co-signers asking him to intervene, or better yet, sponsor a Senate resolution with the same objective."

"Perhaps, Mr. Congressman, someone should remind the president that he took an oath to defend and protect the Constitution."

"I doubt if he has ever read it! Except, of course, for the few sentences he was required to memorize for a grade school civics or American history class. Most politicians, Miss Giblon, and the current president is no exception, regard the Constitution as a barbaric relic fit only for a museum exhibit—long ago hopelessly outdated and totally unsuitable for modern government. True, lip service is occasionally given to the Constitution and the Bill of Rights, but those documents today are regarded as stumbling blocks and obstacles to the methods required today for effective governance."

"In other words, Mr. Congressman, impediments to the mischief of men."

"You got it! Have you ever wondered, Miss Giblon, why our nation with its system of checks and balances handed down to us by the founding fathers is almost always referred to as a democracy when that word is not to be found anywhere in the Declaration of Independence, the Constitution, the Bill of Rights, or in any of the constitutions of any of the states that comprise this union? It's because the framers of those documents knew full well the perils of an unbridled democracy and their intention was to establish a republic, *not* a democracy. As a consequence, the word republic *is* found in those documents, as, of course, it should be, and it means, literally, rule by law—the Constitution. And democracy? The literal interpretation is rule by the people. The popular whim...lynch-mob mentality, sway the masses, ignore the rulebook, situation ethics, do whatever is popular or expedient at the moment!"

"I remember reading that Benjamin Franklin, upon leaving the Constitutional Convention, was asked by a lady on the street, 'What form of government have you given us?' And his reply was, 'A republic, madam...if you can keep it!'"

"Yes, Miss Giblon! Those words spoken well over 200 years ago were never of more significance than right now! If one needs more convincing evidence, all one has to do is recite our Pledge of Allegiance *and pay attention to the words*!

"'I pledge allegiance to the flag of the United States of America and to the...*republic*... for which it stands!'

"OK, end of history lesson. You doubtless already know all of that or you wouldn't be working here.

"Anyway, I have some contacts at the hierarchy of the American Bar Association I can call upon for help, but frankly I don't expect much from that group. Maybe fifty years ago, yes, but I have watched as the years have gone by how their positions have shifted farther and farther to the left and away from constitutional principles. Their flip-flop on the Genocide Convention for example. And speaking of the left, I intend to contact the ACLU and apprise them of this situation."

"The ACLU, Mr. Congressman? I think it would be difficult to find any group anywhere that has done as much to weaken and damage the Constitution as the ACLU!"

"I agree, but maybe, just maybe, they can get something right for a change. My rationale for seeking their support is analogous to the farmer whose abhorrence of snakes was mitigated by his desire to rid the corn crib of rats."

"Do you think we have rats in the body politic of America, Mr. Congressman?"

"Snakes, too…But for the first time, even they can now coexist in peace and contentment."

"Your plate is full, Mr. Congressman. Isn't there something I can do to help?"

"Actually, yes. And my plate is indeed full, as you so aptly describe the situation. In addition to the contacts I have discussed, I also have to begin the process of calling in markers from the most prestigious medical schools as I attempt to lure to our cause the very specialized technical expertise we shall require. Before this day is done, I hope all of these contacts will have been concluded. Then we will both rest easier knowing we've done everything in our power to free Dr. Klinner and advance our investigation into Plum Island.

"What can you do to help, you ask? I'll assign you the joy-filled task of soliciting the support of the ACLU. Ask to speak with the director of the Washington office and explain that it involves a high-profile case of an American citizen being deprived of his civil liberties. Granted, Dr. Klinner is hardly the stereotypical ACLU 'client,' but see what you can do. If I need to be personally involved, that's OK, but see how far you can get. Inform the director, or whomever you have to speak with, it's the office of the Chairman of the Health and Human Services Committee seeking their help."

"No problem, Mr. Congressman. I don't know if 'joy-filled' will aptly describe how I feel talking to the ACLU, but I do know that I will relish the opportunity to engage them once again. I delighted in debating those types when I was at Georgetown. It was fun steering the debates in such a direction so as to require them to reexamine what they thought they knew about the Constitution and the intent of its framers. Most of the ACLU members I encountered were little more than shallow-minded individuals running around parroting their liberal professors.

"When they were challenged with viewpoints requiring a reassessment of their pre-conceived opinions, some of them visibly displayed disillusionment and caved in during the debate. In accordance with the age-old dictum, and I apologize Mr. Congressman for my lack of finesse, 'shit seeks its own level', I can only assume most of them eventually wound up working in the public defender's office."

The smile and accompanying laughter spontaneously erupting from Harry was long overdue. Erin didn't know why she had drifted off on such a tangent, but in retrospect, she was glad that she did. Laughter and a smile at this juncture was a much needed commodity in the office.

"I'm sorry, Mr. Congressman, but it's true. Idealistic young people enroll in the finest colleges seeking a well-rounded education to prepare them for their future careers with assurance they will be exposed to both sides of all issues. If they ever get it figured out, they will discover that instead of being provided with cogent arguments for both sides, they are actually being provided with the same side twice but from different angles. The fortunate ones just swallow their gullibility, assign the deception to the naiveté of youth, and simply get on with their lives. The rest are either too stupid to put the pieces together or are content to spend the rest of their lives vigorously defending their pride and whatever it was they were programmed to think and whatever it is that they think they know."

"I don't envy the lawyer that takes your call, Miss Giblon. It sounds like you are loaded for bear."

"It will be a challenge, I'm sure, but I'll have some fun in the process."

"Well, after you have sufficiently sliced and diced your prey, I have another idea I would like for you to pursue."

"Certainly Mr. Congressman."

"I would like for you to call our ally MacIntosh McAdams and advise him that some additional time is required before we will have a qualified interpretation of the materials we received. I'm sure he'll be eager for some editorial fodder, which, unfortunately, we are unable to provide at this time. Why don't you briefly review our intentions to seek assistance from the Senate Judiciary Committee, the ABA, and, horror of horrors, the ACLU? Then suggest that the creation of a column reminding his readership of the importance of certain constitutional guarantees might be a good idea to fill the interim. A civil liberties primer, if you will."

"I'll get right on it. Will you need any assistance contacting the medical schools?"

"Thanks, but I don't think so at this time. Because of my chairmanship of the committee, most of the people I will need to speak with are almost on a speed-dial basis. I feel confident our requests will be well received, and very soon we will have some of the most brilliant minds America has to offer at our disposal."

Check-Out Time

Wednesday and Thursday found events in the lives of Susan, Cathy, and Toby beginning to move rapidly. Susan continued to present as a model employee at work and truthfully was delighted and excited at the opportunity to review work done over the years by her predecessors. Cathy continued her schedule of relieving Susan at the hospital each morning and staying with Toby until Susan returned in the evening.

As he was making his evening rounds on Wednesday, Dr. Butler informed Susan he was releasing Toby the following day. Susan made plans for her and Cathy to take Toby home after she returned from the facility Thursday afternoon. Dr. Butler also provided Susan with the name, address, and contact information for the Lyme doctor in Birmingham. His office would provide the referral and Toby's records if Susan decided to take Toby there. Susan reflected how unusual it would be for her sister instead of her to have to be responsible for accompanying and transporting Toby to a new doctor in a distant city for evaluation and treatment. Perhaps she could arrange to fly down over the long Labor Day weekend to at least meet the doctor if he would be available.

So many decisions to be made and so many details to be resolved, she thought while pondering just what to do next. She realized the urgency of finding a competent physician to take over Toby's treatment and also of trying to discover as much information as possible about the objectives of Plum Island research while she still had access to the files and records. Instinctively, Susan knew that for whatever reason or reasons her days at the facility were numbered, but the thread of continuity she had discovered while reviewing some of the history of viral research being done at the lab was intriguing.

With her strong academic background in virology, Susan was able to easily identify the direction viral research had taken over the years encompassed by the files she was able to access. Unquestionably, the focus and emphasis had been on the development of programs to engineer the structure of viruses—almost a blueprint, it seems, for the alteration of viruses freely occurring in nature in order to create a recombinant form.

And for what purpose? Susan wondered.

What purpose, indeed? Aren't all viruses, such as the group B Coxsackie virus, which can attack the heart, causing myocarditis and frequently death, nasty enough? And viral meningitis and encephalitis? Or the hemorrhagic Marburg and Ebola viruses?

To her, the research pointed in one direction and one direction only. Instead of engineering viruses to self-destruct or be rendered benign, the emphasis and thrust was clearly the creation of new and even more virulent versions than their root forms.

Have we as a nation lost our collective sanity? Susan wondered. *Hell, it's not just us. Other nations are up to their eyeballs in this kind of stuff too, I'm sure. Russia, China, Iraq, Iran, France, Germany's Insel Reims...I've heard stories. Are we all in a race to try to kill as many people as possible as soon as possible? Maybe this is what the UN leaders have in mind when they talk about reducing the population of the earth to a more sustainable number of less than one billion. What is that, a two-thirds reduction? Or is it 75 percent? One thing is for sure—some of these doomsday bugs they are playing with now could certainly get the job done!*

Thursday provided more clues for Susan's agenda of discovery as she continued reviewing files and data generated by Eliot Steadman and earlier scientists at Plum. Particularly chilling was the review of the Soviets' efforts to combine the deadly Marburg virus with the smallpox virus in order to create an untreatable biological weapon capable of rendering previous smallpox vaccinations ineffectual.

Not to be outdone, the Army's Ft. Detrick, Maryland, lab outsourced the production of viruses to their Pine Bluff Arsenal. There, fertilized chicken eggs could be injected with viruses for germination and then harvesting. The virus plant was known as X1002, and by utilizing conveyor belts and sophisticated mechanization, the workers were able to infect and process over 100,000 eggs per week for Q Fever production alone. Over 100 gallons a week!

Production for other viruses was even higher. For Venezuelan equine encephalitis, VEE, over 250,000 eggs each week would produce in excess of 400 gallons. Whereas production at Ft. Detrick had been limited to ounces, the mechanized processes at Pine Bluff could produce gallons—enough to cripple or kill millions of people. But even with these discoveries, Susan instinctively knew what she had uncovered was only the tip of the iceberg.

How many more combinations? How many more deadly cocktails? she wondered.

Hell, why don't we just take a dozen or so of the most dangerous pathogens known to man and blend them together in a witches' brew straight from the vomit of Satan himself? Let's kill everyone and everything including ourselves!

Would anyone care if they knew what was really going on in these labs? Would anybody give a damn? And even if others knew and were concerned, could anything be done to stop this insanity?

Had the facility at Plum Island been located on a larger land mass, Susan would have wanted to run from it as far as her legs would carry her. As it was, she felt trapped in a catch-22 scenario from hell.

As the afternoon progressed, Susan's thoughts turned more and more to the anticipation of checking Toby out of the hospital and bringing him home. Today would only mark the seventh day Toby had been a patient, but to Susan, it seemed like a month or longer. Of course, Toby would need to return daily for his antibiotics, but the hospital staff was flexible enough so that Cathy could bring Toby in for the thirty-minute infusion on some days or Susan could bring him in the late afternoon after work and, of course, weekends.

Upon arrival at the mainland, Susan briefly entertained the thought of stopping to pick up some kind of a surprise gift for Toby and perhaps some ice cream from Baskin Robbins. She wanted to attempt to make Toby's hospital departure as much of a festive event as possible. And even though much uncertainty and many uncharted waters lay ahead for her and Toby, she at least felt enormous progress had been accomplished during the past week. In her heart, she knew they were on the right track at last with her plans to exit the doomsday lab and for Toby to receive the very best care possible from one of the top Lyme specialists in the entire nation. Uncertainty, yes, but also hope and excitement were on the horizon!

As Susan entered Toby's room, she was delighted to see Toby sitting on the bed totally dressed with an excited smile on his face. Cathy had already packed all of their things, and she, too, was all smiles. Susan hugged Cathy and Toby and then remarked, "Looks like you two guys are ready to blow this popsicle stand."

"Yes, Mommy! I'm ready to go home! The doctor said I could, and Aunt Cathy wants to go too!"

"Well, that's just what we are going to do sweetheart! Would you like to stop on the way and get some ice cream?"

"Yes, Mommy! Let's go!"

"OK…I'll call the nurse and tell her we're ready. As soon as they bring the wheelchair, we will be on our way."

"Thank you, Mommy!"

"For what, sweetie?"

"For taking me home…I don't like it here. I love you, Mommy."

"And I love you, too, sweetie. Soon the doctors and the medicine are going to have you well enough to run and play! Would you like that, Toby?"

"Yes, Mommy, but will I still have to go to school?"

"I'm afraid so, sweetie. You will have to catch up on all the studies you've missed since you've been sick."

"Sis, I'll follow you guys home and help you get moved back in," said Cathy. "Once you're settled, I'll need to get back to my place. I've got laundry to do, and I need to clean up that pig sty."

"What's a pig sty, Aunt Cathy?" asked Toby.

"It's where pigs live, and they are very dirty and messy. They stink, too!"

"I didn't know you had a pig, Aunt Cathy."

As the nurse rolled in Toby's wheelchair, she found two adults laughing and an eight-year-old boy with a big grin on his face. For the moment, a modicum of normalcy existed in that room, and the horrors of Lyme and its associated diseases were relegated to the "I'm not going to think about that now" portion of their brains.

En route home, Susan treated Toby and Cathy to a chocolate nut sundae and a banana split, respectively, while Susan enjoyed a big chocolate milkshake. Toby was able to walk from Susan's car to the ice cream store and back again but not without an element of a stumbling, listing gait. Nevertheless, the mission was accomplished and the mood was indeed as festive as it could be under the circumstances. Toby was glad to see home again, and Susan felt certain that in Toby's mind, his stay in the hospital had seemed very long indeed.

Cathy assisted with the moving back in and she stayed until everything was in its place and Toby was comfortably watching cartoons. The late afternoon hallmark of Lyme fatigue was settling in, and Susan and Cathy both knew Toby would probably need to take a nap soon.

What a contrast, thought Susan. *In just a few months, Toby has gone from a role model for the Energizer Bunny to a role model for a senior citizens' retirement home!*

"Hey, Sis!" exclaimed Cathy. "Before I go, and yes I will be back bright and early in the morning, I wanted to tell you what I found out at church last night and about a phone call I got today."

"Oh, yeah…I remember. You were going to ask about that Birmingham doctor."

"That's right. I've got his name, address, and telephone numbers in my purse."

"Well, let's compare. Dr. Butler came through with a name also. Let's see if they match. What did I do with my purse, Cathy? I think that's where I stuck it."

"How about on top of the fridge? Isn't that where you usually leave it?"

"Not today, apparently. Wait, I see it… it's on top of the microwave. Oh well…OK, I know it's in here somewhere along with about a million other essentials I just can't live without. Here it is…Edward Robinson MD, PhD, PA."

"That's it! The same name the church members provided me last night. He must have quite a reputation! What does PA stand for?"

"Professional Association, Cathy."

"Oh…Well, as long as it's not Professional Ass. We've had enough of those!"

"Yeah, that's for sure. Tell me about it! But I don't think that's going to be a problem with this doctor. According to Dr. Butler, he comes very highly recommended."

"Yeah, and from the church group as well. In fact, let me tell you about today's phone call from one of our members. I think you will find this very interesting."

"Jesus is coming next week to heal everyone?"

"Don't know about that, but the church is going to be providing transportation for Lyme patients in this area to go to see that doctor. Get this—they are going to use the church bus for bi-monthly trips to Birmingham. While in Birmingham, the patients and their caregivers will be staying in the homes of members of a sister church of ours! Isn't that wonderful?"

"Yes, yes it is! Maybe we can work Toby in on some of those missions."

"I'll volunteer to go on the first one, Sis!"

"I love you, Cathy! I've said it before, and I'll say it again! I don't know what Toby and I would do without you! You are truly a Godsend."

"Someday, Susan, I'll convince you that what you've just said is not just an expression. There really is a God and yes, just maybe, I am here by the grace of God to help you in this time of need. But we'll work on that later. By the way, Sis, guess what these church missions to Birmingham are being called?"

"Golly, Sis, I don't know. What?"

"The Lyme-Aid Express! Pretty cool, huh?"

Storm Clouds Gather

FBI Director Frey was increasingly feeling as if his office was operating in a bunker under siege mode. Ever since the nation was rocked to the core by the attacks on September 11, it seemed at every twist and turn his agency was taking flack from yet another quarter for not doing enough to shield America from its enemies. With the asinine color-coded terror alerts changing almost as frequently as traffic signals at a busy intersection, the average American felt unsure and unprepared for whatever eventuality the future held. Unrelenting criticism came from the left, right, and center. More so than any other government agency, including the Office of Homeland Security, the FBI became the focal point for expressions of fear, concern, and paranoia emanating from certain media voices, the clergy, members of academia, and a variety of citizens' groups. The Bureau's policies were questioned at every turn, and Director Frey found himself devoting more and more of his time to defending the Bureau's actions and providing rationale for whatever was or was not resolved to the satisfaction of the critics.

The massacre at the Plum Island ferry was particularly nettlesome, and to Frey's mind, could not have come at a more inopportune time. Adding to his daily stress level had been the recent conference call with the president. Frey had never seen the president so angry, which was, at the least, very disconcerting because he realized full well the political independence of the Bureau ended with Hoover. Frey also knew he didn't want to end up like Hoover. The upcoming committee hearings announced by Congressman McDonald were as of yet an unknown variable but certainly could not be expected to ameliorate existing conditions.

Curiously enough, as Director Frey was pondering these ongoing dilemmas, a call came in from CIA Director Steele.

"Good morning, Director Frey. How are things in your backyard?"

"As a matter of fact, I was just thinking how much more manageable my row boat would be without Congressman McDonald making waves," Frey replied.

"Yeah, here too. That's why I'm calling."

"What's up?"

"We have sources telling us McDonald is casting about for some specialists in the fields of microbiology, virology, epidemiology, and laboratory analysis. He has been contacting some of the top medical schools seeking professional assistance for his committee hearings. Do you know anything about this?"

"No. But I would guess he wants a back-up advisory team to interpret the testimonies of witnesses."

"Yeah, could be, but I've got news for that choir boy—there ain't gonna be any!"

"Witnesses?" asked Frey.

"Yep, I've already talked to Budenz. Whenever McDonald issues those subpoenas, Director Stephens at Plum will petition the courts to have them quashed in the name of national security. Budenz has already spoken to the three judges that make up that district's federal appeals court to inform them of our position. There isn't a chance in hell that even a single employee of the lab will be subpoenaed to testify."

"That's all fine and dandy, but don't you think McDonald's already anticipating the quashing of subpoenas? He might be a pain in our collective asses, but he's no dummy."

"Maybe he's hoping against hope and wants to have a team in place just in case."

"Maybe and maybe not." Frey said doubtfully.

"Yeah, I see what you are saying. Do you think there is a possibility McDonald already has something?" Steele asked.

"I don't see how, Director Steele, unless someone we don't know about made a death bed confession. Those few survivors are in no shape to talk to anyone."

"Well, I think it's a given McDonald's not pulling together that much horsepower for his own edification. The guy was a doctor...he has already been exposed to those areas of medical expertise. What about that new-hire chick?"

"Since the shootings, we have been monitoring her activities. Her supervisor was considering her termination for unpermissioned absenteeism, but lately, according to him, she has been a model employee."

"Why was she absent so much? Was she afraid of a replay at the ferry landing?"

"No, she actually started missing work about three months before that. She claimed her kid was sick. She has an eight-year-old son."

"So the kid got better? What was wrong with him?" Steele asked.

"She told her supervisor it was mono."

"Isn't that a long time to be sick with mono?"

"I don't know, but that's what she told her supervisor. He seemed satisfied with her answer."

"And to the best of your knowledge, Director Frey, she hasn't had any contact with McDonald?"

"None whatsoever. Hell, she may not even know he is her congressman," Frey replied. "She moved there from Birmingham. I'm telling you, this chick is apolitical. Her life is her son, work, and her sister. She doesn't even date!"

"I hope we're not missing something here, Frey. I'm thinking it would be a good idea to find out if that kid really did have mono."

"Are you thinking the kid might have something that was homegrown in that lab, and she developed a severe case of the sour grapes syndrome and wants revenge?"

"Stranger things have happened. How much trouble would it be to find out what the diagnosis really was?"

"It could take some time, Director Steele. We would have to access her health insurance claims to find out who the doctor or doctors were. And then we could possibly encounter some resistance because some of those guys can be pretty damn obstinate about the doctor-patient confidentiality issue. If we have to use subpoenas, it will slow things down even more."

"It might be worth the effort though. I've got a feeling McDonald thinks he has an ace in the hole, and we need to find out what it is. Put that chick under a microscope. She is a potential mole unless McDonald has a psychic on the payroll."

"Do you think she could have somehow removed confidential files from the lab?"

"Not after the McClain vendetta, that's for sure! Excuse the expression, but we corked that place up tighter than a tick! And a tick would be about the largest thing she would be able to get through security. Besides, we know she hasn't had any contact with McDonald."

"Maybe she had information collected before the massacre and just got pissed and sent it to the address for her congressman she dug out of the phone book. Hell, I don't know. We could sit here all day and speculate on the what-ifs. Let's see what McDonald does next while we continue to monitor the new hire."

"And speaking of what McDonald is going to do next, we have already been notified that his Freedom of Information Act request for all information pertinent to the Tuskegee study has been received."

"Not surprising, but that shouldn't be any problem," Frey replied. "All that stuff was blocked and sanitized before it was handed over to the lawyers who were trying to sue on behalf of the survivors. The prolific use of magic markers eliminated any potentially embarrassing future use of those documents. Just make sure McDonald gets copies of the same edited copies. What about FOIA requests for Plum Island? Any sign of those yet?"

"Nope," Steele answered. "And maybe that's why he needs to assemble that team of experts. He's not sure what the hell to ask for yet!"

"We do have a generous supply of magic markers on hand, don't we?"

"You can count on it, Frey. We also have lots of rubber stamps reading 'Request Denied—National Security.' What McDonald will receive will be as beneficial to his hearings as a parchment scroll imprinted with Egyptian hieroglyphics detailing the proper cooking procedure for cow intestines."

"If McDonald's committee subpoenas are blocked because of national security concerns, and his FOIA requests are blocked or blacked out for the same reason, what do we have to worry about? No witnesses, no information. What the hell will they have to investigate? Each other's extramarital affairs?"

"Yes, I agree. But we both realize it would be a very serious mistake to underestimate that son of a bitch, McDonald. We both know we are dealing with something having zero tolerance for error. The integrity of the lab must be maintained and secure at all costs. The American people must never begin to collectively suspect and question the activities and objectives of the bio-labs, and Plum Island, in particular. I don't have to remind you of how much is at stake here."

"Well unless McDonald can pull a rabbit out of his ass, it looks to me like those committee hearings are going to be a great big nonevent. Who else gives a damn? Do any of the other committee members share McDonald's zeal and enthusiasm for investigating Plum? How far would they be willing to go with this thing?"

"Are you kidding? Those guys could care less. Even if a modicum of altruism begins to surface, they will look at the exercise as a futile waste of time…which we will, of course, assure. Their concerns are to engage in politically popular activities ensuring their reelections, especially pork-barrel projects to benefit their constituents. An investigation of Plum Island most assuredly is neither. Nope, if McDonald was not the driving force for the committee, the investigation would fold like a house of cards in a tornado."

Picnicking with the Ticks

Susan Collins relished the opportunity to sleep-in Saturday morning. The week had proven to be the most stressful in her entire life, and a long, peaceful, uninterrupted sleep was what she desperately needed more than anything. Toby, with the aid of the wonderful sleep medication prescribed by Dr. Butler, also slept well with only a short episode of the after-midnight insomnia so common among Lyme patients. Susan awoke briefly at seven, but after determining Toby was still asleep, she drifted off again and slept until nine. With mind and body approaching exhaustion, she probably could have slept another two or three hours had she not been awakened by a ringing telephone that just wouldn't stop.

Susan groggily reached for the phone, not caring that her voice was probably going to sound totally inappropriate for that late in the morning.

Who could that be? Darn, I was sleeping so well! thought Susan as she managed a garbled, "Hello?"

"Good morning," boomed Cathy from the receiver. "Rise and shine, oh sister of mine! You're burning daylight! Get your aching bod out of the bed. We've got places to go and things to do!"

"I was doing one of those things very nicely until you called. Can't you let your worn-out sister sleep in?"

"Not today, sweetheart! You can sleep when you're dead. I've got plans for us, and you and Toby are going to have a blast."

"Can't it wait until tomorrow?"

"Nope! Today is the day! I'm coming over at 10:15, and I expect you and Toby to be ready. It's a beautiful day outside, and we are going on a picky-nicky. God knows you and Toby need to get outside for some sunshine and fresh air. Sometimes I can't remember if it's you or Toby that has Lyme. You both have the poolroom pallor."

"A picnic? Where?"

"We are going to take in the annual Seafood Festival! It starts today down by the water at Ocean Beach Park. The finest restaurants in the area will be offering a variety of delicious seafood from their vendor booths. There'll be arts and crafts and, get this, a sailboat regatta. Tell me Toby wouldn't love that!"

As Cathy excitedly described her plans for them that day, Susan also began thinking about what a really good idea it seemed, and she was reminded afresh how much she loved her sister and how truly special their relationship was.

"OK, Sis, you silver-tongued devil, you. I'll drag Toby out, we'll get ourselves presentable, and we'll see you at 10:15. It sounds like a lot of fun for all of us. What do I need to bring?"

"Just dress appropriately and maybe bring a camera. I figure we'll fill our picnic basket from the seafood vendors."

"It's a date!"

"Oh, Sis, by the way..."

"Yes?"

"Don't forget the repellent!"

"Yeah, and tweezers to pull the little blood suckers off. I'll see you in a little over an hour."

An hour? Thought Susan as she went into Toby's room to wake him. *It will take every bit of that just to get Toby dressed and moving.*

Toby's fatigue level was always the worst early in the morning and late in the afternoon. For sure, some kind of high-energy breakfast would be necessary. Otherwise, Toby would just stay in bed. Susan was amazed at how rapidly Toby's energy levels could fluctuate...but never from low to high. It was always the reverse—more appropriately, from subnormal to super low in an incredibly short time span...almost as if someone suddenly pulled the plug on Toby's energy pack, and down he would go.

"Good morning, sweetie. Are you awake or just playing 'possum?"

Toby moaned and turned over in the bed, moving his eyes away from the sunlight coming through the blinds Susan was opening.

"Wake up, sleepy head. Aunt Cathy's coming over, and we're going on a picnic, and we are going to watch the sailboats!"

Susan moved to sit on the bed to hug and kiss Toby as he began stirring and trying to come awake.

"Doesn't that sound like fun, Toby? Come on, let's get you dressed, and Mommy will make you some breakfast before Aunt Cathy gets here."

"OK, Mommy," Toby mumbled. "My clothes are wet."

Susan's arm and hand wrapped around Toby's back encountered drenched bed covers and a soaking wet shirt adorned with play bears that Toby was wearing.

My God, thought Susan, *is he going to live long enough for us to even get to the park? What kind of disease is this that refuses to relinquish its grip even in the face of an onslaught by one of the most powerful antibiotics known to man? Calm down, Susan! Didn't Dr. Butler explain Toby also had a malarial-type infection? And isn't a hallmark of malaria uncontrollable sweats? Just get Toby in a nice shower and he will feel so much better after getting clean, dry clothes on and a good, nourishing breakfast in his tummy. Once he gets to the park, he will enjoy himself and it will do him a world of good…at least until the dreaded ubiquitous afternoon fatigue sets in. Soon, when we get Toby to the specialist in Birmingham, he will treat Toby's co-infection and the sweats will be gone. Toby's energy levels will recover, and once again he will be a happy, normal eight-year old. Maybe…That's the plan, anyway.*

As usual, Cathy's totally predictable, punctilious self arrived, wearing a big straw hat and equally big grin at precisely 10:15. Also as usual, Susan was not quite ready and was flitting about trying to locate her 'essentials' while simultaneously trying to get Toby ready.

"Give me just a second, Sis," Susan exclaimed. "I can't remember where I put that picnic basket."

"My place, Susan. It's already in the car. Come on, let's go!"

"I'm almost ready….Toby, Aunt Cathy is here. Give her a big hug. We're going to that park you like!"

"How's my favorite nephew this morning? What are you eating?"

"Pancakes and sausage."

"Yummy?"

"I guess," answered Toby as Cathy looked at the plate of food, which appeared to have been pecked at by a small bird.

"Aren't you hungry, sweetheart?"

"Not much…could I have some more juice?"

"Sure, sweetie…we will get some really good food on our picnic. Maybe you will like it better."

"OK, Aunt Cathy…I like to go on picnics, and I like to watch sailboats."

"That's where we are going, sweetheart, if I can just get your mother to put a move on."

Thirty minutes later, they were finally all loaded up in Susan's car and on their way to the park.

"Hey, Sis," remarked Susan as she was backing out of her driveway. "How come every time you have an idea for a road trip, we always wind up taking my car?"

"You need the practice, Susan…. Besides, Toby and I are busy planning our day. Aren't we, sweetie?"

"I want to watch the sailboats, Aunt Cathy."

"We'll be there in just a few minutes. But from the looks of this traffic, a lot of other folks have the same idea."

As Cathy had promised, the day was indeed beautiful. With a cloudless, deep blue sky, low humidity, and a gentle breeze from the sound waters, conditions were perfect for a family outing. As they pulled into an available parking space, Toby's eyes brightened as he saw the beautiful water and the many boats already beginning to appear for the regatta.

"Mommy! Aunt Cathy! Look at all the pretty boats!"

"I know, sweetie….Let's try to find a picnic table close to the water so we can watch the regatta better."

"Mommy, what's a regatta?"

"Well Toby, it's a…well, hmmm…I'm not sure, sweetie."

"Come on, Susan…you know what a regatta is, don't you? Or do you?"

"Golly, I thought I did. Is it like a dog show or a horse show but for boats?"

"No silly, it's a race."

"Are the boats going to race, Aunt Cathy?"

"You bet, sweetie!"

Toby was all grins now as Susan and Cathy exchanged glances and grins of their own.

"Hey guys, I see a vacant table close to the water under that big oak tree. Let's hurry before someone snags it."

"I'll run on down there, Susan, with the picnic basket…you and Toby get your stuff and come on down. If I wait on you slow pokes, someone else will get it."

With that, Cathy took off while Susan helped Toby out of the vehicle. Together they began making their way to the table, which was about 100 yards distant. Toby's steps were unsure and erratic, and it appeared to Susan that his legs could just barely support him. But Toby still managed a trace of a smile because of the excitement of the day, and he was doing his absolute best to make it to that table unassisted. Several minutes later, they were seated with Cathy and began enjoying the view and the picture-perfect day. Toby's breathing, however, was labored after the effort and he was very pale.

"Would you like a soda, Toby?"

"OK, Mommy...I'm thirsty."

"Do you feel OK, honey?"

"My legs are tired, Mommy, and my eyes hurt. But I don't want to go home. Please, Mommy, I like it here. I want to stay."

"We'll stay, sweetie, and we'll have a good time."

"Look you guys," Cathy said. "Here come a lot more boats! There must be at least a hundred or more out there now! Wonder when they will start the race? Can you see the boats OK, Toby? Do you need to stand on the table?"

"OK, Aunt Cathy."

Cathy stood to help little Toby as he attempted to stand on the bench before stepping onto the table. He was able to stand unassisted, but his legs lacked sufficient strength to step up on the table without Cathy's help. Once positioned, Toby was able to stand erect, and he began to watch the boats as they filled the harbor. Susan's heart was heavy as she sadly watched her once strong and healthy son now weakened and emaciated struggling valiantly to enjoy himself.

"Mommy?" Toby asked. "That place I see way out past the boats? Do you see it? Is that where you work, Mommy? Is that the place that makes people sick?"

Cathy glanced to Susan to watch how she would respond to Toby's question while silently expressing gratitude the question was not directed at her.

"Yes, Toby. That's where Mommy works, but not for much longer, sweetie."

"Why, Mommy?"

"Because that place makes people sick, and I'm not going to work anywhere that makes people sick."

"Good. Will you stay home with me?"

"Maybe a little, but Mommy has to work to pay the bills. As soon as you are well, we have to get you back in school. You have a lot of catching up to do."

"Why don't we move back to Birmingham, Susan?" Cathy asked. "You could probably find a job at UAB...maybe not paying as much as this one, but it wouldn't matter. I've got some money saved up, and we could share a place until you could find something. You're probably going to be taking Toby to a doctor there anyway."

"That's probably not a bad idea, Sis, but I couldn't bear the idea of imposing on you."

"Get outta here! The only reason I am here now is to be with you guys! We are the only family we've got. And besides, I can go anywhere. That annuity I purchased with the money from my husband's accidental death settlements will provide me with monthly income for life. It was the smartest thing I've ever done, and it's more than enough to provide for the three of us. Today is not the first time I've thought about going there. I started thinking about Birmingham several weeks ago, and now I think about it every day."

"I know you, Sis…. You're just trying to avoid a trip on the 'Lyme-Aid Express!'"

"Mommy? Aunt Cathy? Are we going to move back home?"

"Maybe, sweetie, but we're just talking. It's not that easy."

"I wouldn't mind, I wasn't sick when I lived there."

Silence prevailed for a few moments as Toby resumed watching the boats, and Susan and Cathy pondered the ramifications of their discussion.

I could do that, thought Susan. *Take Cathy up on her offer and get the hell out of this place. But first I've some unfinished business to take care of. Someone who gives a damn and has the potential to make a difference needs to see what I've uncovered researching the lab's virology programs. Maybe that congressman is for real and the newspaper guy too. If not them, then who? I don't have a clue. Maybe I'm just daydreaming here. Finding something at the lab and then being able to get that something out the door are two very different things.*

Darn Susan! Quit thinking and enjoy the day. This time together is very special…and besides, we've got all that delicious seafood to sample, not to mention lots of arts and crafts. And don't forget the regatta! But we'll probably have to leave about 4 PM and take Toby to the hospital for his infusion. He'll be getting pretty tired by then.

The movement of a tiny dark spot on the back of Toby's white sock caught Susan's attention, and she leaned closer to see what it was.

Is that what I think it is? thought Susan. *Is that a damn tick crawling up Toby's leg?*

"Don't move, Toby, there's a bug on your sock. Mommy's going to get it off."

Toby turned his head to look down while Susan took her car key to flick the bug off his sock and onto the table. As it began to crawl again, Susan, to her horror, was able to discern that it was indeed a tiny tick on the prowl for an unsuspecting victim. *Was* became the operative word as Susan used the point of the car key to pierce the life and a tiny spot of blood out of the arachnid.

"What was it, Mommy? Did it bite me?"

"It was a tick, sweetie, and no, it didn't bite you. Mommy killed it."

"I don't like ticks, Mommy!"

"I know, sweetie…it's OK now."

Susan and Cathy, as if in unison, looked down and carefully inspected themselves for ticks.

"Toby, you just stay on the table until we go to the booths for seafood. The bugs can't get on you there."

"OK, Mommy."

"Well, Cathy, it's usually you that's talking about signs, but this time it's my turn. We are 'Bama bound, girlfriend!"

"Good! I thought you would never ask! I'll be ready whenever you are!"

"I'll see how things go over the next few weeks. I would prefer to wrap up all of Toby's IV therapy before we make any radical changes in our lives. Let's see now…how many are left? Today will make number nine, so that leaves nineteen to go. Two weeks plus five days…so, three weeks it is. I think I can wrap it all up by then, but golly gee, I sure will miss Gallagher and Stephens!"

"You're kidding, aren't you?"

"Yeah!—Miss like a brain tumor!"

The blowing of several very loud fog horns interrupted Susan and Cathy's fantasizing about heading south.

"Look Toby! They are about to start the race! See how the boats are lining up behind the marker buoy?"

"Yes, Mommy! This is fun!"

A few minutes later after another very loud fog-horn blast, the New London Seafood Festival Regatta was officially underway, and young Toby Collins was grinning from ear to ear.

"Thank you, Cathy."

"For what, Sis?"

"For this…I've been so wrapped up in everything going on, I didn't even know such a thing as a New London Seafood Festival even existed. This is wonderful! It's not only therapeutic for Toby, but for you and I as well. We all needed this time together. I really don't know what has been the most beneficial for Toby, nine IV antibiotic infusions or this day in the park by the water. And without you, Sis, it would have never happened!"

"Keep it up, and I'll let you buy my lunch! And speaking of…it's getting close to that time. Is your tummy starting to growl yet?"

"Sorta, but let's wait until most of those boats are almost out of sight because Toby's really enjoying them."

"I tell you what, you guys hold this table and I'll go get us some plates and drinks. Do you know what you want?"

"Yeah, right…I have about as much knowledge of seafood choices in this part of the world as you do. Just whatever looks good. But don't bring anything that looks like an oyster or a clam or has tentacles. You know how I am about those things!"

"OK, Sis, but don't expect fried catfish and hushpuppies. This ain't Alabama!"

"What? No hushpuppies?"

"Mommy, what's a hushpuppy? Do they eat dogs here?"

"No, Toby, they don't eat dogs here…at least I don't think they do," Susan replied. "Cathy, hurry back so you can explain to Toby what a hushpuppy is."

Crowds were beginning to form at the dozen or so seafood vendor booths as Cathy began making her way in their direction. Susan was concerned that because of the crowds, Cathy would be standing in lines for the better part of an hour. After about thirty or forty minutes however, Cathy returned bearing several large sacks of delicious-smelling food.

"Well gee, Sis, did you get enough or will we be hosting a church social after the three of us have sufficiently gorged ourselves?"

"I wasn't sure what you and Toby might like, so I got a little of almost everything. In the bottom of the sacks are some plastic utensils. That big sack has our drinks."

"How about you Toby? Are you getting hungry yet? Aunt Cathy has brought you some wonderful seafood."

"Yes, I'm hungry, Aunt Cathy. Did you bring a hushpuppy?"

"No, but we'll get you some when we get back to Birmingham!"

And so it went with laughter and smiles for the next few hours. Susan, Toby, and Cathy were in the moment, enjoying each other, the beautiful day, and the delicious seafood. Susan was delighted that Toby finally exhibited a semblance of an appetite. She couldn't remember the last time he had enjoyed food this much.

"Hey, Sis!" remarked Cathy, "Do I need to get a farmer's almanac to find out when you are going to be full?"

"Can't help it, Cathy…whatever I'm eating, it's delicious!"

"Well, you still have to be able to walk. I'm not going to roll you! We still have the arts and crafts to take in. And you said you wanted to have Toby at the hospital at 4 PM."

"There about. For sure us girls can't miss arts and crafts. It's definitely a girl thing. Oops….Cathy, we've been enjoying ourselves and not paying attention. Did you check your legs after walking through the grass to get the food?"

"No, but I've got repellent on my legs. Let me see…Oh man, I don't believe this! Look at my socks!"

Cathy stuck out her left leg for Susan to see the two tiny ticks that had ventured as far as the roll at the top of Cathy's sock, inhibited from further encroachment across the bare exposed skin of her leg by the repellent.

"It's a good thing we all wore shorts today," said Cathy as she flicked the invaders off her sock. "If one made it to our skin, I'm sure we would feel it. Would you look at that? There's another one on the other sock! I'm ready whenever you guys are. This is ridiculous!"

"Maybe now we know why the bulk of the crowd is staying around the booths and exhibits—that area is paved. It explains why so many of these tables are still vacant. Just look around."

"Toby, have you had enough to eat?" Susan asked. "We need to leave before the bugs carry us off and have their own picnic."

"But I like it here," Toby said.

"I know, sweetie…so do we, but we are going to go up there where the exhibits are. We don't have to leave the park yet, but we do need to get away from these bugs!"

"OK. Mommy."

Susan was not about to take any chances. Enough was enough. She and Cathy took turns carrying Toby to the relative safety of the pavement and then thoroughly checked each other for the offending predators. Satisfied that everyone was bug free, they began their tour of the arts and crafts exhibits. Even little Toby found a few things for his room that he liked, and Susan didn't hesitate to purchase them. She was so thankful Toby was improving and that she was blessed with a son she could buy things for. A little further along, the trio encountered a display of pictures and crafts representative of what a tourist might encounter at a bazaar in Puerto Vallarta, Cozumel, or Mexico City. Toby was particularly attracted to a painting about a foot square of a colorfully attired matador adroitly flourishing his cape as a raging bull passed close by.

"Mommy! Aunt Cathy! Look at that picture! Can I have that for my room? Please Mommy? I like that!"

Susan glanced at the price tag… $37.50. *What the hell?* she thought. *Toby hasn't been this excited about anything since before he got sick.*

"Do you like that, Toby?" Susan asked him.

"Yes, Mommy…will you get it for me? Please?"

"Well, Toby, you've been such a sweet boy today, and we do need to celebrate your getting out of the hospital. I guess so, if you really like it."

"Oh thank you, Mommy!" said Toby as enthusiastically as his little body could muster. "I love you, Mommy."

Those words spoken by little Toby, combined with the pitiful sight of his frail arms weakly attempting to hug her legs, brought a tear to Susan's eyes, which she quickly wiped away for fear a trickle would become a deluge.

No tears today, Susan! she thought. *We are having fun…the most fun in a long, long time, and nothing but nothing is going to ruin it. Not even those damn ticks!*

"OK, Sis," spoke Cathy, "what about you? I thought I saw a cloud attempting to form. Maybe a nice umbrella with a colorful Latin flavor would be appropriate?"

"I'm OK…Just a little allergy, I guess."

"Yeah, right…"

As they turned to walk on to the next exhibit, Susan took one last look at the items on display, when suddenly something caught her attention and she paused momentarily.

"Hold on just a minute," she told Cathy and Toby as she stepped to a shelf displaying several handbags decorated with floral designs, ornamentations, and vivid colors.

Susan selected a large straw bag from the display adorned with all of the above, including two brass Aztec calendars at least six inches in diameter affixed to each side of the bag. She held the bag closely, examining every inch of the exterior and interior. To Cathy, she appeared totally fixated and almost trancelike.

Time to break the spell, thought Cathy, *before she totally freaks out*.

"You can't be serious!" Cathy exclaimed. "That is the tackiest thing I've ever seen! You're kidding, right?"

"What? What are you talking about? Every girl needs a good bag to put her stuff in! And besides, don't you think it has a festive flair about it?"

"Stuff? That monstrosity has enough room for a litter of the puppies you've been talking about plus the bricks necessary to sink them to the bottom! Get a grip, girl! What are you thinking?"

"I like it," Susan said simply.

"Well, there's plenty to like, that's for sure…that guy, that god, or whatever he is in the middle of the calendar sticking his tongue out for one thing. That's pretty festive, don't you think? Look, Toby…your mother wants a bag with a picture of someone sticking their tongue out. Is that funny or what?"

"OK, you guys can just make fun of me all you want. From today on, that bag is going to be a part of the Collins' household."

"Yes, dear sister, and as soon as I get you home, I'm going to pour the fruit of the vine down your throat until you come to your senses!"

Letters

By 3:30 that afternoon, it was obvious to Susan and Cathy that Toby was becoming fatigued and they needed to leave soon for the hospital. Today would mark Toby's ninth antibiotic infusion, and Susan thought he seemed perceptibly, albeit slightly, better. Anticipating a walk-in, walk-out visit, Susan was completely unprepared for the delays they were to experience upon arrival. The hospital's weekend scheduling shifted all outpatient procedures to the staff in the emergency room. Susan's heart sank when she saw the emergency waiting room filled almost to capacity. The registration clerk apologized for the delay, explaining they would be bringing Toby back to a treatment area as soon as possible. Two hours later, their turn finally arrived but not before exhausted little Toby had fallen asleep. To Susan, he appeared very tired but, nevertheless, she was grateful for the day they had shared together. Toby had a good time…granted not as fun-filled as the day would have been had he been in normal health, but definitely a good day.

As the sisters sat next to each other with Toby asleep and stretched out across their laps, Susan and Cathy couldn't help but observe the crowd in the waiting area.

"Cathy?" Susan whispered. "I don't mean to sound like a snob, but does it look like the majority of these people are representatives of the lowest socio-economic levels?"

"I was wondering, too, Sis. Do you think they are just using the emergency room as a surrogate for a doctor's office?"

"Looks like it to me. I always thought emergency rooms were for trauma victims, car wrecks, heart attacks, that sort of thing…you know."

"Yeah and look around…coughs, sneezing, belly aches, headaches. Some people with pains in arms or legs or backs….hardly what I would consider an emergency, but here they are."

"Wonder if the hospital will get paid for services rendered?"

"I think we already know the answer to that question."

When Toby's name was finally called, Susan cradled her still sleeping son in her arms and carried him into the emergency treatment area. A nurse, upon seeing Toby's limp, unconscious body, rushed over to offer her assistance thinking Toby was suffering from a medical emergency.

"He's just asleep," Susan said softly. "We're here for his daily IV antibiotic infusion."

"You gave me a start there," the nurse replied. "Let's see...bring him over here, and we'll use that gurney behind those curtains. Just let him sleep, if he will, until I get the IV started. Then we'll wake him."

As the nurse reviewed Toby's chart and Dr. Butler's orders, Susan noticed an expression of concern sweeping the nurse's face.

"How long was your son sick before it was determined he had Lyme disease?"

"I don't remember exactly, nurse...months."

"I hear that a lot."

"I can't understand why doctors are not more alert to the symptoms," Susan said.

"Yeah, it makes you wonder, doesn't it?"

"Do you see a lot of Lyme patients?"

"More than any other infectious disease, I suppose...and the numbers are increasing. We're seeing more of it now than ever."

"We were at the seafood festival over at Ocean Beach Park today. I couldn't believe how many ticks there were—they kept getting on our socks."

"I know...I won't even let my kids go out in the woods anymore. We are thinking about moving somewhere else."

"Where would you go?" Susan asked.

"Somewhere there's not a damn government laboratory close by!"

Susan was glad Toby was not awake to hear that remark. She was also hoping her place of employment was not documented somewhere on those pages the nurse had reviewed in Toby's chart. At that moment, Susan felt if her employer was revealed in this environment, she would be very embarrassed, ashamed, and indeed humiliated of her position. A chill swept through Susan as she sat quietly watching the very skilled professional begin Toby's infusion.

THE POISON PLUM

What would this nurse think, thought Susan, *if she knew that the mother of the very sick child before her worked in the very laboratory that incubated the germ trying to kill her son.*

Susan kept looking at the bag containing the antibiotic wishing somehow it could all flow into Toby's body in an instant. She wanted to flee from this place, this town, and this state.

Tear the rear-view mirror off the SUV, point south, floorboard the accelerator, and leave black marks a city block long! And by God before this year is out, that is exactly what we are going to do and we will be gone forever from this hellish place, she thought.

"Did you say something, Ms. Collins?"

"No…I guess I was just thinking aloud. I've got a lot on my mind."

"I would guess so. I certainly wouldn't want to be in your shoes right now."

If only you knew, thought Susan. *If only you knew…*

"The drip looks OK. Let's wake your son now, so I can record his vitals."

Susan was reluctant to wake Toby. She knew it would be difficult for him to get back to sleep later because of the bizarre cycles of insomnia that plagued him. Nevertheless, she did as the nurse requested while hoping his sleeping medication would do the trick when the time came. And speaking of sleep medication, Susan also began hoping Cathy's suggestion of wine later was sincere. Susan was also getting tired, and she realized that last night's wonderful respite of peaceful sleep was just not quite sufficient to allow mind and body to recover from the stress and duress of the week.

Finally, after it seemed they had been in the emergency room for the better part of the night, the nurse began unhooking Toby from the IV bag.

"Well, we're all done for today, Ms. Collins," the nurse said. "You might consider coming tomorrow around noon or 1:00 PM—the crowds are usually not as heavy then…and I wish you and your son the best of luck."

Susan thanked the nurse but began thinking, *There's that "luck" thing again.… Why don't we just hope instead for the best medical care possible for Toby, and leave the 'luck' to those people lined up at the convenience store for lottery tickets?*

"Well it's about time," Cathy said as Toby and Susan exited the treatment area. "I was afraid they were going to keep you both for medical experimentation."

"You can't prove it to me that's not what they're doing."

"Not today, they won't, Sis…let's get on home and pop open that magnum of Merlot I stuck in your fridge this morning."

"God love you, Sis. I'm truly needy, and if you are waiting on me, you are backing up!"

Within fifteen minutes, they were back at Susan's with a tired little boy who said he wasn't hungry and just wanted to go to bed. Susan washed little Toby off with a warm soapy wash cloth and helped him change into clean pajamas. As tired as he seemed, Susan didn't think he needed the sleep aid, but to be on the safe side and to ensure her own restful sleep, she gave him the prescribed dose. Mercifully, as soon as his head hit the pillow, he was gone again.

"Hey, Sis, I brought in your mail," Cathy said. "And there's a cold glass of a dark red liquid in here requiring the wrapping around of your hand."

"Yes, and my lips and my tongue and my throat and my tummy all need the caress of said liquid!" said Susan as she sat down close to Cathy and took her first sip. "Damn, that's good! An excellent choice!"

"Yeah, and good for you too…in moderation, of course. Do you remember that saying Granddaddy always used about anything beneficial? 'It'll do you good and help you, too…'sides the benefits you'll get from it!'"

"I remember," Susan replied. "He was a character, wasn't he? Always quick to offer an opinion about almost anything."

"And speaking of wine," Cathy said. "Did you know turning water into wine for a big wedding party was the first miracle Jesus performed before he began his ministry?"

"Of course I didn't know that," said Susan as she reached for the day's mail. "You know I've never read that book."

"It's true, I even did the math on the quantity involved as described in the scriptures…it was about seventy-six gallons."

"Sounds like a big party or a bunch of drunks. Or maybe both," Susan said. "Now what's this? Here's a letter from my insurance company…I'm not sure I want to open that. And what's this? A letter from UAB in Birmingham? Well, I'll tell you one thing. If it's another solicitation letter from the alumni association seeking contributions, they are going to have to chill on this chick—at least for the time being."

"Are you ready for a refill? Your glass appears precariously low."

"Hit me while I bravely attempt to open and read this letter from the insurance company."

Cathy watched the expression on Susan's face as her eyes darted across the page.

"What the crap is this? Look at this and tell me what you think they're trying to say."

In typical truncated insurance company verbiage, reserved exclusively for policyholder communications, the letter read:

Federated Insurance Companies of Greater New England
One Government Plaza
Hartford, Connecticut

Susan N. Collins
527 Tyler Street
New London, CT

Dear Ms. Collins:

    We are sending you this letter of advisement per our request of the following information from your health care provider.

    Case History and Physical
    Medication Sheet
    Doctor's Progress Notes
    Treatment Notes

We are requiring this information to determine benefits for the patient:

Toby M. Collins

    No Action is required of you at this time, but please be advised certain benefits may be denied subject to a review of your claims.

Sincerely,
Anthony G. Creswell
Case Administrator

"I don't know for sure, Sis, but it looks like they are trying to wiggle out of paying for Toby's treatments," Cathy said after examining the letter.

"That's what I think, too! I was afraid this might happen. I read on the Internet about insurance companies in this part of the country denying benefits for Lyme patients. They don't want to pay for those extended antibiotic treatments."

"Why don't you call Dr. Butler's office for an interpretation…they probably encounter this sort of thing all the time."

"Yeah, I will. That's a good idea. Meanwhile, let's see what's lurking in that UAB envelope. Where's my wine? I thought you were going to bring me a refill?"

"I did. You drank it!"

"Well, barkeep, I guess I need another…can't you see your best patron is thirsty?"

"Right away, mate!"

As Cathy poured her sister's third glass of Merlot, she once again watched Susan's facial expressions go through a metamorphosis of emotion as she rapidly read the letter from her alma mater.

"Oh, my God," Susan exclaimed loudly. "I don't believe what I'm seeing! Oh, my God! This is unbelievable! UAB sent this letter telling me they are honoring a request from Congressman Harry McDonald asking for qualified individuals to assist in a congressional probe into the operations of the laboratory at Plum Island! I was notified because of my academic qualifications as requested by the congressman! Beam me up, Scotty! It doesn't get any weirder than this!"

"You said you would be looking for another job, Sis…Looks like you found it, or rather it found you."

"A job or a death wish? And besides, I'm sure the pay would not be commensurate."

"Have some more wine," Cathy said. "You are starting to make even less sense than usual—and that's a good thing. Let's just get silly tonight. I'll sleep over here tonight and not worry about that driving thing. Toby is sound asleep, so let's just let it all hang out as only sisters can. Those stupid letters will still be here in the morning, and sometimes, just sometimes, the best decisions are made after the decision-making processes have been sufficiently doused the night before with large quantities of alcohol. Sometimes not, but we'll leave that for discussion at a later date. And speaking of making sense, what the hell is that garish, 'South of the Border' garbage bag all about?"

"Ah, oh Sis of mine…ye of little faith. Even as you speak your beloved sister is not idle. My mind has conceived a clever and brilliant grand design, the fruition of which will be revealed shortly for all the world to see and appreciate!"

"Yeah, and you are getting drunk, which, when I last investigated, was our mission here. I will drink to that! Here's to you, Sis…I love you!"

"And I love you, too, Cathy, but you'll see…there really is a grand design. You'll see."

Sunday's Deliberations

First light that Sunday morning in the Collins household revealed a totally drained magnum-sized wine bottle with two wine glasses nearby bearing lipstick marks and wine stains. One of the wine glasses was knocked over on the floor alongside the living room couch where Cathy was sound asleep. In the master bedroom, her sister, Susan, was also sound asleep. The first person to acknowledge the bright new day was Toby, who began attempting to leave a night-sweat-drenched bed to make it to the bathroom. Susan awoke upon hearing Toby moving about, and she too, began stirring.

Time to get up, thought Susan. *I hear Toby…what day is it anyway? Sunday? That's it…Sunday.*

The events of the previous day began spilling into Susan's brain and replaying like clips from a video. She reflected on how beautiful the day had been, and what a good time they'd all had at the park.

And all that wine, she thought, *wonder if it will be a two or three aspirin morning. Whatever…we needed it. Let me see what's going on with Toby, and I'll get Cathy up. Let's get the coffee and breakfast going!*

"Mommy? Is that you?" Toby asked. "My clothes are wet."

"Coming, sweetie…good morning! Mommy will run a nice warm shower for you and we'll get you some dry clothes."

"OK. Mommy. Where's Aunt Cathy?"

"She's still asleep on the couch. We'll get her up for breakfast. How do you feel, sweetie?"

"I'm tired, Mommy. And my head and my eyes hurt. My back and my legs, too, Mommy. Is the medicine going to make me feel better? It hurts to pee…"

"Yes, sweetie, but we will probably get you some new medicine after we get to Birmingham. And you'll have a new doctor, too."

"Will we go soon?"

"Yes, son, we will go pretty soon."

Cathy and Susan put together a much-needed breakfast of pancakes, ham, scrambled eggs, toast with jam, and hot coffee for the adults and orange juice for Toby.

Sufficiently refueled and energized for the day, except for Toby, of course, Susan and Cathy took the opportunity to sit on the patio with a fresh cup of hot coffee each and reflect on the events of the previous day.

"Cathy, I've been thinking about that letter from the insurance company," began Susan, "I do think a call to Dr. Butler's office is in order, but I can't do that from work. Since the massacre, they have banned all personal communications to and from work for security reasons. And besides, if I called from work, God only knows who might be listening in. What if his nurse or office manager said something about Lyme disease?"

"I'll call for you, Sis. Whoever answers won't know I'm not you. Haven't people always told us we sound alike on the phone anyway? No problem. What do you want me to find out?"

"I guess just ask if they know of any reason benefits might be denied."

"I can do that, but what are you going to do about that letter from UAB? Obviously you aren't considering joining the congressman's crusade…please tell me you're not thinking about doing that!"

"What if I am?"

"Oh, my God! Are you crazy? Didn't that wine last night help you at all? What are you going to do, politely ask Gallagher for a leave of absence so you can testify for McDonald's committee?"

"No."

"What then? You can't expect to work there and in Washington at the same time!"

"The only reason I'm going in at all tomorrow is to continue the insurance coverage. And if that's about to be denied anyway, what have I got to lose?"

"How about your life? Storm troopers have already been here once or have you forgotten?"

"Piss on 'em."

"Are you begging for a confrontation? You can't win! Can't you see that?"

"All I can see is they made my son and a lot of other people very sick and even very dead. What do you expect me to do? Turn the other cheek? Let bygones be bygones? Forgive and forget? Roll over and play dead? Piss on 'em!"

"You are scaring me, Susan!"

"I'm scaring myself, Cathy. But not before I was scared shitless by what has been done to my son. I repeat…piss on 'em! May they all rot in hell!"

"I agree, Susan, but 'vengeance is mine' saith the Lord."

"And what is to say the Lord won't use someone like lil' ol' me to exact that vengeance? Huh?"

Cathy stood to embrace her sister as tears began flowing down her cheeks.

"I can't lose you both," she cried, hugging Susan tightly.

"You're not going to lose either one of us. I'm going to do what I have to do, and then we are all going back to Birmingham to live happily ever after. I know it, and I can feel it in my heart, Cathy. It's that sixth sense thing again. I'm going to find a new and wonderful job, and Toby is going to be cured by that new doctor. It will take time, sure it will, but it's going to happen. I just know it."

Susan hugged Cathy back, and it was only her self-imposed resolve and determination that kept her own tears at bay.

"Now…Cathy, shut off the waterworks, and let's get Toby to the hospital before the welfare crowd comes in trying to get drugs. When we are done, it'll be lunchtime, and we can stop at our favorite deli on the way back. They open at 11. It'll be my treat."

"OK, Susan…but you know I'll still worry about you."

"Nothing to worry about! Everything is under control, and I'm right as the rain. Come on. Let's go!"

Susan, Cathy, and Toby were indeed successful in dodging the usual weekend invasion of indigents at the emergency room, and Susan was delighted they only had to wait fifteen minutes before Toby was called back. She was even more delighted that the nurse on duty was a new face. Susan would be spared the humiliation of yesterday's nurse possibly making the connection to Plum Island.

As Susan sat quietly awaiting the completion of Toby's antibiotic infusion, she found her mind racing with her plans for the afternoon after Cathy's departure, as well as for next week. Each time feelings of caution and equivocation attempted to emerge, they were quickly suppressed by her desire for retribution. Courage would be required, but it would be nurtured, sustained, and motivated by her resolve growing stronger with each passing day.

THE POISON PLUM

By 2 PM, Susan, Cathy, and Toby had returned from a delightful lunch at Gino's Deli, and Cathy was preparing to return to her place for the remainder of the day.

"Susan, I'll be here at the usual time in the morning to stay with Toby. I assume you want me to take him in for his antibiotic, so you won't have to when you get home tomorrow afternoon."

"That'd be great, Cathy."

"I'll also call Dr. Butler's office and ask about your insurance."

"When is the church group planning to make their first trip down to Birmingham?"

"I'm not sure, but I plan to go tonight for the Sunday evening services. I'll try to find out."

"Yeah, and be sure to apologize for missing services this morning. I'm sure they will understand if you just tell them you and your sister tied one on, and you were too hung over to make it."

"Ha! That would be a hoot! I'm not sure the members of the Sunday school class would understand, but maybe God would. But speaking of Birmingham, do you want to try to get Toby included in that first group to go?"

"I think the sooner the better—he's got that malarial-type thing going on, and every morning his pjs and bed covers are drenched with sweat."

"Do you want me to call the doctor's office down there and get an appointment for Toby as soon as I get a date from the church group?"

"I guess you'll have to, Cathy. I can't make the call from work, that's a given. By the time I get home, his office is probably already closed."

"I don't mind. I'll just explain that Toby will be part of the group, and maybe they'll be able to work him in."

"You know, Sis, I just feel everything is going to work out for the best. I really do. But I should be ashamed…you've already done so much for Toby and me, and here I am loading you down with even more!"

"Nonsense! What're a few phone calls and a little visiting with my favorite nephew? What else would I be doing with my time?"

"Well since you're feeling so generous and accommodative, I do have one more favor to ask you…"

"Name it."

"If I ever start talking about wanting to return to this little slice of heaven on the Connecticut coast, I want you to whack me on the head with Toby's baseball bat!"

"We'll see, but for now will a hug do? I've got to get on back to my place. That laundry piled up is starting to look like a mini Mount Everest. You too Toby…give Aunt Cathy a hug. I'll see you both bright and early in the morning!"

After Cathy had left, Susan did her best to make sure Toby was comfortable and hoped he would settle in with some television cartoons and kids' shows that would hold his interest for the rest of the afternoon. Susan was indeed on a mission now, and she needed some time to herself. The first order of business would be to locate her sewing kit buried somewhere in the boxes remaining unpacked since the move here from Birmingham. Toby's attention was diverted by his mother's activity, and he didn't understand why she was suddenly pulling boxes from under the beds and out of closets.

"Mommy, are we getting ready to move?"

"Not today, sweetie. Mommy is just looking for something she misplaced."

"What?"

"My sewing kit."

"What do you need it for?"

"You remember that big straw bag Mommy bought yesterday?"

"Yes Mommy…that man sticking out his tongue is funny."

"Well, I'm going to sew some pockets in that bag."

"To put hushpuppies in?"

Susan, laughing now, couldn't resist walking over to the couch to give Toby a big hug and a kiss on the cheek.

"When we get back to Birmingham, Toby, I promise I will take you out for a dinner of fish and hushpuppies. They just sound like puppy dogs, Toby, but they aren't…They're kind of like cornbread but round instead of flat. You'll like them…They're very good."

"OK."

With that, Toby returned to an animated children's movie he was watching, and Susan resumed her search.

Wouldn't you just know it, thought Susan as she finally uncovered her sewing kit. *It's in the very last box! I just hope I've got some thread that matches the liner in that bag.*

For the next two hours, Susan worked intensely inside her new acquisition until she was finally satisfied with her handiwork and ready for the big test.

THE POISON PLUM

Stepping to her computer desk, she retrieved two CDs and carefully inserted them into the neatly sewn and cleverly concealed pockets she'd created behind each Aztec calendar on either side of the bag.

Perfect, she thought as she removed the CDs. *Absolutely perfect! Now I'll take it to work every day appropriately loaded with my 'essentials' that every woman just can't do without until those dum dums we call security guards get used to looking at this monstrosity. And when it's scanned every day on the security belt, those same Aztec calendars are going to show up exactly as they did the day before. The order of the day will be no surprises, and it will be routine as usual at America's defender of livestock health. The model employee may appear to some to perhaps be waxing a bit eccentric with her new Carmen Miranda bag, hoop earrings, and wearing lipstick a brighter red than usual, but other than that...*

Susan was proud of her handiwork, and having finished the project earlier than she had anticipated, she decided to pursue the big stack of newspapers that had accumulated over the past week.

"I need to become more informed about local, national, and world events." mumbled Susan, "Isn't that what Cathy's always telling me?"

Susan began with the oldest paper first, rapidly scanning the pages, mostly just reading headline titles and finding little that motivated her to read deeper.

Same old crap, day in, day out. A world totally screwed up beyond any hope of repair, she thought. *Wars, famines, natural disasters, financial problems...you name it. Man's inhumanity to man...will it ever get any better? Maybe planet Earth will just wobble out of its axis some bright day and careen into the sun. Wait! What is this? Now this is what I'm talking about! Let's read this article, Susan. This looks like it is right up your alley!*

The article suddenly capturing Susan's interest was a wire service story detailing the success of a CDC scientist that had been able to recreate the virus responsible for the flu pandemic of 1918 that killed upwards of 50 million people. The virus, according to the article, was created from scratch by the genius at the CDC. Included in the article for the reader's edification was a block diagram explaining the steps required to engineer such a blessing to mankind. And of course the readers were assured there was nothing to fear because the virus was safely contained in 10 vials securely stored at the CDC in Atlanta.

Wow, thought Susan. *Now that's quite an accomplishment! I can only imagine how proud that doctor's mother must be! Let's see now, the mother calls her son for their weekly telephone visit together, and the conversation goes something like this...*

"Johnny, this is your mother...how are things at the CDC? Is everything OK?"

"Oh, hi, Mom! Yes, better than OK, actually. I just finished recreating that virus that killed all those people in 1918!"

"That's wonderful, son! You mean the virus that caused the great influenza pandemic of 1918?"

"That would be the one, Mom...pretty cool, huh?"

"I'll say...I don't guess you remember, but your great-grandfather was killed by that one after he had visited Europe at the end of World War I."

"You don't say! Well that makes my accomplishment even more symbolic!"

"I'm so proud of you, son!"

"There's more, Mom!"

"More?"

"Yes...the bosses here held a contest to see who could create the most effective virus, and mine won out easily. My nearest competitor was a co-worker who managed to engineer a virus with a projected kill rate of only 100,000 people. And mine could go as high as 50 million! Pretty incredible, don't you think? This puts me in the running for the prestigious annual Dr. Doom Award given to the most promising scientist at the CDC. I've already qualified for an extra week's vacation, and I'm so excited! This year I will be able to enjoy a stay on the beach at Plum Island for an entire week!"

"Oh son, Herman and I are so proud of you. You remember, Herman, don't you? He's your father. At the rate you're going, I just know it won't be long before you will create something with the potential to kill as many as billion people! Just think...a fourth of the world's population! Wouldn't that be wonderful? Got to go now, son. I can't wait to share this good news with Herman. You remember, Herman, don't you son?"

As Susan leaned back on the couch to reflect on the implications of the stunning article she had just read, she silently began wondering what had happened to the moral outrage and righteous indignation that only a few decades ago would have surfaced with a force and a fury sweeping through America after the appearance of such an article.

Have we as a nation become so jaded and our sensibilities so numbed that the deaths of millions of people become just another boring statistic? she thought. *And what of my own growing cynicism? And this macabre sense of humor I have developed seemingly springing suddenly out of nowhere? This is not like you, Susan! Cynical, morbid, and macabre! Maybe you can get a job as a writer for the* Addams Family *cartoon series.*

Susan folded the newspaper, and after a few more minutes of reflection, she moved on to the next in the pile.

After reviewing the next several newspapers, Susan was convinced that a steady diet of such depressing news would eventually result in growing anxieties, increased stress, and suicidal tendencies among the readership. She promised herself she would resist Cathy's urgings to "read the news" and go back to her previous shell of insulation, remaining oblivious to the happenings of the world.

Ah, she thought as she started on the last newspaper in the stack, *here's another article about viruses. Guess I'll just have to read this one also before I begin my self-imposed celibacy. This looks interesting…"Avian Flu Threatens Millions—Global Pandemic Feared!"*

Feared? Why is this virus feared, but the creation of the 1918 flu virus by the goon at the CDC is viewed as a positive development? Let's add that to the list of things that I just don't understand! But let's see now… this one is spread by birds, has already killed hundreds in parts of Asia, and is feared it could quickly spread to the United States in a highly infectious, mutated version…And wipe out a third of the population…Hmmm, sounds yummy. Wait, there's more…The president has requested Congress provide him with the authorization to mobilize the military to forcibly quarantine American citizens. However, some opposed such a move, arguing it would violate the provisions of the Posse Comitatus Act of 1879.

Susan paused for a moment trying to decide which of these two events posed the greatest threat to the security and freedom of the American people—the viral invasion or the military invasion.

Too close to call, she thought. *Looks like we lose either way. And what is that Posse Comitatus Act? I would assume it forbids using the military against American citizens, but it sounds like medical terminology for some female body part.*

"Whatever," she muttered aloud as she angrily tossed the newspapers into the garbage can.

Pep Rally

The streets of the nation's capital were filled to capacity by 8 AM that Monday morning as senators, congressman, Capitol Hill staffers, assorted bureaucrats, and representatives of the media on the prowl were quickly making their ways to their appointed destinations. In the office of Congressman Harry McDonald, however, his entire Washington staff was already gathered in their conference room and most had begun sipping their second cup of coffee. Members of his staff back home in the Second Congressional District were also at their offices and were awaiting the beginning of the conference call linking their offices to Washington. Congressman McDonald entered the conference room precisely at 8 AM, dressed in a dark gray business suit, crisp white shirt, and burgundy tie, looking as strikingly handsome and successful as ever. But Erin Giblon wondered if the other staffers were noticing the changes in his facial features brought about by the incredible stress he had endured. Not only were the brow wrinkles deeper and more pronounced, but it appeared that even the area of graying at his temples had expanded.

"Good morning," Harry began. "I've called you all together to review our progress to date. I realize our workloads and long hours have been difficult schedules to maintain, but I want each and every one of you to know how very much your dedication is appreciated by me and those whom we are trying to help. Not only is your dedication and sacrifice appreciated perhaps more so than you'll ever fully realize, but it's also required, unfortunately, by the development of the current circumstances. For to do any less than we are attempting would be a moral abomination, the stigma of which would simply be too great for any of us to bear. But your hard work has begun producing dividends, and we are now able to identify those areas where significant advancements have been accomplished. At this time, Miss Giblon will report to us on her progress with the

ACLU regarding our solicitation of their support for the release of Dr. Glen Klinner."

"Yes, good morning everyone. I did speak recently with the director of the Washington office of the ACLU. I must admit I was rather surprised by his response to our request. It seems concerns had already been expressed by several members of their executive committee regarding the status of the investigation into Dr. Klinner's role, if any, in the ferry massacre. The announcement by the Justice Department that Dr. Klinner, a U.S. citizen, would be tried for aiding and abetting terrorism under the provisions of the Patriot Act was particularly unsettling to the ACLU hierarchy. In summation, the ACLU has already begun filing legal briefs with the courts alleging violations of Dr. Klinner's civil rights. Yes, pretty amazing, I thought, but just perhaps these recent actions by the government are too brazen for even that crowd to stomach. I thanked the director and offered our support if we could assist in any regard."

"Excellent, Miss Giblon! Let's prepare official correspondence on our congressional letterhead, which I will sign, thanking them for their support of constitutional principles."

"Certainly, Mr. Congressman. I would at this time also like to comment on the response of our friend and ally MacIntosh McAdams of *The Chronicle*. Have any of you seen this morning's issue of *The Chronicle*? No? Well, in the issue, which I just happen to have a copy of here, we find a hard-hitting, very critical column devoted to the plight of Dr. Klinner and his family."

Erin unfolded the paper to display Mac's op-ed piece occupying the top half of the page which included photographs of Attorney General Budenz, Dr. Klinner, and his wife, Fran. Erin held the paper aloft for all to see while she continued her remarks.

"Mr. McAdams first attacked the gullibility of the United States Congress, present company excluded, Mr. Congressman, for hastily supporting the passage of the ill-conceived Patriot Act at the behest of a power-hungry administration in the aftermath of 9/11. 'Err in haste, repent at leisure,' he reminded his readers. Secondly, he was harshly critical of the Senate Judiciary Committee and the American Bar Association for remaining silent throughout this continuing travesty of justice. Thirdly, he offered to his readers what I thought to be an excellent primer on the fundamentals of rule by law as mandated by constitutional restrictions and constraints. I'll leave this issue of the paper in the conference room after our staff meeting for everyone's perusal."

"Well, Miss Giblon, thank you for your report. Very encouraging. Indeed we owe a debt of gratitude to Mr. McAdams for his courage and insightfulness."

"There's more," Erin added. "I have been in contact with Mr. McAdams daily now, communicating via fax, e-mail, and phone. It seems that as of 7:25 AM today, approximately 85 percent of the photographs and images included in the assumed purloined documents have been identified by his staff."

"Eighty-five percent? That's incredible! Any conclusions?"

"We don't know for sure, but it would appear they are ancillary to and supportive of the chronology of the documents we received. For example, there are photographs from Tuskegee, Alabama, with officials identified from the Public Health Service from the thirties and forties. Later on, we have CDC officials at both Tuskegee and Plum Island. Remaining photos are from other bio-labs including, but not limited to, Ft. Detrick, Maryland, the CDC in Atlanta, Ft. Collins, Colorado, and even pictures of conveyor belts moving thousands of eggs at the Army's Pine Bluff, Arkansas, arsenal. I'm not certain what that represents."

"The eggs are for the incubation of viruses, Miss Giblon. In particular, the mass production of the AIDS virus."

"Oh…" responded Erin as the conference room fell deathly silent.

Each and every staffer at that moment paused to reflect on the enormity of what they were hearing. After several moments, Harry broke the silence by asking if Mac would be providing a comprehensive listing of the photographs with supportive explanatory notes.

"Yes, Mr. Congressman…actually he hopes to provide the information retrieved thus far by late this afternoon. Some of the photographs appear to have been taken of individuals and locations in other countries, particularly the former Soviet Union, which may take longer to identify. I advised him we might be able to provide some clues from our office based on the location of the photograph in question relative to the subject matter of the text we hope our imported experts will be able to decipher. And speaking of foreigners in photographs, Mr. McAdams asked me if you were familiar with Operation Paperclip, implemented by our government at the end of World War II."

"Yes, somewhat. Our government was attempting to bring in the best scientists the former enemy or enemies had to offer. The adjective *best* being used in the context of efficacy only, you understand."

"I understand, Mr. Congressman. Well, Mr. McAdams thought you would be interested in the photographs of a certain Erich Traub at the CDC and Plum Island."

"And who is or was Erich Traub?"

"An Operation Paperclip recruit. It appears he was one of the founding fathers of the Plum Island lab, having been brought here from Germany to pattern the lab after those that had existed in the Fatherland. Traub was a former Nazi germ-warfare scientist."

"I'm not surprised."

The congressman is not surprised, thought Erin. *Well, I will be surprised…if I ever get another good night of sleep, that is! I'll be imagining creepy crawlies on my skin and boogey men at the door for the rest of my life! When I get out of here today, I'm going straight for those running shoes, and it's going to be a 10-K for this chick tonight. A nice, hot bubble bath and plenty of vino should get me through the night. Maybe after the committee investigation is completed, I should dust off my passport and reconsider Chile or somewhere…*

"Before we move on to additional encouraging progress, does anyone have anything else to report? No? Well let me conclude our meeting by reporting on my efforts to solicit the support of some members of the Senate Judiciary Committee as well as the American Bar Association. Then I'll provide an update on the response of several medical schools to our request for academically qualified individuals capable of interpreting the large sheath of documents we have received.

"Regarding the Senate Judiciary Committee, I received a quite favorable response from four of the most influential members. We were in agreement on most of the pertinent issues, and I have their assurance that the committee will press for a full Senate resolution condemning the use of the anti-terrorist provisions of the Patriot Act against a United States citizen. In stark contrast, the response I received from the ABA was nil. I think for all practical purposes, we should not assume any support will be forthcoming from that quarter. Again, pretty much as I expected.

"Finally, and most encouraging of all, is the response this office has received from the medical schools to which we sent inquiries. Already we have enthusiastic replies from Emory, Harvard, Johns Hopkins, UAB, Duke, Yale, and the Mayo Clinic. As soon as we select the individuals we deem the most qualified and suitable from the résumés we're receiving, we'll begin the telephone interview process. If they are selected, we will forward an oath of confidentiality and truthfulness for the committee's investigation requiring their signature guarantee of acceptance. Effectively, from that point on, they will have been 'sworn in' and we'll be able to forward copies of the CDs you have produced to each participant for them to begin their research. I think most of these recipients will be in for an eye-opening experience, to say the least.

"At our present rate of progress, I think we can make a public announcement with certainty and confidence that our committee investigation will begin hearings the first week of September, the day after Labor Day, to be precise."

Applause spontaneously erupted at that point and filled the conference room. For Congressman McDonald's staffers, the announcement of a starting date for the committee was analogous to finding out the exact date of the high school prom or the football team's award banquet celebration…or graduation for that matter. It was a rite of passage. They had worked hard, very hard, for a cause in which they all believed. Indeed it was a team effort, and Congressman Harry McDonald was the quarterback for his team.

"That concludes our staff meeting for this morning. Again, I wish to thank each and every one of you for your contributions to our efforts. As we go forward to victory, your continuing efforts individually and collectively will assure our success. Thank you!"

As Erin began collecting her notes in preparation to return to her office, the congressman approached her and quietly asked if she would come to his office. As they together entered Harry's office, he closed the door behind them and moved to sit at his desk while motioning for Erin to take a seat in one of the wingback chairs facing him. She thought the solemn expression she now observed on Harry's face did not match the mood of enthusiasm he had exuded only moments earlier.

What now? she thought. *Has Taliferro of the FBI called to spill the beans about me at the Dubliner that Friday night? Am I about to be canned?*

"Miss Giblon," he began, "I want to thank you again for all you have done. Your assistance has been invaluable. I asked you in because of something that has only recently surfaced that is extremely sensitive to our work here."

That's it! she thought. *That bastard Taliferro! My goose is cooked!*

"What is it, Mr. Congressman?" her voice beginning to sound like a squeak. "You sound disturbed."

"Disturbed? Yes, you could say that, but I think horrified would be a more accurate description."

Erin, pulse now racing, sat quietly waiting for the other shoe to drop.

"Miss Giblon?"

"Yes?"

"Have you ever heard of the Avian Flu virus?"

What? she thought as she gulped and almost coughed as she responded, "Avian Flu? Yes, of course. It's in all the news, or at least the news I read."

"Are you aware of the projections for its spread?"

"So far Asia and parts of Turkey with a potential to spread to the United States?"

"And the projected death toll?"

"No."

"A third of the Earth's total population!"

"What? Are you serious?"

"That's correct…well over a billion people. Are you aware the president has asked Congress for the power to order the military to forcibly quarantine Americans in the event of an outbreak on U.S. soil?"

"No."

"It's true. With not even a single documented case of Avian Flu recorded in the United States, the government and certain media are using alarmist fear tactics to stampede the American people into accepting another massive power grab by the government."

"But is it really a threat to us?"

"If the mutated virus, H5N1 as it's known in the scientific community, is another product of the bio-labs, you bet it's a threat!"

"Are you implying the government might release it deliberately on American citizens? What would that accomplish?"

"That is exactly what I am implying, Miss Giblon! And what would that accomplish? Number one, and of most concern to our objectives, would be the immediate loss of support among the general population for our investigation. The American people would view the bio-labs as their salvation—the potential sources of life-saving vaccines that would be so desperately required. Number two would be the massive expansion and consolidation of power and control by the central government, which as you already know is what the New World Order is all about—power and control. Number three, it would achieve the enormous reduction in the global population so eagerly sought after by the New World Order planners for years. I could probably think of a few more reasons, given the time, but those will do for starters."

"Incredible, Mr. Congressman. But how could such a virus be spread among the population?"

"That's the easy part. Engineer a capsule to contain the virus with a time release mechanism. Plant the capsule in the air conditioning duct work of a U.S. airliner and time the release of the virus to coincide with the airliner's return to the United States from an international flight. Over 200 passengers would be infected and, upon arrival, would proceed to infect thousands, possibly millions. When the source of the contagion is eventually traced it will appear to have been of foreign origin, brought unsuspectingly to our shores by a returning traveler."

Erin sat quietly after the congressman had finished his remarks, too numb to speak. When she finally did speak, her question was simple.

"What do we do?"

"Exactly what we have been doing. We have no control or influence over anything with implications as enormous as what I am describing. Pray to our God for protection and guidance and keep on going. That's all we can do. Well, maybe not completely all—one of the commercially available flu medications is an antiviral that has demonstrated some effectiveness against H5N1. I'll contact some of my practicing physician friends and acquire a supply sufficient for our entire staff and their families. We'll stockpile it and pray we never need it!"

"Sometimes ignorance is bliss, Mr. Congressman. Why are you sharing these concerns with me now? These are things I would rather not know."

"If it happens, I don't want you to be surprised. I want you to keep your focus because you are such a vital, indispensable component of our team effort. Coming events cast their shadows long before, Miss Giblon. I have been studying the goals and modus operandi of the network we loosely term the New World Order for almost two decades now. If there is anything at all I have learned over the ensuing years, it's that to know the mind of your enemy is to anticipate their next move."

"So the shadows you are seeing, metaphorically speaking, are the warning signs of an impending attack, which if it occurs, will precipitate an unprecedented disaster?"

"Possibly, Miss Giblon.... No, let me rephrase that. Quite possibly, Miss Giblon."

Dress Code

Susan Collins arose earlier than usual Monday morning driven by an enthusiasm and eagerness to return to work that for months now had been completely absent from her daily routine. Her newfound zeal, however, was not fueled by expectations of perpetuation of her Plum Island career. Quite the contrary. It was the thought of the imminent termination of those duties, obligations, and ties that had put a spring in her steps and a smile on her face. Dressed in a red silk blouse, full circular skirt emblazoned with vividly colored floral designs, gold sandals, large gold hoop earrings, bright red lipstick and yes, the bag, Susan presented an image of anything but a microbiologist bound for work at America's premier germ-warfare laboratory. Did she care what Gallagher and Stephens might think? Her co-workers? Hardly. This would convey her new image of a woman rejoicing over her son's recovery and her newfound responsibilities at the facility...or at least that's what Susan wanted everyone to think.

I have a doctorate in microbiology from UAB, for goodness sake, she thought. *Am I not deserving of at least some eccentricities and idiosyncrasies? Whatever...as long as they accept and become accustomed to that bag on a daily basis. That's all that matters. Then when the time is right...*

Susan's daydream was interrupted by Cathy's early arrival for another day of caring for Toby while Susan worked.

Cathy, after closing the door, turned to face Susan as Susan loudly exclaimed,

"How do I look?" as she simultaneously twirled in a mini-pirouette and began snapping her fingers to mimic the sound of castanets.

Oh to have a videotape of this moment! thought Susan. *That look on Cathy's face is priceless!*

Susan paused and stood facing Cathy as she held the large, colorful bag in one hand, with her other hand strategically placed on her hip, all the while expressing a broad grin, and awaiting Cathy's response.

THE POISON PLUM

"Well?"

"I thought you were going to work today!"

"Of course I am! Come on, how do I look? Do you like it?"

"You are not going to that job dressed like that! Are you nuts? Have you been back in the wine already?"

"No wine, and no, I'm not nuts! And for the third time, how the hell do I look?"

"Honest injun?"

"Honest injun!"

"You look like a middle-aged school teacher from Alabama on vacation in Tijuana looking for some action!"

"Hmmm...sounds like fun! But not today, I'll be late for work. Love you, Sis! See you about six... Thanks!"

"Hold on just a second! You are not seriously considering hauling that hideosity in there with you, are you?"

"Are you talking about my bag? Of course, I am...how else am I expected to transport my essentials? And besides, what is a hideosity? There is no such word."

"There most certainly is! I just created it. In times of intense emotional excitement, it's perfectly proper to merge adjectives into noun status to get the point across!"

"I love you, Sis. Give me a big hug...I gotta hit the road!"

The stares and nudges among Susan's colleagues began as soon as she exited her SUV and began making her way across the parking lot to the ferry landing. For certain, Susan was the center of attention that Monday morning as her attire contrasted starkly with the normally conservative and staid dress of the facilities' personnel. Never under conditions of permanent employment would Susan ever engage in such an attention-garnering masquerade of lackadaisical flamboyance. Knowing that her time in that environment was sharply limited however, Susan delighted in flaunting a devil-may-care attitude. The security personnel, in particular, were taken aback by the new look of Susan Collins, and scrutinized every aspect of her appearance. The hoop earrings and metal latches of her sandals triggered the metal detectors of course and had to be removed to clear that gauntlet. The bag accomplished the same as it moved along the security belt and through the imaging equipment, triggering alarms and expressions of concern on the faces of Tweedledum and Tweedledee, who operated the device. Seizing the bag, the dynamic duo began their inspection by probing through Susan's essentials and finally unceremoniously and rudely dumping the bag's contents onto the conveyor belt. Their expressions clearly revealed their disdain and lack of patience with Susan's waste of their valuable time.

Good, thought Susan. *Look at my bag inside and out, every morning and every afternoon. Observe the images created by the Aztec calendars each and every time, over and over again, until you just can't stand the sight of that bag any longer.*

One of the guards gruffly ordered Susan to proceed as he looked in the direction of the other while shaking his head. Susan smiled as she took her own good sweet time putting her sandals back on, the hoop earrings back into her ears and yes, slowly repacking her essentials into the bag. The entire episode to Susan was the emotional equivalent of dropping her drawers and mooning the guards and her co-workers.

"Piss on 'em," she mumbled as she proudly walked away, bound for cubicle 11.

Glancing at her watch, Susan began wondering how long it would be before she could expect a visit from the charming Herschel Gallagher.

Surely, she thought, *the word is spreading rapidly throughout the facility...let's see now...hmmm...I would guess in about thirty minutes I will hear the sound of the dork waddling like a penguin to my cubicle. Looking forward to it! Meanwhile, I've got work to do!*

Sure enough, in almost exactly thirty minutes, Susan again felt the presence of someone standing behind her and looking over her shoulder. As she turned and saw that it was indeed Gallagher, she immediately broke into a warm, cheerful smile and said heartily, "Good morning, Mr. Gallagher! How are you this fine Monday morning?"

"It's a little early for Halloween, don't you think Ms. Collins?"

"Oh this?" responded Susan, waiving her hands over her clothes and the bag. "These are just some things I picked up Saturday at the seafood festival. One of the arts and crafts booths had an 'Evening in Old Mexico' theme."

"Ms. Collins, while we do not have an official dress code for our facility, it is generally presumed and expected that our personnel will dress in a manner befitting their employment status."

THE POISON PLUM

"But don't you think, Mr. Gallagher, and especially since the unfortunate event at the ferry, that this place could use a splash of color to lift our spirits? Look around you, Mr. Gallagher… everything is either black, white, or shades of gray. And besides, my cheerful attire reflects my elation at my son's recovery and the assumption of new and exciting responsibilities here at Plum Island. I suppose I am having a difficult time containing my enthusiasm… I can only hope it will be contagious."

With that, Herschel Gallagher abruptly turned and walked away.

"Just like that SOB," Susan muttered to herself. *Not a howdy doody or a kiss my ass, but it doesn't matter. I expected as much. Whatever it takes to get this crowd accustomed to seeing that bag on a regular basis, that's the important part! By Friday, everyone should be sufficiently conditioned, so Friday it is. Just as I am leaving for the weekend…*

Susan had no illusions about the consequences she would face if she were found out. Prison or worse would be her fate. For after all, the courts have never smiled fondly upon those charged and convicted of stealing top-secret government information. For the Rosenbergs, convicted of stealing atomic secrets, it was execution. Certainly, Plum Island was not the nuclear facility at Oak Ridge, Tennessee, but was the information contained within these walls of an even more sensitive and secret nature? A chill swept through Susan's body as she allowed her mind to ponder the possibilities. Copying the files she had access to would pose no problems. Sure the cameras would be watching, but it didn't matter. Susan and the other workers routinely copied files day in and day out as part of their normal routines. But copying a file or multiple files to a CD was one thing, getting that CD through security undetected was another. Susan realized that if caught, she could lose everything forever. Even Toby…

Wipe that tear off your cheek, Susan, she thought. *You're going to do this thing, and you're going to do it Friday. The die is cast, and you have no alternative. You didn't draw first blood, these bastards did. Now suck it up and keep on keeping on. It won't be much longer now. Let's see… it's going to take approximately four CDs to hold all these virology files. Should I try to take out two on Thursday and the remainder on Friday? Nope, that would be double the risk. It's all or nothing. Four on Friday it is. And then what? Do I take them home and hide them under the mattress until I figure out what the hell I'm going to do with them? What if the men in dark suits come and turn my house upside down… again! Too risky! As soon as those CDs come in, they need to go right back out again. And go where? That congressman? That newspaper guy? One of them? Both of them? Do I trust the mail? Wow! These are heavy-duty decisions! Let me think...both the congressman and the newspaper columnist have offices in Washington, but I'm not in Washington. This is New London. But wouldn't that congressman maintain an office in his home district? Even so, what do I do? Walk in with the CDs in a manila envelope, announce that I'm Susan Collins, I work at that bug lab, and would you please see that the congressman gets this package? And what if I'm already under suspicion and being watched 24/7? I can hear it now: "Exactly what was your reason for visiting Congressman McDonald's office, Ms. Collins? And what were the contents of that package you delivered?"*

I'll think about this again tonight after Cathy leaves, and Toby is asleep. And not one word of this will I mention to dear, sweet Cathy. I may sink myself, but no way will I make her an accomplice to my hair-brained schemes.

The day flew by for Susan, and it seemed she had only been at work for a few hours when it was once again time to face the dum dums in security. And, once again, she had to remove her sandals and earrings, and once again one of the guards just had to plunge his fleshy paw into her 'essentials.' But at least this time the contents were not dumped onto the conveyor belt. Susan just smiled broadly and bid them a fond farewell.

"See you tomorrow," she said. "Have a good evening!"

Susan's mind was totally occupied on the ferry ride to the mainland and the ensuing drive home. Events were moving faster now, much faster, and Susan knew she had to stay ahead of the curve. There was too much at stake and too much risk for even the slightest miscalculation. Cathy and Toby both greeted her at the door upon arrival, which for Susan was quite a surprise. Toby was usually in bed every day.

"Well, who do we have here? How are you feeling, sweetie? Give Mommy a big hug! You, too, Sis! What have you two been up to today?"

"Mommy! Aunt Cathy took me to the park with the swings after we left the hospital!"

"No bugs?" Susan asked.

"No bugs, Mommy. We were careful, and I had a great time!"

"That's wonderful, Toby. Are you tired?"

"I was, but I took a nap after we got home."

"How 'bout you, Sis? What's happening?"

"OK, fine…I've been productive."

"I want to hear all about it…I could go for a glass of wine, too. Would you care for one?"

"Not tonight. I've got shopping to do. If I get relaxed, I'll get sleepy, and it'll never get done. Maybe tomorrow."

Susan quickly returned from the kitchen with a small glass of wine, sat on the couch, and promptly propped her feet up on the coffee table.

"Do you still have a job?" Cathy asked.

"Of course I still have a job. Why shouldn't I?"

"Your costume?"

"No problem! Gallagher had to remind me when Halloween was, but that's just the way he is. Nothing to worry about!"

"OK then. Let me tell you about my productive day."

"Golly gee, that wine is fine. Are you sure you don't want a glass?"

"Gotta shop, sorry. Anyway, listen up. I spoke with Dr. Butler's office this morning about your insurance."

"And?"

"They didn't know for sure. I spoke with Joyce, who is in charge of filing insurance for his patients. She said that if a claim is questioned or denied, the company would send you a letter of explanation."

"Isn't that sweet!"

"The only thing she could imagine would be a question regarding his clinical diagnosis of Lyme disease. It is, as you know, unsupported by a positive, confirmatory test result."

"Uh-oh."

"Don't worry about it, Sis. I got you covered."

"Three hundred dollars a day?"

"I said, don't worry about it. Next issue…I spoke with the church members last night, and I have a departure date for the Lyme-Aid Express! Monday after next and returning the following Friday night."

"That soon?"

"Yes, they had already been in touch with the specialist's office in Birmingham. Actually that date was set a week ago."

"Can we get Toby onboard?"

"That's the best news of all. I called Dr. Robinson's office and spoke with his appointment secretary. I explained our situation and asked if there was any way Toby could be worked in with the group that's coming down. She was really nice and told me the doctor would see everyone, even if it meant holding evening appointments. She said he was aware of what had transpired in the Northeast with the government raids and all and would do whatever he could to help those people. Of course, she will need copies of Toby's records, but I've already called Dr. Butler's office back to request those. You'll have to sign a release form, and they will mail them to Dr. Robinson."

"Wow…Sis, you have been productive! Thank you!"

"Piece of cake! I've got a good feeling about all of this, Susan. Everything seems to be coming together, and those folks down there in Birmingham really seem to be on top of things."

Coming together or disintegrating at warp speed? thought Susan as her mind once again began moving forward to Friday.

Later that evening, after Cathy had left, Toby was asleep, and all was quite, Susan reached for the local telephone directory to find the address of Congressman McDonald's local office.

"Hmmm," mused Susan. "120 East Concord Street…that's in the older section of downtown. I wonder if that's the address of the old Abercrombie Building? After work tomorrow, I'll be checking that out."

Show-and-Tell Time

The beginning date of the House Committee on Health and Human Services hearings on Plum Island and related issues was announced with considerable fanfare the following Wednesday morning in Washington. At 9 AM, Congressman McDonald, along with several of the committee's congressional membership, held a news conference that was well attended by representatives of the national media due to the nation's continuing interest in the ferry massacre. Simultaneous announcements were provided to McDonald's congressional district and government offices including the Justice Department, FBI, Department of Homeland Security, and the Central Intelligence Agency.

In addition, subpoenas were issued that day for Martha Johnson, Director of the Plum Island facility; Acting Director Clement Stephens; all department heads; the directors of the CDC in Atlanta, Ft. Detrick, Maryland, and Ft. Collins, Colorado; Attorney General Budenz; Department of Homeland Security Director Dolan; CIA Director Steele; FBI Director Frey; and ATF Director Aderholdt.

Congressman McDonald, completely in his element as chairman of that committee and host of the news conference, once again masterfully presented the justifications for, rationale of, and expected goals of the committee hearings to the media in attendance. In summation, the committee's goals and objectives, as skillfully delineated by the congressman were as follows:

1. Determine the true nature and scope of the work being done at Plum Island and its correlation, if any, with programs in operation at other bio-labs.
2. Determine if possible the motivation for Colonel Gordon McClain's actions.

3. Full and complete exoneration of Colonel Gordon McClain's good name and reputation.
4. Determine if the birthplace of the current and expanding scourge of Lyme disease was the lab at Plum Island.
5. The complete exoneration and release of Dr. Glen Klinner and his wife Fran.

The response of the media to Congressman McDonald's presentation was generally favorable, much to the chagrin of directors Budenz, Dolan, Frey, Steele, and Aderholdt. Even Snodgrass of *The Times* and Lemke of *The Post* exhibited muted responses, due to the completely rational and non-confrontational stated objectives of the committee. MacIntosh McAdams was, of course, grateful for this new opportunity to create another hard-hitting column supportive of the hearings, which was created and edited in time to be published in the next morning's edition of *The Chronicle*. McAdams compared McDonald to a savior on a white horse wielding a sword of righteousness coming to excise a malignancy threatening the body politic of America. Other columnists were less effusive, preferring instead to report the event only and await its outcome to offer their judgments.

Attorney General Budenz would of course have to make the calls he did not particularly relish to the prostituted judges of the appropriate federal district courts telling them to quash the subpoenas for the director and acting director of Plum Island, as well as for all the directors and department heads of the other bio-labs on the grounds of national security.

And it was a given, of course, that a conference call would be held at the completion of the news conference. The only question would be the identity of the initiator. When the phones finally began ringing throughout Washington in the offices of the various agency directors, many were relieved it was CIA Director Steele who had originated the calls instead of the president. After the operator's usual identity verification of the conference call's participants, Director Steele began speaking in his consistently brusque and forthright manner.

"Did everyone watch the choir boy's news conference on C-Span?"

After a unanimous response in the affirmative, Steele continued.

"How many of you received subpoenas?"

"I did," replied FBI Director Frey.

"Me, too," chimed in Director Dolan of Homeland Security.

"Ditto for Helms here."

"And you, Budenz?" asked Steele.

"Yeah! I received a subpoena, and I can't believe the arrogance of that bastard! A piss-ass congressman from who the hell cares Connecticut issuing a subpoena for the attorney general of the United States! Who the hell does he think he is?"

"We're not alone," responded Steele. "Our sources reveal that subpoenas were also issued to all of the directors of the other bio-labs including the CDC in Atlanta."

"Yeah, I'm aware," said Budenz. "The pussies have all been calling my office whimpering about what to do. Now I've got the hassles of having to contact all of those judges in all of those federal districts and clue them in to quash those damn subpoenas."

"And what is that going to look like to the media and the public?" asked Steele. "Quashing subpoenas for Plum Island on the grounds of national security is one thing, but for all the other bio-labs? It's going to look like we are trying to hide something. Which, of course, we are, but that's beside the point."

"I know, Steele, but what choice do we have?" asked Budenz. "Right now, I'm so pissed at McDonald I could slit his damn throat!"

Chuckles erupted from the conference's participants, but it was the vigorous laughter issuing forth from Director Frey that superseded all of the other expressions of humor.

"What the hell is so funny, Frey?" asked Budenz.

"I don't know for sure, Budenz…perhaps it's the mental image of a United States congressman bleeding to death on the steps of the Capitol as the top law-enforcement official of the United States straddles the dying body, clutching a large knife dripping with blood while grinning maniacally."

More laughter erupted from the participants and for a few moments the conference call's direction was interrupted. It was Steele who restored order and the focus of the conference.

"OK, as much as we would all like to see our nemesis turning on the spit like a suckling pig, we need to get back to the business at hand. Let's for a moment reconsider this subpoena thing. For example, what difference does it make if the director of Plum Island gets subpoenaed? What's her name? Martha Johnson? Hell, her appearance would do us more good than harm. She doesn't know shit from Shinola about what is really going on out there. How could she hurt us?

"The same goes for the directors of the other labs. What difference would it make if they all appear? McDonald's going after Plum Island and its connection to Lyme disease. Without any witnesses, he won't even know what questions to ask those other directors. I say we quash the subpoenas for the acting director of Plum, all the department heads and any of the other lesser echelon people or employees that get caught in McDonald's dragnet. Everyone else, including us and especially us, will show. Not only do we show, but we vigorously support and stress the importance of Plum's role in *defending* America from disease and germ warfare. Over and over and over again, we will make it perfectly clear that the objective of Plum Island research is defensive and never offensive. And of course, by extension, that is also the objective of all the other labs. Protection! Protection! Protection! McDonald won't have a leg to stand on…no witnesses, no smoking guns dredged up by the FOIA and all of us patiently explaining to all of those media cameras and recorders that the concerned, well-meaning Congressman is simply confused and is misrepresenting the objectives of America's bio-*defense* laboratories. McDonald will come away looking like a fool, and our positions as defenders of security and freedom for the American people will be stronger than ever."

"That sounds wonderful, Director Steele," replied Frey. "But what about all of the brain horsepower McDonald is importing from the medical schools? What if those people advise McDonald what questions to ask?"

"Who will he ask? Me? You? Martha Johnson?"

"How about Kirkland of the CDC? Lane of Ft. Detrick? Boulware of Ft. Collins? They could sure as hell spill some beans."

"Not to worry…we'll just have a pep rally and a refresher course in obfuscation for those guys prior to the committee investigation. One of the reasons they are directors is their ability to deflect and misdirect, talents kept honed by their constant interactions with the media."

"Look Frey, how do you think those guys in the Federal Reserve System have managed to survive since 1913? We all know that scheme is not federal. There sure as hell aren't any reserves, but it's a system, that's for sure. And what a system it is! Just think…the franchise, granted by those fools in Congress, to splatter ink on paper and convince the gullible American public to accept the printing presses' copious discharge as a money substitute. Look at the face of it and what do you see in that fine print… *This note is legal tender for all debts public and private.* Hell, a note is a debt instrument…the fools are using a debt to pay a debt. We all know where that is going to lead!"

"Yes, Director Steele," interrupted Helms of the Pentagon. "We all know that, but you are digressing. What is your point?"

"My point is, I'm going to buy another hundred ounces of gold as soon as I get off this call. All right, I'm sorry…here's my point. Each time in the past, when some congressman or senator, obviously brighter than the rest, like our friend McDonald, figured out what the fed was really all about and tried to investigate it through the committee route, he was inevitably stonewalled by 'expert' testimony. How many members of Congress are trained economists? How easy is it to have a sophisticated fed chairman pull the wool over everyone's eyes with an endless barrage of financial mumbo jumbo? Have any of you ever looked at the quarterly reviews published by the regional Federal Reserve Banks? Those things are filled with articles laced with the most complicated mathematical formulas you have ever seen, all written and produced by eggheads with doctorates in economics. No one understands the articles and formulas, most assuredly the guy who graduated with honors from the local Rotary Club to become a congressman. Hell, even the authors of those tendentious, erudite articles probably don't understand fully what the shit they have written. My point is, it's all a big shell game. If the members of Congress don't understand economics, which obviously they don't, should we expect them to understand the extremely complicated world of germs, genetic engineering, and biological warfare? Of course not. And I'm still going to put that gold order through!"

"All of us are trained to expect the unexpected," Frey said. "As director of the FBI, I live with it 24/7, which perfectly complements my normal state of paranoia. I agree with what you're saying Steele, but I've got an uneasy feeling about this guy, McDonald. He's not like those others that have swallowed our lies hook, line, and sinker, nor is he like those who expressed a display of opposition and then quickly caved when the struggle became too encompassing. We have all agreed during previous meetings on the degree of tenacity the son of a bitch is capable of exhibiting, and I don't think any of us would dispute his intelligence. McDonald is operating like a man with an ace in the hole. I believe that's obvious, and I believe it would be naïve of us all to think otherwise. On the other hand, we don't have a clue what that ace in the hole could be. Our field agents shadowing the only employee not present at the ferry massacre have nothing of consequence to report. Yesterday, as she was returning home from work, our agents excitedly reported that she stopped briefly at the building in downtown New London where McDonald's district office is located. However, if she even noticed his office, it was not observed by our agents. The building houses a variety of offices and shops, including an optometrist, a travel agency, a small dress shop, some attorneys' offices, and her apparent destination yesterday, an ice cream shop in the courtyard. She purchased a cone and a small container to go, probably for her son who is recovering from mono. Her supervisor at the lab thinks she is a ditzy, flaky broad and keeps her around only because she is eminently qualified academically and they're shorthanded."

"So here we sit," said Dolan. "The director of the FBI thinks McDonald has an ace in the hole or up his sleeve, and even with the combined intelligence gathering capabilities of the CIA and the FBI, we are powerless to even confirm that suspicion, much less identify its source. When we know what the president of Russia had for breakfast and how many orgasms his mistress had last night, but we don't even know what one of our own congressman is up to, something is wrong with that picture. What do we do now? Just show up for the hearings and allow McDonald to put us all on the grill and turn up the heat? I think we need a fail-safe, what-if plan."

"I'll second that, Dolan," responded Budenz. "Just in case Frey's suspicions are correct and McDonald starts pulling out rabbits. A contingency plan prepared well in advance that could be implemented at a moment's notice…or for that matter, shelved at a moment's notice, as conditions dictate."

"We'll work on that," answered Steele. "That's what the CIA does best."

"All right," said General Helms. "We have discussed our plans of deflection and obfuscation for the germ questions, but what are we going to do about that Klinner guy and his wife. I realize the purpose of my subpoena is to question me about Colonel McClain, and somehow McDonald will try to use that testimony to secure the release of Klinner."

"No problem," responded Budenz. "The hearings begin the first Tuesday after Labor Day? What does that give us…almost seven weeks? Everyone knows Klinner is guilty of attempting to foment terrorism. He is guilty, guilty, guilty of aiding and abetting a terrorist act committed against employees of the U.S. government. He must pay for his crimes. He is the sacrificial lamb required to vindicate Colonel McClain while simultaneously satisfying the American citizen's appetite for justice. We have all covered this ground many times before. Our solution is simple—if Klinner is still alive, which is doubtful, just accelerate his trial and conviction. Try him and his wife as a team, which when convicted, will share equal punishment. We all know what the penalty is for treason. End of Klinners, end of problem. Just report to the media the results, not the process."

On that cheery note, another top-drawer, Washington inter-agency conference call drew to a close.

The Arrival of Friday

As if controlled and coordinated by a gigantic metronome, the days of Susan's life ticked by inexorably until the arrival of that fateful Friday. The ritual of daily ferry rides to and from the facility, the arrival and departure of Cathy to provide care for Toby, the antibiotic infusions and any and everything else required to keep the Collins' ship of state on its appointed course continued unabated and unwavering with clockwork precision. And each and every morning as Friday approached, reservations and second thoughts flooded Susan's consciousness as soon as she awoke. Also each and every morning, all the compelling arguments for abandoning her dangerous and brazen scheme were just as quickly dispelled by a visit to Toby's room. The grim picture each day was the same—Toby's flannel pajamas, bed covers, and sheets drenched from the night sweats— the sweet, sick, oppressive odor hanging heavy in the air, permeating every inch of Toby's room… and with every movement, Toby more and more resembling a very old arthritic. Finally, if any further suasion were required of Susan, the expressions of fear and suffering spoke volumes through Toby's sunken and dark-circled eyes, anxiously and silently begging Susan for help.

Susan's movements were almost mechanical when Friday morning finally arrived. She had enjoyed little sleep the night before, awakening frequently to replay over and over in her mind the possible scenarios of what could go wrong. Not one word had Susan mentioned to Cathy of her reckless plan, for she and she alone would bear the consequences if caught.

Just a few more hours, thought Susan as she methodically changed Toby's clothes and bed covers. *Just a few more hours out of the thousands that make up a lifespan. And maybe, after all is said and done, these few will have counted for something significant and contributory rather than just the marking of the passage of time.*

THE POISON PLUM

Cathy arrived as usual at precisely 7 AM, and Susan, after embracing and kissing Toby and hugging Cathy with visibly more emotion than usual, was on her way to her date with destiny.

"I'll be a few minutes later than usual, you guys," she told them. "I'm going to stop again at that really nice ice cream shop in the Abercrombie Building after work and bring home some treats."

"Mommy, could I have some strawberry? I like strawberry!"

"Sure, sweetie, whatever you want. What about you, Sis?"

"No pun here…I'm being serious. How about some lime?"

"You got it. I'll see you guys later. Have fun!"

Appearances, thought Susan as she stepped out into the cool New England morning. *It's all about appearances and perceptions. I have my garish bag, the 'hideosity' as Cathy called it, loaded with my essential needables, my bright red lipstick, flamboyant clothing, earrings, and sandals all topped off with a big broad smile configured to last an entire work day. Who would ever suspect lil' ol' me of being on a mission to discredit and expose one of the most nefarious and cleverly disguised germ-warfare laboratories in the entire world? I only wish I had some of Cathy's faith right about now. If there really is a higher power, I sure could use a heaping portion of that help and strength today!*

Once Susan was seated comfortably on the ferry for the morning ride to Plum Island, she felt a strange calm spreading throughout her body, and her mood shifted to one of reflection. The events of the past several months, which inexorably led to this moment in her life, began replaying over and over in her mind.

Almost like a play, she thought. *Now here we are in the middle of the fourth and final act, and I and all of these people seated around me are the cast of characters in this melodrama. Look at the faces of these people…are they any different from the people we see about us each and every day? They could be our next-door neighbors or the daily crowds admiring the paintings in the Art Institute of Chicago, or the busy shoppers on Fifth Avenue in New York. Do they know what their work is all about? The contributions they're making daily to the coming global pandemics? How many of them understand the grand scheme of the planners who control and design the programs and objectives of the laboratory? They are like little ants, workers laboring tirelessly and efficiently to create a part of the whole, a component of a mechanism, the entirety of which remains unknown and not understood by the makers of the individual parts.*

Granted, thought Susan, *the faces I see around me are on the ship of peons, relatively speaking. The upper-echelon personnel are, of course, onboard the other ferry. But if that higher power Cathy alludes to were to miraculously appear to assign culpability, which ship would sink the deepest? Ship 'A' filled with peons or ship 'B' with the master architects? Would it make any difference to the mind of a supreme being? Are there indeed degrees of culpability, or is it simply wrong is wrong, and sin is sin…period. End of discussion?*

Regardless of who is guilty of what level of malfeasance, Susan in her wildest imagination could never ever understand how anyone for any reason could intellectually prostitute themselves to remain in the employ of a facility dedicated to the production of designer germs. At some point during their employment, naiveté would fade and be replaced with the cold, harsh dawn of realization regarding what is truly going on in these labs.

More weighty issues to discuss with Cathy over another magnum of Merlot some cold winter evening, she thought.

After what seemed like only a few minutes on the ferry, Susan found herself once again facing the fearless defenders of Plum Island's security, Tweedledum and Tweedledee. And just like every other morning and afternoon this week, Susan would go through the ritual of removing her sandals, earrings, and belt. And once again, Dumb and Dumber would fumble around in that large bag after it had passed along the conveyor belt through the screening device.

Getting in this place is not what worries me, thought Susan. *Trying to get out this afternoon, however, could be an entirely different matter.*

Once seated in cubicle 11, Susan tried to the best of her ability to concentrate on the work that had occupied her since her reassignment. As the morning hours faded to afternoon, it became increasingly difficult to maintain even a limited degree of focus and efficiency. With her stress levels rising, Susan became even more nervous and fidgety. Her fingers began trembling, and Susan could feel her heart beating harder in her chest. To a casual observer, Susan probably would have appeared to be suffering from a bladder infection because of her frequent trips to the restroom necessitated by stress-induced urinary tract hyperactivity.

Geez, thought Susan, *I'm falling apart. Shaking like a dog pooping peach pits, as Granddaddy used to say. I've got to get a grip. Can I do this thing or what?*

And then, finally it was time…the appointed hour. For better or worse, the die was cast. The last thing Susan would do that Friday afternoon as she was shutting down the computers would be to insert the four CDs she had copied previously into the pockets she had carefully sewn behind each Aztec calendar on her bag. If she were being watched through the elaborate camera surveillance system, hopefully her movements would only appear to be those of a less than organized female employee hastily stuffing her personal belongings into a carrying bag in preparation for departure and a relaxing weekend.

There! They are in place and secure, she thought. *That only took a few seconds, and I kept my back to the camera. Now throw your makeup kit, hairbrush, and scarf on top of everything else Susan, and let's get the hell out of this place!*

Susan's heart was pounding even harder now as she briskly began moving to the security area for checkout.

Oh shit, thought Susan as she turned the last corner and saw the long line of employees already present and awaiting their turn through security. Not that it would make any difference how quickly Susan cleared security—the ferry wouldn't leave until the last employee had passed through and was aboard. However, it was the thought of standing in that line and slowly shuffling forward until finally it would be her turn that made her stomach tighten. Susan wanted to get it over with as quickly as possible. She wanted to breeze through that area and get seated on the ferry before passing out. Her heart was now pounding like a jackhammer, and she could feel the veins in her temples throbbing.

Can they hear the pounding of my heart? Or see how moist and sweaty my palms are becoming? My hands are trembling…my legs, too. Do they see that?

Susan was certain that if she didn't get out of this place and soon she would simply faint and pass out right here and now in the middle of security.

Think calm, soothing thoughts…deep breaths. Isn't that what the experts tell us to do in stressful situations?

She tried her best to focus on those thoughts as the line inched slowly forward. Soon now, very soon, it would be her turn.

Smile, Susan…appear cavalier and eager for a fun-filled weekend. Just a little bit longer now. You can do it!

It was then that Susan actually looked at the security area and the faces of the guards on duty.

Double shit! What the hell is this? she thought as she realized she didn't recognize the face of one of the guards. *Who the hell is that? I've never seen him before! Oh this is just dandy! All week long, I've been lugging this huge bag conditioning Tweedledum and Tweedledee to expect seeing it every day. Now, half of that equation is missing, having been replaced by an unknown entity of obvious Mongolian extraction!*

Smile! Maybe he will actually be able to speak English, and you two can greet each other with friendly hellos.

With mind racing and heart pounding, it finally became Susan's turn to challenge the gauntlet. She began the ritual of removing her sandals, earrings, and belt and placing those items and the bag on the conveyor belt. Trying to maintain a smile, Susan greeted the new guard with a cheery "hello," which was met with a cold, unresponsive stare. His eyes scanned the display screen as the bulky bag and its contents generated images which caused his brow to furrow and a look of concern to appear on his face. Perhaps it was the peculiar juxtaposition of her essentials… hairbrush, comb, toothpaste, makeup kit, and so forth that created an image on the screen of daggers, automatic pistols, and hand grenades that caught his attention. Or maybe he just didn't like the looks of the guy on the Aztec calendar sticking his tongue out. Susan didn't know and didn't have a clue, but for whatever reason, the mongoloid on duty stopped the conveyor belt and began pawing, prodding, and poking the bag and its contents very aggressively. Susan's heart, by this time, was beating uncontrollably, and she felt it would either burst wide open or stop suddenly from cardiac arrest.

The guard, appearing angry and completely frustrated, suddenly seized Susan's bag and began dumping its contents onto the conveyor belt. Not satisfied with the results so far, he grabbed the bottom of the bag with both hands and shook the bag so vigorously Susan was certain the Aztec calendars would surely fall off. She stood horrified and helpless, watching for and expecting the four purloined CDs to tumble out of her bag onto the belt at any moment. Her breathing was shallow now and her legs were trembling so severely she felt it impossible that they could support her weight for much longer. Not satisfied with the violent shaking he had given the bag, the guard again ran it through the screening device.

THE POISON PLUM

For years into the future, each time Susan would think back on this incident in her life, she would reflect on how and why the CDs had remained securely in their pockets, even after such a violent assault. Easily dislodged after she was safely on the mainland, Susan was at a total loss to explain how they could have remained secure with everything the guard had done to the bag. Almost as equally puzzling was the fact that Susan never again saw that guard. Only that one time at the most critical juncture of her life.

Trancelike, almost as if in a daze, Susan began trying to get her items together. The sandals and belt were not a problem, but she knew it would be impossible to put those earrings back in her ears with her hands shaking so violently. She just tossed them into the bottom of the bag and covered them with the rest of her stuff. She didn't know where the strength came from to walk to the ferry landing. Once seated, she felt her pounding heart would burst her eardrums and blow her eyes right out of their sockets.

Susan tried to calm herself and convince herself that everything was going to be all right now that she was safely out of the facility. However, the calming was slow, very slow, in coming. Her sympathetic nervous system was raging, and she knew one more challenge had to be overcome before this mission could be deemed a success. If only her heart could hold out that long!

Once underway, the soothing rumble of the ferry's engines and the sound of the large vessel moving through the water provided some semblance of calm and solace for Susan. The sounds were pleasing to her jangled nerves and at least they were moving away from the facility and the evil therein. Susan had carefully planned what she would do once safely on the mainland if she managed to get that far. In the glove compartment of her SUV, she had placed a manila envelope of just the proper size to hold four CDs. Also in the glove box was a magic marker to be used to address the envelope once she arrived at her destination and not before.

Oh what a relief, she thought as she carefully buckled her safety belt and locked herself securely in her SUV. *But why can't I stop shaking? Will I be able to drive?*

Once underway, however, her confidence grew as she made her way directly to the Abercrombie Building at 120 East Concord.

I have to move smoothly and expeditiously, but not hurriedly, in case I'm being watched by the goons in the suits. This is, after all, an ice cream run and nothing more.

The Abercrombie Building was probably built in the late 1920s and consisted of two rectangular structures positioned end to end, joined by an enclosed breezeway. Occupying the space between Concord Street and the parallel street of Poindexter, the buildings could be entered through large double doors from either the Concord or Poindexter sides. Circular fountains greeted visitors from either direction as they made their way across the walkways to the entrances. The building, even though old and in many respects outdated, nevertheless reflected a certain charm of a bygone era that citizens of the area desired to preserve.

If one entered the breezeway from the Concord Street side and then walked into the building to the right of the breezeway through another large set of glass and wood frame double doors, the regional office of Congressman Harry McDonald would be the first office on the right. The office door was a single, large wooden door with the old brass lock set and frosted glass neatly lettered with his name, telephone number, and the number of the congressional district. A still-functioning transom above the door and a hinged mail slot completed, in Susan's mind, the mental image of private eye Mike Hammer's office from the old Mickey Spillane novels.

Perfect! thought Susan as she pulled into an easily accessible parking spot on Concord near the walkway to the breezeway. It was then that she removed the manila envelope and began addressing, or more correctly, attempting to address it with the magic marker. Susan had always taken pride in her penmanship, but this afternoon her writing looked like that of a ninety-five-year-old woman with a severe case of Parkinson's.

"God, will I ever stop shaking?" she mumbled as she hastily scribbled:

Congressman Harry McDonald
Urgent and Confidential

She then placed the envelope in her bag, inserted the CDs and folded down the metal clasps.

If I am being followed, she thought, *they had better watch carefully! This is only going to take a few seconds.*

Susan calmly exited her SUV and walked casually down the walkway into the breezeway, immediately turning right. Upon entering the building, the congressman's office, now closed for the weekend, was on her right. Susan, with her right hand, pulled the CD-laden envelope from her bag and deftly slipped it into the mail slot as she continued walking without interruption.

Did anyone see that? she wondered as she casually continued making her way to the end of the building where the ice cream shop was situated in the courtyard. She stopped for a moment to look in the display window of a small dress shop a little further down toward the courtyard and on the opposite side from the congressman's office. Her peripheral vision observed a trim man dressed in a conservative suit entering the building from the direction she had come.

If you are one of them, Dudley Do Right, you are just a tad too late, she thought. *Piss on 'em...next stop is the ice cream shop and a silent celebration of a job well done once I get home.*

As Susan began placing her order for the ice cream, she noticed that she wasn't trembling anymore, and a peaceful calm descended upon her that she hadn't known for a very long time.

The Respite

Congressman McDonald was tired. He couldn't ever remember being as tired as he was Friday afternoon…not even in medical school when four hours of sleep a night sufficed for weeks on end as the grueling schedule of laboratory assignments, constant studying for tests, and classroom lectures continued unabated.

Tired all the way to the bone, he thought. The combination of mental and physical fatigue had seemed to build upon each other, multiplying in a synergistic fashion the deleterious effects of each other. His decision to return to the district for the weekend was a spontaneous one, and it was pure luck that his staff found the single solitary seat available on a flight to New London. Granted, it was a commuter flight, which Harry despised, but nevertheless it was transportation. Tonight, in the arms of his beloved Anna, he would find the solace and comfort he so desperately needed.

A charging of the batteries, he thought as he made his way to the airport. Everyone in the office, especially Harry, had burned the candle at both ends preparing for the committee investigations and attempting to sort through the contents of the mysterious package of documents and photographs they had received.

We are all tired, thought Harry, *and goodness knows when we will be able to even think about taking any more time to rest with the schedules we have looming before us.*

For some strange reason, Harry's mind began wandering back to the days when he was an intern for a time in a hospital in Atlanta. Having only recently graduated from medical school, Harry was filled with the idealism and zeal of youth, eagerly anticipating the dawn of yet another exciting day that would, he was certain, bring him even closer to the brink of a revolutionary new discovery in the field of medicine. Much to Harry's chagrin, that summer internship found

THE POISON PLUM

him linked to a crusty, old backwoods general practitioner who confessed to having delivered over 500 babies during the early years of his practice. He even told of making house calls in a worn out Model A Ford carrying a little black bag filled with alcohol, sutures, hypodermics, and sulfa drugs.

Revolutionary concepts in the practice of medicine may have eluded Harry during that summer in Atlanta, but he certainly learned a lot about life following the old GP up and down the halls of Grady Hospital. An incident occurred one afternoon that Harry seldom thought about anymore, but he always knew it could only be suppressed, not forgotten, as the years passed by. Perhaps it was the overwhelming tiredness causing the long-ago spoken dialogue to re-enter his consciousness now, but for whatever reason, his mind vividly recalled the afternoon of that summer in Atlanta when he and old Dr. Gregory, the attending physician, entered the room of a poor, old, black sharecropper named Moses Johnson.

"How are you feeling today, Moses?" began Dr. Gregory.

"Well, Doc," replied Moses, "Mos' days I'se jus' feel bad. On 'dem udder days, I'se jus' feel mo' worser."

At the time, Harry felt the old black man's comments to be somewhat humorous and insignificant—comments to be laughed off once out of earshot of the patient. Even Dr. Gregory's explanation once they had left the room failed to moderate Harry's perception of insignificance.

"Don't mind ol' Moses…he's eat up with syphilis. Ain't but two neurons left that are firing, and they're held together by a spirochete."

The passage of years since that long ago day in Atlanta caused Harry to look upon the incident in a totally different light. Old Man Johnson, with his limited vocabulary, had spoken with wisdom. If only the young intern had been able to understand and interpret that wisdom. For he was attempting to communicate in the only way he knew how…simplistic and from the heart and very soul of the man.

We listen, but we don't hear, thought Harry. *I heard what the man said, but I didn't understand him. Now I do, and I'm tired, too. Will anyone hear and understand me?*

As soon as Harry arrived at the New London airport and saw Anna's warm, loving smile, his spirits were immediately lifted. She had come to the airport, as always, to meet his flight and Harry thought she had never looked lovelier than she did this Friday evening. Like young lovers, Harry and Anna warmly embraced and kissed. Two strikingly attractive human beings obviously completely in love with and dedicated to each other.

"Oh Harry, I'm so glad you are home. I've missed you so much."

"Same here, sweetheart. I hope we don't have exciting plans for the weekend, except the excitement of your presence, of course. I'm worn out."

"Well, I don't want to put too much of a strain on the old man's heart."

"What a way to go." Harry replied.

"Let's get you home, you crusader of freedom you. I've got a good dinner cooked for us, some wine chilling, and you can relax."

"Sounds wonderful darling!"

"Harry, we need a good long vacation together. How long has it been?"

"I can't remember, Anna. Too long, I'm sure."

"Are the committee hearings still on track to begin the day after Labor Day?"

"Yes."

"Why don't we plan a trip to begin as soon as the hearings are completed? Maybe Switzerland? A chalet in the mountains? A refresher course in skiing?"

"Anna, you certainly know how to tempt a man! It is, of course, impossible to predict exactly how long it will take to successfully complete hearings of that magnitude, but let's begin making plans now to get away. It sounds wonderful, darling!"

"It's a date then! And speaking of the committee hearings, how are things going?"

"Very well, actually. Had we not received the package of information someone fortuitously provided for us, however, we would be bogged down for lack of information and direction and we would be almost entirely dependent upon subpoenaed testimony. As it is, I am almost certain we have indisputable proof that the syphilis research done in Tuskegee, Alabama, many years ago was the springboard for the development of modern day Lyme disease by the CDC and Plum Island."

"I am sure the hundreds of thousands of Lyme disease sufferers nationwide will be pleased to learn the source of their misery has been their own government."

"Yes, quite a generous return on their tax dollars."

"Harry, I am very proud of you and the work you're doing. I know you're trying to help our friends, the Klinners, and the others in this area attacked by the government. And how many throughout America now and in the future that will derive benefit from your efforts, we shall never know the total…but God will. Yes Harry, I am proud. I worry, though. Not a day goes by without some reference in the media to you, the ferry massacre, Colonel Gordon McClain, or your planned committee investigation. I don't possess a fraction of your understanding of the workings of the New World Order, Harry, but I understand enough to know that you have stepped on the toes of a very powerful giant that's now very angry with you. That frightens me, Harry. I realize you and I are just two insignificant human beings powerless and defenseless against the forces that are gathering against us. We are like two little insects that could be squashed at any time by the lumbering giant now awakened to fury and resentment. I used to wonder if it were more difficult for the wife of a busy successful doctor or the wife of a busy, popular, and successful congressman. The demands on your time have always been such that there was precious little left for you and I. But I knew that in the beginning when I agreed to be your wife. I didn't have any illusions, and I accepted the terms of our relationship because I love you. I've always been proud of your work and accomplishments. But Harry, having to work late juggling office visits, surgeries, and hospital rounds is one world. The other world, the one we now occupy, has the same demands on your time, but there is one very significant and distinct difference. The world we're in now has some very sinister and evil entities lurking about that are intent on silencing you. That frightens me, Harry. Yes, I know the truth must be told, but why does it have to be told by the man I love who is now in harm's way?"

Harry could only listen silently to Anna's concerns for he knew in his heart that she was right.

Why indeed, he thought. *What paths and roadways have I traveled in the twists, turns, and vicissitudes of life that have brought me to this juncture? This place of gravity, import, and yes, finality. For me it seems the die was cast eons ago, and all that is left is for me to play out this scene on the stage of life. No change can I make, no alteration of the course is permitted…for all was decided by my maker in some celestial preordination of destiny a very, very long time ago.*

It would be later that evening and after the delicious and romantic dinner and wine by candlelight that Harry would finally begin to leave the stress of Washington behind and relaxation would begin to take its hold. And later still, Anna's passionate lovemaking finally provided what his heart had longed for and he welcomed the long and peaceful sleep awaiting him. Harry slept late the next morning, a luxury conspicuously absent the past several weeks and always absent when he was away in Washington.

He awoke refreshed and relaxed, eager to spend the day with Anna. Perhaps outside at the park down by the water. Or perhaps they would pack a picnic lunch and take a drive through the countryside. Just to be away from Washington, be with Anna, and spend some time outdoors… that would be the ticket!

"Anna, it's a beautiful, clear day outside," he said. "Let's start with breakfast outside on the patio. Maybe later we'll go down to Ocean Beach Park or take a drive out to the countryside for a picnic."

"That sounds wonderful, sweetheart, as long as we are together, and you promise to avoid all telephones and TV or radio news reports!"

"That's a promise!"

Harry was enjoying his second glass of orange juice when he and Anna heard the incessant and impatient ringing of their front door bell interspersed with loud rapping of the doorknocker.

"Who could that possibly be?" asked Harry.

"I don't know, honey, but sit tight and I'll get rid of them," responded Anna as she hastily made her way to the front of the house in her bedroom slippers and housecoat.

Harry listened intently. He could hear muffled female voices but couldn't understand what was being said. Within moments, Anna was quickly returning to the patio loudly announcing from several rooms away, "Harry, it's Francine!"

Francine? thought Harry. *What is she doing here? Our office downtown was scheduled to be closed today. Why isn't she at home with her family enjoying the day?*

"Oh, Mr. Congressman," gushed Francine as she hastily entered the patio area. "I'm so glad you're here. I certainly didn't expect you this weekend, but when I called the Washington office, Erin Giblon told me you were here."

"What is it, Francine? You seem agitated."

"Agitated, Mr. Congressman? More than that! I'm afraid! I'm as nervous as a whore in church!"

"Here, sit down, Francine. Have some coffee or juice and please tell me what is going on."

As Francine took a seat at the patio table, she removed a manila envelope from her purse and slid it across the table to Harry.

"That's what's going on, Mr. Congressman. I went to the office this morning to finish up some correspondence that needed to go out this afternoon, and that envelope was on the floor... obviously where it landed after someone had pushed it through the mail slot in the door."

"What is it, and where is it from?"

"I don't know the answer to either of those questions. All I know is it looks like it was addressed by someone about a hundred years old. I started thinking, is someone playing a prank? Is it anthrax, a bomb, or what? I was afraid to open it, I was afraid to call you, and I was afraid to re-mail it. I feel we are being watched...maybe our telephones are tapped and maybe our mail is searched and censored. Guess I've been listening to you for too long. Anyway, there it is, whatever it is...This girl is too old for all this cloak and dagger stuff!"

"It seems innocuous enough," responded Harry as he casually inspected the envelope. "Let's see what we have here."

With that, both Francine and Anna immediately took several steps back away from the table.

"Harry," Anna said. "Please be careful! Are you sure?"

"I don't see anything to be concerned about," Harry replied as he carefully bent back the metal clasps and began prying open the envelope's flaps.

"Looks like CDs...yes, that's what we have here, some CDs."

"Any note or return address?"

"No...the envelope is empty. Four CDs, and that's it. Francine, please sit down and have some juice...you are looking positively pale! In fact, have some breakfast while I take a look at these."

Anna followed Harry as he walked to their computer, she as curious as he. Within moments, the first CD had loaded and images of dialogue, formulas, and chemical equations and schematics resembling genealogical trees began filling the screen.

"What on earth is that?" Anna said while looking over Harry's shoulder. "A tutorial on understanding Egyptian hieroglyphics?"

"Not exactly, dear Anna, but equally abstruse, I can assure you. I'm not absolutely certain, but that particular image appears to represent a genetically engineered transmutation of the Coxsackie virus over a forty-eight-hour time period."

"Fascinating." spoke Anna somewhat sarcastically, "Does this mean our drive into the countryside is aborted?"

"Not necessarily. Please rejoin Francine and ask her to stay a few more minutes. I may need her help."

Harry's jaw dropped as he moved through the CD file, and the full import of what he was seeing began to register.

God in heaven, he thought. *This is from the work notes of Plum Island scientists. It all appears related to the field of virology. But who and why? Do we have a mysterious and silent benefactor? Unlike the contents of the package received at the Washington office, which chronicled spirochetal research over a period of several decades, this new information appears to represent recent and current work.*

Within moments, Harry had rejoined Anna and Francine at the patio table.

"What is it, Mr. Congressman? Is it important?"

"I think so Francine, but I'll need some help deciphering what is on those CDs. Based on what I've seen, however, I am very grateful you took the action you did bringing those to me. And if I may, I'd like to ask a further favor of you."

"Certainly, Mr. Congressman, whatever you need."

"Right now I need those computer skills you possess. I want you to e-mail the files that are on those discs to our Washington office. I will call Erin Giblon and tell her to expect them."

"Now?"

"Now! This is important. Also, make four copies of those discs. Mail one set to our Washington office regular mail, one set to Washington via Fed Ex, one set via UPS, and take the remaining set home with you. I'll take the originals back on the flight with me after I leave them in the trunk of my car for the rest of the weekend while Anna and I take a little trip together…"

"You are serious…"

"Yes, very."

A Plan

In the arms of Morpheus, thought Susan as she began stretching and yawning trying to wake up. *That's where I have been for the past...what time is it? Hmmm...nine hours! How deliciously decadent. I can't remember a better night of sleep!*

Susan felt relaxed and rested. After a few minutes, as she began coming fully awake, she started wondering if the congressman had been notified about the envelope yet.

"*Naw...probably not. No reason I would think for that office to be open on weekends. It'll be Monday, for sure. Got to get moving though, no matter how good this old bed feels. I've got to get up. Cathy is never late, and she'll be here promptly at noon. I think today we need to devote some time to strategy...I've done my bit to drive the stake in the vampire's heart, and we've got to decide what's next.*"

By eleven, Toby had been bathed, redressed in dry clothes, fed, and his linens changed. He seemed a little better that Saturday morning, displaying more energy, complaining less about aches and pains, and he could walk better. The antibiotics were doing their job, and Toby's otherwise healthy body was responding.

Still a long way to go, thought Susan. *But at least we're going uphill instead of down.*

While reviewing the morning mail, the beige envelope from the Federated Insurance Companies of Greater New England immediately caught her eye.

Why even go through the ritual of opening and reading this missive? she thought. *A dollar to a doughnut, I already know exactly what it says!*

A few moments later, Susan's suspicions were confirmed as she reached the less-than-cheerful conclusions of the letter. In part, it read:

Based upon a careful review of your claims, it has been determined that the diagnosis of Lyme disease and subsequent treatment protocol implemented by your physician is not supported by laboratory test results. As a consequence, benefits will be denied for any charges incurred subsequent to July 30. Should additional test result data supportive of your claim(s) materialize at a later date, we will conduct a review of such data to determine if the reinstatement of benefits is appropriate.

No need to ride that ferry any longer, Susan thought. *Spend tomorrow updating that résumé to send to UAB and draft that letter of resignation…two weeks notice Gallagher…what a shame, just as we're getting to know each other! And you just know I'm going to miss you, old boy. But I'll see you again, Herschel, sweetie. I'll be on the witness stand smiling broadly at you and your cronies as I patiently explain to McDonald's committee what those CD files are really all about. Ain't karma a bitch?"*

A gentle rapping on the front door accompanied by a key turning in the deadbolt signaled the arrival of Cathy for their recently imposed ritual of Saturday visits.

"Is that food I smell?" asked Susan as Cathy entered hugging two bulky sacks from Gino's Deli.

"Us girls have to keep our energy levels up. Where's my sweetheart Toby? I need a big hug!"

"While I can still afford it, Cathy, what is my share of this bacchanalian festival?"

"My treat! Your money is no good today. Crunch and munch, for tomorrow, we may explode from our excesses."

"No argument here! I'm hungry!"

What a blessing, thought Susan as she watched Toby reaching for the food Cathy had brought. *Even Toby's appetite is improved. No weight gain, though. That damn Babesia-what-sis is probably keeping him drained. Soon though, help is coming and it won't be long!*

After everyone had sufficiently gorged themselves, Susan suggested they vacate to the patio to enjoy being outside in the nice weather. Once comfortably seated, Susan proposed they spend a few minutes planning the next several weeks to make certain everyone was on the same page.

"Cathy, you know you are my favorite sister…"

"I'm your *only* sister, you ninny!"

"Oh."

"What is it? Spit it out."

"How serious were you when you told me not to worry about it?"

"That insurance thing? Got you covered. No problem."

"Read this letter."

Cathy's brow wrinkled slightly as she scanned the document.

"So what?" she said as her gaze reverted to Susan's face. "Let's have a show of hands here. Who's surprised?"

"You're serious…"

"Yes, of course I'm serious. Toby comes first. Start a tab, and we'll worry about it later. The only thing that matters is getting your son back!"

"God love you, Sis! But while I've got a tab running, I may as well test the waters, and see what my credit line is."

"Meaning?"

"Well, as you may have surmised, my relationship with my employer has been, shall we say, less than harmonious."

"I'll accept that."

"As a result, I plan to devote tomorrow afternoon to an updating of my résumé to mail to UAB on Monday."

"Hooray!"

"There's more…I will also draft my letter of resignation, which I will submit first thing Monday morning. I'm giving a two-weeks notice."

"So your concern is how big is the kitty to support your tab including not only Toby's treatments but living expenses as well?"

"I'm not exactly destitute, Cathy. Working on it, obviously, but not quite there yet. I've got some savings, which will help."

"Whatever it takes to get you, us, out of Satan's garden, we will do. When I said don't worry about it, I meant it. You are covered, oh sister of mine."

With that affirmation of love and support, Susan lost it and began to cry intensely as she put her arms around Cathy and hugged her tightly. Several minutes elapsed before Susan could regain her composure sufficiently to continue.

"I love you, Sis," blurted Susan. "Toby and I would be up that proverbial creek without a paddle if it weren't for you!"

"I'll get you back," said Cathy, trying to inject a modicum of humor into the tedious situation. "I'll let you pay my nursing home expenses when I finally get there."

"Got you covered!" responded Susan while thinking to herself, *If there's anything left of me after I testify to that committee. But I'd better save that confession to Cathy for another day, that's for sure.*

Under the Microscope

CIA Director Steele and FBI Director Frey had probably spent more time talking to each other in the single month since the ferry massacre than they had the entire previous year. With heightened concern over the direction McDonald's committee investigation might take, their agencies were frantically trying to stay abreast of whatever tack McDonald might choose, with the objective to alter or mute his course of action.

The new hire, Susan Collins, was considered a wild card with unpredictable potential ramifications and surveillance of her activities continued unabated. Controlling, or rather attempting to control, the media was indeed a challenge due to an unrelenting barrage of hostile ink issuing forth from MacIntosh McAdams and certain others of the more conservative journalistic forums. Even some of the liberal media who normally could be counted upon to parrot the New World Order line appeared to balk when faced with the straightforward logic and reasoning offered up by McAdams and others. It was clear that a battle for the minds of the American people was being waged. As the days preceding the beginning of the hearings ticked by, the fury of the raging controversy reached unprecedented, white-hot levels.

Considering the stakes involved, it was no surprise when Frey called Steele to advise him that Susan Collins had given her superiors a two-week notice. The excuse of a sick aunt suffering from a recent stroke back in Birmingham immediately raised suspicions and an investigation was launched to verify or refute Susan's claim. The investigation's outcome coincided with that of a longer running investigation, and for the first time, Frey felt he had finally identified a potentially dangerous enemy outside of the McDonald camp…outside at least for the time being, that is.

On the very last day of Susan's employment at the Plum Island facility, all of the information relative to Susan Collins had been assimilated by the FBI, and yet another telephone conversation occurred between Frey and Steele.

"Good afternoon, Director Steele. This is Director Frey."

"Yes, good afternoon."

"More potential problems."

"What is it? McDonald succeeded in cloning himself?"

"No, but the mystery surrounding the new hire, Susan Collins, at Plum just became more so!"

"There is no aunt in Birmingham?"

"Correct…but there's worse news."

"She has signed on to testify for the McDonald crusade?"

"Not yet, but I suspect it's only a matter of time, Steele."

"Why?"

"Our agents finally got verification of her sick kid's medical diagnosis."

"Let me guess," Steele replied. "It's not mono, as she claimed?"

"Nope. The diagnosis was Lyme disease!"

"Crap on a shingle! We sure as hell don't need the rage and vengeance of a single mom with a kid made sick by her employer. This could easily make our problem much larger!"

"That's for sure," agreed Frey. "I think we can safely toss her supervisor's assessment of her as an innocuous, somewhat klutzy broad out the window. In my mind, she has now become as potentially dangerous as a rattlesnake swimming in your bathwater."

"I agree, but do we have any new information to suggest she has anything tangible McDonald could use?"

"No," Frey replied.

"And she has had no contact with McDonald?"

"That's correct…none."

"Sounds like we need to make absolutely certain she doesn't have a smoking gun in her jewelry box."

"I concur. We will take the necessary steps immediately."

"Thanks for the update, Frey…please advise."

The Return of the Lyme-Aid Express

Susan Collins felt almost euphoric as she began her last ferry ride home from Plum Island to the Connecticut mainland. The two weeks since she had submitted her resignation had gone by smoothly and she was eager to begin a new chapter in her life and Toby's as well. Herschel Gallagher had seemed mildly taken aback by her resignation, but had, for whatever reason, suppressed any overt criticism or sarcasm he may have been harboring. All in all, the transition had been a smooth one, and until her final Friday, she had presented as a model employee if somewhat unconventionally attired. Yes, the large bag had become an essential component of her daily wardrobe, Aztec calendars and all.

Part of Susan's euphoria was obviously the severance from the evil Plum Island bio-lab. The other part was the anticipation of seeing Toby again this evening after his and Cathy's return from the Lyme-Aid Express tour. Toby and Cathy had left for Birmingham as scheduled the previous Monday, and tonight they would return. Granted, each night, the three had visited by phone, but Susan had missed Toby, and her heart ached to hold him. According to Cathy's accounts, the new doctor was an incredibly impressive and accomplished physician who didn't hesitate to aggressively incorporate the most current cutting-edge diagnostic and treatment protocols available for his patients. Indeed, Cathy enthusiastically confirmed that Dr. Robinson was indeed a 'doctor's doctor.' He had, as expected, confirmed Dr. Butler's diagnosis of Lyme and had also confirmed a co-infection of Babesia. So convinced was he of the Babesia infection, he avoided the usual delay of lab results and moved immediately to aggressive treatment using a combination of oral antibiotics and an anti-protozoal drug. Yes, Toby would experience a temporary worsening of his symptoms on this protocol, similar to the Herxheimer reactions but different. More like an overall feeling of malaise, rather than acute symptoms.

THE POISON PLUM

Hopefully, the bus would arrive sometime shortly after eight, which would give Susan time to get settled in and cook a warm, nourishing dinner for the three of them. It would be so good to have Toby back, and the thought of Toby improving dramatically on the new treatments filled Susan's heart with joy.

But instead of the anticipated 8 PM arrival, the church bus, in accordance with a time-honored tradition routinely celebrated by church busses throughout America and proudly exemplified by this particular bus, decided to break down about 200 miles north of Birmingham.

Luckily the breakdown was of short duration, relatively speaking, and not of a terminal nature. Cathy and Toby finally rolled in about 10 PM, and the inaugural journey of the Lyme-Aid Express was declared by all to be a resounding success. Susan was ecstatic to have the two people she loved the most back with her. And soon, very soon, after the relocation to Birmingham, they would always be together as families should.

Dinner was a delightful experience as everyone enjoyed the delicious food and each other's company. Cathy was brimming with stories of their trip, relating the personal experiences and hopes of the other Lyme patients as well as Toby's diagnosis and revised treatment protocols. Susan had little to add as she related the final week of her employment at the lab. All had gone smoothly and as a consequence, there was little to discuss.

Ah, but just wait until I become the star witness of Congressman McDonald's committee investigations, she thought. *Mommy is about to become a celebrity, and the cockroaches, Gallagher, Stephens, and all the rest, are about to perish in the clear, bright, white light of day.*

It was after midnight when most of the food had been eaten and all the stories from the trip had been told. Toby was exhausted and immediately crashed, probably only surviving this long because of the sheer excitement and joy of being with his mother once again. Susan bid Cathy good night, and while hugging her tightly, thanked her again for all she'd done and was doing. Susan had given Toby his sleeping medication immediately after dinner, and she hoped they would each enjoy a long and restful uninterrupted night of sleep.

Hell Is Other People

Precisely at 6 AM, Susan was awakened by a sound from the direction of her front door that seemed to shake the entire house. Her immediate perception was that of a car hitting her house.

"What the hell?" she said, abruptly sitting up in the bed. Within seconds, she heard voices and then a much stronger and louder force struck her house and she heard the front door crash to the living room floor. Terrified, she leapt out of bed and was immediately confronted by the horrifying sight of over a dozen men clad in solid black SWAT team clothing moving rapidly throughout her house. Toby, now awakened by men entering his room, became frightened and began crying loudly. Three agents reached Susan and shoved her back onto the bed while pointing their automatic weapons at her head.

"Don't move bitch! We are in charge here, and we're going to search every inch of this damn property. If you attempt to resist, we will kill you without hesitation."

"My son...he's frightened! Can't you hear him crying?"

"Well that's a good thing, isn't it? It proves he's still alive!"

"But you don't understand...he's very ill. He has Lyme disease."

"And you are going to have lead poisoning if you don't shut the hell up!"

"You bastards! Don't you have any compassion? Any sympathy?"

"Sympathy? You want sympathy, bitch? I'll tell you where you can find sympathy...it's in the dictionary between *shit* and *syphilis*!"

For the better part of four hours, Susan and Toby were once again held hostage in their own home, horrified while the government agents, some in dark suits and glasses and the rest in SWAT gear, turned their house into shambles. That they were searching for something was obvious, but what? Among the confiscated materials were Toby's medical records, Susan's medical books, her laptop computer and discs, and the letter from UAB soliciting volunteers for McDonald's committee. No search warrant was presented, and no explanation or apology was offered.

Susan hugged Toby and held him close for a long time after the last storm trooper had stomped out of what was left of their home. The fact that poor, sick little Toby had been traumatized by the raid was indisputable. How does one explain to a sick little eight-year-old boy about evil men with evil designs on an evil mission? The unsettling event would be seared into Toby's consciousness, never to be forgotten. Their home now was in complete disarray with drawers, shelves, and contents tossed upon the floor, furniture upended and many items broken beyond repair.

How would those scum feel if someone devastated their homes and terrorized their children? thought Susan. *"Be ye careful of the seeds ye sow for as those seeds grow, so shall ye reap!" Isn't that what Cathy was always saying? Something she learned in church? But from whatever source, how very appropriate it seemed!*

Susan recalled how some former president, Reagan, she thought, had once referred to the former Soviet Union as an 'evil empire.' She wondered if the United States had now supplanted the Soviet Union for that dubious distinction.

Later, and before the requisite call to Cathy, came the attempted clean up and restoration of some sense of order. Susan, after getting Toby undressed and in the shower, began cleaning Toby's bed of the urine-and-fecal-matter-covered bed linens while silently making a vow to herself.

Those bastards are going to pay for what they have done here today! I don't know how or when, but I know in the deepest of my heart that Toby and I are going to be vindicated for the evil that has been committed!

Susan knew she would have to calm herself down before calling Cathy. Two full-blown hysterical sisters venting their distress and anguish before an emotionally distraught child would simply be too much for an eight-year-old boy to handle.

Once she was able to walk through the kitchen and find some utensils that were not broken, she prepared some hot chocolate for Toby and herself. She hoped the warm chocolate would exert a calming, soothing influence over him…but just to be on the safe side, she broke apart one of Toby's sleeping pills and poured half of its contents into Toby's drink.

"That should do the trick," she muttered softly. "Personally I would like a nice, big, friendly bottle of valium for just such an occasion!"

The time seemed right to place the call after about thirty minutes and Susan announced to Toby that she was going in the other room to call Cathy to ask her to come over.

"Cathy? This is what's left of your sister...can you come over?"

"What do you mean 'what's left'? Have you already trashed yourself out from celebrating your early retirement by partying too hard?"

"Not exactly. Would you by chance have any plywood or a roll of that heavy clear plastic that builders use over at your place?"

"No, I don't have anything like that. What on earth do you need that stuff for?"

"Well, I guess we'll have to make a trip to the building supply store. My front door is on the floor in the living room."

"What? Are you serious? How did that happen?"

"Rude visitors that didn't knock!"

"What?" responded Cathy excitedly.

"We were raided again...six o'clock this morning. Can you come over and help us?"

"Oh, my God, Susan! Are you and Toby alright?"

"As well as can be expected. No physical trauma anyway..."

"I'll be right there!"

As Susan was awaiting Cathy's arrival, her imagination began running wild. *Why were we raided? What were they looking for? Do they suspect I copied those files? Why on the morning after my last day of employment?*

She had no answers as the mystery grew deeper. Obviously, she was under suspicion, but for what? Had her theft of the files been detected, reprisals, she felt, would have been swift, sudden and harsh. No way would agents have waited two weeks to respond.

A fishing expedition, she thought, *just go in and try to find something, anything. Well, no fish were caught today. They have nothing at all for their efforts. Except my undying hatred and resolve that is. The bastards will pay!*

She heard a sound behind her and, startled, she turned to see Cathy staring at her with eyes wide and full like a deer in the headlights.

"Gee girl! You could give someone a coronary...don't you believe in knocking?"

"On what? Your door is on the floor! Who did this, Susan? The place looks like a tornado blew through. What were they looking for?"

"Your guess is as good as mine! I don't have a clue! No search warrant, no identification, no explanation. Only the promise I would die of lead poisoning if I didn't shut the hell up! Cathy, they held guns to my head the entire time and wouldn't let me off the bed to be with Toby. I could hear him crying, and I knew he was absolutely terrified. They wouldn't let him out of his room and bless his heart, he was so frightened he voided and defecated right there on the bed!"

"What kind of sadistic slime would do such a thing?"

"Goons with guns! What kind of sadistic slime would sit in a laboratory all day trying to engineer germs to be more effective at killing innocent human beings? Just the flip side of the same coin!"

"What are you going to do?"

"Short term or long term?"

"Both."

"Short term, I'm going to ask you to help put this place back together while trying to console Toby. While you are doing that, I am going to get on the phone and try to find a carpenter to fix that door."

"And the long term?"

"What is the time-honored American recourse of action when one has a grievance against the government?"

"Contact your congressman and or your senator and bitch and complain?"

"You got it!"

"Is that all you are going to do, Susan? Bitch and complain?"

"Hardly! Bitching and complaining are just for starters. Now that our home has been reduced to little more than a dung heap by those bastards, I may as well go ahead and tell you. Cathy, I decided weeks ago that I'm going to testify before McDonald's committee."

"Oh, my God! You can't be serious!"

"But I am…serious as a heart attack! Not only am I going to testify, but I am going to be his star witness! Those sons of bitches are going to pay for what they have done to Toby and me!"

"Why don't we just leave, Susan, and go back to Birmingham? Right here and right now! Before somebody does something even more horrible to you and Toby!"

"Appealing idea and a compelling argument, Cathy, but I've never been one to run from a fight, you know that. And I didn't start this one, they did! I'm not going to be intimidated by their terror tactics, and I'll be damned if I'm going to turn tail and run now! Nope! Monday morning, as soon as the congressman's office opens up, I'm going to be standing there!"

"You are really going to go through with this, aren't you, oh stubborn one?"

"Win, lose, or draw…bleed, blister, or bust…to the bitter end!"

"Well, I guess you'll need a babysitter," said Cathy as she reached out to hug Susan, tears now beginning to roll down both their cheeks.

Contact Your Congressman

True to her word, Monday morning found Susan entering the district office of Congressman Harry McDonald within minutes of its opening.

"Good morning," greeted Francine. "I'm Francine Talbot. May I help you?"

"Yes, you may Francine. My name is Susan Collins, and I need to speak with the congressman. It's of a rather urgent nature."

"I'm afraid, Ms. Collins, that the congressman is not in the district. He's in his Washington office. If you will either tell me the nature of your visit or put it in writing, I'll see that it is communicated to him."

"We need to talk now. Would you please get him on the phone?"

"I'm afraid he is very busy at the moment. He and his staff are preparing for a congressional committee investigation. Can you at least tell me what this is concerning?"

"Francine, are you the only employee of this office?"

"Well, yes I am, but what does that have to do with…"

"Francine, did you come in one morning about two weeks ago and find a manila envelope on the floor addressed to the congressman?"

"Well, yes… yes, I did… and I gave the envelope to the congressman."

"And?"

The color was now beginning to drain from Francine's face, and she was becoming visibly nervous and agitated. Who was this Susan Collins, and what did she want? Francine's first thoughts were that Susan must be some kind of government agent, and somehow they had found out about the discs.

What do I do now? thought Francine.

"Francine, it's very important I speak with Congressman McDonald as soon as possible. Up until last Friday, I was an employee of the Plum Island facility, and that envelope and the discs it contained are from me!"

Francine's face was now ashen, and she remained motionless not knowing what to do or say.

"That's not all. I have an eight-year-old son who is very ill with Lyme disease that came from that lab. Our home has been raided and searched twice by government thugs since the massacre at the ferry. Most recently, this past Saturday at 6 AM. What I am telling you is just the tip of the iceberg, Francine, and I'm not kidding. Now will you get the congressman on the phone?"

With that, Francine hastily grabbed for the phone and pushed the speed dial button for Harry's office.

"Oh, Miss Giblon…I'm glad you answered. This is Francine in New London. I have someone here who needs to speak to the congressman. It's urgent. Yes, I know he is very busy, Miss Giblon, but this has to do with those CDs. I know he will want to take this call."

Within moments, Harry was on the line, and Francine briefly explained what was going on before handing the receiver to Susan.

"Ms. Collins, this is Congressman McDonald. How may I be of service?"

"Mr. Congressman, I guess the answer more appropriately should be, how may I be of service to you? Those CDs you have are from me, and until last Friday, I was an employee of Satan's laboratory on Plum Island. Yes, I'm upset. I was the only employee not on the ferry that grim fateful day because I was with my eight-year-old son at a doctor's office trying to find out why he's so sick. I now know that he has Lyme disease, and I also know that it came from Plum Island. But I'm not finished…government goons have raided and ransacked our home, not once, but twice. Once after the massacre and again this past Saturday.

"Pardon my French, Mr. Congressman, but I'm pissed, I'm mad as hell, and I want those bastards to get what they deserve. I have a doctorate in microbiology from UAB in Birmingham, and I think I would be a valuable asset to your committee."

"Do you understand, and can you explain in layman's terms, what is on those discs?"

"That would be a cakewalk, Mr. Congressman…No problem."

"Would you be willing to testify?"

"Hello? I thought you would never ask! But only if I will be able to rant and rave!"

"Perhaps in moderation.... Would you also be willing to come to Washington for a few days so that we could review some of the more pertinent issues?"

"Whatever it would take, Mr. Congressman. Whatever it would take."

"Excellent! The sooner the better. I'll have Francine make all the necessary arrangements. Your transportation and lodging expenses will, of course, be covered. You and Francine can work out a convenient time. Perhaps in a few days?"

"I'll be ready whenever you are, Mr. Congressman."

Erin Giblon had watched intensely the galloping gamut of emotions cascading across Harry's face during the brief time he was on the call, and her curiosity was raging.

"Mr. Congressman! You look like the cat that ate the canary! What was that all about?"

"If that person is who she says she is, Miss Giblon, God is truly smiling on our efforts! What would you say to a potential member of our team that is a former employee of Plum, was the only employee not on the ferry that day, has a PhD in microbiology, has been raided and terrorized by government agents, not once, but twice, has an eight-year-old son sick with Lyme disease, and is the source of the CDs we received?"

"I would say we are either dreaming or hallucinating from overwork! All that sounds too good to be true."

"Yes, I agree, but we are going to find out for sure very soon. Her name is Susan Collins, and Francine is making arrangements to fly her here as soon as possible."

"And I am volunteering here and now for the task of picking her up at Dulles. I can't wait to meet this person! But before I get too excited, do you think she could be a plant?"

"Anything is possible, Miss Giblon, but she certainly sounded sincere to me...almost in a rage with anger. Verifying her claim of being the only employee not on the ferry that day should be easy enough. That's the kind of public interest reporting the media would be certain to emphasize. Perhaps a call to our friend Hank Sturgess at the *New London Ledger* would prove helpful. He should know, he probably wrote the cover story about the massacre."

"Will do, Mr. Congressman!"

Washington

The following Wednesday morning found a very excited and very nervous Susan Collins waving good-bye to her sister, Cathy, and son, Toby, as she boarded a flight to the nation's capital, which had been hastily arranged by Congressman McDonald's staff. Erin Giblon had received rapid confirmation from Hank Sturgess that, yes, an employee by the name of Susan Collins was indeed the only employee not on the ferry that bloody Friday. As a consequence, Harry's office was brimming with excitement, eagerly anticipating the arrival of this mystery lady from New London.

At 10:20 AM, Susan's plane arrived on schedule at Dulles International after an uneventful flight from New London. Shortly thereafter, she found herself at the luggage carousel, awaiting her two pieces of luggage and wondering if she would recognize this Erin Giblon person who was to meet her.

Tall, with dark red hair and conservatively dressed in a blue blazer and matching slacks. Fine, but this is Washington... There must be hundreds of women in this town that match that description.

"Excuse me, Miss, but are you Susan Collins?" came a clear, well-enunciated voice from behind her.

Susan turned to face a tall, strikingly attractive young woman dressed in accordance with the description she had been provided.

"Yes, I'm Susan Collins," she responded somewhat hesitantly, wondering if she were facing the congressman's aide or yet another government agent.

"Welcome to Washington, Ms. Collins," Erin offered with a handshake and warm smile. "I'm Erin Giblon, Congressman McDonald's aide. May I help you with some of your luggage?"

Susan immediately felt as if a load had been lifted. Erin's honesty and sincerity shone through, and Susan felt comfortable and secure in Erin's presence, which was, of course, the usual response of people upon meeting Erin Giblon for the first time.

"The congressman is certainly looking forward to meeting you!" Erin continued. "Truth be told, the entire office has been on tenterhooks anticipating your arrival, including yours truly, which is why I volunteered to meet you at the airport. I hope you are developing an appetite because we all plan to have lunch together before we begin our meeting. Since you are from New London, have you previously met the congressman?"

"No, Miss Giblon, I haven't," responded Susan. "We only recently, well about a year ago actually, moved to New London from Birmingham. Being a single mom totally wrapped up in family and work, I must confess to being totally apolitical. I didn't even know who my congressman was…until recently, that is."

"The circumstances of your situation, Ms. Collins, as I understand them, are truly bewildering. You must obviously feel as if you have been through the proverbial wringer. Of necessity, it requires a lot of courage and conviction on your part just to be here. But please call me Erin…I have a hunch we are going to be spending a lot of time together."

"And please call me Susan."

If Susan felt relieved upon meeting Erin Giblon, she felt almost overwhelmed upon meeting the congressman. Never, but never, did she recall meeting anyone conveying such an imposing presence. His demeanor exuded confidence, superior intelligence, charisma, charm, focus, and resolve, all enhanced by his height, carriage, and remarkable handsomeness. Though it was certainly not the intent of Congressman McDonald, Susan felt an element of intimidation curiously blended with the emotion of admiration when she was in his presence.

Why does he have to be so damn good looking? thought Susan. *How am I ever going to be able to concentrate while he is around? Can't wait to tell Cathy about this man!*

Susan also went through the requisite introductions to each member of Congressman McDonald's staff, and, as a group, they began walking to the House office building's cafeteria. The congressman wasted no time in steering the idle conversations to the heart of the issues at hand.

"Ms. Collins, we sincerely appreciate your taking the time to visit us here in Washington. As you are no doubt well aware, the continuing operations of the laboratory at the Plum Island facility pose a very significant risk to the citizens of these United States and, under proper circumstances, a substantial portion of the world's population as well. It is of the utmost urgency that our committee investigations expose to the congress and the citizens of America the true purpose and objectives of the bio-labs—the production of biological weapons to be used in offensive engagements or experiments. The clear distinction between offensive-oriented research and development and purely defensive objectives must be starkly delineated."

"I certainly agree, Mr. Congressman," responded Susan. "Even as an employee of that facility, I never suspected that the research and experimentation being engaged in was for any purpose other than the amelioration and eradication of diseases primarily affecting animals."

"We all have our thresholds of tolerance and elucidation, Ms. Collins. When was your threshold breached?"

"In retrospect, I would have to say the first raid on my home was the original point of demarcation. My Epiphany and call to arms was the discovery that my beloved son was made critically ill as a result of a pathogen almost certainly engineered at Plum Island. I was in denial at the first suggestions of a link to Plum Island when my son was diagnosed, and as I progressed through the stages of skepticism and doubt to finally reach my present level of conviction, my anger and resolve for vindication and retribution began controlling my every waking moment."

"But Ms. Collins, if, as I understand your motivations, your determination is to incontrovertibly establish a link between the Plum Island lab and Lyme disease, why have you provided us with discs of viral research?"

"Simple. I was facing termination as a result of my frequent absenteeism to be with my son. Realizing the necessity of continuing my health insurance coverage, I somehow convinced my supervisors that my son had only a garden variety case of mono that the doctors had failed to recognize and diagnose. As a result of a correct diagnoses and dramatic improvement in my son's condition, I was committed to devote myself completely to my work and career at Plum. They bought my dog and pony show, and I was reassigned to review work that was in progress at the time of the massacre. I guess it was too much to expect to be assigned to the area of spirochetal research…which is certainly an area I would have given my eye teeth to explore, but it wasn't meant to be. It was the luck of

THE POISON PLUM

the draw that I was assigned to virology. Better than nothing, I thought, and I decided to make the best of the situation. Hence the CDs you have."

"And those alone, Ms. Collins, are sufficient to document the creation and deployment of AIDS and other incredibly virulent viral mutations. We and the American people owe you an enormous debt of gratitude for your courage and conviction. When we present this information in our committee hearings, it will be the equivalent of a nuclear explosion to the consciousness of America."

"Mr. Congressman, does this mean you are going to ignore the link to Lyme in your committee hearings?"

"Quite to the contrary, Ms. Collins, as you will see and appreciate once we complete our lunch and return to the office. I think you will be quite surprised and pleased with what we have to share."

"Mr. Congressman, let me be as direct as I possibly know how. It's my desire and objective to see that lab closed and all the supervisors, top scientists, and their bosses in higher positions of government banished to the most fearsome and dreadful penal facility this nation has to offer for the rest of their damn lives! And when they finally expire, may they rot for eternity in the pit of hell!"

"The latter is a given, Ms. Collins, regardless of our success or failure."

As Harry spoke those words, his thoughts began drifting to the plight of his friends, Glen and Fran Klinner. *The most fearsome and dreadful penal facility this nation has to offer...is it Guantanamo? Is that the hell that has become their fate?* he thought.

The conference room in Harry's office was to be the location for the afternoon's work session, which included Harry, Erin Giblon, and Susan. Harry instructed his aides to hold all of his calls and the original package of documents they had received was removed from the office safe and placed on the conference room table. Once Susan was seated, Harry began to explain the importance of Susan's potential contributions to the committee's investigations.

"Ms. Collins, our office has requested and received confirmations of assistance from individuals who are either currently employed by some of the nations most prestigious medical schools or are recent graduates of those institutions. Their academic credentials qualify them to review and evaluate the information we have and confirm our suspicions about the true nature of the research conducted at Plum. Information such as the discs that you have provided."

"Yes, Mr. Congressman. I, too, was solicited by my alma mater. I would have brought a copy of their letter but the agents seized it during their last raid on my home. I suppose I could request a duplicate be sent from UAB in case you'd like to see it."

"Wonderful, we'd like to have a copy for our files, if you don't mind. But the uniqueness of your contributions to our efforts lies in the fact that you are the only volunteer who is a former employee of the Plum Island facility. Without question, that unique status will substantially enhance the credibility of your testimony before the committee."

"I can assure you, Mr. Congressman, the pleasure will be all mine."

"Perhaps not completely, Ms. Collins. Because of the hand work and dedication of Miss Giblon and other staff members, we shall all derive considerable pleasure, albeit vicariously, from your convincing testimony. Unfortunately however, before we can all gleefully raise our champagne glasses high, much work and preparation remain. But of a more immediate nature, I did promise you at lunch a pleasant surprise when we returned to the office. Miss Giblon, would you please slide that package across to Ms. Collins?

"What you see before you, Ms. Collins, is a package of information our office received not even two weeks ago from an as yet anonymous provider. We would like for you to relax and begin reviewing those files and information. Of necessity, we realize that a complete review would require a considerable amount of time. What we wish to accomplish this afternoon and tomorrow is for you to perform a cursory examination and render an opinion regarding authenticity and worthiness to our efforts."

As Harry continued speaking, Susan began spreading forms and documents across the conference table in front of her. Immediately, she was struck by the perception that every page she saw had to do with spirochetal research and all the documents were at least thirty years old.

"This is incredible, Mr. Congressman! It looks like a cook book for the Lyme germ! And you say the source is anonymous? Do you have any idea where this came from?"

"No. All we know is that one day the package as you see it was delivered by the postal service to our office along with our other routine mail. We have no idea who or what the source may have been. The only clue is the New London postmark. From what we can tell, everything appears authentic, but we can't be certain. And that's where your expertise and academic preparation will prove invaluable. Before we seriously consider using any of that in public display and testimony, we must be absolutely confident and certain of its authenticity, accuracy, and relevance."

"Mr. Congressman, if we make the assumption these documents are genuine, and they certainly appear to be so, we must assume that what you have here came from a disgruntled employee, probably a former employee, considering the ferry massacre, that had a lengthy tenure at Plum. This is fascinating! Yes, I will be delighted to devote whatever time I can muster to sink my teeth into this! I can't wait to watch my supervisors Gallagher and Stephens twist and squirm as I explain the significance of these documents to the committee and the news media. There will be media present, won't there, Mr. Congressman?"

"Yes, Ms. Collins, there will be media present. A lot of media actually. I hope you aren't camera shy?"

"Normally, yes, but under the circumstances, not a snowball's chance in hell! I'm on a mission, Mr. Congressman! And speaking of a mission, before I zero in on what is before me, would there be a possibility of a caffeine infusion? Do you have any coffee, soda pop, or whatever?"

As Susan spoke, she continued pulling papers and pictures out of the large manila folder while spreading them before her like fanning a deck of cards.

"Certainly, Ms. Collins, we have coffee, tea, and variety of soft drinks. Which would you…"

"Holy cow," Susan interrupted loudly, "that's the same damn picture!"

Susan, obviously considerably excited, was now holding a photo from the stack and staring at it. The incredulous look upon her face starkly reflected her shock and surprise.

"Ms. Collins, what is it?" asked Harry. "What's the matter? You look as if you've seen a ghost!"

"A ghost from the past! That same damn picture is proudly displayed on the wall of Director Stephens's office! It caught my attention because it obviously predates the Plum Island facility, and it looks like it was taken somewhere in the South. Definitely not from anywhere around here. Look at those pine trees. That looks like Alabama or Georgia!"

Harry and Erin exchanged smiles and looks of affirmation after seeing the picture and hearing Susan's comments.

"Your powers of observation are absolutely on target, Ms. Collins. That particular picture was taken in front of a Tuskegee Institute building in Tuskegee, Alabama, in the late 1930s. The gentlemen pictured were Public Health Services doctors and the lady was the Institute's resident nurse."

"Tuskegee?" Susan shouted. "So it's all true! Syphilis is the Lyme germ's granddaddy! Those conniving bastards! That's why they withheld treatment from those poor black syphilitics… they wanted to see how long it would take for them to die!"

Big Brother Is Watching

Special agents Hubbard and Stinson had been assigned twelve-hour shifts by their field supervisor to monitor the activities of Susan Collins. Neither could recall a more boring assignment nor understand the objective or reasoning for their mission. Hubbard, in particular, began having serious second thoughts about a continuation of his career with the FBI. Certainly he didn't sign on to spend twelve hours a day shadowing an innocuous appearing middle-aged single mother who apparently was leading an uninspiring and unmitigated boring life.

Where is the excitement in this job? he often thought. *Where are the bad guys? The challenges?*

And then there were the rumors about heavy-handed actions frequently committed by government agents against innocent American citizens, including Susan Collins. The incidents at Ruby Ridge and Waco occurred before Hubbard had joined the Bureau, but their ghosts would appear each time he heard of yet another encroachment upon an individual's civil liberties.

"And what of this preoccupation my superiors have with this Collins woman contacting her congressman? What's the big deal anyway? Isn't that the American way? Don't citizens have the right to contact their elected representatives?"

Hubbard personally didn't participate in the raid on Susan's home last Saturday. But Agent Stinson did, and Hubbard couldn't get him to talk about it. Hubbard even began to wonder if Stinson's silence and reticence was due to the guilt he presently felt resulting from his participation in the raid.

Whatever, he thought. *Too many rumors and too many unanswered questions. Maybe it's time for a career change before I get sucked up into something that turns my stomach totally or compromises whatever remaining integrity I have.*

Having relieved Agent Stinson at their vantage point on Tyler Street several hundred feet from Susan's home at promptly 6 AM, Agent Hubbard had struggled with his boredom by pondering these issues and the qualms of conscience he was now experiencing. Suddenly, a few minutes before 9 AM, he observed Susan Collins briskly walking to her SUV.

Good, he thought. *At least we're going somewhere. Even the Wal-Mart parking lot would beat this!*

Following carefully at a distance to evade detection, Hubbard was surprised when they arrived at Susan's destination, the Abercrombie Building, a few minutes later. Agent Hubbard was careful to enter the building from the Poindexter Street side opposite from the Concord Street entrance where Susan had parked.

Well this should make my supervisor happy, Hubbard thought as he watched her enter Congressman McDonald's district office. *Now at last we have the smoking gun. Threat to society Susan Collins commits heinous crime of contacting her congressman! Truth be known, she's probably going to complain about the way those agents treated her on Saturday. She's probably pissed to high heaven, and who the hell could blame her!*

Nevertheless, Agent Hubbard dutifully reported Susan's actions that Monday to his field supervisor, who in turn reported the development to Director Frey. As interesting as Susan's actions were to Director Frey, it was her trip to the airport on Wednesday to board a flight for Washington that prompted yet another telephone strategy session between Frey, Steele, and Budenz.

"Director Steele, Attorney General Budenz," began Frey. "Our pigeon from Plum, Susan Collins, has flown the coop. Last Monday morning, she was seen visiting McDonald's regional office. This morning, she boarded a flight to Washington, and upon arrival, she was met by McDonald's top aide and taken to his office."

"What does that tell us Frey?" asked Budenz. "Is she so upset as a result of the visit from our friendly agents that she's making a pilgrimage to Washington to demand absolution? Or is she volunteering her services to the committee? Which is it?"

"Who the hell knows?" remarked Steele. "We can only surmise that in her case, the intimidation of our agents failed to produce the usual reactions of fear and submission. Hence her meeting with the congressman to get him to bring those naughty agents to task. As anal as McDonald is, he might try to incorporate her tales of woe and mistreatment into the committee hearings agenda. As far as her 'services' are concerned, what is she going to do? Read tea leaves to the committee? So what if she's a former employee…she doesn't know shit, and McDonald doesn't know shit! He is just on another of his pain-in-the-ass moralistic vendettas and crusades. I'm telling you, he has nothing, nothing, nothing! Those hearings are going to fall apart from day one and be the biggest non-event in Washington history. You mark my words!"

"It's true," said Frey. "Our search of her home turned up not a single shred of evidence that could have been removed from the laboratory and used by McDonald. But I still don't share your confidence in McDonald's impotence. I wish I did…our jobs would be so much easier if McDonald would just fall flat on his face. But it's my concern, gentlemen, that McDonald has something… What, I do not know, but I can assure you, I do not relish the idea of losing my job or going to prison. Maybe the son of a bitch will trot out a quartet of singing ticks from Plum Island! All I know is, we face a formidable enemy possessing more tenacity and perseverance than anyone I've ever seen. Make no mistake, he will successfully launch that committee investigation, and he will ride it to the bitter end. We will be facing a lot of flak for sure, not only from the choir boy but that muckraker McAdams as well. We are collectively out on the proverbial limb without the unequivocal support of the presidency…and we all know if the heat gets turned on, that guy is going to look after number one first and only and turn in whatever direction the political winds are blowing.

"We have to this point covered every base. The Plum Island facility was locked down tight, McClain's image was polished even brighter, the potential threat Klinner is rotting in prison, we have shadowed McDonald and Susan Collins to the best of our abilities, and sensitive subpoenas have been quashed. Now all we can do is wait for the inquisitions to begin and deal with whatever the chief inquisitor dredges up and throws at us."

"Dammit Frey!" roared Budenz. "If you are correct, all that we have done is just not enough! We are on the defensive here, which is an untenable position, as far as I'm concerned!"

"I'm with Budenz," said Steele. "This shit ain't gonna cut it. We've got to come up with something, a plan that can't fail. Count me in as one that has no desire to be canned or imprisoned! We have three weeks and change before hands are placed on a Bible, bright lights are turned on, and every news media in this country is recording for posterity every utterance and subtle nuance. Our asses are on the line if we don't figure out some way to throttle McDonald and shut his freak show down!"

"Let's go on the offensive." Budenz began. "Time the convictions of the Klinners to shortly precede the beginning of the committee hearings. Assure the media is provided with the spin that the Klinners, despite their facade of respectability, are the equivalent of Ethel and Julius Rosenberg to America's security. Assuage the citizens' appetite for justice by providing the requisite sacrificial lambs while simultaneously reinforcing their image of the Plum facility as the first line of defense against horrible diseases threatening America's livestock."

"And after that?" questioned Steele. "What if the Klinners are replaced by our smiling faces in the media's spotlight as McDonald's committee opens up a can of worms? I am not going to risk having my neck placed on the chopping block as a result of something that damn crusade dredges up! I repeat…we need a fail-safe contingency plan to be implemented in a worst-case-scenario situation."

The Commuter

Susan Collins had planned to return to New London the next day. But lying awake in her hotel room that night thinking about the task that lay before her, she realized that a few days a week in Washington would not be sufficient to prepare the detailed exposé required to do justice to the documents the congressman had received. Other volunteers from the medical schools would have no problem in explaining the contents of the CDs Susan had copied, but it was the information relevant to Lyme disease that inspired and motivated Susan.

Whatever it takes, she thought. *I'll just have to beg Cathy for her continuing support and somehow convince Toby that I have to do this thing.*

As Susan reflected back on the incredible journey she and her family had traveled since leaving Birmingham, she realized the events of her life had swirled in increasing intensity like the vortex of liquids flowing through a massive funnel until finally reaching the apex of intensity and discharge.

We're beginning to swirl through the spout of the funnel now, thought Susan, *And soon the contents of that funnel are going to spill out for everyone to see. Instead of going back to New London tomorrow afternoon, I'm going to reschedule and get a flight in on Friday night. I've got to devote as much time as possible to this. I've got one shot for retribution, and this is it. Whatever it takes! I'll call Cathy and Toby tomorrow…they'll understand, I hope!*

So for the weeks leading up to the hearings, Susan assumed the life of a commuter living in one city and working in another. And no, Toby didn't understand why his mother had to be away so much. All he understood was he missed his mother, and he wanted her to come home. Cathy remained supportive and did all she could to provide the necessary surrogate motherhood. Mondays until late Friday afternoons, Susan poured over the documents and photographs with Erin Giblon by her side providing all the assistance she possibly could.

Weekends were spent with Toby and Cathy as Susan adhered to a rigorous schedule of returning on Friday nights and then departing for Washington on early Monday morning flights. While in Washington, Susan was committed to documenting and linking together the logical sequence of events connecting the spirochetal research done in Tuskegee to the development of the engineered Lyme germ at Plum. Everything she needed was at her disposal in those photographs and documents, but the challenge of organizing it all into laymen's terms remained. A combination of projection screen presentations, large placard displays supported by easels, and expert qualified testimony would be required and used. But time was of the essence. All of this information had to be reviewed, assimilated, and organized quickly, concisely, and above all, accurately. Long hours and growing fatigue were to be her lot, but her determination and resolve remained unwavering.

On the Friday before the long Labor Day weekend, Susan and the congressman shared a flight back to New London. The preceding weeks had been long and grueling and they both were very, very tired. All was in readiness, however, and the hearings were to begin as scheduled on the Tuesday following Labor Day. The long weekend would give them each an opportunity to relax and recuperate before the tension-filled hearings got underway. Susan knew she had done her best and felt very secure in her ability to communicate to the audience the genealogy of the germ now wreaking havoc across the northeastern United States. The link to the syphilis spirochete was indisputable. As a result of the government's proven and admitted complicity in the sordid Tuskegee experiments, it was a given that culpability for the Lyme germ's creation would be established beyond a shadow of a doubt.

I've done it, Susan thought as their plane lifted off the runway bound for New London. *I've nailed the bastards once and for all.*

As she settled back into her seat once the captain turned off the Fasten Seatbelts sign, she glanced over at the congressman seated beside her. She wondered what thoughts were going through his mind as the long-awaited hearings rapidly approached. She had watched as he coordinated and directed the efforts of his staff and the volunteers like an architect supervising the construction of a massive building complex until all was completed to perfection.

But what drives this man? thought Susan. *Was it the imprisonment of his friends, the Klinners? The Tasering death of Ben Stegall? The unconscionable and unconsti-*

tutional acts of corrupt and brutal federal agents? The lab at Plum itself? All of the above put together? What? Certainly there was no sign or indication of personal aggrandizement evident. No 'see how wonderful I am and vote for me' with this man. To Susan, Congressman McDonald remained an enigma because he was like no other man she had ever known.

If there is a God, she thought, *please send us some more like him because this world sure could use them!*

Glancing over at the congressman again, she saw him staring out the window at the white, fluffy clouds they were beginning to fly through. He was obviously deep in thought about something.

I'll ask him, thought Susan. *What have I got to lose? And besides, I would like to get to know a little about his personal side…if that's even possible for peons such as myself. God, he seems almost aristocratic at times! But here goes…*

"Mr. Congressman," Susan began. "May I ask you a personal question?"

"Certainly, Ms. Collins. What would you like to know?"

"Well, it's one of those questions that's easy to ask, but I'm not certain the answer could be easy. I would think it possibly could be rather complex, and if so, I apologize."

"Let's give it a try, Ms. Collins…what is your question?"

Swallowing hard, Susan paused for a moment before responding.

"Mr. Congressman? Why do you do it? I mean, what's your motivation or motivations for these committee hearings? It seems to me you have totally committed yourself to a course of action that may or may not be recognized by the average American as beneficial to his or her well being, and, as a result of what I have personally experienced, could even be dangerous."

"All that is necessary for the triumph of evil, Ms. Collins, is for good men to do nothing. No, I'm not trying to trivialize your question with such a succinct reply that could be construed as flippant, but it's true. Succinct but true. I'm doing what I'm doing because it has to be done. It's the right thing to do, and it's the moral thing to do. The diabolical schemes of the New World Order planners must be exposed and opposed. And from what quarter will that exposure and opposition arise? If not our efforts, Ms. Collins, then whose? Just as you were unable to rest until the source of your son's affliction was identified, I shall know no peace until this blight upon mankind is identified and eradicated.

"For you see, we are all adjudged…not only for what we do but for what we don't do. Our actions and inactions. Our sins of omission and our sins of commission. All of us, Ms. Collins…not one exception. Not only here on this earth but in the hereafter as well. So, as you can see from that context, I, you, we, really don't have a choice, do we?"

As Susan sat quietly thinking about the words the congressman had spoken, she began to realize more fully and completely than ever the true dimension of the battle she and the congressman were waging.

It's that simple, she thought. *It really is. It's black against white, good versus evil, wrong versus right, light versus darkness! It's just that simple…it always has been since time immemorial, and it always will be into the infinite future.*

It was then that the realization slowly began dawning upon Susan that she was truly in the presence of a very great man. She felt humbled and honored to be seated by his side. Even more so to be considered an integral component of his committee investigations.

But would this man's greatness, his contributions to mankind, be recognized by this generation? Susan wondered. *Or would it require the inhabitants of some future enlightened generation with the capacity to look back over time and see and judge clearly what had gone before? Probably the latter,* she mused, *Probably the latter…*

For the remainder of the flight, Susan sat quietly with her hands folded in her lap, deep in thought. The congressman resumed staring out the window until finally the silence was broken by the captain's announcement to refasten seat belts for the final descent into New London.

"Ms. Collins," spoke the congressman as he began adjusting his safety belt, "do you have someone meeting you at the airport?"

"Yes, my sister, Cathy, is coming, and she'll have my son, Toby, with her."

"That's good. I would like to meet them, and I would also like for you to meet my wife, Anna, who will be picking me up. Are you and your sister close, Ms. Collins?"

"Yes, very close."

"That's the way it should be. And how is your son now that he's finally receiving treatment?"

"He's better, much better actually, but a lot of problems remain. His new doctor has him on oral antibiotics now and also anti-protozoal therapy for the Babesia. "

"And you feel comfortable with your son's doctor and his treatment protocol?"

"Absolutely! And even though I haven't met the man personally, I still say without equivocation that he is a top-notch professional. Under the circumstances with the area Lyme experts effectively shut down by the government, Dr. Robinson is an absolute Godsend."

"I wish you and your son the best."

"Thank you, Mr. Congressman."

Minutes later, their flight had landed and after retrieving their carry-on luggage, Susan and the congressman began making their way to the terminal building. Susan spotted Cathy and Toby right away, and they rushed to hug and greet each other.

"Toby, sweetheart!" exclaimed Susan as she pulled him to her chest and held him tightly. "Mommy has missed you so much!"

"I've missed you, too, Mommy. You're not going to go away again, are you?"

"Oh sweetie, Mommy doesn't want to! I want to stay here with you and Aunt Cathy. And how is Aunt Cathy? Gimme a hug! Have you two been behaving yourselves? Look, I have someone with me you need to meet! Mr. Congressman, this is my sister, Cathy, and my son, Toby."

"Well hello…actually I believe Cathy and I met a few years ago when I was a guest speaker at her church. It's nice to see you again, Cathy. And this handsome young man must be Toby! Your mother has told me all about you, young man, and how very proud she is of you. Do you know what a really special mother you have, son? In your prayers, you need to always remember to thank God for sending her to you."

Harry McDonald became a hero to young Toby Collins that day. Cathy was flattered that he had remembered her from that casual meeting two years ago, and Susan was even more convinced she was truly in the presence of greatness.

"I see my wife Anna approaching…I want you all to meet her!"

Anna rushed through the crowd, and moments later, she and Harry embraced and kissed as if they had been apart for a very long time.

"Welcome home, darling! I thought today would never arrive!"

"I love you, Anna," Harry said as they continued to embrace and kiss each other.

What a perfectly paired couple, thought Susan. *She is as beautiful as he is handsome! And obviously they absolutely adore each other! Oh, this is so romantic, I think I may cry!*

"Anna, darling, we have some very special people here that I would like you to meet…" Reaching out to take Susan's hand, Harry gently pulled Susan closer to Anna while beginning the introductions.

"This is Susan Collins, the courageous young woman I told you about…a former employee at the Plum lab who has become such an indispensable part of our team. This handsome young man is her son, Toby, who is also imbued with incredible courage. And this fine young lady is Susan's sister, Cathy, who in addition to helping her sister and nephew during these challenging times, somehow finds the time to be quite active in the East Highland Baptist Church. A fine family indeed!"

Swift Injustice

MacIntosh McAdams had spent most of Friday framing a column for the Labor Day edition of *The Chronicle* with the intention of hammering home to his readership the significance of the congressional hearings scheduled to begin the next day. McAdams described the opportunity for exposure of the Plum Island activities as a true watershed event for America and its citizens and stressed that all patriotic Americans should be supportive of and grateful for the heroic and courageous stance of Congressman McDonald. The scientists and their progeny of countless germs were dubbed "The Creatures from Plum Island" and should Americans fail to rally the opposition to a continuation of research at Plum, their indifference would be the equivalent of opening the borders to hordes of Mongolian nomads coming to burn , rape, and pillage our citizens with reckless abandon. The timing of the column was, of course, designed to draw maximum attention to what McAdams described as "the most momentous congressional event of our lifetimes!" The final polishing of his article would be accomplished Saturday morning by noon.

No more than two or three hours, he thought as he arrived early at his office. *I'm going to wrap that puppy up and put it to bed. All work and no play makes Mac a dull boy.... I'm going to be on that golf course no later than 2 PM and get in some R and R while I still can. Next week's gonna be a bitch from hell!*

Mac worked best under stress, but of necessity it must be quiet stress. Distractions such as radio, television, music, or conversations between co-workers were taboo when Mac was working on a column. If his office door was closed and Mac could be seen through the window obviously concentrating on something, every staffer at *The Chronicle* knew to leave him alone. Conversely, if his office door was open, then all knew he could be approached.

At approximately 10 AM, Mac glanced up from his desk to observe a crowd of co-workers beginning to gather in front of a large, wall-mounted plasma television. It was obviously garnering everyone's rapt and solemn attention.

Now what? thought Mac. *Another airplane hit a building? Guess I'd better walk out there and see what the hell is going on. If the president is going to surrender Florida to Castro, maybe he'll stand firm on Alabama and Georgia. I definitely need to know about it!*

"Mac! Hurry! You need to see this!" shouted a coeditor as Mac approached the growing crowd now staring intently at the screen.

Even from a distance, Mac could make out the images of the president flanked by Attorney General Budenz, CIA Director Steele, FBI Director Frey, and Homeland Security Chief Dolan.

Uh-oh, thought Mac. *I don't like the look of this!*

The president was addressing the nation and judging from the very somber expression on his face and the expressions of those surrounding him, the subject was quite serious indeed. His words became more audible to Mac as he drew closer to the screen.

"...and as a result of a very thorough and extensive investigation, the United States military tribunal at Guantanamo, Cuba, operating under the provisions of the Patriot Act, has rendered a verdict in the trial of Dr. Glen Klinner and his wife, Fran Klinner. The Klinners were found guilty of actively and consciously aiding and abetting an act of terrorism against the government of the United States. My fellow Americans, we as a free people must judiciously guard our freedoms and liberties and remain vigilant of any threats to our precious democracy. There is no greater danger to our cherished institutions than an act of treason for it strikes at the very underpinnings of our society.

"It is for these reasons that the penalty for the heinous crime of treason since our nation's inception has always been the ultimate that could be levied by any court. The severity of the penalty is justified by the severity of the crime, which was not limited to those innocent doctors and scientists, as gruesome as that tragedy was, but to each and every one of us as free Americans. The unequivocal verdict of guilty for the malevolent Klinners will allow our nation to begin the necessary healing process as justice will have been served. Consequently, at 9 AM Eastern Standard time and approximately twenty-four hours after the guilty verdict was rendered, the Klinners were simultaneously executed by a military firing squad at our Guantanamo facility. Closure has been achieved, my fellow Americans, thanks to the most efficient terrorism fighting tool our nation has ever possessed—the Patriot Act.

"Let us now move bravely forward, secure in the knowledge that we as a free people will always remain vigilant and will vigorously take whatever actions are required to defend, protect and preserve all that we hold dear. The United States has always been and will continue to be a beacon of freedom for the entire world to envy. Rest assured, my fellow Americans, that with each threat to our American way of life, our nation grows even stronger. Our institutions and principles will continue to prevail, regardless of the efforts of our enemies. Thank you all and may God bless America."

"Yes! And freedom and justice for all, you lying piece of shit!" Mac screamed. "Pap for the masses! Did you people hear that?"

"Mac!" yelled a co-worker. "We're on your side! Calm down! You're going to stroke out!"

"Did you see that?" he bellowed, his face now crimson with rage. "Did you all hear what that son of a bitch said? Do you all realize what this means? Constitutional republic out the damn window and tyrannical oligarchy in! How long before the bastards march goons in here to tell us what we can and cannot print?"

For the next fifteen minutes, Mac stalked around the room like a raging bull, ranting and raving about the government, the administration, the president and his cabinet, the Constitution, and what a travesty of justice the trial had been.

"A kangaroo court...a lynch committee...can't people see that? It's as plain as the nose on your face! The bastards have buried the evidence. The last remaining human being that could have possibly known the mindset of Gordon McClain has been murdered by those cowardly whores!"

Mac's co-workers at *The Chronicle* that day for the most part knew in their hearts that he was right. Indeed a seismic shift determining America's future direction had occurred, and they were all witnesses to it. Most were in awe at the energy, conviction, and ferocity exhibited by MacIntosh McAdams as he stomped furiously and aimlessly around the press room quoting scripture, the Constitution, hurling invectives and epithets, and in general venting his anger and frustration for everyone to see. Then, just as suddenly as it had erupted, the shouting stopped, and Mac quietly walked back to his office and shut the door.

Got to put it all together, he thought. *First, I'll give Erin Giblon a call in case she missed that farce I just saw...then I'll delay finishing that column I've been working on until I write another for tomorrow morning's edition. Get ready, Mr. President and all of your lackeys! Your faithful enemy, MacIntosh McAdams, here at The Chronicle is about to drop a manure truck on your collective asses! No golf game today.... I'm going to write the column of my career, and I'll stay up all night if necessary. Touché you sons of bitches...here it comes!*

Bad News Travels Fastest

Harry and Anna McDonald regarded their rare private time as sacred ground. When at home in New London, televisions and radios were not allowed, and an answering machine screened calls to their unlisted number. Occasionally, the McDonalds would entertain good friends such as the Klinners by inviting them over for a Saturday evening dinner. And once every two months or so on a rotating schedule, the McDonalds would host a Saturday morning Bible study group from their church. As fate would have it, their turn to serve as hosts for the group came on this particular Saturday before the hearings were scheduled to begin. Anna questioned the advisability of hosting the group, feeling very strongly that Harry should instead use the time to rest and collect his thoughts before what was certain to be a very stressful and trying period.

"Sweetheart," Anna began. "Do you really want to have all those people in today? I'm sure everyone would understand if we just cancelled out."

"I'm sure they would, Anna, but I need the comfort I always receive from study of the Holy Scriptures, especially today at this particular juncture of my life. And why, I don't know, but I feel that God has laid it upon my heart to make the study of Revelation 18 our focus today. Especially certain verses I feel are particularly relevant now and I cannot explain why."

"Isn't Revelation 18 the chapter that seemed to describe almost exactly the events of 9/11?"

"Yes," Harry replied.

"But that was then…what is the relevance today?"

"I don't know, Anna. I just know that there's another message in those verses we need to recognize. Perhaps some as yet unforeseen event."

"Let's pray that it not be so. From what I remember of that chapter, it chilled me to the bone!"

By the designated 9:45 AM meeting time, Harry had completed his review of the chapter and knew exactly which verses he felt led to review and study. Fifteen people were present that morning and after everyone was seated and comfortable, Harry opened the meeting with a prayer and then began to explain what he planned to accomplish during the meeting.

"Thank you all for your attendance this morning. Today, I am, with your indulgence, going to deviate from our study guide by revisiting Revelation 18, verses 1 through 5 and verses 8 through 11. As you all will probably recall, we turned to Chapter 18 immediately after the events of 9/11 and were struck by the similarities.... It was as if the words written almost two thousand years ago were leaping from the headlines written that terrible day. I am at a loss to explain my urgency for turning to these passages of scripture at this time. I can only say that I feel God has put it on my heart to do so. As we begin our study, let us prayerfully and humbly beseech our Father to reveal the message these passages could hold for us.

"The entire chapter depicts in graphic detail the complete destruction of Babylon, which has been described in the Bible as both an evil city and an immoral empire. The similarities of the descriptions of Babylon in the Bible and comparisons to the present day city of New York are glaringly obvious to even the most casual of readers. As we begin, imagine in your minds, if you will, the verses are in fact predicting a future time of travail and judgment for that city. Starting with verse 1, John is continuing to describe the visions revealed to him during his exile on the Isle of Patmos sometime around 68 A.D."

And after these things I saw another angel come down from heaven, having great power; and the earth was lightened with his glory. And he cried mightily with a strong voice, saying, Babylon the great is fallen, is fallen, and is become the habitation of devils, and the hold of every foul spirit, and a cage of every unclean and hateful bird.

For all nations have drunk of the wine of the wrath of her fornication, and the kings of the earth have committed fornication with her, and the merchants of the earth are waxed rich through the abundance of her delicacies.

And I heard another voice from heaven, saying, Come out of her, my people, that ye be not partakers of her sins, and that ye receive not of her plagues.

For her sins have reached unto heaven, and God hath remembered her iniquities.

"Now if you are following along in your King James editions, I would like for us to skip ahead to verses 8 through 11. Then we will close with the final verse, 24."

Therefore shall her plagues come in one day, death, and mourning, and famine; and she shall be utterly burned with fire: for strong is the Lord God who judgeth her.

And the kings of the earth, who have committed fornication and lived deliciously with her, shall bewail her, and lament for her, when they shall see the smoke of her burning.

Standing afar off for the fear of her torment, saying, Alas, alas that great city of Babylon, that mighty city! For in one hour is thy judgment come.

And the merchants of the earth shall weep and mourn over her; for no man buyeth their merchandise anymore.

"And now, before we begin our review of what we have read…Anna would you please get that?" Harry said as a ringing phone in the den interrupted the meeting. "I'm sorry for the disruption…let's continue with the reading of the last verse."

And in her was found the blood of prophets, and of saints, and of all that were slain upon the earth.

As Harry lifted his eyes from the pages of his Bible and the verse he had just read aloud, Anna reentered the room, quickly moved to Harry's side and whispered softly…

"Sweetheart, that's Erin on the phone. She sounds upset…says it's urgent."

"Excuse me, everyone," Harry said as he stood to walk to the den. "It seems I have an urgent call. I'll be right back."

The members of the study group, assuming that frequent interruptions of a busy congressman's life were the expected norm, began discussing the scriptures they had reviewed with one another. Harry was only gone for a few moments and returned with a somber, stoic expression on his face, which Anna's darting, perceptive eyes scanned anxiously.

What is it? she wondered as Harry briskly walked to the television and turned it on. As the images began filling the screen, all could see the commentators were discussing some event that had just concluded. The room grew silent as everyone listened intently.

"*...and to recap today's news conference with the president and key members of the administration, the saga of the Plum Island ferry massacre has come to a dramatic conclusion with the announcement that those responsible for inciting Colonel Gordon McClain, Dr. Glen Klinner and his co-conspirator wife, Fran, were found guilty of aiding and abetting a terrorist act against the United States government and were executed today by a firing squad at our military base in Guantanamo, Cuba. These events, stressed the president, bring closure to the speculation and conjecture swirling consistently throughout America since the beginning of the unfolding drama now known as 'Bloody Friday.'*"

"Oh, my God, no!" Anna cried as Harry quickly put his arms around her. "Harry! What have they done with our friends? This can't be happening…tell me this isn't happening!"

Anna buried her face in Harry's chest, sobbing and shaking uncontrollably. Harry held her close in a vain attempt at consolation as he struggled to fight back his own tears and the raging, powerful emotions whipsawing relentlessly throughout his body.

Their guests sat quietly waiting to offer their own condolences of heartfelt Christian sympathy, and each silently offered up his or her own prayers and supplications to the Almighty for the McDonalds and the souls of the Klinners. But most simply realized that the McDonalds needed to be alone during this time of personal crisis and grief. The condolences that were offered were brief; only one or two sentences at the most, as the guests slowly began filing out of the McDonald home.

When the tears finally dried, Harry began speaking softly while continuing to embrace his wife.

"Anna, honey, we did everything humanly possible to secure the release of Glen. We now know Glen and Fran were ruthlessly murdered by the enemy we oppose for the sole purpose of concealing the true activities of the Plum Island lab. We lost in that arena, it's true, and there is nothing we can do to bring the

Klinners back. We have one chance left to vindicate Glen and Fran and hold accountable those responsible for their deaths. One chance and one chance only, Anna, but the one will be sufficient. The evidence we've accumulated for the committee hearings is powerful, compelling, and irrefutable. It's true that the decay of our nation is far advanced, but that decay is not so far advanced that the findings of a congressional committee will be rendered impotent. No conspiracy, no matter how clever and devious, can withstand the light of day shed on their plots and nefarious schemes."

"I want to be with you when you let the sunlight in next week," Anna said. "I want to see the look on their faces when you confront them with the proof you have! When you return to Washington tomorrow evening, darling, I want to be by your side on that plane. And throughout next week, every single day, I want to be in the audience of that committee room praying unceasingly for your triumph over our enemies. And every night I will be with you holding you in my arms…I will do everything in my power to strengthen and support you darling."

America's Response

For the average American going about his or her daily rat-race routine, the news of the Klinners' execution was received in a more or less ho-hum blasé manner. Justice had been served, the door had been closed on that episode of our nation's history, and it was time to move on. Most did not fully understand or appreciate the issues involved and few were willing to expend the time and energy required to delve deeper into the issues at stake. For the portions of the media providing editorial analysis, comment and conjecture, most were content to offer to their readers or viewers a synopsis of events in chronological order, beginning with the illustrious career of Colonel Gordon McClain and concluding with the execution of the Klinners. At the far-left liberal end of the political spectrum, represented by the likes of Snodgrass of *The Times* and Lemke at *The Post*, the universal theme was that more government control and surveillance would be required in the future to keep America safe from her enemies. The Patriot Act was lauded as the most progressive advancement America had ever seen for providing and ensuring domestic security, but obviously more needed to be done legislatively. Reminding their audience that the world was becoming an increasingly dangerous place, they championed for an "essential" national identity program with cards supported by a central computer data bank and complete abolition of all private ownership of firearms, including long guns and those traditionally used for hunting fowl, small game, and deer.

All provisions of the Patriot Act were to be reviewed and strengthened in as many areas as possible and especially the money laundering and bank secrecy sections. To eliminate terrorist funding, specifically their primary source of illegal narcotics trafficking, it was recommended that the reporting provisions for currency transactions of $10,000 or more be reduced immediately to a new threshold of $1,000 or more and the fines and penalties imposed for noncompliance increased dramatically. The congressional hearings planned by Congressman McDonald were denounced as an anachronistic throwback to the days of witch hunts, the avatar of regressive thought, and a total waste of taxpayer monies.

Editorial opinion from the opposite end of the political spectrum, including of course MacIntosh McAdams, stressed that a government grown beyond its constitutionally mandated boundaries was the problem and certainly not the solution. Support for McDonald and his hearings, even among the more conservative media, ranged from overwhelming (McAdams and a limited number of others) to tepid, with most endorsing a moderately cautious, wait-and-see attitude.

In the first of two columns prepared by McAdams for *The Chronicle* to appear consecutively, he forcefully and adamantly called outright for the impeachment of the president and the resignations of Attorney General Budenz, CIA Director Steele, FBI Director Frey, and Chief of Homeland Security Dolan. America could no longer tolerate the high crimes and misdemeanors committed by these high-ranking government officials, McAdams charged. Nor could it tolerate their flagrant violations of the U.S. Constitution. In sentence after sentence, paragraph after paragraph, Mac relentlessly exhorted his readers to contact their respective representatives in Congress and demand that impeachment proceedings begin in the House of Representatives immediately. Failure of the elected representatives to rise to this challenge and defend the Constitution would surely result in a renaming of that formally august body to the "House of Reprehensibles!"

Mac reviewed for his readers the constitutional provisions for impeachment of public officials and also cited examples in American history, including that of President Clinton. Reminding readers that dead men tell no tales, McAdams recounted how certain individuals posing varying degrees of impediments to the progress of the New World Order met untimely fates and died under mysterious circumstances. The list included former Secretary of War James Forrestal, Senator Joseph McCarthy, General George Patton, President John F. Kennedy, FBI Director J. Edgar Hoover, Dr. Martin Luther King, Jr., and almost but not quite, former Alabama Governor George Wallace. McAdams even threw in Marilyn Monroe for good measure.

The significance of the elimination of Glen and Fran Klinner was obvious. At the conclusion of the article was printed a petition for impeachment, which Mac encouraged his readers to sign and distribute.

The Hearings — Day One

Susan Collins was on pins and needles the morning the committee hearings were to commence. Bidding Toby and Cathy an emotional farewell, Susan boarded an early flight to Dulles for what was certain to be the beginning of the most exciting and challenging period of her entire life. Susan's testimony wouldn't be required that first day, and technically her presence was unnecessary. So, she elected to spend Monday night, Labor Day, in New London with Toby and Cathy. Her flight schedule would allow her to arrive in Washington in plenty of time for her to arrive at the hearings before they officially began at 9 AM, as it was her intention not to miss even a single minute of the proceedings.

Not knowing quite what to expect, Susan, after clearing security, entered the large hearing room Tuesday morning and was astounded at the large assemblage of media present. Her seating was pre-assigned and assured, which was a very good thing, considering there was not even room to stand. Media personnel and equipment occupied the floor space surrounding the committee staff and also circled the perimeter of the room. As Susan took her seat, she could see the congressman and committee members arranging their notes and conferring with one another. Seated in the witness area, Susan identified Budenz, Frey, Steele, and Dolan. It was at that moment the awesome reality of the situation that was about to unfold gripped Susan.

No turning back now, she thought. *Not for us and not for them. This is real and now. No more prevarication, no more equivocation. It's show-and-tell time!*

Susan's heart was thumping as the 9 AM hour arrived, and Congressman McDonald stood proudly erect to bring the hearings to order.

I've never seen anyone appear so brave and resolute, Susan thought as Harry hammered the gavel and called for attention.

"Ladies and gentlemen," he began. "Members of congress, the current administration, selected witnesses, and members of the media, I, as chairman of the

House Health and Human Services Committee, call to order this investigative committee for the purpose of determining the true objective of the research and programs being implemented at the government's Animal Disease Research Center located on Plum Island, New York. We shall endeavor to demonstrate in these hearings that taxpayer monies are being wrongfully utilized at the Plum Island facility for the purpose of genetically engineering germs to be used in biological-warfare programs.

"Furthermore," Harry continued as murmurs of excitement rippled through the audience and the media, "we will demonstrate unequivocally that these programs, operating in secrecy and under direct contradiction to the stated objectives of the facility, have resulted in the dissemination of at least one such genetically engineered pathogen amongst the general population of the United States. And that, ladies and gentlemen, would be the germ that causes Lyme disease."

Gasps of shock and surprise erupted as Harry spoke, and for several moments bedlam prevailed until Harry could hammer the proceedings back to order.

Susan thought that the congressman was certainly not wasting any time with unnecessary niceties.

These hearings are going to be brutal, she thought. *He is going straight for the jugular in a scorched-earth, take-no-hostages approach. This guy ain't pussyfooting around!*

"At this time, I would like to call our first witness before the committee. Attorney General Budenz, would you please take the witness stand?"

As Budenz stood to comply with the congressman's request, Susan noted that he was a stocky man in his late fifties, almost completely bald, and bearing a totally inscrutable expression.

Let's see if that stoicism makes it through the first five minutes, thought Susan. *A dollar to a doughnut that hard-ass facade cracks once the congressman turns up the heat!*

"Mr. Budenz," Harry began forcefully as he turned to squarely face the attorney general. "Your appearance here today is a result of a subpoena issued by this committee requiring your presence. Is that correct, Mr. Budenz?"

"Yes, that would be correct," he replied.

"Mr. Budenz, this committee also issued subpoenas for Mr. Clement Stephens, acting director of the Plum Island facility, and all the department heads working under him."

"Yes," Budenz interrupted. "I am well aware of the subpoena power of a congressional committee."

"Then you are no doubt aware that this committee, because of the overlapping research of programs implemented at the other bio-labs, subpoenaed Director Kirkland of the CDC, Director Lane of Ft. Detrick, and Director Boulware of Ft. Collins. And you obviously are also aware that all of those subpoenas were quashed as a result of a formal request to quash issued by your office to the appropriate federal district judges."

Silence gripped the hearing room as McDonald and Budenz stared intently at each other, Budenz's face remaining emotionless.

"What is the objective of the research being done at Plum Island as you understand it, Mr. Budenz?"

"We all know the answer to that question, Mr. Congressman. The facility exists to protect America's livestock from disease."

"Livestock...?"

"Yes."

"So are you telling this committee that the research and programs implemented by the scientists at Plum are defensive in nature?"

"Of course," replied Budenz, a trace of irritation beginning to appear in his voice.

"So, Mr. Budenz, by your own admission, the work is relatively benign...chickens, pigs, cows, turkeys...that sort of thing?"

More silence followed as McDonald and Budenz continued staring at one another as if they were the only human beings in the massive room.

"Mr. Budenz, why were those subpoenas quashed? Would you please explain this to the committee?"

"National security."

"National security, you say? Would you please explain how this committee could possibly jeopardize national security by asking questions about diseases that affect chickens, pigs, cows, and turkeys?"

"America's food supply must be protected from our enemies."

"So if this committee were to ask a department head at Plum what is being done to protect our cattle from hoof-and-mouth disease, his or her testimony might in some way be used by our enemies?"

"Something like that."

"But aren't research findings provided on a continuous basis to the various veterinary and medical journals for dissemination to the interested public, pharmaceutical companies, and so forth?"

"Mr. Congressman, let me remind you that I am the attorney general of the United States. I am the chief law enforcement officer of this nation. Whether or not current laboratory research is provided to appropriate media is beyond my purview!"

"Mr. Budenz, is it your practice to issue directives to quash subpoenas concerning matters beyond your purview?"

That did it! thought Susan. *Blankness is now replaced with a scowl. McDonald is drawing blood, and the arrogant SOB wants revenge.*

McDonald continued, "Were those subpoenas quashed because you know and I know that research at Plum Island and the other bio-labs is not limited to purely defensive research? Those facilities are aggressively engineering and creating germs to be used offensively against human beings."

"That is ridiculous!"

"Is it? Let me remind *you* of something, Mr. Budenz. You are under oath, and you are testifying before a committee of the United States Congress that has the power to declare you in contempt and recommend your impeachment to the full House of Representatives. Before these hearings are completed, your assertion of national security will be revealed for what it really is…*a euphemism for controlled obfuscation!*"

Budenz's face was now crimson as he angrily stood, fists clenched, glaring at his accuser. A frenzy of activity among the media resulted in Harry again having to hammer the proceedings back to order.

MacIntosh McAdams was front-row-center in the media section and having the time of his life. Watching lying bureaucrats squirm and wiggle when confronted with the truth was his cup of tea, providing instant gratification and justification for the endless hours and sweat of putting together column after column of exposure and exhortation.

"Gig the pig, McDonald! Ram the spit down his lying throat!" mumbled Mac under his breath.

"Mr. Budenz," Harry continued, "in light of what I have just reminded you and before I call our next witness, would you care to recant any of your testimony?"

"Of course not!" Budenz roared angrily.

"Fine, so be it. You are excused for now, Mr. Budenz, but you are still under subpoena to this committee."

Harry continued, "Director Dolan of Homeland Security, would you please take the witness stand?"

Dolan? Ha! Another puppet and front man for the New World Order hierarchy, thought Mac. *Homeland Insecurity would be more like it! What does McDonald think he's gonna get out of these guys but rubber stamp answers?*

"Director Dolan…shortly after 9/11, the operations of the Plum Island Animal Disease Research Center were transferred from the Department of Agriculture to the Department of Homeland Security. Is that correct?"

"Yes, that is correct."

"And as the Director of Homeland Security, it is your responsibility to have a working knowledge of the operations of the Plum Island facility…unlike our previous witness."

"That would also be correct."

"Fine. And would you please tell this committee exactly what types of programs are being conducted at Plum Island?"

"Certainly, Mr. Congressman. They relate to the studies of diseases that affect our domestic livestock population."

"That sounds wonderful, Director Dolan. I'm reassured to hear that. Are there now or have there ever been programs at Plum Island designed to develop germs to be used in biological warfare?"

"Absolutely not. Assertions of that nature are directly attributable to the lunatic fringe and conspiracy theorists segments of our society, unfortunately."

"Would it be possible for such programs to exist and escape detection?"

"Certainly not. All functions and operations of Plum Island are continuously monitored by our agency."

"So there is absolutely no way rogue scientists could surreptitiously develop biological weapons at the Plum Island lab?"

"No way!"

"And Director, correspondingly, would it be logical to assume if such programs did exist and were operated and controlled by directives from a higher level of government, they would still be unable to evade your scrutiny, and you would be aware of their existence?"

"I can assure you no such programs as you describe exist at Plum Island."

"I have no further questions at this time, Director Dolan, but further testimony will be required. You remain under subpoena to this committee."

Susan Collins was incredulous.

How can human beings lie so glibly? she wondered. *I can't wait to see the looks on their faces after I begin my testimony tomorrow. I only wish Stephens and Gallagher were here. I know they are just amoral employees following orders, and these creeps are some of their bosses, but still…*

Mac began daydreaming during the brief lull at the completion of Dolan's testimony.

How appropriate and efficient an old fashioned Mexican firing squad would be in this situation! mused Mac. *Budenz, Frey, Dolan, and Steele standing blindfolded side by side in front of a stuccoed brick wall, nervously awaiting the order to fire and the volley of bullets that would end their lives… Colonel McClain had the right idea, just not enough targets!*

"The committee now calls CIA Director Steele to the witness stand," Harry began anew. "Director Steele, you are the Director of the most powerful and efficient intelligence-gathering organization in the entire world, are you not?"

"Well, Mr. Congressman…thank you for the compliment. Yes, I am."

The higher their position, the more arrogant the bastards become! thought Mac. *This guy's the most ferocious tiger of the litter. He could slit your throat in a New York second and smile while you bled out!*

"Director Steele," Harry continued, "As director of the CIA you are aware of all essential and significant activities of this government and others that affect the security of the United States. Is that correct?"

"That would be an understatement."

"So your knowledge is quite comprehensive?"

"Quite."

"That's what we want to hear, Director. A witness that knows what is going on and why. Would you please explain to this committee and the media why the

U.S. government operating clandestinely and secretively is using the biological research laboratories at Plum Island, Ft. Detrick, the CDC, Ft. Collins, and others to develop and culture germs that, if unleashed, have the capability of killing millions of innocent people?"

"The U.S. government, Congressman McDonald, is not clandestinely and secretively developing germs to harm civilian populations. But the enemies of our republic *are* engaged in such activities because they seek to destroy us. In order to develop vaccines and effective treatment protocols for the weapons in their germ arsenals, we need to study and research every potentially lethal pathogen known to exist."

"So if a pathogen is only marginally lethal, for example, we will devote time and resources to try to find a way to make it more lethal?"

"Certainly. We have to understand that our enemies are engaged in exactly that kind of research. If we are able to discover how they may have been successful, odds are we will be able to develop strategies of protection for our citizens. The research at our labs is purely defensive, Mr. Congressman."

"Purely defensive, Director?"

"Yes."

McAdams took the opportunity to gaze about the room to observe the expressions on the faces of the media in attendance.

Look at Snodgrass and Lemke, he thought. *Their smug, supercilious smirks reflect their convictions that McDonald's boat is not even going to leave the dock. In their minds, these hearings are already over before they have even begun, and McDonald is finished because he doesn't have a leg to stand on. Just look at the rest of these bozos...they don't have a clue. Tomorrow's the day though. Their worlds and the worlds of those "Four Horsemen of the Apocalypse" up there are going to be rocked big time. McDonald is setting those witnesses up just like the pins in a bowling alley!*

And indeed, if unbiased objective observers were to judge the effectiveness of the congressman's efforts at the completion of that first day, all would unanimously agree that not only was McDonald wasting taxpayer monies with his hearings, but he was wasting the time of the dedicated public servants Budenz, Frey, Steele, and Dolan.

Interviewing Frey was especially painful and difficult for the congressman because of the long-standing, deep-rooted animosity that prevailed between the two men. McDonald was one of the members of Congress that took Frey to task

THE POISON PLUM

for the Bureau's gruesome actions at Ruby Ridge. An FBI sharpshooter with cold-blooded precision had killed a mother by shooting her in the head as she stood on the porch of their cabin, holding her baby in her arms.

"Unconscionable! Cold-blooded murder!" the Congressman had roared from the floor of the House of Representatives. The Waco incident, an even more ghastly event from recent American history, had a fulminant Harry McDonald demanding from his fellow members of congress the courage and unity to impeach the then attorney general and Director Frey.

"What does it take?" Harry had said angrily as he addressed the full Congress.

"Heavily armed agents of the FBI and the military use tanks equipped with flame throwers to massacre and incinerate men, women, and children at the Waco religious compound and you sit here in this legislative chamber as if frozen with impotence. In the name of Almighty God, where is your angst? Where is your demonstration of responsibility as a United States congressman? Is there a man or woman among you with the backbone to stand erect and declare enough is enough?"

Frey, always an elitist and always an arrogant but cunning adversary had felt the stings and barbs of McDonald's attacks far more frequently than he would have preferred. To Frey, McDonald with his silly, outdated patriotic fetishes was a disgusting and anachronistic obstacle to the logical progression of the New World Order.

"I wish I could blast that son of a bitch McDonald back to the nineteenth century where he belongs!" said Frey to Budenz on more than one occasion. "Better yet, the eighteenth century. He would fit right in!"

Frey hated McDonald, the man, and everything he stood for with a bitterness and vindictiveness that seethed beneath the surface. And therein was the distinction between the two…Frey hated McDonald, the man, but McDonald hated not Frey, the man, but the evil that he did.

"Director Frey," Harry began. "Would you please tell this committee what your understanding is of the mission of the Plum Island facility?"

"Mr. Congressman, the previous witnesses have rather succinctly, I believe, related very clearly to the committee the purposes and objectives of that lab's research. As my field is law enforcement, I certainly do not believe I am in any position to contribute to the clarity of their testimony."

Yeah right! thought McAdams. *And are you sleepy from staying up all night with your cronies rehearsing what lies you were going to tell this committee?*

"I see," continued Harry. "And in your role as a law enforcement agent, exactly what are your directives and obligations regarding Plum Island?"

"The nature of the research being done there is essential to the national security of the nation. I will see to it that never again will the security and protection of that facility or any similar facilities be compromised by a terrorist attack, whether foreign or domestic."

"Are you telling this committee, Director Frey, that Colonel Gordon McClain was a terrorist?"

Oops, thought Mac as the hearing room suddenly became very quiet. *An unrehearsed question Frey.... How are you going to deal with this one?*

"Certainly not!" Frey boomed. "We all know Colonel McClain was a very sick man and was cleverly manipulated by the real terrorists—Dr. Glen Klinner and his co-conspirator wife."

"And we all know that, do we, Director?"

"Of course! Don't you read the news, McDonald? An appropriately convened military tribunal found Klinner and his wife guilty of treason, and they were executed for their crimes."

"Appropriately convened you say? Director Frey, upon assuming your responsibilities at the Bureau, did you take an oath to protect and defend the Constitution?"

"Of course I did!"

"Have you ever read that document?"

"Of course I have!" Frey responded, obviously irritated.

"Then you obviously did not understand what you read. There are no provisions in that document for trying American citizens with military tribunals. That type of government tyranny was addressed in an earlier document—the Declaration of Independence. Perhaps you have heard of that little bit of nostalgia, Director?"

"Dammit, McDonald!" screamed Frey. "You've got to get your head out of the past! There are no absolutes, don't you know that? We live in difficult times with unprecedented challenges to our nation...we must adapt to those challenges with strategies that will get the job done. We can't expect outdated procedures that worked for our forefathers to work now!"

THE POISON PLUM

"Really, Director Frey? Let me remind you our nation experienced difficult times and unprecedented challenges during the first terrorist attacks…the invasion and tyranny of the British forces. Those 'outdated procedures' as you refer to them, Director Frey, worked very well for our young nation, allowing us to repel the British without compromising the civil liberties of our citizens. And these 'procedures' continued to function very well for our nation throughout the decades until prostituted by the corruption of the New World Order planners, schemers, and conspirators. Before these hearings are completed, Director, this committee will have revealed to the entire world exactly who the real terrorists and threats to our precious freedoms and institutions truly are. Further testimony will be required of you, Director Frey, and you are still under subpoena."

Like a cat playing with a mouse! thought Susan. *No…more like a jungle tiger toying with his quarry before pouncing for the kill. The congressman knows exactly what he's doing by giving those creeps enough rope to hang themselves. All we need now is a good sturdy yardarm to hang them from. Tomorrow morning, 9 AM sharp, with the help of the volunteers from the medical schools, we will begin construction. Let's see now, today's session will be devoted to testimony from those four plus a few deputy directors from each agency. The congressman has already told us not to expect any breakthroughs from today's hearings. We should only expect those guys to present a united front and cover each other's asses…tomorrow and Thursday we will present our Lyme disease road show, which should scare the hell out of everyone in this room and pull the ropes tighter around the necks of the guilty. Friday…oh yes, let us not forget Friday… That's the day we will have visitors—sick, crippled, and dying Lyme patients from a hundred miles around. Wheelchairs, walkers, IV drip poles.… Oh I can just see it now! Signs, posters, banners, heart-wrenching testimonials! And the media—they should have a field day. It's sure to be a circus! I hope little Toby will be watching me on C-Span every single day, and I hope somehow he will understand that I'm here because of him."*

By four that afternoon, all the day's witnesses had been called to the stand, and all had stood firm in their testimony of support for the research of the biolabs. And also by four, Susan had pledged herself to never again trust any high-ranking government official on any matter whatsoever. In her mind, their capacity to lie, distort, and mislead was simply incredible. The witnessing of their testimony laced with perfidy and mendacity shook her to the core.

All Susan wanted that afternoon was to leave the hearing room and find refuge in a hot bath, a quiet dinner alone, and a phone visit with Toby, whom she was already missing. Politely declining an opportunity to join Erin Giblon later for dinner, Susan checked into her hotel and made the hot, relaxing bath first on her agenda. Tomorrow would be a big day for her, indeed the most important of her life, and she needed to relax, collect her thoughts, and review her outline. It was basically in Susan's lap tomorrow. True, she would be assisted by testimony from several of the volunteers, but the hearings were to follow the format she has constructed over the weeks while reviewing the documents Harry's office has received.

Lyme 101, she had often thought to herself as she studied the progression of development of the Lyme pathogen from the early days of spirochetal research at the Tuskegee Institute.

Step by step, this is how it's done if you want to cripple, maim, and slowly kill your fellow man, she thought while sinking into the hot bathwater. *After I complete my testimony by Thursday afternoon, even your average high school biology student could have a good working knowledge of how our government was able to genetically engineer a spirochete. Oh the diabolical cleverness of it all.... It's not your benevolent, caring government that's responsible for your misery and afflictions. It's those darn naughty ticks on a rampage. Mother Nature...she just can't be trusted!*

While waiting for room service to arrive, Susan took the opportunity to put in a call to Cathy and Toby and was surprised when little Toby answered the phone.

"Well, hello, sweetie.... I didn't expect you to answer! Aren't you the young man of the house!"

"Mommy!" Toby shouted into the receiver. "I saw you on TV!"

"You did?"

"Yes, Mommy...you were sitting there listening to those men talk."

"That's right, sweetie, I was. I want you to watch again tomorrow and see those men watching Mommy talk."

"What are you going to talk about?"

"That bad ol' place where I used to work."

THE POISON PLUM

"Mommy, I didn't like those men Mr. McDonald was talking to. They aren't nice men. Are they going to hurt you?"

"No, sweetie, they aren't," she told Toby...and then, thinking to herself, *at least not on TV!*

"I miss you, sweetie, and I'll call you again tomorrow night."

"OK, Mommy. I miss you, too. When are you coming home?"

"I'll fly home Friday night. In the meantime, I want you to be a good boy for Aunt Cathy."

"I will. Aunt Cathy wants to talk to you."

"Love you, Toby!"

"Hey, Sis!" answered Cathy, "Have you slain the evil dragon yet?"

"I don't get my lance until tomorrow but don't forget to tune in...same tick time, same tick channel! Did you listen to those lying bastards, Cathy? Can you believe it?"

"I just want you to do your thing...vent your spleen, salute the flag, nail them to the cross, whatever. Get it over with, get out of there, and let's go back to Birmingham as soon as possible. You are sticking your head and butt into a hornets' nest!"

"Tell me about it...but when I'm done, it's going to be their asses in the hornets' nest. They deserve every sting they get, too!"

"I know you are on a vendetta, Susan, and I can't blame you after all the crap you and Toby have been through. I cannot, however, stop worrying about you. I just can't rationalize my fears away. Those are some bad, bad characters you are up against. Brave and courageous you are, but Joan of Arc you ain't. I just want all of this drama and intrigue to be over with, and I want us to be a normal family again."

"Ditto here...please try not to worry. This will all be over soon. Just take care of Toby. I'll call in every night, and I'll see you both on Friday."

The Hearings —Day Two

Budenz, Frey, Dolan, and Steele arrived Wednesday morning, obviously pleased with the way things were going. As they approached the hearing room, Budenz was all smiles, remarking to Frey how pathetic McDonald's efforts were.

"All that imported brain power and nobody to interview…except us, of course. What a shame! I predict McDonald folds before the day is over and adjourns the committee lest he become the laughing stock of Congress."

"I've said it before, and I'll say it again," Frey replied. "Don't count the choir boy out until it's obvious he can't get off the canvas."

"Nonsense, Frey! McDonald's goose is cooked…let's stick a fork in it and get the hell out of here. We've all got better things to do than sit around and watch that self-anointed defender of the Constitution strutting around trying to rally the masses with chimerical fabrications of dark conspiracies."

As Budenz spoke those words, they entered the hearing room and were startled to see the lighting had been dimmed and a large screen at the back of the room was displaying an image from a powerful overhead projector.

"What the hell is this?" Budenz asked, his eyes glancing back and forth from the screen to Frey, Dolan, and Steele.

"Damned if I know," Frey said. "What have those people in that picture got to do with anything? And look at that old car. Man, that picture has got to be fifty or sixty years old!"

"Hey guys," interrupted Dolan. "I've seen that picture before! It's hanging on the wall in Director Stephens's office at Plum!"

Perplexed, the four men moved to their pre-assigned seating as Congressman McDonald took the microphone and gaveled the hearings to order.

"Ladies and gentlemen," he began, "I am Congressman Harry McDonald, and I am calling to order this investigative committee hearing of the House Health and Human Services Committee. Today we will continue our investigation of the government's so-called Animal Disease Research Center at Plum Island, New York. Our first witness and moderator of today's session is a single mother from New London, Connecticut. She holds a doctorate degree in microbiology from the University of Alabama in Birmingham and is a former employee of the Plum Island lab. Indeed, she is one of only a few surviving employees of that facility due to her absence the day of the ferry massacre. In what is to be the ultimate irony, her absence that day was attributable to her eight-year-old son's serious illness, later correctly diagnosed as Lyme disease. Her name is Susan Collins. At this time I would like to turn these proceedings over to her and our select team of infectious disease specialists who have so generously provided their services to this committee. Ms. Collins?"

"Thank you, Mr. Congressman. I am grateful for this opportunity to address this committee. I, like most people, I assume, regarded the work being done at the Plum Island Facility to be essential to the health and preservation of our nation's livestock. It was only after I had encountered the horror and agony of my critically ill eight-year-old son's undiagnosed disease that I began to question the true objective of the research and development being done at Plum. Not only did lay people suggest that my son had Lyme disease, but that the source of that disease was my employer. Incredulous at first, I nevertheless began searching for answers. Today I stand before you with a confirmed diagnosis of Lyme disease for my son and a total conviction that the germ that has ravaged his body and countless other unfortunates had its origin at Plum Island. With the assistance of photographs and official documents from Plum, the CDC, the Public Health Service, and others anonymously provided to this committee, we will clearly explain the origin and development of the biological warfare agent known as Lyme disease.

"Every story and every mystery has a beginning. The beginning of the Lyme germ is no exception. Our story begins with the photograph you see projected on the screen. That, ladies and gentlemen, is from 1938 and depicts a group of doctors and a nurse from the Public Health Service standing in front of a building at the Tuskegee Institute in Tuskegee, Alabama. That same photograph is hanging on the wall of the office of the acting director of Plum Island, Mr. Clement Stephens. Why you ask? Because those doctors were in Tuskegee to study the long-term effects of untreated syphilis among the black population of Macon County,

Alabama. Syphilis, as many of you already know, is caused by a bacterium known scientifically as a spirochete. Lyme disease is also caused by a spirochete. As we shall see over the next two days, it was the initial spirochetal experimentation done at Tuskegee under the auspices of the PHS, and later the CDC, that paved the way for that germ's refinement into the Lyme germ by the scientists at Plum."

The hearing room suddenly burst into a bedlam of chatter and activity while the television media frantically jockeyed for the best positions to capture the expressions of Congressman McDonald and the pertinent witnesses. Turning to Frey, Dolan, and Steele, an angry Budenz cursing under his breath demanded to know what was going on.

"You damn fools! So much for McDonald not having shit! What the hell does she mean, 'anonymously provided'? Steele! Frey! Where the hell were your people? One thumb up their butts, the other in their mouths and swapping hands every thirty seconds? How in the hell could anyone get anything out of that place? We had enough security to choke a piss ant! And how could anyone get anything to McDonald? He and that damn bitch up there that is about to slit our throats were under a microscope! Dammit to hell!"

MacIntosh McAdams smiled as he watched the facial expressions and obvious agitation of the "Four Horsemen of the Apocalypse" revealing their anguish.

Ah, ain't payback a bitch, he thought. *The kitty cat is coming out of the bag, boys, and he is coming to claw and gnaw your testicles off! It's a beautiful thing! I'm glad I'm alive to see this! And lookie yonder over there in the press section.... I do believe Mr. Snodgrass and Mr. Lemke be looking a little green around the gills. Tsk, tsk! Hang 'em all high and let the buzzards pluck their damn eyes out!*

Once again, Harry had to gavel the tumultuous proceedings back to order before Susan could continue.

"The government of the United States, acting through the Public Health Service and later the CDC, conducted inhumane experiments on hundreds of poor, illiterate black sharecroppers in the Tuskegee area. The government doctors deliberately withheld beneficial treatments, including penicillin, in order to study the long-term effects of untreated syphilis on the human body. The subjects were told they had 'bad blood,' and if they would cooperate with the government doctors and consent to tests and exams until they died, they would receive a burial stipend of $50. The subjects were never told they had syphilis. What is so shocking and horrible about this entire program is that it continued even after the development of penicillin until an investigative journalist blew the whistle in 1972. The ensuing moral outrage forced the termination of the Nazi-like experimentation, as well it should have. Initially, the Justice Department tried to block requests for information submitted under the Freedom of Information Act and failed. Were you with the Justice Department then, Mr. Budenz? No? Well, finally in 1974, the government consented to its long-standing culpability and paid 10 million dollars to the survivors and heirs of the syphilis experiments. After this committee proves beyond a shadow of a doubt the government's culpability in the creation of the Lyme germ, will apologies be made and compensation afforded to the victims and their heirs? If 10 million 1974 dollars were necessary to assuage several hundred poor and mostly illiterate black people, how many millions or billions of current dollars would be required to mitigate the suffering of hundreds of thousands of Lyme victims and their families? Do you have your calculator, Mr. Budenz? Mr. Dolan? Mr. Steele?"

If Budenz could have leapt to the witness stand and choked Susan to death that exact moment, he would have done it with his bare hands and without remorse. Never before had he hated another human being so intensely and with good reason. Budenz knew he was finished. Whatever McDonald had was going to drive nails in his coffin. His career was over and he would be damned lucky to avoid a prison sentence. And he knew he would not be able to rely on the president to bail him out of this quagmire. The president would be too busy trying to cover his own ass and would willingly toss Budenz and the others to the wolves.

"I'll not detail the horrors of untreated syphilis," Susan continued. "I'll leave those gruesome details to the medical journals. Nor will I attempt to detail the horrors of Lyme disease, both treated and untreated. Suffice it to say that an illness that tortures the human existence endlessly by night and day to the terminal point of suicide or serious consideration thereof, is a very serious disease indeed. However, with the assistance of the materials this committee was provided, I *will* review the progression of research done at Tuskegee as it was dutifully reported by the doctors to their superiors at the Public Health Service and the CDC. We should be able to complete this exposé of the true intent of the syphilis experiments by early afternoon, and then we will continue with an examination of the research transferred to the Plum Island lab for refinement into a biological weapon."

It doesn't get any better than this! thought a gleeful MacIntosh McAdams. *How many years have I waited for just such a moment as this? How many columns have I written railing for accountability in government? How many years have I endured waiting for someone, anyone, to ride up on a white horse and smite the enemy? And would you look at this? A single mother with an eight-year-old son sick with Lyme disease simultaneously taking on Budenz, Frey, Steele, and Dolan! God in heaven, thank you for letting me live long enough to experience this glorious day of Epiphany!*

By the time the hearings adjourned for lunch, Susan and her team, with the aid of the purloined official documents and photos properly sequenced and interspersed with explanatory dialog, had done a masterful job of putting the true purpose and objective of the dreadful experiments into proper context and perspective. And also by the time of the break, Budenz, Steele, Frey, and Dolan were each desperately trying to fabricate a way out of the deepening imbroglio that was rapidly pulling them closer and closer to the total repudiation of any remaining vestige of personal and professional credibility they may have previously enjoyed. To avoid being overheard, the four left the hearing room and occupied a small, vacant office down the hall for the duration of the lunch break.

"OK, guys," began Budenz. "What the hell are we going to do now? By the end of this day the president will be so far up our collective asses, we won't be able to blink our eyes! Not only do we not know what else McDonald has in those documents obviously smuggled out of Plum, we don't have the foggiest idea who took them out!"

"It sure as hell wasn't Collins," interrupted Frey. "She wasn't even born when most of those documents were created!"

"What difference does it make where they came from?" said Steele. "The only thing that matters now is how we are going to deal with these cards as they are played. Maybe that syphilis shit was removed about the time that Buxton guy was in those hearings with Senator Kennedy…hell maybe even some employee at Plum was sympathetic to those blacks…you know, civil rights and all that stuff that was going on back then…the sixties and seventies, Martin Luther King, Jr., and all the rest. Maybe this is the worst of it. Let's don't jump out the window just yet. This stuff is all ancient history at this point. Hell, everyone knows what happened…the government program was discovered, exposed, apologized for, and compensation was paid. End of story…old news. Let's just keep a cool stool and see what else they've got. We'll deal with it then. Maybe we don't have a problem, after all. Proving the Tuskegee story is no problem. It's already been done. Proving a link to Lyme and Plum is another matter."

Returning to the hearing room after the break, the attendees were stunned to see a gigantic photo of a swastika and the very personification of evil, Adolph Hitler, on the projection screen. This began a slide show narrated by the congressman documenting the atrocious human experiments performed on prisoners of war and Jews by the Nazi doctors and germ-warfare scientists during World War II. Dozens of pictures of captured Nazis known to have collaborated in the experiments and ghastly scenes from Buchenwald, Auschwitz, and other facilities were shown. One could almost smell the stench of rotting flesh as the images of bulldozers pushing piles of naked, horribly emaciated bodies into vast yawning graves were projected.

Sparing the attendees further mental anguish and discomfort, Harry interrupted the gruesome slide show long enough to provide a review of the government's "Operation Paperclip" program implemented at the conclusion of World War II, identifying participants such as Werner Von Braun. Harry made it clear that all of these highly talented doctors and scientists were brought to our shores to perpetuate the work they previously performed for Nazi Germany. At the conclusion of his remarks, the image of Erich Traub and accompanying Department of Defense documents filled the screen. He then explained that Erich Traub was a Nazi germ-warfare scientist who was brought to the United States by Operation Paperclip and employed by the CDC to serve as a founding father of the lab at Plum Island. Obviously the attending news media personnel were considerably agitated by this latest revelation as the ensuing pandemonium once again required Harry to gavel the proceedings back to order. Once a semblance of order had been restored, Susan Collins again took the witness stand and began the laborious process, with the assistance of the volunteers, of meshing and explaining the chain of research leading from the Tuskegee experiments to the Public Health Service, then to the CDC, and finally, the ultimate recipient, the lab at Plum Island. Step by step, for the next several hours until the afternoon adjournment, laboratory notes and worksheets, inter-departmental and inter-agency communications, directives, and analysis were projected onto the screen. Each document was interpreted and explained by the expert witnesses.

The understanding that there was purpose and direction to the research became glaringly obvious. Like a gigantic jigsaw puzzle, the pieces were carefully assembled by Susan Collins and her team. The developing image, amorphous in the beginning, began revealing a horrific picture almost too terrible to contemplate.

The evening news commentators, providing a summation of the days events to their viewers, began speculating wildly on what tomorrow's proceedings would reveal. The perceived mindset of most Americans that the execution of the Klinners ended the mystery of the ferry massacre was no longer dominant. With the unfolding drama revealing lies, intrigue, cover-ups, and murder, the American people waited with baited breath for the next installment.

The Hearings—Day Three

The excitement generated by the hearings the previous day ensured another standing-room-only crowd for Thursday. As word of the proceedings spread throughout the news media, additional journalists arrived, and with no space available, they began occupying the halls leading to and from the hearing room. Representatives of major foreign media also appeared, including the official news source for the Arab world, *Al Jazeera*. The smug looks of self-assuredness worn by Budenz, Steele, Frey, and Dolan had been replaced with somber, morose expressions as they realized McDonald's arsenal of damaging information was certainly not limited to the already well-exposed Tuskegee experiments.

Let's see those four ambulatory anal orifices try to lie their way out of this! thought a delighted MacIntosh McAdams.

Hell, McDonald's opening the flood gates! This sewage is going to sweep through the White House like a tidal wave. The president will have to employ every PR guy and spin doctor he can find just to avoid impeachment!

The morning session, again moderated by Susan after the congressman's opening remarks, began focusing on the specific objectives of the genetic engineering of the syphilis spirochete as revealed by the documents. Admittedly complex and highly technical, the information nevertheless was rendered relevant to the lay person by Susan's masterful explanation of what the recombinant techniques, as they are known in the scientific community, were designed to accomplish. Perhaps most revealing was the explanation of the engineering of the protective protein sheath that shielded the spirochete from detection by antibiotics and the body's immune system. By appearing to be part of the host's own body, the spirochete was able to render itself invisible for all practical purposes. Indeed, this was the most significant difference between the easily treated syphilis spirochete and the designer Lyme spirochete, which is almost impossible to completely eradicate. The lab notes of the scientists responsible for this talented bit of creativity revealed the exultation that prevailed among them for their successful craftsmanship. In an effusive communication from the then department head at the Plum lab to the director of the CDC, the department head gloated:

"Now that all barriers to known efficacious treatment modalities have been blocked by the clever adaptation of the protein shroud, we feel that an ideal biological weapon has been created. It will certainly kill, cripple, or render impotent a substantial percentage of any population in which it is deployed. By the use of insects serving as the transmission vectors, the true identity of those responsible will remain hidden, leaving the victims to falsely assume they have been sickened by a previously undiscovered naturally occurring germ. Our department is now cultivating ticks which we will be able to provide for the initial human testing at your direction."

Susan brought the dimmed lighting back up to normal after the display of that document, which mercifully coincided with the lunch break. The well-lit hearing room revealed an audience temporarily awestruck attempting to comprehend the full significance of what had been disclosed during that morning session. Only after several moments had elapsed did they slowly and quietly begin moving out of the hearing room for lunch.

Operation Aerotick

The excitement was electric by the time Congressman McDonald called the hearings to order for the afternoon. First to appear on the projection screen were photographs of specially fitted Army DC-3 airplanes. The accompanying letter from a Pentagon official to the directors of the Plum Island facility and the CDC explained the aircraft had been modified and refitted as requested, and all was ready for the first drop. Further documents projected for the audience's perusal included detailed weather projections from the National Weather Service for the coastline of Connecticut during the spring of 1975. Document after document meticulously detailed the preparation of the Plum Island lab, the CDC, and the Army as coordinated by the Pentagon for the event planned for the coast that spring. On the morning of May 1, 1975, preparations were finally completed for a clandestine military operation dubbed "Operation Aerotick." Two specially fitted DC-3 aircraft took off from Bradley Field at Windsor Locks, and with the enhancement of the prevailing wind flow, began releasing their poisonous cargo on the unsuspecting population below.

Susan explained that several hundred thousand ticks infected with the Lyme germ were dropped from the aircraft on the coastal residents of Connecticut that day, unleashing an epidemic that is currently the fastest growing infectious disease in America, second only to AIDS.

"And indeed," she continued, "much debate exists regarding the true infection rate of Lyme as many thousand cases go undiagnosed. It is the opinion of this committee that the actual Lyme infection growth rate already exceeds that of AIDS. As the infected ticks began assimilating into the terrain below, they began searching, as all ticks do, for a warm mammal host to begin their feeding. The indigenous deer population, which was substantial, provided immediate gratification for many. Others found hosts in children and young adults frequently involved in outdoor activities. As humans became infected and sought professional treatment for their symptoms, the area's clinics, emergency rooms, and physicians' offices began experiencing a substantial influx of area residents complaining of headaches, fatigue, and muscle and joint pain. A substantial number of those cases were dutifully reported to the CDC for informational reporting purposes. As we shall see from the following slides, the information reported was time sequenced and geographically delineated in order to render an accurate demographic representation of the spread of infection. By calculating the existing population statistics and correlating those numbers with the quantity of ticks used for transmission of the germ, the scientists were able to ascertain with some degree of certainty, the ratio of the exposed human population to the infected tick population required to produce a desired per capita infection rate."

Closing remarks for the afternoon were provided by the congressman in a very focused, logical, and didactic presentation leaving no doubts that a sinister biological experiment had been conducted clandestinely by the U.S. government for many decades. It was also clearly revealed that not only were unsuspecting black victims of syphilis callously used as guinea pigs, but U.S. soldiers; residents of Panama City, Florida; San Francisco; and certainly residents of Connecticut and Rhode Island as well. In order to put a human face on this tragedy, Harry explained tomorrow's session would be devoted to the many Lyme disease patients who would be coming to the hearings to testify.

As the attendees of the session that afternoon departed, they unquestionably knew deep in their hearts that events had transpired in their America forever altering their perception of the nation they thought they knew. September 11th was an overt, sudden attack. Unsettling? Yes! But soon to be forgotten and shoved into the trash bin of history? No! But this was different. A decay, an erosion, an attack from within.... Planned, coordinated, and executed by individuals at the very highest levels of government holding the de facto trust of millions of Americans. It was nothing less than an evil, invisibly growing malignancy, surreptitiously rotting away the very underpinnings of America's foundations.

The Hearings—Day Four: The Living Dead

A morbid curiosity, albeit unspoken, permeated the committee's hearing room on Friday. The attendees had withstood the lengthy testimony revealing exactly how horrible and devastating this mysterious disease Lyme could be to its human host. Now, as if in a macabre version of show-and-tell time, they wanted to see first-hand, living examples of what the Lyme germ could do to a human being. They were not to be disappointed.

From near and far they came. Some with their stumbling, ataxic gait, some on crutches, and others in wheelchairs with attached IV antibiotic drip poles. Their grim-faced caregivers by their sides, the human faces of the Lyme tragedy filled to capacity the allocated spaces in the room and overflowed into the adjacent hallways and clogged the sidewalks in front of the congressional building. The stronger ones carried signs and placards pleading their plight as they paraded up and down the sidewalks seizing the opportunity to be heard and seen.

"Lyme Disease…Coming Soon to a Neighborhood Near You!" read one sign. "Plum Ticked Off!" read another. "Why Are We Forgotten?" "America's Denied and Ignored Epidemic!" "Why Won't Someone Help Us?" "The *Tick*-ing Lyme Bomb!" read others.

As the congressman opened the hearings and began introducing the representatives of the various Lyme disease support groups that were scheduled to testify, Susan Collins felt a growing dread and anxiety that became momentarily overwhelming.

My God! Would you look at those poor wretches? she thought. *These are the people that antibiotics failed to cure! Am I looking at the fate of my Toby only a year or two from now?*

One by one, as the victims began to testify, their heart-wrenching, impassioned statements and pleas echoed a common theme of endless misdiagnoses, failed antibiotic therapy, and confused and unsupportive caregivers. In emotional, gut-twisting, back-to-back testimonials, a bleak canvas was painted of neglect bordering on the criminal, involving doctors, insurance companies, the CDC, the social security system, and employers quick to seize upon a diagnosis of depression to justify a sickened employee's termination. Most of these people had lost every single thing most humans would cherish and hold dear—health, financial security, mobility, mental acuity, and, in many cases, loved ones who were so close before their illnesses.

Absent from the hearings that day were the tumultuous outbursts occurring so frequently in previous sessions. A reverential silence prevailed allowing even the faintest utterance from a witness to be heard. *Quiet as a church mouse*, thought Mac. *You could hear a pin drop. Finally, something that succeeds in garnering Americans' undivided attention! What a curious breed, we Americans…we can drink our beer while eating our pizzas and not blink an eye as we watch television film footage of floods, tsunamis, earthquakes, famines, bombings, mass murders, etc., but when it appears we could be brought to the brink of death by a tiny tick biting us in the ass while we are barbequing a steak, all of a sudden, it's personal. We sit up and pay attention!*

In his closing remarks, Harry passionately thanked the Lyme volunteers for their personal sacrifices in attending the hearing. He solemnly pledged to do everything in his power as a congressman to ameliorate their suffering as expeditiously as possible. And then, almost as an afterthought, another bombshell was dropped. He announced that beginning Monday, the committee would reveal to the nation the true source of the AIDS epidemic and those responsible for its creation.

At the close of the hearings that Friday afternoon, every person on Congressman McDonald's staff was drained emotionally and physically. Most of the attendees wished they didn't know now what they didn't know at the start of all this and the "Four Horsemen of the Apocalypse" wished everything from the ferry massacre forward would be consumed and eradicated in some gigantic realignment of time. With heads bowed, Budenz, Frey, Dolan, and Steele made their way out of the hearing room at the conclusion of the last witness's testimony and Harry's closing remarks. Enduring a gamut of catcalls, ridicule, sneers, boos, and obscenities, they finally entered their waiting limousine for the trip to the Pentagon where a very-high-level strategy meeting with General Helms awaited.

"Did you guys hear what that son of bitch said?" Budenz began when the limo door closed behind him. "Lyme disease is bad enough, but it's only the tip of the iceberg! Is it possible he has something on AIDS? How in hell could that be possible?"

"We wrote him off before on Lyme, remember?" Frey replied with the same amount of agitation. "I told you not to underestimate the bastard!"

"I don't know about you guys," Steele injected, "but I don't relish the idea of coming down next week to sit around like ducks in a shooting gallery so McDonald can shoot us in the ass. This shit has got to stop. We can't risk it!"

"Stop it how?" Budenz shouted back. "Tell Washington Power and Light to pull the plug on the building? Write McDonald a nice letter asking him politely not to talk about AIDS in the name of national security? Charge him with being a homophobe?"

"Whatever, guys," Steele continued. "After we've finished meeting with Helms, some kind of plan has got to be on the table, or we collectively are going to the Hotel Sodomy!"

Susan Collins breathed a sigh of relief when the hearings finally ground to a close on Friday afternoon. She knew, even after the long and tiring day, that her efforts had not been in vain. Her skillful presentations laced with analytically cogent and descriptive dialogue had drawn blood from the enemy, piercing their veil of obfuscation. But as fulfilling as that realization was, she missed Toby and Cathy. Above all else, Susan wanted the hearings completed, and the villains sentenced and condemned to eternal damnation, scorn, and ridicule. She wanted her life back. The congressman, of necessity, had scheduled a news conference for Saturday afternoon in New London to explain and update the constituents regarding the progress of the hearings. Susan had politely declined an invitation to join the congressman at the news conference, feeling that her presence was not essential and would be considered redundant. Besides, she preferred to spend her precious time with Toby and Cathy. Next week was certain to be even more challenging and stressful considering the subject matter to be reviewed. Yes, Susan had agonized over the possibility of a connection being made between the contents of those viral research files she had smuggled out and her employment at Plum. Would her life be in jeopardy if a causal link were established or suspected? Could she ever breathe easy or rest assured in the coming months or even years that some sort of retribution would not be forthcoming from those she was certain to expose? Susan knew she didn't want to spend the rest of her life looking over her shoulder, but she also knew she had one chance and one chance only to expose those nefarious schemes and damn the consequences.

For the trip back to New London, Susan shared a flight with the congressman and his wife. Harry took the opportunity to share with Susan his pleasure at how the hearings had progressed and also his eager anticipation of the week to come. If the exposure of the government's involvement in the creation of the Lyme germ created a seismic shift, the exposure of the government's involvement in the creation and dissemination of the AIDS virus would be the equivalent of a 9.2 on the Richter scale.

The weekend for Susan would be short, too short, in fact. The congressman had already scheduled a return flight to Washington for the three of them on Sunday evening at 6:15.

Too little time to visit with Toby and Cathy, thought Susan. *But soon it will all be over, and the chips will fall where they may. I've done my part above and beyond the call of duty...my conscience is assuaged, and whatever happens is whatever happens!*

Cathy and Toby were already waiting when Susan's flight arrived at 8:50 PM. Susan wasted no time in getting to Toby as soon as she could get off the plane. As she pulled him to her, hugging him tightly, Susan could see in his face the fatigue that continued to sap his energy.

No wonder, she thought, *The little guy is running on adrenaline with excitement, waiting to see his mother. Usually he is in bed by seven, totally exhausted!*

"Sweetie, I've missed you so much! You, too, Sis!"

"I've missed you, too, Mommy! Please don't go back to that place!"

"Oh, sweetie...Mommy doesn't want to go back. I have to one more time, and then we'll all be together again."

"Mommy, I hope so. You were gone for long, long time!"

"I know, sweetie. It has been a long time, but soon what I have to do will be all over, and Mommy will come home to you and Aunt Cathy. Then we are going back home to Birmingham. Would you like that?"

THE POISON PLUM

"Yes, Mommy. I like that doctor, and he is going to give me medicine to make me feel better."

With that, a tear began rolling down Susan's cheek as she turned to give Cathy a hug.

"Welcome back, Sis. We watched you every day on C-Span. Looks like you turned over some apple carts!"

"More like a manure truck, I'm thinking…judging from the expressions on those guys' faces."

"Mommy, those men are mad at you!"

"I know, sweetie," Susan replied. "And I am mad at them."

"Why?" Toby asked, looking up at her with innocent eyes.

"Because those are some of the men that made you sick."

"How Mommy?"

"When you get a little older, I'll explain."

"Why can't you tell me now?"

"Because you wouldn't understand. I promise I will tell you everything when you get a little older."

"OK, Mommy. I love you!"

"And I love you, too, sweetie!"

Susan, Cathy, and Toby stayed together that weekend enjoying each other's company and excitedly made plans for the return to Birmingham. For Susan, the end of the tunnel was in sight. Another week of testimony at the hearings, two at the most, and her mission would be accomplished. She had no idea what the grinding wheels of justice might eventually do to those men and institutions that had now become her nemesis. That was not her concern now. She had done her part, indeed, the best she could have done. The rest was now in the hands of fate.

Saturday was another picture-perfect day on the coast of Connecticut. An absolutely delightful time to be outside as much as possible, so Susan organized an outing for the three of them that included sandwiches from Gino's, a visit to Ocean Beach Park to enjoy the boats, a walking tour of some of the quaint shops downtown, and, finally, a late-afternoon treat of ice cream from the shop in the Abercrombie Building. Little Toby was so excited and happy to be with his mother, his enthusiasm belied the fatigue encroaching heavier and heavier with each passing hour. Susan knew she had to get him home for a shower and food by six because he could only hold out for about ten hours. Beddy-bye by seven.

Once Toby was asleep, Susan and Cathy shared a bottle of their favorite Merlot and discussed the progress of the hearings and their plans for returning to Birmingham.

"Susan," Cathy mused, "I guess after all that stuff in Washington is over, you are going to be some kind of celebrity. But do you think you are going to be an employable celebrity? You know how some employers feel about whistleblowers. Do you think UAB would hire you?"

"If they have crap swept under the rug they are trying to keep hidden, the answer is hell no! On the other hand, if their research is ethical and performed with the objective of preserving and protecting the health of mankind, the answer is yes. An emphatic yes!"

"So may we assume, given your impeccable academic credentials, your employment application to UAB will be the equivalent of a litmus test for that institution?"

"I guess…I suppose…. Hell, I don't know. How did we get off on that? Is there another bottle of wine in the kitchen? I think that one had a hole in the bottom."

Another bottle was procured, and the sisters stayed up until almost midnight talking about everything and nothing, relaxing and enjoying their time together. Susan called it a night about 12:30 after looking in on Toby and verifying he was sleeping soundly. She was looking forward to a rock-solid eight hours of sound, restful sleep.

Her wonderful plan went well until 4 AM. Susan was then suddenly awaked from one of the deepest sleeps she had ever experienced by shrill, piercing screams emanating from Cathy's bedroom.

Oh, my God, thought Susan as she quickly jumped up from the bed. *Is someone trying to kill Cathy?*

She rushed to Cathy's room and flipped on the light, unsure of what was awaiting her in the darkness. As the overhead light illumined the room, Susan saw that her sister was sitting up in the bed, face in her hands, crying and shaking uncontrollably. Susan immediately leapt onto the bed and pulled Cathy to her.

"What's wrong, Cathy?" she blurted. "What's wrong? What is it?"

"Susan, don't leave! Promise you won't! You've got to stay here!" And then more hysterical crying as Cathy grabbed Susan and hugged her tightly.

THE POISON PLUM

"What do you mean?" Susan asked anxiously as Cathy continued sobbing. "What is it? Tell me what's wrong. Did you have a bad dream?"

Unable to speak, Cathy clung to her sister for several minutes until Susan realized Cathy would just have to cry it out before any coherent conversation could be attempted. Finally, Cathy, face drenched with tears, began trying to dry her eyes on the sheets as she tried to talk.

"Oh, Susan! It was horrible! The most horrible thing I have ever seen! And it was so real! I was right there! I could even smell the burning flesh!"

"What on earth are you talking about?"

"The airplane! And it was you! You were on that plane!"

"What are you saying?" Susan said, trying to calm her sister. "You just had a dream."

"No! No, it was not just a dream! It was real, and it was you! You can't get on that plane tomorrow. I won't let you! I'll do anything to stop you. Susan you can't get on that plane! I could see the number…part of it anyway. The last two numbers were 21."

Cathy began crying again and hugged Susan even tighter.

"I don't want to lose you! Please don't go!"

A chill settled over Susan as Cathy continued crying and trembling.

Grandfather, she thought, *this kind of thing happened to Grandfather all the time. He would see things that would happen days, weeks, or months later. Oh, my God! This is really spooky!*

"Cathy," Susan said to her sister. "Everything will look different in the morning. It was just a dream! I can't let the congressman down…I've got to go back to Washington."

"Take a later flight! You can't get on that one! And you've got to warn the congressman. Oh, Susan, it was so real. Where are your tickets? Look at the number! Look at the damn flight number!"

Susan didn't want to get out of that bed to get her purse, but she knew she had to. Bringing her purse back to Cathy's room, she sat on the edge of the bed and anxiously pulled the flight tickets out of her bag.

"What is the number, Susan? What is the number? Tell me!"

Susan slowly opened the envelope and began scanning the itinerary for the flight number.

"…SkyTran flight number 2347, departure Dulles International, Friday 7:10 PM, EST, arrive New London 8:50 PM. SkyTran flight 17…*21*! Departure New London Sunday 6:15 PM, arrive Dulles International 7:55 PM!"

Susan was trembling and her face was ashen as she placed the envelope and the tickets on the bedcovers. There was a long silence as the sisters held hands and desperately searched each other's eyes seeking some kind of solution to this terrifying dilemma. Finally, Cathy squeezed Susan's hands and said, "You've got to warn the congressman! You've got to find some way to tell him."

"How? He won't believe any of this! He's too practical and driven by his obsession to see those hearings conducted to their conclusion!"

"You've got to try!"

Getting back to sleep was impossible for Cathy and Susan that morning. Finally, about 7 AM, Susan, with a heavy heart and a confused mind, just got up and began cooking breakfast for everyone. Little Toby came into the kitchen as she was scrambling some eggs.

"Mommy, I heard Aunt Cathy crying last night. What was wrong?"

"Well good morning, sweetie. I didn't know you were up. Did I wake you?"

"Aunt Cathy did, but I went back to sleep. Is she sick?"

"No, sweetie…she's fine. She just had a bad ol' dream. That's all."

"What was it about?"

What was it about, indeed! thought Susan. *I'll add that one to the big long list of questions I've already promised my son I'll answer someday.*

"It was a scary dream Toby…the kind that grown-ups have sometimes. Little boys don't need to know about such things."

"Will I have to have scary dreams when I grow up? I don't want to, Mommy."

Scary dreams? The way this world is going? she thought.

"I hope not, sweetie. Maybe they won't happen anymore by the time you are grown."

"Mommy, my pajamas are wet again," Toby said, as Susan noticed him shivering from the cold.

"Oh, I'm sorry, sweetie. Mommy will get you some dry clothes, and then you can have a nice warm breakfast."

"Thank you, Mommy. I love you."

After breakfast, admittedly feeling somewhat foolish, Susan made the necessary phone call to cancel her 6:15 flight to Washington and rescheduled for a later flight at 10:28.

"Not much sleep for this girl," she remarked to Cathy, feeling somewhat foolish after talking to the ticket agent.

"Well, Susan, I'll share a little secret with you," Cathy said. "I prefer you sleepy to dead! Now, get back on that telephone and call the congressman."

At 9 AM, respectful of the Congressman's privacy and his need for rest and seclusion, Susan made the call she dreaded to the very core of her being.

"Hello?" answered Anna.

"Mrs. McDonald, this is Susan Collins. I am so sorry to bother you this morning, but I must speak to the congressman. It's urgent."

"Oh yes, Ms. Collins. He'll take your call, please hold."

Susan's pulse quickened as the seconds ticked by, and she nervously awaited the sound of Harry's voice filling the receiver.

"Ms. Collins? I'm here. Is there a problem?"

"Mr. Congressman, I'm so sorry to disturb you, but something has happened that I think you need to know about. I only hope you won't think I'm crazy!"

"Crazy? No, I don't think so. What is it, Ms. Collins?"

"It seems certain members of my family...Oh, God, this really sounds crazy. Please forgive me, Mr. Congressman. Certain members of my family have been able to see things that haven't happened yet. You know, dreams, visions, that sort of thing."

"Joel 2:28... *and your sons and your daughters shall prophesy, your old men shall dream dreams, your young men shall see visions.* Yes, I remember that passage. It's from the Old Testament, Ms. Collins."

"My sister had a terrible dream last night. She dreamt there was a horrible tragedy involving an airplane flight I was on. Mr. Congressman, in the dream she could see the last two digits of the flight number...*21!* The last two digits of tonight's flight number are *21! 1721!*"

Susan was totally unprepared for the Congressman's response to her plea for caution—laughter...bold, hearty, and healthy, booming from the receiver!

"Old Testament, Ms. Collins, Old Testament! Granted, I don't particularly like to fly, but neither do I particularly enjoy driving an automobile. And you know the statistics Ms. Collins…air travel is proven many times safer per capita than automobile transportation. I really don't think we have anything to worry about, especially with this beautiful weather. But if it would make you feel any better, why don't you schedule a later flight? Unfortunately, Anna and I can't afford that luxury. I've got to get back in time to complete more preparations for Monday's hearings. I don't think you or your sister are crazy, Ms. Collins, nor do I think there is anything to be concerned about. Thank you for the warning, but I'll risk it. I'll see you back in Washington."

Susan felt like a bumbling nincompoop as she managed a stuttering apology and good-bye. Turning to face Cathy, all she could manage to say was, "He wouldn't listen. He laughed it off!"

Cathy wept.

Fly the Friendly Skies of ...

SkyTran commuter flight number 1721 bound for Washington, D.C. with a crew of four and sixty-two passengers, disappeared from the air traffic controller's radar screens at approximately 6:22 PM. Eyewitness accounts reported the plane exploding into flames shortly after takeoff, scattering fiery debris throughout the air. The bulk of the fuselage, enveloped in a gigantic fireball, crashed to earth in a vacant field about eight miles from the end of the runway. There were no survivors.

Two men returning to New London from a day of fishing in Long Island Sound gave sworn depositions of seeing two fiery streaks of light travel from the ground up to the plane, exploding upon contact. Their credentials of having been battle veterans of the first Gulf War and familiar with surface-to-air missiles were discounted because of the empty beer cans that were observed in their boat. It was subsequently explained the late afternoon sun can sometimes cause unusual reflections and rays of light to appear, especially near water.

The official findings of the FAA and the National Transportation Safety Board confirmed a fuel leak in the starboard engine compartment as well as concomitant pilot error.

The president of the United States, in his weekly radio address to the nation, commented on the progress of the war on terror in Iraq, Iran, and Afghanistan, but never mentioned the tragic loss of a dedicated and prominent U.S. congressman.

The hearings Congressman McDonald had started were postponed for one week to allow for a period of mourning and transition.

Susan Collins, deciding not to tempt fate further, never boarded the 10:28 flight to Washington.

OMEGA

I am Alpha and Omega, the beginning and the end, the first and the last.
Revelation 22:13

In what would later be described by MacIntosh McAdams as an unparalleled modern display of celestial synchronicity, Omega's earthly birth miraculously coincided with the fiery crash of SkyTran flight number 1721 and the untimely death of Congressman Harry McDonald.

Spawned in the warm, tropical waters about seventy-five miles north of Devil's Island off the coast of French Guiana, Omega quickly grew into a tropical depression keenly observed by the National Hurricane Center. The combination of an unusually warm winter and record high ocean temperatures throughout the Caribbean Sea, the Gulf of Mexico, and the Gulf Coast of the United States had resulted in a hurricane season shattering all records for frequency and intensity. Earlier storms bearing the pre-assigned names of Alton, Bonnie, Carl and Doreen wreaked havoc throughout the Caribbean as they meandered their way to America's Gulf Coast. Once there, they triggered a wave of destruction and chaos stretching from Miami to Tampa; Panama City; Mobile, Alabama; and Lake Charles, Louisiana. It seemed to storm-weary Americans that as soon as one storm had expended its fury, another was born to begin its inexorable journey to America's shores.

Later in the season, New Orleans and Gulfport, Mississippi, were to again feel the brunt of an extremely large and powerful Category 5 hurricane, which relentlessly hammered the area with extensive flooding, property damage, and countless loss of life. Emergency preparedness agencies, FEMA included, were woefully unprepared and incapable of coping with back-to-back disasters, unprecedented in the country's history. By the time the National Hurricane Center ran out of pre-assigned names and began using the Greek alphabet, the southern portion of the U.S. from the eastern coast of Florida to Corpus Christi, Texas, and 150 miles inland resembled a war zone. Pensacola, Florida, had been hit with an enormously destructive Category 4 storm only to be followed in a very short three weeks by a Category 5 dashing the hopes and spirits of the survivors. The same story of misery and suffering could be told of Tampa, Destin, Miami, Key West, and Mobile. Hurricane-ravaged survivors watched with trepidation the formation of the tropical depression bearing the name of the last letter in the Greek alphabet. They anxiously hoped and prayed that this storm, like its namesake, would be the last of the season to torment America.

Churning her way through the warm waters of the West Indies, Omega moved in a west, northwesterly direction, passing between Barbados to the north and Trinidad Tobago to the south. As Omega moved into the eastern Caribbean bringing torrential rains to the Lesser Antilles, she continued fueling her insatiable appetite for energy from the record-setting warm water temperatures of the region. Within nine hours of being designated a tropical depression, Omega was declared a dangerous hurricane with a core expanding rapidly and wind speeds approaching 130 miles per hour.

Omega's ultimate direction seemed uncertain for several hours as hurricane surveillance aircraft and satellite imagery indicated that Jamaica seemed to be the initial target of this rapidly developing storm. As hurricane warnings were issued for Kingston and Port au Prince, the storm's forward motion slowed unexpectedly for several hours in the Caribbean while she continued growing in intensity, seemingly girding herself for the destruction she had yet to inflict. Shifting inexplicably to the north after passing between Kingston and Port au Prince, Omega was a direct hit on Guantanamo Bay, Cuba. By the time of landfall on that far eastern tip of Cuba, the storm's recorded wind speeds were in excess of 175 miles per hour, and she had earned the dubious distinction of becoming the fifth storm of the season to achieve Category 5 status. Ironically, prior to Omega's arrival, pressure had been steadily building in the United States for the closure of the Guantanamo facility due to the many lurid stories of prisoner mistreatment during the Iraq War. Man's indecision and hesitancy was replaced, however, with God's decision and judgment as Omega literally removed all vestiges of Guantanamo from the face of the earth.

Fear of Omega now increased rapidly as the storm continued to grow in size and intensity, and the news reports of damage and numerous lives lost began filtering to America's shores. A sizeable portion of America's hurricane-weary citizens breathed a collective sigh of relief when it became apparent the hurricane's path would not be into the Gulf of Mexico and ultimately the already battered U.S. Gulf Coast.

Instead, Omega began a north, northwesterly route, ultimately pulverizing Nassau and the gambling center of Paradise Island with a direct hit. By this time, wind gusts had been recorded in excess of 200 miles per hour, and Omega's forward motion had intensified to 18 miles per hour. Hurricane watches were issued for the entire eastern seaboard of Florida, with its governor issuing mandatory evacuations for Cape Canaveral, Daytona Beach, and Jacksonville. Like a gigantic pinwheel, Omega, with her outer bands spinning in an ever widening counter-clockwise motion, seemed to propel herself with even more fury and intensity as the tips of those bands touched land and ratcheted Omega's core up the eastern shoreline of America. As if delaying her most destructive vengeance, she passed by Charleston, Cape Hatteras, Norfolk, and Richmond, inundating each city with torrential rains and hurricane-force winds.

With an estimated diameter of over 250 miles and sustained winds in excess of 185 miles per hour, there was no doubt in any rational person's mind that Omega was indeed an unprecedented, extremely dangerous killer storm destined to rewrite the record books.

And if Omega's size and fury were almost incomprehensible, so too was her forward motion, which accelerated the further north she traveled. Her speed of thirty-six miles per hour, reached after passing Myrtle Beach, drastically reduced the preparedness times for individuals within the projected cone of impact. Compounding the urgency for the evacuation of major population areas was the abrupt dashing of hopes for those in the New York City area, when Omega suddenly shifted her north, northeasterly course after passing Atlantic City. A course, which if continued after passing Atlantic City, would have taken her farther into the Atlantic Ocean, away from America's coast and well to the east of Nova Scotia. Instead, the sudden shift described in an emergency warning issued early Wednesday morning at 1:45 AM by the National Hurricane Center caught most New Yorkers totally off guard, if not soundly asleep. With less than five hours before a projected direct hit on New York City, evacuation for most quickly became impossible as the few available exit routes rapidly clogged and vehicular traffic ground to a halt. The mayor of New York, in an emotionally

THE POISON PLUM

charged 2:30 AM news conference, implored everyone to remain calm and stay in their homes and apartments, emphasizing that panic would only exacerbate the already perilous conditions prevailing.

Susan, little Toby, and Cathy had fortuitously left New London about noon on the Monday morning following the Sunday crash of Congressman McDonald's flight. Consciously or subconsciously, Susan had made the decision to "vote with her feet."

"No," she had told Cathy. "I'm not getting on that later flight! And furthermore, I'm not returning to Washington to testify again! The hearings are probably going to fall apart anyway without the leadership of Congressman McDonald. And while I'm naming things I'm not going to do, I may as well state the obvious. I'm not going to continue living in Connecticut, and furthermore we need to get the hell out of Dodge as soon as possible! I've pushed the envelope to the brink, and, if I keep up this cloak-and-dagger spying crap, sooner or later it will be me in the government's crosshairs—if I'm not there already!"

"You don't have to convince me, Sis!" Cathy had responded. "Mentally, I'm already packing my bags. I've said it before, and I'll say it again…if you are waiting on me, dear heart, you are backing up! We, and especially you, oh fearless one, have literally been hugging hell by staying here. Let's just get out now, take our essentials, and we'll worry about our furniture later. Maybe, just maybe, Uncle Thomas will let us have his garage apartment until we can decide what we're going to do…if it's still vacant, that is."

By late afternoon of their second day of driving, the sisters had stopped at a large truck stop on the Interstate for gas and food. In the restaurant, everyone's attention was focused on the news report being broadcast on every television set, documenting the latest developments concerning Hurricane Omega.

"I don't understand," Susan said to Cathy. "What's the big deal? Everyone knows hurricanes fizzle out the further north they go. Those northerners don't have a clue! They should try to ride out just one of those monsters we've seen. And what is a nor'easter anyway? Just a bunch of rain and some wind. So what?"

"Just one more reason to be glad we're gone," Cathy responded. "Who knows? The wind might blow hard enough up there to fill your mouth up with flying ticks if you were outside!"

After some laughter and a tasty meal even Toby enjoyed, the sisters once again continued their journey south. It was almost midnight when the exhausted trio finally arrived in Birmingham. After securing accommodations at a Red Roof Inn near the Interstate, they all enjoyed a solid eight hours of sound, restful sleep.

With their energies and focus devoted to just getting out of New London and making their way safely to Birmingham, the sisters had dismissed any further concerns about Omega and consequently were oblivious to the drama that had unfolded during the night along America's eastern seaboard. Oblivious, that is, until Cathy turned on the television in her room as they were preparing for breakfast on Wednesday morning.

"Susan! Come here quick! Look at this! That hurricane is knocking the crap out of New York!"

"No way!" Susan shouted from the bathroom of her adjoining room. "Hurricanes don't travel that far north. Get off the Sci-Fi Channel."

"There might be some folks at the National Hurricane Center that would disagree with you! Look at this!"

As Susan entered Cathy's room, grim-faced news commentators and representatives of the NWS were anxiously describing to the viewing audience the magnitude of the catastrophe now unfolding in New York City.

From the onset, a massive storm surge, estimated to be as high as fifty feet, had swept across Coney Island, which immediately toppled the scaffolding of the roller coasters and swept aside the Ferris wheels as if they were children's matchstick toys. The low-lying areas of Staten Island, Brooklyn, Queens, Kennedy International, and lower Manhattan were turned into flood zones of rapidly rising waters threatening the lives of the over two million inhabitants trapped like rats on a sinking ship.

As the waters of the Hudson and the East rivers rose, the island of Manhattan rapidly became a no-man's land. First to flood were the subways, entombing the helpless victims attempting to escape in a watery grave. For those unfortunate ones scurrying about the streets of New York seeking shelter before the rising waters overcame them, a fate of a different sort awaited. Incredibly, the hurricane-force winds actually intensified in a whiplash fashion after encountering the massive skyscrapers. The resulting atmospheric pressure differentials blew out thousands and thousands of windows filling the air with shards of lethal glass flying at more than 200 miles per hour, which literally shredded the bodies of those exposed.

By noon, New York City had become a statistic…a worst nightmare come true. It was the greatest natural disaster ever recorded on North American soil. Property damage was estimated in the hundreds of billions of dollars and emergency management personnel grimly estimated over one million lives were probably lost.

The president of the United States, in an emergency news conference before the nation, asked for American's prayers, understanding, and patience as the difficult issues facing the country going forward were identified and addressed. As if the property damage and loss of life were not traumatizing enough, Americans would soon have to grapple with the unstated but implicitly implied stark reality of a major disruption of the principal financial services sector of the nation.

As horrific as these unfolding developments were to New York, sadly and unbeknownst to all, the nation's woes were just beginning. For a little over seventy miles away and slightly to the northwest, a small island, with its low-lying buildings and sparse vegetation, bore the brunt of the most intense portion of the hurricane…the ferocious northwest quadrant.

From his home in Groton near the coastline of Connecticut, the acting director of the Plum Island facility, Mr. Clement Stephens, had received a frantic 4 AM phone call from the official in charge of maintenance and security at the island. The Stephens' household, like the thousands of others in the region, had already been awakened early Wednesday morning by the severe weather alarms and sirens that had been activated to alert the population to the approaching storm. After securing his own home to the best of his ability, Director Stephens had turned his thoughts to the Plum Island lab even before the frantic call came in.

Granted, he reasoned, *power had failed, and some containment areas had been breached after Hurricane Bob hit in 1991, but surely after installing the new generators and state-of-the-art containment system safeguards, there was nothing to fear from this latest interloper. It would rain, and the wind would blow, but in the morning, the sun would again shine brightly on Plum Island. After this brief interruption, we will all go back to the work in progress.*

Shattering his self-imposed illusion of assuredness were the hastily spoken words of the supervisor in charge of the lab's safety and security.

"We're starting to flood, Director Stephens! The water is already over my boots in the main building!"

"My God, man, start the pumps!"

"What with? We lost power about 2:30 and then about thirty minutes ago we lost the generators! Hell, they are under water! I'm standing on a desk in the lobby of the main entrance, and I swear to God, man, I can see the water rising with my flashlight!"

"Are you saying the refrigeration is off in the containment areas?"

"Get the picture, Stephens! No power, no lights, no refrigeration, and the water is rising three inches per minute!"

"You've got to get out of there!"

"No shit, but how? Flap my arms and fly? The last damn ferry left at 10 PM and the four of us are stranded. We're the skeleton crew, remember?"

"Listen! Whatever you guys do, defend those containment systems! Whatever you have to do…portable generators, barricade the doors! Whatever it takes! Under no circumstances can we allow a major breach to occur! My God man, you know the consequences! Call me back in thirty minutes with a…. Hello? Can you hear me? Hello?"

Several minutes later, Director Stephens sat quietly and dejectedly with his cell phone in his lap, finally realizing after repeated call attempts that further communication with Plum Island that night was impossible. Stephens's wife, lantern in hand, entered the den and asked her husband what was wrong.

"Oh, nothing much," he replied as he stood and closed his cell phone, seemingly staring right through her. "The lid was just blown off a simmering pressure cooker in Hell's kitchen, that's all. Nothing to worry about."

All human life on Plum Island was extinguished that incredible night as the full force and fury of Omega relentlessly pounded the government's facility until the final crushing blow of the massive storm surge broke apart and washed away every man-made structure that had formerly blighted the serenity of the island. And, as if by the offering of human life in some twisted macabre sacrifice of atonement, different life forms were then catapulted to activity, dissemination, procreation, and prominence. The winds, swirling waters, and warm temperatures were all churning together to create a perfect embryo-like environment for the unleashed myriad of viruses and bacteria spilling out of Hell's kitchen. The Level 4 biological hazard reactor on Plum Island had just experienced a biological meltdown, the severity of which would, by comparison, pale into insignificance the nuclear meltdown at Chernobyl.

As Omega continued her swath of devastation throughout the northeastern United States, temporarily surviving New Yorkers began attempting to come to some semblance of understanding of the magnitude of the tragedy that had befallen them. With all areas of the city flooded to the fourth-floor level of most buildings, those able to observe the prevailing conditions from their vantage points at higher elevations were shocked at the ghastly scene unfolding below them. As far as the eye could see in any direction, thousands of corpses of men, women, and children floated on the surface of the floodwaters. Floating caskets, which had bobbed up out of the many graveyards like corks out of a bottle, contributed to the unmitigated horror. There was no power, no transportation, no potable water, and no emergency services. Every hospital within the core area of the storm was damaged beyond any hope of a speedy repair. The attending doctors and nurses were helpless to save most of the elderly and critically ill patients who were destined to die over the next several hours. It would be many long hours before the first attempts at rescue by boat and helicopter would begin. Sadly, like Hurricane Katrina, those efforts would prove to be too little, too late.

As darkness descended upon the stricken city, an eerie calm settled across the area. An occasional flashlight could be seen in some of the buildings and even an occasional lantern. But for the most part, the city was plunged into utter darkness and total silence except for the muffled crying of children emanating from some of the buildings.

Daylight brought clear skies over the city and temperatures rapidly rising into the mid-nineties. The absence of any breeze and 90 percent humidity only contributed to the already miserable conditions prevailing. By noon, the baking sun had accelerated the decay of exposed bodies and the sickening odor of rotting flesh began to permeate the air. As evening approached, one could see the New York skyline illuminated by dozens of fires which had erupted and were being fueled by broken natural gas pipelines and ruptured gasoline and oil storage tanks. Receding waters from the highest elevations revealed thousands of automobiles stranded along the few evacuation routes, their passengers drowned from the powerful storm surge that had totally engulfed their vehicles.

Remaining New Yorkers were trapped in a sea of fires, death, destruction, and stench with no hope of fresh water and fresh supplies of food any time soon.

It was a bleak situation rapidly deteriorating into a hopeless, impossible situation for the survivors.

At area hospitals and clinics far enough away to have escaped the destruction of Omega's storm surge, doctors and nurses braced for the inevitable. Over the next several hours, there would be hundreds, if not thousands, of hurricane victims seeking shelter and emergency medical care. And, as the network of emergency services and personnel began springing to life, the first of Omega's exodus of victims poured into the emergency rooms.

"Routine stuff but at high volume," commented one very busy emergency physician to his nurse. "Cuts, scrapes, contusions, dehydration, exhaustion, stress-induced heart attacks…we can handle it! Once all the beds are filled, we will just start shipping them out to other hospitals. No problem."

Within hours, however, the routine of standard emergency room care suddenly began to shift as new patients arrived presenting with a bewildering array of symptoms and complaints, which baffled attending doctors and nurses.

"If I didn't know better," one doctor remarked, "I would swear that guy we just saw had anthrax!"

"I've never seen it," responded his nurse, "but I've never seen smallpox either. And I'll be damned, but I think that woman in 3A has it!"

What began as a trickle in the hospitals evolved into a deluge over the next twenty-four hours. Many cases remained undiagnosed, but the confirmed cases chilled the health care providers to the bone.

West Point was the first to report Ebola. Newburgh confirmed smallpox. Poughkeepsie reported a weapons-grade form of anthrax. Danbury, Connecticut, West Nile encephalitis; Kingston, drug-resistant tuberculosis; Waterbury, Connecticut, tularemia; Hartford, *Yersinia Pestis*—the plague!

From *A* to *Z*, they were all represented. It was a veritable alphabet soup of bacteria and viruses, many long thought dormant, reappearing in one giant devil's cocktail to once again plague mankind. Patients began dying in droves; their communicable diseases rapidly infecting the health care workers valiantly trying to stave off the grim reaper. Like a raging-out-of-control wildfire, the crème de la crème of Plum Island's productions swept through the northeastern United States and extended their relentless march into Canada.

Once it was obvious what was happening, mandatory evacuations and quarantines began in an effort to contain the spread of the virulent germs. Riots broke out in many cities as Americans, distrustful of their government, which had been responsible for this catastrophe, resisted efforts at relocation and quarantine. Health care workers failed to show up for their shifts, and doctors hastily closed their offices, not wanting to be yet another statistic. In droves, the able and capable ones began to flee to the west and south, defying orders to submit to quarantine. With their families sick and dying and they themselves becoming ill, members of the military and National Guard that had been mobilized to conduct evacuations and enforce quarantines began leaving their posts in hordes. Chaos became the order of the day; it was every man for himself.

Fundamentalist preachers, seeking comfort and guidance from the scriptures, began quoting and interpreting Revelation 6, Chapter 8:

And I looked, and behold a pale horse: and his name that sat on him was Death, and Hell followed with him. And power was given unto them over the fourth part of the earth, to kill with sword, and with hunger, and with death, and with the beasts of the earth.

And of course the "beasts of the earth," as explained by the Bible scholars, was literally translated as "living creatures"...the germs. True believers throughout the world excitedly began wondering in amazement if the Fourth Horseman of the Apocalypse as revealed to the apostle John while in exile on the Isle of Patmos circa 68 A.D. was indeed galloping across America's landscape.

Many Americans who were fortunate enough to have been unexposed to Omega's swath of destruction and who had also escaped infection by the germ invasion, found themselves entangled in a storm of an entirely different nature as the financial meltdown began.

The heart of the world's financial center, New York City, had stopped beating. The shutdown of the New York Federal Reserve Bank and the stock and commodity exchanges cumulatively triggered a wave of defaults that ripped through the money capitals and bourses of the world like a hot knife through butter, with losses quickly aggregating into the trillions. With the check clearing functions of the Federal Reserve no longer operational, average Americans suddenly found themselves unable to pay for simple essentials. Their stores of wealth, represented by digits totaling the sums of their personal, IRA, and 401-K plans, became irretrievably lost bits and bytes of information swallowed into the black hole of cyberspace by the destruction of the computers entrusted with their storage.

With the flooding of the sub-basement vaults of the New York Federal Reserve Bank, the vast gold reserves of the world's central banks became inaccessible. The majority of international trade and commerce dependent upon those reserves for the settlement of transactions ground to a screeching halt. America quickly became a barter nation on the brink of anarchy. Basic human emotions surfaced and rose to prominence. It was Hurricane Katrina devastation and emotions to the nth power. Do unto your fellow man before he can do unto you. Gold, silver, guns, ammunition, potable water, emergency medical supplies, and food were the items in demand.

Canada, our friendly neighbor to the north, suddenly became less friendly and abruptly closed the border with the United States in an attempt to control the spread of disease. Previous outstanding concerns about a tidal wave of illegal immigrants pouring across America's border from Mexico evaporated when Mexico's government, following Canada's lead, closed their borders, allowing only Mexican nationals back into their country as they frantically fled the legacy of Omega.

With the borders closed, all international flights grounded, and international trade and commerce at a standstill, America became an island unto itself. The next great financial depression had begun, which would ultimately make the Great Depression of 1929–1939 look like a Sunday School picnic.

The former king of the world's currencies, the U.S. dollar, rapidly began losing its status as the premier reserve currency of the world. In response to an overwhelming demand from foreign holders of the U.S. currency that America mobilize its massive gold reserves at the Fort Knox Depository to stabilize the currency, the surviving members of Congress hastily approved a plan to return to a gold-backed dollar. To dispel rumors that had circulated for years, members of Congress ordered the first audit in decades of the Fort Knox reserves to provide the required assurance of legitimacy, that yes, America indeed had the gold bullion necessary to restore confidence in the beleaguered dollar.

Sadly, those hopes of a quick fix for the struggling dollar were promptly dashed when the congressional committee, after finally gaining access to the vaults of Fort Knox over the strenuous objections of what was left of the Treasury Department, discovered what many observers had suspected for years. Plainly and simply, the only gold found at that location was in the teeth of the guards bravely defending the empty vaults, as they had done for years. Decades of government profligacy, coupled with misguided schemes such as the Lend Lease programs to rebuild Europe at the end of World War II, bribes to Japan, continuous wars and military skirmishes, and the redemption of U.S. dollars for gold by foreigners in the sixties and seventies until Nixon finally slammed the gold window shut, had all taken their toll on the once massive cache of gold that had been the envy of the world. Ounce by ounce, bar by bar, it had all been sold, traded, and frittered away throughout the years until now, for the entire world to see, the unbacked dollar was nothing more than a piece of high-quality paper with ink smeared on it.

When the New York Stock Exchange attempted to reopen six months later, the Dow Jones Industrial Average stood at 600. This average, when adjusted for inflation, was even lower than the 41 recorded at the depth of the previous depression in July of 1932.

Attempting to restore some semblance of stability, officials of the exchange scrapped the calculation of the Dow average designed decades earlier by Charles Dow and substituted a complex series of formulas incorporating the euro, the dollar, and the Japanese yen. The century-old Dow Jones Industrial Average had been replaced. Its successor became the DEY, the *DEY Industrial Average*.

America's status as a world power had toppled. The U.S. dollar's status as the reserve currency of the world had toppled. America, for all practical purposes, had been relegated to third-world country status as all her warts, blemishes, and dirty laundry were paraded before the court of world opinion.

For many years, a nagging recurring question had troubled Bible students and scholars as they struggled to interpret the scriptures in the aftermath of evolving world conditions.

How, they questioned, had the Bible prophets of the Old Testament failed to see the coming arrival of the unquestionable superpower of the world, the United States, after the conclusion of World War II? How could those revered prophets, inspired in their unerring prophecies by the very word and direction of Almighty God, have failed to see the coming arrival on the world stage a nation as powerful as America? That there was no reference to the United States in End-Time prophecy was both problematic and puzzling to the serious students of the Bible. To suggest and ascribe a potential for errors and inaccuracies in the centuries-old prophecies was tantamount to heresy and only served to heighten the intensity of the raging debate.

After Omega, America reeled from a population loss of over 100 million people, and chronic health problems afflicted another 50 million people. The economy was in shambles; lawlessness and anarchy were the order of the day, and America had reverted to an agrarian, barter-based society. The Bible scholars finally had their answer. The prophets of old had not erred at all. The United States was not mentioned at the arrival of the hour of destiny of that great celestial clock because she had become too weak and insignificant to have merited any acknowledgment whatsoever.

This is not the end.